THE OXFORD BOOK OF
GOTHIC TALES

Chris Baldick is a lecturer in English at Lancaster University. His previous publications include *In Frankenstein's Shadow: Myth, Monstrosity, and Nineteenth-Century Writing* (1987), *The Concise Oxford Dictionary of Literary Terms* (1990), and an introduction to the World's Classics edition of C. R. Maturin's Gothic tale, *Melmoth the Wanderer*.

The
Oxford Book of
GOTHIC
TALES

Edited by

CHRIS BALDICK

Oxford   New York

OXFORD UNIVERSITY PRESS

1993

Oxford University Press, Walton Street, Oxford OX2 6DP
Oxford New York Toronto
Delhi Bombay Calcutta Madras Karachi
Kuala Lumpur Singapore Hong Kong Tokyo
Nairobi Dar es Salaam Cape Town
Melbourne Auckland Madrid

and associated companies in
Berlin Ibadan

Oxford is a trade mark of Oxford University Press

First published 1992
First issued as an Oxford University Press paperback 1993

British Library Cataloguing in Publication Data
Data available

Library of Congress Cataloging in Publication Data
Data available
ISBN 0–19–283117–8

1 3 5 7 9 10 8 6 4 2

Printed in Great Britain by
Clays Ltd.
Bungay, Suffolk

To Grace and Ken Curtis

ACKNOWLEDGEMENTS

I AM indebted to several friends and colleagues for their suggestions, advice, and encouragement; among them being Peter Currie, Pamela Jackson, John Sears, John and Kathryn Simons, and Peter Wright. Special thanks are due to Alison Easton, Niall Martin, and Lien van der Leij for their valuable help in bibliographical research; to Julie Walker for checking the proofs; to Alison Milbank for her advice on Sheridan Le Fanu and other aspects of Gothickry; and to Keith and Jagoda Hanley for supporting the later stages of work on this book with their unfailing hospitality.

I should also like to thank Alan Carter and other members of staff of the Bodleian Library, Oxford, and the staffs of the National Library of Scotland, Edinburgh, and the British Library, London, for their assistance.

CONTENTS

Contents

III. THE TWENTIETH CENTURY

INTRODUCTION

THIS book can claim to be the first attempt to exhibit, along the full extent of its career from the eighteenth century to the present day, a tradition of short fiction specifically designated as 'Gothic'. Although some of the tales reprinted here could also be counted under various other related headings—as ghost stories, as horror stories, as tales of terror, of the macabre, of the supernatural, or the uncanny—the fictional tradition represented in this collection is not adequately described by any of these familiar labels. The category of the Gothic tale overlaps at some points with its neighbouring fictional types, but still retains special features of its own which can and do thrive outside the particular conventions of, say, the ghost story. One of the aims of this introductory account will be to characterize those distinctive properties of the Gothic tale, bringing to a somewhat clearer definition the often nebulous associations that we draw upon when we use such a phrase as 'Gothic horror'.

The term 'Gothic' has become firmly established as the name for one sinister corner of the modern Western imagination, but it seems to work by intuitive suggestion rather than by any agreed precision of reference. There are several difficulties of usage involved in the term itself, of which the most obvious today is the incompatibility between the literary and architectural senses: whereas 'Gothic' in architectural contexts refers to a style of European architecture and ornament that flourished from the late twelfth to the fifteenth century, it is used in its literary and cinematic senses to describe works that appeared in an entirely different medium several hundreds of years later. A term thus applied simultaneously to the products of two such widely differing ages (to say nothing of the cultural gulf between Chartres cathedral and a sensationalist magazine story) would seem to require some qualification attached to it; and, indeed, it is the sensible practice of architectural historians to distinguish from the Gothic of the late Middle Ages the Neo-Gothic or Gothic Revival style of the nineteenth century. In a more logical world, we might have learned to adopt a clearer designation of this kind for the 'Gothic' of modern literature and cinema; but, of course, it is far too late to undo our inherited confusions, and even if we were able to do so, we would only run up against further difficulties rendering 'Neo-Gothic fiction' or some such nomenclature just as unsatisfactory. But before we can see our way through such further tangles, we will need to look back into the common source of these divergent senses of 'Gothic'.

In its earliest sense, the word is simply the adjective denoting the language and ethnic identity of the Goths: the Germanic peoples, first heard of upon the shores of the Baltic, whose later maraudings and migrations from the third to the fifth century AD took them across southern Europe from the Black Sea to the Iberian peninsula, fatally weakening the Roman empire in the face of further 'barbarian' incursions. Long after they disappeared into the ethnic melting-pots of the northern Mediterranean, their fearful name was taken and used to prop up one side of that set of cultural oppositions by which the Renaissance and its heirs defined and claimed possession of European civilization: Northern versus Southern, Gothic versus Graeco-Roman, Dark Ages versus the Age of Enlightenment, medieval versus modern, barbarity versus civility, superstition versus Reason. As revised by northern Protestant nationalisms, the 'map' of these contraries would be turned about so that the southern Catholic cultures could be represented as the barbarously superstitious antagonist; but the essential shape of the polarity would persist as the founding mythology of modern Europe and its internal tensions. In the drastic simplifications of such a scheme, a telescoping of historical periods that merged the 'Dark Ages' of Rome's decline with the more flourishing condition of the later Middle Ages, lumping together the Ostrogothic warrior of the third century with the learned Parisian monk of the thirteenth, was not considered an anachronism so much as a necessary verdict on centuries of unproductive pre-history. So although the Goths themselves never constructed a single Gothic cathedral, nor composed any Gothic fiction, these later senses of Gothic still have a recognizable meaning by virtue of their polar opposition to the 'Classical' architectural and literary traditions derived from Greece and Rome. Accordingly, by the late eighteenth century 'Gothic' was commonly used to mean 'medieval, therefore barbarous', in a largely unquestioned equation of civilization with classical standards. The early literary sense of Gothic is founded upon this usage, denoting, as in the subtitle of Horace Walpole's *The Castle of Otranto: A Gothic Story* (1764), a tale concerned with the brutality, cruelty, and superstition of the Middle Ages. The assumed superiority of specifically classical culture then tends to be eroded by the challenge of the Romantic Movement, but there remain other terms of opposition—the modern, the enlightened, the rational— which serve to hold the pejorative sense of Gothic in its place. Unlike

'Romantic', then, 'Gothic' in its literary usage never becomes a positive term of cultural revaluation, but carries with it (even among antiquarian enthusiasts for medieval art, such as Walpole, the Aikins, and their followers) an identification of the medieval with the barbaric. A Gothic novel or tale will almost certainly offend classical tastes and rational principles, but it will not do so by urging any positive view of the Middle Ages. In this important respect literary Gothicism differs crucially from serious medieval revivalism of the kind found in the mature phase of the Gothic Revival in architecture: here, the views of the Catholic convert Augustus Welby Pugin and of John Ruskin effected in the nineteenth century a rehabilitation of the Middle Ages as the great age of Faith and of social responsibility, radically revising the term 'Gothic' to mean 'Christian' in contradistinction to the corruptly pagan tradition of the Renaissance. The term 'Neo-Gothic' used for the Victorian architectural style so endorsed would be entirely unsuitable for the literary Gothickry of Pugin's or Ruskin's contemporaries, because the implied valuations of medieval life are so different in either case. Such a contrast helps to clarify the fact that the most troublesome aspect of the term 'Gothic' is, indeed, that literary Gothic is really anti-Gothic.

The anti-Gothicism of Gothic, by which I mean its ingrained distrust of medieval civilization and its representation of the past primarily in terms of tyranny and superstition, has taken several forms, from the vigilant Protestant xenophobia so strongly evident in the first half-century of Gothic writing, to the rationalist feminism of Angela Carter's fiction. In whatever form, it has persisted as a major element of the tradition, even though its significance has tended to be disguised by the apparent indulgence of archaic superstitions and barbarous energies. At first sight, Gothic fiction may appear, as it did to many anxious readers in the late eighteenth century, as some sort of irresponsible relapse into the old delusions of a benighted age, nostalgically glamorizing the worst features of a past from which we have thankfully escaped. Some attraction to the imagined vitality of past ages is indeed always there in Gothic, but this appeal consists principally in the imaginative freedoms and symbolic possibilities of discarded folk beliefs, not in any faith actually attached to them. When Gothic fiction has employed the ghostly apparitions and omens of archaic lore (and it has not always needed their aid at all), it has at the same time placed them under strong suspicion as part of a cruelly repressive and deluded past. There is often a kind of homeopathic principle at work here, in the way that Gothic writers have borrowed the fables and nightmares of a past age in order to repudiate their authority: just as the consciously Protestant pioneers of the Gothic novel raise the old ghosts of Catholic Europe only to exorcize them, so in a later age the fiction of Angela Carter has exploited the power of a patriarchal folklore, all the better to expose and dispel its grip upon us. In the early days of Gothic writing, the strong anxiety among both critics and practitioners of Gothic fiction about the risks of dabbling in bygone superstition, and especially about the permissible use of supernatural incidents was animated by a watchful Protestant fear of popery and its imaginative snares. It is no accident at all that Gothic fiction first emerged and established itself within the British and Anglo-Irish middle class, in a society which had through generations of warfare, political scares, and popular martyrology persuaded itself that its hard-won liberties could at any moment be snatched from it by papal tyranny and the ruthless wiles of the Spanish Inquisition. At the foundation of Gothic literature's anti-Gothic sentiment lies this nightmare of being dragged back to the persecutions of the Counter-Reformation; and so the novels and tales of the early Gothic writers are peopled by scheming Franciscan poisoners, depraved abbesses, fearsome Inquisitors, and diabolical murderers from every monastic order, plotting against helpless maidens who have been forced against their wills into the hypocrisies of a conventual regime. Symptomatic of this nightmare world is the familiar contortion by which the Gothic writer has to provide for the hero and heroine of the tale some reassuring Protestant credentials by making them, although Roman Catholic, secretly immune from the impostures of their own faith. The differences often observed between competing schools of early Gothic fiction on the grounds of their deployment of explicable or inexplicable supernatural effects disappear into unanimity on the matter of Catholic superstition, which is relentlessly satirized and condemned.

The distrust which Gothicism shows towards the bugbears of a discarded mythology may be highlighted helpfully by contrast with the principles of the orthodox ghost story. In spite of their consanguinity and their many mutual borrowings, the two traditions can be seen as mutually opposed on this point. There is a very familiar model followed by many ghost stories in English from the early twentieth century: this usually begins with an assembly of gentlemen gathered at a dinner-table or in a London club, debating the existence of spirits. Then a nervous-looking member of the company pipes up with his first-hand account of the inexplicable occurrences at a country house he has rented for a weekend, where the spooky goings-on have reached the point at which the servants have given notice. At the close of his narrative, the materialist doubters are silenced, and some moralizing is made to the effect that there are more things in heaven and earth, Horatio, than are dreamt of in the narrow secular philosophies of bolshevists, suffragettes, and the other democratic do-gooders of this rationalist age. My little travesty does no justice to many more sophisticated writers who have worked in this genre, but readers who have browsed at any length in ghost-lore will immediately recognize the type and its conventions. The ostensible point of the ghost story (even when the author may privately be an unbeliever) is to convince the sceptical reader of the palpable existence of phantoms. The conservative tendency of such tales lies in their dedication to overcoming modern scepticism on behalf of an older belief which has been foolishly abandoned. Gothic fiction, on the other hand, usually shows no such respect for the wisdom of the past, and indeed tends to portray former ages as prisons of delusion.

This survey of the difficulties involved in the term 'Gothic' in literature has so far considered the two problems of its anachronistic origins and its possible confusion with more positive medievalist senses to which it is in fact hostile. There remains a further warning to be made against any inflexible identification of Gothic with specifically medieval settings. As this tradition of fiction has evolved, it has adapted the archaic atmosphere of early Gothic fiction, with its usual time of action in the late Middle Ages or the early modern period, to later periods, even in some cases to the writer's own time. It has done this by abstracting certain leading features of these original Gothic settings, retaining especially the enclosed spaces of the old building, with further associations of the past's destructive cruelty. The modern time of writing which is set against the Gothic past eventually comes round to being the past of succeeding generations of readers and writers; and so by the 1930s we find F. M. Mayor and Isak Dinesen both setting their stories in the early nineteenth century, now become a 'Gothic' period itself, its customs cruelly repressive in twentieth-century eyes. In principle and in practice it is perfectly possible to have a Gothic story set in the author's own time, provided that the tale focuses upon a relatively enclosed space in which some antiquated barbaric code still prevails. For instance, Conan Doyle's story 'The Adventure of the Speckled Band' is set at a time within the living memory of all its first readers, but within an ancestral mansion locked into an archaic form of domestic tyranny. Dislodged from the specific association with the Middle Ages which gave it its name, the Gothic has become in such ways a mobile form, and so has generated significant traditions where there are no medieval castles at all, in the Americas.

Before attempting any summary definition of the Gothic tale as I have understood it in making the selections for this book, it will be worth reviewing briefly the emergence of Gothic fiction in its widest sense; because the Gothic tale, unlike the relatively free-standing genre of the ghost story, initially derives from and is thereafter partly entangled with the tradition of the longer Gothic novel or romance. Some of the most important practitioners of Gothic and semi-Gothic fiction, notably Ann Radcliffe and the Brontë sisters, never published short stories, and some others have kept their Gothic work and their shorter fiction separate. As a result, our usual understanding and recognition of Gothic effects in shorter tales depends partly upon conventions originating and continuing outside the short-story tradition itself, which is to some extent a supplementary and junior line: an additional wing belatedly built on to the larger ruined house of Gothic fiction, although still well worth exploring for its own sake.

The tradition began with the attention attracted by Walpole's *Castle of Otranto* in the 1760s. This short novel, set in the thirteenth century, concerns the efforts of Manfred, a tyrannical Italian prince, to produce an heir to the title and estate which his grandfather has usurped. Following the strange death of his son, he decides to continue the family line by taking his son's fiancée Isabella in marriage. Aided by the gallant peasant boy Theodore (who later turns out to be the rightful heir of Otranto), Isabella resists, and the enraged Manfred pursues her through the castle until he mistakenly stabs his own daughter Matilda to death. Theodore is restored to the title by the intervention of the gigantic ghost of his ancestor Prince Alfonso the Good, whose statue had earlier crushed Manfred's son. Walpole was inspired to produce this novel by his antiquarian explorations among old ballads and romances, and he offered his work to the public (at first under the guise of a translation from the Italian) as a modest experiment in resurrecting the imaginative liberties of medieval romance, against the realistic constraints of a contemporary fictional code which frowned upon his supernatural marvels. Judged by the standards of Walpole's successors it is a rather clumsy production, but it did establish for them a fruitful combination of themes, motifs, and settings: the merciless determination of the feudal tyrant to continue his family line, the threat of dynastic extinction, the confinement and persecution of a vulnerable heroine in a sinister labyrinthine building. These were to become the standard materials of Gothic as the tradition took shape.

Taking their cue from Walpole, several other antiquarian hobbyists took to composing pseudo-medieval works: in verse, the craze called forth the poetical forgeries of the tragic prodigy Thomas Chatterton, while in prose it generated the transient genre of the Gothic 'fragment'—an incomplete narrative presented as if the result of an antiquarian discovery among partially destroyed manuscripts. The Gothic fragment, which is the forerunner of the Gothic tale proper, ingeniously exploits the aesthetic principle behind the appeal of ruined buildings, by suggesting a lost whole which the reader's imagination is then invited to reconstruct. This device of the tantalizingly incomplete text—a crumbling parchment or fatally interrupted narrative—was to be incorporated into the far more substantial works of the greatest early Gothic novelist, Ann Radcliffe. Her full-length novels *The Romance of the Forest* (1792), *The Mysteries of Udolpho* (1794), and *The Italian* (1797) all combine more successfully the elements earlier assembled by Walpole. Again the endangered heroine is brought under the malevolent power of a sinister aristocrat in the gloomy chambers of an old castle or abbey, although the time of the action is brought forward into the sixteenth and seventeenth centuries. She developed the leisurely construction of suspense and brooding atmosphere, apparently abandoning her heroes and heroines to the most frightful of fates for several chapters before returning to permit their escape through some damp subterranean passage. Such prolonged teasing of the reader's anxieties was possible only in the three-volume novel, and it was in this form that Gothic fiction dominated the circulating libraries for the next fifteen or twenty years, before Walter Scott's new mode of historical fiction displaced it. There were, however, shorter and less expensive forms of Gothic reading-matter: several magazines in this period offered serialized Gothic romances and, more rarely, the occasional self-contained tale; while at the lower end of the market there were the popular chapbooks known from their covers as 'bluebooks' and sometimes nicknamed 'shilling shockers'. The first decade of the nineteenth century witnessed a brisk trade in these sixpenny, thirty-six page pamphlets with their condensed reworkings and outright plagiarisms of Gothic novels. Lifting as much as they could from the novels of Radcliffe and her imitators, the bluebook hack-writers compressed their tales into a breakneck narration that frequently degenerated into a plot-summary interspersed with choice incidents of violent outrage, in the more frantic sensationalist style of M. G. Lewis's novel *The Monk* (1796). The hectic confusion of this manner can be seen here in 'The Vindictive Monk', and a more assured exercise in abridged

Radcliffean imitation in 'The Ruins of the Abbey of Fitz-Martin'.

Although many literary historians are satisfied to regard Gothic as a closed episode after the appearance of C. R. Maturin's rambling novel *Melmoth the Wanderer* in 1820, the tradition in fact survives through the nineteenth century and beyond, following two intertwined courses of evolution. On the one hand, it infiltrates and contributes powerfully to the mainstream of the Victorian novel, distinctly colouring the atmosphere of major works by Charlotte Brontë and by Charles Dickens, whose characters Bertha Mason and Miss Havisham are unmistakably and unforgettably Gothic figures; and it resurfaces in the 1860s within the modern settings of 'sensation novels' by Sheridan Le Fanu, Mary Elizabeth Braddon, and Wilkie Collins, appearing once again towards the close of the century in more overtly Gothic works by Stevenson, Wilde, and Bram Stoker. On the other hand, it adapts itself to the emergent form of the magazine tale as the modern genre that we recognize as 'the short story' takes shape. This second development is in some ways the more remarkable, requiring as it did a thoroughgoing reformulation of Gothic conventions away from the protracted suspense of Ann Radcliffe's work and from the disorderly multiplication of incidents found in Lewis, Maturin, and others, towards a far more tightly concentrated effect, of a kind that the fragment-writers and the bluebook summarizers had failed to refine. Although the somewhat expansive stories of Sheridan Le Fanu have an honourable place in this process, the writer who almost single-handedly carried through the necessary transformation was Edgar Allan Poe. If there is one work that announces the true arrival of the Gothic tale, its convincing emergence from cruder beginnings, it is his story 'The Fall of the House of Usher'. Poe's deliberate dedication to economy and consistency of effect in his writings produced in this tale a remarkably crystallized pattern for the future evolution of Gothic fiction. His new formula involved not only the stripping down of a cumbersome conventional machinery to its essential elements but an accompanying clarification and highlighting of a theme long familiar to Gothic writing and to the surrounding culture of Romantic sensationalism, although hitherto left hovering in the shadows: that of the decline and extinction of the old family line. Perfectly harmonizing the terminal involution of the Usher family with the final crumbling of its mansion—of 'house' as dynasty with house as habitation—Poe ensured that whereas before him the keynote of Gothic fiction had been cruelty, after him it would be decadence.

There is no space here to prolong the story of Gothic fiction beyond these founding and defining stages, except to notice that among Poe's achievements was the successful translation of Gothic into American literature, if not exactly on to American soil. The full 'grounding' of Gothic in particular territories and their special customs would later be accomplished by writers of the 'local color' movement, notably George Washington Cable. This transatlantic appropriation, though, guaranteed for the Gothic tale an extended life in the flourishing short-story tradition of the United States, as the many American tales in this collection should illustrate. By the middle of the twentieth century there even came to be talk of a 'Southern Gothic' movement in the most fertile region of the States—a group usually understood to include, among others, William Faulkner and Eudora Welty (with some writers like Flannery O'Connor whose work inclines more to the 'grotesque' than to Gothic proper). So pronounced did this tendency become, in both North and South, that Leslie Fiedler in his provocative critical study *Love and Death in the American Novel* (1960) was tempted to conclude that the central tradition of fiction in the United States had been predominantly Gothic from first to last. And although Fiedler was speaking of the literature of white America, his view would seem to have been confirmed subsequently by the appearance of the most outstanding Gothic work of recent years, the novel *Beloved* (1987) by the African-American writer Toni Morrison.

Drawing together some of the characteristics of Gothic fiction already suggested in this brief account of its evolution, I can now summarize what I have understood, in selecting the contents of this collection, a Gothic tale to be. For the Gothic effect to be attained, a tale should combine a fearful sense of inheritance in time with a claustrophobic sense of enclosure in space, these two dimensions reinforcing one another to produce an impression of sickening descent into disintegration. This is, of course, too abstract a formula to capture the real accumulation of physical and historical associations by which we actually recognize the conventions of Gothic; so it may be translated into more concrete terms by noting that typically a Gothic tale will invoke the tyranny of the past (a family curse, the survival of archaic forms of despotism and of superstition) with such weight as to stifle the hopes of the present (the liberty of the heroine or hero) within the dead-end of physical incarceration (the dungeon, the locked room, or simply the confinements of a family house closing in upon itself). Even more concisely, although at the risk of losing an important series of connected meanings, we could just say that Gothic fiction is characteristically obsessed with old buildings as sites of human decay. The Gothic castle or house is not just an old and sinister building; it is a house of degeneration, even of decomposition, its living-space darkening and contracting into the dying-space of the mortuary and the tomb. Although Gothic fiction can work with other kinds of enclosed space, if these are sufficiently isolated and introverted—convents, prisons, schools, madhouses, even small villages—it is still the dark mansion that occupies its central ground. Doubling as both fictional setting and as dominant symbol, the house reverberates for us with associations which are simultaneously psychological and historical. As a kind of folk-psychology set in stone, the Gothic house is readily legible to our post-Freudian culture, so we can recognize in its structure the crypts and cellars of repressed desire, the attics and belfries of neurosis, just as we accept Poe's invitation to read the haunted palace of the poem in his tale as the allegory of a madman's head. Less often remarked, however, despite all the signs thrown out by Gothic fiction—from the status of its characters to the very decor of its settings—is the mansion's historical resonance. Some further commentary may help to bring out this rather neglected dimension of the Gothic.

It is customary to account for the appeal of Gothic fiction by reference to a set of universal and timeless dreads usually referred to as 'our deepest fears'. And some such common repertoire of shared anxieties, including the fear of death, of decay, and of confinement, is almost certainly involved in both the creation of Gothic works and the reader's response to them. The difficulty with this generalizing claim, though, is that Gothic writing summons up these fears only within its own peculiar framework of conventions, whose special features cannot be explained directly by any nameless dread that Gothic has in common with very different fictional forms like the folk-tale, the ancient myth, or most modern horror stories. Unlike the fear of death, Gothic fiction is neither immemorial nor global, but belongs specifically to the modern age of Europe and the Americas since the end of the eighteenth century; and it is marked by this limited location and history in ways that help differentiate it further from the generality of fearful narratives. Prominent among its special features is a preoccupation with the inherited powers and corruptions of feudal aristocracy, and with similar lineages and agencies of archaic authority, which can include the pseudo-aristocracies of the American South and the monastic hierarchies of the Roman Catholic Church. So while it would be possible to concoct a passable horror story about the misdeeds of, say, a dangerously sadistic bank manager or dentist, one would not be writing a Gothic tale unless one linked the subject-matter in some way to the antiquated tyrannies and dynastic corruptions of an aristocratic power or at least of a proud old provincial family. Moulding our common existential dread into the more particular shapes of Gothic fiction, then, is a set of 'historical fears' focusing upon the memory of an age-old regime of oppression and persecution which threatens still to fix its dead hand upon us. As the brief account of early Gothic fiction given above should already have suggested, these fears first took the form of nervous Protestant fascination with Catholic aristocrats and monks; but as this sectarian alarm subsided, the Gothic tradition continued to feed upon the sinister allure of noble dynasties or lesser family autocracies. It is a middle-class tradition, and its anxiety may be characterized briefly as a fear of historical reversion; that is, of the nagging possibility that the despotisms buried by the modern age may prove to be yet undead.

In this context it may be worth speculating that the figure of the vampire (which has hardly any prominence in early Gothic writing) probably carries a greater importance in twentieth-century mythology than it ever did for Transylvanian villagers in centuries past, and that this is because it encapsulates for a more democratic age a fantasy model of decadent aristocratic cruelty which we need to sacrifice over and over again. Those millions of us who descend, however remotely, from peasant stock rather than from the blood of princes must, it seems, derive some necessary reassurance from these fictional rites of exorcism. The mainstream non-vampiric traditions of Gothic fiction give us something similar, to the extent that they re-enact and implicitly celebrate the extinction of their fearsome dynastic houses. Just why we should feel any need to reassure ourselves may seem to be the real mystery here: after all, the Bastille fell long ago, and, as Jane Austen reminded the readers of Gothic novels in *Northanger Abbey*, it is not so easy these days to be kidnapped and assassinated by an Italian count. One kind of answer to this riddle may be indicated by considering the noticeable prominence of women in the Gothic tradition, as popular and influential authors, as central fictional characters, and as devoted readers. Gothic fiction has long been presided over by Ann Radcliffe and her female successors, commonly employing the Radcliffean model of the heroine enclosed in the master's house: a formula persistently re-worked in the popular variety of women's fiction still known as the 'Gothic romance', whose descent can be traced back through Daphne du Maurier's *Rebecca* and Charlotte Brontë's *Jane Eyre*. It is more than likely that this enduring adoption of Gothic fiction by women has to do with the relative failure of modern societies to ensure for women the kind of economic, legal, and personal security that are enjoyed as the post-absolutist rights of man. And if the liberties of women are felt to be more precarious in these public senses, their traditional sphere of the domestic interior will often come to appear less as a refuge than as the most imprisoning space of all, where there may survive the most archaic of tyrannies. As Charlotte Perkins Stetson's tale 'The Yellow Wall-Paper' reminds us, in its combination of personal testimony and feminist fable, the imprisoning house of Gothic fiction has from the very beginning been that of patriarchy, in both its earlier and its expanded feminist senses. Developing the principle more widely, we can conclude that while the existential fears of Gothic may concern our inability to escape our decaying bodies, its historical fears derive from our inability finally to convince ourselves that we have really escaped from the tyrannies of the past. The price of liberty, as the old saying tells us, is eternal vigilance; and in Gothic fiction we find this vigilance running beyond the sober assessment of dangers into a lurid form of fatalism for which paranoia is often not too strong a term. Gothic fiction is a way of exercising such anxieties, but also of allaying them by imagining the worst before it can happen, and giving it at least a safely recognizable form.

In my choice of tales for this collection, I have set out to present not only the best and the most strikingly characteristic of shorter Gothic works but at the same time some sort of evolutionary sequence through which the reader can trace developments across more than two hundred years of this tradition. The tales are accordingly arranged in their chronological order. Readers who are likely to be impatient with the historical curiosities to be found in the opening section, and who wish to spend time only on works of some literary accomplishment may prefer to skip straight to the second section, or even to Poe's 'Fall of the House of Usher', although they will be missing some rather startling entertainment.

This selection has been guided by the conception of Gothic fiction sketched out in the last few pages, and represents an attempt, perverse as it may be, to put together for the first time a relatively pure line of shorter Gothic writing. I am aware, however, that a broader definition of Gothic is possible, and have at some points slackened the line to accommodate this view. An example is the inclusion of Isak Dinesen's story 'The Monkey'. This does not quite meet my own entry requirements, but since Dinesen herself, by including it in her *Seven Gothic Tales*, classified it for us as Gothic (in her sense, as melancholy, fantastical, and Romantic in setting), I am happy to give it the benefit of the doubt, especially as it is so fascinating and so well written. I had also decided to exclude parodies, partly because so many Gothic tales are already half-way to sending themselves up; but in the time-honoured fashion of anthologists I have in the end broken my own rule in favour of Bret Harte's irresistible 'Selina Sedilia'. Although this collection has an international scope, with two stories from France and three from Latin America, it is dominated by writing from Britain, Ireland, and the United States; I would have preferred it otherwise, but it does seem that Gothic travels only with great difficulty across cultural borders. Within the constraints of the chronological arrangement, I hope to have found some acceptable balance between shorter and longer tales, between the subtle and the sensational, and between little-known pieces and old favourites. Some of the tales found in the first portion of the book reappear here for the first time since their original publication. Others in the later sections, such as Conan Doyle's 'Adventure of the Speckled Band' or Faulkner's 'A Rose for Emily', will have been seen before by many readers in different contexts, but may now appear to take on a changed complexion alongside their new neighbours in the many-windowed house of Gothic fiction.

I

Beginnings

ANNA LAETITIA AIKIN

Sir Bertrand: A Fragment

...After this adventure, Sir Bertrand turned his steed towards the north, hoping to cross these dreary moors before the curfew. But ere he had proceeded half his journey, he was bewildered by the different tracks, and not being able, as far as the eye could reach, to espy any object but the brown heath surrounding him, he was at length quite uncertain which way he should direct his course. Night overtook him in this situation. It was one of those nights when the moon gives a faint glimmering of light through the thick black clouds of a lowering sky. Now and then she suddenly emerged in full splendor from her veil; and then instantly retired behind it, having just served to give the forlorn Sir Bertrand a wide extended prospect over the desolate waste. Hope and native courage a while urged him to push forwards, but at length the increasing darkness and fatigue of body and mind overcame him; he dreaded moving from the ground he stood on, for fear of unknown pits and bogs, and alighting from his horse in despair, he threw himself on the ground. He had not long continued in that posture when the sullen toll of a distant bell struck his ears—he started up, and turning towards the sound discerned a dim twinkling light. Instantly he seized his horse's bridle, and with cautious steps advanced towards it. After a painful march he was stopt by a moated ditch surrounding the place from whence the light proceeded; and by a momentary glimpse of moon-light he had a full view of a large antique mansion, with turrets at the corners, and an ample porch in the centre. The injuries of time were strongly marked on every thing about it. The roof in various places was fallen in, the battlements were half demolished, and the windows broken and dismantled. A draw-bridge, with a ruinous gate-way at each end, led to the court before the building—He entered, and instantly the light, which proceeded from a window in one of the turrets, glided along and vanished; at the same moment the moon sunk beneath a black cloud, and the night was darker than ever. All was silent—Sir Bertrand fastened his steed under a shed, and approaching the house traversed its whole front with light and slow footsteps—All was still as death—He looked in at the lower windows, but could not distinguish a single object through the impenetrable gloom. After a short parley with himself, he entered the porch, and seizing a massy iron knocker at the gate, lifted it up, and hesitating, at length struck a loud stroke. The noise resounded through the whole mansion with hollow echoes. All was still again—He repeated the strokes more boldly and louder—another interval of silence ensued—A third time he knocked, and a third time all was still. He then fell back to some distance that he might discern whether any light could be seen in the whole front—It again appeared in the same place and quickly glided away as before—at the same instant a deep sullen toll sounded from the turret. Sir Bertrand's heart made a fearful stop—He was a while motionless; then terror impelled him to make some hasty steps towards his steed—but shame stopt his flight; and urged by honour, and a resistless desire of finishing the adventure, he returned to the porch; and working up his soul to a full readiness of resolution, he drew forth his sword with one hand, and with the other lifted up the latch of the gate. The heavy door, creaking upon its hinges, reluctantly yielded to his hand—he applied his shoulder to it and forced it open—he quitted it and stept forward—the door instantly shut with a thundering clap. Sir Bertrand's blood was chilled—he turned back to find the door, and it was long ere his trembling hands could seize it—but his utmost strength could not open it again. After several ineffectual attempts, he looked behind him, and beheld, across a hall, upon a large staircase, a pale bluish flame which cast a dismal gleam of light around. He again summoned forth his courage and advanced towards it—It retired. He came to the foot of the stairs, and after a moment's deliberation ascended. He went slowly up, the flame retiring before him, till he came to a wide gallery—The flame proceeded along it, and he followed in silent horror, treading lightly, for the echoes of his footsteps startled him. It led him to the foot of another staircase, and then vanished—At the same instant another toll sounded from the turret—Sir Bertrand felt it strike upon his heart. He was now in total darkness, and with his arms extended, began to ascend the second stair-case. A dead cold hand met his left hand and firmly grasped it, drawing him forcibly forwards—he endeavoured to disengage himself, but could not—he made a furious blow with his sword, and instantly a loud shriek pierced his ears, and the dead hand was left powerless in his—He dropt it, and rushed forwards with a desperate valour. The stairs were narrow and winding, and interrupted by frequent breaches, and loose fragments of stone. The stair-case grew narrower and narrower, and at length terminated in a low iron grate. Sir Bertrand pushed it open—it led to an intricate winding passage, just large enough to admit a person on his hands and knees. A faint glimmering of light served to show the nature of the place. Sir Bertrand entered—A deep hollow groan resounded from a distance through the vault—He went forwards, and proceeding beyond the first turning, he discerned the same blue flame which had before conducted him. He followed it. The vault, at length, suddenly opened into a lofty gallery, in the midst of which a figure appeared, compleatly armed, thrusting forwards the bloody stump of an arm, with a terrible frown and menacing gesture, and brandishing a sword in his hand. Sir Bertrand undauntedly sprung forwards; and aiming a fierce blow at the figure, it instantly vanished, letting fall a massy iron key. The flame now rested upon a pair of ample folding doors at the end of the gallery. Sir Bertrand went up to it, and applied the key to a brazen lock—with difficulty he turned the bolt—instantly the doors flew open, and discovered a large apartment, at the end of which was a coffin rested upon a bier, with a taper burning on each side of it. Along the room on both sides were gigantic statues of black marble, attired in the Moorish habit, and holding enormous sabres in their right hands. Each of them reared his arm, and advanced one leg forwards, as the knight entered; at the same moment the lid of the coffin flew open, and the bell tolled. The flame still glided forwards, and Sir Bertrand resolutely followed, till he arrived within six paces of the coffin. Suddenly, a lady in a shrowd and black veil rose up in it, and stretched out her arms towards him—at the same time the statues clashed their sabres and advanced. Sir Bertrand flew to the lady and clasped her in his arms—she threw up her veil and kissed his lips; and instantly the whole building shook as with an earthquake, and fell asunder with a horrible crash. Sir Bertrand was thrown into a sudden trance, and on recovering, found himself seated on a velvet sofa, in the most magnificent room he had ever seen, lighted with innumerable tapers, in lustres of pure crystal. A sumptuous banquet was set in the middle. The doors opening to soft music, a lady of incomparable beauty, attired with amazing splendor entered, surrounded by a troop of gay nymphs more fair than the Graces—She advanced to the knight, and falling on her knees thanked him as her deliverer. The nymphs placed a garland of laurel upon his head, and the lady led him by the hand to the banquet, and sat beside him. The nymphs placed themselves at the table, and a numerous train of servants entering, served up the feast; delicious music playing all the time. Sir Bertrand could not speak for

astonishment—he could only return their honours by courteous looks
and gestures. After the banquet was finished, all retired but the lady,
who leading back the knight to the sofa, addressed him in these
words: ---

RICHARD CUMBERLAND

The Poisoner of Montremos

A Portuguese gentleman, who I shall beg leave to describe no otherwise than by the name of Don Juan, was lately brought to trial for poisoning his half sister by the same father, after she was with child by him. This gentleman had for some years before his trial led a very solitary life at his castle in the neighbourhood of Montremos, a town on the road between Lisbon and Badajos, the frontier garrison of Spain. I was shown his castle, as I passed through that dismal country, about a mile distant from the road, in a bottom surrounded with cork trees, and never saw a more melancholy habitation. The circumstances which made against this gentleman were so strong, and the story was in such general circulation in the neighbourhood where he lived, that although he laid out the greatest part of a considerable income in acts of charity, nobody even entered his gates to thank him for his bounty, or solicit relief, except one poor father of the Geronzmiter convent in Montremos, who was his confessor, and acted as his almoner at discretion.

A charge of so black a nature, involving the crime of incest as well as murder, at length reached the ears of justice, and a commission was sent to Montremos to make enquiry into the case. The supposed criminal made no attempt to escape, but readily attended the summons of the commissioners.

Upon the trial it came out upon the confession of the prisoner, as well as from the deposition of witnesses, that Don Juan had lived from his infancy in the family of a rich merchant in Lisbon, who carried on a considerable trade and correspondence in the Brasils. Don Juan being allowed to take this merchant's name, it was generally supposed that he was his natural son, and a clandestine affair of love having been carried on between him and the merchant's daughter Josepha, who was an only child, she became pregnant, and a medicine being administered to her by the hands of Don Juan, she died in a few hours after, with all the symptoms of a person who had taken poison. The mother of the young lady survived her death but a few days, and the father threw himself into a convent of Mendicants,

7

making over by deed of gift the whole of his property to the supposed murderer.

In this account there seemed a strange obscurity of facts, for some made strongly to the crimination of Don Juan, and the last mentioned circumstance was of so contradictory a nature as to throw the whole into perplexity; and therefore to compel the prisoner to a farther elucidation of the case, it was thought proper to interrogate him by torture.

Whilst this was preparing, Don Juan, without betraying the least alarm upon what was going forward, told his judges he would save them and himself some trouble if they would receive his confession upon certain points to which he should truly speak, but beyond which all the tortures of the world could not force one syllable.

He said he was not the son, as was supposed, of the merchant, with whom he lived, nor allied to the deceased Josepha any otherwise than by the tenderest ties of mutual affection and a promise of marriage, which, however, he acknowledged had not been solemnized. That he was the son of a gentleman of considerable fortune in the Brasils, who left him an infant in the care of the merchant in question; that the merchant for reasons best known to himself chose to call him by his own name, and this being done in his infancy he was taught to believe that he was an orphan youth the son of a distant relation of the person who had adopted him; he begged his judges therefore to observe that he never understood Josepha to be his sister; that as to her being with child by him he acknowledged it, and prayed God forgiveness for an offence which it had been his intention to repair by marriage; that with respect to the medicine he certainly did give it to her with his own hands, for that she was sick in consequence of her pregnancy, and being afraid of creating alarm or suspicion in her parents, had required him to order certain drugs from an apothecary, as if for himself, which he accordingly did, and he verily believed they were faithfully mixed, inasmuch as he stood by the man while he prepared the medicine, and saw every ingredient separately put in.

The judges thereupon asked him if he would take it on his conscience to say the lady did not die by poison. Don Juan bursting into tears for the first time, answered, to his eternal sorrow, he knew she did die by poison. Was that poison contained in the medicine she took?—It was.—Did he impute the crime of mixing the poison in the medicine to the apothecary, or did he take it on himself?—Neither the apothecary nor himself was guilty.—Did the lady from a principle of shame (he was then asked) commit the act of suicide, and infuse the poison without his knowledge? He started into horror at the question, and took God to witness that she was innocent of the deed.

The judges seemed now confounded, and for a time abstained from any farther interrogatories, debating the matter amongst themselves by whispers, when one of them observed to the prisoner, that according to his confession he had said she did die by poison, and yet by the answers he had now given it should seem as if he meant to acquit every person on whom suspicion could possibly rest; there was, however, one interrogatory left, which, unnatural as it was, he would just put to him for form's sake only, before they proceeded to greater extremities, and that question involved the father or mother of the lady.—Did he mean to impute the horrid intention of murdering their child to the parents? No, replied the prisoner, in a firm tone of voice, I am certain no such intention ever entered the hearts of the unhappy parents, and I should be the worst of sinners if I imputed it to them. The judges upon this declared with one voice he was trifling with the court, and gave orders for the rack; they would, however, for the last time, demand of him, if he knew who it was that did poison Josepha, to which he answered, without hesitation, that he did know, but that no tortures should force him to declare it. As to life he was weary of it, and they might dispose of it as they saw fit.

They now took this peremptory recusant, and stripping him of his upper garments laid him on the rack; a surgeon was called in, who kept his fingers on his pulse, and the executioners were directed to begin their tortures; they had given him one severe stretch by ligatures fixed to his extremities, and passed over an axle which was turned by a windlass; the strain on his muscles and joints by the action of this infernal engine was dreadful, and nature spoke her sufferings by a horrid crash in every limb; the sweat started in large drops upon his face and bosom, yet the man was firm amid the agonies of the machine, not a groan escaped, and the head, who was superintendant of the hellish work, declared they might encrease his tortures upon the next tug, for that his pulse had not varied a stroke, nor abated of its strength in the smallest degree.

The tormentors had now begun a second operation with more violence than the former, which their devilish ingenuity had contrived to vary, so as to extort acuter pains from the application of the engine to parts that had not yet had a full share of the agony; when suddenly a monk rushed into the chamber and called out to the judges to desist from torturing that innocent man, and take the confession of the murderer from his own lips. Upon a signal from the judges, the executioner let go the engine at once, and the joints snapped audibly

9

into their sockets with the elasticity of a bow. Nature sunk under the revulsion, and Don Juan fainted on the rack. The monk immediately with a loud voice exclaimed, 'Inhuman wretches, delegates of hell, and agents of the devil, make ready your engine for the guilty, and take off your bloody hands from the innocent, for behold (and so saying he threw back his cowl) the father and the murderer of Josepha!'

The whole assembly started with astonishment; the judges stood aghast, and even the daemons of torture rolled their eye-balls on the monk with horror and dismay.

'If you are willing, says he to the judges, to receive my confession whilst your tormentors are preparing the rack for the vilest criminal ever stretched upon it, hear me. If not, set your engine to work without further enquiry, and glut your appetites with human agonies, which once in your lives you may now inflict with justice.'

Proceed, said the senior judge.

'That guiltless sufferer who now lies insensible before my eyes (said the monk) is the son of an excellent father, who was once my dearest friend. He was confided to my charge, being then an infant, and my friend followed his fortunes to our settlements in the Brasils. He resided there twenty years without visiting Portugal once in the time; he remitted to me many sums of money on his son's account; at this time a hellish thought arose in my mind, which the distress of my affairs, and a passion for extravagance inspired of converting the property of my charge to my own account. I imparted these suggestions to my unhappy wife, who is now at her accompt; let me do her justice to confess she withstood them firmly for a time; still fortune frowned upon me, and I was failing in my credit every hour; ruin stared me in the face, and nothing stood between me and immediate disgrace but this infamous expedient.

'At length persuasion, menaces, and the impending pressure of necessity conquered her virtue, and she acceded to the fraud. We agreed to adopt the infant as the orphan son of a relation of our name; I maintained a correspondence with his father by letters pretending to be written by the son, and I supported my family in a splendid extravagance by the assignments I received from the Brasils. At length the father of Don Juan died, and by will bequeathed his fortune to me in failure of his son and his heir. I had already advanced so far in guilt, that the temptation of this contingency met with no resistance in my mind, and I determined upon removing this bar to my ambition, and proposed to my wife to secure the prize which fortune had hung within our reach, by the assassination of the heir. She revolted from the idea with horror, and for some time her thoughts remained in so disturbed a state, that I did not think it prudent to renew the attack. After some time the agent of the deceased arrived in Lisbon, from the Brasils, and as he was privy to my correspondence, it became necessary for me to discover to Don Juan who he was, and also what fortune he was entitled to. In this crisis, threatened with shame and detection on one hand, and tempted by avarice, pride, and the devil on the other, I won over my reluctant wife to a participation of my crime, and we mixed that dose with poison which we believed was intended for Don Juan, but which in fact was destined for our only child. She took it, Heaven discharged its vengeance on our heads, and we saw our daughter expire in agonies before our eyes, with the bitter aggravation of a double murder, for the child was alive within her. Are there words in language to express our lamentations? Are there tortures even in the reach of your invention to compare with those we felt? Wonderful were the struggles of nature in the heart of our expiring child. She bewailed us, she consoled us, nay, she even forgave us. To Don Juan we made immediate confession of our guilt, and conjured him to inflict that punishment upon us which justice demanded, and our crimes deserved. It was in this dreadful moment that our daughter with her last breath, by the most solemn adjurations, exacted and obtained a promise from Don Juan not to expose her parents to a public execution by disclosing what had passed. Alas! alas! we see too plainly how he has kept his word. Behold he dies a martyr to honour! Your infernal tortures have destroyed him.'

No sooner had the monk pronounced these words in a loud and furious tone, than the wretched Don Juan drew a sigh; a second would have followed, but Heaven no longer could tolerate the agonies of innocence, and stopped his heart for ever.

The monk had fixed his eyes upon him, ghastly with horror, as he stretched out his mangled limbs at life's last gasp. 'Accursed monsters, (he exclaimed) may God requite his murder on your souls at the great day of judgement! His blood be on your heads ye ministers of darkness! For me, if heavenly vengeance is not yet appeased by my contrition, in the midst of flames my aggrieved soul will find some consolation in the thought, that you partake of its torments.'

Having uttered this in a voice scarce human, he plunged a knife to his heart, and whilst his blood spirted on the pavement, dropped dead upon the body of Don Juan, and expired without a groan.

ANONYMOUS

The Friar's Tale

In several convents situated among the mountains which divide France and Italy, a custom prevails that does honour to human nature: in these sequestered cloisters, which are often placed in the most uninhabited parts of the Alps, strangers and travellers are not only hospitably entertained, but a breed of dogs are trained to go in search of wanderers, and are every morning sent from the convent with an apparatus fastened to their collars, containing some refreshment, and a direction to travellers to follow the sagacious animal: many lives are by this means preserved in this wild romantic country. During my last visit to the south of France, I made a trip into this mountainous region, and at the convent of ——, where I was at first induced to prolong my stay by the majestic scenery of its environs; as that became familiar, I was still more forcibly detained by the amiable manners of the reverend father, who was at that time superior of that monastery. From him I received the following pathetic narrative, which I shall deliver, as nearly as I can recollect in his own words:

'About twenty years ago, (said the venerable old man) I was then in the fifty-seventh year of my age, and second of my priority over this house, a most singular event happened through the sagacity of one of these dogs, to which I became myself a witness. Not more than a dozen leagues from hence, there lived a wealthy gentleman, the father of Matilda, who was his only child, and whose history I am going to relate. In the same village lived also Albert, a youth possessed of all the world deems excellent in man, except one single article, which was the only object of regard in the eyes of Matilda's father. Albert, with a graceful person, cultivated mind, elegance of manners, and captivating sweetness of disposition, was poor in fortune; and Matilda's father was blind to every other consideration; blind to his daughter's real happiness, and a stranger to the soul-delighting sensation of raising worth and genius, depressed by poverty, to affluence and independence. Therefore, on Matilda's confession of unalterable attachment to her beloved Albert, the cruel father resolved to take advantage of the power which the laws here give a man, to dispose both of his daughter and his wealth at pleasure; the latter he resolved to bequeath to his nephew Conrad, and Matilda was sent to a neighbouring convent; where, after a year's probation, she was to be compelled to renounce both Albert and the world.

'Conrad, whose artful insinuations had long worked on the weak mind of this misguided father, was not content with having thus separated these lovers, but by inciting persecution from the petty creditors of Albert, drove him from his home; and after many fruitless endeavours to communicate with his lost mistress, he fled for sanctuary to this convent. Here (said the hoary monk) I became acquainted with the virtues of that excellent young man, for he was our guest about ten months.

'In all this time, Matilda passed her days in wretchedness and persecution. The abbess of the convent, sister Theresa, who, to the disgrace of her profession, and our holy church, disguised the disposition of a devil in the garment of a saint, became the friend and minister of Conrad's wicked purposes, and never ceased to persecute Matilda by false reports concerning Albert, urging her to turn her thoughts from him to that heavenly spouse to whom she was about to make an everlasting vow. Matilda scorned her artifice, and love for Albert resisted every effort of the abbess to shake her confidence in his fidelity.

'She was in the last week of her noviciate, when her father became dangerously ill, and desired once more to see her. Conrad used every endeavour to prevent it, but in vain; she was sent for; and the interview was only in the presence of Conrad and the nurse: but when the dying father perceived the altered countenance of his once-beloved child, his heart condemned him; he reflected that the wealth which he was going to quit for ever belonged to her, and not to Conrad, and he resolved to expiate his cruelty by cancelling the will, and consenting to the union of Albert and Matilda. Having made a solemn declaration of his purpose, he called for the will; then taking Matilda's hand in one of his, and presenting the fatal writing with the other, he said, "Forgive thy father!—Destroy this paper, and be happy; so be my sins forgiven in heaven!" The joy of his heart at this first effort of benevolence, was too much for his exhausted spirits, and he expired as he uttered the last words, letting fall the will which he was going to deliver.

'Matilda's gentle soul was torn with contending passions; she had lost her father at the moment when he had bestowed fresh life; and, in the contest betwixt joy and grief, she sunk on the lifeless corpse, in an agony of gratitude and filial tenderness.

'Meanwhile Conrad did not let slip this opportunity to compleat his plan, which, by the dying words of his uncle, had been so nearly defeated. He secured the will, and corrupted the nurse by promises and bribes never to reveal what she had witnessed; half persuading the interested, doating old woman, that it was only the effect of delirium in the deceased. This idea was but too well supported by the first question of Matilda, who exclaimed, as she came to herself, "Where am I?—sure 'tis a dream! my father could not say I should be happy; he could not bid me tear that fatal will!—Speak, am I really awake, or does my fancy mock me with such sounds?" The artful Conrad assured her that nothing of the kind had passed, telling her, that her father had only mentioned Albert's name to curse him; and, with his last breath, commanded her to take the veil at the expiration of the week. All this the perjured nurse confirmed; and then Matilda, being perfectly recovered, first saw the horrors of her situation. It was in vain for her to deny what they asserted, or remonstrate against their combined perfidy. She was presently, by force, conveyed to her nunnery, in a state of mind much easier to imagine than describe.

'Here she was more violently than ever attacked by Theresa's persecution, who urged, with increasing vehemence, the pretended positive commands of her dying father; and, by the advice of Conrad, used severities of conventual discipline, which almost deprived the devoted victim of her reason; still pleading that *religion* justified her conduct. Can it be wondered that such cruel treatment should, at length, disturb the piety and faith of poor Matilda; and induce her to exclaim, with presumptuous bitterness, against the institutions of our church, and brand the sacred ordinances of our religion with unjust suspicions?

'"Why," said she, "why are these massy gates permitted to exist; why are these hated walls, sad prisons of innocence and youth, where fraud and cruelty have power, and to torture and confine the helpless?—Religion is the plea; Religion which should bring peace, and not affliction to its votaries; then surely that religion which justifies these gloomy dungeons must be false, and I will abjure it; yes, I will fly to happier regions, where prisons are allotted only to the guilty; there no false vows are exacted, but Albert and Matilda may yet be happy."

'The possibility of an escape had never before presented itself, and, indeed, it could never have occurred but to one whose reason was disordered, for she well knew that the doors were secured by many bars and locks, and that the keys were always deposited beneath the pillow of the abbess.

'Her imagination was now too much heated to attend to any obstacles, and with a mixture of foresight, inspired by insanity, she packed up all her little ornaments of value, carelessly drew on her cloaths, and put in her pocket some bread and provision which had been left in her cell; then wrapping round her elegant form one of the blankets from the bed, she lighted a taper, and fearless walked towards the cloister door, idly expecting that it would fly open of its own accord to innocence like her's.—And now, methinks I see her with hair dishevelled, face pale and wan, her large black eyes wildly staring, and the whole of her ghastly figure, lighted by the feeble glimmer of her taper, majestically stalking through the gloomy-vaulted hall. Arrived at the great door, she found it partly open, and, scarcely believing what she saw, she quickly glided through it; but, as she passed, an iron bar, which she had not observed, and which projected at the height of her forehead, slightly grazed her temple; and though she scarcely felt the wound, yet it added new horrors to her look, by covering her ghostly face with streaks of blood.

'Although Matilda had never considered the improbability of passing this door, she now reflected with wonder how she had passed it, and fear of a discovery began to operate, as she, with more cautious steps, moved silently through the cloister, towards the outer gate; at which, when she approached, she heard Theresa's voice whispering these words: "Adieu! dear Conrad;—but remember that your life, as well as mine, depend on the secresy of our conduct." Then tenderly embracing each other, a man ran swiftly from her, and the abbess, turning round, stood motionless with horror at the bloody spectre firmly approaching. The guilty mind of Theresa could only suppose the horrid vision to be the departed spirit of one whom she thought her cruelties had murdered; and while the panic seized her whole frame, a gust of wind from the gate extinguishing the taper, Matilda seemed to vanish, as she resolutely pushed through the postern door still open.

'Theresa was too well hackneyed in the ways of vice to let fear long take possession of her prudence: the night was dark, and it would have been in vain to pursue the phantom, if her recovering courage had suggested it; she therefore resolved to fasten both the doors, and return in silence to her own apartment, waiting in all the perturbation of anxiety and guilt, till morning should explain this dreadful mystery.

'Meanwhile Matilda, conscious of her innocence, and rejoicing in her escape, pursued a wandering course through the unfrequented paths of this mountainous district, during three whole days and nights; partly supporting her fatigue by the provisions she had taken with her, but more from a degree of insanity, which gave her powers beyond her natural strength; yet in her distracted mind, this last instance of Theresa's wickedness, had excited a disgust and loathing, bordering on fury, against every religious or monastic institution.'

The monk had proceeded thus far, when he was called away to attend the duties of his convent, and promised to continue the narrative at his return.

*   *   *

The father soon returned, and proceeded with his narrative as follows:

'During the whole twelve months of Matilda's noviciate, no intercourse of any kind had passed betwixt her and Albert, who continued under the protection of this house, alike ignorant of her father's death, and of all the other transactions which I have now related: yet knowing that the term of her probation was about to expire, he resolved once more to attempt some means of gaining admittance to her convent. With this view he made a journey thither in the disguise of a peasant; and on the very morning on which his mistress had escaped, he presented himself at the gate.

'Conrad, who had, by letter from the abbess, been informed that her prisoner was fled, was desired to come immediately, and devise some excuse to the sisters for what had happened; for, although both to Conrad and Theresa the fact was evident enough, yet the sister nuns were distracted in conjectures: till, by one of those artful stretches of assurance which consummate villainy finds it easy to exert, Conrad recommended a plausible expedient.—And now *religion* (that constant comfort of the good, and powerful weapon of the wicked) presented itself as the only resource in this emergency. Theresa was taught to say, for the present, that she had no doubt the sinful reluctance of Matilda to receive the veil had excited the wrath of heaven; and that she was miraculously snatched away, or, perhaps, annihilated, to prevent the dreadful profanation of the holy ceremony at which she must that day have assisted.

'This plan had been settled, and Conrad was going, with all haste, in pursuit of the fugitive, when, at the outer gate, he met the pretended peasant.—The penetrating eye either of love or hatred soon discover a friend or enemy, however carefully disguised—Conrad and Albert knew each other—Instantly the flames of hatred, jealousy, and fury, kindled in their bosoms; and Conrad, seizing Albert by the throat, exclaimed, "I have caught the villain, the sacrilegious ravisher!" A severe struggle ensued, in which Conrad drew his sword; but Albert, who had no weapon, dexterously wrenched the instrument from the hand of Conrad, and plunged it in his bosom— The villain fell; while Albert fled with the utmost precipitation from the bloody scene, and returned in the evening to this convent.

'How shall I describe (said the good old monk) the contrast betwixt the looks of our unhappy youth at this moment, and on the preceding morning when he left us!—Then innocence, faintly enlightened by a gleam of hope, smiled in his features, as he chearfully bid us adieu, and said, "Perhaps I may again hear tidings of Matilda;—should the will of heaven deny me happiness with her, I will come back resigned, and dedicate my future life to holy meditation void of guilt."—But now, he returned breathless and pale, his hands besmeared with blood, his limbs trembling; he could only utter in faultering words, "Save me, reverend fathers! save me from justice, from myself, if possible!—Behold a murderer!"

'Some hours elapsed before we could collect from him the circumstances of a crime which had produced this extreme degree of horror and compunction in a mind so virtuous and innocent as that of Albert; and having heard the whole, in which he took all the blame to his own hasty conduct, we promised him protection; and endeavoured, though in vain, for two whole days to speak comfort to his troubled mind, and to inspire confidence in the boundless mercy of his God. On the third day, we were diverted from this arduous task by the return and behaviour of one of our dogs; the poor animal, who had been out all day, was restless, and shewed evident marks of a desire that we should accompany him to the relief of some poor wretch, who was unable to reach the convent.

'Father Jerome and I resolved to follow him; and we proceeded about half a mile, when we turned from the beaten track, guided by our dog, to a retired glen where human feet had hardly ever trod before. Here, on a rock which projected over a dreadful precipice, sat an unhappy, half-distracted object;—I need not tell you it was Matilda. She had crept, with wondrous difficulty, up a steep ascent to a ledge of rock which overhung a fearful chasm:—the very recollection of the place freezes my blood! When we first discovered her she was eagerly clinging to a branch of yew, which grew from a fissure in the rock above, and which half shaded her melancholy figure.

'The dog followed her steps; but Jerome and I, unable to ascend a

17

path so dangerous, stood, unobserved by her, at a little distance, on the opposite side of the glen.

'When Matilda first perceived the dog, she looked with wildness round her; then fixing her eyes with tenderness on the animal, she said, "Are you returned to me again?—and are you now my friend?—Fie! fie upon it! shall even dogs seduce the helpless!—Perhaps you repent of what you would have done.—You look piteously!—Poor brute! you know I followed you all the day long, and would have followed you for ever, but you led me to a detested convent!—thither Matilda will not go—Why should *you* lead me to a prison?—A dog cannot plead *religion* in excuse for treachery!"

'She paused; then taking a rosary of pearls from her side, she fantastically wound it about the dog's neck, saying, "I have a boon to ask, and thus I bribe you; these precious beads are your's: now guide me to the top of this high mountain, that I may look about me, and see all the world!—Then I shall know whether my Albert still be living—Ah no! it cannot be! for then Matilda would be happy! and that can never, never be!" She then burst into a flood of tears, which seemed to give her some relief.

'When I thought she was sufficiently composed, Jerome and I discovered ourselves. On this she shrieked, and hid her face; but, calling to her, I said, "Albert is still alive." She looked at us, till, by degrees, she had wildly examined us from head to foot; then turning to the dog, she seized him by the throat, and would have dashed him down the precipice, saying, "Ah, traitor! is it thus thou hast betrayed me?"—But the animal struggled and got from her. She then firmly looked at us, and cried, "Here I am safe, deceitful monsters! safe from the tyranny of your religious persecution; for if you approach one single step, I plunge into this yawning gulph, and so escape your power.—Ha! ha! ha!" Then, recovering from a frantic laugh, she said, "Yet tell me, did you not say that Albert lives? Oh! that such words had come from any lips but those of a false monk.—I know your arts; with *you* such falsehoods are religious frauds; this is a pious lie, to ensnare a poor helpless linnet to its cage: but I tell you, cunning priests! here I defy you; nor will I ever quit this rock, till Albert's voice assures me I may do it safely."

'You will easily imagine (continued the monk) the situation of Jerome and myself. Ignorant then of the manner in which Matilda had escaped, we could only know from her words and actions that it was she herself, and that her senses were impaired; perplexed how to entice her from this perilous retreat, and knowing that one false step would dash her headlong down the dreadful chasm that parted us, at length I said, "Gentle maid, be comforted; Albert and Matilda may yet be happy." Then leaving Jerome concealed among the bushes to watch the poor lunatic, I hastened to the convent to relate what I had seen.

'Meanwhile Matilda, looking with vacant stare around her, from time to time repeated my words, *"Albert and Matilda may yet be happy!"* then pausing, she seemed delighted with the sound re-echoed from the rocks, again repeating, *"Albert and Matilda may yet be happy!"* still varying the modulations of her voice, as joy, grief, doubt, despair, or hope alternately prevailed in her disordered mind.'

At this interesting period of the narrative, the venerable father was a second time called out, and promised to conclude his story when he returned.

*   *   *

I will not long detain you, resumed the reverend friar, with the effect my narrative had on the dejected Albert, how he at first exclaimed, 'Can there be comfort for a guilty wretch like Albert?' and eagerly ran towards the place; then moved more calmly on my representing how fatal might be surprise to one in so dangerous a situation; and, at length, shrinking back as he approached the spot, and turning to me, he said, 'Father, I will go no further! Heaven has ordained, as a punishment for the murder I have committed, that I should become a witness to the shocking death of the poor lost Matilda; at my approach, in frantic extacy, she will quit her hold, and perish before my sight.' I urged him to proceed, but it was in vain, he sat down on a bank, and was silently wrapt in an agony of irresolution, when he heard, at a little distance, the well known voice of the poor lunatic, still repeating my words, *'Albert and Matilda may yet be happy!'* Roused by the sound, he started up, and cautiously advancing, he exclaimed, 'Just heaven, fulfil those words, and let them indeed be happy!'

Matilda knew the voice, and carefully treading a path, which would have seemed impracticable to one possessed of reason, she descended from the ledge on which she sat, and approached with cautious steps; but at the sight of Albert, she flew impetuously forward, till, seeing me, she as suddenly ran back, and would have again retreated to the rock, shrieking, 'It is all illusion! priestcraft! it is no real Albert, and I am betrayed!' We pursued, and caught her; then finding my religious garb augmented the disorder of her mind, I withdrew, leaving only Albert to calm her needless fears.

But no persuasion even from him could induce her to come within view of the convent gates; I provided, therefore, accommodations for her in the cottage of a labourer, at some little distance; where, for many days, her delirium continued, while a fever threatened a speedy dissolution. During this period, Albert was labouring under all the anxiety which his situation could inspire: the deed he had committed sat heavy on his soul, and he dared not hope for an event, which his own guilty thoughts reproached him with having not deserved.

At length the crisis of the fever shewed signs of a recovery, and now his joy was without bounds, even the blood of Conrad seemed a venial crime, and he triumphed in the anticipation of reward for all he had suffered: but this happiness was of short duration, for at that time I received a letter from the abbess Theresa, demanding back the fugitive, whose retreat she had discovered. This requisition I knew I must obey; and giving the letter to Albert, I was going to explain the necessity of my compliance, when he burst out in bitter execrations against this and all religious houses; cursing their establishment as a violation of the first law of nature, which commands an intercourse between the sexes.

Having heard with a mixture of patience, pity, and resentment, all that his rage or disappointment could suggest, I answered nearly in these words, beginning calmly, but by degrees assuming all the authority the case required: 'My son, blame not the pious institutions of our holy church, sanctified by the observance of many ages; nor impiously arraign the mysterious decrees of providence, which often produces good from evil. This sacred edifice has been consecrated like many others by our pious ancestors, for purposes honourable to heaven, and useful to mankind; these hospitable doors are ever open to distress; and the chief object of our care is to discover and relieve it. This holy mansion has long been an asylum against the oppression of human laws, which drove thee from thine home; and, but a few days since thou thyself blessed an institution which saved the wretched Matilda, perishing with madness. Nay, at this very moment, its mercy shelters from the hand of justice, a murderer! yet thy presumption dares deny its general use, from thine own sense of partial inconvenience, and execrates monastic institutions, because by a separation of the sexes, lewdness and sensuality are checked: but know, short sighted youth, that the world will not remain unpeopled, because a few of its members consecrate their lives to holy meditation; nor shall the human species become extinct, because Albert and Matilda cannot be united to propagate a race of infidels and murderers.' I stopped, for I perceived the gentle Albert was touched with my rebuke; and falling on his knees, he cried in the emphatic words of scripture, 'Father! I have sinned against heaven, and in thy sight.' 'It is enough, my son, I replied, and now I will compassionate your situation; I will do more, for though I cannot detain Matilda longer than till she is well enough to be removed; yet in that time (if heaven approve my endeavours) I may contribute to your happiness, by interceding with her father, and should I fail in the attempt, this roof, which thy hasty passion has profaned, shall yet be a refuge to thee from despair; and I will strive to raise thy thoughts above the trifling disappointments of a transitory world.'

I could not wait the reply of Albert, (said the prior) being at this time called out to welcome the arrival of a stranger, who they said was dangerously ill; and who proved to be no other than the wounded Conrad. He, in a few words, explained the motive of his visit, telling me, that immediately after the rencounter, dreading that awful presence in which no secret is concealed, and to which he apprehended he was summoned by his own sword in the injured hand of Albert, he had vowed, if heaven would grant him life, to repair the wrongs he had committed. He had already executed a deed, resigning all the fortune of her father in favour of Matilda; he had declared his guilty commerce with Theresa, that she might prevent, or suffer punishment; he had paid all the debts of Albert, and justified his character to the world; and finally, he had resolved to implore the prayers of myself, and the venerable fathers of this house, to make him worthy of becoming one of our holy order; that if he lived he might be useful; or if he died he might be happy.

The prior then concluded this interesting narrative, by saying, that Albert and Matilda were united, and are still blessed in each others virtues, improved by difficulties thus surmounted; that Theresa had too far profaned the laws of heaven to have any confidence in religion, and died by her own hands; but that Conrad recovered slowly from his wound, and, after living many years an honour to the order he professed, he died in peace: the faithful dog (he said) was the favourite companion of Albert and Matilda, who had begged him from the convent, and encouraged him to pursue his task of discovering travellers who had lost their way, but whom he now brought to the hospitable mansion of this virtuous pair.

He then briefly hinted arguments in favour of monastic institutions; yet liberally allowing that the religion of his country might in certain points be wrong, and knowing me to be a protestant, I suppose that he acknowledged more than I ought in justice to his candour to relate. For this reason I have purposely suppressed the name and situation of his convent; but I shall ever remember these words, with which he finished this discourse. 'True religion (said he) howsoever it may vary in outward ceremonies, or articles of faith, will always teach you to do good, to love and help each other; it will teach you that no sin, however secret, can long remain concealed; and that when the world and all its vanities have palled the sated appetite, you must seek refuge in conscious innocence, or a sincere repentance.'

'JUVENIS'

Raymond: A Fragment

Night had diffused her darkness o'er the earth, and the moon darted her pale rays on the murmuring rivulet, which twined its narrow road through the fertile meads that surrounded the humble cottage of the unhappy Raymond, who was pensively reclining on a bench at the door of his cot. The melodious harmony of the nightingale, which at intervals floated with dulcet sweetness on the evening air; the universal silence which prevailed, and seemed (if I may so say) 'to waft the soul to realms unknown' together with his own melancholy thoughts, inspired Raymond with a degree of enthusiasm which he had never before experienced. When the sweet notes of the night-bird echoed along the dreary expanse he caught the harmonious sound, and when it died away expectantly waited for a repetition. His thoughts roved to the remembrance of past felicity, when he was blessed with the company of his much lamented and adored wife. His fancy represented her seated by him as she was wont, and at that delusive moment he forgot his miseries, and thought himself again blessed with his beloved companion: but when the visionary image had disappeared, and awful reality presented herself to his view, he exclaimed, with a voice half-stifled by the agitation of his soul—

'And are those truly happy days never to be repeated? Is she lost to me for ever! Oh, let me not indulge the heart-piercing thought!' Then suddenly recollecting himself—'But what if she were to be restored to me—if I were once more to possess my lovely Miranda— and she to be bereft of that chastity, in the possession of which she was torn from me, tenfold unhappiness would be my portion! I should be miserable to eternity! The thought rends my very soul! Oh, God! why am I thus afflicted?' His agitated frame would not permit him to proceed, until after a short time, becoming more calm, he said, 'But what have I done? I have presumptuously questioned the great decree of Heaven, and thereby have justly merited its divine displeasure! Be calm; be calm, my soul! tear not my heart-strings thus with thy vague surmises; I *may*—Oh! the ecstatic thought adds fresh vigour to my nearly exhausted strength: it pours into my aching

23

heart the sweet balsam of comfort!—I may once more possess my loved Miranda: I may press her panting bosom to mine own, chaste and unpolluted. But, oh! the thought seems almost impossible!—Yet, hold! there is an almighty being above, to whom nothing is impossible, although it appears so to my weak eye of mortality. To him I commit myself, and to his decree I patiently bow.'

Thus said Raymond: after which he seemed to have gained an ascendancy over despair, and sunk into a profound thoughtfulness.

He had not continued thus long before the air became tremulous, and the dull aspect of the heavens seemed to portend an approaching storm; thick clouds were rapidly collecting, and grew fast upon the horizon. The nightingale, affrighted, fled for shelter within her leafy nest; and the owlet, with dismal note, commenced her nightly wailing. Raymond was still buried in thought, when a distant and faint shriek assailed his ears. He started up; and, laying his hand on his sword, rushed into an adjoining mead, in the direction from whence he imagined the sound proceeded. He had not gone far before it was repeated in a more heart-rending sound, and seemed to be uttered by a person at the verge of despair. It almost froze the soul of Raymond.

Not until that moment did he notice the dreadful aspect of the elements; and, however regardless of the awful scene which he foresaw must infallibly ensue, he proceeded with eager inquiry, in order, if possible, to give succour to the person distressed. The voice seemed to be that of a female, and this discovery roused a sensation within him which again prompted him to proceed.

The thunder now began awfully to murmur from a distance, and the lightning streaked with fire the prominent clouds which rolled terrifically over the head of Raymond. The sky was so overshadowed with black vapours and impenetrable mists that they obscured every object, except when at intervals the moon-beams, darting between a cavity in the clouds, gave Raymond a melancholy opportunity of beholding the dreary prospect before him. He found himself to be entangled in an unknown path, and knew not how to proceed. He stopped to consider what he should do; and, after some conflict between his regard for his safety and his humanity, he determined to make the best way he could back to his mournful cottage, rather than still further bewilder himself in an unknown place.

He was turning round, in order to prosecute his intention, when a vivid flash of lightning, succeeded by a dreadful clap of thunder, burst over the spot on which he was standing, and seemed to rend the firmament. He stood appalled; never had dread seized him in so powerful a degree before; and he had scarcely recovered from the shock it had occasioned, when another shriek, much louder than either of the former, assailed his ears. The sound seemed to issue from a spot not far distant. He knew not which track to pursue, and was bewildered in a place, the labyrinths of which he was totally unacquainted with. His senses were confounded; and he, a second time, questioned himself whether it would be more advisable to proceed or return. He felt a peculiar *something* throb within his breast prompting him to the former: it was not merely a common sensation which he now experienced; a sensation which must naturally arise from the desire of dispensing succour to the unhappy; but a something, he knew not what, blended with that which rendered all return impracticable. He felt as if his own happiness were implicated with the present adventure; and, scarcely had he determined to proceed, when he perceived a light burst from a place at no great distance. He had not the least doubt but that the dreadful shrieks he had heard must have proceeded from thence. He grasped his sword, ejaculated a prayer to the director of all events, and rushed with alacrity to the place whence the light issued. The rain now poured from the swoln clouds with tremendous fury, and the hoarse thunder resounded reiteratedly along the perturbed vault of heaven. Raymond, undaunted by the rage of the storm, rushed on, totally occupied with the hope of giving his feeble aid to the piteous mourner.

It was not long ere his twinkling guide conducted him to the front of an ancient tower, whose walls were tottering under the decay of time. The light remained visible at the broken casement from whence he first observed it, and he traversed around the moss-covered walls in order to find an entrance. It was not long before he perceived one, to his great joy, open. As he was about to enter, a loud peal of thunder shook the hoary pile to its foundation; and he, ejaculating another prayer to Heaven, entered with a firm step the massy portal. He proceeded along a dark passage, which conveyed him into a spacious court-yard. The aspect of the place, although greatly decayed, still retained its native grandeur.

Whilst Raymond stood musing on the extraordinary adventure, which had drawn him thus far from his home, he perceived another light issue from a small casement, and almost instantly disappear. A violent crash now broke upon the prevailing silence, and seemed to convulse the earth. The sound indicated it to be the falling of armour. The dread it occasioned in the mind of Raymond can better be conceived than described: however, his ruffled spirit soon overcame the shock; and, by the assistance of a sudden flash of lightning, he perceived a small door situated at the extremity of the place in which he was. This was an entrance into the small turret from whence the light had before appeared and vanished. He advanced firmly towards it, and found it fast; but, on applying his strength, it flew open, and its harsh creaking hinges gave a doleful jar. He now found himself at the foot of a mouldering stair-case, and was ascending it when he distinctly heard foot-steps from above, and, almost instantly afterwards, two successive shrieks resounded through the tottering edifice. The sound, thrilling as it was, added fresh vigour to the soul of Raymond, since it confirmed the object of his solicitude to be in the turret in which he was; and, quickening his pace up the crazy steps, he soon arrived at a landing-place.

The first object that presented itself, was an old suit of armour lying on the ground, which had evidently just fallen down and occasioned the sound just mentioned. Raymond approached it: but judge his horror, his astonishment, when he, assisted by the rays of a glimmering lamp, perceived it still to confine within its rusty frame the skeleton of a human being. The sight sickened him; he recoiled with disgust, and proceeded onwards, muttering a prayer for the soul of the poor departed mortal.

In a few moments he arrived in a large Gothic chamber, in which a dreary lamp was suspended from the ceiling. But upon his entrance into this gloomy chamber, a tremendous clap of thunder burst over the edifice, and appalled him. A secret impulse directed his attention to a small door at the further end of the room. He distinctly heard footsteps from within, and a faint voice exclaim, 'Oh, spare me! spare me!' which was succeeded by a deep and convulsive groan. He sprang towards the door, which being only a-jar permitted him to enter; but oh, what a dreadful spectacle presented itself to the astonished Raymond. He beheld a man, brandishing, exultingly, a dagger, reeking with blood, over the body of a female, who had fallen a victim to his barbarity. His savage triumph was not long lived; for Raymond soon gave him that reward he so justly deserved, and thus, revenging the death of the murdered female, sent his loaded soul to expiate his mortal crimes in the regions of eternal misery.

He now approached the corpse of the unfortunate fair. On beholding her distorted countenance, a sudden shivering seized him, his strength failed him; he tottered a few paces back, and fell senseless to the floor.—It was Miranda.

ANONYMOUS

The Parricide Punished

The following very singular adventure is related as a fact in La Nouvelle Bibliothèque de Société; *and is said to have happened in one of the provinces of France. It is related in a letter to a friend.*

The adventure which I am going to relate to you, my dear friend, is of so strange and dreadful a nature, that you are the only person to whom I must ever disclose the secret.

The nuptials of Mademoiselle de Vildac were celebrated yesterday; at which, as a neighbour, custom and good manners required my attendance. You are acquainted with M. de Vildac: he has a countenance which never pleased me; his eyes have often a wild and suspicious glare, a something which has given me disagreeable sensations for which I could no way account. I could not help observing yesterday, that, in the midst of joy and revelry, he partook not of pleasure: far from being penetrated with the happiness of his new son and daughter, the delight of others seemed to him a secret torment.

The feast was held at his ancient castle; and, when the hour of rest arrived, I was conducted to a chamber immediately under the Old Tower at the north end. I had just fallen into my first sleep, when I was awakened and alarmed by a heavy kind of noise over head. I listened, and heard very distinctly the foot-steps of some one slowly descending, and dragging chains that clanked upon the stairs. The noise approached, and presently my chamber door was opened; the clanking of the chains redoubled, and he who bore them went towards the chimney. There were a few embers half extinguished; these he scraped together, and said, in a sepulchral voice, 'Alas! how long it is since I have seen a fire.' I own, my friend, I was terrified: I seized my sword, looked between my curtains, and saw, by the glimmer of the embers, a withered old man, half naked, with a bald head, and a white beard. He put his trembling hands to the wood, which began to blaze, and soon afterwards turned towards the door by which he entered, fixed his eyes with horror upon the floor, as if he beheld something most horrible, and exclaimed with agony, 'God! God!'

My emotions caused my curtains to make a noise, and he turned affrighted. 'Who is there?' said he. 'Is there any one in that bed?'— 'Yes,' I replied; 'and who are you?' Contending passions would not for a while suffer him to speak; at length he answered, 'I am the most miserable of men. This, perhaps, is more than I ought to say: but it is so long, so many years, since I have seen or spoken to a human being, that I cannot resist. Fear nothing; come towards the fire; listen to my sorrows, and for a moment soften my sufferings.'

My fear gave place to pity; I sat down by him. My condescension and my feelings moved him; he took my hand, bathed it with tears, and said, 'Generous man! let me desire you first to satisfy my curiosity. Tell me why you lodge in this chamber, where no man has lodged before for so many years; and what mean the rejoicings I have heard? what extraordinary thing has happened to-day in the castle?'

When I had informed him of the marriage of Vildac's daughter, he lifted up his hands to heaven—'Has Vildac a daughter! and is she married! Almighty God grant she may be happy! grant she may never know guilt!' He paused for a moment: 'Learn who I am,' said he. 'You see, you speak to—the father of Vildac—the cruel Vildac! Yet, what right have I to complain?—Should I—should I call man or tiger cruel?'—'What!' exclaimed I with astonishment, 'is Vildac your son? Vildac! the monster! shut you from the sight of man! load you with chains! And lives there such a wretch?'

'Behold,' said he, 'the power, the detestable power of riches! The hard and pitiless heart of my unhappy son is impenetrable to every tender sentiment: impenetrable to love and friendship, he is also deaf to the cries of nature; and, to enjoy my lands, has hung these eating irons on me.

'He went one day to visit a neighbouring young nobleman, who had lately lost his father; him he saw encircled by his vassals, and occupied in receiving their homage and their rents: the sight made a shocking impression upon the imagination of Vildac, which had long been haunted with a strong desire to enjoy his future patrimony. I observed, at his return, a degree of thoughtfulness and gloom about him that was unusual. Five days afterwards I was seized during the night, carried off naked by three men masked, and lodged in this tower. I know not by what means Vildac spread the report of my death; but I guessed, by the tolling of the bells, and funeral dirges, more solemn than for inferior persons, they were performed for my interment. The idea was horrid; and I entreated most earnestly to speak, but for a moment, to my son, but in vain; those who brought me my food, no doubt, supposed me a criminal, condemned to perish in prison. It is now twenty years since I was first confined here. I perceived this morning that my door was not secured, and I waited till night to profit by the accident: yet I do not wish to escape; but the liberty of a few yards is much to a prisoner.'

'No,' cried I, 'you shall quit that dishonourable habitation. Heaven has destined me to be your deliverer, defender, support, and guide. Every body sleeps; now is the time; let us begone.'

'It must not be,' said he, after a moment's silence. 'Solitude has changed my ideas, and my principles. Happiness is but opinion. Now that I am enured to suffer, why should I fly from my fate? What is there for me to wish in this world? The die is thrown, and this tower must be my tomb!'

'Surely you dream!' answered I. 'Let us not lose time; the night is advanced: we shall presently have but a moment. Come!'

'I am affected,' replied he, 'but cannot profit by your kindness. Liberty has no charms for my small remains of life. Shall I dishonour my son; or which way has his daughter given me offence, to whom I was never known, by whom I was never seen? This sweet innocent sleeps happily in the arms of her husband, and shall I overwhelm her with infamy? Yet, might I but behold her! might I but lock her in these feeble arms, and bedew her bosom with my tears!—'Tis in vain! It cannot be! I never must look upon her!

'Adieu! Day begins to break, and we shall be surprised. I will return to my prison.'

'No,' said I, stopping him; 'I will not suffer that. Slavery has enfeebled your soul; I must inspire you with courage. Let us be gone; we will afterwards examine whether it be proper to make the matter public. My house, my friends, my fortune, are at your service. No one shall know who you are; and, since it is necessary, Vildac's crime shall be concealed. What do you fear?'

'Nothing! I am all gratitude. But, oh, no! it cannot be! here I must remain.'

'Well, act as you please; but if you refuse to fly with me, I will go immediately to the governor of the province, tell him who you are, and return, armed with his authority and his power, to wrest you from the barbarity of an inhuman child.'

'Beware what you do! abuse not my confidence. Leave me to perish.—You know me not. I am a monster! Day and the blessed sun would sicken at my sight. Infamous I am, and covered with guilt—guilt most horrible!—Turn your eyes upon that wall; behold these boards; sprinkled with blood, a father's blood;—murdered by his son; by me!—Ha! look! behold! do you not see him! he stretches

29

forth his bleeding arms! he begs for pity! the vital stream flows out! he falls! he groans! Oh horror! madness! despair!'

The miserable wretch fell convulsed with terror to the floor; and when fear and passion in part subsided, he durst not turn his guilty eyes towards me, where I stood transfixed with horror. As soon as he had the power, he approached the door—'Farewell,' said he, 'be innocent, if you would be happy! The wretch who so lately moved your pity, is now become detestable to you, as well as to himself: he goes unlamented to the dungeon, whence alive he shall never return!'

I had neither the power to speak or move. The castle was become a place most abominable; and I departed on the morning. I must leave the neighbourhood; I cannot bear the sight of Vildac, nor the remembrance of this night.—How, my friend, is it possible that humanity can produce wickedness so intolerable and unnatural!

ANONYMOUS

The Ruins of the Abbey of Fitz-Martin

The Abbey of Fitz-Martin had been once famous for its riches and grandeur, and, as a monastery, was dedicated to St Catherine; but the subsequent irregularity of its order, together with the despotic tyranny of one of its ancient lords, had stripped it by slow but sure degrees of all its former wealth and consequence; insomuch, that the haughty Baron had, under unjust pretences, demanded heavy contributions, to assist in carrying on the war between the first Edward and the nearly subdued Scots. His only excuse for such an open violation of ecclesiastic rights, was grounded on a discovery he pretended he had made, of one of the nuns having broken the sacred rules of her profession, by a disregard to her vows of vestal celibacy. The haughty Baron seized greedily this circumstance, as the means of succeeding in his ambitious designs, and determined to humble the pride and insolence of the superiors, since the land belonged originally to his ancestors, and was transmitted to himself with powers to exact homage and fee from the heads of the monastery for this only part of their dependance on laical jurisdiction. For this latter purpose, the Baron, as Lord Patron of the holy community, entered the abbey, and demanded from the superiors not only a large subsidy of money, but an acknowledgement of their obedience; and, to cover his injustice, pretended it was designed for the further prosecution of the Holy Wars.

The superiors proudly refused compliance, and, in angry tones, threatened an appeal to Rome, with a dreadful anathema on the head of the daring violator, if he persisted in his presumptions. But the Baron knew the surety of his proceedings, and, with a smile of malicious triumph, exposed his knowledge of the crimes of Sister St Anna, even relating at full his acquaintance with the proof of her lapse from that sacred vow, which for ever enjoined the community of a monastery to celibacy. The fathers of the order, when summoned to the council, heard the account with confusion and dismay, and entreated time to search into the truth of the Baron's assertions. The crafty Baron knew the advantage he had over them; and, to increase

31

their fears of the dreaded exposure, quitted the abbey, in haughty and forbidding silence, without deigning to answer their petitions.

The unhappy community of the once proud monastery of St Catherine, at length, harassed by their dread of an exposure, and the total loss of all their wealth, by multiplied and never ceasing demands, became dependant on its tyrannic Baron, who kept the monks in such entire and arbitrary subjection, that in the course of a very few years, the abbey became nearly quite forsaken by its once imperious masters; when, at length, the Baron having disclosed to the King the dissolute manners of the order, and supplying Edward also with a large sum of money, that Monarch unknowingly rewarded his treachery with the hereditary possession of the abbey, and all its tenures, revenues and riches.

The Baron, therefore, took undisputed possession of his new acquisition, which he soon transformed into a princely habitation. But tradition says, that its imperious master did not, though surrounded by the possession of a mine of wealth, enjoy that expected ease, and inward happiness, which the gratification of his lawless wishes led him to hope for. For he is reported ever after to have been subject to gloomy passions, and melancholy abstractions of mind, which often ended in vehement paroxisms of madness. An imperfectly handed tradition still existed, which related, that the spectre of St Anna, the unhappy instrument of his destruction to the monastery, had repeatedly appeared to the Baron, to warn him of his heinous offences, and even accuse him as the cause of her ruin, and subsequent punishment by death. Certain it is, that various reports and conjectures had arisen in the minds of the ignorant; some tending to involve the Baron in the guilt of being the unknown seducer of Anna, for the purpose of completing his avaricious designs. But the real truth of her destiny was totally involved in silence; as, soon after the Baron had exposed to the superiors his knowledge of her dereliction, she had suddenly disappeared from the community, nor was ever heard of after. Whatever was in reality her dreadful end is still unknown. But the Baron lived not long to enjoy the splendor of his ill-gained riches. He was heard to confess, that peace of mind was for ever banished from his heart; and, though lying on the downy couches of luxury, yet did he never after enjoy a calm undisturbed conscience. His death was the departure of guilty horror, and alarm for the future; and he quitted the world with curses and execrations on himself, leaving no child to inherit the abbey, which descended to his next heir; who, being every way unlike his uncle, refused to reside in a place that had been obtained by fraud and injustice. From this period the abbey, for near a century and a half, had acknowledged several lords, but was seldom honored, for any length of time, by the presence of its possessors, who were in general eager to shun a place, whose traditional history teemed with dark and mysterious records. The owners of the abbey were too superiorly gifted with Fortune's treasures, and the spectred traditions of St Anna kept them from ever approaching its decayed towers. Its lands, therefore, remaining untilled, soon added increase to the surrounding forests, and were suffered to become useless, and over-run with the luxuriance of uncultivated nature.

The last owner deceased, was a distant relation of the present inheritor, Sir Thomas Fitz-Martin, who was driven by severe misfortune, and the loss of a most amiable wife, to seek its long-deserted ruins, to hide himself and family from the dreadful consequences of an over-ruling fate which no human wisdom could avert, but in the hoped-for security of this long-forgotten retreat. Yet the suddenness of his journey, its long and fatiguing continuance, together with the gloomy, remote, and even terrific habitation he was speedily approaching, began to raise fears and doubts in the minds of the domestics, who shrunk back, declaring it impossible to venture into so terrific and ruinous a place. Sir Thomas had never but once seen it, and that many years since, and even shuddered as he again reviewed its dreary and frowning exterior, and half wished that his haste had not led him to chuse so desolate a place for his future abode. At that moment the carriage suddenly stopping, at some little distance from an open avenue that led immediately to the abbey, Owen demanded if he was to proceed further, or if his Honor had not better turn into another path, and seek the nearest way out of the dismal forest; 'for surely, my Lord will never think of entering yon frightful old ruin, which, I dare say, will fall, and crush us alive beneath its humble battlements: or perhaps we shall have to encounter a battle with an army of ghosts and hobgoblins, who will dispute our right of admission within their tottering territories.'

'Peace, I command you,' exclaimed Sir Thomas. 'I thought you, at least, possessed more courage, than to admit the impression of such idle fears as even your female companions would blush to express. The seat of my ancestors, though long deserted and now perhaps destitute of every comfort, has, I will vouch for it, nothing that can justly alarm or excite cowardice in the minds of my servants. If, however, yourself, or any of your companions, fear to enter with your lord the building he has chosen for his future abode, they have free permission to remain with the carriage till day-light, whilst I and my daughter will alone seek our admission within a mansion that hereafter shall become our chief residence.'

Sir Thomas, at length descending from the vehicle, walked, with cautious inspection, a considerable way beneath the walls, before he arrived at the heavy gates of entrance. They were, however, securely closed, and resisted his attempts to force them, with an obstinacy that surprised him. Calling loudly to his terror-stricken people, he commanded them, on their approach, to join their efforts with his; but the gates proved the strength of their interior holds, and none of the fastenings yielded to their attacks. Tired with this fruitless labour, yet wondering at the security with which they were barricaded, Sir Thomas paused once more, and in that interval the idea flashed on his mind, that the abbey might possibly be inhabited; though well he knew he had given no one permission to enter its precincts; and the traditional terrors of the place he thought were a sufficient guard against all unknown intruders. Yet it was not unlikely, that if it were indeed inhabited, it was become the dreadful haunt of banditti, to whom the lonely situation of the forest rendered it a very favorable concealment for the practice of their daring profession. For a moment this fearful supposition rendered Sir Thomas undecided, and he remained irresolute how to proceed, from the dread of exposing his family to more real dangers than the imaginary ones of Owen, till a violent flash of lightning ended his doubts; as it glanced in an instant on the walls of the abbey, and displayed its tottering turrets and broken casements. It shewed also, at no great distance, a small postern, whose weak state seemed to promise greater success; and they determined to try it if they could not here find a more willing admission. The postern was extremely old, and seemed only held by the bolt of the lock, which soon gave way to the attack of the travellers; and crossing beneath a heavy Gothic arch, they found themselves within the area of the first court. Sir Thomas, followed by his trembling attendants, was hastening forward, till recollecting the females in the carriage were left unguarded, he ordered one of the men to return instantly, and await with them the event of their lord's bold adventure to gain shelter within the ruin. Owen summoned up a sort of desperate courage, and declared his intention of attending his master: and lighting a torch, he followed his calm and undaunted conductor, who now advanced with caution through the wide area of a second court, which, being covered with crumbling fragments of the ruins, rendered his advances difficult, and even dangerous. At length he reached a flight of steps, that seemed to lead to the grand portal of entrance. Sir Thomas, however, determined to ascend; and Owen, though tottering beneath his own weight with terrors, dared not interpose his resistance: his trembling hand held the light to the great folding doors, and Sir Thomas, after some efforts, burst them open, and entered what appeared an immense hall, terminating in vistas of huge pillars, whose lofty heads, like the roof they supported, were impervious to the faint rays of the torch, and enveloped in an awful and misty gloom, beyond expression impressive and solemn, and creating astonishing sensations in the startled beholder.

At length Sir Thomas's progress was stopped by some steps, that led up to a Gothic door, which, with no little difficulty, he forced back, and entering its dark precincts, found himself within a large antique room, with the forms of several crumbling pieces of furniture, which, from the number of its raised couches, now covered with blackness, seemed evidently the remnants of a chamber that had once been stately and magnificent. Sir Thomas examined it well. The walls, though dripping with damp, seemed tolerably entire, and to promise security from the dangers of the night; and as he had as yet seen nothing to excite alarm or dread, he hastened to the carriage, and declared to its inmates his resolution. The females knowing that, as they had proceeded thus far, to retract from their fearful enterprise was now become impracticable, obeyed with trembling and reluctant steps, and, supported by their male companions, slowly advanced; whilst Sir Thomas, taking Rosaline in his arms, conveyed her to the abbey.

Owen and Rowland, who had, by the command of their master, cut down several branches from the forest, now set them alight within the wide spreading hearth, whose brisk and crackling blaze soon dispelled the damp and glooms of a dreary chamber, and at length compelled even the long-stretched countenances of the females to relax into something like a smile; and the remembered fatigue and danger of their perilous journey through the forest, when compared with their present shelter, and the comforts of a welcome and plentiful meal, succeeded at last in making a very visible alteration. The repast being ended, Sir Thomas commanded Owen to place before the fire some of the strongest couches he could find, and cover them with packages, and compose themselves to rest. The servants, who had dreaded the thoughts of being obliged to pass the night in the chamber, were grateful for this considerate permission; and reclining themselves on the couches, they soon forgot the terrors and dangers they had felt, and became alike insensible to their forlorn situation, and to the storm which howled without, and now shook the trembling fabric, with each fresh gust of wind that assailed its ruined towers.

Sir Thomas was the first of the slumbering travellers that awoke.

Convinced that it was day, from a ray of light that shone through a broken window shutter, he hastened to arise; for, since he was assured he should sleep no more, he resolved not to disturb his wearied domestics, but use the present interval to search the abbey. He proceeded to a large folding door on the west side, which he concluded must have been the grand entrance; but he declined, for the present, any further examination of the outside of the building; and turning to the left, advanced to a folding door, deeply fixed within a Gothic portal, which opening harshly to his efforts, let him, with astonishment, into a long suit of rooms, which, notwithstanding their silent, deserted, ruinous state, he was rejoiced to find might again be rendered habitable, and in a little time even convenient and comfortable.

They were eight in number, and still retained many remnants of furniture, which, though covered with mildew and dust, and crumbling to tatters, evidently witnessed the splendor of its former owner. He was satisfied that these chambers would amply answer his present wants, and rejoiced to find them in such a state as to make their repair not only possible but easy.

Proceeding forward through this vast extent of chambers, Sir Thomas felt that every former surmise of robbers was at an end, as he had as yet met with not a single circumstance that could in any degree confirm it. He was now hastening back to his family, who, should they have awoke, might experience no inconsiderable alarm.

Having descended for this purpose, he found himself, as he turned on the left, in a long but narrow gallery or passage; passing forward, he opened with much labor several old doors, in hopes they would bring him into a passage leading into the great hall or church; but they only presented a number of weak and dangerous recesses, perhaps formerly cells of the monastery, whose flooring was so much decayed, and in some places fallen in, as to render further progress impossible. Quitting the fruitless search, he proceeded to the extreme end, where he met with a stronger door, which occasioned him no small manual exercise to unclose, when, to his surprise, a violent scream rung upon his ears; and, as he threw open the arched door, he beheld his terrified party, who, awaked by the noise of his forcing of the portal, had rushed into the arms of the men, to whom they clung, shrieking for protection against nothing less than a legion of armed spectres, whom their affrighted fancies had in an instant conjured from their graves.

'I have,' said Sir Thomas, 'explored the chief apartments of the abbey, and rejoice to find them every way beyond my expectations.

Workmen, and other necessary persons shall be instantly engaged for the repair of this ancient and long-neglected mansion, which, as I mean to make it perfectly habitable, I have now only to assure all present, that the seat of my family has nothing to excite just terror, or encourage misconceptions relating to beings that never had existence.'

As soon as their small repast was ended, Sir Thomas desired Owen to take one of the horses, and find the nearest way to the next town; for a supply of food was become necessary. Sir Thomas went, followed by Owen, round the southern angle of the abbey, where they had a full view of a portal more ruinous than the one they had quitted, and which presented a long and dreary continuation of those parts of the building once dedicated to conventual occupation, and were now crumbling into dust. 'Now,' said Sir Thomas, 'mount your horse, and proceed down yonder avenue, which will conduct you to the next town; and likewise inquire for one Norman Clare, who was steward to these estates; explain to him my present situation, and that I require his attendance; and give him full commission to engage such workmen as shall be needful for the full repair.'

Owen immediately obeyed; and lashing his steed into a fast trot, soon arrived within sight of a poor but neat-looking cottage, with a venerable looking old man sitting beneath a spreading oak, who had seen the intruder as he gallopped out of the forest, with surprise strongly marked in his face. 'Pray,' said Owen, as he rode up to the cottage, 'can you inform me if there be one Norman Clare living in this neighbourhood?'

The old man started back with increased surprise, exclaiming, 'And pray what is thy business with Norman Clare?' The simple-hearted Owen entered into a full detail of his mission, adding, 'if such a person as Norman was alive, his master, Sir Thomas, Lord of Fitz-Martin's abbey and lands, demanded his assistance at the above named mansion.'

'If thou requirest to be acquainted with him, thou shalt not further waste thy labor; for truly I am Norman Clare; and since I find thou art real flesh and blood, thou shalt enter with me my lonely dwelling, and welcome shalt thou be to share its homely fare.' Owen alighted joyfully from his panting steed, and entered with his host the well-arranged cottage. 'Here, good dame!' exclaimed Norman to his aged partner, 'I have brought you a stranger, who, coming from the old abbey yonder, must needs lack something to cheer his spirits.'

Owen then entered at large upon the whole of his late journey, and its termination at the abbey. 'What!' cried Blanche, 'lie in such a

37

place as the haunted abbey! Mercy on us! friend, does your master know that it has not been inhabited for more than an hundred years; and does he not know, that it is all over so full of goblins and spectres, that nobody will ever set a foot near it? And, moreover, the ghost of Anna is seen every night, walking down the great long aisles of the church up to the altar, where it kneels till the clock strikes twelve, when it goes out of the great doors, which fly open at its approach, and walks to the great south tower, where it utters three loud shrieks; when the old wicked Baron's ghost is forced to come, as soon as these are heard; and Anna drives him with a fire-brand in one hand, and a dead child in the other, all over the ruins, till they come to the chamber where the Baron used to sleep after he treacherously got possession of the abbey. Dismal yells, and dying groans, are then heard to echo through all the apartments, and blazing lights thrown about the great north bed-chamber, till the great turret clock, that has never for many a weary long year been touched by mortal hands, tolls heavily two, and sometimes three strokes upon the bell.'

'Nonsense, nonsense,' interrupted Norman, with a wink, meant to silence the loquacity of Blanche, 'you see all these idle terrors are done away. Did not Sir Thomas and his family sleep there last night, and is not Mr Owen here alive to tell us so?' Poor Owen, a coward at heart, sat trembling every joint as he listened to the extravagances of Blanche, and gave implicit belief to all the wild incoherences she uttered. At length, Owen, aided by a flaggon of ale, which inspired him with something like resolution, once more braved the terrific dangers of the abbey, and mounting his horse, (well stored with many comforts provided by Norman,) he gallopped down the avenue leading towards the abbey.

The next day, Norman, followed by a parcel of workmen, brought with him all his paper accounts, and monies, the produce of the rents, which he had faithfully hoarded up for the lord of the demesne whenever he thought proper to claim it.

One half of the range of the west front in a month's time was rendered perfectly safe; and having undergone a complete repair, the apartments soon began to lose much of their desolate and forlorn appearance. Three chambers were fitted up for the future residence of the steward; but it was a work of long entreaty before Sir Thomas could prevail on the venerable old Norman to take possession of them.

The lovely Rosaline (the Baron's only daughter) had at this period arrived at the age of sixteen, and having no society, but the inmates of the abbey, nor accustomed to any other, would dispense with the forms of rank, and, seating herself by the brisk wood fire that blazed on the hearth, listen attentively to the talkative Blanche's terrible narratives of spectres and supernatural appearances.

Rosaline would, at times, anxiously attend to these dreadful stories; as the tales of Blanche were generally terrific in the extreme, and always finished with the history of the Baron and the nun; who, she affirmed, still haunted the ruins of the abbey. The story of Sister Anna had made a deep impression on her memory; and having often wished for a clear and true account of what was the end of the unfortunate nun, had determined to search among the ruins, in hopes that some discoveries might be made, that would lead to a development of her death. But as this enterprise could not so well be performed alone, she made Jannette her confidant, who readily promised obedience.

As they proceeded from the abbey, Rosaline failed not to examine every nook and corner that crossed her way. Sometimes she ventured up the broken steps of a broken tower, whose lofty battlements no longer reared their proud heads, that lay extended in the area. She ascended the first story, and through the heavy arch had a full view of the south tower. Rosaline bade Jannette observe it, and asked if she had courage to enter it.—'Indeed, my lady,' she replied, 'I never behold that tower, but it makes me tremble. It was there, they say, that poor Anna was confined; and I dare hardly look at it. Besides, my lady, you see it is more ruinous than this; nor is it safe to be approached. Surely, Madam, you do not mean to make the trial?'

'If, as you say, that was the prison of poor Anna, it is there only I may hope to find some documents relative to her fate. I am, therefore, resolved to proceed. But for you, Jannette, stay where you are: I shall not require a further attendance than your remaining within hearing.'

Rosaline descended the broken steps, and proceeded towards the tower, whilst Jannette, not daring to advance, stood trembling, entreating her young lady to forego her dangerous enterprise: but Rosaline having as yet found nothing to gratify her search, resolved not to yield to the light fears of Jannette: she therefore proceeded, and arrived at the full sight of the south tower: its black and frowning aspect, together with its weak, tottering situation, at first aroused a momentary feeling of terror; but youthful hope encouraged her to venture, and she approached the old Gothic door, which gave her a sight of an iron grating that was fixed in the wall.

To the left she beheld a flight of stairs that led to the upper stories;

but these were too weak to admit her ascent in safety to the top; she therefore gave over the design, and turned again to the iron grating. As she caught the first view of the alarming objects within, her mind, unprepared for the sudden shock, endured a momentary suspension, and she fell, nearly fainting, against the wall. The power of calling for aid was gone, and, for a few seconds, she was unable to support herself.

The terrific spectacle that had so powerfully affected Rosaline, as she caught a view of the interior of this forlorn ruin, was a deep narrow cell, whose walls were hung with mouldering trappings of black. The only light that was admitted within, proceeded from an iron grate fixed in the amazing thickness of the wall. Around this gloomy place were fixed, in all directions, the horrific emblems of death; and which ever way the desolate inhabitant of this dreary cell turned, images of horror, shocking to nature, met the tortured view, in the terrific state and eyeless sockets of the ghastly skull bones that hung in grim appalling array. In the middle of the cell, upon a raised pedestal, stood the mouldering relics of a coffin, which had been once covered with a velvet pall, but which now hung in tatters down its sides. At one corner was a small hillock, that appeared the sad resting place of the distracted penitent; for that this was the severe prison of penance and contrition, every superstitious emblem of monkish torture that surrounded the walls plainly bore testimony of. A crucifix, and broken hour-glass, still remained, covered with dust, upon a small altar, beneath an arched recess; whilst the floor was strewed with skulls and human bones.

After the first momentary shock had subsided, Rosaline arose, and stood irresolute to proceed in researches. Her alarms were strong, but her curiosity was, if possible, stronger. She felt she should never be able voluntarily again to enter this tremendous place; and she debated whether her courage would support her, should she pursue further the daring adventure. 'Perhaps,' said she, 'this was, indeed, the final end of the unhappy sister. Alas! poor unfortunate, this too, surely was alike your prison, and the cause of your lingering death. Yet wherefore am I thus anxious to solve the mystery of her death? Dare I lift the pall from that horrific spectacle? What if my spirits fail me, and I sink, overcome with dread, in this charnel house of death. May not my senses forsake me in the trial? or is it not very likely that terror may bereave me of my reason?—Shall I enter?'

Either her senses were indeed confused, or perhaps her mind, wrought to a certain pitch, led her to fancy more than reality; for, as the last word dropped from her lips, she started, and thought she heard it feebly repeated by an unknown voice, which slowly pronounced, 'Enter!'

Rosaline trembled, and not exactly aware of her intentions, unfastened the grate, and threw back the rattling chains that were hooked on the staples without the cell. The grate opened with ease, and swung on its hinges with little or no resistance; and Rosaline, with an imagination distempered, and misled by the hopes of discovering something she came in search of, that would repay her fears, descended the indented declivity, and with trembling steps staggered two or three paces from the grating; but again became irresolute, and terrified from her purpose, she stopped. 'Dare I,' she faintly ejaculated, 'dare I raise the mysterious lid of that horrific coffin?'

'Dare to do so!' replied a voice, that sounded hollow along the dreaded vault; and Rosaline, whose terror now had suspended the faculty of feeling, though not of life, actually moved towards the coffin, as if performing some dreadful rite, that she found she had not a power to resist. Impelled with a notion of that superior agency which she dared not disobey, and not exactly sensible of what she did, she fearfully cast aside the lid, which, as she touched, fell crumbling to the ground; and turning aside her head, her hand fell within the coffin; and in her fright she grasped something moist and clammy, which she brought away. Shrieking wildly, she rushed from the scene of terror, and precipitating herself through the tower-gate, fell fainting into the arms of Jannette; who, pale and terrified, called aloud for help, as she supported her insensible lady. Norman, who had long been impatient at the stay of his mistress, and alarmed for her safety, was hastening down the ruins, when the cries of Jannette assailed his ears, and had arrived at the scene of terror as Rosaline began to open her eyes.

'Holy Virgin protect the lady,' he exclaimed. 'Hast thou seen any thing? or do these pale looks proceed from some fall which may have bruised thy tender form among the ruins?'

'Oh no, good Norman, not so,' feebly and wildly ejaculated Rosaline. 'The tower! the dreadful tower!' 'The tower! sayst thou, my lady? Mercy on me! Have you been so hardy as to venture into that dismal place!'

Rosaline, as she gradually recovered, felt a perfect recollection of the late horrid scene, and recalling the awful voice she had heard, which she doubted not proceeded from some supernatural agency, she no sooner beheld Norman, than she darted towards her chamber, regardless of the terrors of the old steward or Jannette.

As soon as she entered her room, she drew from the folds of her

ANONYMOUS

robe the relics she had unknowingly grasped from the coffin. On examination, it seemed to be some folded papers; but in so decayed a condition, that they threatened to drop in pieces with the touch.

She carefully unfolded the parcel, and found it to contain the story of the unfortunate Anna; but many of the lines were totally extinct, and only here and there a few that could be distinguished. At length, in another packet she discovered a more perfect copy of the preceding ones, which, from the style of its writing, evidently proved them to be the labor of some of the monks, who had, from the papers discovered in the cell of her confinement, been enabled to trace the truth of her melancholy story and sufferings, in which the Baron was but too principally concerned.

Rosaline, retrimming her lamp, and seating herself nearer the table, took up the monk's copy, and began, not without difficulty, to read the melancholy story of

The Bleeding Nun of St Catherine's.

It was in the reign of Edward the First, that, in an old dilapidated mansion, lived the poor but proud Sir Emanfred, descended of an illustrious house, whose noble progenitors had with the Conqueror settled in England, upon the establishment of their royal master.

In the two succeeding centuries, however, great changes had taken place, and many events had reduced the once powerful and splendid ancestors of Sir Emanfred to little more than a military dependance. The proud nature of the Knight shrunk from the consequences of the total ruin of his house; and, indignant at the disgraceful and humiliating change of his circumstances, he hastily quitted the gay triumphs of the British court, because his fallen fortunes and wasted patrimony no longer enabled him to vie, in the splendor of his appearance and expenditure, with the rest of the nobles of the kingdom. In the gloomy shades of his forsaken mansion, he buried himself from all the joys of social intercourse: nor was his melancholy habitation ever after disturbed by the sounds of festive cheerfulness, or the smile of contentment. Morose in temper from his disappointments of fortune, and too proud to stoop to such honorable recourses, as might have in time procured for him the re-establishment of his decayed house, he disdained all pecuniary acquirements, and determined to build his hope of future greatness on an alliance of his only child with the splendid and noble lord of Osmand. But the lovely Anna, brought up in total seclusion, and unacquainted with the manners of the world, happily free from the ambitious and haughty passions of her stern sire, had unconsciously rendered obedience to his commands impossible, and shrunk in horror from the dreaded proposal of an union with Lord Osmand; for, alas! she had not a heart to bestow, nor a hand to give away. Anna, the beautiful and enchanting Anna, whose years scarce numbered seventeen, had known the exquisite pain and pleasures of a secret love; and, in the simple innocence of an unsuspecting mind, had given her heart, her soul, her all to a——*Stranger*.

Anna had never known a mother's tenderness, nor experienced a father's sheltering protection; the artless dictates of her too susceptible heart were her only guides and monitors; and, during the long absence of her sire, her soul first felt the pleasing emotions of love for an unknown but graceful Stranger, whom she had first beheld in the shades of a melancholy but romantic wood, that adjoined equally her father's domain, and the vast forest of St Catherine's monastery, where she had often been accustomed to roam, and where she had first met the fascinating Vortimer, who but too soon betrayed the unconscious maid into a confession that his fervent love was not displeasing, and that to him, and him only, she had resigned her heart, beyond even a wish for its recall. The mind of Anna was incapable of restraining the soft thrilling ecstasies of a first infant passion. The Stranger urged his suit with all the melting, all the prevailing, eloquence of an enraptured lover, and all the outward blandishments of feeling and sincerity. Unacquainted with the world's deceits, poor Anna listened to his fervent vows with downcast, blushing timidity, and pleased acceptance. Each secret meeting more firmly linked her chains: her very soul was devoted to the Stranger, whom, as yet, she knew not by any other title than the simple name of Vortimer. In a moment fatally destructive to her repose, when love had blinded reason, and the artless character of Anna but too successfully aided the purposes of the Stranger, he obtained not only complete possession of her affections, but of her person also.

At midnight, in the ruined chapel of Sir Emanfred's gloomy edifice, the Stranger had prevailed on the innocent Anna to meet him, and ratify his wishes. A monk of a distant convent waited in the chapel; and the inauspicious nuptials were performed; and Anna became a bride, without knowing by what title she must in future call herself.

Scarcely had three months of happiness and love passed over her head, when a storm, dreadful and unexpected, threatened for ever to annihilate the bright prospect of felicity.

The sudden arrival of a hasty messenger from the Knight alarmed the trembling Anna; and scarce had she perused the purport of his arrival, than with a faint shriek, and a stifled cry of agony, she fell to the ground, as she feebly exclaimed, 'Lost, undone, and wretched Anna! destruction and death await thee!'

The Stranger read the fatal paper that contained the harsh mandate of his Anna's father: his brow became contracted, and his countenance overcast with apparent gloom and sorrow, as he perused the unwelcome information of the Knight's arrival, on the morrow, at his castle, to celebrate the nuptials of his daughter with the lord of Osmand, who accompanied him. For a time a gloomy silence pervaded his lips; and Anna vainly cast her tearful, imploring eyes to him for succour and protection. At length, starting from a deep reverie, he caught her in his arms, as she was sinking to the ground, and kissing her cold and quivering lips, bade her take comfort, and abide with patience the arrival of her sire; adding, that in three weeks he would return, and openly claim her as his wife; when the mystery that had so long enveloped his name and title in secrecy should be unravelled, and his adored Anna be restored to affluence and splendor. Again embracing her, he hurried precipitately from the place; and Anna— the ruined hapless Anna—never saw him more—****

Here many lines became defaced, as the ink had rotted through the vellum, and all traces of writing were totally lost in mildew and obscurity. At length she was able to continue as follows:

Ferocious rage filled the soul of the Knight, and darkened his features, as prostrate at his feet lay, overwhelmed in grief and tears, the imploring Anna. 'Spare me!' she cried, 'Oh, sire! spare your wretched child—she cannot marry the lord of Osmand!'

Fury flashed in the eyes of the stern Sir Emanfred, on hearing these words of his daughter. At length the burst of rage found vent, he seized the arm of the trembling Anna, and placing her hand forcibly in that of Sir Osmand's, commanded her to prepare herself, in three days, to become his bride, or meet the curses of an angry father, and be driven from his sight for ever.

Driven to despair, and now vainly calling on the mysterious Stranger to shield her from the direful fate that awaited her, or the still more dreadful vengeance of her unrelenting father, the hapless Anna wildly flew to the gloomy wood, in the forlorn hope that there, once more, she might behold the lord of all her love and fondest wishes. In three weeks he had promised to reclaim her; but, alas! they had already expired, and no Stranger had appeared. The fourth week of his absence came: it passed away, but he came not; and now but three days remained between her and her hateful nuptials. Wildly she wandered through the gloomy wood, and vainly cast her eyes in hopeless anguish on all around her: no Stranger met her sight: he came not to rescue his forlorn bride from the rude grasp of impending misery and destruction. Night came on; the hours passed away unheeded, yet still she quitted not the solemn shades of the dreary grove. The bell of midnight sounded; she started at the melancholy toll, and fear and awe possessed her sickening fancy. She hurried through the wood, and reached in silence her chamber; but sleep visited not the wretched Anna.

Again, as the hour of suffering drew still nigher, she threw herself in supplication before the gloomy Knight, and besought him to spare her but one week longer, ere he linked her to misery and woe; hoping by this delay to procure time for the Stranger, and give him yet another chance, ere it was too late, to save her, and claim his affianced bride. But, inexorably bent on the union of his child with Lord Osmand, the Knight, in anger, cast her from his knees, and threatened to overwhelm her with his most tremendous curses, if she did not meet Lord Osmand at the altar before the sixth hour of the early morrow had chimed upon the bell.

Poor Anna shrunk from the angry glances of the enraged Knight; despair and anguish seized her soul. The Stranger never came; he had forgotten his solemn vows, neglected his promise, and abandoned her to her fate. Whither could she fly? How was she to avoid the choice of miseries that equally pursued her? Either she must perjure her soul to false oaths, or meet the dreadful alternative of a parent's dire malediction.—Oh! whither, lost and wretched Anna! canst thou fly! Upon the pillow of her tear-bedewed couch she vainly laid her head, to seek a momentary oblivion of her sorrow in repose. Something lay upon her pillow—It was a paper curiously folded.— With fearful, trembling expectation she hastily opened the envelope, and read, 'The Stranger guards his love; and though unseen, and yet forbidden, to reclaim his lovely bride, now watches over her safety, and awaits the precious moment when he shall hasten on the wings of love to restore his Anna to happiness and liberty. If then she would preserve herself for her unknown friend, let her instantly fly to the monastery of St Catherine's, where she may remain in security till demanded by her adoring

VORTIMER.'

The unhappy maid perused the fatal lines with unsuspecting belief and joyful ecstasy; and, in compliance with the Stranger's mysterious

45

warning, escaped at midnight from her father's mansion; and took refuge in the cloisters of St Catherine.

The haughty lady abbess received the forlorn wanderer with cold civility and suspicious scrutiny. The unfortunate Anna had, in the simple innocence of her heart, confided to the superior her mournful tale, nor left one circumstance untold that could excite her pity, save her marriage with the Stranger, for whom she now began to feel unusual fears, and dreadful forebodings of evil to herself; for a month had glided away at the abbey, and yet he came not.

The Knight, with dreadful rage, discovered his daughter's flight; but vainly sought again to restore her to his power. He never saw her more; nor knew the sad conclusion of the unhappy Anna's destiny; who, deceived and terrified by the threats, expostulations, and commands, of the lady abbess, and the father confessors of the monastery, was at length betrayed into her own destruction; for the merciless abbess threatened to return her to her lord, and to her father, if she longer refused to take the vow of monastic life.

Despair and horror now seized the suffering victim of bigotry and paternal tyranny. Another and another month elapsed, and hope no longer could support her—the cruel stranger never came. At the gates of her prison, she was told, waited her father, with a powerful band, to force her from the abbey into the arms of a hated husband; and only the alternative of instantly taking the veil, could save her from the misery that pursued her. In a wild agony of terror, that had totally bereft her of her reason, she faintly bade them save her from her father's vengeance.

That instant the sacred, irrevocable vow was administered, and all its binding forms complied with by the lost St Anna, who, in the terror of her father, had for a moment forgot her previous engagements with the Stranger—forgot that she must, in a little time, become, perhaps, a wretched mother, and now was a still more wretched nun.*****

Here again the papers were totally useless, as Rosaline could only make out here and there a word, by which it appeared, that the Baron Fitzmartin had accused the order, with breaking the vow of celibacy. At length she read as follows:

With difficulty he was prevailed upon to suspend his proceedings against the abbey till the succeeding morrow, whilst the holy sisterhood endured the most persecuting examination from the lady abbess. No signs of guilt, however, were found; and the fathers, rejoicing in their expected security, were debating on an ample defiance to the Baron, when news was brought that Sister St Anna had fallen senseless on the steps of the grand altar, and had been with difficulty removed to her cell. Thither the abbess instantly hastened; and as the insensible nun lay still reclined on her mattress, her outer garment unlaced to admit of respiration, the disfigurement of her person first forcibly struck the lady mother with suspicion. She started, frowned; then looked again; conviction flashed upon her eyes; and, regardless of pity for the still lifeless state of the hapless Anna, she commanded all to quit the cell, and send instantly the father abbot to her. The father hastily obeyed, and entered. The lady abbess murmured in a hollow voice, as frowns of fury darted from her now terrific countenance: 'Behold the guilty wretch that, with impious sacrilege, hath defiled our holy sanctuary, and brought destruction on the glory of our house's fame!—Say, holy father, how must we dispose of the accursed apostate?'

Before the abbot could reply, the unfortunate Anna awoke from the counterfeit of death's repose, and, wildly casting her eyes around her cell, beheld the forms of her inveterate destroyers. Their fierce and angry looks of dreadful inquiry were bent upon the terrified nun, who, sickened with an unusual apprehension and dismay, whilst the abbot, fixing on the trembling Anna an increasing look of penetrating sternness, in a hollow, deep-toned voice, that sunk to her appalled heart, thus exclaimed: 'What punishment too terrible can await that guilty wretch who with sacrilege defiles our holy order?—say, lost one of God, art thou not guilty?'

Sinking on her knees, of every hope of life bereft, the unhappy Anna drooped her head to avoid the terrible scrutiny of truths pronounced, and looks unanswerable. No chance of escape was left her; she dared not prevaricate; and only with a groan of agony she feebly exclaimed—'I am, indeed!—Have mercy, holy father, as you shall hereafter expect to receive mercy from our heavenly Judge, on my involuntary crime!' She then turned to the frowning abbess her beseeching eyes, and piteously added, as she clung around her knees, 'Spare, oh gracious mother, spare a repentant daughter!'

In the countenances of her terrific judges poor Anna read the horrid mandate of her fate; for against the sacred order of the sisterhood she had sinned beyond atonement by any other punishment than death—Death the most horrible and excruciating! Vainly then she knelt, and clung to the robe of the abbess; she had slandered with sacrilege the purity of God's anointed house; its ministers and sacred devotees were sullied with a stain, that only the blood of a victim could wash away. Nor was the plea of marriage to a knight, who evidently never meant to claim her, admitted as the slightest expiation of her perjured vows to the abbey, and the disgrace she had brought on its sanctified inmates. Her horrid crimes demanded instant punishment: and the dreadful vengeance of the insulted members of the church could only be appeased by the immediate extirpation of the heinous apostate. To dispose of the unfortunate nun for ever, beyond the possibility of her being produced as a living evidence of the Baron's censure, and the abbey's shame, was now become an event absolutely necessary to the safety and welfare of the order: the claims of mercy, or the melting pleadings of pity, were alike disregarded for the stronger interest of the more immediate triumph of the abbey over its avowed and implacable enemy: and the father abbot, with the lady mother, having exhausted on the lost fair one the dreadful thunders of the church's vengeance, forcibly tore themselves from her distracted grasp, and prepared to inflict the terrific punishments that awaited their despairing victim, who, shrieking vainly for aid, and calling piteously on the Stranger for rescue and protection from her horrid fate, was borne by the tormentors from her cell to the dungeon of the south tower.

At the hour of midnight they dragged the miserable victim from her bed, and deep in the horrific dungeons of the prison plunged the distracted nun!—Groans, sighs, and shrieks, alternately rung echoing round the rugged walls: the torturing horrors of famine awaited the unfortunate nun; no pity alleviated her misery; and in the centre of the place stood the coffin destined for her; whilst round the walls and floor, in all directions, were strewed the ghastly ensigns of woe and torment. A faint glimmering lamp, suspended from the massy bars of the roof (as if with a refinement of cruelty unequalled, to blast the sight of the victim, and shut out every contemplation but her immediate fate) served to shew her the horrors that overwhelmed her, and the terrific engines of her tortures. The implements of confession were placed on the lid of her coffin; for the fathers denied her even the last consolation of absolution; but these she only in moments of short intellect would use, when distracted sentences, and wild, unfinished exclamations and appeals were all that it produced, sufficiently depictive of the horrors of her fate.

Two days of lingering sufferings had passed, and the third was nearly closed. Shut from life, and light, and every means of existence, the pangs of hunger seized the frantic sufferer, and the perils of premature childbirth writhed her anguished frame. Shrieks of despair rang through the building, and echoed to the vault of heaven. Hark! again that soul-appalling cry!—Inhuman fiends, is mercy dead within you!—Is there no touch of pity in your obdurate souls!—And thou too, remorseless betrayer of trusting innocence, hear ye not yon soul-appalling cry of her thy fatal love has destroyed?—Hark! again she calls on thy unpitying name; and now, in the bitterness of her soul's sufferings, she curses thee, and imprecates heaven's just vengeance on thy perjured head! Heaven hears the awful appeal!—it will avenge thee, suffering Anna! Now sink to death appeased.—Again the shrieks—Sure it is her last! The holy sisterhood, appalled, fly wildly from the dreadful tower; but vainly supplicate the mercy of their superiors for its dying inmate. Nature is exhausted, and hark, again the groans grow fainter! Short breathed murmurs proclaim the welcome dissolution of life. The soul, though confined with the suffering frame within the massy bars of her prison, at length has burst its bonds—It mounts from death, and in a moment is freed for ever. A short prayer addressed to the throne of mercy, releases the sufferer, and wafts her soul from the persecution of the wicked. The cruel strife has ceased—Poor Anna is at rest—her voice is heard no more. In the coffin of penitence she laid her suffering form; perhaps, it will never be removed from thence. Her guilty judges tremble at the place, nor dare their unhallowed footsteps approach the sacred dust.

Again the papers were useless, but it seemed, by what she could make out, that the haughty Baron triumphed over the Fathers of the Abbey, to the entire seclusion of the order. At length she came to the following passage, which concluded the manuscript.

The vengeance of heaven hung heavily over the conscience of the wicked Baron, nor was he suffered ever after to partake of happiness. It was on the third evening after his removal from his castle to the abbey he had plundered, that, retiring earlier than usual to his unwelcome couch, he tried in the arms of sleep to lose the remembrance of his crimes, and the terrible vengeance they inflicted on his guilty conscience. The sullen bell had tolled the hour of midnight ere he could compose his mind to repose. On this night, however, unusual restlessness pervaded his frame; nor could he for some time close in forgetfulness his eye-lids. At length a kind of unwilling stupor lulled for a moment his tortured spirits, and he slept. Not long did the balmy deity await him: troubled groans of anguish sounded through the apartment, and piercing shrieks rung bitterly in his ears. Starting in horror, he wildly raised himself, half bent, on his couch, and drew aside his curtains. The chamber was in total darkness, and every taper seemed suddenly to have been extinguished. At that moment the heavy bell of the abbey clock struck one. A freezing awe stole over the senses of the Baron: he in vain attempted to call his attendants; for speech was denied him; and a suspense of trembling horror had chilled his soul. His blood ran cold to its native source; his hair stood erect, and his countenance was distorted; for, as his eyes turned wildly, he beheld, standing close to the side of his bed, the pale figure of a female form, thinly clothed in the habiliments of a nun, and bearing in one hand a taper, whilst the other arm supported the ghastly form of a dead infant reclining on her breast. The countenance of the figure was pale, wan, and horrible to behold; for from its motionless eyes no spark of life proceeded; but they were fixed in unmoving terrific expression on the appalled Baron. At length a hollow-sounding voice pronounced through the closed lips of the spectre, 'O false, false Vortimer! accursed and rejected of thy Maker! knowest thou not the shadowy form that stands before thee? knowest thou not thy wretched bride? seest thou not the murdered infant thou hast destroyed?—From the deep bosom of immensity, the yawning horrors of the grave, the spirit of St Anna comes to call for vengeance and retribution; for know, the curses of her latest moments, when writhing beneath the agonies, the torments of death, and devouring hunger, that she then called upon thy head, were heard; and never shalt thou, guilty wretch! enjoy one quiet moment more. My mangled form, as now thou seest me, and dreams for ever of affright and terror, shall haunt thy thoughts with horror; nor shall even the grave rescue thee from the tortures I await to inflict.—Farewell—farewell till next we meet. In the grove where first thy perjured soul won on my happy, unsuspecting nature, and drew my youthful heart from parental duty and obedience, there shalt thou again behold me!'

Suddenly the eyes of the spectre became animated—Oh! then what flashes of appalling anger darted their orbits on the horror-struck Vortimer! three dreadful shrieks rung pealing through the chamber, now filled with a blaze of sulphureous light. The spectre suddenly became invisible, and the Baron fell senseless on his couch.

ISAAC CROOKENDEN
Sceloni — locks up Calini
— Kills Holbrug, (rival #2)
almost kills
rival

The Vindictive Monk *or* The Fatal Ring
becomes monk   Calini (his own son!)
A + C held

The young *Calini* was descended of a good family; was heir to great and still-increasing wealth; was the last representative of an honorable house; and the delight and admiration not only of his doting parent, but of every body who knew him. He possessed every grace of mental perfection; for his education had been conducted on so liberal a plan, that a clear, just, and accurate perception had been the happy result of his juvenile studies. His person was every way answerable to the above delineation of his mind. His make exhibited the truest symmetry; and his countenance beamed with masculine dignity, corrected with a gracious condescension.

Although *Calini* was reared up in the principles of the *Romish* church, that did not hinder him from seeing some of its absurdities; and therefore, while some of the votaries placed the essence of their religion in a gaudy exhibition of pompous ceremonies, his consisted in a steady, uniform system of good actions; an undeviating rectitude of conduct, prompted by the motive of his present and everlasting interest, as well as by the intrinsic beauty of benevolence. Such was the youth, whom we have selected for the hero of these memoirs. One day his father (as the youth had ever considered him), took him aside, and spake as follows—

'The substance of what I am now going to unfold, I once thought I should have buried in oblivion; but, upon mature deliberation, I am come to a determination of entrusting you with it. You have always been thought to be my son. This is the moment to undeceive you. You are *not* my child!'—'Not your son!' exclaimed the youth, in the utmost astonishment; 'whose then can I be?'—'That you will never probably know,' replied Signor *Calini*. 'But you have not many obligations to your parents, who left you to perish in your infancy. My story excites your astonishment. Listen attentively, while I disclose the circumstance which induced me to bring you up as my own offspring. About twenty years ago, as I was landing from a gondola, one dark night, on the northern shores of the Adriatic, after I had returned from visiting one of my estates, my sight was struck with a white bundle within a foot from the waves; on examining which, I

51

found it contained an infant. It was yourself; and I resolved that the direful intentions of those who left you should not only be frustrated, but I would adopt you as my son, two of mine having recently died. When I got home, I examined the bundle more accurately, and was surprised to see this ring. (Here he presented one to the astonished youth) You see, it is of a peculiar make; there is some name underneath. (The young man turned it, and saw the word *Ollorini* engraved on it) I beg, that from this day you would wear it, to remind you of the singular event; and be assured, my dear boy, although you are not the natural issue of my own loins, yet I shall always feel for you a father's tenderness.'

Here Signor *Calini* concluded his narration, and left his auditor overwhelmed with astonishment. The barbarity of his real parents affected him severely; but the kindness of the signor afforded him a continual source of the most pleasing sensation.

A short time after this wondrous disclosure, young *Calini* (for so we shall still call him) had been to visit a young lady, to whom he was sincerely attached; and was now returning home on horseback. The night was far advanced, and very threatning. His road lay through a dark wood; in the midst of which, he was seized by two men, who dragged him along, 'till they came to the ruins of an old castle, where they halted, 'till one, who had a lamp, sought for a door, and at length told his comrade he had found it. They then led our hero through a long intricate passage; at the end of which they unbolted a heavy iron door, and entered a gloomy stone dungeon. A strong chain, which was fastened to an enormous staple in the wall, discovered to the youth the horrors which awaited him. 'Here,' said one of the ruffians, 'here is your habitation, 'till you resign all pretensions to lady *Alexa*.' Our young lover now saw through the whole affair. He had been seized by order of a rival; but who this rival was, he had no means of judging. The inhuman monsters chained him to the wall, and, without speaking another word, left the dungeon. This mysterious event we shall now unfold:

There lived, in the neighbourhood of *Calini*, a man called *Sceloni*; of a gloomy character, and who was never seen once to smile; he was dependant on a nobleman, and had, from motives of self-interest, engaged to administer to his lewd propensities. This nobleman was enamoured of the very same lady our hero loved. Seeing no possibility of supplanting him in her affection, he called in the aid of the dark *Sceloni*, to whom he promised great pecuniary rewards, if he would dispatch his rival, and secure to him the possession of *Alexa*. The avaricious *Italian* undertook to perform what he required. For this purpose, he way-laid the youth on his return from *Alexa*'s house, as we have observed. But as he did not wish to embrue his hands in blood, if it could be done without, he had conveyed him to the ruins of the castle, whose intricate windings he well knew. Here he meant to keep him, 'till he should be able to extort an oath from him, that he would for ever resign all pretensions to *Alexa*. When he left the dungeon, he went directly to his employer, and told him the rival of his love was removed beyond the possibility of again being formidable. Signor *Holbruzi* took these words to mean no less than the death of the youth; and therefore he reaped the golden reward he aimed at.

But, notwithstanding this, *Alexa* was decidedly against his suit; and as she could not but be surprised at *Calini*'s unaccountable absence, as well as very much affected at it; she not only conceived additional disgust at *Holbruzi*'s addresses, but began to be suspicious of some base design having been executed against *Calini*. In the mean time, that unfortunate youth was suffering the severest extremities of imprisonment, and calling in vain on his dear *Alexa*. He was visited in the dungeon frequently by *Sceloni*, who endeavoured, by every means in his power, to make him resign all pretensions to *Alexa*; but he was steady in his refusal; nor did he yield, even when he was threatened with assassination. *Calini* was as unsuccessful in trying to discover the name and quality of his rival, as *Sceloni* was in extorting a resignation of *Alexa*.

After *Sceloni* had quitted the dungeon, the miserable youth began to reflect anew on his unhappy situation. He saw no probability of being united to the beloved object of his soul; why then not resign her? There was something in this word which seemed to imply cowardice, and he pertinaciously objected it. *Holbruzi* finding *Alexa* so little disposed to favor his passion, was resolved to possess her at all events. He ordered *Sceloni* to force her from her home, and bring her to his palace; which, under cover of a dark night, he effected.

Alexa was left an orphan at an early age; and, after her parents' death, she was reared up by a tender aunt, who loved her as her own child; but having a very slender income, necessity had obliged her to part with an estate in *Piedmont*, and she had purchased a small but neat villa in the neighborhood of *Naples*, where she resided with her beloved niece. The young *Calini* had found them out in their retirement, and had made his addresses to the fair *Alexa*; which at first was discouraged by the aunt, not as she had any objection to the youth; on the contrary, she was convinced he was worthy of her niece; but she knew the girl was his inferior in point of fortune. Yet when she found how firm he had taken hold of *Alexa*'s heart, and likewise heard of the liberal sentiments of signor *Calini*, she no longer opposed the mutual bias of their young and innocent hearts.

Things were in this situation, when *Calini* discontinued so unaccountably (to them at least) his visits. This circumstance, severe as it was to the young lady, was also felt by the aunt, who had conceived the greatest friendship for him. But her sorrows were unspeakably acute, when one night several ruffians broke into the house, and tore away her beloved *Alexa*. These were the cruel *Sceloni* and his emissaries, who conveyed her to the monster *Holbruzi*, as already related. But that lascivious wretch did not yet find his end answered. The persecuted maid was enabled to make a vigorous resistance to his meretricious wishes. Force he could have employed; but this he determined to delay, 'till every other method had been tried. He thought no way so likely to weaken her virtuous resolutions, as to let her know that her union with *Calini* was impossible, as that being was no longer an inhabitant of earth. This fatal intelligence overwhelmed her unfortunate breast with fresh despair, and rendered *Holbruzi* more than ever an object of disgust and abhorrence. His pride was severely mortified by her fixed dislike and undisguised contempt. In this unseasonable moment, *Sceloni* solicited a new supply for his late services in bringing *Alexa* to his palace. *Holbruzi*, smarting with the indifference of that female, answered sternly, that his trifling services had already been more than sufficiently rewarded; and, after rebuking him sharply for his avarice, absolutely refused to give him another *carlin* (fourpence of our money).

Sceloni seemed all humility, but he quitted the palace with a soul full of revenge; to accomplish which, he concerted a deep-laid scheme. He retired to the outskirts of the city, wrote to *Holbruzi* that he was leaving for his monastery (for this wretch was of an holy order), and going to a different part of the world; but conjured him to release the young *Calini* (who he confessed was alive, but imprisoned), and he described a dungeon where the youth was *not*. After he had sent this letter, he provided himself with a brace of pistols, and repaired to that very dungeon which he had mentioned in his letter as the prison of *Calini*. Here he threw himself on the ground, and personating the distress of that unfortunate youth, waited deliberately for *Holbruzi*'s arrival; for he never doubted but that vindictive tyrant would come to sacrifice *Calini* with his own hand. He was not deceived in his conjecture. When that monster received the monk's letter, his countenance bespoke the savage passions it inspired. 'What!' said he, 'my detested rival living! This

[handwritten marginalia: Rival true to told Alexa) who resists]

[handwritten marginalia: Rival from Sceloni]

night he breathes his last.' He accordingly stole away that very evening, muffled up in a disguise, with a lamp in one hand, and a dagger in the other, through the dark passages of the ruins. *Sceloni* heard him coming, and uttered a groan, on purpose to direct his steps to the dungeon where he was. *Sceloni* soon heard the door unfastened, and he kept his finger close to the trigger. *Holbruzi* cautiously advanced the light, and then entered. The subtle *Sceloni* lay as if he was in a disturbed sleep. *Holbruzi* drew near; and as he bent over him, exclaimed, 'favored minion! Wilt thou ever more rival me in love? Thou sleepest. Awake in—' he would have said *death*; but at this moment the pseudo-*Calini* pressed the trigger, and dismissed his soul from this world.

But *Sceloni* was not yet satisfied; his revengeful soul thirsted for more blood. He considered, that if *Calini* had resigned *Alexa*, that maid, out of revenge, might have yielded to *Holbruzi*; and consequently he should not have met with that mortifying refusal from him, which had stimulated him to take the bloody means that he had just executed. His vindictive spirit resolving upon a double revenge, marked *Calini* for a second victim. No sooner had he made this horrible determination, but, snatching up the lamp (which had not been extinguished in falling), and the yet bloodless dagger, he rushed out of the dungeon into that of the destined youth, fully resolved to accomplish his dreadful purpose. The report of the pistol, as it was at a considerable distance from him, and vented in a close-pent dungeon, did not reach his auditory nerves; and he was yet in a deep slumber, with his right hand on his breast. *Sceloni* drew near to strike; but, on observing the position of his hand, stooped down to remove it. The rays of the light discovered the ring, which his supposed father desired him to wear. It excited *Sceloni*'s curiosity. He gently drew it off, and examined it by the lamp. Each moment furnished new alarm to his terrified mind. His face assumed an ashy paleness; his joints trembled with amazement and horror; but when he turned it up, and saw the engraved name of 'Ollorini' upon it, his horror and astonishment was complete. He hastily threw away the dagger; and awaking the youth, interrogated him about the mysterious ring. He could only relate what his supposed father had told him. This was enough. *Sceloni,* while convulsive sobs burst from his torn bosom, could only exclaim, 'I am your father.' The astonished youth looked up, and thought his reason was unsettled; but seeing his tears and groans, he knew not what to think. At length, he desired him to give some indubitable proof that he was his father. 'I will, my son, I will do it,' answered *Sceloni*; 'but this is not a proper place for conversa-

55

tion; let me unbind you from these ignominious chains!' He then freed the youth from his fetters; and they left the dungeon together, and retired to a small house, where, after they had entered a private room, he addressed the wondering impatient youth as follows:—

'Although, in reciting those circumstances which prove you to be my son, I must criminate myself; yet I shall not hesitate to do it, as I am sensible that you have more virtue than to conspire against the life of your father.' Here he paused a moment; for he recollected, that he himself had conspired against the life of his son. At length, he proceeded. 'My real name is *Dictori*. I was brought up under very indulgent parents. My natural temper, which was violent in the extreme, was put into a hot-bed, by the unreasonable and fatal indulgence of those parents. 'Tis that indulgence which has caused my ruin. If they had done their duty, and restrained, by due correction, the impetuosity of my natural temper, I should not have been a prey to those destructive passions of my nature, which have since acted as gourds to prick me forward down the slippery path of vice. I was early attached to a lady, whose name was *Mariana Vicenza*; but my native pride was severely wounded, when I discovered that she not only beheld me with indifference, but with a fixed dislike. I now, through obstinacy, advanced my suit with more eagerness than ever; when it would have been more honorable silently to withdraw it. However, her parents obliged her to accept of my hand at the altar. As I never could forgive the little affection she had shown for me, I soon began to retaliate upon her after marriage. Among other passions which I vented upon her without mercy, the demon of jealousy began to agitate my restless breast with its hydra horrors. I thought it very probable that she, who was forced to marry a man whom she did not like, should entertain in his absence one she did. My suspicions were strengthened by seeing this very ring upon her finger, which I apprehended was given her by her gallant. I went so far as to believe you was his child. In a frenzy of rage, I murdered my wife, and committed you to the waves, together with the detested and fatal ring. I have had proof since, that that very ring was given her before marriage by an uncle who had gone beyond sea; that he had his name engraved on it, which was *Ollorini*. As I was afraid to stay in that part, I came to *Naples*, and became a monk of the order of St *Francis*. Spare me the rest!'

This truly wonderful relation affected the astonished youth a great deal.

But we must take leave of *Calini* a little while to look after the lovely persecuted *Alexa*. That unfortunate maid was ready to abandon herself to despair. Torn away from her peaceful retreat by ruffians, at the dreadful, the horror-working hour of midnight, to fall a prey to the unbridled lust of a lewd barbarian! Separated from her dear aunt! Torn too from the fond, the protecting arms of the youth she sighed for! what can exceed her misery, wretched captive as she then was in the most hated mansion of the nefarious monster *Holbruzi?* for she as yet knew nothing of the sanguinary scenes which had been exhibited in the castle-ruins. The savage *Holbruzi*, when he left his house at midnight, had consigned the wretched maid to one of his trusty servants, who executed with relentless rigor the confidence reposed in him. We now, for a short time, turn from the unhappy beauty, to see the mournful effect which her loss had upon her disconsolate aunt. That distressed matron, now separated by cruel fate from a beloved niece, in whom her very existence seemed to be wrapt up, experienced the most poignant anguish that can possibly be imagined. She wrung her aged hands in wild despair, and in frantic accents called on her far-off niece, her dear *Alexa*. While she was in the heighth of her lamentation, a knocking at the door was heard. For a considerable time she was afraid to open it, least, in so doing, she should let in those who ravished from her embraces her beloved niece, and thereby become herself a victim of their savage fury. But while she hesitated what to do, she heard a voice at the door requesting admission; the cadence of which she thought she remembered, though her distress would not permit her to be certain to whom it belonged. She however assumed courage sufficient to open it, when *Calini* directly rushed in. As he knew nothing of *Alexa* being at *Holbruzi*'s detested mansion, he, as soon as he left the monk, repaired to her residence, though not without dreadful apprehensions for her safety, occasioned by the silence of *Sceloni*, on his asking after her.

It may perhaps be thought strange, that the monk should not have told his son where she was; seeing he knew she was at *Holbruzi*'s palace. But, if we consider that he had been some time absent from *Naples*, and that he knew so much of that villain as to think it probable that he had murdered that maid, before he intended to assassinate her lover, we shall cease to wonder at his conduct. Add to this, that if he had discovered to *Calini* that *Alexa* was at *Holbruzi*'s mansion, it would naturally have introduced an inquiry into that monster's mysterious absence—an inquiry which would doubtless have directed the finger of suspicion to himself. This was what the monk dreaded should transpire. He had already dipped his hands so deep in blood, that his conscience was always pointing to the gibbet, or the inquisitorial torture. He had therefore preserved an obstinate silence respecting *Alexa*; and our hero, unable to endure the tortures of suspense, flew upon the pinions of indescribable anxiety to her aunt's, as already mentioned.

When *Calini* asked for *Alexa*, all her grief was renewed; and she told the distracted lover the real truth. 'Dragged away at midnight!' exclaimed our frantic hero. 'I am the football of destiny. Why did I not die in my prison?' In a little time, however, he became more calm; and he vowed to discover her, if it was within the verge of possibility.

The reputed father of our hero received his foster son with the greatest joy imaginable, and heard with astonishment and horror the circumstances which had happened to him. He was, however, severely afflicted at the loss of the amiable *Alexa*; for that lovely maid stood very high both in his esteem and affection; and he had beheld the growing love which the youth evinced for her with cheerful approbation. It excited his utmost surprise to think who could possibly have stolen her from her peaceful home. He little thought that it was the machinations of one who often partook of his hospitality, and had been a frequent visitor at his festive board. But this very consideration enabled our hero to trace out her persecutor, and her present prison. He recollected *Holbruzi* being at his father's, as he then thought him; as likewise, that he was always exceedingly discourteous to himself, the occasion of which he had in vain attempted to unravel; but now it appeared plain enough. *Calini* considered also, that he knew perfectly well of his love for *Alexa*, as also the place of that young lady's residence. When therefore he, in his cooler moments, put all these circumstances together, the suspicions they excited were so strong, that our unfortunate youth found it impossible to think otherways than that he must be certainly somehow concerned, if not a principal agent in the removal of the unfortunate girl.

Influenced by this supposition, he determined to go directly to the palace of *Holbruzi*, to see if the beloved of his soul was really there. But, upon second thoughts, he resolved to await all night; and set spies in the mean time about the house, to discover, if possible, the secret transactions going forward in it. The spies brought him intelligence, that they saw a young lady superficially through one of the windows, leaning upon her arm in a melancholy posture, and that she appeared to be in extreme distress. This was sufficient to stimulate our hero to instant exertion. He directly went, with a desperate determination, well armed; resolving, if they denied him admission, to force the door. But the servant admitted him upon the first summons, expecting it was his master. Our hero instantly rushed up stairs; and hearing a female scream, he broke into the room, and beheld his beloved *Alexa*, struggling in the embraces of a ruffian; whom he severely wounded, and rescued the lovely maid.

How was she rejoiced to see her dear, her loved *Calini*!

Sceloni had the satisfaction of seeing them happy before he retired for life to his monastery.

He now found no difficulty in being united to his dear *Alexa*; whose marriage was celebrated amid an amazing multitude of admiring spectators.

The monk, after this, was never seen beyond the walls of his convent; but passed his life in the most rigorous penance.

II

The Nineteenth Century

ANONYMOUS

The Astrologer's Prediction *or* The Maniac's Fate

$\mathbb{R}$eginald, sole heir of the illustrious family of Di Venoni, was remarkable, from his earliest infancy, for a wild enthusiastic disposition. His father, it was currently reported, had died of an hereditary insanity; and his friends, when they marked the wild mysterious intelligency of his eye, and the determined energy of his aspect, would often assert that the dreadful malady still lingered in the veins of young Reginald. Whether such was the case or not, certain it is, that his mode of existence was but ill calculated to eradicate any symptoms of insanity. Left at an early age to the guidance of his mother, who since the death of her husband had lived in the strictest seclusion, he experienced but little variety to divert or enliven his attention. The gloomy château in which he resided was situated in Swabia on the borders of the Black Forest. It was a wild isolated mansion, built after the fashion of the day in the gloomiest style of Gothic architecture. At a distance rose the ruins of the once celebrated Castle of Rudstein, of which at present but a mouldering tower remained; and, beyond, the landscape was terminated by the deep shades and impenetrable recesses of the Black Forest.

Such was the spot in which the youth of Reginald was immured. But his solitude was soon to be relieved by the arrival of an unexpected resident. On the anniversary of his eighteenth year, an old man, apparently worn down with age and infirmity, took up his abode at the ruined tower of Rudstein. He seldom stirred out during the day; and from the singular circumstance of his perpetually burning a lamp in the tower, the villagers naturally enough concluded that he was an emissary of the devil. This report soon acquired considerable notoriety; and having at last reached the ears of Reginald through the medium of a gossiping gardener, his curiosity was awakened, and he resolved to introduce himself into the presence of the sage, and ascertain the motives of his singular seclusion. Impressed with this resolution he abruptly quitted the château of his mother, and bent his steps towards the ruined tower, which was situated at a trifling distance from his estate. It was a gloomy night, and the spirit of the storm seemed abroad on the wings of the wind. As the clock from the village church struck twelve, he gained the ruin; and ascending the time-worn staircase, that tottered at each step he took, reached with some labour the apartment of the philosopher. The door was thrown open, and the old man was seated by the grated casement. His appearance was awfully impressive. A long white beard depended from his chin, and his feeble frame with difficulty sustained a horoscope that was directed to the heavens. Books, written in unknown characters of cabalism, were promiscuously strewed about the floor; and an alabaster vase, engraved with the sign of the Zodiac, and circled by mysterious letters, was stationed on the table. The appearance of the Astrologer himself was equally impressive. He was habited in a suit of black velvet, fancifully embroidered with gold, and belted with a band of silver. His thin locks hung streaming in the wind, and his right hand grasped a wand of ebony. On the entrance of a stranger he rose from his seat, and bent a scrutinizing glance on the anxious countenance of Reginald.

'Child of ill-starred fortunes!' he exclaimed in a hollow tone, 'dost thou come to pry into the secrets of futurity? Avoid me, for thy life, or, what is dearer still, thine eternal happiness! for I say unto thee, Reginald Di Venoni, it is better that thou hadst never been born, than permitted to seal thy ruin in a spot which, in after years, shall be the witness of thy fall.'

The countenance of the Astrologer as he uttered these words was singularly terrific, and rung in the ears of Reginald like his death-knell. 'I am innocent, father!' he falteringly replied, 'nor will my disposition suffer me to perpetrate the sins you speak of.'—'Hah!' resumed the prophet, 'man is indeed innocent, till the express moment of his damnation; but the star of thy destiny already wanes in the heaven, and the fortunes of the proud family of Venoni must decline with it. Look to the west! Yon planet that shines so brightly in the night-sky, is the star of thy nativity. When next thou shalt behold it, shooting downward like a meteor through the hemisphere, think on the words of the prophet and tremble. A deed of blood will be done, and thou art he that shall perpetrate it!'

At this instant the moon peeped forth from the dun clouds that lagged slowly in the firmament, and shed a mild radiance upon the earth. To the west, a single bright star was visible. It was the star of Reginald's nativity. He gazed with eyes fixed in the breathless intensity of expectation, and watched it till the passing clouds concealed its radiance from his view. The Astrologer, in the meantime, had resumed his station at the window. He raised the horoscope to heaven. His frame seemed trembling with convulsion. Twice he passed his hand across his brow, and shuddered as he beheld the aspect of the heavens. 'But a few days,' he said, 'are yet left me on earth, and then shall my spirit know the eternal repose of the grave. The star of my nativity is dim and pale. It will never be bright again, and the aged one will never know comfort more. Away!' he continued, motioning Reginald from his sight, 'disturb not the last moments of a dying man; in three days return, and under the base of this ruin inter the corpse that you will find mouldering within. Away!'

Impressed with a strange awe, Reginald could make no reply. He remained as it were entranced; and after the lapse of a few minutes rushed from the tower, and returned in a state of disquietude to the gloomy château of his mother.

The three days had now elapsed, and, faithful to his promise, Reginald pursued his route back to the tower. He reached it at nightfall, and tremblingly entered the fatal apartment. All within was silent, but his steps returned a hollow echo as he passed. The wind sighed around the ruin, and the raven from the roofless turrets had already commenced his death-song. He entered. The Astrologer, as before, was seated by the window, apparently in profound abstraction, and the horoscope was placed by his side. Fearful of disturbing his repose, Reginald approached with caution. The old man stirred not. Emboldened by so unexpected a silence, he advanced and looked at the face of the Astrologer. It was a corpse he gazed on,—the relic of what had once been life. Petrified with horror at the sight, the memory of his former promise escaped him, and he rushed in agony from the apartment.

For many days the fever of his mind continued unabated. He frequently became delirious, and in the hour of his lunacy was accustomed to talk of an evil spirit that had visited him in his slumbers. His mother was shocked at such evident symptoms of derangement. She remembered the fate of her husband; and implored Reginald, as he valued her affection, to recruit the agitation of his spirits by travel. With some difficulty he was induced to quit the home of his infancy. The expostulations of the countess at last prevailed, and he left the Château Di Venoni for the sunny climes of Italy.

Time rolled on; and a constant succession of novelty had produced so beneficial an effect, that scarcely any traces remained of the once mysterious and enthusiastic Venoni. Occasionally his mind was disturbed and gloomy, but a perpetual recurrence of amusement diverted the influence of past recollection, and rendered him at least as tranquil as it was in the power of his nature to permit. He continued for years abroad, during which time he wrote frequently to his mother, who still continued at the Château Di Venoni, and at last announced his intention of settling finally at Venice. He had remained but a few months in the city, when, at the gay period of the Carnival, he was introduced, as a foreign nobleman, to the beautiful daughter of the Doge. She was amiable, accomplished, and endowed with every requisite to ensure permanent felicity. Reginald was charmed with her beauty, and infatuated with the excelling qualities of her mind. He confessed his attachment, and was informed with a blush that the affection was mutual. Nothing, therefore, remained but application to the Doge; who was instantly addressed on the subject, and implored to consummate the felicity of the young couple. The request was attended with success, and the happiness of the lovers was complete.

On the day fixed for the wedding, a brilliant assemblage of beauty thronged the ducal palace of St Mark. All Venice crowded to the festival; and, in the presence of the gayest noblemen of Italy, Reginald Count Di Venoni received the hand of Marcelia, the envied daughter of the Doge. In the evening, a masqued festival was given at the palace; but the young couple, anxious to be alone, escaped the scene of revelry, and hurried in their gondola to the château that was prepared for their reception.

It was a fine moonlight night. The mild beams of the planets sparkled on the silver bosom of the Adriatic, and the light tones of music, 'by distance made more sweet', came wafted on the western gale. A thousand lamps, from the illuminated squares of the city, reflected their burnished hues along the wave, and the mellow chaunt of the gondoliers kept time to the gentle splashing of their oars. The hearts of the lovers were full, and the witching spirit of the hour passed with all its loveliness into their souls. On a sudden a deep groan escaped the overcharged heart of Reginald. He had looked to the western hemisphere, and the star which, at that moment, flashed brightly in the horizon, reminded him of the awful scene which he had witnessed at the tower of Rudstein. His eye sparkled with delirious brilliancy; and had not a shower of tears come opportunely to his relief, the consequence might have been fatal. But the affectionate caresses of his young bride succeeded for the present in soothing his agitation, and restoring his mind to its former tranquil temperament.

A few months had now elapsed from the period of his marriage, and the heart of Reginald was happy. He loved Marcelia, and was tenderly beloved in return. Nothing, therefore, remained to complete his felicity but the presence of his mother, the Countess. He wrote accordingly to intreat that she would come and reside with him at Venice, but was informed by her confessor in reply, that she was dangerously ill, and requested the immediate attendance of her son. On the receipt of this afflicting intelligence he hurried with Marcelia to the Château Di Venoni. The countess was still alive when he entered, and received him with an affectionate embrace. But the exertion of so unexpected an interview with her son, was too great for the agitated spirits of the parent, and she expired in the act of folding him to her arms.

From this moment the mind of Reginald assumed a tone of the most confirmed dejection. He followed his mother to the grave, and was observed to smile with unutterable meaning as he returned home from the funeral. The Château Di Venoni increased the native depression of his spirits, and the appearance of the ruined tower never failed to imprint a dark frown upon his brow. He would wander for days from his home, and when he returned, the moody expression of his countenance alarmed the affection of his wife. She did all in her power to assuage his anguish, but his melancholy remained unabated. Sometimes, when the fit was on him, he would repulse her with fury; but, in his gentler moments, would gaze on her as on a sweet vision of vanished happiness.

He was one evening wandering with her through the village, when his conversation assumed a more dejected tone than usual. The sun was slowly setting, and their route back to the château lay through the churchyard where the ashes of the countess reposed. Reginald seated himself with Marcelia by the grave, and plucking a few wild flowers from the turf, exclaimed, 'Are you not anxious to join my mother, sweet girl? She has gone to the land of the blest—to the land of love and sunshine! If we are happy in this world, what will be our state of happiness in the next? Let us fly to unite our bliss with hers, and the measure of our joy will be full.' As he uttered these words his eye glared with delirium, and his hand seemed searching for a weapon. Marcelia, alarmed at his appearance, hurried him from the spot, and clasping his hand in hers, drew him gently onward.

The sun in the meantime had sunk, and the stars of evening came out in their glory. Brilliant above all shone the fatal western planet, the star of Reginald's nativity. He observed it with horror, and pointed it out to the notice of Marcelia. 'The hand of heaven is in it!' he mentally exclaimed, 'and the proud fortunes of Venoni hasten to a close.' At this instant the ruined tower of Rudstein appeared in sight, with the moon shining full upon it. 'It is the place,' resumed the maniac, 'where a deed of blood must be done, and I am he that must perpetrate it! But fear not, my poor girl,' he added, in a milder tone, while the tears sprang to his eyes, 'thy Reginald cannot harm thee; he may be wretched, but he never shall be guilty!' With these words he reached the château, and threw himself on his couch in restless anxiety of mind.

Night waned, morning dawned on the upland hills of the scenery, and with it came a renewal of Reginald's disorder. The day was stormy, and in unison with the troubled feeling of his spirit. He had been absent from Marcelia since day break, and had given her no promise of return. But as she was seated at twilight near the lattice, playing on her harp a favourite Venetian canzonet, the folding doors flew open, and Reginald made his appearance. His eye was red, with the deepest—the deadliest madness, and his whole frame seemed unusually convulsed. ' 'Twas not a dream,' he exclaimed, 'I have seen her and she has beckoned us to follow.' 'Seen her, seen who?' said Marcelia, alarmed at his phrenzy. 'My mother,' replied the maniac. 'Listen while I repeat the horrid narrative. Methought as I was wandering in the forest, a sylph of heaven approached, and revealed the countenance of my mother, I flew to join her but was withheld by a sage who pointed to the western star. On a sudden loud shrieks were heard, and the sylph assumed the guise of a demon. Her figure towered to an awful height, and she pointed in scornful derision to thee; yes, to thee, my Marcelia. With rage she drew thee towards me. I seized—I murdered thee; and hollow groans broke on the midnight gale. The voice of the fiendish Astrologer was heard shouting as from a charnel house, "The destiny is accomplished, and the victim may retire with honour." Then; methought, the fair front of heaven was obscured, and thick gouts of clotted, clammy blood showered down in torrents from the blackened clouds of the west. The star shot through the air, and—the phantom of my mother again beckoned me to follow.'

The maniac ceased, and rushed in agony from the apartment. Marcelia followed and discovered him leaning in a trance against the wainscot of the library. With gentlest motion she drew his hand in hers, and led him into the open air. They rambled on, heedless of the gathering storm, until they discovered themselves at the base of the tower of Rudstein. Suddenly the maniac paused. A horrid thought seemed flashing across his brain, as with giant grasp he seized Marcelia in his arms, and bore her to the fatal apartment. In vain she shrieked for help, for pity. 'Dear Reginald, it is Marcelia who speaks, you cannot surely harm her.' He heard—he heeded not, nor once staid his steps, till he reached the room of death. On a sudden his countenance lost its wildness, and assumed a more fearful, but composed look of determined madness. He advanced to the window, and gazed on the stormy face of heaven. Dark clouds flitted across the horizon, and hollow thunder echoed awfully in the distance. To the west the fatal star was still visible, but shone with sickly lustre. At this instant a flash of lightning re-illuminated the whole apartment, and threw a broad red glare upon a skeleton, that mouldered upon the floor. Reginald observed it with affright, and remembered the unburied Astrologer. He advanced to Marcelia, and pointing to the rising moon, 'A dark cloud is sailing by,' he shudderingly exclaimed, 'but ere the full orb again shines forth, thou shalt die, I will accompany thee in death, and hand in hand will we pass into the presence of our mother.' The poor girl shrieked for pity, but her voice was lost in the angry ravings of the storm. The cloud in the meantime sailed on, —it approached—the moon was dimmed, darkened, and finally buried in its gloom. The maniac marked the hour, and rushed with a fearful cry towards his victim. With murderous resolution he grasped her throat, while the helpless hand and half strangled articulation, implored his compassion. After one final struggle the hollow death rattle announced that life was extinct, and that the murderer held a corpse in his arms. An interval of reason now occurred, and on the partial restoration of his mind, Reginald discovered himself the unconscious murderer of Marcelia. Madness—deepest madness again took possession of his faculties. He laughed—he shouted aloud with the unearthly yellings of a fiend, and in the raging violence of his delirium, hurled himself headlong from the summit of the tower.

In the morning the bodies of the young couple were discovered, and buried in the same tomb. The fatal ruin of Rudstein still exists; but is now commonly avoided as the residence of the spirits of the departed. Day by day it slowly crumbles to earth, and affords a shelter for the night raven, or the wild beasts of the forests. Superstition has consecrated it to herself, and the tradition of the country has invested it with all the awful appendages of a charnel house. The wanderer who passes at night-fall, shudders while he surveys its utter desolation, and exclaims as he journies on, 'Surely this is a spot where guilt may thrive in safety, or bigotry weave a spell to enthrall her misguided votaries.'

PETRUS BOREL

Andreas Vesalius the Anatomist

I. CHALYBARIUM

At that peaceful hour of night when a city comes to resemble a graveyard, a single crooked little sidestreet—one of Madrid's minor arteries—still throbbed with a violently feverish pulse. This restless street in the otherwise slumbering city was the *Callejuela casa del Campo*. At one end of it was found a prosperous residence inhabited by a foreigner: a Fleming. The stained-glass windows were lit up from within, casting their light obliquely across the dark façade of the house opposite, so that in the gloom it seemed to be sprinkled with fires and burning nets, and with tracery of gold.

The gates of this mansion were wide open, disclosing a spacious porch with its groined arch and pendant keystone, at the foot of a great stone stairway with balustrades elaborately carved like the ivory of a fan and all strewn with sweet-smelling flowers.

The walls were, to put it fancifully, in their carnival dress, all bedecked and tricked out with tapestries, velvets, and glittering candelabra.

A few halberdiers patrolled to and fro at the entrance.

Occasionally, when the yells of the crowd gathering outside subsided, the sweet and lively harmonies of music could be heard at the foot of the stairs, calling forth echoes in the resounding archway.

The whole palace was alive with celebrations, but outside a common rabble was howling and milling at the gates; these were the groundlings from the lowest gutter. Sometimes they sent up a frightful cheering, and sometimes snorts of mockery, which were taken up by one group after another in the darkness, and died away like the satanic laughter of thunderclouds.

'The doctor has chosen a fine wedding day—a Saturday, feast of the Sabbath. A sorcerer couldn't do better,' said a toothless old crone squatting in a gateway.

'Too true, my dear; and, by God, if all his dead victims came back here, they could make a ring around Madrid.'

'What a sight that would be,' replied the crone, 'if all the poor Castilians who've been picked to pieces by this torturer—God preserve them—turned up to get back their skins!'

'I've been told,' said a little bearded man squeezing up on tiptoes from out of the crowd, 'that he often dines on cutlets that never came from the butcher's.'
— cannibal?

'It's true, it's true!'

'No, no, it's a lie!' cried a tall young man stuck up against a trellis window, 'all lies! Go and ask Rivadeneyra the butcher.'

'Silence! You, pipe down!' cried still louder a man wrapped in a brown cape with his hat pulled down over his eyes. 'Don't you all recognize him? It's Enrique Zapata, the torturer's apprentice, sticking up for his master. I'll bet if you searched his doublet you'd find a hand or a leg.'

'Just think of it! That old cannibal getting his hands on a young bride!' said the crone. 'If I were King Philip, I'd stop the monster from—'
/ conflict

'Oh yes?' said the stranger in the brown cape, 'even when Philip the Second protects this Flemish dog? Just yesterday, Torrijos, the baker from La Cebada, went missing; and no doubt he's ended up in the wedding cake. It's an outrage! We must put a stop to it!'

'What's the king doing, protecting him?' the people complained. 'He should burn him alive.'

Then some monks joined in, from the monastery of Our Lady of Atocha, recently founded by Father Garcia de Loaysa, Inquisitor-General and archbishop of Seville, and Father Juan Hurtado de Mendoza, confessor to Emperor Charles V. They added mildly: 'Christians! This man is a heretic! a sorcerer! a Fleming! He deserves to die!' And the chorus was joined by all the monks of the royal monastery of San Geronimo.

'Death to him!' shouted the mob, pushing back the halberdiers and cursing in their faces.

'Death to him!' responded the gentleman in the cape.

'Death to him!' yelled the monks, brandishing their crucifixes and stirring up the rabble. 'Put him to death! Start up the fire!'

Suddenly the gathering storm broke. Murderous threats filled the air as the crowd hurled itself against the gates, led by a monk brandishing a torch. But the halberdiers, supported by Enrique Zapata and several more students, firmly stood their ground and forced this unruly and bellowing rabble into retreat. The response

71

was a renewed uproar: they clattered away with bells, knives, and pans, raising a thunder that was agonizing, deafening, a whole symphony of murder.

II. SALTATIO, TURBA, MORS

Within the mansion, the hearty merrymaking and bantering went on, and nobody bothered themselves at all about the din outside, it being the custom to greet the marriage of an old man and a young bride with some such revelry.

In the gallery where the guests were leaving their robes, a brown cape was hung up at the entrance. The bride was dancing with a dashing cavalier who had as yet put in only a fleeting appearance at the party. They seemed to be more occupied in whispering together than in dancing. The bridegroom was at the other end of the room, flirting with the little daughter of one of his relatives.

The great ballroom opened on to a balcony overlooking a courtyard. It was crowded with guests: ladies, knights, aged relatives, and duennas; and all of them, under the pretext of breathing in some fresh night air, were out there to unleash their spiteful mockery. There was a hubbub of conversation, a chorus of many voices, high-pitched, deep, hoarse, and trembling; a gallery of sweet faces and sour faces, creased by broad laughter or lit up by malicious smirks, and revealing sets of teeth like ivory keyboards or like crenellated turrets, or like serrated arches.

'And who's the good-looking cavalier our bride is simpering over?'

'How wicked you are, senorita!'

'Ha, ha! Just look at Don Vesalius over there, giving himself airs in his scarlet stockings and black doublet. Devil take me if his legs inside his boots don't look just like pens in an inkwell! Look at him cavorting with that plump and rosy Amalia de Cárdenas. Doesn't he look to you like Old Father Time?'

'Or like Death dancing with Life.'

'Holbein's dance.'

'Tell me, Olivares, what can he give her?'

'A lesson in anatomy.'

'A topic for conversation.'

'Thanks for the bride!'

'Now the saraband is finished, watch him kiss cousin Amalia's hand.'

'This is no bourgeois wedding, it's a brilliant occasion.'

'But where's the bride?'

'And where's our dashing cavalier?'

'Don Vesalius is fussing about looking for her. Sniff her out, you old fox!'

'Go on, then, Olivares, ask him—he's supposed to be a sorcerer—what Maria is doing just now.'

'Careful, my friend; we mustn't get our fingers burned.'

The dancing began once more. Vesalius asked Amalia for another dance, but she just pouted prettily and then laughed behind his back. The bride was no longer in the ballroom, nor was the brown cape to be found in the gallery. But in one gloomy corridor there was the sound of footsteps, and of these words:

'Quickly, Maria, cover yourself with this cape. We must leave!'

'Alderán, I can't.'

'Can I leave you to be the prey of Vesalius? No—you belong to me! While I'm away you betray me; I hear about it; I come in haste, this very morning, mingling in with the celebrations; I take you aside all alone, and now that I ask you to leave with me, you refuse! Oh no, Maria, you're deluding yourself. Come, we still have time. Break off this shameful alliance, and we shall be happy: I will be yours entirely, yours alone and forever! Come, Maria!'

'Alderán, my family has imposed this yoke on me, and I must submit. But you will still be my lover all the same, as I will always be yours! What does this man matter? What is he but another valet, a screen to hide our secret love? Leave me, leave me, and adieu!'

'Very well. So you refuse, Maria. Go and defile yourself with this man, then. You carry out your wishes, as I shall carry out my own. Begone!' Flung from his embrace, she hurried from the gallery back to the ballroom.

Alderán paused for a few moments, as if overwhelmed. He cursed, stamped his foot, then suddenly vanished into the night.

Meanwhile the crowd at the gates had swollen like floodwater in a storm. The tumult grew fiercer, and the frenzy more alarming. Renewing the boldness of its first attempt, the rabble edged closer and closer to the halberdiers, laughing in their faces. Again they snarled their curses and their threats of death; they threw stones at the windows, and they smeared the walls with ox blood and dung. Suddenly the crowd opened up to make way for a dishevelled woman who howled like a dog at the moon. It was La Torrija, the baker's wife, crying out for her husband and demanding vengeance.

The word went round on all sides: 'It's La Torrija, the baker's wife.' The mob observed a compassionate silence as La Torrija sobbed and howled. Then the man in the brown cape got up on the steps and shouted: 'Friends, justice must be done! Those who fail to follow me now are cowards. Vengeance! Death to Vesalius! Death to the sorcerer!'

The response was a volley of stones flung at the windows and at the halberdiers, who retreated as far as the stairway. The crowd spilled into the porch, threw itself against the fixed pikes and smashed them. It had clambered up the stairs and was breaking open the door of the ballroom when the sound of galloping was heard in the distance. 'Run for your lives—it's the Guard!' Seized with panic, the mob tumbled down the stairs, disappeared down corridors, or leaped out of the windows. A few brave souls stood their ground and waited alone.

'In the name of the King, disperse!'

'The King is there to put murderers, heretics, and sorcerers to death. Death to the Fleming!'

'In the King's name, disperse!'

Then the guardsmen rode into the porch. They were met by sticks of furniture raining down on them, whereupon they shot their muskets, bringing down the boldest of the rioters. With a cry of pain, the man in the brown cape clutched his side. The survivors took flight along with the wounded, leaving behind five corpses lying on the ground.

A gloomy silence quickly descended on the mansion and the street. The watchmen carried off the bodies of the fallen, while the guests slipped away nervously through a back door. The gates were bolted shut, the lamps were snuffed out, in deathly contrast to the evening's vitality. Only in one wing of Vesalius's mansion did two windows blaze on in the darkness.

III. QUOD LEGI NON POTEST

Through the broken panels of the ballroom door, Maria had seen the man in the brown cape shot down by musket-fire, and had swooned at the sound of his piercing cry. She had been carried to her room and placed on a couch where she had been laid out unconscious for a long time. Kneeling down beside her, the tearful and trembling Vesalius was kissing her hands and her brow.

'How do you feel, Maria, my love?'

'Better—but is the trouble all over?'

'Yes, that ugly rabble has been seen to. What can these people have against me? I live in peaceful seclusion, unassumingly passing my time with dull anatomical research for the good of humanity, the advancement of science, and the greater glory of God. These people are demanding my head, believing me to be a sorcerer. Everyone in this city who goes missing is supposed to have been abducted by me, Vesalius, for my experiments. The common people will always be gross and stupid—the ungrateful brutes! And such is the fate in store for those of us who devote our lives to them, who show the way forward, or who have something new to say. They crucified Jesus of Nazareth and laughed in Christopher Columbus's face. The people will always be gross and stupid—ungrateful brutes!'

'You must cast aside these dismal thoughts, Vesalius; although, to be honest, this latest bloodletting is not going to win you their love.'

'Oh, what does the people's love matter, after all, so long as I have yours? Oh you do love me, don't you? You love me a little?'

'How can you still ask me such questions?'

'I know I'm old, Maria, and age is beset by doubts. I know I don't have a gallant manner, that I'm broken down by my long nights of work, and that I've become nearly as gaunt as one of the skeletons in my workshop; but my heart is young and eager. Don't you see, there's nothing stale in the passion I feel for you: the skin may be old, but the soul I bring you is new. I have met many women in my time, but I swear to you not one has sparked such a fire in me! What a fate—having to reach this decrepitude before knowing the violent force of love! Maria, you will get used to seeing the crude frame that imprisons my youthful soul: under the bark of the ancient oak tree, the sap is boiling!'

Maria threw an arm round his neck and lightly kissed his bald pate and white beard. Vesalius wept with joy.

Time for bed! A time of ecstasy, throbbing with shame and rapture, when souls unite, and desire is aroused and then drowned! Bedtime, with all its delights and its deceptions! Time of painful paradox, which is sometimes the hour of our death . . .

The bride gracefully threw off her wedding gown and her jewels, like a rose emerging from its leaves. She was a Castilian beauty such as one sees in one's dreams! Awkwardly, Vesalius too doffed his festive garments and revealed his hideous figure—like a mummy unpeeling its wrappings!

The lamp was abruptly blown out, and the curtain-rings rattled on their rods. A deep calm prevailed, which was now and then loudly broken; but nobody heard Maria cry out . . .

Then, far into the night, there were caresses and kisses that went unanswered, then grumbling and reproach, as the learned professor of anatomy repeated in a shaking voice:

'Oh, don't you go thinking this is weakness, Maria! It's the violence of my love that leaves me shattered. Your beauty paralyses me with shame, as I seem to be touching something holy, so great is my love for you, Maria! No, you mustn't imagine that this is impotence. In the morning I'll show you, in twenty authors—in Mundinus, in Galienus, in my master Gonthierus Andernaci, the chief physician to Francis I of France—and you'll see that, on the contrary, it's potency and excessive love; I love you that much, Maria!'

We can only assume that this excessive love was unrelenting, for only a few days had gone by before Maria moved into an isolated suite of rooms in another wing of the mansion, accompanied by the professor's devoted old housekeeper, now transformed into his wife's duenna. The old owl no longer saw his turtle-dove except at mealtimes, when they treated each other with the chilly politeness that prevails between strangers.

Once again, Vesalius was wedded to his research. Immersed in his studies, he shuttled back and forth from the laboratory to the lecture-hall, from the lecture-hall to the laboratory.

Here is a lesson you should draw from this, all you young women ripe for marriage: if you have a strongly passionate nature, make sure, if you can help it, never to marry a university professor, nor a member of the literary academy, and especially not one of the demigods of the forty-strong Académie Française with its everlasting dictionary.

IV. NIDUS ADULTERATUS

After about four years, the lady Maria, who had not made her customary appearance at the table for several days, sent for her husband. Vesalius was at her side in an instant, and found her sprawled on her bed in a state of collapse, her features deadly pale with rings around her eyes, her voice a lifeless whisper. Drawing up a chair, Vesalius sat down and leaned over to hear her. Maria, feeling a warm breath on her face, opened her eyes, recognized Vesalius, and said with an agonized sigh:

'Andreas, you are my lord and master. I feel weaker with every passing moment. Soon I shall be kneeling at the feet of God, the strictest of judges. And I am impure! I have sinned so much against you; but this sinner begs forgiveness. Do not be angry with me. You are a wise man, my husband and my master: let me bare my soul to you!'

'Senora, you are not as ill as you seem to believe. It is your mind that is afflicted.'

'No one knows an illness better than the patient herself. Something inside me says that my time is almost come. You are my husband and my good lord; listen, and forgive me, for in some things I am not to blame. We both made our vows at the altar, and we have both been unfaithful: I, because I was young and too full of life; and you, because your hair turned white from studying and your body broke down with work. Oh, misery!—to be reduced to cursing my youth! Oh, Vesalius, if only you knew what it is to be a young woman, if you knew what we go through, Vesalius, you would forgive me! Be calm, now, and listen: I tell you I am an adulteress, that I have betrayed you shamefully. The crimes I have committed, Andreas! I have brought my lovers under your roof, made them drunk with your wine, stuffed them with your food; and while you were asleep or buried in your studies I joined them in laughing at you. Our filthy vices took advantage of your good nature. You were the butt of all our mockery. How vile it was! This very bed, now to be my deathbed, still shudders with our lascivious abandon. God is summoning me, and I am dying! If you spurn me now . . .'

Her voice was drowned in sobbing. Then, after a moment of silence, she spoke more clearly:

'I have already been punished, bitterly and grievously. An adulteress always makes herself repulsive, dragging her filth around with her. Since we were married, I have had three lovers, but I had each one only once. When I gave way to their cravings after prolonged entreaty, when I offered up my body to them, sharing this bed . . . Yes, a guilty wife is truly disgusting! In the morning, when I awoke, I was alone! And I never saw them again! Can anyone be punished more cruelly than that? Crime and punishment are bound up with one another, and each crime calls forth its own torment. Have pity on me, Andreas, and let me confess everything, that I may gain remission of my sins. Let me tell you, I loved the last one with a reckless, insane passion. Losing him is killing me; forsaken by him, I can live no longer! Now I have confessed all. In the name of Our Lady of Atocha, in the name of San Isodro Labrador, in the name of San Andreas, your patron saint, in the name of my father, forgive this weak woman who has so grievously trespassed against you. Let me be purified by your blessing. Oh, give me your pardon! I am dying . . .'

She seized his hand, covering it with kisses and with tears. Vesalius snatched it away, pushed back his chair, and said resolutely:

'Get up, Maria, and follow me.'

'I am sinking fast; I cannot.'

'I told you to follow me.'

Struggling to get up, Maria wrapped herself in a gown and staggered along behind Vesalius, who went down the great stairway, crossed the courtyard, and opened a little lattice door which led into a small building lit by high stone-framed windows. The door closed behind them, and the bolts on the inside creaked into their fastenings.

V. OPIFICINA

We are within Vesalius's workshop or laboratory: a large square room with a vaulted ceiling, paved and walled with stone. The furnishings consisted of a few dirty, greasy tables, some work-benches, a couple of wash-tubs, one cupboard, and a few storage chests. A number of cauldrons were laid out around the fireplace, the wide mantel of which descended straight from the vaulted ceiling. Hanging from the chimney-hook was a pan boiling up over the heat of the fire. The benches were so overladen with chopped-up corpses that you risked treading on scraps of flesh or amputated limbs. The professor himself would crush muscles and cartilage under his sandals. A skeleton was hung up on the door, which would creak open and shut like a chandler's shop sign agitated by a wintry gale. The ceiling and the walls were covered with ribs, backbones, skeletons, and carcasses; some of them were human, but most came from monkeys and pigs—the animals whose form most closely resembles human bone-structure. These had been of assistance in Vesalius's researches; and it should be said that he was the first to make anatomy a true science, the first who dared to dissect corpses (even those of orthodox Christians) and work on them publicly. Not until about 1315, well before this time, had the world been treated to the new spectacle of dissected cadavers—three of them, exhibited by Mundinus, a professor at Bologna. This daring outrage had never been repeated, the Church having formally prohibited the practice as sacrilegious. Frightened off by this latest papal edict from Boniface VII, Mundinus himself could hardly draw any benefit at all from his discoveries. Among the ancients, contact with a corpse, or even the bare sight of one was held to be so indelible a pollution that the most vigorous of solemn ablutions and other rites of expiation could scarcely expunge it. In the Middle Ages, to dissect a creature 'made in God's image' was considered a blasphemy worthy of the gallows.

VI. ENODATIO = freeing from Knot ⟶ denouement

'So now what do you want of me here in your laboratory, Vesalius?' said Maria tearfully. 'What do you want of me? I can't stay in here: the foul stench of these bodies is choking me. Open the door and let me out—I can't bear this!'

'I don't care about that. It's your turn to listen to me. You had three lovers, am I right?'

'Yes, my lord.'

'And you made them drunk on my wine?'

'Yes, my lord.'

'Well, the wine was contaminated. Your duenna mixed into it some opium—a narcotic—and you went into a long and deep sleep, didn't you?'

'Yes, my lord, and when I awoke I was alone.'

'Alone, indeed?'

'Yes, and I never saw them again.'

'Never! Very good. Now come with me . . . !'

Taking her arm, he dragged her to the other end of the room, where he opened a chest, in which there hung a complete skeleton, its bones all properly connected and as white as ivory.

'Do you recognize this man?'

'What, these bones?'

'Do you recognize this doublet and brown cape?'

'Yes, my lord, it belongs to the cavalier Alderán!'

'Look more closely, senora. Now do you recognize the dashing cavalier who wore this cape, and who danced with you so gallantly at our wedding?'

'Alderán!' Maria uttered a shriek fit to wake the dead.

'As you can see, madame, this has at least been of great benefit to science', he said, turning to her coldly, 'and so, you see, science is greatly indebted to you.'

Then, with a sneer, he led her along to a kind of reliquary or glass showcase that displayed a miraculously preserved human skeleton: the arteries were filled with a red liquid, and the veins with a liquid of blue, so that this bony frame seemed to be wrapped in silken webs. It was not hard to recognize, since some tufts of beard and hair were still attached to it.

'This one, madame, do you recall him? Just look at his fine beard and blond hair.'

'Fernando!! You killed him?'

'Until now, without having dissected any living bodies, we have had

79

only a vague and incomplete notion of the circulation of the blood or of the action of the muscles; but thanks to you, senora, Vesalius has stripped away these veils and won eternal glory.'

Then, grabbing her by her hair, he dragged her over to a huge chest and heaved up its heavy lid, forcing her head down to look inside.

'And now look at this! This was your last one, wasn't he?'

The chest contained a number of jars in which pieces of flesh were immersed in alcohol.

'Pedro, Pedro! And so you killed him too!'

'Yes, him too!'

Then with a frightful deathly gasp, Maria slumped to the floor.

The next day, a funeral procession set off from the mansion. The gravediggers who lowered the coffin into the crypt of Santa Maria la Mayor remarked to each other that it was heavy but hollow-sounding, and that the sound it made when it dropped was not that of a body.

That night, through the lattice of the laboratory door, you could have caught sight of Andreas Vesalius at his work-bench, dissecting the body of a beautiful woman, whose blond hair trailed down to the floor.

VII. AFFABULATIO

At the fabulously wealthy court of Madrid, overflowing with the treasures of Columbus and dominating the whole of Europe, Andreas Vesalius basked in his glory, his riches, and his position of high esteem. Balancing himself between Philip II and the Inquisition, he encouraged the study of anatomy as far as he possibly could, until he was plunged into a series of dreadful calamities by an official denunciation.

While he was conducting a public autopsy upon the body of a nobleman, the heart appeared to give a beat under the very blade of his scalpel. Nursing a bitter grudge against the scientist, the Inquisition accused him of murder and demanded the death penalty. Only with great difficulty could Philip manage to commute the sentence to a pilgrimage to the Holy Land. Vesalius made his way to Palestine in the company of Malatesta, the leader of the Venetian army. After braving all the hazards of this perilous journey, he was shipwrecked on the return voyage by a storm off the coast of Zante, where he died of hunger on the 15 October 1564. The Venetian Republic, mourning the recent premature death of his disciple Gabrielle Fallopius, had just appointed him to the University of Padua.

If Boerhave and Albinus are to be credited, Andreas Vesalius perished a victim of the constant ridicule with which he mocked the ignorance, the fripperies, and the immorality of the Spanish monks and of the Inquisition—which was only too glad of the opportunity to rid itself of this troublesome scholar.

Andreas Vesalius's great work on anatomy, *De humani corporis fabrica*, was published in Basel in 1562, embellished by illustrations attributed to his friend Titian.

J. WADHAM

Lady Eltringham *or* The Castle of Ratcliffe Cross

Lady Eltringham was wandering alone through the mysterious and gloomy passages of a wing of the castle of Ratcliffe Cross, one evening, in the last summer that ever the golden sun flashed upon the blood-stained banner of chivalry, when her attention was suddenly attracted to the prisoners ward, the only part of the castle she had never visited. 'Here, perhaps I shall find' said she, as her raven eyes pursued the object of her search, 'some traces that may lead me to discover who and why so many sufferers send their heavy groans even to my bedchamber; and often, very often in the night have my dreams been disturbed by the noise of their blood-stained manacles and piteous sighs!'

Scarce had she entered the massy portals of the dungeon, when she heard a rustling in a hidden corner of the vault, and at the same time a sigh almost inaudible told her she had reached the incarcerated victims of her lord's tyranny.

A shriek burst upon the ears of the affrighted Lady Eltringham, which soon died along the walls, driving a host of innumerable bats from their mouldering recesses. It came from the last victim that ever the iron key of solitude and barbarity turned upon. Lady Eltringham approached the pallet of the prisoner, and endeavoured to console his insufferable anguish by protesting that it was the presence of a friend and not an enemy.

'Oh, how that voice resembles the sound and melody of hers, the faithless but lovely form of my earliest attachment!' exclaimed the sunken voice of the exhausted wretch, writhing beneath the infliction of his approaching tortures, and then turning and starting as the moon's rays fell upon the dark eyes of the rosy-faced Lady Eltringham, he broke forth in the following incoherent strain:

'Oh, dearest lady! art thou too, a prisoner? So fair a flower thrown upon this wild and arid waste?—but that cannot be; the assassins who came reeking with blood from the scaffold, and placed on me these heavy chains, would have been beheaded had they disobeyed the orders of their savage master. To-morrow's sun will shine through yonder grated window, but it will light upon a corpse. My heart has ceased to beat;—I counted its vibrations till they were no more. When I heard you approach, I took it for the executioner, who with his poisoned chalice I had expected to find entering my cell. Every night my spirit is torn from its earthly dwelling to flit about in the solitude of these porches. Mine may be the next; but if I die by the agency of the tyrant, I will haunt him in his dreams, in the whitest garment of the tomb, and wherever the midnight bell is heard by him, there will I follow, and remind him of my presence.'

'I am the wife of that tyrant,' said the drooping Lady Eltringham, 'whose decrees I so often hear are put into execution;—but no victim has forfeited life whose cell I have been enabled to trace out. Take repose until the morrow, when your captivity is at an end.'

Scarcely had she made her departure, and hurried to the chamber of her lord, who had retired early to rest; when the slow and heavy steps of the executioner accompanied by two priests, and a train of attendants, startled the object of their visit from the cold and damp recess into which his bed of straw was thrown and littered about, and held to his lips the poisoned bowl.

With a supernatural grasp he snatched the bowl from their hands and drank the contents, exclaiming as he fell upon the stone floor of his cell, 'Such an end is better than the tortures of your master!' and instantly was he dragged away by his remorseless executioners to the vault for the reception of those who suffered by their hands.

The next morning the beautiful Lady Eltringham wandered to the dungeon whose inmate she had promised freedom;—all was solitude and gloom, not even the low and distant sounds of melancholy—or the stifled sighs of the patriot, were heard, so unlike the hell it appeared the preceding night.—At length, after great exertion and fatigue, she came to the crumbling pillars frowning at the entrance of the ponderous archway; here she took from her bosom the secret key to unloose the shackles of the object of her sympathy.—Suddenly, on beholding no trace of the prisoner, she cried out in extasies of joy,—'He has escaped—all around tells me so—and he again is free!'

The next night as the turrets of the castle shook with the peal of the midnight bell,—a cold perspiration ran across the heart of the affrighted lady with the dark locks, as she went restless to the chamber of her lord, and her imagination suddenly carried her back to those hours when she alone enjoyed happiness!—then the light, the gay, the beautiful,—at her own sweet will; but now the slave to the passions of a remorseless tyrant.

The melancholy sound of the old monkish bell had scarcely died away, and sleep closed the portals leading to the aching heart of Lady Eltringham, when the crumbling walls of the castle shook as if an earthquake had opened its oblivious jaws, and had commenced crunching its foundation.

Quickly through the gloom hurried the form who met its death by the blood decree of the tyrant, to his bedside, and drawing the tapestry apart gazed motionless on its inmates.—Lady Eltringham sprang up in an erect position; when, judge her horror and alarm, when she gazed upon the form of her early lover!—for a beautiful embossed pen which she had worked with silk and given as a pledge of her affections,—suddenly fell from the folds of the enveloping shroud with its thousand recollections.

The unfortunate Lady Eltringham was that night dressed for the sepulchre; her lord died beneath the blazing sun of the Asian Isles, but still the lover of Lady E— haunts the Black towers of Ratcliffe Cross.

EDGAR ALLAN POE

The Fall of the House of Usher

Son cœur est un luth suspendu;
Sitôt qu'on le touche il résonne.
DE BÉRANGER

During the whole of a dull, dark, and soundless day in the autumn of the year, when the clouds hung oppressively low in the heavens, I had been passing alone, on horseback, through a singularly dreary tract of country; and at length found myself, as the shades of the evening drew on, within view of the melancholy House of Usher. I know not how it was—but, with the first glimpse of the building, a sense of insufferable gloom pervaded my spirit. I say insufferable; for the feeling was unrelieved by any of that half-pleasurable, because poetic, sentiment, with which the mind usually receives even the sternest natural images of the desolate or terrible. I looked upon the scene before me—upon the mere house, and the simple landscape features of the domain—upon the bleak walls—upon the vacant eye-like windows—upon a few rank sedges—and upon a few white trunks of decayed trees—with an utter depression of soul which I can compare to no earthly sensation more properly than to the after-dream of the reveller upon opium—the bitter lapse into everyday life—the hideous dropping off of the veil. There was an iciness, a sinking, a sickening of the heart—an unredeemed dreariness of thought which no goading of the imagination could torture into aught of the sublime. What was it—I paused to think—what was it that so unnerved me in the contemplation of the House of Usher? It was a mystery all insoluble; nor could I grapple with the shadowy fancies that crowded upon me as I pondered. I was forced to fall back upon the unsatisfactory conclusion, that while, beyond doubt, there *are* combinations of very simple natural objects which have the power of thus affecting us, still the analysis of this power lies among considerations beyond our depth. It was possible, I reflected, that a mere different arrangement of the particulars of the scene, of the details of the picture, would be sufficient to modify, or perhaps to annihilate its capacity for sorrowful impression; and, acting upon this idea, I reined my horse to the precipitous brink of a black and lurid tarn that lay in unruffled lustre by the dwelling, and gazed down—but with a shudder even more thrilling than before—upon the remodelled and inverted images of the grey sedge, and the ghastly tree-stems, and the vacant and eye-like windows.

Nevertheless, in this mansion of gloom I now proposed to myself a sojourn of some weeks. Its proprietor, Roderick Usher, had been one of my boon companions in boyhood; but many years had elapsed since our last meeting. A letter, however, had lately reached me in a distant part of the country—a letter from him—which, in its wildly importunate nature, had admitted of no other than a personal reply. The MS gave evidence of nervous agitation. The writer spoke of acute bodily illness—of a mental disorder which oppressed him— and of an earnest desire to see me, as his best, and indeed his only personal friend, with a view of attempting, by the cheerfulness of my society, some alleviation of his malady. It was the manner in which all this, and much more, was said—it was the apparent *heart* that went with his request—which allowed me no room for hesitation; and I accordingly obeyed forthwith what I still considered a very singular summons.

Although, as boys, we had been even intimate associates, yet I really knew little of my friend. His reserve had been always excessive and habitual. I was aware, however, that his very ancient family had been noted, time out of mind, for a peculiar sensibility of temperament, displaying itself, through long ages, in many works of exalted art, and manifested, of late, in repeated deeds of munificent yet unobtrusive charity, as well as in a passionate devotion to the intricacies, perhaps even more than to the orthodox and easily recognisable beauties, of musical science. I had learned, too, the very remarkable fact, that the stem of the Usher race, all time-honoured as it was, had put forth, at no period, any enduring branch; in other words, that the entire family lay in the direct line of descent, and had always, with very trifling and very temporary variation, so lain. It was this deficiency, I considered, while running over in thought the perfect keeping of the character of the premises with the accredited character of the people, and while speculating upon the possible influence which the one, in the long lapse of centuries, might have exercised upon the other—it was this deficiency, perhaps, of collateral issue, and the consequent undeviating transmission, from sire to son, of the patrimony with the name, which had, at length, so identified the two as to merge the original title of the estate in the quaint and equivocal appellation of the 'House of Usher'—an appellation which seemed to include, in the minds of the peasantry who used it, both the family and the family mansion.

I have said that the sole effect of my somewhat childish experiment —that of looking down within the tarn—had been to deepen the first singular impression. There can be no doubt that the consciousness of the rapid increase of my superstition—for why should I not so term it?—served mainly to accelerate the increase itself. Such, I have long known, is the paradoxical law of all sentiments having terror as a basis. And it might have been for this reason only, that, when I again uplifted my eyes to the house itself, from its image in the pool, there grew in my mind a strange fancy—a fancy so ridiculous, indeed, that I but mention it to show the vivid force of the sensations which oppressed me. I had so worked upon my imagination as really to believe that about the whole mansion and domain there hung an atmosphere peculiar to themselves and their immediate vicinity—an atmosphere which had no affinity with the air of heaven, but which had reeked up from the decayed trees, and the grey wall, and the silent tarn—a pestilent and mystic vapour, dull, sluggish, faintly discernible, and leaden-hued.

Shaking off from my spirit what *must* have been a dream, I scanned more narrowly the real aspect of the building. Its principal feature seemed to be that of an excessive antiquity. The discoloration of ages had been great. Minute *fungi* overspread the whole exterior, hanging in a fine tangled web-work from the eaves. Yet all this was apart from any extraordinary dilapidation. No portion of the masonry had fallen; and there appeared to be a wild inconsistency between its still perfect adaptation of parts, and the crumbling condition of the individual stones. In this there was much that reminded me of the specious totality of old woodwork which has rotted for long years in some neglected vault, with no disturbance from the breath of the external air. Beyond this indication of extensive decay, however, the fabric gave little token of instability. Perhaps the eye of a scrutinising observer might have discovered a barely perceptible fissure, which, extending from the roof of the building in front, made its way down the wall in a zigzag direction, until it became lost in the sullen waters of the tarn.

Noticing these things, I rode over a short causeway to the house. A servant in waiting took my horse, and I entered the Gothic archway of the hall. A valet, of stealthy step, thence conducted me, in silence, through many dark and intricate passages in my progress to the *studio* of his master. Much that I encountered on the way contributed, I know not how, to heighten the vague sentiments of which I have already spoken. While the objects around me—while the carvings of the ceilings, the sombre tapestries of the walls, the ebon blackness of the floors, and the phantasmagoric armorial trophies which rattled as

I strode, were but matters to which, or to such as which, I had been accustomed from my infancy—while I hesitated not to acknowledge how familiar was all this—I still wondered to find how unfamiliar were the fancies which ordinary images were stirring up. On one of the staircases, I met the physician of the family. His countenance, I thought, wore a mingled expression of low cunning and perplexity. He accosted me with trepidation and passed on. The valet now threw open a door and ushered me into the presence of his master.

The room in which I found myself was very large and lofty. The windows were long, narrow, and pointed, and at so vast a distance from the black oaken floor as to be altogether inaccessible from within. Feeble gleams of encrimsoned light made their way through the trellised panes, and served to render sufficiently distinct the more prominent objects around; the eye, however, struggled in vain to reach the remoter angles of the chamber, or the recesses of the vaulted and fretted ceiling. Dark draperies hung upon the walls. The general furniture was profuse, comfortless, antique, and tattered. Many books and musical instruments lay scattered about, but failed to give any vitality to the scene. I felt that I breathed an atmosphere of sorrow. An air of stern, deep, and irredeemable gloom hung over and pervaded all.

Upon my entrance, Usher arose from a sofa on which he had been lying at full length, and greeted me with a vivacious warmth which had much in it, I at first thought, of an overdone cordiality—of the constrained effort of the *ennuyé* man of the world. A glance, however, at his countenance, convinced me of his perfect sincerity. We sat down; and for some moments, while he spoke not, I gazed upon him with a feeling half of pity, half of awe. Surely, man had never before so terribly altered, in so brief a period, as had Roderick Usher! It was with difficulty that I could bring myself to admit the identity of the wan being before me with the companion of my early boyhood. Yet the character of his face had been at all times remarkable. A cadaverousness of complexion; an eye large, liquid, and luminous beyond comparison; lips somewhat thin and very pallid, but of a surpassingly beautiful curve; a nose of a delicate Hebrew model, but with a breadth of nostril unusual in similar formations; a finely moulded chin, speaking, in its want of prominence, of a want of moral energy; hair of a more than web-like softness and tenuity; these features, with an inordinate expansion above the regions of the temple, made up altogether a countenance not easily to be forgotten. And now in the mere exaggeration of the prevailing character of these features, and of the expression they were wont to convey, lay so much of change that I doubted to whom I spoke. The now ghastly pallor of the skin, and the now miraculous lustre of the eye, above all things startled and even awed me. The silken hair, too, had been suffered to grow all unheeded, and as, in its wild gossamer texture, it floated rather than fell about the face, I could not, even with effort, connect its arabesque expression with any idea of simple humanity.

In the manner of my friend I was at once struck with an incoherence—an inconsistency; and I soon found this to arise from a series of feeble and futile struggles to overcome an habitual trepidancy—an excessive nervous agitation. For something of this nature I had indeed been prepared, no less by his letter, than by reminiscences of certain boyish traits, and by conclusions deduced from his peculiar physical conformation and temperament. His action was alternately vivacious and sullen. His voice varied rapidly from a tremulous indecision (when the animal spirits seemed utterly in abeyance) to that species of energetic concision—that abrupt, weighty, unhurried, and hollow-sounding enunciation—that leaden, self-balanced and perfectly modulated guttural utterance, which may be observed in the lost drunkard, or the irreclaimable eater of opium, during the periods of his most intense excitement.

It was thus that he spoke of the object of my visit, of his earnest desire to see me, and of the solace he expected me to afford him. He entered, at some length, into what he conceived to be the nature of his malady. It was, he said, a constitutional and a family evil, and one for which he despaired to find a remedy—a mere nervous affection, he immediately added, which would undoubtedly soon pass off. It displayed itself in a host of unnatural sensations. Some of these, as he detailed them, interested and bewildered me; although, perhaps, the terms, and the general manner of the narration had their weight. He suffered much from a morbid acuteness of the senses; the most insipid food was alone endurable; he could wear only garments of certain texture; the odours of all flowers were oppressive; his eyes were tortured by even a faint light; and there were but peculiar sounds, and these from stringed instruments, which did not inspire him with horror.

To an anomalous species of terror I found him a bounden slave. 'I shall perish,' said he, 'I *must* perish in this deplorable folly. Thus, thus, and not otherwise, shall I be lost. I dread the events of the future, not in themselves, but in their results. I shudder at the thought of any, even the most trivial, incident, which may operate upon this intolerable agitation of soul. I have, indeed, no abhorrence of danger, except in its absolute effect—in terror. In this unnerved—

in this pitiable condition—I feel that the period will sooner or later arrive when I must abandon life and reason together, in some struggle with the grim phantasm, FEAR.'

I learned, moreover, at intervals, and through broken and equivocal hints, another singular feature of his mental condition. He was enchained by certain superstitious impressions in regard to the dwelling which he tenanted, and whence, for many years, he had never ventured forth—in regard to an influence whose suppositious force was conveyed in terms too shadowy here to be re-stated—an influence which some peculiarities in the mere form and substance of his family mansion, had, by dint of long sufferance, he said, obtained over his spirit—an effect which the *physique* of the grey walls and turrets, and of the dim tarn into which they all looked down, had, at length, brought about upon the *morale* of his existence.

He admitted, however, although with hesitation, that much of the peculiar gloom which thus afflicted him could be traced to a more natural and far more palpable origin—to the severe and long-continued illness—indeed to the evidently approaching dissolution—of a tenderly beloved sister—his sole companion for long years—his last and only relative on earth. 'Her decease,' he said, with a bitterness which I can never forget, 'would leave him (him the hopeless and the frail) the last of the ancient race of the Ushers.' While he spoke, the Lady Madeline (for so was she called) passed slowly through a remote portion of the apartment, and, without having noticed my presence, disappeared. I regarded her with an utter astonishment not unmingled with dread—and yet I found it impossible to account for such feelings. A sensation of stupor oppressed me, as my eyes followed her retreating steps. When a door, at length, closed upon her, my glance sought instinctively and eagerly the countenance of the brother—but he had buried his face in his hands, and I could only perceive that a far more than ordinary wanness had overspread the emaciated fingers through which trickled many passionate tears.

The disease of the Lady Madeline had long baffled the skill of her physicians. A settled apathy, a gradual wasting away of the person, and frequent although transient affections of a partially cataleptical character, were the unusual diagnosis. Hitherto she had steadily borne up against the pressure of her malady, and had not betaken herself finally to bed; but, on the closing in of the evening of my arrival at the house, she succumbed (as her brother told me at night with inexpressible agitation) to the prostrating power of the destroyer; and I learned that the glimpse I had obtained of her person would thus probably be the last I should obtain—that the lady, at least while living, would be seen by me no more.

For several days ensuing, her name was unmentioned by either Usher or myself: and during this period I was busied in earnest endeavours to alleviate the melancholy of my friend. We painted and read together; or I listened, as if in a dream, to the wild improvisations of his speaking guitar. And thus, as a closer and still closer intimacy admitted me more unreservedly into the recesses of his spirit, the more bitterly did I perceive the futility of all attempt at cheering a mind from which darkness, as if an inherent positive quality, poured forth upon all objects of the moral and physical universe, in one unceasing radiation of gloom.

I shall ever bear about me a memory of the many solemn hours I thus spent alone with the master of the House of Usher. Yet I should fail in any attempt to convey an idea of the exact character of the studies, or of the occupations, in which he involved me, or led me the way. An excited and highly distempered ideality threw a sulphureous lustre over all. His long improvised dirges will ring for ever in my ears. Among other things, I hold painfully in mind a certain singular perversion and amplification of the wild air of the last waltz of Von Weber. From the paintings over which his elaborate fancy brooded, and which grew, touch by touch, into vagueness at which I shuddered the more thrillingly, because I shuddered knowing not why;—from these paintings (vivid as their images now are before me) I would in vain endeavour to educe more than a small portion which should lie within the compass of merely written words. By the utter simplicity, by the nakedness of his designs, he arrested and overawed attention. If ever mortal painted an idea, that mortal was Roderick Usher. For me at least—in the circumstances then surrounding me—there arose out of the pure abstractions which the hypochondriac contrived to throw upon his canvas, an intensity of intolerable awe, no shadow of which felt I ever yet in the contemplation of the certainly glowing yet too concrete reveries of Fuseli.

One of the phantasmagoric conceptions of my friend, partaking not so rigidly of the spirit of abstraction, may be shadowed forth, although feebly, in words. A small picture presented the interior of an immensely long and rectangular vault or tunnel, with low walls, smooth, white, and without interruption or device. Certain accessory points of the design served well to convey the idea that this excavation lay at an exceeding depth below the surface of the earth. No outlet was observed in any portion of its vast extent, and no torch, or other artificial source of light was discernible; yet a flood of intense rays rolled throughout, and bathed the whole in a ghastly and inappropriate splendour.

I have just spoken of that morbid condition of the auditory nerve which rendered all music intolerable to the sufferer, with the exception of certain effects of stringed instruments. It was, perhaps, the narrow limits to which he thus confined himself upon the guitar, which gave birth, in great measure, to the fantastic character of his performances. But the fervid *facility* of his *impromptus* could not be so accounted for. They must have been, and were, in the notes, as well as in the words of his wild fantasias (for he not unfrequently accompanied himself with rhymed verbal improvisations), the result of that intense mental collectedness and concentration to which I have previously alluded as observable only in particular moments of the highest artificial excitement. The words of one of these rhapsodies I have easily remembered. I was, perhaps, the more forcibly impressed with it, as he gave it, because, in the under or mystic current of its meaning, I fancied that I perceived, and for the first time, a full consciousness on the part of Usher, of the tottering of his lofty reason upon her throne. The verses, which were entitled 'The Haunted Palace', ran very nearly, if not accurately, thus:

I

In the greenest of our valleys,
     By good angels tenanted,
Once a fair and stately palace—
     Radiant palace—reared its head.
In the monarch Thought's dominion—
     It stood there!
Never seraph spread a pinion
     Over fabric half so fair.

II

Banners yellow, glorious, golden,
     On its roof did float and flow;
(This—all this—was in the olden
     Time long ago)
And every gentle air that dallied,
     In that sweet day,
Along the ramparts plumed and pallid,
     A winged odour went away.

III

Wanderers in that happy valley
     Through two luminous windows saw

Spirits moving musically
  To a lute's well tunèd law,
Round about a throne, where sitting
  (Porphyrogene!)
In state his glory well befitting,
  The ruler of the realm was seen.

IV

And all with pearl and ruby glowing
  Was the fair palace door,
Through which came flowing, flowing, flowing
  And sparkling evermore,
A troop of Echoes whose sweet duty
  Was but to sing,
In voices of surpassing beauty,
  The wit and wisdom of their king.

V

But evil things, in robes of sorrow,
  Assailed the monarch's high estate;
(Ah, let us mourn, for never morrow
  Shall dawn upon him, desolate!)
And, round about his home, the glory
  That blushed and bloomed
Is but a dim-remembered story
  Of the old time entombed.

VI

And travellers now within that valley,
  Through the red-litten windows, see
Vast forms that move fantastically
  To a discordant melody;
While, like a rapid ghastly river,
  Through the pale door,
A hideous throng rush out forever,
  And laugh—but smile no more.

I well remember that suggestions arising from this ballad, led us into a train of thought wherein there became manifest an opinion of Usher's which I mention not so much on account of its novelty (for other men[1] have thought thus), as on account of the pertinacity with which he maintained it. This opinion, in its general form, was that of the sentience of all vegetable things. But, in his disordered fancy, the idea had assumed a more daring character, and trespassed, under

[1] Watson, Dr Percival, Spallanzani, and especially the Bishop of Landaff.

certain conditions, upon the kingdom of inorganization. I lack words to express the full extent, or the earnest *abandon* of his persuasion. The belief, however, was connected (as I have previously hinted) with the grey stones of the home of his forefathers. The conditions of the sentience had been here, he imagined, fulfilled in the method of collocation of these stones—in the order of their arrangement, as well as in that of the many *fungi* which overspread them, and of the decayed trees which stood around—above all, in the long undisturbed endurance of this arrangement, and in its reduplication in the still waters of the tarn. Its evidence—the evidence of the sentience—was to be seen, he said, (and I here started as he spoke) in the gradual yet certain condensation of an atmosphere of their own about the waters and the walls. The result was discoverable, he added, in that silent, yet importunate and terrible influence which for centuries had moulded the destinies of his family, and which made *him* what I now saw him—what he was. Such opinions need no comment, and I will make none.

Our books—the books which, for years, had formed no small portion of the mental existence of the invalid—were, as might be supposed, in strict keeping with this character of phantasm. We pored together over such works as the *Ververt et Chartreuse* of Gresset; the *Belphegor* of Machiavelli; the *Heaven and Hell* of Swedenborg; the *Subterranean Voyage of Nicholas Klimm* by Holberg; the *Chiromancy* of Robert Flud, of Jean D'Indaginé, and of De la Chambre; the *Journey into the Blue Distance* of Tieck; and the *City of the Sun* of Campanella. One favourite volume was a small octavo edition of the *Directorium Inquisitorum*, by the Dominican Eymeric de Gironne; and there were passages in *Pomponius Mela*, about the old African Satyrs and Ægipans, over which Usher would sit dreaming for hours. His chief delight, however, was found in the perusal of an exceedingly rare and curious book in quarto Gothic—the manual of a forgotten church—the *Vigiliæ Mortuorum Chorum Ecclesiæ Maguntinæ*.

I could not help thinking of the wild ritual of this work, and of its probable influence upon the hypochondriac, when, one evening, having informed me abruptly that the Lady Madeline was no more, he stated his intention of preserving her corpse for a fortnight (previously to its final interment), in one of the numerous vaults within the main walls of the building. The wordly reason, however, assigned for this singular proceeding, was one which I did not feel at liberty to dispute. The brother had been led to his resolution (so he told me) by consideration of the unusual character of the malady of the deceased, of certain obtrusive and eager inquiries on the part of her medical men, and of the remote and exposed situation of the burial-ground of the family. I will not deny that when I called to mind the sinister countenance of the person whom I met upon the staircase, on the day of my arrival at the house, I had no desire to oppose what I regarded as at best but a harmless, and by no means unnatural, precaution.

At the request of Usher, I personally aided him in the arrangements for the temporary entombment. The body having been encoffined, we two alone bore it to its rest. The vault in which we placed it (and which had been so long unopened that our torches, half smothered in its oppressive atmosphere, gave us little opportunity for investigation) was small, damp, and entirely without means of admission for light; lying, at great depth, immediately beneath that portion of the building in which was my own sleeping apartment. It had been used, apparently, in remote feudal times, for the worst purpose of a donjon-keep, and, in later days, as a place of deposit for powder, or some other highly combustible substance, as a portion of its floor, and the whole interior of a long archway through which we reached it, were carefully sheathed with copper. The door, of massive iron, had been, also, similarly protected. Its immense weight caused an unusually sharp grating sound, as it moved upon its hinges.

Having deposited our mournful burden upon tressels within this region of horror, we partially turned aside the yet unscrewed lid of the coffin, and looked upon the face of the tenant. A striking similitude between the brother and sister now first arrested my attention; and Usher, divining, perhaps, my thoughts, murmured out some few words from which I learned that the deceased and himself had been twins, and that sympathies of a scarcely intelligible nature had always existed between them. Our glances, however, rested not long upon the dead—for we could not regard her unawed. The disease which had thus entombed the lady in the maturity of youth, had left, as usual in all maladies of a strictly cataleptical character, the mockery of a faint blush upon the bosom and the face, and that suspiciously lingering smile upon the lip which is so terrible in death. We replaced and screwed down the lid, and, having secured the door of iron, made our way, with toil, into the scarcely less gloomy apartments of the upper portion of the house.

And now, some days of bitter grief having elapsed, an observable change came over the features of the mental disorder of my friend. His ordinary manner had vanished. His ordinary occupations were neglected or forgotten. He roamed from chamber to chamber with hurried, unequal, and objectless step. The pallor of his countenance had assumed, if possible, a more ghastly hue—but the luminousness of his eye had utterly gone out. The once occasional huskiness of his tone was heard no more; and a tremulous quaver, as if of extreme terror, habitually characterized his utterance. There were times, indeed, when I thought his unceasingly agitated mind was labouring with some oppressive secret, to divulge which he struggled for the necessary courage. At times, again, I was obliged to resolve all into the mere inexplicable vagaries of madness, for I beheld him gazing upon vacancy for long hours, in an attitude of the profoundest attention, as if listening to some imaginary sound. It was no wonder that his condition terrified—that it infected me. I felt creeping upon me, by slow yet certain degrees, the wild influences of his own fantastic yet impressive superstitions.

It was, especially, upon retiring to bed late in the night of the seventh or eighth day after the placing of the Lady Madeline within the donjon, that I experienced the full power of such feelings. Sleep came not near my couch—while the hours waned and waned away. I struggled to reason off the nervousness which had dominion over me. I endeavoured to believe that much, if not all of what I felt, was due to the bewildering influence of the gloomy furniture of the room—of the dark and tattered draperies, which, tortured into motion by the breath of a rising tempest, swayed fitfully to and fro upon the walls, and rustled uneasily about the decorations of the bed. But my efforts were fruitless. An irrepressible tremor gradually pervaded my frame; and, at length, there sat upon my very heart an incubus of utterly causeless alarm. Shaking this off with a gasp and a struggle, I uplifted, myself upon the pillows, and, peering earnestly within the intense darkness of the chamber, hearkened—I know not why, except that an instinctive spirit prompted me—to certain low and indefinite sounds which came, through the pauses of the storm, at long intervals, I knew not whence. Overpowered by an intense sentiment of horror, unaccountable yet unendurable, I threw on my clothes with haste (for I felt that I should sleep no more during the night), and endeavoured to arouse myself from the pitiable condition into which I had fallen, by pacing rapidly to and fro through the apartment.

I had taken but few turns in this manner, when a light step on an adjoining staircase arrested my attention. I presently recognised it as that of Usher. In an instant afterwards he rapped, with a gentle touch, at my door, and entered, bearing a lamp. His countenance was, as usual, cadaverously wan—but, moreover, there was a species of mad hilarity in his eyes—an evidently restrained *hysteria* in his whole demeanour. His air appalled me—but anything was preferable to the solitude which I had so long endured, and I even welcomed his presence as a relief.

'And you have not seen it?' he said abruptly, after having stared about him for some moments in silence—'you have not then seen it?—but, stay! you shall.' Thus speaking, and having carefully shaded his lamp, he hurried to one of the casements, and threw it freely open to the storm.

The impetuous fury of the entering gust nearly lifted us from our feet. It was, indeed, a tempestuous yet sternly beautiful night, and one wildly singular in its terror and its beauty. A whirlwind had apparently collected its force in our vicinity; for there were frequent and violent alterations in the direction of the wind; and the exceeding density of the clouds (which hung so low as to press upon the turrets of the house) did not prevent our perceiving the lifelike velocity with which they flew careering from all points against each other, without passing away into the distance. I say that even their exceeding density did not prevent our perceiving this—yet we had no glimpse of the moon or stars—nor was there any flashing forth of the lightning. But the under surfaces of the huge masses of agitated vapour, as well as all terrestrial objects immediately around us, were glowing in the unnatural light of a faintly luminous and distinctly visible gaseous exhalation which hung about and enshrouded the mansion.

'You must not—you shall not behold this!' said I, shudderingly, to Usher, as I led him, with a gentle violence, from the window to a seat. 'These appearances, which bewilder you, are merely electrical phenomena not uncommon—or it may be that they have their ghastly origin in the rank miasma of the tarn. Let us close this casement;— the air is chilling and dangerous to your frame. Here is one of your favourite romances. I will read, and you shall listen;—and so we will pass away this terrible night together.'

The antique volume which I had taken up was the *Mad Trist* of Sir Launcelot Canning; but I had called it a favourite of Usher's more in sad jest than in earnest; for, in truth, there is little in its uncouth and unimaginative prolixity which could have had interest for the lofty and spiritual ideality of my friend. It was, however, the only book immediately at hand; and I indulged a vague hope that the excite- ment which now agitated the hypochondriac, might find relief (for the history of mental disorder is full of similar anomalies) even in the extremeness of the folly which I should read. Could I have judged, indeed, by the wild overstrained air of vivacity with which he hearkened, or apparently hearkened, to the words of the tale, I might well have congratulated myself upon the success of my design.

I had arrived at that well-known portion of the story where Ethelred, the hero of the Trist, having sought in vain for peaceable admission into the dwelling of the hermit, proceeds to make good an entrance by force. Here, it will be remembered, the words of the narrative run thus:

'And Ethelred, who was by nature of a doughty heart, and who was now mighty withal, on account of the powerfulness of the wine which he had drunken, waited no longer to hold parley with the hermit, who, in sooth, was of an obstinate and maliceful turn, but, feeling the rain upon his shoulders, and fearing the rising of the tempest, uplifted his mace outright, and, with blows, made quickly room in the plankings of the door for his gauntleted hand; and now pulling therewith sturdily, he so cracked, and ripped, and tore all asunder, that the noise of the dry and hollow-sounding wood alarmed and reverberated throughout the forest.'

At the termination of this sentence I started, and for a moment, paused; for it appeared to me (although I at once concluded that my excited fancy had deceived me)—it appeared to me that, from some very remote portion of the mansion, there came, indistinctly, to my ears, what might have been, in its exact similarity of character, the echo (but a stifled and dull one certainly) of the very cracking and ripping sound which Sir Launcelot had so particularly described. It was, beyond doubt, the coincidence alone which had arrested my attention; for, amid the rattling of the sashes of the casements, and the ordinary commingled noises of the still increasing storm, the sound, in itself, had nothing, surely, which should have interested or disturbed me. I continued the story:

'But the good champion Ethelred, now entering within the door, was sore enraged and amazed to perceive no signal of the maliceful hermit; but, in the stead thereof, a dragon of a scaly and prodigious demeanour, and of a fiery tongue, which sate in guard before a palace of gold, with a floor of silver; and upon the wall there hung a shield of shining brass with this legend enwritten—

> Who entereth herein, a conqueror hath bin;
> Who slayeth the dragon, the shield he shall win;

and Ethelred uplifted his mace, and struck upon the head of the dragon, which fell before him, and gave up his pesty breath, with a shriek so horrid and harsh, and withal so piercing, that Ethelred had fain to close his ears with his hands against the dreadful noise of it, the like whereof was never before heard.'

Here again I paused abruptly, and now with a feeling of wild amazement—for there could be no doubt whatever that, in this instance, I did actually hear (although from what direction it proceeded I found it impossible to say) a low and apparently distant, but harsh, protracted, and most unusual screaming or grating sound— the exact counterpart of what my fancy had already conjured up for the dragon's unnatural shriek as described by the romancer.

Oppressed, as I certainly was, upon the occurrence of the second and most extraordinary coincidence, by a thousand conflicting sensations, in which wonder and extreme terror were predominant, I still retained sufficient presence of mind to avoid exciting, by any observation, the sensitive nervousness of my companion. I was by no means certain that he had noticed the sounds in question; although, assuredly, a strange alteration had, during the last few minutes, taken place in his demeanour. From a position fronting my own, he had gradually brought round his chair, so as to sit with his face to the door of the chamber; and thus I could but partially perceive his features, although I saw that his lips trembled as if he were murmuring inaudibly. His head had dropped upon his breast—yet I knew that he was not asleep, from the wide and rigid opening of the eye as I caught a glance of it in profile. The motion of his body, too, was at variance with this idea—for he rocked from side to side with a gentle yet constant and uniform sway. Having rapidly taken notice of all this, I resumed the narrative of Sir Launcelot, which thus proceeded:

'And now, the champion, having escaped from the terrible fury of the dragon, bethinking himself of the brazen shield, and of the breaking up of the enchantment which was upon it, removed the carcass from out of the way before him, and approached valorously over the silver pavement of the castle to where the shield was upon the wall; which in sooth tarried not for his full coming, but fell down at his feet upon the silver floor, with a mighty great and terrible ringing sound.'

No sooner had these syllables passed my lips, than—as if a shield of brass had indeed, at the moment, fallen heavily upon a floor of silver—I became aware of a distinct, hollow, metallic, and clangorous, yet apparently muffled reverberation. Completely unnerved, I leaped to my feet; but the measured rocking movement of Usher was undisturbed. I rushed to the chair in which he sat. His eyes were bent fixedly before him, and throughout his whole countenance there reigned a stony rigidity. But, as I placed my hand upon his shoulder, there came a strong shudder over his whole person; a sickly smile quivered about his lips; and I saw that he spoke in a low, hurried, and gibbering murmur, as if unconscious of my presence.

Bending closely over him, I at length drank in the hideous import of his words.

'Not hear it?—yes, I hear it, and *have* heard it. Long—long—long—many minutes, many hours, many days, have I heard it— yet I dared not—oh, pity me, miserable wretch that I am!—I dared not—I *dared* not speak! *We have put her living in the tomb!* Said I not that my senses were acute? I *now* tell you that I heard her first feeble movements in the hollow coffin. I heard them—many, many days ago—yet I dared not—*I dared not speak!* And now—tonight—Ethelred—ha! ha!—the breaking of the hermit's door, and the death-cry of the dragon, and the clangour of the shield!—say, rather, the rending of her coffin, and the grating of the iron hinges of her prison, and her struggles within the coppered archway of the vault! Oh whither shall I fly? Will she not be here anon? Is she not hurrying to upbraid me for my haste? Have I not heard her footstep on the stair? Do I not distinguish that heavy and horrible beating of her heart? MADMAN!' here he sprang furiously to his feet, and shrieked out his syllables, as if in the effort he were giving up his soul—'MADMAN! I TELL YOU THAT SHE NOW STANDS WITHOUT THE DOOR!'

As if in the superhuman energy of his utterance there had been found the potency of a spell—the huge antique panels to which the speaker pointed, threw slowly back, upon the instant, their ponderous and ebony jaws. It was the work of the rushing gust—but then without those doors there DID stand the lofty and enshrouded figure of the Lady Madeline of Usher. There was blood upon her white robes, and the evidence of some bitter struggle upon every portion of her emaciated frame. For a moment she remained trembling and reeling to and fro upon the threshold, then with a low moaning cry, fell heavily inward upon the person of her brother, and in her violent and now final death-agonies, bore him to the floor a corpse, and a victim to the terrors he had anticipated.

From that chamber, and from that mansion, I fled aghast. The storm was still abroad in all its wrath as I found myself crossing the old causeway. Suddenly there shot along the path a wild light, and I turned to see whence a gleam so unusual could have issued; for the vast house and its shadows were alone behind me. The radiance was that of the full, setting, and blood-red moon which now shone vividly through that once barely discernible fissure of which I have before spoken as extending from the roof of the building, in a zigzag direction, to the base. While I gazed, this fissure rapidly widened—there came a fierce breath of the whirlwind—the entire orb of the satellite burst at once upon my sight—my brain reeled as I saw the mighty walls rushing asunder—there was a long tumultuous shouting sound like the voice of a thousand waters—and the deep and dank tarn at my feet closed sullenly and silently over the fragments of the 'HOUSE OF USHER'.

SHERIDAN LE FANU

A Chapter in the History of a Tyrone Family

Being a Tenth Extract from the Legacy of the Late
Francis Purcell, P. P. of Drumcoolagh

𝔍NTRODUCTION. In the following narrative, I have endeavoured to give as nearly as possible the *'ipsissima verba'* of the valued friend from whom I received it, conscious that any aberration from *her* mode of telling the tale of her own life, would at once impair its accuracy and its effect. Would that, with her words, I could also bring before you her animated gesture, her expressive countenance, the solemn and thrilling air and accent with which she related the dark passages in her strange story; and, above all, that I could communicate the impressive consciousness that the narrator had seen with her own eyes, and personally acted in the scenes which she described; these accompaniments, taken with the additional circumstance, that she who told the tale was one far too deeply and sadly impressed with religious principle, to misrepresent or fabricate what she repeated as fact, gave to the tale a depth of interest which the events recorded could hardly, themselves, have produced. I became acquainted with the lady from whose lips I heard this narrative, nearly twenty years since, and the story struck my fancy so much, that I committed it to paper while it was still fresh in my mind, and should its perusal afford you entertainment for a listless half hour, my labour shall not have been bestowed in vain. I find that I have taken the story down as she told it, in the first person, and, perhaps, this is as it should be. She began as follows.

My maiden name was Richardson,* the designation of a family of some distinction in the county of Tyrone. I was the younger of two daughters, and we were the only children. There was a difference in our ages of nearly six years, so that I did not, in my childhood, enjoy

* I have carefully altered the names as they appear in the original MSS, for the reader will see that some of the circumstances recorded are not of a kind to reflect honour upon those involved in them; and, as many are still living, in every way honoured and honourable, who stand in close relation to the principal actors in this drama, the reader will see the necessity of the course which we have adopted.

that close companionship which sisterhood, in other circumstances, necessarily involves; and while I was still a child, my sister was married. The person upon whom she bestowed her hand, was a Mr Carew, a gentleman of property and consideration in the north of England. I remember well the eventful day of the wedding; the thronging carriages, the noisy menials, the loud laughter, the merry faces, and the gay dresses. Such sights were then new to me, and harmonized ill with the sorrowful feelings with which I regarded the event which was to separate me, as it turned out, for ever, from a sister whose tenderness alone had hitherto more than supplied all that I wanted in my mother's affection. The day soon arrived which was to remove the happy couple from Ashtown-house. The carriage stood at the hall-door, and my poor sister kissed me again, and again, telling me that I should see her soon. The carriage drove away, and I gazed after it until my eyes filled with tears, and, returning slowly to my chamber, I wept more bitterly, and so to speak more desolately, than ever I had done before. My father had never seemed to love, or to take an interest in me. He had desired a son, and I think he never thoroughly forgave me my unfortunate sex. My having come into the world at all as his child, he regarded as a kind of fraudulent intrusion, and, as his antipathy to me had its origin in an imperfection of mine, too radical for removal, I never even hoped to stand high in his good graces. My mother was, I dare say, as fond of me as she was of any one; but she was a woman of a masculine and a worldly cast of mind. She had no tenderness or sympathy for the weaknesses, or even for the affections of woman's nature, and her demeanour towards me was peremptory, and often even harsh. It is not to be supposed, then, that I found in the society of my parents much to supply the loss of my sister. About a year after her marriage, we received letters from Mr Carew, containing accounts of my sister's health, which, though not actually alarming, were calculated to make us seriously uneasy. The symptoms most dwelt upon, were loss of appetite and cough. The letters concluded by intimating that he would avail himself of my father and mother's repeated invitation to spend some time at Ashtown, particularly as the physician who had been consulted as to my sister's health had strongly advised a removal to her native air. There were added repeated assurances that nothing serious was apprehended, as it was supposed that a deranged state of the liver was the only source of the symptoms which seemed to intimate consumption. In accordance with this announcement, my sister and Mr Carew arrived in Dublin, where one of my father's carriages awaited them, in readiness to start upon whatever day or hour they might choose for their departure. It was arranged that Mr Carew was, as soon as the day upon which they were to leave Dublin was definitely fixed, to write to my father, who intended that the two last stages should be performed by his own horses, upon whose speed and safety far more reliance might be placed than upon those of the ordinary *post-horses*, which were, at that time, almost without exception, of the very worst order. The journey, one of about ninety miles, was to be divided; the larger portion to be reserved for the second day. On Sunday, a letter reached us, stating that the party would leave Dublin on Monday, and, in due course, reach Ashtown upon Tuesday evening. Tuesday came: the evening closed in, and yet no carriage appeared; darkness came on, and still no sign of our expected visitors. Hour after hour passed away, and it was now past twelve; the night was remarkably calm, scarce a breath stirring, so that any sound, such as that produced by the rapid movement of a vehicle, would have been audible at a considerable distance. For some such sound I was feverishly listening. It was, however, my father's rule to close the house at nightfall, and the window-shutters being fastened, I was unable to reconnoitre the avenue as I would have wished. It was nearly one o'clock, and we began almost to despair of seeing them upon that night, when I thought I distinguished the sound of wheels, but so remote and faint as to make me at first very uncertain. The noise approached; it became louder and clearer; it stopped for a moment. I now heard the shrill screaking of the rusty iron, as the avenue gate revolved on its hinges; again came the sound of wheels in rapid motion.

'It is they,' said I, starting up, 'the carriage is in the avenue.' We all stood for a few moments, breathlessly listening. On thundered the vehicle with the speed of a whirlwind; crack went the whip, and clatter went the wheels, as it rattled over the uneven pavement of the court; a general and furious barking from all the dogs about the house, hailed its arrival. We hurried to the hall in time to hear the steps let down with the sharp clanging noise peculiar to the operation, and the hum of voices exerted in the bustle of arrival. The hall-door was now thrown open, and we all stepped forth to greet our visitors. The court was perfectly empty; the moon was shining broadly and brightly upon all around; nothing was to be seen but the tall trees with their long spectral shadows, now wet with the dews of midnight. We stood gazing from right to left, as if suddenly awakened from a dream; the dogs walked suspiciously, growling and snuffing about the court, and by totally and suddenly ceasing their former loud barking, as also by carrying their tails between their legs, expressing the predominance of fear. We looked one upon the other in perplexity and dismay, and I think I never beheld more pale faces assembled. By my father's direction, we looked about to find anything which might indicate or account for the noise which we had heard; but no such thing was to be seen—even the mire which lay upon the avenue was undisturbed. We returned to the house, more panic struck than I can describe. On the next day, we learned by a messenger, who had ridden hard the greater part of the night, that my sister was dead. On Sunday evening, she had retired to bed rather unwell, and, on Monday, her indisposition declared itself unequivocally to be malignant fever. She became hourly worse, and, on Tuesday night, a little after midnight, she expired.* I mention this circumstance, because it was one upon which a thousand wild and fantastical reports were founded, though one would have thought that the truth scarcely required to be improved upon; and again, because it produced a strong and lasting effect upon my spirits, and indeed, I am inclined to think, upon my character. I was, for several years after this occurrence, long after the violence of my grief subsided, so wretchedly low-spirited and nervous, that I could scarcely be said to live, and during this time, habits of indecision, arising out of a listless acquiescence in the will of others, a fear of encountering even the

---

* The residuary legatee of the late Francis Purcell, who has the honour of selecting such of his lamented old friend's manuscripts as may appear fit for publication, in order that the lore which they contain may reach the world before scepticism and utility have robbed our species of the precious gift of credulity, and scornfully kicked before them, or trampled into annihilation, those harmless fragments of picturesque superstition, which it is our object to preserve, has been subjected to the charge of dealing too largely in the marvellous; and it has been half insinuated that such is his love for *diablerie*, that he is content to wander a mile out of his way, in order to meet a fiend or a goblin, and thus to sacrifice all regard for truth and accuracy to the idle hope of affrighting the imagination, and thus pandering to the bad taste of his reader. He begs leave, then, to take this opportunity of asserting his perfect innocence of all the crimes laid to his charge, and to assure his reader that he never *pandered to his bad taste*, nor went one inch out of his way to introduce witch, fairy, devil, ghost, or any other of the grim fraternity of the redoubted Raw-head and bloody-bones. His province, touching these tales, has been attended with no difficulty and little responsibility; indeed, he is accountable for nothing more than an alteration in the names of persons mentioned therein, when such a step seemed necessary, and for an occasional note, whenever he conceived it possible, innocently, to edge in a word. These tales have been *written down*, as the heading of each announces, by the Revd Francis Purcell, P. P. of Drumcoolagh; and in all the instances, which are many, in which the present writer has had an opportunity of comparing the manuscript of his departed friend with the actual traditions which are current amongst the families whose fortunes they pretend to illustrate, he has uniformly found that whatever of supernatural occurred in the story, so far from having been exaggerated by him, had been rather softened down, and, wherever it could be attempted, accounted for.

She became desirable heiress

slightest opposition, and a disposition to shrink from what are commonly called amusements, grew upon me so strongly, that I have scarcely even yet, altogether overcome them. We saw nothing more of Mr Carew. He returned to England as soon as the melancholy rites attendant upon the event which I have just mentioned were performed; and not being altogether inconsolable, he married again within two years; after which, owing to the remoteness of our relative situations, and other circumstances, we gradually lost sight of him. I was now an only child; and, as my elder sister had died without issue, it was evident that, in the ordinary course of things, my father's property, which was altogether in his power, would go to me, and the consequence was, that before I was fourteen, Ashtown-house was besieged by a host of suitors; however, whether it was that *I* was too young, or that none of the aspirants to my hand stood sufficiently high in rank or wealth, I was suffered by both parents to do exactly as I pleased; and well was it for me, as I afterwards found that fortune, or, rather Providence, had so ordained it, that I had not suffered my affections to become in any degree engaged, for my mother would never have suffered any *silly fancy* of mine, as she was in the habit of styling an attachment, to stand in the way of her ambitious views; views which she was determined to carry into effect, in defiance of every obstacle, and in order to accomplish which, she would not have hesitated to sacrifice anything so unreasonable and contemptible as a girlish passion.

When I reached the age of sixteen, my mother's plans began to develope themselves, and, at her suggestion, we moved to Dublin to sojourn for the winter, in order that no time might be lost in disposing of me to the best advantage. I had been too long accustomed to consider myself as of no importance whatever, to believe for a moment that I was in reality the cause of all the bustle and preparation which surrounded me, and being thus relieved from the pain which a consciousness of my real situation would have inflicted, I journeyed towards the capital with a feeling of total indifference.

My father's wealth and connection had established him in the best society, and, consequently, upon our arrival in the metropolis, we commanded whatever enjoyment or advantages its gaieties afforded. The tumult and novelty of the scenes in which I was involved did not fail considerably to amuse me, and my mind gradually recovered its tone, which was naturally cheerful. It was almost immediately known and reported that I was an heiress, and of course my attractions were pretty generally acknowledged. Among the many gentlemen whom it was my fortune to please, one, ere long, established himself in my mother's good graces, to the exclusion of all less important aspirants. However, I had not understood, or even remarked his attentions, nor, in the slightest degree, suspected his or my mother's plans respecting me, when I was made aware of them rather abruptly by my mother herself. We had attended a splendid ball, given by Lord M——, at his residence in Stephen's-green, and I was, with the assistance of my waiting-maid, employed in rapidly divesting myself of the rich ornaments which, in profuseness and value, could scarcely have found their equals in any private family in Ireland. I had thrown myself into a lounging chair beside the fire, listless and exhausted, after the fatigues of the evening, when I was aroused from the reverie into which I had fallen, by the sound of footsteps approaching my chamber, and my mother entered.

'Fanny, my dear,' said she, in her softest tone. 'I wish to say a word or two with you before I go to rest. You are not fatigued, love, I hope?'

'No, no, madam, I thank you,' said I, rising at the same time from my seat with the formal respect so little practised now.

'Sit down, my dear,' said she, placing herself upon a chair beside me; 'I must chat with you for a quarter of an hour or so. Saunders (to the maid), you may leave the room; do not close the room door, but shut that of the lobby.'

This precaution against curious ears having been taken as directed, my mother proceeded.

'You have observed, I should suppose, my dearest Fanny; indeed you *must* have observed, Lord Glenfallen's marked attentions to you?'

'I assure you, madam,' I began.

'Well, well, that is all right,' interrupted my mother; 'of course you must be modest upon the matter; but listen to me for a few moments, my love, and I will prove to your satisfaction that your modesty is quite unnecessary in this case. You have done better than we could have hoped, at least, so very soon. Lord Glenfallen is in love with you. I give you joy of your conquest,' and saying this, my mother kissed my forehead.

'In love with me!' I exclaimed, in unfeigned astonishment.

'Yes, in love with you,' repeated my mother; 'devotedly, distractedly in love with you. Why, my dear, what is there wonderful in it; look in the glass, and look at these,' she continued, pointing with a smile to the jewels which I had just removed from my person, and which now lay a glittering heap upon the table.

'May there not,' said I, hesitating between confusion and real alarm; 'is it not possible that some mistake may be at the bottom of all this?'

'Mistake! dearest; none,' said my mother. 'None, none in the world; judge for yourself; read this, my love,' and she placed in my hand a letter, addressed to herself, the seal of which was broken. I read it through with no small surprise. After some very fine complimentary flourishes upon my beauty and perfections, as, also, upon the antiquity and high reputation of our family, it went on to make a formal proposal of marriage, to be communicated or not to me at present, as my mother should deem expedient; and the letter wound up by a request that the writer might be permitted, upon our return to Ashtown-house, which was soon to take place, as the spring was now tolerably advanced, to visit us for a few days, in case his suit was approved.

'Well, well, my dear,' said my mother, impatiently; 'do you know who Lord Glenfallen is?'

'I do, madam,' said I rather timidly, for I dreaded an altercation with my mother.

'Well, dear, and what frightens you?' continued she; 'are you afraid of a title? What has he done to alarm you? he is neither old nor ugly.'

I was silent, though I might have said, 'He is neither young nor handsome.'

'My dear Fanny,' continued my mother, 'in sober seriousness you have been most fortunate in engaging the affections of a nobleman such as Lord Glenfallen, young and wealthy, with first-rate, yes, acknowledged *first-rate* abilities and of a family whose influence is not exceeded by that of any in Ireland—of course you see the offer in the same light that I do—indeed I think you *must*.'

This was uttered in no very dubious tone. I was so much astonished by the suddenness of the whole communication that I literally did not know what to say.

'You are not in love?' said my mother, turning sharply, and fixing her dark eyes upon me, with severe scrutiny.

'No, madam,' said I, promptly; horrified, as what young lady would not have been, at such a query.

'I am glad to hear it,' said my mother, dryly. 'Once, nearly twenty years ago, a friend of mine consulted me how he should deal with a daughter who had made what they call a love match, beggared herself, and disgraced her family; and I said, without hesitation, take no care of her, but cast her off; such punishment I awarded for an offence committed against the reputation of a family not my own; and what I advised respecting the child of another, with full as small compunction I would *do* with mine. I cannot conceive anything more unreasonable or intolerable than that the fortune and the character of a family should be marred by the idle caprices of a girl.'

She spoke this with great severity, and paused as if she expected some observation from me. I, however, said nothing.

'But I need not explain to you, my dear Fanny,' she continued, 'my views upon this subject; you have always known them well, and I have never yet had reason to believe you likely, voluntarily, to offend me, or to abuse or neglect any of those advantages which reason and duty tell you should be improved—come hither, my dear, kiss me, and do not look so frightened. Well, now, about this letter, you need not answer it yet; of course you must be allowed time to make up your mind; in the mean time I will write to his lordship to give him my permission to visit us at Ashtown—good night, my love.'

And thus ended one of the most disagreeable, not to say astounding, conversations I had ever had; it would not be easy to describe exactly what were my feelings towards Lord Glenfallen; whatever might have been my mother's suspicions, my heart was perfectly disengaged; and hitherto, although I had not been made in the slightest degree acquainted with his real views, I had liked him very much, as an agreeable, well-informed man, whom I was always glad to meet in society; he had served in the navy in early life, and the polish which his manners received in his after intercourse with courts and cities had not served to obliterate that frankness of *manner* which belongs proverbially to the sailor. Whether this apparent candour went deeper than the outward bearing I was yet to learn; however there was no doubt that as far as I had seen of Lord Glenfallen, he was, though perhaps not so young as might have been desired in a lover, a singularly pleasing man, and whatever feeling unfavourable to him had found its way into my mind, arose altogether from the dread, not an unreasonable one, that constraint might be practised upon my inclinations. I reflected, however, that Lord Glenfallen was a wealthy man, and one highly thought of and although I could never expect to love him in the romantic sense of the term, yet I had no doubt but that, all things considered, I might be more happy with him than I could hope to be at home. When next I met him it was with no small embarrassment, his tact and good breeding, however, soon reassured me, and effectually prevented my awkwardness being remarked upon; and I had the satisfaction of leaving Dublin for the country with the full conviction that nobody, not even those most intimate with me, even suspected the fact of Lord Glenfallen's having made me a

formal proposal. This was to me a very serious subject of self gratula-
tion, for, besides my instinctive dread of becoming the topic of the
speculations of gossip, I felt that if the situation which I occupied in
relation to him were made publicly known, I should stand committed
in a manner which would scarcely leave me the power of retraction.
The period at which Lord Glenfallen had arranged to visit Ashtown-
house was now fast approaching, and it became my mother's wish to
form me thoroughly to her will, and to obtain my consent to the
proposed marriage before his arrival, so that all things might proceed
smoothly without apparent opposition or objection upon my part;
whatever objections, therefore, I had entertained were to be subdued;
whatever disposition to resistance I had exhibited or had been supposed to feel, were to be completely eradicated before he made his
appearance, and my mother addressed herself to the task with a
decision and energy against which even the barriers, which her
imagination had created, could hardly have stood. If she had, however, expected any determined opposition from me, she was agreeably
disappointed; my heart was perfectly free, and all my feelings of
liking and preference were in favour of Lord Glenfallen, and I well
knew that in case I refused to dispose of myself as I was desired, my
mother had alike the power and the will to render my existence as
utterly miserable as any, even the most ill-assorted marriage could
possibly have done. You will remember, my good friend, that I was
very young and very completely under the controul of my parents,
both of whom, my mother particularly, were unscrupulously determined in matters of this kind, and willing, when voluntary obedience
on the part of those within their power was withheld, to compel a
forced acquiescence by an unsparing use of all the engines of the
most stern and rigorous domestic discipline. All these combined, not
unnaturally, induced me to resolve upon yielding at once, and without
useless opposition, to what appeared almost to be my fate. The
appointed time was come, and my now accepted suitor arrived; he
was in high spirits, and, if possible, more entertaining than ever. I
was not, however, quite in the mood to enjoy his sprightliness; but
whatever I wanted in gaiety was amply made up in the triumphant
and gracious good humour of my mother, whose smiles of benevolence and exultation were showered around as bountifully as the
summer sunshine. I will not weary you with unnecessary prolixity. Let
it suffice to say, that I was married to Lord Glenfallen with all the
attendant pomp and circumstance of wealth, rank, and grandeur.
According to the usage of the times, now humanely reformed, the
ceremony was made until long past midnight, the season of wild,

uproarious, and promiscuous feasting and revelry. Of all this I have a painfully vivid recollection, and particularly of the little annoyances inflicted upon me by the dull and coarse jokes of the wits and wags who abound in all such places, and upon all such occasions. I was not sorry, when, after a few days, Lord Glenfallen's carriage appeared at the door to convey us both from Ashtown; for any change would have been a relief from the irksomeness of ceremonial and formality which the visits received in honour of my newly acquired titles hourly entailed upon me. It was arranged that we were to proceed to Cahergillagh, one of the Glenfallen estates, lying, however, in a southern county, so that a tedious journey (then owing to the impracticability of the roads,) of three days intervened. I set forth with my noble companion, followed by the regrets of some, and by the envy of many, though God knows I little deserved the latter; the three days of travel were now almost spent, when passing the brow of a wild heathy hill, the domain of Cahergillagh opened suddenly upon our view. It formed a striking and a beautiful scene. A lake of considerable extent stretching away towards the west, and reflecting from its broad, smooth waters, the rich glow of the setting sun, was overhung by steep hills, covered by a rich mantle of velvet sward, broken here and there by the grey front of some old rock, and exhibiting on their shelving sides, their slopes and hollows, every variety of light and shade; a thick wood of dwarf oak, birch, and hazel skirted these hills, and clothed the shores of the lake, running out in rich luxuriance upon every promontory, and spreading upward considerably upon the side of the hills.

'There lies the enchanted castle,' said Lord Glenfallen, pointing towards a considerable level space intervening between two of the picturesque hills, which rose dimly around the lake. This little plain was chiefly occupied by the same low, wild wood which covered the other parts of the domain; but towards the centre a mass of taller and statelier forest trees stood darkly grouped together, and among them stood an ancient square tower, with many buildings of an humbler character, forming together the manor-house, or, as it was more usually called, the court of Cahergillagh. As we approached the level upon which the mansion stood, the winding road gave us many glimpses of the time-worn castle and its surrounding buildings; and seen as it was through the long vistas of the fine old trees, and with the rich glow of evening upon it, I have seldom beheld an object more picturesquely striking. I was glad to perceive, too, that here and there the blue curling smoke ascended from stacks of chimneys now hidden by the rich, dark ivy, which, in a great measure, covered the building; other indications of comfort made themselves manifest as we approached; and indeed, though the place was evidently one of considerable antiquity, it had nothing whatever of the gloom of decay about it.

'You must not, my love,' said Lord Glenfallen, 'imagine this place worse than it is. I have no taste for antiquity, at least I should not choose a house to reside in because it is old. Indeed I do not recollect that I was even so romantic as to overcome my aversion to rats and rheumatism, those faithful attendants upon your noble relics of feudalism; and I much prefer a snug, modern, unmysterious bed-room, with well-aired sheets, to the waving tapestry, mildewed cushions, and all the other interesting appliances of romance; how-ever, though I cannot promise you all the discomfort generally pertaining to an old castle, you will find legends and ghostly lore enough to claim your respect; and if old Martha be still to the fore, as I trust she is, you will soon have a supernatural and appropriate anecdote for every closet and corner of the mansion; but here we are—so, without more ado, welcome to Cahergillagh.'

We now entered the hall of the castle, and while the domestics were employed in conveying our trunks and other luggage which we had brought with us for immediate use to the apartments which Lord Glenfallen had selected for himself and me, I went with him into a spacious sitting room, wainscoted with finely polished black oak, and hung round with the portraits of various of the worthies of the Glenfallen family. This room looked out upon an extensive level covered with the softest green sward, and irregularly bounded by the wild wood I have before mentioned, through the leafy arcade formed by whose boughs and trunks the level beams of the setting sun were pouring; in the distance, a group of dairy maids were plying their task, which they accompanied throughout with snatches of Irish songs which, mellowed by the distance, floated not unpleasingly to the ear; and beside them sat or lay, with all the grave importance of conscious protection, six or seven large dogs of various kinds; farther in the distance, and through the cloisters of the arching wood, two or three ragged urchins were employed in driving such stray kine as had wandered farther than the rest to join their fellows. As I looked upon this scene which I have described, a feeling of tranquillity and happiness came upon me, which I have never experienced in so strong a degree; and so strange to me was the sensation that my eyes filled with tears. Lord Glenfallen mistook the cause of my emotion, and taking me kindly and tenderly by the hand he said, 'Do not suppose, my love, that it is my intention to *settle* here, whenever you desire to leave this, you have only to let me know your wish and it shall be complied with, so I must entreat of you not to suffer any circumstances which I can controul to give you one moment's uneasiness; but here is old Martha, you must be introduced to her, one of the heirlooms of our family.'

A hale, good-humoured, erect, old woman was Martha, and an agreeable contrast to the grim, decrepit hag, which my fancy had conjured up, as the depository of all the horrible tales in which I doubted not this old place was most fruitful. She welcomed me and her master with a profusion of gratulations, alternately kissing our hands and apologizing for the liberty, until at length Lord Glenfallen put an end to this somewhat fatiguing ceremonial, by requesting her to conduct me to my chamber if it were prepared for my reception. I followed Martha up an old-fashioned, oak stair-case into a long, dim passage at the end of which lay the door which communicated with the apartments which had been selected for our use; here the old woman stopped, and respectfully requested me to proceed. I accordingly opened the door and was about to enter, when something like a mass of black tapestry as it appeared disturbed by my sudden approach, fell from above the door, so as completely to screen the aperture; the startling unexpectedness of the occurrence, and the rustling noise which the drapery made in its descent, caused me involuntarily to step two or three paces backwards, I turned, smiling and half ashamed to the old servant, and said, 'You see what a coward I am.' The woman looked puzzled, and without saying any more, I was about to draw aside the curtain and enter the room, when upon turning to do so, I was surprised to find that nothing whatever interposed to obstruct the passage. I went into the room, followed by the servant woman, and was amazed to find that it, like the one below, was wainscoted, and that nothing like drapery was to be found near the door.

'Where is it,' said I; 'what has become of it?'

'What does your ladyship wish to know?' said the old woman.

'Where is the black curtain that fell across the door, when I attempted first to come to my chamber,' answered I.

'The cross of Christ about us,' said the old woman, turning suddenly pale.

'What is the matter, my good friend,' said I; 'you seem frightened.'

'Oh, no, no, your ladyship,' said the old woman, endeavouring to conceal her agitation; but in vain, for tottering towards a chair, she sunk into it, looking so deadly pale and horror-struck that I thought every moment she would faint.

'Merciful God, keep us from harm and danger,' muttered she at length.

'What can have terrified you so,' said I, beginning to fear that she had seen something more than had met my eye, 'you appear ill, my poor woman.'

'Nothing, nothing, my lady,' said she, rising; 'I beg your ladyship's pardon for making so bold; may the great God defend us from misfortune.'

'Martha,' said I, 'something *has* frightened you very much, and I insist on knowing what it is; your keeping me in the dark upon the subject will make me much more uneasy than any thing you could tell me; I desire you, therefore, to let me know what agitates you; I command you to tell me.'

'Your ladyship said you saw a black curtain falling across the door when you were coming into the room,' said the old woman.

'I did,' said I; 'but though the whole thing appears somewhat strange I cannot see any thing in the matter to agitate you so excessively.'

'It's for no good you saw that, my lady,' said the crone; 'something terrible is coming; it's a sign, my lady—a sign that never fails.'

'Explain, explain what you mean, my good woman,' said I, in spite of myself, catching more than I could account for, of her superstitious terror.

'Whenever something—something *bad* is going to happen to the Glenfallen family, some one that belongs to them sees a black handkerchief or curtain just waved or falling before their faces; I saw it myself, continued she, lowering her voice, 'when I was only a little girl, and I'll never forget it; I often heard of it before, though I never saw it till then, nor since, praised be God; but I was going into Lady Jane's room to waken her in the morning; and sure enough when I got first to the bed and began to draw the curtain, something dark was waved across the division, but only for a moment; and when I saw rightly into the bed, there was she lying cold and dead, God be merciful to me; so, my lady, there is small blame to me to be daunted when any one of the family sees it, for it's many's the story I heard of it, though I saw it but once.'

I was not of a superstitious turn of mind; yet I could not resist a feeling of awe very nearly allied to the fear which my companion had so unreservedly expressed; and when you consider my situation, the loneliness, antiquity, and gloom of the place, you will allow that the weakness was not without excuse. In spite of old Martha's boding predictions, however, time flowed on in an unruffled course; one little incident, however, though trifling in itself, I must relate as it serves to make what follows more intelligible. Upon the day after my arrival, Lord Glenfallen of course desired to make me acquainted with the house and domain; and accordingly we set forth upon our ramble; when returning, he became for some time silent and moody, a state so unusual with him as considerably to excite my surprise, I endeavoured by observations and questions to arouse him—but in vain; at length as we approached the house, he said, as if speaking to himself, ''twere madness—madness—madness,' repeating the word bitterly—'sure and speedy ruin.' There was here a long pause; and at length turning sharply towards me in a tone very unlike that in which he had hitherto addressed me, he said, 'Do you think it possible that a woman can keep a secret?'

'I am sure,' said I, 'that women are very much belied upon the score of talkativeness, and that I may answer your question with the same directness with which you put it; I reply that I *do* think a woman can keep a secret.'

'But I do not,' said he, dryly.

We walked on in silence for a time; I was much astonished at his unwonted abruptness; I had almost said rudeness. After a considerable pause he seemed to recollect, himself, and with an effort resuming his sprightly manner, he said, 'well, well, the next thing to keeping a secret well is, not to desire to possess one—talkativeness and curiosity generally go together; now I shall make test of you in the first place, respecting the latter of these qualities. I shall be your *Bluebeard*—tush, why do I trifle thus; listen to me, my dear Fanny, I speak now in solemn earnest; what I desire is, intimately, inseparably, connected with your happiness and honour as well as my own; and your compliance with my request will not be difficult; it will impose upon you a very trifling restraint during your sojourn here, which certain events which have occurred since our arrival, have determined me shall not be a long one. You must promise me, upon your sacred honour, that you will visit *only* that part of the castle which can be reached from the front entrance, leaving the back entrance and the part of the building commanded immediately by it, to the menials, as also the small garden whose high wall you see yonder; and never at any time seek to pry or peep into them, nor to open the door which communicates from the front part of the house through the corridor with the back. I do not urge this in jest or in caprice, but from a solemn conviction that danger and misery will be the certain consequences of your not observing what I prescribe. I cannot explain myself further at present—promise me, then, these things as you hope for peace here and for mercy hereafter.'

I did make the promise as desired, and he appeared relieved; his manner recovered all its gaiety and elasticity, but the recollection of the strange scene which I have just described dwelt painfully upon my mind. More than a month passed away without any occurrence worth recording; but I was not destined to leave Cahergillagh without further adventure; one day intending to enjoy the pleasant sunshine in a ramble through the woods, I ran up to my room to procure my bonnet and shawl; upon entering the chamber, I was surprised and somewhat startled to find it occupied; beside the fireplace and nearly opposite the door, seated in a large, old-fashioned elbow-chair, was placed the figure of a lady; she appeared to be nearer fifty than forty, and was dressed suitably to her age, in a handsome suit of flowered silk; she had a profusion of trinkets and jewellery about her person, and many rings upon her fingers; but although very rich, her dress was not gaudy or in ill taste; but what was remarkable in the lady was, that although her features were handsome, and upon the whole pleasing, the pupil of each eye was dimmed with the whiteness of cataract, and she was evidently stone blind. I was for some seconds so surprised at this unaccountable apparition, that I could not find words to address her.

'Madam,' said I, 'there must be some mistake here—this is my bed-chamber.'

'Marry come up,' said the lady, sharply; '*your* chamber! Where is Lord Glenfallen?'

'He is below, madam,' replied I; 'and I am convinced he will be not a little surprised to find you here.'

'I do not think he will,' said she; 'with your good leave, talk of what you know something about; tell him I want him; why does the minx dilly dally so?'

In spite of the awe which this grim lady inspired, there was something in her air of confident superiority which, when I considered our relative situations, was not a little irritating.

'Do you know, madam, to whom you speak?' said I.

'I neither know nor care,' said she; 'but I presume that you are some one about the house, so, again, I desire you, if you wish to continue here, to bring your master hither forthwith.'

'I must tell you madam,' said I, 'that I am Lady Glenfallen.'

'What's that?' said the stranger, rapidly.

'I say, madam,' I repeated, approaching her, that I might be more distinctly heard, 'that I am Lady Glenfallen.'

'It's a lie, you trull,' cried she, in an accent which made me start, and, at the same time, springing forward, she seized me in her grasp and shook me violently, repeating, 'it's a lie, it's a lie,' with a rapidity

116

Lord G
says
she
is
mad

and vehemence which swelled every vein of her face; the violence of her action, and the fury which convulsed her face, effectually terrified me, and disengaging myself from her grasp, I screamed as loud as I could for help; the blind woman continued to pour out a torrent of abuse upon me, foaming at the mouth with rage, and impotently shaking her clenched fists towards me. I heard Lord Glenfallen's step upon the stairs, and I instantly ran out; as I past him I perceived that he was deadly pale, and just caught the words, 'I hope that demon has not hurt you?' I made some answer, I forget what, and he entered the chamber, the door of which he locked upon the inside; what passed within I know not; but I heard the voices of the two speakers raised in loud and angry altercation. I thought I heard the shrill accents of the woman repeat the words, 'let her look to herself'; but I could not be quite sure. This short sentence, however, was, to my alarmed imagination, pregnant with fearful meaning; the storm at length subsided, though not until after a conference of more than two long hours. Lord Glenfallen then returned, pale and agitated. 'That unfortunate woman,' said he, 'is out of her mind; I dare say she treated you to some of her ravings, but you need not dread any further interruption from her, I have brought her so far to reason. She did not hurt you, I trust.'

'No, no,' said I; 'but she terrified me beyond measure.' 'Well,' said he, 'she is likely to behave better for the future, and I dare swear that neither you nor she would desire after what has passed to meet again.'

This occurrence, so startling and unpleasant, so involved in mystery, and giving rise to so many painful surmises, afforded me no very agreeable food for rumination. All attempts on my part to arrive at the truth were baffled; Lord Glenfallen evaded all my enquiries, and at length peremptorily forbid any further allusion to the matter. I was thus obliged to rest satisfied with what I had actually seen, and to trust to time to resolve the perplexities in which the whole transaction had involved me. Lord Glenfallen's temper and spirits gradually underwent a complete and most painful change; he became silent and abstracted, his manner to me was abrupt and often harsh, some grievous anxiety seemed ever present to his mind; and under its influence his spirits sunk and his temper became soured. I soon perceived that his gaiety was rather that which the stir and excitement of society produces, than the result of a healthy habit of mind; and every day confirmed me in the opinion, that the considerate good nature which I had so much admired in him was little more than a mere manner; and to my infinite grief and surprise, the gay, kind, open-hearted nobleman who had for months followed and flattered me, was rapidly assuming the form of a gloomy, morose, and singularly selfish man; this was a bitter discovery, and I strove to conceal it from myself as long as I could, but the truth was not to be denied, and I was forced to believe that Lord Glenfallen no longer loved me, and that he was at little pains to conceal the alteration in his sentiments. One morning after breakfast, Lord Glenfallen had been for some time walking silently up and down the room, buried in his moody reflections, when pausing suddenly, and turning towards me, he exclaimed,

'I have it, I have it; we must go abroad and stay there, too, and if that does not answer, why—why we must try some more effectual expedient. Lady Glenfallen, I have become involved in heavy embarrassments; a wife you know must share the fortunes of her husband, for better for worse, but I will waive my right if you prefer remaining here—here at Cahergillagh; for I would not have you seen elsewhere without the state to which your rank entitled you; besides it would break your poor mother's heart,' he added, with sneering gravity, 'so make up your mind—Cahergillagh or France, I will start if possible in a week, so determine between this and then.'

He left the room and in a few moments I saw him ride past the window, followed by a mounted servant; he had directed a domestic to inform me that he should not be back until the next day. I was in very great doubt as to what course of conduct I should pursue, as to accompanying him in the continental tour so suddenly determined upon, I felt that it would be a hazard too great to encounter; for at Cahergillagh I had always the consciousness to sustain me, that if his temper at any time led him into violent or unwarrantable treatment of me, I had a remedy within reach, in the protection and support of my own family, from all useful and effective communication with whom, if once in France, I should be entirely debarred. As to remaining at Cahergillagh in solitude, and for aught I knew, exposed to hidden dangers, it appeared to me scarcely less objectionable than the former proposition; and yet I feared that with one or other I must comply, unless I was prepared to come to an actual breach with Lord Glenfallen; full of these unpleasing doubts and perplexities, I retired to rest. I was wakened after having slept uneasily for some hours, by some person shaking me rudely by the shoulder; a small lamp burned in my room, and by its light, to my horror and amazement, I discovered that my visitant was the self-same blind, old lady who had so terrified me a few weeks before. I started up in the bed, with a view to ring the bell, and alarm the domestics, but she instantly anticipated me by saying, 'Do not be frightened, silly girl; if I had wished to harm you I could have done it while you were sleeping, I need not have wakened you; listen to me, now, attentively and fearlessly; for what I have to say, interests you to the full as much as it does me; tell me, here, in the presence of God, did Lord Glenfallen marry you, *actually marry* you?—speak the truth, woman.'

'As surely as I live and speak,' I replied, 'did Lord Glenfallen marry me in presence of more than a hundred witnesses.'

'Well,' continued she, 'he should have told you *then*, before you married him, that he had a wife living, which wife I am; I feel you tremble—tush! do not be frightened. I do not mean to harm you— mark me now—you are *not* his wife. When I make my story known you will be so, neither in the eye of God nor of man; you must leave this house upon tomorrow; let the world know that your husband has another wife living; go, you, into retirement, and leave him to justice, which will surely overtake him. If you remain in this house after tomorrow you will reap the bitter fruits of your sin,' so saying, she quitted the room, leaving me very little disposed to sleep.

Here was food for my very worst and most terrible suspicions; still there was not enough to remove all doubt. I had no proof of the truth of this woman's statement. Taken by itself there was nothing to induce me to attach weight to it; but when I viewed it in connection with the extraordinary mystery of some of Lord Glenfallen's proceedings, his strange anxiety to exclude me from certain portions of the mansion, doubtless, lest I should encounter this person—the strong influence, nay, command, which she possessed over him, a circumstance clearly established by the very fact of her residing in the very place, where of all others, he should least have desired to find her—her thus acting, and continuing to act in direct contradiction to his wishes; when, I say, I viewed her disclosure in connection with all these circumstances, I could not help feeling that there was at least a fearful veri-similitude in the allegations which she had made. Still I was not satisfied, nor nearly so; young minds have a reluctance almost insurmountable to believing upon any thing short of unquestionable proof, the existence of premeditated guilt in any one whom they have ever trusted; and in support of this feeling I was assured that if the assertion of Lord Glenfallen, which nothing in this woman's manner had led me to disbelieve, were true, namely, that her mind was unsound, the whole fabric of my doubts and fears must fall to the ground. I determined to state to Lord Glenfallen freely and accurately the substance of the communication which I had just heard, and in his words and looks to seek for its proof or refutation;

119

full of these thoughts I remained wakeful and excited all night, every moment fancying that I heard the step, or saw the figure of my recent visitor towards whom I felt a species of horror and dread which I can hardly describe. There was something in her face, though her features had evidently been handsome, and were not, at first sight, unpleasing, which, upon a nearer inspection, seemed to indicate the habitual prevalence and indulgence of evil passions, and a power of expressing mere animal anger, with an intenseness that I have seldom seen equalled, and to which an almost unearthly effect was given by the convulsive quivering of the sightless eyes. You may easily suppose that it was no very pleasing reflection to me to consider, that whenever caprice might induce her to return, I was within the reach of this violent, and, for aught I knew, insane woman, who had, upon that very night, spoken to me in a tone of menace, of which her mere words, divested of the manner and look with which she uttered them, can convey but a faint idea. Will you believe me when I tell you that I was actually afraid to leave my bed in order to secure the door, lest I should again encounter the dreadful object lurking in some corner or peeping from behind the window curtains, so very a child was I in my fears.

The morning came, and with it Lord Glenfallen. I knew not, and indeed I cared not, where he might have been; my thoughts were wholly engrossed by the terrible fears and suspicions which my last night's conference had suggested to me; he was, as usual, gloomy and abstracted, and I feared in no very fitting mood to hear what I had to say with patience, whether the charges were true or false. I was, however, determined not to suffer the opportunity to pass, or Lord Glenfallen to leave the room, until, at all hazards, I had unburdened my mind.

'My Lord,' said I, after a long silence, summoning up all my firmness, 'my lord, I wish to say a few words to you upon a matter of very great importance, of very deep concernment to you and to me.' I fixed my eyes upon him to discern, if possible, whether the announcement caused him any uneasiness, but no symptom of any such feeling was perceptible.

'Well, my dear,' said he, 'this is, no doubt, a very grave preface, and portends, I have no doubt, something extraordinary—pray let us have it without more ado.'

He took a chair, and seated himself nearly opposite to me.

'My lord,' said I, 'I have seen the person who alarmed me so much a short time since, the blind lady, again, upon last night'; his face, upon which my eyes were fixed, turned pale, he hesitated for a moment, and then said—

'And did you, pray madam, so totally forget or spurn my express command, as to enter that portion of the house from which your promise, I might say, your oath, excluded you—answer me that?' he added, fiercely.

'My lord,' said I, 'I have neither forgotten your *commands*, since such they were, nor disobeyed them. I was, last night, wakened from my sleep, as I lay in my own chamber, and accosted by the person whom I have mentioned—how she found access to the room I cannot pretend to say.'

'Ha! this must be looked to,' said he, half reflectively; 'and pray,' added he, quickly, while in turn he fixed his eyes upon me, 'what did this person say, since some comment upon her communication forms, no doubt, the sequel to your preface.'

'Your lordship is not mistaken,' said I, 'her statement was so extraordinary that I could not think of withholding it from you; she told me, my lord, that you had a wife living at the time you married me, and that she was that wife.'

Lord Glenfallen became ashy pale, almost livid; he made two or three efforts to clear his voice to speak, but in vain, and turning suddenly from me, he walked to the window; the horror and dismay, which, in the olden time, overwhelmed the woman of Endor, when her spells unexpectedly conjured the dead into her presence, were but types of what I felt, when thus presented with what appeared to be almost unequivocal evidence of the guilt, whose existence I had before so strongly doubted. There was a silence of some moments, during which it were hard to conjecture whether I or my companion suffered most. Lord Glenfallen soon recovered his self command; he returned to the table, again sat down and said—

'What you have told me has so astonished me, has unfolded such a tissue of motiveless guilt, and in a quarter from which I had so little reason to look for ingratitude or treachery, that your announcement almost deprived me of speech; the person in question, however, has one excuse, her mind is, as I told you before, unsettled. You should have remembered that, and hesitated to receive as unexceptionable evidence against the honour of your husband, the ravings of a lunatic. I now tell you that this is the last time I shall speak to you upon this subject, and, in the presence of the God who is to judge me, and as I hope for mercy in the day of judgment, I swear that the charge thus brought against me, is utterly false, unfounded, and ridiculous; I defy the world in any point to taint my honour; and, as I have never taken the opinion of madmen touching your character or morals, I think it but fair to require that you will evince a like tenderness for me; and now, once for all, never again dare to repeat to me your insulting suspicions, or the clumsy and infamous calumnies of fools. I shall instantly let the worthy lady who contrived this somewhat original device, understand fully my opinion upon the matter—good morning'; and with these words he left me again in doubt, and involved in all horrors of the most agonizing suspense. I had reason to think that Lord Glenfallen wreaked his vengeance upon the author of the strange story which I had heard, with a violence which was not satisfied with mere words, for old Martha, with whom I was a great favourite, while attending me in my room, told me that she feared her master had ill used the poor, blind, Dutch woman, for that she had heard her scream as if the very life were leaving her, but added a request that I should not speak of what she had told me to any one, particularly to the master.

'How do you know that she is a Dutch woman?' inquired I, anxious to learn anything whatever that might throw a light upon the history of this person, who seemed to have resolved to mix herself up in my fortunes.

'Why, my lady,' answered Martha, 'the master often calls her the Dutch hag, and other names you would not like to hear, and I am sure she is neither English nor Irish; for, whenever they talk together, they speak some queer foreign lingo, and fast enough, I'll be bound; but I ought not to talk about her at all; it might be as much as my place is worth to mention her—only you saw her first yourself, so there can be no great harm in speaking of her now.'

'How long has this lady been here?' continued I.

'She came early on the morning after your ladyship's arrival,' answered she; 'but do not ask me any more, for the master would think nothing of turning me out of doors for daring to speak of her at all, much less to *you*, my lady.'

I did not like to press the poor woman further; for her reluctance to speak on this topic was evident and strong. You will readily believe that upon the very slight grounds which my information afforded, contradicted as it was by the solemn oath of my husband, and derived from what was, at best, a very questionable source, I could not take any very decisive measure whatever; and as to the menace of the strange woman who had thus unaccountably twice intruded herself into my chamber, although, at the moment, it occasioned me some uneasiness, it was not, even in my eyes, sufficiently formidable to induce my departure from Cahergillagh.

A few nights after the scene with I have just mentioned, Lord Glenfallen having, as usual, early retired to his study, I was left alone in the parlour to amuse myself as best I might. It was not strange that my thoughts should often recur to the agitating scenes in which I had recently taken a part; the subject of my reflections, the solitude, the silence, and the lateness of the hour, as also the depression of spirits to which I had of late been a constant prey, tended to produce that nervous excitement which places us wholly at the mercy of the imagination. In order to calm my spirits, I was endeavouring to direct my thoughts into some more pleasing channel, when I heard, or thought I heard, uttered, within a few yards of me, in an odd half-sneering tone, the words, 'There is blood upon your ladyship's throat.' So vivid was the impression, that I started to my feet, and involuntarily placed my hand upon my neck. I looked around the room for the speaker, but in vain. I went then to the room-door, which I opened, and peered into the passage, nearly faint with horror, lest some leering, shapeless thing should greet me upon the threshold. When I had gazed long enough to assure myself that no strange object was within sight.

'I have been too much of a rake, lately; I am racking out my nerves,' said I, speaking aloud, with a view to reassure myself. I rang the bell, and, attended by old Martha, I retired to settle for the night. While the servant was, as was her custom, arranging the lamp which I have already stated always burned during the night in my chamber, I was employed in undressing, and, in doing so, I had recourse to a large looking-glass which occupied a considerable portion of the wall in which it was fixed, rising from the ground to a height of about six feet; this mirror filled the space of a large pannel in the wainscoting opposite the foot of the bed. I had hardly been before it for the lapse of a minute, when something like a black pall was slowly waved between me and it.

'Oh, God! there it is,' I exclaimed wildly. 'I have seen it again, Martha—the black cloth.'

'God be merciful to us, then!' answered she, tremulously crossing herself. 'Some misfortune is over us.'

'No, no, Martha,' said I, almost instantly recovering my collectedness; for, although of a nervous temperament, I had never been superstitious. 'I do not believe in omens. You know, I saw, or fancied I saw, this thing before, and nothing followed.'

'The Dutch lady came the next morning,' replied she.

'Methinks, such an occurrence scarcely deserved a supernatural announcement,' I replied.

'She is a strange woman, my lady,' said Martha, 'and she is not *gone* yet—mark my words.'

'Well, well, Martha,' said I, 'I have not wit enough to change your opinions, nor inclination to alter mine; so I will talk no more of the matter. Good-night,' and so I was left to my reflections. After lying for about an hour awake, I at length fell into a kind of doze; but my imagination was still busy, for I was startled from this unrefreshing sleep by fancying that I heard a voice close to my face exclaim as before, 'There is blood upon your ladyship's throat.' The words were instantly followed by a loud burst of laughter. Quaking with horror, I awakened, and heard my husband enter the room. Even this was a relief. Scared as I was, however, by the tricks which my imagination had played me, I preferred remaining silent, and pretending to sleep, to attempting to engage my husband in conversation, for I well knew that his mood was such, that his words would not, in all probability, convey anything that had not better be unsaid and unheard. Lord Glenfallen went into his dressing-room, which lay upon the right-hand side of the bed. The door lying open, I could see him by himself, at full length upon a sofa, and, in about half an hour, I became aware, by his deep and regularly drawn respiration, that he was fast asleep. When slumber refuses to visit one, there is something peculiarly irritating, not to the temper, but to the nerves, in the consciousness that some one is in your immediate presence, actually enjoying the boon which you are seeking in vain; at least, I have always found it so, and never more than upon the present occasion. A thousand annoying imaginations harassed and excited me, every object which I looked upon, though ever so familiar, seemed to have acquired a strange phantom-like character, the varying shadows thrown by the flickering of the lamp-light, seemed shaping them-selves into grotesque and unearthly forms, and whenever my eyes wandered to the sleeping figure of my husband, his features appeared to undergo the strangest and most demoniacal contortions. Hour after hour was told by the old clock, and each succeeding one found me, if possible, less inclined to sleep than its predecessor. It was now considerably past three; my eyes, in their involuntary wanderings, happened to alight upon the large mirror which was, as I have said, fixed in the wall opposite the foot of the bed. A view of it was commanded from where I lay, through the curtains, as I gazed fixedly upon it. I thought I perceived the broad sheet of glass shifting its position in relation to the bed; I rivetted my eyes upon it with intense scrutiny; it was no deception, the mirror, as if acting of its own impulse moved slowly aside, and disclosed a dark aperture in the wall, nearly as large as an ordinary door; a figure evidently stood in this; but the light was too dim to define it accurately. It stepped cautiously into the chamber, and with so little noise, that had I not actually seen it, I do not think I should have been aware of its presence. It was arrayed in a kind of woollen night-dress, and a white handkerchief or cloth was bound tightly about the head; I had no difficulty spite of the strangeness of the attire in recognising the blind woman whom I so much dreaded. She stooped down, bringing her head nearly to the ground, and in that attitude she remained motionless for some moments, no doubt in order to ascertain if any suspicious sound were stirring. She was apparently satisfied by her observations, for she immediately recommenced her silent progress towards a ponderous mahogany dressing table of my husband's; when she had reached it, she paused again, and appeared to listen attentively for some minutes; she then noiselessly opened one of the drawers from which, having groped for some time, she took something which I soon perceived to be a case of razors; she opened it and tried the edge of each of the two instruments upon the skin of her hand; she quickly selected one, which she fixed firmly in her grasp; she now stooped down as before, and having listened for a time, she, with the hand that was disengaged, groped her way into the dressing room where Lord Glenfallen lay fast asleep. I was fixed as if in the tremendous spell of a night mare. I could not stir even a finger; I could not lift my voice; I could not even breathe, and though I expected every moment to see the sleeping man murdered, I could not even close my eyes to shut out the horrible spectacle, which I had not the power to avert. I saw the woman approach the sleeping figure, she laid the unoccupied hand lightly along his clothes, and having thus ascertained his identity, she, after a brief interval, turned back and again entered my chamber; here she bent down again to listen. I had now not a doubt but that the razor was intended for my throat; yet the terrific fascination which had locked all my powers so long, still continued to bind me fast. I felt that my life depended upon the slightest ordinary exertion, and yet I could not stir one joint from the position in which I lay, nor even make noise enough to waken Lord Glenfallen. The murderous woman now, with long, silent steps, approached the bed; my very heart seemed turning to ice; her left hand, that which was disengaged, was upon the pillow; she gradually slid it forward towards my head, and in an instant, with the speed of lightning, it was clutched in my hair, while, with the other hand, she dashed the razor at my throat. A slight inaccuracy saved me from instant death; the blow fell short, the point of the razor grazing my throat; in a moment I know not how, I found myself at the other side of the bed uttering shriek after shriek; the wretch was, however, determined if possible to murder me; scrambling along by the curtains, she rushed round the bed towards me; I seized the handle of the door to make my escape; it was, however, fastened; at all events I could not open it, from the mere instinct of recoiling terror, I shrunk back into a corner—she was now within a yard of me—her hand was upon my face—I closed my eyes fast, expecting never to open them again, when a blow, inflicted from behind by a strong arm, stretched the monster senseless at my feet; at the same moment the door opened, and several domestics, alarmed by my cries, entered the apartment. I do not recollect what followed, for I fainted. One swoon succeeded another so long and death-like, that my life was considered very doubtful. At about ten o'clock, however, I sunk into a deep and refreshing sleep, from which I was awakened at about two, that I might swear my deposition before a magistrate, who attended for that purpose. I, accordingly, did so, as did also Lord Glenfallen; and the woman was fully committed to stand her trial at the ensuing assizes. I shall never forget the scene which the examination of the blind woman and of the other parties afforded. She was brought into the room in the custody of two servants; she wore a kind of flannel wrapper which had not been changed since the night before; it was torn and soiled, and here and there smeared with blood, which had flowed in large quantities from a wound in her head; the white handkerchief had fallen off in the scuffle; and her grizzled hair fell in masses about her wild and deadly pale countenance. She appeared perfectly composed, however, and the only regret she expressed throughout, was at not having succeeded in her attempt, the object of which she did not pretend to conceal. On being asked her name, she called herself the Countess Glenfallen, and refused to give any other title.

'The woman's name is Flora Van-Kemp,' said Lord Glenfallen.

'It *was*, it *was*, you perjured traitor and cheat,' screamed the woman; and then there followed a volley of words in some foreign language. 'Is there a magistrate here?' she resumed; 'I am Lord Glenfallen's wife—I'll prove it—write down my words. I am willing to be hanged or burned, so *he* meets his deserts. I did try to kill that doll of his; but it was he who put it into my head to do it—two wives were too many—I was to murder her, or she was to hang me—listen to all I have to say.'

Here Lord Glenfallen interrupted.

'I think, sir,' said he, addressing the magistrate, 'that we had better proceed to business, this unhappy woman's furious recriminations but waste our time; if she refuses to answer your questions, you had better, I presume, take my depositions.'

'And are you going to swear away my life, you black perjured murderer?' shrieked the woman. 'Sir, sir, sir, you must hear me,' she continued, addressing the magistrate, 'I can convict him—he bid me murder that girl, and then when I failed, he came behind me, and struck me down, and now he wants to swear away my life—take down all I say.'

'If it is your intention,' said the magistrate, 'to confess the crime with which you stand charged, you may, upon producing sufficient evidence, criminate whom you please.'

'Evidence!—I have no evidence but myself,' said the woman. 'I will swear it all—write down my testimony—write it down, I say—we shall hang side by side, my brave Lord—all your own handy-work, my gentle husband.' This was followed by a low, insolent, and sneering laugh, which, from one in her situation, was sufficiently horrible.

'I will not at present hear anything,' replied he, 'but distinct answers to the questions which I shall put to you upon this matter.'

'Then you shall hear nothing,' replied she sullenly, and no inducement or intimidation could bring her to speak again.

Lord Glenfallen's deposition and mine were then given, as also those of the servants who had entered the room at the moment of my rescue; the magistrate then intimated that she was committed, and must proceed directly to gaol, whither she was brought in a carriage of Lord Glenfallen's, for his lordship was naturally by no means indifferent to the effect which her vehement accusations against himself might produce, if uttered before every chance hearer whom she might meet with between Cahergillagh and the place of confinement whither she was dispatched.

During the time which intervened between the committal and the trial of the prisoner, Lord Glenfallen seemed to suffer agonies of mind which baffle all description, he hardly ever slept, and when he did, his slumbers seemed but the instruments of new tortures, and his waking hours were, if possible, exceeded in intensity of terrors by the dreams which disturbed his sleep. Lord Glenfallen rested, if to lie in the mere attitude of repose were to do so, in his dressing-room, and thus I had an opportunity of witnessing, far oftener than I wished it, the fearful workings of his mind; his agony often broke out into such fearful paroxysms that delirium and total loss of reason appeared to be impending; he frequently spoke of flying from the country, and bringing with him all the witnesses of the appalling scene upon which the prosecution was founded; then again he would fiercely lament that the blow which he had inflicted had not ended all.

The assizes arrived, however, and upon the day appointed, Lord

Glenfallen and I attended in order to give our evidence. The cause was called on, and the prisoner appeared at the bar. Great curiosity and interest were felt respecting the trial, so that the court was crowded to excess. The prisoner, however, without appearing to take the trouble of listening to the indictment, pleaded guilty, and no representations on the part of the court availed to induce her to retract her plea. After much time had been wasted in a fruitless attempt to prevail upon her to reconsider her words, the court proceeded according to the usual form to pass sentence. This having been done, the prisoner was about to be removed, when she said in a low, distinct voice.—

'A word—a word, my Lord:—is Lord Glenfallen here in the court?' On being told that he was, she raised her voice to a tone of loud menace, and continued—

'Hardress, Earl of Glenfallen, I accuse you here in this court of justice of two crimes—first, that you married a second wife, while the first was living, and again, that you prompted me to the murder, for attempting which I am to die—secure him—chain him—bring him here.'

There was a laugh through the court at these words, which were naturally treated by the judge as a violent extemporary recrimination, and the woman was desired to be silent.

'You won't take him, then,' she said, 'you won't try him? You'll let him go free?'

It was intimated by the court that he would certainly be allowed 'to go free', and she was ordered again to be removed. Before, however, the mandate was executed, she threw her arms wildly into the air, and uttered one piercing shriek so full of preternatural rage and despair, that it might fitly have ushered a soul into those realms where hope can come no more. The sound still rang in my ears, months after the voice that had uttered it was for ever silent. The wretched woman was executed in accordance with the sentence which had been pronounced.

For some time after this event, Lord Glenfallen appeared, if possible, to suffer more than he had done before, and altogether, his language, which often amounted to half confessions of the guilt imputed to him, and all the circumstances connected with the late occurrences, formed a mass of evidence so convincing that I wrote to my father, detailing the grounds of my fears, and imploring him to come to Cahergillagh without delay, in order to remove me from my husband's control, previously to taking legal steps for a final separation. Circumstanced as I was, my existence was little short of

Lord G
promise
to
explain
all

intolerable, for, besides the fearful suspicions which attached to my husband, I plainly perceived that if Lord Glenfallen were not relieved, and that speedily, insanity must supervene. I therefore expected my father's arrival, or at least a letter to announce it, with indescribable impatience.

About a week after the execution had taken place, Lord Glenfallen one morning met me with an unusually sprightly air—

'Fanny,' said he, 'I have it now for the first time, in my power to explain to your satisfaction every thing which has hitherto appeared suspicious or mysterious in my conduct. After breakfast come with me to my study, and I shall, I hope, make all things clear.'

This invitation afforded me more real pleasure than I had experienced for months; something had certainly occurred to tranquillize my husband's mind, in no ordinary degree, and I thought it by no means impossible that he would, in the proposed interview, prove himself the most injured and innocent of men. Full of this hope I repaired to his study at the appointed hour; he was writing busily when I entered the room, and just raising his eyes, he requested me to be seated. I took a chair as he desired, and remained silently awaiting his leisure, while he finished, folded, directed, and sealed his letter; laying it then upon the table, with the address downward, he said—

'My dearest Fanny, I know I must have appeared very strange to you and very unkind—often even cruel; before the end of this week I will show you the necessity of my conduct; how impossible it was that I should have seemed otherwise. I am conscious that many acts of mine must have inevitably given rise to painful suspicions—suspicions, which indeed, upon one occasion you very properly communicated to me. I have gotten two letters from a quarter which commands respect, containing information as to the course by which I may be enabled to prove the negative of all the crimes which even the most credulous suspicion could lay to my charge. I expected a third by this morning's post, containing documents which will set the matter for ever at rest, but owing, no doubt, to some neglect, or, perhaps, to some difficulty in collecting the papers, some inevitable delay, it has not come to hand this morning, according to my expectation. I was finishing one to the very same quarter when you came in, and if a sound rousing be worth anything, I think I shall have a special messenger before two days have passed. I have been thinking over the matter within myself, whether I had better imperfectly clear up your doubts by submitting to your inspection the two letters which I have already received, or wait till I can triumphantly vindicate myself by the production of the documents which I have already mentioned, and I have, I think, not unnaturally decided upon the latter course; however, there is a person in the next room, whose testimony is not without its value—excuse me for one moment.'

So saying, he arose and went to the door of a closet which opened from the study, this he unlocked, and half opening the door, he said, 'It is only I,' and then slipped into the room, and carefully closed and locked the door behind him. I immediately heard his voice in animated conversation; my curiosity upon the subject of the letter was naturally great, so smothering any little scruples which I might have felt, I resolved to look at the address of the letter which lay as my husband had left it, with its face upon the table. I accordingly drew it over to me, and turned up the direction. For two or three moments I could scarce believe my eyes, but there could be no mistake—in large characters were traced the words, 'To the Archangel Gabriel in heaven.' I had scarcely returned the letter to its original position, and in some degree recovered the shock which this unequivocal proof of insanity produced, when the closet door was unlocked, and Lord Glenfallen re-entered the study, carefully closing and locking the door again upon the outside.

'Whom have you there?' inquired I, making a strong effort to appear calm.

'Perhaps,' said he musingly, 'you might have some objection to seeing her, at least for a time.'

'Who is it?' repeated I.

'Why,' said he, 'I see no use in hiding it—the blind Dutchwoman; I have been with her the whole morning. She is very anxious to get out of that closet, but you know she is odd, she is scarcely to be trusted.'

A heavy gust of wind shook the door at this moment with a sound as if something more substantial were pushing against it.

'Ha, ha, ha!—do you hear her,' said he, with an obstreperous burst of laughter. The wind died away in a long howl, and Lord Glenfallen, suddenly checking his merriment, shrugged his shoulders, and muttered—

'Poor devil, she has been hardly used.'

'We had better not tease her at present with questions,' said I, in as unconcerned a tone as I could assume, although I felt every moment as if I should faint.

'Humph! may be so,' said he, 'well, come back in an hour or two, or when you please, and you will find us here.'

He again unlocked the door, and entered with the same precautions which he had adopted before, locking the door upon the inside, and as I hurried from the room, I heard his voice again exerted as if in eager parley. I can hardly describe my emotions; my hopes had been raised to the highest, and now in an instant, all was gone—the dreadful consummation was accomplished—the fearful retribution had fallen upon the guilty man—the mind was destroyed—the power to repent was gone. The agony of the hours which followed what I would still call my *awful* interview with Lord Glenfallen, I cannot describe; my solitude was, however, broken in upon by Martha, who came to inform me of the arrival of a gentleman, who expected me in the parlour. I accordingly descended, and to my great joy, found my father seated by the fire. This expedition, upon his part, was easily accounted for: my communications had touched the honour of the family. I speedily informed him of the dreadful malady which had fallen upon the wretched man. My father suggested the necessity of placing some person to watch him, to prevent his injuring himself or others. I rang the bell, and desired that one Edward Cooke, an attached servant of the family, should be sent to me. I told him distinctly and briefly, the nature of the service required of him, and, attended by him, my father and I proceeded at once to the study; the door of the inner room was still closed, and everything in the outer chamber remained in the same order in which I had left it. We then advanced to the closet door, at which we knocked, but without receiving any answer. We next tried to open the door, but in vain—it was locked upon the inside; we knocked more loudly, but in vain. Seriously alarmed, I desired the servant to force the door, which was, after several violent efforts, accomplished, and we entered the closet. Lord Glenfallen was lying on his face upon a sofa.

'Hush,' said I, 'he is asleep'; we paused for a moment.

'He is too still for that,' said my father; we all of us felt a strong reluctance to approach the figure.

'Edward,' said I, 'try whether your master sleeps.'

The servant approached the sofa where Lord Glenfallen lay; he leant his ear towards the head of the recumbent figure, to ascertain whether the sound of breathing was audible; he turned towards us, and said—

'My lady, you had better not wait here, I am sure he is dead!'

'Let me see the face,' said I, terribly agitated, 'you *may* be mistaken.'

The man then, in obedience to my command, turned the body round, and, gracious God! what a sight met my view—he was, indeed, perfectly dead. The whole breast of the shirt, with its lace frill, was drenched with gore, as was the couch underneath the spot where he lay. The head hung back, as it seemed almost severed from the body by a frightful gash, which yawned across the throat. The instrument which had inflicted it, was found under his body. All, then, was over; I was never to learn the history in whose termination I had been so deeply and so tragically involved.

The severe discipline which my mind had undergone was not bestowed in vain. I directed my thoughts and my hopes to that place where there is no more sin, nor danger, nor sorrow.

Thus ends a brief tale, whose prominent incidents many will recognize as having marked the history of a distinguished family, and though it refers to a somewhat distant date, we shall be found not to have taken, upon that account, any liberties with the facts, but in our statement of all the incidents, to have rigorously and faithfully adhered to the truth.

NATHANIEL HAWTHORNE

Rappaccini's Daughter

A young man, named Giovanni Guasconti, came, very long ago, from the more southern region of Italy, to pursue his studies at the University of Padua. Giovanni, who had but a scanty supply of gold ducats in his pocket, took lodgings in a high and gloomy chamber of an old edifice which looked not unworthy to have been the palace of a Paduan noble, and which, in fact, exhibited over its entrance the armorial bearings of a family long since extinct. The young stranger, who was not unstudied in the great poem of his country, recollected that one of the ancestors of this family, and perhaps an occupant of this very mansion, had been pictured by Dante as a partaker of the immortal agonies of his Inferno. These reminiscences and associations, together with the tendency to heartbreak natural to a young man for the first time out of his native sphere, caused Giovanni to sigh heavily as he looked around the desolate and ill-furnished apartment.

'Holy Virgin, signor!' cried old Dame Lisabetta, who, won by the youth's remarkable beauty of person, was kindly endeavoring to give the chamber a habitable air, 'what a sigh was that to come out of a young man's heart! Do you find this old mansion gloomy? For the love of Heaven, then, put your head out of the window, and you will see as bright sunshine as you have left in Naples.'

Guasconti mechanically did as the old woman advised, but could not quite agree with her that the Paduan sunshine was as cheerful as that of southern Italy. Such as it was, however, it fell upon a garden beneath the window and expended its fostering influences on a variety of plants, which seemed to have been cultivated with exceeding care.

'Does this garden belong to the house?' asked Giovanni.

'Heaven forbid, signor, unless it were fruitful of better pot herbs than any that grow there now,' answered old Lisabetta. 'No; that garden is cultivated by the own hands of Signor Giacomo Rappaccini, the famous doctor, who, I warrant him, has been heard of as far as Naples. It is said that he distils these plants into medicines that are as potent as a charm. Oftentimes you may see the signor doctor at work, and perchance the signora, his daughter, too, gathering the strange flowers that grow in the garden.'

The old woman had now done what she could for the aspect of the chamber; and, commending the young man to the protection of the saints, took her departure.

Giovanni still found no better occupation than to look down into the garden beneath his window. From its appearance, he judged it to be one of those botanic gardens which were of earlier date in Padua than elsewhere in Italy or in the world. Or, not improbably, it might once have been the pleasure-place of an opulent family; for there was the ruin of a marble fountain in the centre, sculptured with rare art, but so wofully shattered that it was impossible to trace the original design from the chaos of remaining fragments. The water, however, continued to gush and sparkle into the sunbeams as cheerfully as ever. A little gurgling sound ascended to the young man's window, and made him feel as if the fountain were an immortal spirit that sung its song unceasingly and without heeding the vicissitudes around it, while one century embodied it in marble and another scattered the perishable garniture on the soil. All about the pool into which the water subsided grew various plants, that seemed to require a plentiful supply of moisture for the nourishment of gigantic leaves, and, in some instances, flowers gorgeously magnificent. There was one shrub in particular, set in a marble vase in the midst of the pool, that bore a profusion of purple blossoms, each of which had the lustre and richness of a gem; and the whole together made a show so resplendent that it seemed enough to illuminate the garden, even had there been no sunshine. Every portion of the soil was peopled with plants and herbs, which, if less beautiful, still bore tokens of assiduous care, as if all had their individual virtues, known to the scientific mind that fostered them. Some were placed in urns, rich with old carving, and others in common garden pots; some crept serpent-like along the ground or climbed on high, using whatever means of ascent was offered them. One plant had wreathed itself round a statue of Vertumnus, which was thus quite veiled and shrouded in a drapery of hanging foliage, so happily arranged that it might have served a sculptor for a study.

While Giovanni stood at the window he heard a rustling behind a screen of leaves, and became aware that a person was at work in the garden. His figure soon emerged into view, and showed itself to be that of no common laborer, but a tall, emaciated, sallow, and sickly-looking man, dressed in a scholar's garb of black. He was beyond the middle term of life, with gray hair, a thin, gray beard, and a face singularly marked with intellect and cultivation, but which could never, even in his more youthful days, have expressed much warmth of heart.

Nothing could exceed the intentness with which this scientific gardener examined every shrub which grew in his path: it seemed as if he was looking into their inmost nature, making observations in regard to their creative essence, and discovering why one leaf grew in this shape and another in that, and wherefore such and such flowers differed among themselves in hue and perfume. Nevertheless, in spite of this deep intelligence on his part, there was no approach to intimacy between himself and these vegetable existences. On the contrary, he avoided their actual touch or the direct inhaling of their odors with a caution that impressed Giovanni most disagreeably; for the man's demeanor was that of one walking among malignant influences, such as savage beasts, or deadly snakes, or evil spirits, which, should he allow them one moment of license, would wreak upon him some terrible fatality. It was strangely frightful to the young man's imagination to see this air of insecurity in a person cultivating a garden, that most simple and innocent of human toils, and which had been alike the joy and labor of the unfallen parents of the race. Was this garden, then, the Eden of the present world? And this man, with such a perception of harm in what his own hands caused to grow,—was he the Adam?

The distrustful gardener, while plucking away the dead leaves or pruning the too luxuriant growth of the shrubs, defended his hands with a pair of thick gloves. Nor were these his only armor. When, in his walk through the garden, he came to the magnificent plant that hung its purple gems beside the marble fountain, he placed a kind of mask over his mouth and nostrils, as if all this beauty did but conceal a deadlier malice; but, finding his task still too dangerous, he drew back, removed the mask, and called loudly, but in the infirm voice of a person affected with inward disease,—

'Beatrice! Beatrice!'

'Here am I, my father. What would you?' cried a rich and youthful voice from the window of the opposite house—a voice as rich as a tropical sunset, and which made Giovanni, though he knew not why, think of deep hues of purple or crimson and of perfumes heavily delectable. 'Are you in the garden?'

'Yes, Beatrice,' answered the gardener, 'and I need your help.'

Soon there emerged from under a sculptured portal the figure of a young girl, arrayed with as much richness of taste as the most splendid of the flowers, beautiful as the day, and with a bloom so deep and vivid that one shade more would have been too much. She looked redundant with life, health, and energy; all of which attributes were bound down and compressed, as it were, and girdled tensely, in their luxuriance, by her virgin zone. Yet Giovanni's fancy must have grown morbid while he looked down into the garden; for the impression which the fair stranger made upon him was as if here were another flower, the human sister of those vegetable ones, as beautiful as they, more beautiful than the richest of them, but still to be touched only with a glove, nor to be approached without a mask. As Beatrice came down the garden path, it was observable that she handled and inhaled the odor of several of the plants which her father had most sedulously avoided.

'Here, Beatrice,' said the latter, 'see how many needful offices require to be done to our chief treasure. Yet, shattered as I am, my life might pay the penalty of approaching it so closely as circumstances demand. Henceforth, I fear, this plant must be consigned to your sole charge.'

'And gladly will I undertake it,' cried again the rich tones of the young lady, as she bent towards the magnificent plant and opened her arms as if to embrace it. 'Yes, my sister, my splendor, it shall be Beatrice's task to nurse and serve thee; and thou shalt reward her with thy kisses and perfumed breath, which to her is as the breath of life.'

Then, with all the tenderness in her manner that was so strikingly expressed in her words, she busied herself with such attentions as the plant seemed to require; and Giovanni, at his lofty window, rubbed his eyes and almost doubted whether it were a girl tending her favorite flower, or one sister performing the duties of affection to another. The scene soon terminated. Whether Dr Rappaccini had finished his labors in the garden, or that his watchful eye had caught the stranger's face, he now took his daughter's arm and retired. Night was already closing in; oppressive exhalations seemed to proceed from the plants and steal upward past the open window; and Giovanni, closing the lattice, went to his couch and dreamed of a rich flower and beautiful girl. Flower and maiden were different, and yet the same, and fraught with some strange peril in either shape.

But there is an influence in the light of morning that tends to rectify whatever errors of fancy, or even of judgment, we may have incurred during the sun's decline, or among the shadows of the night, or in the less wholesome glow of moonshine. Giovanni's first movement, on starting from sleep, was to throw open the window and gaze down into the garden which his dreams had made so fertile of mysteries. He was surprised and a little ashamed to find how real and matter-of-fact an affair it proved to be, in the first rays of the sun which gilded the dew-drops that hung upon leaf and blossom, and, while giving a brighter beauty to each rare flower, brought everything within the limits of ordinary experience. The young man rejoiced that, in the heart of the barren city, he had the privilege of overlooking this spot of lovely and luxuriant vegetation. It would serve, he said to himself, as a symbolic language to keep him in communion with Nature. Neither the sickly and thoughtworn Dr Giacomo Rappaccini, it is true, nor his brilliant daughter, were now visible; so that Giovanni could not determine how much of the singularity which he attributed to both was due to their own qualities and how much to his wonder-working fancy; but he was inclined to take a most rational view of the whole matter.

In the course of the day he paid his respects to Signor Pietro Baglioni, professor of medicine in the university, a physician of eminent repute to whom Giovanni had brought a letter of introduction. The professor was an elderly personage, apparently of genial nature, and habits that might almost be called jovial. He kept the young man to dinner, and made himself very agreeable by the freedom and liveliness of his conversation, especially when warmed by a flask or two of Tuscan wine. Giovanni, conceiving that men of science, inhabitants of the same city, must needs be on familiar terms with one another, took an opportunity to mention the name of Dr Rappaccini. But the professor did not respond with so much cordiality as he had anticipated.

'Ill would it become a teacher of the divine art of medicine,' said Professor Pietro Baglioni, in answer to a question of Giovanni, 'to withhold due and well-considered praise of a physician so eminently skilled as Rappaccini; but, on the other hand, I should answer it but scantily to my conscience were I to permit a worthy youth like yourself, Signor Giovanni, the son of an ancient friend, to imbibe erroneous ideas respecting a man who might hereafter chance to hold your life and death in his hands. The truth is, our worshipful Dr Rappaccini has as much science as any member of the faculty—with perhaps one single exception—in Padua, or all Italy; but there are certain grave objections to his professional character.'

'And what are they?' asked the young man.

'Has my friend Giovanni any disease of body or heart, that he is so inquisitive about physicians?' said the professor, with a smile. 'But as for Rappaccini, it is said of him—and I, who know the man well, can answer for its truth—that he cares infinitely more for science than for mankind. His patients are interesting to him only as subjects for some new experiment. He would sacrifice human life, his own among the rest, or whatever else was dearest to him, for the sake of adding so much as a grain of mustard seed to the great heap of his accumulated knowledge.'

'Methinks he is an awful man indeed,' remarked Guasconti, mentally recalling the cold and purely intellectual aspect of Rappaccini. 'And yet, worshipful professor, is it not a noble spirit? Are there many men capable of so spiritual a love of science?'

'God forbid,' answered the professor, somewhat testily; 'at least, unless they take sounder views of the healing art than those adopted by Rappaccini. It is his theory that all medicinal virtues are comprised within those substances which we term vegetable poisons. These he cultivates with his own hands, and is said even to have produced new varieties of poison, more horribly deleterious than Nature, without the assistance of this learned person, would ever have plagued the world withal. That the signor doctor does less mischief than might be expected with such dangerous substances is undeniable. Now and then, it must be owned, he has effected, or seemed to effect, a marvellous cure; but, to tell you my private mind, Signor Giovanni, he should receive little credit for such instances of success,—they being probably the work of chance,—but should be held strictly accountable for his failures, which may justly be considered his own work.'

The youth might have taken Baglioni's opinions with many grains of allowance had he known that there was a professional warfare of long continuance between him and Dr Rappaccini, in which the latter was generally thought to have gained the advantage. If the reader be inclined to judge for himself, we refer him to certain black-letter tracts on both sides, preserved in the medical department of the University of Padua.

'I know not, most learned professor,' returned Giovanni, after musing on what had been said of Rappaccini's exclusive zeal for science,—'I know not how dearly this physician may love his art; but surely there is one object more dear to him. He has a daughter.'

'Aha!' cried the professor, with a laugh. 'So now our friend Giovanni's secret is out. You have heard of this daughter, whom all the young men in Padua are wild about, though not half a dozen have ever had the good hap to see her face. I know little of the Signora Beatrice save that Rappaccini is said to have instructed her deeply in his science, and that, young and beautiful as fame reports her, she is already qualified to fill a professor's chair. Perchance her father destines her for mine! Other absurd rumors there be, not worth talking about or listening to. So now, Signor Giovanni, drink off your glass of lachryma.'

Guasconti returned to his lodgings somewhat heated with the wine he had quaffed, and which caused his brain to swim with strange fantasies in reference to Dr Rappaccini and the beautiful Beatrice. On his way, happening to pass by a florist's, he bought a fresh bouquet of flowers.

Ascending to his chamber, he seated himself near the window, but within the shadow thrown by the depth of the wall, so that he could look down into the garden with little risk of being discovered. All beneath his eye was a solitude. The strange plants were basking in the sunshine, and now and then nodding gently to one another, as if in acknowledgment of sympathy and kindred. In the midst, by the shattered fountain, grew the magnificent shrub, with its purple gems clustering all over it; they glowed in the air, and gleamed back again out of the depths of the pool, which thus seemed to overflow with colored radiance from the rich reflection that was steeped in it. At first, as we have said, the garden was a solitude. Soon, however,—as Giovanni had half hoped, half feared, would be the case,—a figure appeared beneath the antique sculptured portal, and came down between the rows of plants, inhaling their various perfumes as if she were one of those beings of old classic fable that lived upon sweet odors. On again beholding Beatrice, the young man was even startled to perceive how much her beauty exceeded his recollection of it; so brilliant, so vivid, was its character, that she glowed amid the sunlight, and, as Giovanni whispered to himself, positively illuminated the more shadowy intervals of the garden path. Her face being now more revealed than on the former occasion, he was struck by its expression of simplicity and sweetness,—qualities that had not entered into his idea of her character, and which made him ask anew what manner of mortal she might be. Nor did he fail again to observe, or imagine, an analogy between the beautiful girl and the gorgeous shrub that hung its gemlike flowers over the fountain,—a resemblance which Beatrice seemed to have indulged a fantastic humor in heightening, both by the arrangement of her dress and the selection of its hues.

Approaching the shrub, she threw open her arms, as with a passionate ardor, and drew its branches into an intimate embrace—so intimate that her features were hidden in its leafy bosom and her glistening ringlets all intermingled with the flowers.

'Give me thy breath, my sister,' exclaimed Beatrice; 'for I am faint with common air. And give me this flower of thine, which I separate with gentlest fingers from the stem and place it close beside my heart.'

With these words the beautiful daughter of Rappaccini plucked one of the richest blossoms of the shrub, and was about to fasten it in her bosom. But now, unless Giovanni's draughts of wine had bewildered his senses, a singular accident occurred. A small orange-colored reptile, of the lizard or chameleon species, chanced to be creeping along the path, just at the feet of Beatrice. It appeared to Giovanni,—but, at the distance from which he gazed, he could scarcely have seen anything so minute,—it appeared to him, however, that a drop or two of moisture from the broken stem of the flower descended upon the lizard's head. For an instant the reptile contorted itself violently, and then lay motionless in the sunshine. Beatrice observed this remarkable phenomenon, and crossed herself, sadly, but without surprise; nor did she therefore hesitate to arrange the fatal flower in her bosom. There it blushed, and almost glimmered with the dazzling effect of a precious stone, adding to her dress and aspect the one appropriate charm which nothing else in the world could have supplied. But Giovanni, out of the shadow of his window, bent forward and shrank back, and murmured and trembled.

'Am I awake? Have I my senses?' said he to himself. 'What is this being? Beautiful shall I call her, or inexpressibly terrible?'

Beatrice now strayed carelessly through the garden, approaching closer beneath Giovanni's window, so that he was compelled to thrust his head quite out of its concealment in order to gratify the intense and painful curiosity which she excited. At this moment there came a beautiful insect over the garden wall; it had, perhaps, wandered through the city, and found no flowers or verdure among those antique haunts of men until the heavy perfumes of Dr Rappaccini's shrubs had lured it from afar. Without alighting on the flowers, this winged brightness seemed to be attracted by Beatrice, and lingered in the air and fluttered about her head. Now, here it could not be but that Giovanni Guasconti's eyes deceived him. Be that as it might, he fancied that, while Beatrice was gazing at the insect with childish delight, it grew faint and fell at her feet; its bright wings shivered; it was dead—from no cause that he could discern, unless it were the atmosphere of her breath. Again Beatrice crossed herself and sighed heavily as she bent over the dead insect.

An impulsive movement of Giovanni drew her eyes to the window. There she beheld the beautiful head of the young man—rather a Grecian than an Italian head, with fair, regular features, and a glistening of gold among his ringlets—gazing down upon her like a being that hovered in mid-air. Scarcely knowing what he did, Giovanni threw down the bouquet which he had hitherto held in his hand.

'Signora,' said he, 'there are pure and healthful flowers. Wear them for the sake of Giovanni Guasconti.'

'Thanks, signor,' replied Beatrice, with her rich voice, that came forth as it were like a gush of music, and with a mirthful expression half childish and half woman-like. 'I accept your gift, and would fain recompense it with this precious purple flower; but if I toss it into the air it will not reach you. So Signor Guasconti must even content himself with my thanks.'

She lifted the bouquet from the ground, and then, as if inwardly ashamed at having stepped aside from her maidenly reserve to respond to a stranger's greeting, passed swiftly homeward through the garden. But few as the moments were, it seemed to Giovanni, when she was on the point of vanishing beneath the sculptured portal, that his beautiful bouquet was already beginning to wither in her grasp. It was an idle thought; there could be no possibility of distinguishing a faded flower from a fresh one at so great a distance.

For many days after this incident the young man avoided the window that looked into Dr Rappaccini's garden, as if something ugly and monstrous would have blasted his eyesight had he been betrayed into a glance. He felt conscious of having put himself, to a certain extent, within the influence of an unintelligible power by the communication which he had opened with Beatrice. The wisest course would have been, if his heart were in any real danger, to quit his lodgings and Padua itself at once; the next wiser, to have accustomed himself, as far as possible, to the familiar and daylight view of Beatrice—thus bringing her rigidly and systematically within the limits of ordinary experience. Least of all, while avoiding her sight, ought Giovanni to have remained so near this extraordinary being that the proximity and possibility even of intercourse should give a kind of substance and reality to the wild vagaries which his imagination ran riot continually in producing. Guasconti had not a deep heart—or, at all events, its depths were not sounded now; but he had a quick fancy, and an ardent southern temperament, which rose every instant to a higher fever pitch. Whether or no Beatrice possessed those terrible attributes, that fatal breath, the affinity with those so beautiful and deadly flowers which were indicated by what Giovanni had witnessed, she had at least instilled a fierce and subtle poison into his system. It was not love, although her rich beauty was a

141

madness to him; nor horror, even while he fancied her spirit to be imbued with the same baneful essence that seemed to pervade her physical frame; but a wild offspring of both love and horror that had each parent in it, and burned like one and shivered like the other. Giovanni knew not what to dread; still less did he know what to hope; yet hope and dread kept a continual warfare in his breast, alternately vanquishing one another and starting up afresh to renew the contest. Blessed are all simple emotions, be they dark or bright! It is the lurid intermixture of the two that produces the illuminating blaze of the infernal regions.

Sometimes he endeavored to assuage the fever of his spirit by a rapid walk through the streets of Padua or beyond its gates: his footsteps kept time with the throbbings of his brain, so that the walk was apt to accelerate itself to a race. One day he found himself arrested; his arm was seized by a portly personage, who had turned back on recognizing the young man and expended much breath in overtaking him.

'Signor Giovanni! Stay, my young friend!' cried he. 'Have you forgotten me? That might well be the case if I were as much altered as yourself.'

It was Baglioni, whom Giovanni had avoided ever since their first meeting, from a doubt that the professor's sagacity would look too deeply into his secrets. Endeavoring to recover himself, he stared forth wildly from his inner world into the outer one and spoke like a man in a dream.

'Yes; I am Giovanni Guasconti. You are Professor Pietro Baglioni. Now let me pass!'

'Not yet, not yet, Signor Giovanni Guasconti,' said the professor, smiling, but at the same time scrutinizing the youth with an earnest glance. 'What! did I grow up side by side with your father? and shall his son pass me like a stranger in these old streets of Padua? Stand still, Signor Giovanni; for we must have a word or two before we part.'

'Speedily, then, most worshipful professor, speedily,' said Giovanni with feverish impatience. 'Does not your worship see that I am in haste?'

Now, while he was speaking there came a man in black along the street, stooping and moving feebly like a person in inferior health. His face was all overspread with a most sickly and sallow hue, but yet so pervaded with an expression of piercing and active intellect that an observer might easily have overlooked the merely physical attributes and have seen only this wonderful energy. As he passed, this person exchanged a cold and distant salutation with Baglioni, but fixed his eyes upon Giovanni with an intentness that seemed to bring out whatever was within him worthy of notice. Nevertheless, there was a peculiar quietness in the look, as if taking merely a speculative, not a human interest, in the young man.

'It is Dr Rappaccini!' whispered the professor when the stranger had passed. 'Has he ever seen your face before?'

'Not that I know,' answered Giovanni, starting at the name.

'He *has* seen you! he must have seen you!' said Baglioni, hastily. 'For some purpose or other, this man of science is making a study of you. I know that look of his! It is the same that coldly illuminates his face as he bends over a bird, a mouse, or a butterfly, which, in pursuance of some experiment, he has killed by the perfume of a flower; a look as deep as Nature itself, but without Nature's warmth of love. Signor Giovanni, I will stake my life upon it, you are the subject of one of Rappaccini's experiments!'

'Will you make a fool of me?' cried Giovanni passionately. '*That*, signor professor, were an untoward experiment.'

'Patience! patience!' replied the imperturbable professor. 'I tell thee, my poor Giovanni, that Rappaccini has a scientific interest in thee. Thou hast fallen into fearful hands! And the Signora Beatrice,—what part does she act in this mystery?'

But Guasconti, finding Baglioni's pertinacity intolerable, here broke away, and was gone before the professor could again seize his arm. He looked after the young man intently and shook his head.

'This must not be,' said Baglioni to himself. 'The youth is the son of my old friend, and shall not come to any harm from which the arcana of medical science can preserve him. Besides, it is too insufferable an impertinence in Rappaccini, thus to snatch the lad out of my own hands, as I may say, and make use of him for his infernal experiments. This daughter of his! It shall be looked to. Perchance, most learned Rappaccini, I may foil you where you little dream of it!'

Meanwhile Giovanni had pursued a circuitous route, and at length found himself at the door of his lodgings. As he crossed the threshold he was met by old Lisabetta, who smirked and smiled, and was evidently desirous to attract his attention; vainly, however, as the ebullition of his feelings had momentarily subsided into a cold and dull vacuity. He turned his eyes full upon the withered face that was puckering itself into a smile, but seemed to behold it not. The old dame, therefore, laid her grasp upon his cloak.

'Signor! signor!' whispered she, still with a smile over the whole breadth of her visage, so that it looked not unlike a grotesque carving in wood, darkened by centuries. 'Listen, signor! There is a private entrance into the garden!'

'What do you say?' exclaimed Giovanni, turning quickly about, as if an inanimate thing should start into feverish life. 'A private entrance into Dr Rappaccini's garden?'

'Hush! hush! not so loud!' whispered Lisabetta, putting her hand over his mouth. 'Yes; into the worshipful doctor's garden, where you may see all his fine shrubbery. Many a young man in Padua would give gold to be admitted among those flowers.'

Giovanni put a piece of gold into her hand.

'Show me the way,' said he.

A surmise, probably excited by his conversation with Baglioni, crossed his mind, that this interposition of old Lisabetta might perchance be connected with the intrigue, whatever were its nature, in which the professor seemed to suppose that Dr Rappaccini was involving him. But such a suspicion, though it disturbed Giovanni, was inadequate to restrain him. The instant that he was aware of the possibility of approaching Beatrice, it seemed an absolute necessity of his existence to do so. It mattered not whether she were angel or demon; he was irrevocably within her sphere, and must obey the law that whirled him onward, in ever-lessening circles, towards a result which he did not attempt to foreshadow; and yet, strange to say, there came across him a sudden doubt whether this intense interest on his part were not delusory; whether it were really of so deep and positive a nature as to justify him in now thrusting himself into an incalculable position; whether it were not merely the fantasy of a young man's brain, only slightly or not at all connected with his heart.

He paused, hesitated, turned half about, but again went on. His withered guide led him along several obscure passages, and finally undid a door, through which, as it was opened, there came the sight and sound of rustling leaves, with the broken sunshine glimmering among them. Giovanni stepped forth, and, forcing himself through the entanglement of a shrub that wreathed its tendrils over the hidden entrance, stood beneath his own window in the open area of Dr Rappaccini's garden.

How often is it the case that, when impossibilities have come to pass and dreams have condensed their misty substance into tangible realities, we find ourselves calm, and even coldly self-possessed, amid circumstances which it would have been a delirium of joy or agony to anticipate! Fate delights to thwart us thus. Passion will choose his own time to rush upon the scene, and lingers sluggishly behind when an appropriate adjustment of events would seem to summon his appearance. So was it now with Giovanni. Day after day his pulses had throbbed with feverish blood at the improbable idea of an interview with Beatrice, and of standing with her, face to face, in this very garden, basking in the Oriental sunshine of her beauty, and snatching from her full gaze the mystery which he deemed the riddle of his own existence. But now there was a singular and untimely equanimity within his breast. He threw a glance around the garden to discover if Beatrice or her father were present, and, perceiving that he was alone, began a critical observation of the plants.

The aspect of one and all of them dissatisfied him; their gorgeousness seemed fierce, passionate, and even unnatural. There was hardly an individual shrub which a wanderer, straying by himself through a forest, would not have been startled to find growing wild, as if an unearthly face had glared at him out of the thicket. Several also would have shocked a delicate instinct by an appearance of artificialness indicating that there had been such commixture, and, as it were, adultery, of various vegetable species, that the production was no longer of God's making, but the monstrous offspring of man's depraved fancy, glowing with only an evil mockery of beauty. They were probably the result of experiment, which in one or two cases had succeeded in mingling plants individually lovely into a compound possessing the questionable and ominous character that distinguished the whole growth of the garden. In fine, Giovanni recognized but two or three plants in the collection, and those of a kind that he well knew to be poisonous. While busy with these contemplations he heard the rustling of a silken garment, and, turning, beheld Beatrice emerging from beneath the sculptured portal.

Giovanni had not considered with himself what should be his deportment; whether he should apologize for his intrusion into the garden, or assume that he was there with the privity at least, if not by the desire, of Dr Rappaccini or his daughter; but Beatrice's manner placed him at his ease, though leaving him still in doubt by what agency he had gained admittance. She came lightly along the path and met him near the broken fountain. There was surprise in her face, but brightened by a simple and kind expression of pleasure.

'You are a connoisseur in flowers, signor,' said Beatrice, with a smile, alluding to the bouquet which he had flung her from the window. 'It is no marvel, therefore, if the sight of my father's rare collection has tempted you to take a nearer view. If he were here, he could tell you many strange and interesting facts as to the nature and habits of these shrubs; for he has spent a lifetime in such studies, and this garden is his world.'

'And yourself, lady,' observed Giovanni, 'if fame says true,—you likewise are deeply skilled in the virtues indicated by these rich blossoms and these spicy perfumes. Would you deign to be my instructress, I should prove an apter scholar than if taught by Signor Rappaccini himself.'

'Are there such idle rumors?' asked Beatrice, with the music of a pleasant laugh. 'Do people say that I am skilled in my father's science of plants? What a jest is there! No; though I have grown up among these flowers, I know no more of them than their hues and perfume; and sometimes methinks I would fain rid myself of even that small knowledge. There are many flowers here, and those not the least brilliant, that shock and offend me when they meet my eye. But pray, signor, do not believe these stories about my science. Believe nothing of me save what you see with your own eyes.'

'And must I believe all that I have seen with my own eyes?' asked Giovanni, pointedly, while the recollection of former scenes made him shrink. 'No, signora; you demand too little of me. Bid me believe nothing save what comes from your own lips.'

It would appear that Beatrice understood him. There came a deep flush to her cheek; but she looked full into Giovanni's eyes, and responded to his gaze of uneasy suspicion with a queenlike haughtiness.

'I do so bid you, signor,' she replied. 'Forget whatever you may have fancied in regard to me. If true to the outward senses, still it may be false in its essence; but the words of Beatrice Rappaccini's lips are true from the depths of the heart outward. Those you may believe.'

A fervor glowed in her whole aspect and beamed upon Giovanni's consciousness like the light of truth itself; but while she spoke there was a fragrance in the atmosphere around her, rich and delightful, though evanescent, yet which the young man, from an indefinable reluctance, scarcely dared to draw into his lungs. It might be the odor of the flowers. Could it be Beatrice's breath which thus embalmed her words with a strange richness, as if by steeping them in her heart? A faintness passed like a shadow over Giovanni and flitted away; he seemed to gaze through the beautiful girl's eyes into her transparent soul, and felt no more doubt or fear.

The tinge of passion that had colored Beatrice's manner vanished; she became gay, and appeared to derive a pure delight from her communion with the youth not unlike what the maiden of a lonely island might have felt conversing with a voyager from the civilized world. Evidently her experience of life had been confined within the limits of that garden. She talked now about matters as simple as the daylight or summer clouds, and now asked questions in reference to the city, or Giovanni's distant home, his friends, his mother, and his sisters—questions indicating such seclusion, and such lack of familiarity with modes and forms, that Giovanni responded as if to an infant. Her spirit gushed out before him like a fresh rill that was just catching its first glimpse of the sunlight and wondering at the reflections of earth and sky which were flung into its bosom. There came thoughts, too, from a deep source, and fantasies of a gemlike brilliancy, as if diamonds and rubies sparkled upward among the bubbles of the fountain. Ever and anon there gleamed across the young man's mind a sense of wonder that he should be walking side by side with the being who had so wrought upon his imagination, whom he had idealized in such hues of terror, in whom he had positively witnessed such manifestations of dreadful attributes,—that he should be conversing with Beatrice like a brother, and should find her so human and so maidenlike. But such reflections were only momentary; the effect of her character was too real not to make itself familiar at once.

In this free intercourse they had strayed through the garden, and now, after many turns among its avenues, were come to the shattered fountain, beside which grew the magnificent shrub, with its treasury of glowing blossoms. A fragrance was diffused from it which Giovanni recognized as identical with that which he had attributed to Beatrice's breath, but incomparably more powerful. As her eyes fell upon it, Giovanni beheld her press her hand to her bosom as if her heart were throbbing suddenly and painfully.

'For the first time in my life,' murmured she, addressing the shrub, 'I had forgotten thee.'

'I remember, signora,' said Giovanni, 'that you once promised to reward me with one of these living gems for the bouquet which I had the happy boldness to fling to your feet. Permit me now to pluck it as a memorial of this interview.'

He made a step towards the shrub with extended hand; but Beatrice darted forward, uttering a shriek that went through his heart like a dagger. She caught his hand and drew it back with the whole force of her slender figure. Giovanni felt her touch thrilling through his fibres.

'Touch it not!' exclaimed she, in a voice of agony. 'Not for thy life! It is fatal!'

Then, hiding her face, she fled from him and vanished beneath the sculptured portal. As Giovanni followed her with his eyes, he beheld the emaciated figure and pale intelligence of Dr Rappaccini, who had been watching the scene, he knew not how long, within the shadow of the entrance.

No sooner was Guasconti alone in his chamber than the image of Beatrice came back to his passionate musings, invested with all the witchery that had been gathering around it ever since his first glimpse of her, and now likewise imbued with a tender warmth of girlish womanhood. She was human; her nature was endowed with all gentle and feminine qualities; she was worthiest to be worshipped; she was capable, surely, on her part, of the height and heroism of love. Those tokens which he had hitherto considered as proofs of a frightful peculiarity in her physical and moral system were now either forgotten, or, by the subtle sophistry of passion transmitted into a golden crown of enchantment, rendering Beatrice the more admirable by so much as she was the more unique. Whatever had looked ugly was now beautiful; or, if incapable of such a change, it stole away and hid itself among those shapeless half ideas which throng the dim region beyond the daylight of our perfect consciousness. Thus did he spend the night, nor fell asleep until the dawn had begun to awake the slumbering flowers in Dr Rappaccini's garden, whither Giovanni's dreams doubtless led him. Up rose the sun in his due season, and, flinging his beams upon the young man's eyelids, awoke him to a sense of pain. When thoroughly aroused, he became sensible of a burning and tingling agony in his hand—in his right hand—the very hand which Beatrice had grasped in her own when he was on the point of plucking one of the gemlike flowers. On the back of that hand there was now a purple print like that of four small fingers, and the likeness of a slender thumb upon his wrist.

Oh, how stubbornly does love,—or even that cunning semblance of love which flourishes in the imagination, but strikes no depth of root into the heart,—how stubbornly does it hold its faith until the moment comes when it is doomed to vanish into thin mist! Giovanni wrapped a handkerchief about his hand and wondered what evil thing had stung him, and soon forgot his pain in a reverie of Beatrice.

After the first interview, a second was in the inevitable course of what we call fate. A third; a fourth; and a meeting with Beatrice in the garden was no longer an incident in Giovanni's daily life, but the whole space in which he might be said to live; for the anticipation and memory of that ecstatic hour made up the remainder. Nor was it otherwise with the daughter of Rappaccini. She watched for the youth's appearance, and flew to his side with confidence as unreserved as if they had been playmates from early infancy—as if they were such playmates still. If, by any unwonted chance, he failed to come at

the appointed moment, she stood beneath the window and sent up
the rich sweetness of her tones to float around him in his chamber
and echo and reverberate throughout his heart: 'Giovanni! Giovanni!
Why tarriest thou? Come down!' And down he hastened into that
Eden of poisonous flowers.

But, with all this intimate familiarity, there was still a reserve in
Beatrice's demeanor, so rigidly and invariably sustained that the idea
of infringing it scarcely occurred to his imagination. By all appreci-
able signs, they loved; they had looked love with eyes that conveyed
the holy secret from the depths of one soul into the depths of the
other, as if it were too sacred to be whispered by the way; they had
even spoken love in those gushes of passion when their spirits darted
forth in articulated breath like tongues of long-hidden flame; and yet
there had been no seal of lips, no clasp of hands, nor any slightest
caress such as love claims and hallows. He had never touched one of
the gleaming ringlets of her hair; her garment—so marked was the
physical barrier between them—had never been waved against him
by a breeze. On the few occasions when Giovanni had seemed
tempted to overstep the limit, Beatrice grew so sad, so stern, and
withal wore such a look of desolate separation, shuddering at itself,
that not a spoken word was requisite to repel him. At such times he
was startled at the horrible suspicions that rose, monster-like, out of
the caverns of his heart and stared him in the face; his love grew thin
and faint as the morning mist, his doubts alone had substance. But,
when Beatrice's face brightened again after the momentary shadow,
she was transformed at once from the mysterious, questionable being
whom he had watched with so much awe and horror; she was now
the beautiful and unsophisticated girl whom he felt that his spirit
knew with a certainty beyond all other knowledge.

A considerable time had now passed since Giovanni's last meeting
with Baglioni. One morning, however, he was disagreeably surprised
by a visit from the professor, whom he had scarcely thought of for
whole weeks, and would willingly have forgotten still longer. Given
up as he had long been to a pervading excitement, he could tolerate
no companions except upon condition of their perfect sympathy with
his present state of feeling. Such sympathy was not to be expected
from Professor Baglioni.

The visitor chatted carelessly for a few moments about the gossip
of the city and the university, and then took up another topic.

'I have been reading an old classic author lately,' said he, 'and met
with a story that strangely interested me. Possibly you may remember
it. It is of an Indian prince, who sent a beautiful woman as a present

to Alexander the Great. She was as lovely as the dawn and gorgeous as the sunset; but what especially distinguished her was a certain rich perfume in her breath—richer than a garden of Persian roses. Alexander, as was natural to a youthful conqueror, fell in love at first sight with this magnificent stranger; but a certain sage physician, happening to be present, discovered a terrible secret in regard to her.'

'And what was that?' asked Giovanni, turning his eyes downward to avoid those of the professor.

'That this lovely woman,' continued Baglioni, with emphasis, 'had been nourished with poisons from her birth upward, until her whole nature was so imbued with them that she herself had become the deadliest poison in existence. Poison was her element of life. With that rich perfume of her breath she blasted the very air. Her love would have been poison—her embrace death. Is not this a marvellous tale?'

'A childish fable,' answered Giovanni, nervously starting from his chair. 'I marvel how your worship finds time to read such nonsense among your graver studies.'

'By the by,' said the professor, looking uneasily about him, 'what singular fragrance is this in your apartment? Is it the perfume of your gloves? It is faint, but delicious; and yet, after all, by no means agreeable. Were I to breathe it long, methinks it would make me ill. It is like the breath of a flower; but I see no flowers in the chamber.'

'Nor are there any,' replied Giovanni, who had turned pale as the professor spoke; 'nor, I think, is there any fragrance except in your worship's imagination. Odors, being a sort of element combined of the sensual and the spiritual, are apt to deceive us in this manner. The recollection of a perfume, the bare idea of it, may easily be mistaken for a present reality.'

'Ay; but my sober imagination does not often play such tricks,' said Baglioni; 'and, were I to fancy any kind of odor, it would be that of some vile apothecary drug, wherewith my fingers are likely enough to be imbued. Our worshipful friend Rappaccini, as I have heard, tinctures his medicaments with odors richer than those of Araby. Doubtless, likewise, the fair and learned Signora Beatrice would minister to her patients with draughts as sweet as a maiden's breath; but woe to him that sips them!'

Giovanni's face evinced many contending emotions. The tone in which the professor alluded to the pure and lovely daughter of Rappaccini was a torture to his soul; and yet the intimation of a view of her character, opposite to his own, gave instantaneous distinctness to a thousand dim suspicions, which now grinned at him like so many demons. But he strove hard to quell them and to respond to Baglioni with a true lover's perfect faith.

'Signor professor,' said he, 'you were my father's friend; perchance, too, it is your purpose to act a friendly part towards his son. I would fain feel nothing towards you save respect and deference; but I pray you to observe, signor, that there is one subject on which we must not speak. You know not the Signora Beatrice. You cannot, therefore, estimate the wrong—the blasphemy, I may even say—that is offered to her character by a light or injurious word.'

'Giovanni! my poor Giovanni!' answered the professor, with calm expression of pity, 'I know this wretched girl far better than yourself. You shall hear the truth in respect to the poisoner Rappaccini and his poisonous daughter; yes, poisonous as she is beautiful. Listen; for, even should you do violence to my gray hairs, it shall not silence me. That old fable of the Indian woman has become a truth by the deep and deadly science of Rappaccini and in the person of the lovely Beatrice.'

Giovanni groaned and hid his face.

'Her father,' continued Baglioni, 'was not restrained by natural affection from offering up his child in this horrible manner as the victim of his insane zeal for science; for, let us do him justice, he is as true a man of science as ever distilled his own heart in an alembic. What, then, will be your fate? Beyond a doubt you are selected as the material of some new experiment. Perhaps the result is to be death; perhaps a fate more awful still. Rappaccini, with what he calls the interest of science before his eyes, will hesitate at nothing.'

'It is a dream,' muttered Giovanni to himself; 'surely it is a dream.'

'But,' resumed the professor, 'be of good cheer, son of my friend. It is not yet too late for the rescue. Possibly we may even succeed in bringing back this miserable child within the limits of ordinary nature, from which her father's madness has estranged her. Behold this little silver vase! It was wrought by the hands of the renowned Benvenuto Cellini, and is well worthy to be a love gift to the fairest dame in Italy. But its contents are invaluable. One little sip of this antidote would have rendered the most virulent poisons of the Borgias innocuous. Doubt not that it will be as efficacious against those of Rappaccini. Bestow the vase, and the precious liquid within it, on your Beatrice, and hopefully await the result.'

Baglioni laid a small, exquisitely wrought silver vial on the table and withdrew, leaving what he had said to produce its effect upon the young man's mind.

'We will thwart Rappaccini yet,' thought he, chuckling to himself, as he descended the stairs; 'but, let us confess the truth of him, he is a wonderful man—a wonderful man indeed; a vile empiric, however, in his practice, and therefore not to be tolerated by those who respect the good old rules of the medical profession.'

Throughout Giovanni's whole acquaintance with Beatrice, he had occasionally, as we have said, been haunted by dark surmises as to her character; yet so thoroughly had she made herself felt by him as a simple, natural, most affectionate, and guileless creature, that the image now held up by Professor Baglioni looked as strange and incredible as if it were not in accordance with his own original conception. True, there were ugly recollections connected with his first glimpses of the beautiful girl; he could not quite forget the bouquet that withered in her grasp, and the insect that perished amid the sunny air, by no ostensible agency save the fragrance of her breath. These incidents, however, dissolving in the pure light of her character, had no longer the efficacy of facts, but were acknowledged as mistaken fantasies, by whatever testimony of the senses they might appear to be substantiated. There is something truer and more real than what we can see with the eyes and touch with the finger. On such better evidence had Giovanni founded his confidence in Beatrice, though rather by the necessary force of her high attributes than by any deep and generous faith on his part. But now his spirit was incapable of sustaining itself at the height to which the early enthusiasm of passion had exalted it; he fell down, grovelling among earthly doubts, and defiled therewith the pure whiteness of Beatrice's image. Not that he gave her up; he did but distrust. He resolved to institute some decisive test that should satisfy him, once for all, whether there were those dreadful peculiarities in her physical nature which could not be supposed to exist without some corresponding monstrosity of soul. His eyes, gazing down afar, might have deceived him as to the lizard, the insect, and the flowers; but if he could witness, at the distance of a few paces, the sudden blight of one fresh and healthful flower in Beatrice's hand, there would be room for no further question. With this idea he hastened to the florist's and purchased a bouquet that was still gemmed with the morning dew-drops.

It was now the customary hour of his daily interview with Beatrice. Before descending into the garden, Giovanni failed not to look at his figure in the mirror,—a vanity to be expected in a beautiful young man, yet, as displaying itself at that troubled and feverish moment, the token of a certain shallowness of feeling and insincerity of character. He did gaze, however, and said to himself that his features had never before possessed so rich a grace, nor his eyes such vivacity, nor his cheeks so warm a hue of superabundant life.

'At least,' thought he, 'her poison has not yet insinuated itself into my system. I am no flower to perish in her grasp.'

With that thought he turned his eyes on the bouquet, which he had never once laid aside from his hand. A thrill of indefinable horror shot through his frame on perceiving that those dewy flowers were already beginning to droop; they wore the aspect of things that had been fresh and lovely yesterday. Giovanni grew white as marble, and stood motionless before the mirror, staring at his own reflection there as at the likeness of something frightful. He remembered Baglioni's remark about the fragrance that seemed to pervade the chamber. It must have been the poison in his breath! Then he shuddered— shuddered at himself. Recovering from his stupor, he began to watch with curious eye a spider that was busily at work hanging its web from the antique cornice of the apartment, crossing and recrossing the artful system of interwoven lines—as vigorous and active a spider as ever dangled from an old ceiling. Giovanni bent towards the insect, and emitted a deep, long breath. The spider suddenly ceased its toil; the web vibrated with a tremor originating in the body of the small artisan. Again Giovanni sent forth a breath, deeper, longer, and imbued with a venomous feeling out of his heart: he knew not whether he were wicked, or only desperate. The spider made a convulsive gripe with his limbs and hung dead across the window.

'Accursed! accursed!' muttered Giovanni, addressing himself. 'Hast thou grown so poisonous that this deadly insect perishes by thy breath?'

At that moment a rich, sweet voice came floating up from the garden.

'Giovanni! Giovanni! It is past the hour! Why tarriest thou? Come down!'

'Yes,' muttered Giovanni again. 'She is the only being whom my breath may not slay! Would that it might!'

He rushed down, and in an instant was standing before the bright and loving eyes of Beatrice. A moment ago his wrath and despair had been so fierce that he could have desired nothing so much as to wither her by a glance; but with her actual presence there came influences which had too real an existence to be at once shaken off: recollections of the delicate and benign power of her feminine nature, which had so often enveloped him in a religious calm; recollections of many a holy and passionate outgush of her heart, when the pure fountain had been unsealed from its depths and made visible in its transparency to his mental eye; recollections which, had Giovanni known how to estimate them, would have assured him that all this ugly mystery was but an earthly illusion, and that, whatever mist of evil might seem to have gathered over her, the real Beatrice was a heavenly angel. Incapable as he was of such high faith, still her presence had not utterly lost its magic. Giovanni's rage was quelled into an aspect of sullen insensibility. Beatrice, with a quick spiritual sense, immediately felt that there was a gulf of blackness between them which neither he nor she could pass. They walked on together, sad and silent, and came thus to the marble fountain and to its pool of water on the ground, in the midst of which grew the shrub that bore gem-like blossoms. Giovanni was affrighted at the eager enjoyment—the appetite, as it were—with which he found himself inhaling the fragrance of the flowers.

'Beatrice,' asked he, abruptly, 'whence came this shrub?'

'My father created it,' answered she, with simplicity.

'Created it! created it!' repeated Giovanni. 'What mean you, Beatrice?'

'He is a man fearfully acquainted with the secrets of Nature,' replied Beatrice; 'and, at the hour when I first drew breath, this plant sprang from the soil, the offspring of his science, of his intellect, while I was but his earthly child. Approach it not!' continued she, observing with terror that Giovanni was drawing nearer to the shrub. 'It has qualities that you little dream of. But I, dearest Giovanni,—I grew up and blossomed with the plant and was nourished with its breath. It was my sister, and I loved it with a human affection; for, alas!—hast thou not suspected it?—there was an awful doom.'

Here Giovanni frowned so darkly upon her that Beatrice paused and trembled. But her faith in his tenderness reassured her, and made her blush that she had doubted for an instant.

'There was an awful doom,' she continued, 'the effect of my father's fatal love of science, which estranged me from all society of my kind. Until Heaven sent thee, dearest Giovanni, oh, how lonely was thy poor Beatrice!'

'Was it a hard doom?' asked Giovanni, fixing his eyes upon her.

'Only of late have I known how hard it was,' answered she tenderly. 'Oh, yes; but my heart was torpid, and therefore quiet.'

Giovanni's rage broke forth from his sullen gloom like a lightning flash out of a dark cloud.

'Accursed one!' cried he, with venomous scorn and anger. 'And, finding thy solitude wearisome, thou hast severed me likewise from all the warmth of life and enticed me into thy region of unspeakable horror!'

'Giovanni!' exclaimed Beatrice, turning her large bright eyes upon his face. The force of his words had not found its way into her mind; she was merely thunderstruck.

'Yes, poisonous thing!' repeated Giovanni, beside himself with passion. 'Thou hast done it! Thou hast blasted me! Thou hast filled my veins with poison! Thou hast made me as hateful, as ugly, as loathsome and deadly a creature as thyself—a world's wonder of hideous monstrosity! Now, if our breath be happily as fatal to ourselves as to all others, let us join our lips in one kiss of unutterable hatred, and so die!'

'What has befallen me?' murmured Beatrice, with a low moan out of her heart. 'Holy Virgin, pity me, a poor heart-broken child!'

'Thou,—dost thou pray?' cried Giovanni, still with the same fiendish scorn. 'Thy very prayers, as they come from thy lips, taint the atmosphere with death. Yes, yes; let us pray! Let us to church and dip our fingers in the holy water at the portal! They that come after us will perish as by a pestilence! Let us sign crosses in the air! It will be scattering curses abroad in the likeness of holy symbols!'

'Giovanni,' said Beatrice, calmly, for her grief was beyond passion, 'why dost thou join thyself with me thus in those terrible words? I, it is true, am the horrible thing thou namest me. But thou,—what hast thou to do, save with one other shudder at my hideous misery to go forth out of the garden and mingle with thy race, and forget there ever crawled on earth such a monster as poor Beatrice?'

'Dost thou pretend ignorance?' asked Giovanni, scowling upon her. 'Behold! this power have I gained from the pure daughter of Rappaccini.'

There was a swarm of summer insects flitting through the air in search of the food promised by the flower odors of the fatal garden. They circled round Giovanni's head, and were evidently attracted towards him by the same influence which had drawn them for an instant within the sphere of several of the shrubs. He sent forth a breath among them, and smiled bitterly at Beatrice as at least a score of the insects fell dead upon the ground.

'I see it! I see it!' shrieked Beatrice. 'It is my father's fatal science! No, no, Giovanni; it was not I! Never! never! I dreamed only to love thee and be with thee a little time, and so to let thee pass away, leaving but thine image in mine heart; for, Giovanni, believe it, though my body be nourished with poison, my spirit is God's creature, and craves love as its daily food. But my father,—he has united us in this fearful sympathy. Yes; spurn me, tread upon me, kill me! Oh, what is death after such words as thine? But it was not I. Not for a world of bliss would I have done it.'

Giovanni's passion had exhausted itself in its outburst from his lips. There now came across him a sense, mournful, and not without tenderness, of the intimate and peculiar relationship between Beatrice and himself. They stood, as it were, in an utter solitude, which would be made none the less solitary by the densest throng of human life. Ought not, then, the desert of humanity around them to press this insulated pair closer together? If they should be cruel to one another, who was there to be kind to them? Besides, thought Giovanni, might there not still be a hope of his returning within the limits of ordinary nature, and leading Beatrice, the redeemed Beatrice, by the hand? O, weak, and selfish, and unworthy spirit, that could dream of an earthly union and earthly happiness as possible, after such deep love had been so bitterly wronged as was Beatrice's love by Giovanni's blighting words! No, no; there could be no such hope. She must pass heavily, with that broken heart, across the borders of Time—she must bathe her hurts in some fount of paradise, and forget her grief in the light of immortality, and *there* be well.

But Giovanni did not know it.

'Dear Beatrice,' said he, approaching her, while she shrank away as always at his approach, but now with a different impulse, 'dearest Beatrice our fate is not yet so desperate. Behold! there is a medicine, potent, as a wise physician has assured me, and almost divine in its efficacy. It is composed of ingredients the most opposite to those by which thy awful father has brought this calamity upon thee and me. It is distilled of blessed herbs. Shall we not quaff it together, and thus be purified from evil?'

'Give it me!' said Beatrice, extending her hand to receive the little silver vial which Giovanni took from his bosom. She added, with a peculiar emphasis, 'I will drink; but do thou await the result.'

She put Baglioni's antidote to her lips; and, at the same moment, the figure of Rappaccini emerged from the portal and came slowly towards the marble fountain. As he drew near, the pale man of science seemed to gaze with a triumphant expression at the beautiful youth and maiden, as might an artist who should spend his life in achieving a picture or a group of statuary and finally be satisfied with his success. He paused; his bent form grew erect with conscious power; he spread out his hands over them in the attitude of a father imploring a blessing upon his children; but those were the same hands that had thrown poison into the stream of their lives. Giovanni trembled. Beatrice shuddered nervously, and pressed her hand upon her heart.

'My daughter,' said Rappaccini, 'thou art no longer lonely in the world. Pluck one of those precious gems from thy sister shrub and bid thy bridegroom wear it in his bosom. It will not harm him now. My science and the sympathy between thee and him have so wrought within his system that he now stands apart from common men, as thou dost, daughter of my pride and triumph, from ordinary women. Pass on, then, through the world, most dear to one another and dreadful to all besides!'

'My father,' said Beatrice, feebly,—and still as she spoke she kept her hand upon her heart,—'wherefore didst thou inflict this miserable doom upon thy child?'

'Miserable!' exclaimed Rappaccini. 'What mean you, foolish girl? Dost thou deem it misery to be endowed with marvellous gifts against which no power nor strength could avail an enemy—misery, to be able to quell the mightiest with a breath—misery, to be as terrible as thou art beautiful? Wouldst thou, then, have preferred the condition of a weak woman, exposed to all evil and capable of none?'

'I would fain have been loved, not feared,' murmured Beatrice, sinking down upon the ground. 'But now it matters not. I am going, father, where the evil which thou hast striven to mingle with my being will pass away like a dream—like the fragrance of these poisonous flowers, which will no longer taint my breath among the flowers of Eden. Farewell, Giovanni! Thy words of hatred are like lead within my heart; but they, too, will fall away as I ascend. Oh, was there not, from the first, more poison in thy nature than in mine?'

To Beatrice,—so radically had her earthly part been wrought upon by Rappaccini's skill,—as poison had been life, so the powerful antidote was death; and thus the poor victim of man's ingenuity and of thwarted nature, and of the fatality that attends all such efforts of perverted wisdom, perished there, at the feet of her father and Giovanni. Just at that moment Professor Pietro Baglioni looked forth from the window, and called loudly, in a tone of triumph mixed with horror, to the thunderstricken man of science,—

'Rappaccini! Rappaccini! and is *this* the upshot of your experiment!'

BRET HARTE

Selina Sedilia

BY MISS M. E. B–DD–N AND MRS H–N–Y W–D.

CHAPTER I

The sun was setting over Sloperton Grange, and reddened the windows of the lonely chamber in the western tower, supposed to be haunted by Sir Edward Sedilia, the founder of the Grange. In the dreamy distance arose the gilded mausoleum of Lady Felicia Sedilia, who haunted that portion of Sedilia Manor known as 'Stiff-uns Acre'. A little to the left of the Grange might have been seen a mouldering ruin, known as 'Guy's Keep', haunted by the spirit of Sir Guy Sedilia, who was found, one morning, crushed by one of the fallen battlements. Yet, as the setting sun gilded these objects, a beautiful and almost holy calm seemed diffused about the Grange.

The Lady Selina sat by an oriel window overlooking the park. The sun sank gently in the bosom of the German Ocean, and yet the lady did not lift her beautiful head from the finely curved arm and diminutive hand which supported it. When darkness finally shrouded the landscape, she started, for the sound of horse-hoofs clattered over the stones of the avenue. She had scarcely risen before an aristocratic young man fell on his knees before her.

'My Selina!'

'Edgardo! You here?'

'Yes, dearest.'

'And—you—you—have—seen nothing?' said the lady in an agitated voice and nervous manner, turning her face aside to conceal her emotion.

'Nothing—that is, nothing of any account,' said Edgardo. 'I passed the ghost of your aunt in the park, noticed the spectre of your uncle in the ruined keep, and observed the familiar features of the spirit of your great grandfather at his post. But nothing beyond these trifles, my Selina. Nothing more, love, absolutely nothing.'

The young man turned his dark liquid orbs fondly upon the ingenuous face of his betrothed.

'My own Edgardo!—and you still love me? You still would marry me in spite of this dark mystery which surrounds me? In spite of the fatal history of my race? In spite of the ominous predictions of my aged nurse?'

'I would, Selina;' and the young man passed his arm around her yielding waist. The two lovers gazed at each other's faces in unspeakable bliss. Suddenly Selina started.

'Leave me, Edgardo! leave me! A mysterious something—a fatal misgiving—a dark ambiguity—an equivocal mistrust oppresses me. I would be alone!'

The young man arose, and cast a loving glance on the lady. 'Then we will be married on the seventeenth.'

'The seventeenth,' repeated Selina, with a mysterious shudder.

They embraced and parted. As the clatter of hoofs in the courtyard died away, the Lady Selina sank into the chair she had just quitted.

'The seventeenth,' she repeated slowly, with the same fatal shudder. 'Ah!—what if he should know that I have another husband living? Dare I reveal to him that I have two legitimate and three natural children? Dare I repeat to him the history of my youth? Dare I confess that at the age of seven I poisoned my sister, by putting verdigris in her cream tarts—that I threw my cousin from a swing at the age of twelve? That the lady's-maid who incurred the displeasure of my girlhood now lies at the bottom of the horsepond? No! no! he is too pure—too good—too innocent, to hear such improper conversation!' and her whole body writhed as she rocked to and fro in a paroxysm of grief.

But she was soon calm. Rising to her feet, she opened a secret panel in the wall, and revealed a slow-match ready for lighting.

'This match,' said the Lady Selina, 'is connected with a mine beneath the western tower, where my three children are confined; another branch of it lies under the parish church, where the record of my first marriage is kept. I have only to light this match and the whole of my past life is swept away!' She approached the match with a lighted candle.

But a hand was laid upon her arm, and with a shriek the Lady Selina fell on her knees before the spectre of Sir Guy.

CHAPTER II

'Forbear, Selina,' said the phantom in a hollow voice.

'Why should I forbear?' responded Selina haughtily, as she recovered her courage. 'You know the secret of our race?'

'I do. Understand me—I do not object to the eccentricities of your youth. I know the fearful fate which, pursuing you, led you to poison your sister and drown your lady's maid. I know the awful doom which I have brought upon this house! But if you make away with these children——'

'Well?' said the Lady Selina hastily.

'They will haunt you!'

'Well, I fear them not,' said Selina, drawing her superb figure to its full height.

'But what place are they to haunt? The ruin is sacred to your uncle's spirit. Your aunt monopolizes the park, and, I must be allowed to state, not unfrequently trespasses upon the grounds of others. The horsepond is frequented by the spirit of your maid, and your murdered sister walks these corridors. To be plain, there is no room at Sloperton Grange for another ghost. I cannot have them in my room—for you know I don't like children. Think of this, rash girl, and forbear! Would you, Selina,' said the phantom mournfully, 'would you force your great grandfather's spirit to take lodgings elsewhere?'

Lady Selina's hand trembled; the lighted candle fell from her nerveless fingers.

'No,' she cried passionately, 'never!' and fell fainting to the floor.

CHAPTER III

Edgardo galloped rapidly towards Sloperton. When the outline of the Grange had faded away in the darkness, he reined his magnificent steed beside the ruins of Guy's Keep.

'It wants but a few minutes of the hour,' he said, consulting his watch by the light of the moon. 'He dared not break his word. He will come.' He paused, and peered anxiously into the darkness. 'But come what may, she is mine,' he continued, as his thoughts reverted fondly to the fair lady he had quitted. 'Yet if she knew all. If she knew that I were a disgraced and ruined man—a felon and an outcast. If she knew that at the age of fourteen I murdered my Latin tutor and forged my uncle's will. If she knew that I had three wives already, and that the fourth victim of misplaced confidence and my unfortunate peculiarity is expected to be at Sloperton by tonight's train with her baby. But no; she must not know it. Constance must not arrive. Burke the Slogger must attend to that.

'Ha! here he is! Well?'

These words were addressed to a ruffian in a slouched hat, who suddenly appeared from Guy's Keep.

'I be's here, measter,' said the villain, with a disgracefully low accent and complete disregard of grammatical rules.

'It is well. Listen: I'm in possession of facts that will send you to the gallows. I know of the murder of Bill Smithers, the robbery of the toll-gate keeper, and the making away of the youngest daughter of Sir Reginald de Walton. A word from me, and the officers of justice are on your track.'

Burke the Slogger trembled.

'Hark ye! serve my purpose, and I may yet save you. The 5.30 train from Clapham will be due at Sloperton at 9.25. *It must not arrive!*'

The villain's eyes sparkled as he nodded at Edgardo.

'Enough—you understand; leave me!'

CHAPTER IV

About half a mile from Sloperton Station the South Clapham and Medway line crossed a bridge over Sloperton-on-Trent. As the shades of evening were closing, a man in a slouched hat might have been seen carrying a saw and axe under his arm, hanging about the bridge. From time to time he disappeared in the shadow of its abutments, but the sound of a saw and axe still betrayed his vicinity. At exactly nine o'clock he reappeared, and crossing to the Sloperton side, rested his shoulder against the abutment and gave a shove. The bridge swayed a moment, and then fell with a splash into the water, leaving a space of one-hundred feet between the two banks. This done, Burke the Slogger—for it was he—with a fiendish chuckle seated himself on the divided railway track and awaited the coming of the train.

A shriek from the woods announced its approach. For an instant Burke the Slogger saw the glaring of a red lamp. The ground trembled. The train was going with fearful rapidity. Another second and it had reached the bank. Burke the Slogger uttered a fiendish laugh. But the next moment the train leaped across the chasm, striking the rails exactly even, and, dashing out the life of Burke the Slogger, sped away to Sloperton.

The first object that greeted Edgardo as he rode up to the station on the arrival of the train, was the body of Burke the Slogger hanging on the cow-catcher; the second was the the face of his deserted wife looking from the windows of a second-class carriage.

CHAPTER V

A nameless terror seemed to have taken possession of Clarissa, Lady Selina's maid, as she rushed into the presence of her mistress.

'Oh, my lady, such news!'

'Explain yourself,' said her mistress, rising.

'An accident has happened on the railway, and a man has been killed.'

'What—not Edgardo!' almost screamed Selina.

'No, Burke the Slogger, your ladyship!'

'My first husband!' said Lady Selina, sinking on her knees. 'Just Heaven, I thank thee!'

CHAPTER VI

The morning of the seventeenth dawned brightly over Sloperton. 'A fine day for the wedding,' said the sexton to Swipes, the butler of Sloperton Grange. The aged retainer shook his head sadly. 'Alas! there's no trusting in signs!' he continued. 'Seventy-five years ago, on a day like this, my young mistress——' but he was cut short by the appearance of a stranger.

'I would see Sir Edgardo,' said the newcomer impatiently.

The bridegroom, who, with the rest of the wedding train, was about stepping into the carriage to proceed to the parish church, drew the stranger aside.

'It's done!' said the stranger, in a hoarse whisper.

'Ah! and you buried her?'

'With the others!'

'Enough. No more at present. Meet me after the ceremony, and you shall have your reward.'

The stranger shuffled away, and Edgardo returned to his bride. 'A trifling matter of business I had forgotten, my dear Selina; let us proceed,' and the young man pressed the timid hand of his blushing bride as he handed her into the carriage. The cavalcade rode out of the courtyard. At the same moment, the deep bell on Guy's Keep tolled ominously.

CHAPTER VII

Scarcely had the wedding train left the Grange than Alice Sedilia, youngest daughter of Lady Selina, made her escape from the western tower, owing to a lack of watchfulness on the part of Clarissa. The innocent child, freed from restraint, rambled through the lonely corridors, and finally, opening a door, found herself in her mother's boudoir. For some time she amused herself by examining the various ornaments and elegant trifles with which it was filled. Then, in pursuance of a childish freak, she dressed herself in her mother's laces and ribbons. In this occupation she chanced to touch a peg which proved to be a spring that opened a secret panel in the wall. Alice uttered a cry of delight as she noticed what, to her childish fancy, appeared to be the slow-match of a firework. Taking a lucifer match in her hand she approached the fuse. She hesitated a moment. What would her mother and her nurse say?

Suddenly the ringing of the chimes of Sloperton parish church met her ear. Alice knew that the sound signified that the marriage party had entered the church, and that she was secured from interruption. With a childish smile upon her lips, Alice Sedilia touched off the slow-match.

*   *   *

CHAPTER VIII

At exactly two o'clock on the seventeenth, Rupert Sedilia, who had just returned from India, was thoughtfully descending the hill towards Sloperton Manor. 'If I can prove that my aunt, Lady Selina, was married before my father died, I can establish my claim to Sloperton Grange,' he uttered, half aloud. He paused, for a sudden trembling of the earth beneath his feet, and a terrific explosion, as of a park of artillery, arrested his progress. At the same moment he beheld a dense cloud of smoke envelop the churchyard of Sloperton, and the western tower of the Grange seemed to be lifted bodily from its foundation. The air seemed filled with falling fragments, and two dark objects struck the earth close at his feet. Rupert picked them up. One seemed to be a heavy volume bound in brass.

A cry burst from his lips.

'The Parish Records.' He opened the volume hastily. It contained the marriage of Lady Selina to 'Burke the Slogger'.

The second object proved to be a piece of parchment. He tore it open with trembling fingers. It was the missing will of Sir James Sedilia!

CHAPTER IX

When the bells again rang on the new parish church of Sloperton it was for the marriage of Sir Rupert Sedilia and his cousin, the only remaining members of the family.

Five more ghosts were added to the supernatural population of Sloperton Grange. Perhaps this was the reason why Sir Rupert sold the property shortly afterward, and that for many years a dark shadow seemed to hang over the ruins of Sloperton Grange.

GEORGE WASHINGTON CABLE

Jean-ah Poquelin

In the first decade of the present century, when the newly established American Government was the most hateful thing in Louisiana—when the Creoles were still kicking at such vile innovations as the trial by jury, American dances, anti-smuggling laws, and the printing of the Governor's proclamation in English—when the Anglo-American flood that was presently to burst in a crevasse of immigration upon the delta had thus far been felt only as slippery seepage which made the Creole tremble for his footing—there stood, a short distance above what is now Canal Street, and considerably back from the line of villas which fringed the river-bank on Tchoupitoulas Road, an old colonial plantation-house half in ruin.

It stood aloof from civilization, the tracts that had once been its indigo fields given over to their first noxious wildness, and grown up into one of the horridest marshes within a circuit of fifty miles.

The house was of heavy cypress, lifted up on pillars, grim, solid, and spiritless, its massive build a strong reminder of days still earlier, when every man had been his own peace officer and the insurrection of the blacks a daily contingency. Its dark, weather-beaten roof and sides were hoisted up above the jungly plain in a distracted way, like a gigantic ammunition-wagon stuck in the mud and abandoned by some retreating army. Around it was a dense growth of low water willows, with half a hundred sorts of thorny or fetid bushes, savage strangers alike to the 'language of flowers' and to the botanist's Greek. They were hung with countless strands of discolored and prickly smilax, and the impassable mud below bristled with *chevaux de frise* of the dwarf palmetto. Two lone forest-trees, dead cypresses, stood in the centre of the marsh, dotted with roosting vultures. The shallow strips of water were hid by myriads of aquatic plants, under whose coarse and spiritless flowers, could one have seen it, was a harbor of reptiles, great and small, to make one shudder to the end of his days.

The house was on a slightly raised spot, the levee of a draining canal. The waters of this canal did not run; they crawled, and were full of big, ravening fish and alligators, that held it against all comers.

Such was the home of old Jean Marie Poquelin, once an opulent indigo planter, standing high in the esteem of his small, proud circle of exclusively male acquaintances in the old city; now a hermit, alike shunned by and shunning all who had ever known him. 'The last of his line,' said the gossips. His father lies under the floor of the St Louis Cathedral, with the wife of his youth on one side, and the wife of his old age on the other. Old Jean visits the spot daily. His half-brother—alas! there was a mystery; no one knew what had become of the gentle, young half-brother, more than thirty years his junior, whom once he seemed so fondly to love, but who, seven years ago, had disappeared suddenly, once for all, and left no clew of his fate.

They had seemed to live so happily in each other's love. No father, mother, wife to either, no kindred upon earth. The elder a bold, frank, impetuous, chivalric adventurer; the younger a gentle, studious, book-loving recluse; they lived upon the ancestral estate like mated birds, one always on the wing, the other always in the nest.

There was no trait in Jean Marie Poquelin, said the old gossips, for which he was so well known among his few friends as his apparent fondness for his 'little brother'. 'Jacques said this,' and 'Jacques said that'; he 'would leave this or that, or any thing to Jacques,' for Jacques was a scholar, and 'Jacques was good,' or 'wise', or 'just,' or 'far-sighted,' as the nature of the case required; and 'he should ask Jacques as soon as he got home,' since Jacques was never elsewhere to be seen.

It was between the roving character of the one brother, and the bookishness of the other, that the estate fell into decay. Jean Marie, generous gentleman, gambled the slaves away one by one, until none was left, man or woman, but one old African mute.

The indigo-fields and vats of Louisiana had been generally abandoned as unremunerative. Certain enterprising men had substituted the culture of sugar; but while the recluse was too apathetic to take so active a course, the other saw larger, and, at that time equally respectable profits, first in smuggling, and later in the African slave-trade. What harm could he see in it? The whole people said it was vitally necessary, and to minister to a vital public necessity—good enough, certainly, and so he laid up many a doubloon, that made him none the worse in the public regard.

One day old Jean Marie was about to start upon a voyage that was to be longer, much longer, than any that he had yet made. Jacques had begged him hard for many days not to go, but he laughed him off, and finally said, kissing him:

'*Adieu, 'tit frère.*'

'No,' said Jacques, 'I shall go with you.'

They left the old hulk of a house in the sole care of the African mute, and went away to the Guinea coast together.

Two years after, old Poquelin came home without his vessel. He must have arrived at his house by night. No one saw him come. No one saw 'his little brother'; rumor whispered that he, too, had returned, but he had never been seen again.

A dark suspicion fell upon the old slave-trader. No matter that the few kept the many reminded of the tenderness that had ever marked his bearing to the missing man. The many shook their heads. 'You know he has a quick and fearful temper'; and 'why does he cover his loss with mystery?' 'Grief would out with the truth.'

'But,' said the charitable few, 'look in his face; see that expression of true humanity.' The many did look in his face, and, as he looked in theirs, he read the silent question: 'Where is thy brother Abel?' The few were silenced, his former friends died off, and the name of Jean Marie Poquelin became a symbol of witchery, devilish crime, and hideous nursery fictions.

The man and his house were alike shunned. The snipe and duck hunters forsook the marsh, and the wood-cutters abandoned the canal. Sometimes the hardier boys who ventured out there snake-shooting heard a low thumping of oar-locks on the canal. They would look at each other for a moment half in consternation, half in glee, then rush from their sport in wanton haste to assail with their gibes the unoffending, withered old man who, in rusty attire, sat in the stern of a skiff, rowed homeward by his white-headed African mute.

'O Jean-ah Poquelin! O Jean-ah! Jean-ah Poquelin!'

It was not necessary to utter more than that. No hint of wickedness, deformity, or any physical or moral demerit: merely the name and tone of mockery: 'Oh, Jean-ah Poquelin!' and while they tumbled one over another in their needless haste to fly, he would rise carefully from his seat, while the aged mute, with downcast face, went on rowing, and rolling up his brown fist and extending it toward the urchins, would pour forth such an unholy broadside of French imprecation and invectives as would all but craze them with delight.

Among both blacks and whites the house was the object of a thousand superstitions. Every midnight, they affirmed, the *feu follet* came out of the marsh and ran in and out of the rooms, flashing from window to window. The story of some lads, whose word in ordinary statements was worthless, was generally credited, that the night they camped in the woods, rather than pass the place after dark, they saw, about sunset, every window blood-red, and on each of the four chimneys an owl sitting, which turned his head three times round, and moaned and laughed with a human voice. There was a bottomless well, everybody professed to know, beneath the sill of the big front door under the rotten veranda; whoever set his foot upon that threshold disappeared forever in the depth below.

What wonder the marsh grew as wild as Africa! Take all the Faubourg Ste Marie, and half the ancient city, you would not find one graceless dare-devil reckless enough to pass within a hundred yards of the house after nightfall.

The alien races pouring into old New Orleans began to find the few streets named for the Bourbon princes too strait for them. The wheel of fortune, beginning to whirl, threw them off beyond the ancient corporation lines, and sowed civilization and even trade upon the lands of the Graviers and Girods. Fields became roads, roads streets. Everywhere the leveller was peering through his glass, rodsmen were whacking their way through willow-brakes and rose-hedges, and the sweating Irishmen tossed the blue clay up with their long-handled shovels.

'Ha! that is all very well,' quoth the Jean-Baptistes, feeling the reproach of an enterprise that asked neither co-operation nor advice of them, 'but wait till they come yonder to Jean Poquelin's marsh; ha! ha! ha!' The supposed predicament so delighted them, that they put on a mock terror and whirled about in an assumed stampede, then caught their clasped hands between their knees in excess of mirth and laughed till the tears ran; for whether the street-makers mired in the marsh, or contrived to cut through old 'Jean-ah's' property, either event would be joyful. Meantime a line of tiny rods, with bits of white paper in their split tops, gradually extended its way straight through the haunted ground, and across the canal diagonally.

'We shall fill that ditch,' said the men in mud-boots, and brushed close along the chained and padlocked gate of the haunted mansion. Ah, Jean-ah Poquelin, those were not Creole boys, to be stampeded with a little hard swearing.

He went to the Governor. That official scanned the odd figure with no slight interest. Jean Poquelin was of short, broad frame, with a bronzed leonine face. His brow was ample and deeply furrowed. His eye, large and black, was bold and open like that of a war-horse, and his jaws shut together with the firmness of iron. He was dressed in a suit of Attakapas cottonade, and his shirt unbuttoned and thrown back from the throat and bosom, sailor-wise, showed a herculean breast, hard and grizzled. There was no fierceness or defiance in his look, no harsh ungentleness, no symptom of his unlawful life or violent temper; but rather a peaceful and peaceable fearlessness. Across the whole face, not marked in one or another feature, but as it were laid softly upon the countenance like an almost imperceptible veil, was the imprint of some great grief. A careless eye might easily overlook it, but, once seen, there it hung—faint, but unmistakable.

The Governor bowed.

'*Parlez-vous français?*' asked the figure.

'I would rather talk English, if you can do so,' said the Governor.

'My name, Jean Poquelin.'

'How can I serve you, Mr Poquelin?'

'My 'ouse is yond'; *dans le marais là-bas*.'

The Governor bowed.

'Dat *marais* billong to me.'

'Yes, sir.'

'To me; Jean Poquelin; I hown 'im meself.'

'Well, sir?'

'He don't billong to you; I get him from me father.'

'That is perfectly true, Mr Poquelin, as far as I am aware.'

'You want to make strit pass yond'?'

'I do not know, sir; it is quite probable; but the city will indemnify you for any loss you may suffer—you will get paid, you understand.'

'Strit can't pass dare.'

'You will have to see the municipal authorities about that, Mr Poquelin.'

A bitter smile came upon the old man's face.

'*Pardon, Monsieur,* you is not *le Gouverneur?*'

'Yes.'

'*Mais,* yes. You har *le Gouverneur*—yes. Veh-well. I come to you. I tell you, strit can't pass at me 'ouse.'

'But you will have to see—'

'I come to you. You is *le Gouverneur*. I know not the new laws. I ham a Fr-r-rench-a-man! Fr-rench-a-man have something *aller au contraire*—he come at his *Gouverneur*. I come at you. If me not had been bought from me king like *bossals* in the hold time, ze king gof—France would-a-show *Monsieur le Gouverneur* to take care his men to make strit in right places. *Mais*, I know; we billong to *Monsieur le Président*. I want you do somesin for me, eh?'

'What is it?' asked the patient Governor.

'I want you tell *Monsieur le Président*, strit—can't—pass—at—me—'ouse.'

'Have a chair, Mr Poquelin'; but the old man did not stir. The

Governor took a quill and wrote a line to a city official, introducing Mr Poquelin, and asking for him every possible courtesy. He handed it to him, instructing him where to present it.

'Mr Poquelin,' he said, with a conciliatory smile, 'tell me, is it your house that our Creole citizens tell such odd stories about?'

The old man glared sternly upon the speaker, and with immovable features said:

'You don't see me trade some Guinea nigga'?'

'Oh, no.'

'You don't see me make some smugglin'?'

'No, sir; not at all.'

'But, I am Jean Marie Poquelin. I mine me hown bizniss. Dat all right? Adieu.'

He put his hat on and withdrew. By and by he stood, letter in hand, before the person to whom it was addressed. This person employed an interpreter.

'He says,' said the interpreter to the officer, 'he come to make you the fair warning how you muz not make the street pas' at his 'ouse.'

The officer remarked that 'such impudence was refreshing'; but the experienced interpreter translated freely.

'He says: "Why you don't want?"' said the interpreter.

The old slave-trader answered at some length.

'He says,' said the interpreter, again turning to the officer, 'the marass is a too unhealth' for peopl' to live.'

'But we expect to drain his old marsh; it's not going to be a marsh.'

'*Il dit*'—The interpreter explained in French.

The old man answered tersely.

'He says the canal is a private,' said the interpreter.

'Oh! *that* old ditch; that' s to be filled up. Tell the old man we're going to fix him up nicely.'

Translation being duly made, the man in power was amused to see a thunder-cloud gathering on the old man's face.

'Tell him,' he added, 'by the time we finish, there'll not be a ghost left in his shanty.'

The interpreter began to translate, but—

'*J' comprends, J' comprends*,' said the old man, with an impatient gesture, and burst forth, pouring curses upon the United States, the President, the Territory of Orleans, Congress, the Governor and all his subordinates, striding out of the apartment as he cursed, while the object of his maledictions roared with merriment and rammed the floor with his foot.

'Why, it will make his old place worth ten dollars to one,' said the official to the interpreter.

''Tis not for de worse of de property,' said the interpreter.

'I should guess not,' said the other, whittling his chair,—'seems to me as if some of these old Creoles would liever live in a crawfish hole than to have a neighbor.'

'You know what make old Jean Poquelin make like that? I will tell you. You know—'

The interpreter was rolling a cigarette, and paused to light his tinder; then, as the smoke poured in a thick double stream from his nostrils, he said, in a solemn whisper:

'He is a witch.'

'Ho, ho, ho!' laughed the other.

'You don't believe it? What you want to bet?' cried the interpreter, jerking himself half up and thrusting out one arm while he bared it of its coat-sleeve with the hand of the other. 'What you want to bet?'

'How do you know?' asked the official.

'Dass what I goin' to tell you. You know, one evening I was shooting some *grosbec*. I killed three; but I had trouble to find them, it was becoming so dark. When I have them I start' to come home; then I got to pas' at Jean Poquelin's house.'

'Ho, ho, ho!' laughed the other, throwing his leg over the arm of his chair.

'Wait,' said the interpreter. 'I come along slow, not making some noises; still, still—'

'And scared,' said the smiling one.

'*Mais*, wait. I get all pas' the 'ouse. "Ah!" I say; "all right!" Then I see two thing' before! Hah! I get as cold and humide, and shake like a leaf. You think it was nothing? There I see, so plain as can be (though it was making nearly dark), I see Jean—Marie—Po-que-lin walkin' right in front, and right there beside of him was something like a man—but not a man—white like paint!—I dropp' on the grass from scared—they pass'; so sure as I live 'twas the ghos' of Jacques Poquelin, his brother!'

'Pooh!' said the listener.

'I'll put my han' in the fire,' said the interpreter.

'But did you never think,' asked the other, 'that that might be Jack Poquelin, as you call him, alive and well, and for some cause hid away by his brother?'

'But there har' no cause!' said the other, and the entrance of third parties changed the subject.

Some months passed and the street was opened. A canal was first dug through the marsh, the small one which passed so close to Jean Poquelin's house was filled, and the street, or rather a sunny road, just touched a corner of the old mansion's dooryard. The morass ran dry. Its venomous denizens slipped away through the bulrushes; the cattle roaming freely upon its hardened surface trampled the super-abundant undergrowth. The bellowing frogs croaked to westward. Lilies and the flower-de-luce sprang up in the place of reeds; smilax and poison-oak gave way to the purple-plumed iron-weed and pink spiderwort; the bindweeds ran everywhere, blooming as they ran, and on one of the dead cypresses a giant creeper hung its green burden of foliage and lifted its scarlet trumpets. Sparrows and red-birds flitted through the bushes, and dewberries grew ripe beneath. Over all these came a sweet, dry smell of salubrity which the place had not known since the sediments of the Mississippi first lifted it from the sea.

But its owner did not build. Over the willow-brakes, and down the vista of the open street, bright new houses, some singly, some by ranks, were prying in upon the old man's privacy. They even settled down toward his southern side. First a wood-cutter's hut or two, then a market gardener's shanty, then a painted cottage, and all at once the faubourg had flanked and half surrounded him and his dried-up marsh.

Ah! then the common people began to hate him. 'The old tyrant!' 'You don't mean an old *tyrant*?' 'Well, then, why don't he build when the public need demands it? What does he live in that unneighbourly way for?' 'The old pirate!' 'The old kidnapper!' How easily even the most ultra Louisianians put on the imported virtues of the North when they could be brought to bear against the hermit. 'There he goes, with the boys after him! Ah! ha! ha! Jean-ah Poquelin! Ah! Jean-ah! Aha! aha! Jean-ah Marie! Jean-ah Poquelin! The old villain!' How merrily the swarming Américains echo the spirit of persecution! 'The old fraud,' they say—'pretends to live in a haunted house, does he? We'll tar and feather him some day. Guess we can fix him.'

He cannot be rowed home along the old canal now; he walks. He has broken sadly of late, and the street urchins are ever at his heels. It is like the days when they cried: 'Go up, thou bald-head,' and the old man now and then turns and delivers ineffectual curses.

To the Creoles—to the incoming lower class of superstitious Germans, Irish, Sicilians, and others—he became an omen and embodiment of public and private ill-fortune. Upon him all the vagaries of their superstitions gathered and grew. If a house caught fire, it was imputed to his machinations. Did a woman go off in a fit, he had bewitched her. Did a child stray off for an hour, the mother shivered with the apprehension that Jean Poquelin had offered him to strange gods. The house was the subject of every bad boy's invention who loved to contrive ghostly lies. 'As long as that house stands we shall have bad luck. Do you not see our pease and beans dying, our cabbages and lettuce going to seed and our gardens turning to dust, while every day you can see it raining in the woods? The rain will never pass old Poquelin's house. He keeps a fetich. He has conjured the whole Faubourg St Marie. And why, the old wretch? Simply because our playful and innocent children call after him as he passes.'

A 'Building and Improvement Company,' which had not yet got its charter, 'but was going to,' and which had not, indeed, any tangible capital yet, but 'was going to have some,' joined the 'Jean-ah Poquelin' war. The haunted property would be such a capital site for a market-house! They sent a deputation to the old mansion to ask its occupant to sell. The deputation never got beyond the chained gate and a very barren interview with the African mute. The President of the Board was then empowered (for he had studied French in Pennsylvania and was considered qualified) to call and persuade M. Poquelin to subscribe to the company's stock; but—,

'Fact is, gentlemen,' he said at the next meeting, 'it would take us at least twelve months to make Mr Pokaleen understand the rather original features of our system, and he wouldn't subscribe when we'd done; besides, the only way to see him is to stop him on the street.'

There was a great laugh from the Board; they couldn't help it. 'Better meet a bear robbed of her whelps,' said one.

'You're mistaken as to that,' said the President. 'I did meet him, and stopped him, and found him quite polite. But I could get no satisfaction from him; the fellow wouldn't talk in French, and when I spoke in English he hoisted his old shoulders up, and gave the same answer to every thing I said.'

'And that was—?' asked one or two, impatient of the pause.

'That it "don't worse w'ile?"'

One of the Board said: 'Mr President, this market-house project, as I take it, is not altogether a selfish one; the community is to be benefited by it. We may feel that we are working in the public interest [the Board smiled knowingly], if we employ all possible means to oust this old nuisance from among us. You may know that at the time the street was cut through, this old Poquelann did all he could to prevent it. It was owing to a certain connection which I had with that affair that I heard a ghost story [smiles, followed by a sudden dignified check]—ghost story, which, of course, I am not going to relate; but I *may* say that my profound conviction, arising from a prolonged study of that story, is, that this old villain, John Poquelann, has his brother locked up in that old house. Now, if this is so, and we can fix it on him, I merely *suggest* that we can make the matter highly useful. I don't know, he added, beginning to sit down, 'but that it is an action we owe to the community—hem!'

'How do you propose to handle the subject?' asked the President.

'I was thinking,' said the speaker, 'that, as a Board of Directors, it would be unadvisable for us to authorize any action involving trespass; but if you, for instance, Mr President, should, as it were, for mere curiosity, *request* some one, as, for instance, our excellent Secretary, simply as a personal favor, to look into the matter—this is merely a suggestion.'

The Secretary smiled sufficiently to be understood that, while he certainly did not consider such preposterous service a part of his duties as secretary, he might, notwithstanding, accede to the President's request; and the Board adjourned.

Little White, as the Secretary was called, was a mild, kind-hearted little man, who, nevertheless, had no fear of any thing, unless it was the fear of being unkind.

'I tell you frankly,' he privately said to the President, 'I go into this purely for reasons of my own.'

The next day, a little after nightfall, one might have descried this little man slipping along the rear fence of the Poquelin place, preparatory to vaulting over into the rank, grass-grown yard, and bearing himself altogether more after the manner of a collector of rare chickens than according to the usage of secretaries.

The picture presented to his eye was not calculated to enliven his mind. The old mansion stood out against the western sky, black and silent. One long, lurid pencil-stroke along a sky of slate was all that was left of daylight. No sign of life was apparent; no light at any window, unless it might have been on the side of the house hidden from view. No owls were on the chimneys, no dogs were in the yard.

He entered the place, and ventured up behind a small cabin which stood apart from the house. Through one of its many crannies he easily detected the African mute crouched before a flickering pine-knot, his head on his knees, fast asleep.

He concluded to enter the mansion, and, with that view, stood and scanned it. The broad rear steps of the veranda would not serve him; he might meet some one midway. He was measuring, with his eye, the proportions of one of the pillars which supported it, and estimating the practicability of climbing it, when he heard a footstep. Some one dragged a chair out toward the railing, then seemed to change his mind and began to pace the veranda, his footfalls resounding on the dry boards with singular loudness. Little White drew a step backward, got the figure between himself and the sky, and at once recognized the short, broad-shouldered form of old Jean Poquelin.

He sat down upon a billet of wood, and, to escape the stings of a whining cloud of mosquitoes, shrouded his face and neck in his handkerchief, leaving his eyes uncovered.

He had sat there but a moment when he noticed a strange, sickening odor, faint, as if coming from a distance, but loathsome and horrid.

Whence could it come? Not from the cabin; not from the marsh, for it was as dry as powder. It was not in the air; it seemed to come from the ground.

Rising up, he noticed, for the first time, a few steps before him a narrow footpath leading toward the house. He glanced down it—ha! right there was some one coming—ghostly white!

Quick as thought, and as noiselessly, he lay down at full length against the cabin. It was bold strategy, and yet, there was no denying it, little White felt that he was frightened. 'It is not a ghost,' he said to himself. 'I *know* it cannot be a ghost'; but the perspiration burst out at every pore, and the air seemed to thicken with heat. 'It is a living man,' he said in his thoughts. 'I hear his footstep, and I hear old Poquelin's footsteps, too, separately, over on the veranda. I am not discovered; the thing has passed; there is that odor again; what a smell of death! Is it coming back? Yes. It stops at the door of the cabin. Is it peering in at the sleeping mute? It moves away. It is in the path again. Now it is gone.' He shuddered. 'Now, if I dare venture, the mystery is solved.' He rose cautiously, close against the cabin, and peered along the path.

The figure of a man, a presence if not a body—but whether clad in some white stuff or naked, the darkness would not allow him to determine—had turned, and now, with a seeming painful gait, moved slowly from him. 'Great Heaven! can it be that the dead do walk?' He withdrew again the hands which had gone to his eyes. The dreadful object passed between two pillars and under the house. He listened. There was a faint sound as of feet upon a staircase; then all was still except the measured tread of Jean Poquelin walking on the veranda, and the heavy respirations of the mute slumbering in the cabin.

The little Secretary was about to retreat; but as he looked once more toward the haunted house a dim light appeared in the crack of a closed window, and presently old Jean Poquelin came, dragging his chair, and sat down close against the shining cranny. He spoke in a low, tender tone in the French tongue, making some inquiry. An answer came from within. Was it the voice of a human? So unnatural was it—so hollow, so discordant, so unearthly—that the stealthy listener shuddered again from head to foot; and when something stirred in some bushes near by—though it may have been nothing more than a rat—and came scuttling through the grass, the little Secretary actually turned and fled. As he left the enclosure he moved with bolder leisure through the bushes; yet now and then he spoke aloud: 'Oh, oh! I see, I understand!' and shut his eyes in his hands.

How strange that henceforth little White was the champion of Jean Poquelin! In season and out of season—wherever a word was uttered against him—the Secretary, with a quiet, aggressive force that instantly arrested gossip, demanded upon what authority the statement or conjecture was made; but as he did not condescend to explain his own remarkable attitude, it was not long before the disrelish and suspicion which had followed Jean Poquelin so many years fell also upon him.

It was only the next evening but one after his adventure that he made himself a source of sullen amazement to one hundred and fifty boys, by ordering them to desist from their wanton hallooing. Old Jean Poquelin, standing and shaking his cane, rolling out his long-drawn maledictions, paused and stared, then gave the secretary a courteous bow and started on. The boys, save one, from pure astonishment, ceased; but a ruffianly little Irish lad, more daring than any had yet been, threw a big hurtling clod, that struck old Poquelin between the shoulders and burst like a shell. The enraged old man wheeled with uplifted staff to give chase to the scampering vagabond; and—he may have tripped, or he may not, but he fell full length. Little White hastened to help him up, but he waved him off with a fierce imprecation and staggering to his feet resumed his way homeward. His lips were reddened with blood.

Little White was on his way to the meeting of the Board. He would have given all he dared spend to have staid away, for he felt both too fierce and too tremulous to brook the criticisms that were likely to be made.

'I can't help it, gentlemen; I can't help you to make a case against the old man, and I'm not going to.'

'We did not expect this disappointment, Mr White.'

'I can't help that, sir. No, sir; you had better not appoint any more investigations. Somebody'll investigate himself into trouble. No, sir; it isn't a threat, it is only my advice, but I warn you that whoever takes the task in hand will rue it to his dying day—which may be hastened, too.'

The President expressed himself surprised.

'I don't care a rush,' answered little White, wildly and foolishly. 'I don't care a rush if you are, sir. No, my nerves are not disordered; my head's as clear as a bell. No, I'm *not* excited.'

A Director remarked that the Secretary looked at though he had waked from a nightmare.

'Well, sir, if you want to know the fact, I have; and if you choose to cultivate old Poquelin's society you can have one, too.'

'White,' called a facetious member, but White did not notice. 'White,' he called again.

'What?' demanded White, with a scowl.

'Did you see the ghost?'

'Yes, sir; I did,' cried White, hitting the table, and handing the President a paper which brought the Board to other business.

The story got among the gossips that somebody (they were afraid to say little White) had been to the Poquelin mansion by night and beheld something appalling. The rumor was but a shadow of the truth, magnified and distorted as is the manner of shadows. He had seen skeletons walking, and had barely escaped the clutches of one by making the sign of the cross.

Some madcap boys with an appetite for the horrible plucked up courage to venture through the dried marsh by the cattle-path, and come before the house at a spectral hour when the air was full of bats. Something which they but half saw—half a sight was enough—sent them tearing back through the willow-brakes and acacia bushes to their homes, where they fairly dropped down, and cried:

'Was it white?' 'No—yes—nearly so—we can't tell—but we saw it.' And one could hardly doubt, to look at their ashen faces, that they had, whatever it was.

'If that old rascal lived in the country we come from,' said certain Américains, 'he'd have been tarred and feathered before now, wouldn't he, Sanders?'

'Well, now he just would.'

'And we'd have rid him on a rail, wouldn't we?'

'That's what I allow.'

'Tell you what you *could* do.' They were talking to some rollicking Creoles who had assumed an absolute necessity for doing *something*. 'What is it you call this thing where an old man marries a young girl, and you come out with horns and—'

'*Charivari?*' asked the Creoles.

'Yes, that's it. Why don't you shivaree him?' Felicitous suggestion. Little White, with his wife beside him, was sitting on their doorsteps on the sidewalk, as Creole custom had taught them, looking toward the sunset. They had moved into the lately-opened street. The view was not attractive on the score of beauty. The houses were small and scattered, and across the flat commons, spite of the lofty tangle of weeds and bushes, and spite of the thickets of acacia, they needs must see the dismal old Poquelin mansion, tilted awry and shutting out the declining sun. The moon, white and slender, was hanging the tip of its horn over one of the chimneys.

'And you say,' said the Secretary, 'the old black man has been going by here alone? Patty, suppose old Poquelin should be concocting some mischief; he don't lack provocation; the way that clod hit him the other day was enough to have killed him. Why, Patty, he dropped as quick as *that!* No wonder you haven't seen him. I wonder if they haven't heard something about him up at the drug-store. Suppose I go and see.'

'Do,' said his wife.

She sat alone for half an hour, watching that sudden going out of the day peculiar to the latitude.

'That moon is ghost enough for one house,' she said, as her husband returned. 'It has gone right down the chimney.'

'Patty,' said little White, 'the drug-clerk says the boys are going to shivaree old Poquelin tonight. I'm going to try to stop it.'

'Why, White,' said his wife, 'you'd better not. You'll get hurt.'

'No, I'll not.'

'Yes, you will.'

'I'm going to sit out here until they come along. They're compelled to pass right by here.'

'Why, White, it may be midnight before they start; you're not going to sit out here till then.'

'Yes, I am.'

'Well, you're very foolish,' said Mrs White in an undertone, looking anxious, and tapping one of the steps with her foot.

They sat a very long time talking over little family matters.

'What's that?' at last said Mrs White.

'That's the nine-o'clock gun,' said White, and they relapsed into a long-sustained, drowsy silence.

'Patty, you'd better go in and go to bed,' said he at last.

'I'm not sleepy.'

'Well, you're very foolish,' quietly remarked little White, and again silence fell upon them.

'Patty, suppose I walk out to the old house and see if I can find out any thing.'

'Suppose,' said she, 'you don't do any such—listen!'

Down the street arose a great hubbub. Dogs and boys were howling and barking; men were laughing, shouting, groaning, and blowing horns, whooping, and clanking cow-bells, whinnying, and howling, and rattling pots and pans.

'They are coming this way,' said little White. 'You had better go into the house, Patty.'

'So had you.'

'No. I'm going to see if I can't stop them.'

'Why, White!'

'I'll be back in a minute,' said White, and went toward the noise.

In a few moments the little Secretary met the mob. The pen hesitates on the word, for there is a respectable difference, measurable only on the scale of the half century, between a mob and a *charivari*. Little White lifted his ineffectual voice. He faced the head of the disorderly column, and cast himself about as if he were made of wood and moved by the jerk of a string. He rushed to one who seemed, from the size and clatter of his tin pan, to be a leader. '*Stop these fellows, Bienvenu, stop them just a minute, till I tell them something.*' Bienvenu turned and brandished his instruments of discord in an imploring way to the crowd. They slackened their pace, two or three hushed their horns and joined the prayer of little White and Bienvenu for silence. The throng halted. The hush was delicious.

'Bienvenu,' said little White, 'don't shivaree old Poquelin tonight; he's—'

'My fwang,' said the swaying Bienvenu, 'who tail you I goin' to chahivahi somebody, eh? You sink bickause I make a little playfool wiz zis tin pan zat I am *dhonk*?'

'Oh, no, Bienvenu, old fellow, you're all right. I was afraid you might not know that old Poquelin was sick, you know, but you're not going there, are you?'

'My fwang, I vay soy to tail you zat you ah dhonk as de dev'. I am *shem* of you. I ham ze servan' of ze *publique*. Zese *citoyens* goin' to wickwest Jean Poquelin to give to the Ursuline' two hondred fifty dolla'—'

'*Hé quoi!*' cried a listener, '*Cinq cent piastres, oui!*'

'*Oui!*' said Bienvenu, 'and if he wiffuse we make him some lit' *musique*; ta-ra-ta!' He hoisted a merry hand and foot, then frowning, added: 'Old Poquelin got no bizniz dhink s'much w'isky.'

'But, gentlemen,' said little White, around whom a circle had gathered, 'the old man is very sick.'

'My faith!' cried a tiny Creole, 'we did not make him to be sick.

W'en we have say we going make *le charivari*, do you want that we hall tell a lie? My faith! 'sfools!'

'But you can shivaree somebody else,' said desperate little White.

'*Oui!*' cried Bienvenu, '*et chahivahi* Jean-ah Poquelin tomo'w!'

'Let us go to Madame Schneider!' cried two or three, and amid huzzas and confused cries, among which was heard a stentorian Celtic call for drinks, the crowd again began to move.

'*Cent piastres pour l'hôpital de charité!*'

'Hurrah!'

'One hongred dolla' for Charity Hospital!'

'Hurrah!'

'Whang!' went a tin pan, the crowd yelled, and Pandemonium gaped again. They were off at a right angle.

Nodding, Mrs White looked at the mantle-clock.

'Well, if it isn't away after midnight.'

The hideous noise down street was passing beyond earshot. She raised a sash and listened. For a moment there was silence. Some one came to the door.

'Is that you, White!'

'Yes.' He entered. 'I succeeded, Patty.'

'Did you?' said Patty, joyfully.

'Yes. They've gone down to shivaree the old Dutchwoman who married her step-daughter's sweetheart. They say she has got to pay a hundred dollars to the hospital before they stop.'

The couple retired, and Mrs White slumbered. She was awakened by her husband snapping the lid of his watch.

'What time?' she asked.

'Half-past three. Patty, I haven't slept a wink. Those fellows are out yet. Don't you hear them?'

'Why, White, they're coming this way!'

'I know they are,' said White, sliding out of bed and drawing on his clothes, 'and they're coming fast. You'd better go away from that window, Patty! My! what a clatter!'

'Here they are,' said Mrs White, but her husband was gone. Two or three hundred men and boys pass the place at a rapid walk straight down the broad, new street, toward the hated house of ghosts. The din was terrific. She saw little White at the head of the rabble brandishing his arms and trying in vain to make himself heard; but they only shook their heads, laughing and hooting the louder, and so passed, bearing him on before them.

Swiftly they pass out from among the houses, away from the dim oil lamps of the street, out into the broad starlit commons, and enter the willowy jungles of the haunted ground. Some hearts fail and their owners lag behind and turn back, suddenly remembering how near morning it is. But the most part push on, tearing the air with their clamor.

Down ahead of them in the long, thicket-darkened way there is—singularly enough—a faint, dancing light. It must be very near the old house; it is. It has stopped now. It is a lantern, and is under a well-known sapling which has grown up on the wayside since the canal was filled. Now it swings mysteriously to and fro. A goodly number of the more ghost-fearing give up the sport; but a full hundred move forward at a run, doubling their devilish howling and banging.

Yes; it is a lantern, and there are two persons under the tree. The crowd draws near—drops into a walk; one of the two is the old African mute; he lifts the lantern up so that it shines on the other; the crowd recoils; there is a hush of all clangor, and all at once, with a cry of mingled fright and horror from every throat, the whole throng rushes back, dropping every thing, sweeping past little White and hurrying on, never stopping until the jungle is left behind, and then to find that not one in ten has been the cause of the stampede, and not one of the tenth is certain what it was.

There is one huge fellow among them who looks capable of any villainy. He finds something to mount on, and, in the Creole *patois*, calls a general halt. Bienvenu sinks down, and, vainly trying to recline gracefully, resigns the leadership. The herd gather round the speaker; he assures them that they have been outraged. Their right peaceably to traverse the public streets has been trampled upon. Shall such encroachments be endured? It is now daybreak. Let them go now by the open light of day and force a free passage of the public highway!

A scattering consent was the response, and the crowd, thinned now and drowsy, straggled quietly down toward the old house. Some drifted ahead, others sauntered behind, but every one, as he again neared the tree, came to a stand-still. Little White sat upon a bank of turf on the opposite side of the way looking very stern and sad. To each newcomer he put the same question:

'Did you come here to go to old Poquelin's?'

'Yes.'

'He's dead.' And if the shocked hearer started away he would say: 'Don't go away.'

'Why not?'

'I want you to go to the funeral presently.'

If some Louisianian, too loyal to dear France or Spain to understand English, looked bewildered, some one would interpret for him; and presently they went. Little White led the van, the crowd trooping after him down the middle of the way. The gate, that had never been seen before unchained, was open. Stern little White stopped a short distance from it; the rabble stopped behind him. Something was moving out from under the veranda. The many whisperers stretched upward to see. The African mute came very slowly toward the gate, leading by a cord in the nose a small brown bull, which was harnessed to a rude cart. On the flat body of the cart, under a black cloth, were seen the outlines of a long box.

'Hats off, gentlemen,' said little White, as the box came in view, and the crowd silently uncovered.

'Gentlemen,' said little White, 'here come the last remains of Jean Marie Poquelin, a better man, I'm afraid, with all his sins,—yes, a better—a kinder man to his blood—a man of more self-forgetful goodness—than all of you put together will ever dare to be.'

There was a profound hush as the vehicle came creaking through the gate; but when it turned away from them toward the forest, those in front started suddenly. There was a backward rush, then all stood still again staring one way; for there, behind the bier, with eyes cast down and labored step, walked the living remains—all that was left—of little Jacques Poquelin, the long-hidden brother—a leper, as white as snow.

Dumb with horror, the cringing crowd gazed upon the walking death. They watched, in silent awe, the slow *cortège* creep down the long, straight road and lessen on the view, until by and by it stopped where a wild, unfrequented path branched off into the undergrowth toward the rear of the ancient city.

'They are going to the *Terre aux Lépreux*,' said one in the crowd. The rest watched them in silence.

The little bull was set free; the mute, with the strength of an ape, lifted the long box to his shoulder. For a moment more the mute and the leper stood in sight, while the former adjusted his heavy burden; then, without one backward glance upon the unkind human world, turning their faces toward the ridge in the depths of the swamp known as the Leper's Land, they stepped into the jungle, disappeared, and were never seen again.

ROBERT LOUIS STEVENSON

Olalla

'Now,' said the doctor, 'my part is done, and, I may say, with some vanity, well done. It remains only to get you out of this cold and poisonous city, and to give you two months of pure air and an easy conscience. The last is your affair. To the first I think I can help you. It falls indeed rather oddly; it was but the other day the Padre came in from the country; and as he and I are old friends, although of contrary professions, he applied to me in a matter of distress among some of his parishioners. This was a family—but you are ignorant of Spain, and even the names of our grandees are hardly known to you; suffice it then, that they were once great people, and are now fallen to the brink of destitution. Nothing now belongs to them but the residencia, and certain leagues of desert mountain, in the greater part of which not even a goat could support life: But the house is a fine old place, and stands at a great height among the hills, and most salubriously; and I had no sooner heard my friend's tale than I remembered you. I told him I had a wounded officer, wounded in the good cause, who was now able to make a change; and I propose that his friends should take you for a lodger. Instantly the Padre's face grew dark, as I had maliciously foreseen it would. It was out of the question, he said. Then let them starve, said I, for I have no sympathy with tatterdemalion pride. Thereupon we separated, not very content with one another; but yesterday, to my wonder, the Padre returned and made a submission: the difficulty, he said, he had found upon enquiry to be less than he had feared; or, in other words, these proud people had put their pride in their pocket. I closed with the offer; and, subject to your approval, I have taken rooms for you in the residencia. The air of these mountains will renew your blood; and the quiet in which you will there live is worth all the medicines in the world.'

'Doctor,' said I, 'you have been throughout my good angel, and your advice is a command. But tell me, if you please, something of the family with which I am to reside.'

'I am coming to that,' replied my friend; 'and, indeed, there is a difficulty in the way. These beggars are, as I have said, of very high descent and swollen with the most baseless vanity; they have lived for some generations in a growing isolation, drawing away, on either hand, from the rich who had now become too high for them, and from the poor, whom they still regarded as too low; and even today, when poverty forces them to unfasten their door to a guest, they cannot do so without a most ungracious stipulation. You are to remain, they say, a stranger; they will give you attendance, but they refuse from the first the idea of the smallest intimacy.'

I will not deny that I was piqued, and perhaps the feeling strengthened my desire to go, for I was confident that I could break down that barrier if I desired. 'There is nothing offensive in such a stipulation,' said I; 'and I even sympathize with the feeling that inspired it.'

'It is true they have never seen you,' returned the doctor politely; 'and if they knew you were the handsomest and the most pleasant man that ever came from England (where I am told that handsome men are common, but pleasant ones not so much so), they would doubtless make you welcome with a better grace. But since you take the thing so well, it matters not. To me, indeed, it seems discourteous. But you will find yourself the gainer. The family will not much tempt you. A mother, a son, and a daughter; an old woman said to be halfwitted, a country lout, and a country girl, who stands very high with her confessor, and is, therefore,' chuckled the physician, 'most likely plain; there is not much in that to attract the fancy of a dashing officer.'

'And yet you say they are high-born,' I objected.

'Well, as to that, I should distinguish,' returned the doctor. 'The mother is; not so the children. The mother was the last representative of a princely stock, degenerate both in parts and fortune. Her father was not only poor, he was mad: and the girl ran wild about the residencia till his death. Then, much of the fortune having died with him, and the family being quite extinct, the girl ran wilder than ever, until at last she married, Heaven knows whom; a muleteer some say, others a smuggler; while there are some who upheld there was no marriage at all, and that Felipe and Olalla are bastards. The union, such as it was, was tragically dissolved some years ago; but they live in such seclusion, and the country at that time was in so much disorder, that the precise manner of the man's end is known only to the priest—if even to him.'

'I begin to think I shall have strange experiences,' said I.

'I would not romance, if I were you,' replied the doctor; 'you will find, I fear, a very grovelling and commonplace reality. Felipe, for instance, I have seen. And what am I to say? He is very rustic, very cunning, very loutish, and I should say, an innocent; the others are probably to match. No, no, señor commandante, you must seek congenial society among the great sights of our mountains; and in these at least, if you are at all a lover of the works of nature, I promise you will not be disappointed.'

The next day Felipe came for me in a rough country cart, drawn by a mule; and a little before the stroke of noon, after I had said farewell to the doctor, the innkeeper, and different good souls who had befriended me during my sickness, we set forth out of the city by the eastern gate, and began to ascend into the sierra. I had been so long a prisoner, since I was left behind for dying after the loss of the convoy, that the mere smell of the earth set me smiling. The country through which we went was wild and rocky, partially covered with rough woods, now of the corktree, and now of the great Spanish chestnut, and frequently intersected by the beds of mountain torrents. The sun shone, the wind rustled joyously, and we had advanced some miles, and the city had already shrunk into an inconsiderable knoll upon the plain behind us, before my attention began to be diverted to the companion of my drive. To the eye, he seemed but a diminutive, loutish, well-made country lad, such as the doctor had described, mighty quick and active, but devoid of any culture; and this first impression was with most observers final. What began to strike me was his familiar, chattering talk; so strangely inconsistent with the terms on which I was to be received; and partly from his imperfect enunciation, partly from the sprightly incoherence of the matter, so very difficult to follow clearly without an effort of the mind. It is true I had before talked with persons of a similar mental constitution; persons who seemed to live (as he did) by the senses, taken and possessed by the visual object of the moment and unable to discharge their minds of that impression. His seemed to me (as I sat, distantly giving ear) a kind of conversation proper to drivers, who pass much of their time in a great vacancy of the intellect and threading the sights of a familiar country. But this was not the case of Felipe; by his own account, he was a homekeeper; 'I wish I was there now,' he said; and then, spying a tree by the wayside, he broke off to tell me that he had once seen a crow among its branches.

'A crow?' I repeated, struck by the ineptitude of the remark, and thinking I had heard imperfectly.

But by this time he was already filled with a new idea; hearkening with a rapt intentness, his head on one side, his face puckered; and he struck me rudely, to make me hold my peace. Then he smiled and shook his head.

'What did you hear?' I asked.

'Oh, it is all right,' he said; and began encouraging his mule with cries that echoed unhumanly up the mountain walls.

I looked at him more closely. He was superlatively well built, light, and lithe and strong; he was well-featured; his yellow eyes were very large, though, perhaps, not very expressive; take him altogether, he was a pleasant looking lad, and I had no fault to find with him, beyond that he was of a dusky hue, and inclined to hairiness; two characteristics that I disliked. It was his mind that puzzled and yet attracted me. The doctor's phrase—an innocent—came back to me; and I was wondering if that were, after all, the true description, when the road began to go down into the narrow and naked chasm of a torrent. The waters thundered tumultuously in the bottom; and the ravine was filled full of the sound, the thin spray, and the claps of wind, that accompanied their descent. The scene was certainly impressive; but the road was in that part very securely walled in; the mule went steadily forward; and I was astonished to perceive the paleness of terror in the face of my companion. The voice of that wild river was inconstant, now sinking lower as if in weariness, now doubling its hoarse tones; momentary freshets seemed to swell its volume, sweeping down the gorge, raving and booming against the barrier walls; and I observed it was at each of these accessions to the clamour that my driver more particularly winced and blanched. Some thoughts of Scottish superstition and the river Kelpie passed across my mind; I wondered if perchance the like were prevalent in that part of Spain; and turning to Felipe, sought to draw him out.

'What is the matter?' I asked.

'Oh, I am afraid,' he replied.

'Of what are you afraid?' I returned. 'This seems one of the safest places on this very dangerous road.'

'It makes a noise,' he said, with a simplicity of awe that set my doubts at rest.

The lad was but a child in intellect; his mind was like his body, active and swift, but stunted in development; and I began from that time to regard him with a measure of pity, and to listen at first with indulgence, and at last even with pleasure, to his disjointed babble.

By about four in the afternoon we had crossed the summit of the mountain line, said farewell to the western sunshine, and began to go down upon the other side, skirting the edge of many ravines and moving through the shadow of dusky woods. There rose upon all sides the voice of falling water, not condensed and formidable as in the gorge of the river, but scattered and sounding gaily and musically from glen to glen. Here, too, the spirits of my driver mended, and he began to sing aloud in a falsetto voice, and with a singular bluntness of musical perception, never true either to melody or key, but wandering at will, and yet somehow with an effect that was natural and pleasing, like that of the song of birds. As the dusk increased, I fell more and more under the spell of this artless warbling, listening and waiting for some articulate air, and still disappointed; and when at last I asked him what it was he sang—'Oh,' cried he, 'I am just singing!' Above all, I was taken with a trick he had of unweariedly repeating the same note at little intervals; it was not so monotonous as you would think, or, at least, not disagreeable; and it seemed to breathe a wonderful contentment with what is, such as we love to fancy in the attitude of trees, or the quiescence of a pool.

Night had fallen dark before we came out upon a plateau, and drew up a little after, before a certain lump of superior blackness which I could only conjecture to be the residencia. Here, my guide, getting down from the cart, hooted and whistled for a long time in vain; until at last an old peasant man came towards us from somewhere in the surrounding dark, carrying a candle in his hand. By the light of this I was able to perceive a great arched doorway of a moorish character: it was closed by iron-studded gates, in one of the leaves of which Felipe opened a wicket. The peasant carried off the cart to some out-building; but my guide and I passed through the wicket, which was closed again behind us; and by the glimmer of the candle, passed through a court, up a stone stair, along a section of an open gallery, and up more stairs again, until we came at last to the door of a great and somewhat bare apartment. This room, which I understood was to be mine, was pierced by three windows, lined with some lustrous wood disposed in panels, and carpeted with the skins of many savage animals. A bright fire burned in the chimney, and shed abroad a changeful flicker; close up to the blaze there was drawn a table, laid for supper; and in the far end a bed stood ready. I was pleased by these preparations, and said so to Felipe; and he, with the same simplicity of disposition that I had already remarked in him, warmly re-echoed my praises. 'A fine room,' he said; 'a very fine room. And fire, too; fire is good; it melts out the pleasure in your bones. And the bed,' he continued, carrying over the candle in that direction—'see what fine sheets—how soft, how smooth, smooth,' and he passed his hand again and again over their texture, and then laid down his head and rubbed his cheeks among them with a grossness of content that somehow offended me. I took the candle from his hand (for I feared he would set the bed on fire) and walked back to the supper table, where, perceiving a measure of wine, I poured out a cup and called to him to come and drink of it. He started to his feet at once and ran to me with a strong expression of hope; but when he saw the wine, he visibly shuddered.

'Oh, no,' he said, 'not that, that is for you. I hate it.'

'Very well, señor,' said I; 'then I will drink to your good health, and to the prosperity of your house and family. Speaking of which,' I added, after I had drunk, 'shall I not have the pleasure of laying my salutations in person at the feet of the señora, your mother?'

But at these words all the childishness passed out of his face and was succeeded by a look of indescribable cunning and secrecy. He backed away from me at the same time, as though I were an animal about to leap or some dangerous fellow with a weapon, and when he had got near the door, glowered at me sullenly with contracted pupils. 'No,' he said at last, and the next moment was gone noiselessly out of the room; and I heard his footing die away downstairs as light as rainfall, and silence closed over the house.

After I had supped I drew up the table nearer to the bed and began to prepare for rest; but in the new position of the light, I was struck by a picture on the wall. It represented a woman, still young. To judge by her costume and the mellow unity which reigned over the canvas, she had long been dead; to judge by the vivacity of the attitude, the eyes and the features, I might have been beholding in a mirror the image of life. Her figure was very slim and strong, and of a just proportion; red tresses like a crown over her brow; her eyes, of a very golden brown, held mine with a look; and her face, which was perfectly shaped, was yet marred by a cruel, sullen, and sensual expression. Something in both face and figure, something exquisitely intangible, like the echo of an echo, suggested the features and bearing of my guide; and I stood a while, unpleasantly attracted and wondering at the oddity of the resemblance. The common carnal stock of that race, which had been originally designed for such high dames as the one now looking on me from the canvas, had fallen to baser uses, wearing country clothes, sitting on the shaft and holding the reins of a mule cart, to bring home a lodger. Perhaps an actual link subsisted; perhaps some scruple of the delicate flesh that was once clothed upon with the satin and brocade of the dead lady, now winced at the rude contact of Felipe's frieze.

The first light of the morning shone full upon the portrait, and, as I lay awake, my eyes continued to dwell upon it with growing complacency; its beauty crept about my heart insidiously, silencing my scruples one after another; and while I knew that to love such a woman were to sign and seal one's own sentence of degeneration, I still knew that, if she were alive, I should love her. Day after day the double knowledge of her wickedness and of my weakness grew clearer. She came to be the heroine of many daydreams, in which her eyes led on to, and sufficiently rewarded, crimes. She cast a dark shadow on my fancy; and when I was out in the free air of heaven, taking vigorous exercise and healthily renewing the current of my blood, it was often a glad thought to me that my enchantress was safe in the grave, her wand of beauty broken, her lips closed in silence, her philtre spilt. And yet I had a half-lingering terror that she might not be dead after all, but rearisen in the body of some descendant.

Felipe served my meals in my own apartment; and his resemblance to the portrait haunted me. At times it was not; at times, upon some change of attitude or flash of expression, it would leap out upon me like a ghost. It was above all in his ill-tempers that the likeness triumphed. He certainly liked me; he was proud of my notice, which he sought to engage by many simple and childlike devices; he loved to sit close before my fire, talking his broken talk or singing his odd, endless, wordless songs, and sometimes drawing his hand over my clothes with an affectionate manner of caressing that never failed to cause in me an embarrassment of which I was ashamed. But for all that, he was capable of flashes of causeless anger and fits of sturdy sullenness. At a word of reproof, I have seen him upset the dish of which I was about to eat, and this not surreptitiously, but with defiance; and similarly at a hint of inquisition. I was not unnaturally curious, being in a strange place and surrounded by strange people; but at the shadow of a question, he shrank back, lowering and dangerous. Then it was that, for a fraction of a second, this rough lad might have been the brother of the lady in the frame. But these humours were swift to pass; and the resemblance died along with them.

In these first days I saw nothing of any one but Felipe, unless the portrait is to be counted; and since the lad was plainly of weak mind, and had moments of passion, it may be wondered that I bore his dangerous neighbourhood with equanimity. As a matter of fact, it was for some time irksome; but it happened before long that I obtained over him so complete a mastery as set my disquietude at rest.

It fell in this way. He was by nature slothful, and much of a vagabond, and yet he kept by the house, and not only waited upon my wants, but laboured every day in the garden or small farm to the south of the residencia. Here he would be joined by the peasant whom I had seen on the night of my arrival, and who dwelt at the far end of the enclosure, about half a mile away, in a rude outhouse; but it was plain to me that, of these two, it was Felipe who did most; and though I would sometimes see him throw down his spade and go to sleep among the very plants he had been digging, his constancy and energy were admirable in themselves, and still more so since I was well assured they were foreign to his disposition and the fruit of an ungrateful effort. But while I admired, I wondered what had called forth in a lad so shuttle-witted this enduring sense of duty. How was it sustained? I asked myself, and to what length did it prevail over his instincts? The priest was possibly his inspirer. But the priest came one day to the residencia; I saw him both come and go after an interval of close upon an hour, from a knoll where I was sketching, and all that time Felipe continued to labour undisturbed in the garden.

At last, in a very unworthy spirit, I determined to debauch the lad from his good resolutions and, waylaying him at the gate, easily persuaded him to join me in a ramble. It was a fine day, and the woods to which I led him were green and pleasant and sweet-smelling and alive with the hum of insects. Here he discovered himself in a fresh character, mounting up to heights of gaiety that abashed me, and displaying an energy and grace of movement that delighted the eye. He leaped, he ran round me in a mere glee; he would stop, and look and listen, and seemed to drink in the world like a cordial; and then he would suddenly spring into a tree with one bound, and hang and gambol there like one at home. Little as he said to me, and that of not much import, I have rarely enjoyed more stirring company; the sight of his delight was a continual feast; the speed and accuracy of his movements pleased me to the heart; and I might have been so thoughtlessly unkind as to make a habit of these walks, had not chance prepared a very rude conclusion to my pleasure. By some swiftness or dexterity the lad captured a squirrel in a treetop. He was then some way ahead of me, but I saw him drop to the ground and crouch there, crying aloud for pleasure like a child. The sound stirred my sympathies, it was so fresh and innocent; but as I bettered my pace to draw near, the cry of the squirrel knocked upon my heart. I have heard and seen much of the cruelty of lads, and above all of peasants; but what I now beheld struck me into a passion of anger. I thrust the fellow aside, plucked the poor brute out of his hands, and with swift mercy killed it. Then I turned upon the torturer, spoke to him long out of the heat of my indignation, calling him names at which he seemed to wither; and at length, pointing toward the residencia, bade him begone and leave me, for I chose to walk with men, not with vermin. He fell upon his knees and, the words coming to him with more clearness than usual, poured out a stream of the most touching supplications, begging me in mercy to forgive him, to forget what he had done, to look to the future. 'Oh, I try so hard,' he said, 'O, commandante, bear with Felipe this once, he will never be a brute again!' Thereupon, much more affected than I cared to show, I suffered myself to be persuaded, and at last shook hands with him and made it up. But the squirrel, by way of penance, I made him bury; speaking of the poor thing's beauty, telling him what pains it had suffered, and how base a thing was the abuse of strength. 'See, Felipe,' said I, 'you are strong indeed, but in my hands you are as helpless as that poor thing of the trees. Give me your hand in mine. You cannot remove it. Now suppose that I were cruel like you, and took a pleasure in pain. I only tighten my hold, and see how you suffer.' He screamed aloud, his face stricken ashy and dotted with needle points of sweat; and when I set him free, he fell to the earth and nursed his hand and moaned over it like a baby. But he took the lesson in good part; and whether from that, or from what I had said to him, or the higher notion he now had of my bodily strength, his original affection was changed into a doglike, adoring fidelity.

Meanwhile I gained rapidly in health. The residencia stood on the crown of a stony plateau; on every side the mountains hemmed it about; only from the roof, where was a bartizan, there might be seen between two peaks, a small segment of plain, blue with extreme distance. The air in these altitudes moved freely and largely; great clouds congregated there, and were broken up by the wind and left in tatters on the hilltops; a hoarse, and yet faint rumbling of torrents rose from all round; and one could there study all the ruder and more ancient characters of nature in something of their pristine force. I delighted from the first in the vigorous scenery and changeful weather; nor less in the antique and dilapidated mansion where I dwelt. This was a large oblong, flanked at two opposite corners by bastion-like projections, one of which commanded the door, while both were loopholed for musketry. The lower storey was, besides, naked of windows, so that the building, if garrisoned, could not be carried without artillery. It enclosed an open court planted with pomegranate trees. From this a broad flight of marble stairs ascended to an open gallery, running all round and resting, towards the court, on slender pillars. Thence again, several enclosed stairs led to the upper storeys of the house, which were thus broken up into distinct divisions. The windows, both within and without, were closely shuttered; some of the stonework in the upper parts had fallen; the roof in one place had been wrecked in one of the flurries of wind which were common in these mountains; and the whole house, in the strong, beating sunlight, and standing out above a grove of stunted corktrees, thickly laden and discoloured with dust, looked like the sleeping palace of the legend. The court, in particular, seemed the very home of slumber. A hoarse cooing of doves haunted about the eaves; the winds were excluded, but when they blew outside, the mountain dust fell here as thick as rain, and veiled the red bloom of the pomegranates; shuttered windows and the closed doors of numerous cellars, and the vacant arches of the gallery, enclosed it; and all day long the sun made broken profiles on the four sides, and paraded the shadow of the pillars on the gallery floor. At the ground level there was, however, a certain pillared recess, which bore the marks of human habitation. Though it was open in front upon the court, it was yet provided with a chimney, where a wood fire would be always prettily blazing; and the tile floor was littered with the skins of animals.

It was in this place that I first saw my hostess. She had drawn one of the skins forward and sat in the sun, leaning against a pillar. It was her dress that struck me first of all, for it was rich and brightly coloured, and shone out in that dusty courtyard with something of the same relief as the flowers of the pomegranates. At a second look it was her beauty of person that took hold of me. As she sat back— watching me, I thought, though with invisible eyes—and wearing at the same time an expression of almost imbecile good-humour and contentment, she showed a perfectness of feature and a quiet nobility of attitude that were beyond a statue's. I took off my hat to her in passing, and her face puckered with suspicion as swiftly and lightly as a pool ruffles in the breeze; but she paid no heed to my courtesy. I went forth on my customary walk a trifle daunted, her idol-like impassivity haunting me; and when I returned, although she was still in much the same posture, I was half surprised to see that she had moved as far as the next pillar, following the sunshine. This time, however, she addressed me with some trivial salutation, civilly enough conceived, and uttered in the same deepchested, and yet indistinct and lisping tones, that had already baffled the utmost niceness of my hearing from her son. I answered rather at a venture; for not only did I fail to take her meaning with precision, but the sudden disclosure of her eyes disturbed me. They were unusually large, the iris golden like Felipe's, but the pupil at that moment so distended that they seemed almost black; and what affected me was not so much their size as (what was perhaps its consequence) the singular insignificance of their regard. A look more blankly stupid I have never met. My eyes dropped before it even as I spoke, and I went on my way upstairs to my own room, at once baffled and embarrassed. Yet, when I came there and saw the face of the portrait, I was again reminded of the miracle of family descent. My hostess was, indeed, both older and fuller in person; her eyes were of a different colour; her face, besides, was not only free from the ill-significance that offended and attracted me in the painting; it was devoid of either good or bad—a moral blank expressing literally naught. And yet there was a likeness, not so much speaking as immanent, nor so much in any particular feature as upon the whole. It should seem, I thought, as if when the master set his signature to that grave canvas, he had not only caught the image of one smiling and false-eyed woman, but stamped the essential quality of a race.

From that day forth, whether I came or went, I was sure to find the señora seated in the sun against a pillar, or stretched on a rug before the fire; only at times she would shift her station to the top round of the stone staircase, where she lay with the same nonchalance right across my path. In all these days, I never knew her to display the least spark of energy beyond what she expended in brushing and rebrushing her copious copper-coloured hair, or in lisping out, in the rich and broken hoarseness of her voice, her customary idle salutations to myself. These, I think, were her two chief pleasures, beyond that of mere quiescence. She seemed always proud of her remarks, as though they had been witticisms; and, indeed, though they were empty enough, like the conversation of many respectable persons, and turned on a very narrow range of subjects, they were never meaningless or incoherent; nay, they had a certain beauty of their own, breathing, as they did, of her entire contentment. Now she would speak of the warmth, in which (like her son) she greatly delighted; now of the flowers of the pomegranate trees, and now of the white doves and long-winged swallows that fanned the air of the court. The birds excited her. As they raked the eaves in their swift flight, or skimmed sidelong past her with a rush of wind, she would sometimes stir and sit up a little, and seem to awaken from her doze of satisfaction. But for the rest of her days she lay luxuriously folded on herself and sunk in sloth and pleasure. Her invincible content at first annoyed me, but I came gradually to find repose in the spectacle, until at last it grew to be my habit to sit down beside her four times in the day both coming and going, and to talk with her sleepily, I scarce knew of what. I had come to like her dull almost animal neighbourhood; her beauty and her stupidity soothed and amused me. I began to find a kind of transcendental good sense in her remarks, and her unfathomable good nature moved me to admiration and envy. The liking was returned; she enjoyed my presence half-consciously, as a man in deep meditation may enjoy the babbling of a brook. I can scarce say she brightened when I came, for satisfaction was written on her face eternally, as on some foolish statue's; but I was made conscious of her pleasure by some more intimate communication than the sight. And one day, as I sat within reach of her on the marble step, she suddenly shot forth one of her hands and patted mine. The thing was done, and she was back in her accustomed attitude, before my mind had received intelligence of the caress; and when I turned to look her in the face I could perceive no answerable sentiment. It was plain she attached no moment to the act, and I blamed myself for my own more uneasy consciousness.

The sight and (if I may so call it) the acquaintance of the mother confirmed the view I had already taken of the son. The family blood had been impoverished, perhaps by long inbreeding, which I knew to be a common error among the proud and the exclusive. No decline, indeed, was to be traced in the body, which had been handed down unimpaired in shapeliness and strength, and the faces of today were struck as sharply from the mint as the face of two centuries ago that smiled upon me from the portrait. But the intelligence (that more precious heirloom) was degenerate; the treasure of ancestral memory ran low; and it had required the potent, plebeian crossing of a muleteer or mountain contrabandista to raise, what approached hebetude in the mother, into the active oddity of the son. Yet of the two, it was the mother I preferred. Of Felipe, vengeful and placable, full of starts and shyings, inconstant as a hare, I could even conceive as a creature possibly noxious. Of the mother I had no thoughts but those of kindness. And indeed, as spectators are apt ignorantly to take sides, I grew something of a partisan in the enmity which I perceived to smoulder between them. True, it seemed mostly on the mother's part. She would sometimes draw in her breath as he came near, and the pupils of her vacant eyes would contract as if with horror or fear. Her emotions, such as they were, were much upon the surface and readily shared; and this latent repulsion occupied my mind, and kept me wondering on what grounds it rested, and whether the son was certainly in fault.

I had been about ten days in the residencia, when there sprang up a high and harsh wind, carrying clouds of dust. It came out of malarious lowlands, and over several snowy sierras. The nerves of those on whom it blew were strung and jangled; their eyes smarted with the dust; their legs ached under the burden of their body; and the touch of one hand upon another grew to be odious. The wind, besides, came down the gullies of the hills and stormed about the house with a great, hollow buzzing and whistling that was wearisome to the ear and dismally depressing to the mind. It did not so much blow in gusts as with the steady sweep of a waterfall, so that there was no remission of discomfort while it blew. But higher upon the mountain it was probably of a more variable strength, with accesses of fury; for there came down at times a far-off wailing, infinitely grievous to hear; and at times, on one of the high shelves or terraces, there would start up and then disperse a tower of dust, like the smoke of an explosion.

I no sooner awoke in bed than I was conscious of the nervous tension and depression of the weather, and the effect grew stronger as the day proceeded. It was in vain that I resisted; in vain that I set forth upon my customary morning's walk; the irrational, unchanging fury of the storm had soon beat down my strength and wrecked my temper; and I returned to the residencia, glowing with dry heat and foul and gritty with dust. The court had a forlorn appearance; now and then a glimmer of sun fled over it; now and then the wind swooped down upon the pomegranates and scattered the blossoms, and set the window shutters clapping on the wall. In the recess the señora was pacing to and fro with a flushed countenance and bright eyes; I thought, too, she was speaking to herself, like one in anger. But when I addressed her with my customary salutation she only replied by a sharp gesture and continued her walk. The weather had distempered even this impassive creature; and as I went on upstairs I was the less ashamed of my own discomposure.

All day the wind continued; and I sat in my room and made a feint of reading, or walked up and down and listened to the riot overhead. Night fell and I had not so much as a candle. I began to long for some society and stole down to the court. It was now plunged in the blue of the first darkness, but the recess was redly lighted by the fire. The wood had been piled high and was crowned by a shock of flames, which the draught of the chimney brandished to and fro. In this strong and shaken brightness the señora continued pacing from wall to wall with disconnected gestures, clasping her hands, stretching forth her arms, throwing back her head as in appeal to Heaven. In these disordered movements the beauty and grace of the woman showed more clearly; but there was a light in her eye that struck on me unpleasantly; and when I had looked on awhile in silence, and seemingly unobserved, I turned tail as I had come, and groped my way back again to my own chamber.

By the time Felipe brought my supper and lights, my nerve was utterly gone; and, had the lad been such as I was used to seeing him, I should have kept him (even by force had that been necessary) to take off the edge from my distasteful solitude. But on Felipe, also, the wind had exercised its influence. He had been feverish all day; now that the night had come he was fallen into a low and tremulous humour that reacted on my own. The sight of his scared face, his starts and pallors and sudden hearkenings, unstrung me; and when he dropped and broke a dish, I fairly leaped out of my seat.

'I think we are all mad today,' said I, affecting to laugh.

'It is the black wind,' he replied dolefully. 'You feel as if you must do something, and you don't know what it is.'

I noted the aptness of the description; but, indeed, Felipe had sometimes a strange felicity in rendering into words the sensations of the body. 'And your mother, too,' said I, 'she seems to feel this weather much. Do you not fear she may be unwell?'

He stared at me a little, and then said, 'No,' almost defiantly and the next moment, carrying his hand to his brow, cried out lamentably on the wind and the noise that made his head go round like a millwheel. 'Who can be well?' he cried; and indeed, I could only echo his question, for I was disturbed enough myself.

I went to bed early, wearied with daylong restlessness, but the poisonous nature of the wind, and its ungodly and unintermittent uproar, would not suffer me to sleep. I lay there and tossed, my nerves and senses on the stretch. At times I would doze, dream horribly, and wake again; and these snatches of oblivion confused me as to time. But it must have been late on in the night, when I was suddenly startled by an outbreak of pitiable and hateful cries. I leaped from my bed, supposing I had dreamed; but the cries still continued to fill the house, cries of pain, I thought, but certainly of rage also, and so savage and discordant that they shocked the heart. It was no illusion; some living thing, some lunatic or some wild animal, was being foully tortured. The thought of Felipe and the squirrel flashed into my mind, and I ran to the door, but it had been locked from the outside; and I might shake it as I pleased, I was a fast prisoner. Still the cries continued. Now they would dwindle down into a moaning that seemed to be articulate, and at these times I made sure they must be human; and again they would break forth and fill the house with ravings worthy of hell. I stood at the door and gave ear to them, till at last they died away. Long after that I still lingered and still continued to hear them mingle in fancy with the storming of the wind; and when at last I crept to my bed, it was with a deadly sickness and a blackness of horror on my heart.

It was little wonder if I slept no more. Why had I been locked in? What had passed? Who was the author of these indescribable and shocking cries? A human being? It was inconceivable. A beast? The cries were scarce quite bestial; and what animal, short of a lion or a tiger, could thus shake the solid walls of the residencia? And while I was thus turning over the elements of the mystery, it came into my mind that I had not yet set eyes upon the daughter of the house. What was more probable than that the daughter of the señora, and the sister of Felipe, should be herself insane? Or, what more likely than that these ignorant and half-witted people should seek to manage an afflicted kinswoman by violence? Here was a solution; and yet when I called to mind the cries (which I never did without a shuddering chill) it seemed altogether insufficient: not even cruelty could wring such cries from madness. But of one thing I was sure: I could not live in a house where such a thing was half conceivable and not probe the matter home and, if necessary, interfere.

The next day came, the wind had blown itself out, and there was nothing to remind me of the business of the night. Felipe came to my bedside with obvious cheerfulness; as I passed through the court, the señora was sunning herself with her accustomed immobility; and when I issued from the gateway, I found the whole face of nature austerely smiling, the heavens of a cold blue, and sown with great cloud islands, and the mountainside mapped forth into provinces of light and shadow. A short walk restored me to myself, and renewed within me the resolve to plumb this mystery; and when, from the vantage of my knoll, I had seen Felipe pass forth to his labours in the garden, I returned at once to the residencia to put my design in practice. The señora appeared plunged in slumber; I stood a while and marked her, but she did not stir; even if my design was indiscreet, I had little to fear from such a guardian; and turning away, I mounted to the gallery and began my explorations of the house.

All morning I went from one door to another, and entered spacious and faded chambers, some rudely shuttered, some receiving their full charge of daylight, all empty and unhomely. It was a rich house, on which Time had breathed his tarnish and dust had scattered disillusion. The spider swung there; the bloated tarantula scampered on the cornices; ants had their crowded highways on the floor of halls of audience; the big and foul fly, that lives on carrion and is often the messenger of death, had set up his nest in the rotten woodwork, and buzzed heavily about the rooms. Here and there a stool or two, a couch, a bed, or a great carved chair remained behind, like islets on the bare floors, to testify of man's bygone habitation; and everywhere the walls were set with the portraits of the dead. I could judge, by these decaying effigies, in the house of what a great and what a handsome race I was then wandering. Many of the men wore orders on their breasts and had the port of noble offices; the women were all richly attired; the canvases most of them by famous hands. But it was not so much these evidences of greatness that took hold upon my mind, even contrasted, as they were, with the present depopulation and decay of that great house. It was rather the parable of family life that I read in this succession of fair faces and shapely bodies. Never before had I so realized the miracle of the continued race, the creation and recreation, the weaving and changing and handing down of fleshly elements. That a child should be born of its mother, that it should grow and clothe itself (we know not how) with humanity, and put on inherited looks, and turn its head with the manner of one ascendant, and offer its hand with the gesture of another, are wonders dulled for us by repetition. But in the singular unity of look, in the common features and common bearing, of all these painted generations on the walls of the residencia, the miracle started out and looked me in the face. And an ancient mirror falling opportunely in my way, I stood and read my own features a long while, tracing out on either hand the filaments of descent and the bonds that knit me with my family.

At last, in the course of these investigations, I opened the door of a chamber that bore the marks of habitation. It was of large proportions and faced to the north, where the mountains were most wildly figured. The embers of a fire smouldered and smoked upon the hearth, to which a chair had been drawn close. And yet the aspect of the chamber was ascetic to the degree of sternness; the chair was uncushioned; the floor and walls were naked; and beyond the books which lay here and there in some confusion, there was no instrument of either work or pleasure. The sight of books in the house of such a family exceedingly amazed me; and I began with a great hurry, and in momentary fear of interruption, to go from one to another and hastily inspect their character. They were of all sorts, devotional, historical, and scientific, but mostly of a great age and in the Latin tongue. Some I could see to bear the marks of constant study; others had been torn across and tossed aside as if in petulance or disapproval. Lastly, as I cruised about that empty chamber, I espied some papers written upon with pencil on a table near the window. An unthinking

curiosity led me to take one up. It bore a copy of verses, very roughly
metred in the original Spanish, and which I may render somewhat
thus:

> Pleasure approached with pain and shame,
> Grief with a wreath of lilies came.
> Pleasure showed the lovely sun;
> Jesu dear, how sweet it shone!
> Grief with her worn hand pointed on,
> Jesu dear, to thee!

Shame and confusion at once fell on me; and, laying down the
paper, I beat an immediate retreat from the apartment. Neither
Felipe nor his mother could have read the books nor written these
rough but feeling verses. It was plain I had stumbled with sacrilegious
feet into the room of the daughter of the house. God knows, my own
heart most sharply punished me for my indiscretions. The thought
that I had thus secretly pushed my way into the confidence of a girl
so strangely situated, and the fear that she might somehow come to
hear of it, oppressed me like guilt. I blamed myself besides for my
suspicions of the night before; wondered that I should ever have
attributed these shocking cries to one of whom I now conceived as of
a saint, spectral of mien, wasted with maceration, bound up in the
practices of a mechanical devotion, and dwelling in a great isolation of soul with her incongruous relatives; and as I leaned on the
balustrade of the gallery and looked down into the bright close of
pomegranates and at the gaily dressed and somnolent woman, who
just then stretched herself and delicately licked her lips as in the very
sensuality of sloth, my mind swiftly compared the scene with the cold
chamber looking northward on the mountains, where the daughter
dwelt.

That same afternoon, as I sat upon my knoll, I saw the Padre enter
the gates of the residencia. The revelation of the daughter's character
had struck home to my fancy, and almost blotted out the horrors of
the night before; but at sight of this worthy man the memory revived.
I descended, then, from the knoll, and making a circuit among the
woods, posted myself by the wayside to await his passage. As soon as
he appeared I stepped forth and introduced myself as the lodger of
the residencia. He had a very strong, honest countenance, on which
it was easy to read the mingled emotions with which he regarded
me, as a foreigner, a heretic, and yet one who had been wounded
for the good cause. Of the family at the residencia he spoke with
reserve, and yet with respect. I mentioned that I had not yet seen the

daughter, whereupon he remarked that that was as it should be, and looked at me a little askance. Lastly, I plucked up courage to refer to the cries that had disturbed me in the night. He heard me out in silence, and then stopped and partly turned about, as though to mark beyond doubt that he was dismissing me.

'Do you take tobacco powder?' said he, offering his snuffbox; and then, when I had refused, 'I am an old man,' he added, 'and I may be allowed to remind you that you are a guest.'

'I have, then, your authority,' I returned, firmly enough, although I flushed at the implied reproof, 'to let things take their course, and not to interfere?'

He said 'Yes,' and with a somewhat uneasy salute turned and left me where I was. But he had done two things: he had set my conscience at rest, and he had awakened my delicacy. I made a great effort, once more dismissed the recollection of the night, and fell once more to brooding on my saintly poetess. At the same time, I could not quite forget that I had been locked in, and that night when Felipe brought me my supper I attacked him warily on both points of interest.

'I never see your sister,' said I casually.

'Oh, no,' said he, 'she is a good, good girl,' and his mind instantly veered to something else.

'Your sister is pious, I suppose?' I asked in the next pause.

'Oh!' he cried, joining his hands with extreme fervour, 'a saint, it is she that keeps me up.'

'You are very fortunate,' said I, 'for the most of us, I am afraid, and myself among the number, are better at going down.'

'Señor,' said Felipe earnestly, 'I would not say that. You should not tempt your angel. If one goes down, where is he to stop?'

'Why, Felipe,' said I, 'I had no guess you were a preacher, and I may say a good one; but I suppose that is your sister's doing?'

He nodded at me with round eyes.

'Well, then,' I continued, 'she has doubtless reproved you for your sin of cruelty?'

'Twelve times!' he cried; for this was the phrase by which the odd creature expressed the sense of frequency. 'And I told her you had done so—I remembered that,' he added proudly—'and she was pleased.'

'Then, Felipe,' said I, 'what were those cries that I heard last night? for surely they were cries of some creature in suffering.'

'The wind,' returned Felipe, looking in the fire.

I took his hand in mine, at which, thinking it to be a caress, he smiled with a brightness of pleasure that came near disarming my resolve. But I trod the weakness down. 'The wind,' I repeated; 'and yet I think it was this hand,' holding it up, 'that had first locked me in.' The lad shook visibly, but answered never a word. 'Well,' said I, 'I am a stranger and a guest. It is not my part either to meddle or to judge in your affairs; in these you shall take your sister's counsel, which I cannot doubt to be excellent. But in so far as concerns my own, I will be no man's prisoner, and I demand that key.' Half an hour later my door was suddenly thrown open, and the key tossed ringing on the floor.

A day or two after I came in from a walk a little before the point of noon. The señora was lying lapped in slumber on the threshold of the recess; the pigeons dozed below the eaves like snowdrifts; the house was under a deep spell of noontide quiet; and only a wandering and gentle wind from the mountain stole round the galleries, rustled among the pomegranates, and pleasantly stirred the shadows. Something in the stillness moved me to imitation, and I went very lightly across the court and up the marble staircase. My foot was on the topmost round, when a door opened, and I found myself face to face with Olalla. Surprise transfixed me; her loveliness struck to my heart; she glowed in the deep shadow of the gallery a gem of colour; her eyes took hold upon mine and clung there, and bound us together like the joining of hands; and the moments we thus stood face to face, drinking each other in, were sacramental and the wedding of souls. I know not how long it was before I awoke out of a deep trance, and, hastily bowing, passed on into the upper stair. She did not move, but followed me with her great thirsting eyes; and as I passed out of sight it seemed to me as if she paled and faded.

In my own room, I opened the window and looked out, and could not think what change had come upon that austere field of mountains that it should thus sing and shine under the lofty heaven. I had seen her—Olalla! And the stone crags answered Olalla! and the dumb, unfathomable azure answered, Olalla! The pale saint of my dreams had vanished for ever; and in her place I beheld this maiden on whom God had lavished the richest colours and the most exuberant energies of life, whom He had made active as a deer, slender as a reed, and in whose great eyes He had lighted the torches of the soul. The thrill of her young life, strung like a wild animal's, had entered into me; the force of soul that had looked out from her eyes and conquered mine, mantled about my heart and sprang to my lips in singing. She passed through my veins: she was one with me.

I will not say that this enthusiasm declined; rather my soul held out in its ecstasy as in a strong castle, and was there beseiged by cold and sorrowful considerations. I could not doubt but that I loved her at first sight, and already with a quivering ardour that was strange to my experience. What then was to follow? She was the child of an afflicted house, the señora's daughter, the sister of Felipe; she bore it even in her beauty. She had the lightness and swiftness of the one, swift as an arrow, light as dew; like the other, she shone on the pale background of the world with the brilliancy of flowers. I could not call by the name of brother that halfwitted lad, nor by the name of mother that immovable and lovely thing of flesh, whose silly eyes and perpetual simper now recurred to my mind like something hateful. As if I could not marry, what then? She was helplessly unprotected; her eyes, in that single and long glance which had been all our intercourse, had confessed a weakness equal to my own; but in my heart I knew her for the student of the cold northern chamber, and the writer of the sorrowful lines; and this was a knowledge to disarm a brute. To flee was more than I could find courage for; but I registered a vow of unsleeping circumspection.

As I turned from the window, my eyes alighted on the portrait. It had fallen dead, like a candle after sunrise; it followed me with eyes of paint. I knew it to be like, and marvelled at the tenacity of type in that declining race; but the likeness was swallowed up in difference. I remembered how it had seemed to me a thing unapproachable in the life, a creature rather of the painter's craft than of the modesty of nature, and I marvelled at the thought, and exulted in the image of Olalla. Beauty I had seen before, and not been charmed, and I had been often drawn to women who were not beautiful except to me; but in Olalla all that I desired and had not dared to imagine was united.

I did not see her the next day, and my heart ached and my eyes longed for her, as men long for morning. But the day after, when I returned, about my usual hour, she was once more on the gallery, and our looks once more met and embraced. I would have spoken, I would have drawn near to her; but strongly as she plucked at my heart, drawing me like a magnet, something yet more imperious withheld me; and I could only bow and pass by; and she, leaving my salutation unanswered, only followed me with her noble eyes.

I had now her image by rote, and as I conned the traits in memory it seemed as if I read her very heart. She was dressed with something of her mother's coquetry, and love of positive colour. Her robe, which I knew she must have made with her own hands, clung about her with a cunning grace. After the fashion of that country, besides, her bodice stood open in the middle, in a long slit, and here, in spite of the poverty of the house, a gold coin, hanging by a ribbon, lay on her brown bosom. These were proofs, had any been needed, of her inborn delight in life and her own loveliness. On the other hand, in her eyes that hung upon mine, I could read depth beyond depth of passion and sadness, lights of poetry and hope, blacknesses of despair, and thoughts that were above the earth. It was a lovely body, but the inmate, the soul, was more than worthy of that lodging. Should I leave this incomparable flower to wither unseen on these rough mountains? Should I despise the great gift offered me in the eloquent silence of her eyes? Here was a soul immured; should I not burst its prison? All side considerations fell off from me; were she the child of Herod I swore I should make her mine; and that very evening I set myself, with a mingled sense of treachery and disgrace, to captivate the brother. Perhaps I read him with more favourable eyes, perhaps the thought of his sister always summoned up the better qualities of that imperfect soul; but he had never seemed to be so amiable, and his very likeness to Olalla, while it annoyed, yet softened me.

A third day passed in vain—an empty desert of hours. I would not lose a chance, and loitered all afternoon in the court where (to give myself a countenance) I spoke more than usual with the señora. God knows it was with a most tender and sincere interest that I now studied her; and even as for Felipe, so now for the mother, I was conscious of a growing warmth of toleration. And yet I wondered. Even while I spoke with her, she would doze off into a little sleep, and presently awake again without embarrassment; and this composure staggered me. And again, as I marked her make infinitesimal changes in her posture, savouring and lingering on the bodily pleasure of the movement, I was driven to wonder at this depth of passive sensuality. She lived in her body; and her consciousness was all sunk into and disseminated through her members, where it luxuriously dwelt. Lastly, I could not grow accustomed to her eyes. Each time she turned on me these great beautiful and meaningless orbs, wide open to the day, but closed against human inquiry—each time I had occasion to observe the lively changes of her pupils which expanded and contracted in a breath—I know not what it was came over me, I can find no name for the mingled feeling of disappointment, annoyance, and distaste that jarred along my nerves. I tried her on a variety of subjects, equally in vain; and at last led the talk to her daughter. But even there she proved indifferent; said she was pretty, which (as with children) was her highest word of commendation, but was plainly incapable of any higher thought and when I remarked that

Olalla seemed silent, merely yawned in my face and replied that speech was of no great use when you had nothing to say. 'People speak much, very much,' she added, looking at me with expanded pupils; and then again yawned, and again showed me a mouth that was as dainty as a toy. This time I took the hint, and, leaving her to her repose, went up into my own chamber to sit by the open window, looking on the hills and not beholding them, sunk in lustrous and deep dreams, and hearkening in fancy to the note of a voice that I had never heard.

I awoke on the fifth morning with a brightness of anticipation that seemed to challenge fate. I was sure of myself, light of heart and foot, and resolved to put my love incontinently to the touch of knowledge. It should lie no longer under the bonds of silence, a dumb thing, living by the eye only, like the love of beasts; but should now put on the spirit, and enter upon the joys of the complete human intimacy. I thought of it with wild hopes, like a voyager to El Dorado; into that unknown and lovely country of her soul, I no longer trembled to adventure. Yet when I did encounter her, the same force of passion descended on me and at once submerged my mind; speech seemed to drop away from me like a childish habit; and I but drew near to her as the giddy man draws near to the margin of a gulf. She drew back from me a little as I came; but her eyes did not waver from mine, and these lured me forward. At last, when I was already within reach of her, I stopped. Words were denied me; if I advanced I could but clasp her to my heart in silence; and all that was sane in me, all that was still unconquered, revolted against the thought of such an accost. So we stood for a second, all our life in our eyes, exchanging salvos of attraction and yet each resisting; and then, with a great effort of the will, and conscious at the same time of a sudden bitterness of disappointment, I turned and went away in the same silence.

What power lay upon me that I could not speak? And she, why was she also silent? Why did she draw away before me dumbly, with fascinated eyes? Was this love? or was it a mere brute attraction, mindless and inevitable, like that of the magnet for the steel? We had never spoken, we were wholly strangers; and yet an influence, strong as the grasp of a giant, swept us silently together. On my side it filled me with impatience; and yet I was sure that she was worthy; I had seen her books, read her verses, and thus, in a sense, divined the soul of my mistress. But on her side it struck me almost cold. Of me she knew nothing but my bodily favour; she was drawn to me as stones fall to the earth; the laws that rule the earth conducted her, unconsenting, to my arms; and I drew back at the thought of such a bridal and began to be jealous for myself. It was not thus that I desired to be loved. And then I began to fall into a great pity for the girl herself. I thought how sharp must be her mortification, that she, the student, the recluse, Felipe's saintly monitress, should have thus confessed an overweening weakness for a man with whom she had never exchanged a word. And at the coming of pity, all other thoughts were swallowed up; and I longed only to find and console and reassure her; to tell her how wholly her love was returned on my side, and how her choice, even if blindly made, was not unworthy.

The next day it was glorious weather; depth upon depth of blue over-canopied the mountains; the sun shone wide; and the wind in the trees and the many falling torrents in the mountains filled the air with delicate and haunting music. Yet I was prostrated with sadness. My heart wept for the sight of Olalla, as a child weeps for its mother. I sat down on a boulder on the verge of the low cliffs that bound the plateau to the north. Thence I looked down into the wooded valley of a stream, where no foot came. In the mood I was in, it was even touching to behold the place untenanted; it lacked Olalla; and I thought of the delight and glory of a life passed wholly with her in that strong air, and among these rugged and lovely surroundings, at first with a whimpering sentiment, and then again with such a fiery joy that I seemed to grow in strength and stature, like a Samson.

And then suddenly I was aware of Olalla drawing near. She appeared out of a grove of corktrees, and came straight towards me; and I stood up and waited. She seemed in her walking a creature of such life and fire and lightness as amazed me; yet she came quietly and slowly. Her energy was in the slowness; but for inimitable strength, I felt she would have run, she would have flown to me. Still, as she approached, she kept her eyes lowered to the ground; and when she had drawn quite near, it was without one glance that she addressed me. At the first note of her voice I started. It was for this I had been waiting; this was the last test of my love. And lo, her enunciation was precise and clear, not lisping and incomplete like that of her family; and the voice, though deeper than usual with women, was still both youthful and womanly. She spoke in a rich chord; golden contralto strains mingled with hoarseness, as the red threads were mingled with the brown among her tresses. It was not only a voice that spoke to my heart directly, but it spoke to me of her. And yet her words immediately plunged me back upon despair.

'You will go away,' she said, 'today.'

Her example broke the bonds of my speech, I felt as lightened of a weight, or as if a spell had been dissolved. I know not in what words I answered; but, standing before her on the cliffs, I poured out the whole ardour of my love, telling her I lived upon the thought of her, slept only to dream of her loveliness, and would gladly forswear my country, my language, and my friends, to live for ever by her side. And then, strongly commanding myself, I changed the note; I reassured, I comforted her: I told her I had divined in her a pious and heroic spirit, with which I was worthy to sympathize, and which I longed to share and lighten. 'Nature,' I told her, 'was the voice of God, which men disobey at peril; and if we were thus dumbly drawn together, ay, even as by a miracle of love, it must imply a divine fitness in our souls; we must be made,' I said—'made for one another. We should be mad rebels,' I cried out—'mad rebels against God, not to obey this instinct.'

She shook her head. 'You will go today,' she repeated, and then with a gesture, and in a sudden, sharp note—'no, not today,' she cried, 'tomorrow!'

But at this sign of relenting, power came in upon me in a tide. I stretched out my arms and called upon her name; and she leaped to me and clung to me. The hills rocked about us, the earth quailed; a shock as of a blow went through me and left me blind and dizzy. And the next moment she had thrust me back, broken rudely from my arms, and fled with the speed of a deer among the corktrees.

I stood and shouted to the mountains; I turned and went back towards the residencia, walking upon air. She sent me away, and yet I had but to call upon her name and she came to me. These were but the weaknesses of girls, from which even she, the strongest of her sex, was not exempted. Go? Not I, Olalla—oh, not I, Olalla! A bird sang near by; and in that season birds were rare. It bade me be of good cheer. And once more the whole countenance of nature, from the ponderous and stable mountains down to the lightest leaf and the smallest darting fly in the shadow of the groves, began to stir before me and to put on the lineaments of life and wear a face of awful joy. The sunshine struck upon the hills, strong as a hammer on the anvil, and the hills shook; the earth, under that vigorous insolation, yielded up heady scents; the woods smouldered in the blaze. I felt the thrill of travail and delight run through the earth. Something elemental, something rude, violent, and savage, in the love that sang in my heart, was like a key to nature's secrets; and the very stones that rattled under my feet appeared alive and friendly. Olalla! Her touch had quickened, and renewed, and strung me up to the old pitch of concert with the rugged earth, to a swelling of the soul that men learned to forget in their polite assemblies. Love burned in me like rage; tenderness waxed fierce; I hated, I adored, I pitied, I revered her with ecstasy. She seemed the link that bound me in with dead things on the one hand, and with our pure and pitying God upon the other; a thing brutal and divine, and akin at once to the innocence and to the unbridled forces of the earth.

My head thus reeling, I came into the courtyard of the residencia, and the sight of the mother struck me like a revelation. She sat there, all sloth and contentment, blinking under the strong sunshine, branded with a passive enjoyment, a creature set quite apart, before whom my ardour fell away like a thing ashamed. I stopped a moment, and, commanding such shaken tones as I was able, said a word or two. She looked at me with her unfathomable kindness; her voice in reply sounded vaguely out of the realm of peace in which she slumbered, and there fell on my mind, for the first time, a sense of respect for one so uniformily innocent and happy, and I passed on in a kind of wonder at myself, that I should be so much disquieted.

On my table there lay a piece of the same yellow paper I had seen in the north room; it was written on with pencil in the same hand, Olalla's hand, and I picked it up with a sudden sinking of alarm, and read: 'If you have any kindness for Olalla, if you have any chivalry for a creature sorely wrought, go from here today; in pity, in honour, for the sake of Him who died, I supplicate that you shall go.' I looked at this a while in mere stupidity, then I began to awaken to a weariness and horror of life; the sunshine darkened outside on the bare hills, and I began to shake like a man in terror. The vacancy thus suddenly opened in my life unmanned me like a physical void. It was not my heart, it was not my happiness, it was life itself that was involved. I could not lose her. I said so, and stood repeating it. And then, like one in a dream, I moved to the window, put forth my hand to open the casement, and thrust it through the pane. The blood spurted from my wrist; and with an instantaneous quietude and command of myself, I pressed my thumb on the little leaping fountain and reflected what to do. In that empty room there was nothing to my purpose; I felt, besides, that I required assistance. There shot into my mind a hope that Olalla herself might be my helper, and I turned and went downstairs, still keeping my thumb upon the wound.

There was no sign of either Olalla or Felipe, and I addressed myself to the recess, whither the señora had now drawn quite back and sat dozing close before the fire, for no degree of heat appeared too much for her.

'Pardon me,' said I, 'if I disturb you, but I must apply to you for help.'

She looked up sleepily and asked me what it was, and with the very words I thought she drew in her breath with a widening of the nostrils and seemed to come suddenly and fully alive.

'I have cut myself,' I said, 'and rather badly. See!' And I held out my two hands from which the blood was oozing and dripping.

Her great eyes opened wide, the pupils shrank into points; a veil seemed to fall from her face, and leave it sharply expressive and yet inscrutable. And as I still stood, marvelling a little at her disturbance, she came swiftly up to me, and stooped and caught me by the hand; and the next moment my hand was at her mouth, and she had bitten me to the bone. The pang of the bite, the sudden spurting of blood, and the monstrous horror of the act, flashed through me all in one, and I beat her back; and she sprang at me again and again, with bestial cries, cries that I recognized, such cries as had awakened me on the night of the high wind. Her strength was like that of madness; mine was rapidly ebbing with the loss of blood; my mind besides was whirling with the abhorrent strangeness of the onslaught, and I was already forced against the wall, when Olalla ran betwixt us, and Felipe, following at a bound, pinned down his mother on the floor.

A trancelike weakness fell upon me; I saw, heard, and felt, but I was incapable of movement. I heard the struggle roll to and fro upon the floor, the yells of that catamount ringing up to Heaven as she strove to reach me. I felt Olalla clasp me in her arms, her hair falling on my face, and, with the strength of a man, raise and half drag, half carry me upstairs into my own room, where she cast me down upon the bed. Then I saw her hasten to the door and lock it, and stand an instant listening to the savage cries that shook the residencia. And then, swift and light as a thought, she was again beside me, binding up my hand, laying it in her bosom, moaning and mourning over it with dovelike sounds. They were not words that came to her, they were sounds more beautiful than speech, infinitely touching, infinitely tender; and yet as I lay there, a thought stung to my heart, a thought wounded me like a sword, a thought, like a worm in a flower, profaned the holiness of my love. Yes, they were beautiful sounds, and they were inspired by human tenderness; but was their beauty human?

All day I lay there. For a long time the cries of that nameless female thing, as she struggled with her halfwitted whelp, resounded through the house, and pierced me with despairing sorrow and disgust. They were the death cry of my love; my love was murdered; it was not only dead, but an offence to me; and yet, think as I pleased, feel as I must, it still swelled within me like a storm of sweetness, and my heart melted at her looks and touch. This horror that had sprung out, this doubt upon Olalla, this savage and bestial strain that ran not only through the whole behaviour of her family, but found a place in the very foundations and story of our love—though it appalled, though it shocked and sickened me, was yet not of power to break the knot of my infatuation.

When the cries had ceased, there came a scraping at the door, by which I knew Felipe was without; and Olalla went and spoke to him—I know not what. With that exception, she stayed close beside me, now kneeling by my bed and fervently praying, now sitting with her eyes upon mine. So then, for these six hours I drank in her beauty, and silently perused the story in her face. I saw the golden coin hover on her breaths; I saw her eyes darken and brighten, and still speak no language but that of an unfathomable kindness; I saw the faultless face, and, through the robe, the lines of the fault-less body. Night came at last, and in the growing darkness of the chamber, the sight of her slowly melted; but even then the touch of her smooth hand lingered in mine and talked with me. To lie thus in deadly weakness and drink in the traits of the beloved, is to reawake to love from whatever shock of disillusion. I reasoned with myself, and I shut my eyes on horrors, and again I was very bold to accept the worst. What mattered it, if that imperious sentiment survived; if her eyes still beckoned and attached me; if now, even as before, every fibre of my dull body yearned and turned to her? Late on in the night some strength revived in me, and I spoke:

'Olalla,' I said, 'nothing matters; I ask nothing; I am content; I love you.'

She knelt down awhile and prayed, and I devoutly respected her devotions. The moon had begun to shine in upon one side of each of the three windows, and make a misty clearness in the room, by which I saw her indistinctly. When she rearose she made the sign of the cross.

'It is for me to speak,' she said, 'and for you to listen. I know; you can but guess. I prayed, how I prayed for you to leave this place. I begged it of you, and I know you would have granted me even this; or if not, oh, let me think so!'

'I love you,' I said.

'And yet you have lived in the world,' she said; after a pause, 'you are a man and wise; and I am but a child. Forgive me, if I seem to teach, who am as ignorant as the trees of the mountain; but those who learn much do but skim the face of knowledge; they seize the laws, they conceive the dignity of the design—the horror of the living fact fades from their memory. It is we who sit at home with evil who remember, I think, and are warned and pity. Go, rather, go now, and keep me in mind. So I shall have a life in the cherished places of your memory: a life as much my own as that which I lead in this body.'

'I love you,' I said once more; and reaching out my weak hand, took hers, and carried it to my lips and kissed it. Nor did she resist, but winced a little, and I could see her look upon me with a frown that was not unkindly, only sad and baffled. And then it seemed she made a call upon her resolution; plucked my hand towards her, herself at the same time leaning somewhat forward, and laid it on the beating of her heart. 'There,' she cried, 'you feel the very footfall of my life. It only moves for you; it is yours. But is it even mine? It is mine indeed to offer you, as I might take the coin from my neck, as I might break a live branch from a tree and give it you. And yet not mine! I dwell, or I think I dwell (if I exist at all), somewhat apart, an impotent prisoner, and carried about and deafened by a mob that I disown. This capsule, such as throbs against the sides of animals, knows you at a touch for its master; ay, it loves you! But my soul, does my soul? I think not; I know not, fearing to ask. Yet when you spoke to me, your words were of the soul; it is of the soul that you ask—it is only from the soul that you would take me.'

'Olalla,' I said, 'the soul and the body are one, and mostly so in love. What the body chooses, the soul loves; where the body clings, the soul cleaves; body for body, soul to soul, they come together at God's signal; and the lower part (if we can call aught low) is only the footstool and foundation of the highest.'

'Have you,' she said, 'seen the portraits in the house of my fathers? Have you looked at my mother or at Felipe? Have your eyes never rested on that picture that hangs by your bed? She who sat for it died ages ago; and she did evil in her life. But, look again: there is my hand to the least line, there are my eyes and my hair. What is mine, then, and what am I? If not a curve in this poor body of mine (which you love, and for the sake of which you dotingly dream that you love me), not a gesture that I can frame, not a tone of my voice, not any look from my eyes, no, not even now when I speak to him I love, but has belonged to others? Others, ages dead, have wooed other men with my eyes; other men have heard the pleading of the same voice that now sounds in your ears. The hands of the dead are in my bosom; they move me, they pluck me, they guide me; I am a puppet at their command; and I but reinform features and attributes that have long been laid aside from evil in the quiet of the grave. Is it me you love, friend? or the race that made me? The girl who does not know and cannot answer for the least portion of herself? or the stream of which she is a transitory eddy, the tree of which she is the passing fruit? The race exists; it is old, it is very young, it carries its eternal destiny in its bosom; upon it, like waves upon the sea, individual succeeds to individual, mocked with a semblance of self-control, but they are nothing. We speak of the soul, but the soul is in the race.'

'You fret against the common law,' I said. 'You rebel against the voice of God, which He had made so winning to convince, so imperious to command. Hear it, and how it speaks between us! Your hand clings to mine, your heart leaps at my touch, the unknown elements of which we are compounded awake and run together at a look; the clay of the earth remembers its independent life and yearns to join us; we are drawn together as the stars are turned about in space; or as the tides ebb and flow, by things older and greater than we ourselves.'

'Alas!' she said, 'what can I say to you? My fathers, eight hundred years ago, ruled all this province: they were wise, great, cunning, and cruel; they were a picked race of the Spanish; their flags led in war; the king called them his cousin; the people, when the rope was slung for them or when they returned and found their hovels smoking, blasphemed their name. Presently a change began. Man has risen; if he has sprung from the brutes, he can descend again to the same level. The breath of weariness blew on their humanity and cords relaxed; they began to go down; their minds fell on sleep, their passions awoke in gusts, heady and senseless like the wind in the gutters of the mountains; beauty was still handed down, but no longer the guiding wit nor the human heart; the seed passed on, it was wrapped in flesh, the flesh covered the bones, but they were the bones and the flesh of brutes, and their mind was as the mind of flies. I speak to you as I dare; but you have seen for yourself how the wheel has gone backward with my doomed race. I stand, as it were, upon a little rising ground in this desperate descent, and see both before and behind, both what we have lost and to what we are condemned, to go farther downward. And shall I—I that dwell apart in the house of the dead, my body, loathing its ways—shall I repeat the spell? Shall I bind another spirit, reluctant as my own, into this bewitched and tempest-broken tenement that I now suffer in? Shall I hand down this cursed vessel of humanity, charge it with fresh life as with fresh poison, and dash it, like a fire, in the faces of posterity? But my vow has been given; the race shall cease from off the earth. At this hour my brother is making ready; his foot will soon be on the stair; and you will go with him and pass out of my sight for ever. Think of me sometimes as one to whom the lesson of life was very harshly told, but who heard it with courage; as one who loved you indeed, but who hated herself so deeply that her love was hateful to her; as one who sent you away and yet would have longed to keep you for ever; who had no dearer hope than to forget you, and no greater fear than to be forgotten.'

She had drawn towards the door as she spoke, her rich voice sounding softer and farther away; and with the last word she was gone, and I lay alone in the moonlit chamber. What I might have done had not I lain bound by my extreme weakness, I know not; but as it was there fell upon me a great and blank despair. It was not long before there shone in at the door the ruddy glimmer of a lantern, and Felipe coming, charged me without a word upon his shoulders, and carried me down to the great gate, where the cart was waiting. In the moonlight the hills stood out sharply, as if they were of cardboard; on the glimmering surface of the plateau, and from among the low trees which swung together and sparkled in the wind, the great black cube of the residencia stood out bulkily, its mass only broken by three dimly lighted windows in the northern front above the gate. They were Olalla's window, and as the cart jolted onwards I kept my eyes fixed upon them till, where the road dipped into a valley, they were lost to my view for ever. Felipe walked in silence beside the shafts, but from time to time he would check the mule and seem to look back upon me; and at length drew quite near and laid his hand upon my head. There was such kindness in the touch, and such a simplicity, as of the brutes, that tears broke from me like the bursting of an artery.

'Felipe,' I said, 'take me where they will ask no questions.'

He said never a word, but he turned his mule about, end for end, retraced some part of the way we had gone, and, striking into another path, led me to the mountain village, which was, as we say in Scotland, the kirkton of that thinly peopled district. Some broken memories dwell in my mind of the day breaking over the plain, of the cart stopping, of arms that helped me down, of a bare room into which I was carried, and of a swoon that fell upon me like sleep.

The next day and the days following the old priest was often at my side with his snuffbox and prayer book, and after a while, when I began to pick up strength, he told me that I was now on a fair way to recovery, and must as soon as possible hurry my departure; whereupon, without naming any reason, he took snuff and looked at me sideways. I did not affect ignorance; I knew he must have seen Olalla.

'Sir,' said I, 'you know that I do not ask in wantonness. What of that family?'

He said they were very unfortunate; that it seemed a declining race, and that they were very poor and had been much neglected.

'But she has not,' I said. 'Thanks, doubtless, to yourself, she is instructed and wise beyond the use of women.'

'Yes,' he said, 'the señorita is well-informed. But the family has been neglected.'

'The mother?' I queried.

'Yes, the mother too,' said the Padre, taking snuff. 'But Felipe is a well-intentioned lad.'

'The mother is odd?' I asked.

'Very odd,' replied the priest.

'I think, sir, we beat about the bush,' said I. 'You must know more of my affairs than you allow. You must know my curiosity to be justified on many grounds. Will you not be frank with me?'

'My son,' said the old gentleman, 'I will be very frank with you on matters within my competence; on those of which I know nothing it does not require much discretion to be silent. I will not fence with you, I take your meaning perfectly; and what can I say, but that we are all in God's hands, and that His ways are not as our ways? I have even advised with my superiors in the Church, but they, too, were dumb. It is a great mystery.'

'Is she mad?' I asked.

'I will answer you according to my belief. She is not,' returned the Padre, 'or she was not. When she was young—God help me, I fear I neglected that wild lamb—she was surely sane; and yet, although it did not run to such heights, the same strain was already notable; it had been so before her in her father, ay, and before him, and this inclined me, perhaps, to think too lightly of it. But these things go on growing, not only in the individual but in the race.'

'When she was young,' I began, and my voice failed me for a moment, and it was only with a great effort that I was able to add, 'was she like Olalla?'

'Now God forbid!' exclaimed the Padre. 'God forbid that any man should think so slightingly of my favourite penitent. No, no; the señorita (but for her beauty, which I wish most honestly she had less of) has not a hair's resemblance to what her mother was at the same age. I could not bear to have you think so; though, Heaven knows, it were, perhaps, better that you should.'

At this, I raised myself in bed and opened my heart to the old man; telling him of our love and of her decision, owning my own horrors, my own passing fancies, but telling him that these were at an end, and with something more than a purely formal submission, appealing to his judgement.

He heard me very patiently and without surprise; and when I had done, he sat for some time silent. Then he began: 'The Church,' and instantly broke off again to apologize. 'I had forgotten my child, that you were not a Christian,' said he. 'And indeed, upon a point so highly unusual, even the Church can scarce be said to have decided. But would you have my opinion? The señorita is, in a matter of this kind, the best judge; I would accept her judgement.'

On the back of that he went away, nor was he thenceforward so assiduous in his visits; indeed, even when I began to get about again, he plainly feared and deprecated my society, not as in distaste but much as a man might be disposed to flee from the riddling sphynx. The villagers, too, avoided me; they were unwilling to be my guides upon the mountain. I thought they looked at me askance, and I made sure that the more superstitious crossed themselves on my approach. At first I set this down to my heretical opinions; but it began at length to dawn upon me that if I was thus redoubted it was because I had stayed at the residencia. All men despise the savage notions of such peasantry; and yet I was conscious of a chill shadow that seemed to fall and dwell upon my love. It did not conquer, but I may not deny that it restrained my ardour.

Some miles westward of the village there was a gap in the sierra, from which the eye plunged direct upon the residencia, and thither it became my daily habit to repair. A wood crowned the summit, and just where the pathway issued from its fringes, it was overhung by a considerable shelf of rock, and that, in its turn, was surmounted by a crucifix of the size of life and more than usually painful in design. This was my perch; thence, day after day, I looked down upon the plateau and the great old house, and could see Felipe, no bigger than a fly, going to and fro about the garden. Sometimes mists would draw across the view, and be broken up again by mountain winds; sometimes the plain slumbered below me in unbroken sunshine; it would sometimes be all blotted out by rain. This distant post, these interrupted sights of the place where my life had been so strangely changed, suited the indecision of my humour. I passed whole days there, debating with myself the various elements of our position; now leaning to the suggestions of love, now giving an ear to prudence, and in the end halting irresolute between the two.

One day, as I was sitting on my rock, there came by that way a somewhat gaunt peasant wrapped in a mantle. He was a stranger, and plainly did not know me even by repute; for, instead of keeping the other side, he drew near and sat down beside me, and we had soon fallen in talk. Among other things he told me he had been a muleteer, and in former years had much frequented these mountains; later on, he had followed the army with his mules, had realized a competence, and was now living retired with his family.

'Do you know that house?' I inquired at last, pointing to the residencia, for I readily wearied of any talk that kept me from the thought of Olalla.

He looked at me darkly and crossed himself.

'Too well,' he said, 'it was there that one of my comrades sold himself to Satan; the Virgin shield us from temptations! He has paid the price; he is now burning in the reddest place in Hell!'

A fear came upon me; I could answer nothing; and presently the man resumed, as if to himself: 'Yes,' he said, 'oh yes, I know it. I have passed its doors. There was snow upon the pass, the wind was driving it; sure enough there was death that night upon the mountains, but there was worse beside the hearth. I took him by the arm, señor, and dragged him to the gate; I conjured him, by all he loved and respected, to go forth with me; I went on my knees before him in the snow, and I could see he was moved by my entreaty. And just then she came out on the gallery and called him by his name; and he turned, and there was she standing with a lamp in her hand and smiling on him to come back. I cried out aloud to God, and threw my arms about him, but he put me by and left me alone. He had made his choice; God help us. I would pray for him, but to what end? There are sins that not even the Pope can loose.'

'And your friend,' I asked, 'what became of him?'

'Nay, God knows,' said the muleteer. 'If all be true that we hear, his end was like his sin, a thing to raise the hair.'

'Do you mean that he was killed?' I asked.

'Sure enough, he was killed,' returned the man. 'But how? Ay, how? But these are things that it is sin to speak of.'

'The people of that house . . .' I began.

But he interrupted me with a savage outburst. 'The people?' he cried. 'What people? There are neither men nor women in that house of Satan's! What? have you lived here so long and never heard?' And here he put his mouth to my ear and whispered, as if even the fowls of the mountain might have overheard and been stricken with horror.

What he told me was not true, nor was it even original; being, indeed, but a new edition, vamped up again by village ignorance and superstition, of stories nearly as ancient as the race of man. It was rather the application that appalled me. In the old days, he said, the Church would have burned out that nest of basilisks; but the arm of the Church was now shortened; his friend Miguel had been unpunished by the hands of men, and left to the more awful judgement of an offended God. This was wrong; but it should be so no more. The Padre was sunk in age; he was even bewitched himself; but the eyes of his flock were now awake to their own danger; some day—ay, and before long—the smoke of that house should go up to Heaven.

He left me filled with horror and fear. Which way to turn I knew not; whether first to warn the Padre, or to carry my ill-news direct to the threatened inhabitants of the residencia. Fate was to decide for me, for, while I was still hesitating, I beheld the veiled figure of a woman drawing near to me up the pathway. No veil could deceive my penetration; by every line and every movement I recognized Olalla; and keeping hidden behind a corner of the rock, I suffered her to gain the summit. Then I came forward. She knew me and paused, but did not speak; I, too, remained silent, and we continued for some time to gaze upon each other with a passionate sadness.

'I thought you had gone,' she said at length. 'It is all that you can do for me—to go. It is all I ever asked of you. And you still stay. But do you know that every day heaps up the peril of death, not only on your head, but on ours? A report has gone about the mountain; it is thought you love me, and the people will not suffer it.'

I saw she was already informed of her danger, and I rejoiced at it. 'Olalla,' I said, 'I am ready to go this day, this very hour, but not alone.'

She stepped aside and knelt down before the crucifix to pray, and I stood by and looked now at her and now at the object of her adoration, now at the living figure of the penitent, and now at the ghastly daubed countenance, the painted wounds, and the projected ribs of the image. The silence was only broken by the wailing of some large birds that circled sidelong, as if in surprise or alarm, about the summit of the hills. Presently Olalla rose again, turned towards me, raised her veil, and, still leaning with one hand on the shaft of the crucifix, looked upon me with a pale and sorrowful countenance.

'I have laid my hand upon the cross,' she said. 'The Padre says you are no Christian; but look up for a moment with my eyes, and behold the face of the Man of Sorrows. We are all such as He was—the inheritors of sin; we must all bear and expiate a past which was not ours; there is in all of us—ay, even in me—a sparkle of the divine. Like Him, we must endure for a little while, until morning returns bringing peace. Suffer me to pass on upon my way alone; it is thus that I shall be least lonely, counting for my friend Him who is the friend of all the distressed; it is thus that I shall be the most happy, having taken my farewell of earthly happiness, and willingly accepted sorrow for my portion.'

I looked at the face of the crucifix, and, though I was no friend to images, and despised that imitative and grimacing art of which it was a rude example, some sense of what the thing implied was carried home to my intelligence. The face looked down upon me with a painful and deadly contraction; but the rays of glory encircled it, and reminded me that the sacrifice was voluntary. It stood there, crowning the rock, as it still stands on so many highway sides, vainly preaching to passers-by, an emblem of sad and noble truths; that pleasure is not an end, but an accident; that pain is the choice of the magnanimous; that it is best to suffer all things and do well. I turned and went down the mountain in silence; and when I looked back for the last time before the wood closed about my path, I saw Olalla still leaning on the crucifix.

THOMAS HARDY

Barbara of the House of Grebe

It was apparently an idea, rather than a passion, that inspired Lord Uplandtowers' resolve to win her. Nobody ever knew when he formed it, or whence he got his assurance of success in the face of her manifest dislike of him. Possibly not until after that first important act of her life which I shall presently mention. His matured and cynical doggedness at the age of nineteen, when impulse mostly rules calculation, was remarkable, and might have owed its existence as much to his succession to the earldom and its accompanying local honours in childhood, as to the family character; an elevation which jerked him into maturity, so to speak, without his having known adolescence. He had only reached his twelfth year when his father, the fourth Earl, died, after a course of the Bath waters.

Nevertheless, the family character had a great deal to do with it. Determination was hereditary in the bearers of that escutcheon, sometimes for good, sometimes for evil.

The seats of the two families were about ten miles apart, the way between them lying along the now old, then new, turnpike-road connecting Havenpool and Warborne with the city of Melchester; a road which, though only a branch from what was known as the Great Western Highway, is probably, even at present, as it has been for the last hundred years, one of the finest examples of a macadamized turnpike-track that can be found in England.

The mansion of the Earl, as well as that of his neighbour, Barbara's father, stood back about a mile from the highway, with which each was connected by an ordinary drive and lodge. It was along this particular highway that the young Earl drove on a certain evening at Christmastide some twenty years before the end of the last century, to attend a ball at Chene Manor, the home of Barbara and her parents Sir John and Lady Grebe. Sir John's was a baronetcy created a few years before the breaking out of the Civil War, and his lands were even more extensive than those of Lord Uplandtowers himself, comprising this Manor of Chene, another on the coast near, half the Hundred of Cockdene, and well-enclosed lands in several other parishes, notably Warborne and those contiguous. At this time Barbara was barely seventeen, and the ball is the first occasion on which we have any tradition of Lord Uplandtowers attempting tender relations with her; it was early enough, God knows.

An intimate friend—one of the Drenkhards—is said to have dined with him that day, and Lord Uplandtowers had, for a wonder, communicated to his guest the secret design of his heart.

'You'll never get her—sure; you'll never get her!' this friend had said at parting. 'She's not drawn to your lordship by love: and as for thought of a good match, why, there's no more calculation in her than in a bird.'

'We'll see,' said Lord Uplandtowers impassively.

He no doubt thought of his friend's forecast as he travelled along the highway in his chariot; but the sculptural repose of his profile against the vanishing daylight on his right hand would have shown his friend that the Earl's equanimity was undisturbed. He reached the solitary wayside tavern called Lornton Inn—the rendezvous of many a daring poacher for operations in the adjoining forest; and he might have observed, if he had taken the trouble, a strange post-chaise standing in the halting-space before the inn. He duly sped past it, and half-an-hour after through the little town of Warborne. Onward, a mile further, was the house of his entertainer.

At this date it was an imposing edifice—or, rather, congeries of edifices—as extensive as the residence of the Earl himself, though far less regular. One wing showed extreme antiquity, having huge chimneys, whose substructures projected from the external walls like towers; and a kitchen of vast dimensions, in which (it was said) breakfasts had been cooked for John of Gaunt. Whilst he was yet in the forecourt he could hear the rhythm of French horns and clarionets, the favourite instruments of those days at such entertainments.

Entering the long parlour, in which the dance had just been opened by Lady Grebe with a minuet—it being now seven o'clock, according to the tradition—he was received with a welcome befitting his rank, and looked round for Barbara. She was not dancing, and seemed to be preoccupied—almost, indeed, as though she had been waiting for him. Barbara at this time was a good and pretty girl, who never spoke ill of any one, and hated other pretty women the very least possible. She did not refuse him for the country-dance which followed, and soon after was his partner in a second.

The evening wore on, and the horns and clarionets tootled merrily. Barbara evinced towards her lover neither distinct preference nor aversion; but old eyes would have seen that she pondered something. However, after supper she pleaded a headache, and disappeared. To pass the time of her absence, Lord Uplandtowers went into a little room adjoining the long gallery, where some elderly ones were sitting by the fire—for he had a phlegmatic dislike of dancing for its own sake—and, lifting the window-curtains, he looked out of the window into the park and wood, dark now as a cavern. Some of the guests appeared to be leaving even so soon as this, two lights showing themselves as turning away from the door and sinking to nothing in the distance.

His hostess put her head into the room to look for partners for the ladies, and Lord Uplandtowers came out. Lady Grebe informed him that Barbara had not returned to the ball-room: she had gone to bed in sheer necessity.

'She has been so excited over the ball all day,' her mother continued, 'that I feared she would be worn out early . . . But sure, Lord Uplandtowers, you won't be leaving yet?'

He said that it was near twelve o'clock, and that some had already left.

'I protest nobody has gone yet,' said Lady Grebe.

To humour her he stayed till midnight, and then set out. He had made no progress in his suit; but he had assured himself that Barbara gave no other guest the preference, and nearly everybody in the neighbourhood was there.

''Tis only a matter of time,' said the calm young philosopher.

The next morning he lay till near ten o'clock, and he had only just come out upon the head of the staircase when he heard hoofs upon the gravel without; in a few moments the door had been opened, and Sir John Grebe met him in the hall, as he set foot on the lowest stair.

'My lord—where's Barbara—my daughter?'

Even the Earl of Uplandtowers could not repress amazement. 'What's the matter, my dear Sir John,' says he.

The news was startling, indeed. From the Baronet's disjointed explanation Lord Uplandtowers gathered that after his own and the other guests' departure Sir John and Lady Grebe had gone to rest without seeing any more of Barbara; it being understood by them that she had retired to bed when she sent word to say that she could not join the dancers again. Before then she had told her maid that she would dispense with her services for this night; and there was evidence to show that the young lady had never lain down at all, the bed remaining unpressed. Circumstances seemed to prove that the deceitful girl had feigned indisposition to get an excuse for leaving the ball-room, and that she had left the house within ten minutes, presumably during the first dance after supper.

'I saw her go,' said Lord Uplandtowers.

'The devil you did!' says Sir John.

'Yes.' And he mentioned the retreating carriage-lights, and how he was assured by Lady Grebe that no guest had departed.

'Surely that was it!' said the father. 'But she's not gone alone, d'ye know!'

'Ah—who is the young man?'

'I can on'y guess. My worst fear is my most likely guess. I'll say no more. I thought—yet I would not believe—it possible that you was the sinner. Would that you had been! But 'tis t'other, 'tis t'other, by Heaven! I must e'en up and after 'em!'

'Whom do you suspect?'

Sir John would not give a name, and, stultified rather than agitated, Lord Uplandtowers accompanied him back to Chene. He again asked upon whom were the Baronet's suspicions directed; and the impulsive Sir John was no match for the insistence of Uplandtowers.

He said at length, 'I fear 'tis Edmond Willowes.'

'Who's he?'

'A young fellow of Shottsford-Forum—a widow-woman's son,' the other told him, and explained that Willowes's father, or grandfather, was the last of the old glass-painters in that place, where (as you may know) the art lingered on when it had died out in every other part of England.

'By God that's bad—mighty bad!' said Lord Uplandtowers, throwing himself back in the chaise in frigid despair.

They despatched emissaries in all directions; one by the Melchester Road, another by Shottsford-Forum, another coastwards.

But the lovers had a ten-hours' start; and it was apparent that sound judgement had been exercised in choosing as their time of flight the particular night when the movements of a strange carriage would not be noticed, either in the park or on the neighbouring highway, owing to the general press of vehicles. The chaise which had been seen waiting at Lornton Inn was, no doubt, the one they had escaped in; and the pair of heads which had planned so cleverly thus far had probably contrived marriage ere now.

The fears of her parents were realized. A letter sent by special messenger from Barbara, on the evening of that day, briefly informed them that her lover and herself were on the way to London, and before this communication reached her home they would be united as husband and wife. She had taken this extreme step because she loved her dear Edmond as she could love no other man, and because she had seen closing round her the doom of marriage with Lord

Uplandtowers, unless she put that threatened fate out of possibility by doing as she had done. She had well considered the step beforehand, and was prepared to live like any other country-townsman's wife if her father repudiated her for her action.

'Damn her!' said Lord Uplandtowers, as he drove homeward that night. 'Damn her for a fool!'—which shows the kind of love he bore her.

Well; Sir John had already started in pursuit of them as a matter of duty, driving like a wild man to Melchester, and thence by the direct highway to the capital. But he soon saw that he was acting to no purpose; and by and by, discovering that the marriage had actually taken place, he forebore all attempts to unearth them in the City, and returned and sat down with his lady to digest the event as best they could.

To proceed against this Willowes for the abduction of our heiress was, possibly, in their power; yet, when they considered the now unalterable facts, they refrained from violent retribution. Some six weeks passed, during which time Barbara's parents, though they keenly felt her loss, held no communication with the truant, either for reproach or condonation. They continued to think of the disgrace she had brought upon herself; for, though the young man was an honest fellow, and the son of an honest father, the latter had died so early, and his widow had had such struggles to maintain herself, that the son was very imperfectly educated. Moreover, his blood was, as far as they knew, of no distinction whatever, whilst hers, through her mother, was compounded of the best juices of ancient baronial distillation, containing tinctures of Maundeville, and Mohun, and Syward, and Peverell, and Culliford, and Talbot, and Plantagenet, and York, and Lancaster, and God knows what besides, which it was a thousand pities to throw away.

The father and mother sat by the fireplace that was spanned by the four-centred arch bearing the family shields on its haunches, and groaned aloud—the lady more than Sir John.

'To think this should have come upon us in our old age!' said he.

'Speak for yourself!' she snapped through her sobs, 'I am only one-and-forty! . . . Why didn't ye ride faster and overtake 'em!'

In the meantime the young married lovers, caring no more about their blood than about ditch-water, were intensely happy—happy, that is, in the descending scale which, as we all know, Heaven in its wisdom has ordained for such rash cases; that is to say, the first week they were in the seventh heaven, the second in the sixth, the third week temperate, the fourth reflective, and so on; a lover's heart after possession being comparable to the earth in its geologic stages, as described to us sometimes by our worthy President; first a hot coal, then a warm one, then a cooling cinder, then chilly—the simile shall be pursued no further. The long and the short of it was that one day a letter, sealed with their daughter's own little seal, came into Sir John and Lady Grebe's hands; and, on opening it, they found it to contain an appeal from the young couple to Sir John to forgive them for what they had done, and they would fall on their naked knees and be most dutiful children for evermore.

Then Sir John and his lady sat down again by the fireplace with the four-centred arch, and consulted, and re-read the letter. Sir John Grebe, if the truth must be told, loved his daughter's happiness far more, poor man, than he loved his name and lineage; he recalled to his mind all her little ways, gave vent to a sigh; and, by this time acclimatized to the idea of the marriage, said that what was done could not be undone, and that he supposed they must not be too harsh with her. Perhaps Barbara and her husband were in actual need; and how could they let their only child starve?

A slight consolation had come to them in an unexpected manner. They had been credibly informed that an ancestor of plebeian Willowes was once honoured with intermarriage with a scion of the aristocracy who had gone to the dogs. In short, such is the foolishness of distinguished parents, and sometimes of others also, that they wrote that very day to the address Barbara had given them, informing her that she might return home and bring her husband with her; they would not object to see him, would not reproach her, and would endeavour to welcome both, and to discuss with them what could best be arranged for their future.

In three or four days a rather shabby post-chaise drew up at the door of Chene Manor-house, at sound of which the tender-hearted baronet and his wife ran out as if to welcome a prince and princess of the blood. They were overjoyed to see their spoilt child return safe and sound—though she was only Mrs Willowes, wife of Edmond Willowes of nowhere. Barbara burst into penitential tears, and both husband and wife were contrite enough, as well they might be, considering that they had not a guinea to call their own.

When the four had calmed themselves, and not a word of chiding had been uttered to the pair, they discussed the position soberly, young Willowes sitting in the background with great modesty till invited forward by Lady Grebe in no frigid tone.

'How handsome he is!' she said to herself. 'I don't wonder at Barbara's craze for him.'

He was, indeed, one of the handsomest men who ever set his lips on a maid's. A blue coat, murrey waistcoat, and breeches of drab set off a figure that could scarcely be surpassed. He had large dark eyes, anxious now, as they glanced from Barbara to her parents and tenderly back again to her; observing whom, even now in her trepidation, one could see why the *sang froid* of Lord Uplandtowers had been raised to more than lukewarmness. Her fair young face (according to the tale handed down by old women) looked out from under a grey conical hat, trimmed with white ostrich-feathers, and her little toes peeped from a buff petticoat worn under a puce gown. Her features were not regular: they were almost infantine, as you may see from miniatures in possession of the family, her mouth showing much sensitiveness, and one could be sure that her faults would not lie on the side of bad temper unless for urgent reasons.

Well, they discussed their state as became them, and the desire of the young couple to gain the goodwill of those upon whom they were literally dependent for everything induced them to agree to any temporizing measure that was not too irksome. Therefore, having been nearly two months united, they did not oppose Sir John's proposal that he should furnish Edmond Willowes with funds sufficient for him to travel a year on the Continent in the company of a tutor, the young man undertaking to lend himself with the utmost diligence to the tutor's instructions, till he became polished outwardly and inwardly to the degree required in the husband of such a lady as Barbara. He was to apply himself to the study of languages, manners, history, society, ruins, and everything else that came under his eyes, till he should return to take his place without blushing by Barbara's side.

'And by that time,' said worthy Sir John, 'I'll get my little place out at Yewsholt ready for you and Barbara to occupy on your return. The house is small and out of the way; but it will do for a young couple for a while.'

'If 'twere no bigger than a summer-house it would do!' says Barbara.

'If 'twere no bigger than a sedan-chair!' says Willowes. 'And the more lonely the better.'

'We can put up with the loneliness,' said Barbara, with less zest. 'Some friends will come, no doubt.'

All this being laid down, a travelled tutor was called in—a man of many gifts and great experience,—and on a fine morning away tutor and pupil went. A great reason urged against Barbara accompanying her youthful husband was that his attentions to her would naturally be such as to prevent his zealously applying every hour of his time to learning and seeing—an argument of wise prescience, and unanswerable. Regular days for letter-writing were fixed, Barbara and her Edmond exchanged their last kisses at the door, and the chaise swept under the archway into the drive.

He wrote to her from Le Havre, as soon as he reached that port, which was not for seven days, on account of adverse winds; he wrote from Rouen, and from Paris; described to her his sight of the King and Court at Versailles, and the wonderful marblework and mirrors in that palace; wrote next from Lyons; then, after a comparatively long interval, from Turin, narrating his fearful adventures in crossing Mont Cenis on mules, and how he was overtaken with a terrific snowstorm, which had well-nigh been the end of him, and his tutor, and his guides. Then he wrote glowingly of Italy; and Barbara could see the development of her husband's mind reflected in his letters month by month; and she much admired the forethought of her father in suggesting this education for Edmond. Yet she sighed sometimes—her husband being no longer in evidence to fortify her in her choice of him—and timidly dreaded what mortifications might be in store for her by reason of this *mésalliance*. She went out very little; for on the one or two occasions on which she had shown herself to former friends she noticed a distinct difference in their manner, as though they should say, 'Ah, my happy swain's wife; you're caught!'

Edmond's letters were as affectionate as ever; even more affectionate, after a while, than hers were to him. Barbara observed this growing coolness in herself; and like a good and honest lady was horrified and grieved, since her only wish was to act faithfully and uprightly. It troubled her so much that she prayed for a warmer heart, and at last wrote to her husband to beg him, now that he was in the land of Art, to send her his portrait, ever so small, that she might look at it all day and every day, and never for a moment forget his features.

Willowes was nothing loth, and replied that he would do more than she wished: he had made friends with a sculptor in Pisa, who was much interested in him and his history; and he had commissioned this artist to make a bust of himself in marble, which when finished he would send her. What Barbara had wanted was something immediate; but she expressed no objection to the delay; and in his next communication Edmond told her that the sculptor, of his own choice, had decided to extend the bust to a full-length statue, so anxious was he to get a specimen of his skill introduced to the notice of the English aristocracy. It was progressing well, and rapidly.

Meanwhile, Barbara's attention began to be occupied at home with Yewsholt Lodge, the house that her kind-hearted father was preparing for her residence when her husband returned. It was a small place on the plan of a large one—a cottage built in the form of a mansion, having a central hall with a wooden gallery running round it, and rooms no bigger than closets to support this introduction. It stood on a slope so solitary, and surrounded by trees so dense, that the birds who inhabited the boughs sang at strange hours, as if they hardly could distinguish night from day.

During the progress of repairs at this bower Barbara frequently visited it. Though so secluded by the dense growth, it was near the high road, and one day while looking over the fence she saw Lord Uplandtowers riding past. He saluted her courteously, yet with mechanical stiffness, and did not halt. Barbara went home, and continued to pray that she might never cease to love her husband. After that she sickened, and did not come out of doors again for a long time.

The year of education had extended to fourteen months, and the house was in order for Edmond's return to take up his abode there with Barbara, when, instead of the accustomed letter for her, came one to Sir John Grebe in the handwriting of the said tutor, informing him of a terrible catastrophe that had occurred to them at Venice. Mr Willowes and himself had attended the theatre one night during the Carnival of the preceding week, to witness the Italian comedy, when, owing to the carelessness of one of the candle-snuffers, the theatre had caught fire, and been burnt to the ground. Few persons had lost their lives, owing to the superhuman exertions of some of the audience in getting out the senseless sufferers; and, among them all, he who had risked his own life the most heroically was Mr Willowes. In re-entering for the fifth time to save his fellow-creatures some fiery beams had fallen upon him, and he had been given up for lost. He was, however, by the blessing of Providence, recovered, with the life still in him, though he was fearfully burnt; and by almost a miracle he seemed likely to survive, his constitution being wondrously sound. He was, of course, unable to write, but he was receiving the attention of several skilful surgeons. Further report would be made by the next mail or by private hand.

The tutor said nothing in detail of poor Willowes's sufferings, but as soon as the news was broken to Barbara she realized how intense they must have been, and her immediate instinct was to rush to his side, though, on consideration, the journey seemed impossible to her. Her health was by no means what it had been, and to post across Europe at that season of the year, or to traverse the Bay of Biscay in a sailing-craft, was an undertaking that would hardly be justified by the result. But she was anxious to go till, on reading to the end of the letter, her husband's tutor was found to hint very strongly against such a step if it should be contemplated, this being also the opinion of the surgeons. And though Willowes's comrade refrained from giving his reasons, they disclosed themselves plainly enough in the sequel.

The truth was that the worst of the wounds resulting from the fire had occurred to his head and face—that handsome face which had won her heart from her,—and both the tutor and the surgeons knew that for a sensitive young woman to see him before his wounds had healed would cause more misery to her by the shock than happiness to him by her ministrations.

Lady Grebe blurted out what Sir John and Barbara had thought, but had had too much delicacy to express.

'Sure, 'tis mighty hard for you, poor Barbara, that the one little gift he had to justify your rash choice of him—his wonderful good looks—should be taken away like this, to leave 'ee no excuse at all for your conduct in the world's eyes . . . Well, I wish you'd married t'other—that do I!' And the lady sighed.

'He'll soon get right again,' said her father soothingly.

Such remarks as the above were not often made; but they were frequent enough to cause Barbara an uneasy sense of self-stultification. She determined to hear them no longer; and the house at Yewsholt being ready and furnished, she withdrew thither with her maids, where for the first time she could feel mistress of a home that would be hers and her husband's exclusively, when he came.

After long weeks Willowes had recovered sufficiently to be able to write himself, and slowly and tenderly he enlightened her upon the full extent of his injuries. It was a mercy, he said, that he had not lost his sight entirely; but he was thankful to say that he still retained full vision in one eye, though the other was dark for ever. The sparing manner in which he meted out particulars of his condition told Barbara how appalling had been his experience. He was grateful for her assurance that nothing could change her; but feared she did not fully realize that he was so sadly disfigured as to make it doubtful if she would recognize him. However, in spite of all, his heart was as true to her as it ever had been.

Barbara saw from his anxiety how much lay behind. She replied that she submitted to the decrees of Fate, and would welcome him in any shape as soon as he could come. She told him of the pretty retreat in which she had taken up her abode, pending their joint occupation of it, and did not reveal how much she had sighed over the information that all his good looks were gone. Still less did she say that she felt a certain strangeness in awaiting him, the weeks they had lived together having been so short by comparison with the length of his absence.

Slowly drew on the time when Willowes found himself well enough to come home. He landed at Southampton, and posted thence towards Yewsholt. Barbara arranged to go out to meet him as far as Lornton Inn—the spot between the Forest and the Chase at which he had waited for night on the evening of their elopement. Thither she drove at the appointed hour in a little pony-chaise, presented her by her father on her birthday for her especial use in her new house; which vehicle she sent back on arriving at the inn, the plan agreed upon being that she should perform the return journey with her husband in his hired coach.

There was not much accommodation for a lady at this wayside tavern; but, as it was a fine evening in early summer, she did not mind—walking about outside, and straining her eyes along the highway for the expected one. But each cloud of dust that enlarged in the distance and drew near was found to disclose a conveyance other than his post-chaise. Barbara remained till the appointment was two hours passed, and then began to fear that owing to some adverse wind in the Channel he was not coming that night.

While waiting she was conscious of a curious trepidation that was not entirely solicitude, and did not amount to dread; her tense state of incertitude bordered both on disappointment and on relief. She had lived six or seven weeks with an imperfectly educated yet handsome husband whom now she had not seen for seventeen months, and who was so changed physically by an accident that she was assured she would hardly know him. Can we wonder at her compound state of mind?

But her immediate difficulty was to get away from Lornton Inn, for her situation was becoming embarrassing. Like too many of Barbara's actions, this drive had been undertaken without much reflection. Expecting to wait no more than a few minutes for her husband in his post-chaise, and to enter it with him, she had not hesitated to isolate herself by sending back her own little vehicle. She now found that, being so well known in this neighbourhood, her excursion to meet her long-absent husband was exciting great interest. She was conscious that more eyes were watching her from the inn-windows than met her own gaze. Barbara had decided to get home by hiring whatever kind of conveyance the tavern afforded, when, straining her eyes for the last time over the now darkening highway, she perceived yet another dust-cloud drawing near. She paused; a chariot ascended to the inn, and would have passed had not its occupant caught sight of her standing expectantly. The horses were checked on the instant.

'You here—and alone, my dear Mrs Willowes?' said Lord Upland-towers, whose carriage it was.

She explained what had brought her into this lonely situation; and, as he was going in the direction of her own home, she accepted his offer of a seat beside him. Their conversation was embarrassed and fragmentary at first; but when they had driven a mile or two she was surprised to find herself talking earnestly and warmly to him: her impulsiveness was in truth but the natural consequence of her late existence—a somewhat desolate one by reason of the strange marriage she had made; and there is no more indiscreet mood than that of a woman surprised into talk who has long been imposing upon herself a policy of reserve. Therefore her ingenuous heart rose with a bound into her throat when, in response to his leading questions, or rather hints, she allowed her troubles to leak out of her. Lord Uplandtowers took her quite to her own door, although he had driven three miles out of his way to do so; and in handing her down she heard from him a whisper of stern reproach: 'It need not have been thus if you had listened to me!'

She made no reply, and went indoors. There, as the evening wore away, she regretted more and more that she had been so friendly with Lord Uplandtowers. But he had launched himself upon her so un-expectedly: if she had only foreseen the meeting with him, what a careful line of conduct she would have marked out! Barbara broke into a perspiration of disquiet when she thought of her unreserve, and, in self-chastisement, resolved to sit up till midnight on the bare chance of Edmond's return; directing that supper should be laid for him, improbable as his arrival till the morrow was.

The hours went past, and there was dead silence in and round about Yewsholt Lodge, except for the soughing of the trees; till, when it was near upon midnight, she heard the noise of hoofs and wheels approaching the door. Knowing that it could only be her husband, Barbara instantly went into the hall to meet him. Yet she stood there not without a sensation of faintness, so many were the changes since their parting! And, owing to her casual encounter with Lord Upland-towers, his voice and image still remained with her, excluding Edmond, her husband, from the inner circle of her impressions.

But she went to the door, and the next moment a figure stepped inside, of which she knew the outline, but little besides. Her husband was attired in a flapping black cloak and slouched hat, appearing altogether as a foreigner, and not as the young English burgess who had left her side. When he came forward into the light of the lamp, she perceived with surprise, and almost with fright, that he wore a mask. At first she had not noticed this—there being nothing in its colour which would lead a casual observer to think he was looking on anything but a real countenance.

He must have seen her start of dismay at the unexpectedness of his appearance, for he said hastily: 'I did not mean to come in to you like this—I thought you would have been in bed. How good you are, dear Barbara!' He put his arm round her, but he did not attempt to kiss her.

'O Edmond—it *is* you?—it must be?' she said, with clasped hands, for though his figure and movement were almost enough to prove it, and the tones were not unlike the old tones, the enunciation was so altered as to seem that of a stranger.

'I am covered like this to hide myself from the curious eyes of the inn-servants and others,' he said, in a low voice. 'I will send back the carriage and join you in a moment.'

'You are quite alone?'

'Quite. My companion stopped at Southampton.'

The wheels of the post-chaise rolled away as she entered the dining-room, where the supper was spread; and presently he rejoined her there. He had removed his cloak and hat, but the mask was still retained; and she could now see that it was of special make, of some flexible material like silk, coloured so as to represent flesh; it joined naturally to the front hair, and was otherwise cleverly executed.

'Barbara—you look ill,' he said, removing his glove, and taking her hand.

'Yes—I have been ill,' said she.

'Is this pretty little house ours?'

'O—yes.' She was hardly conscious of her words, for the hand he had ungloved in order to take hers was contorted, and had one or two of its fingers missing; while through the mask she discerned the twinkle of one eye only.

'I would give anything to kiss you, dearest, now at this moment!' he continued, with mournful passionateness. 'But I cannot—in this guise. The servants are abed, I suppose?'

'Yes,' said she. 'But I can call them? You will have some supper?'

He said he would have some, but that it was not necessary to call anybody at that hour. Thereupon they approached the table, and sat down, facing each other.

Despite Barbara's scared state of mind, it was forced upon her notice that her husband trembled, as if he feared the impression he was producing, or was about to produce, as much as, or more than, she. He drew nearer, and took her hand again.

'I had this mask made at Venice,' he began, in evident embarrassment. 'My darling Barbara—my dearest wife—do you think you—will mind when I take it off? You will not dislike me—will you?'

'O Edmond, of course I shall not mind,' said she. 'What has happened to you is our misfortune; but I am prepared for it.'

'Are you sure you are prepared?'

'O yes! You are my husband.'

'You really feel quite confident that nothing external can affect you?' he said again, in a voice rendered uncertain by his agitation.

'I think I am—quite,' she answered faintly.

He bent his head. 'I hope, I hope you are,' he whispered.

In the pause which followed, the ticking of the clock in the hall seemed to grow loud; and he turned a little aside to remove the mask. She breathlessly awaited the operation, which was one of some tediousness, watching him one moment, averting her face the next; and when it was done she shut her eyes at the dreadful spectacle that was revealed. A quick spasm of horror had passed through her; but though she quailed she forced herself to regard him anew, repressing the cry that would naturally have escaped from her ashy lips. Unable to look at him longer, Barbara sank down on the floor beside her chair, covering her eyes.

'You cannot look at me!' he groaned in a hopeless way. 'I am too terrible an object even for you to bear! I knew it; yet I hoped against it. O, this is a bitter fate—curse the skill of those Venetian surgeons who saved me alive! . . . Look up, Barbara,' he continued beseechingly; 'view me completely; say you loathe me, if you do loathe me, and settle the case between us for ever!'

His unhappy wife pulled herself together for a desperate strain. He was her Edmond; he had done her no wrong; he had suffered. A momentary devotion to him helped her, and lifting her eyes as bidden she regarded this human remnant, this *écorché*, a second time. But the sight was too much. She again involuntarily looked aside and shuddered.

'Do you think you can get used to this?' he said. 'Yes or no! Can you bear such a thing of the charnel-house near you? Judge for yourself, Barbara. Your Adonis, your matchless man, has come to this!'

The poor lady stood beside him motionless, save for the restlessness of her eyes. All her natural sentiments of affection and pity were driven clean out of her by a sort of panic; she had just the same sense of dismay and fearfulness that she would have had in the presence of an apparition. She could nohow fancy this to be her chosen one—the man she had loved; he was metamorphosed to a specimen of another species. 'I do not loathe you,' she said with trembling. 'But I am so horrified—so overcome! Let me recover myself. Will you sup now? And while you do so may I go to my room to—regain my old feeling for you? I will try, if I may leave you awhile? Yes, I will try!'

Without waiting for an answer from him, and keeping her gaze carefully averted, the frightened woman crept to the door and out of the room. She heard him sit down to the table, as if to begin supper; though, Heaven knows, his appetite was slight enough after a reception which had confirmed his worst surmises. When Barbara had ascended the stairs and arrived in her chamber she sank down, and buried her face in the coverlet of the bed.

Thus she remained for some time. The bedchamber was over the dining-room, and presently as she knelt Barbara heard Willowes thrust back his chair, and rise to go into the hall. In five minutes that figure would probably come up the stairs and confront her again; it,—this new and terrible form, that was not her husband's. In the loneliness of this night, with neither maid nor friend beside her, she lost all self-control, and at the first sound of his footstep on the stairs, without so much as flinging a cloak round her, she flew from the room, ran along the gallery to the back staircase, which she descended, and, unlocking the back door, let herself out. She scarcely was aware what she had done till she found herself in the greenhouse, crouching on a flower-stand.

Here she remained, her great timid eyes strained through the glass upon the garden without, and her skirts gathered up, in fear of the field-mice which sometimes came there. Every moment she dreaded to hear footsteps which she ought by law to have longed for, and a voice that should have been as music to her soul. But Edmond Willowes came not that way. The nights were getting short at this season, and soon the dawn appeared, and the first rays of the sun. By daylight she had less fear than in the dark. She thought she could meet him, and accustom herself to the spectacle.

So the much-tried young woman unfastened the door of the hot-house, and went back by the way she had emerged a few hours ago. Her poor husband was probably in bed and asleep, his journey having been long; and she made as little noise as possible in her entry. The house was just as she had left it, and she looked about in the hall for his cloak and hat, but she could not see them; nor did she perceive the small trunk which had been all that he brought with him, his heavier baggage having been left at Southampton for the road-waggon. She summoned courage to mount the stairs; the bedroom-door was open as she had left it. She fearfully peeped round; the bed had not been pressed. Perhaps he had lain down on the dining-room sofa. She descended and entered; he was not there. On the table beside his unsoiled plate lay a note, hastily written on the leaf of a pocket-book. It was something like this:

My ever-beloved Wife.—The effect that my forbidding appearance has produced upon you was one which I foresaw as quite possible. I hoped against it, but foolishly so. I was aware that no *human* love could survive such a catastrophe. I confess I thought yours *divine*; but, after so long an absence, there could not be left sufficient warmth to overcome the too natural first aversion. It was an experiment, and it has failed. I do not blame you; perhaps, even, it is better so. Good-bye. I leave England for one year. You will see me again at the expiration of that time, if I live. Then I will ascertain your true feeling; and, if it be against me, go away for ever.

E.W.

On recovering from her surprise, Barbara's remorse was such that she felt herself absolutely unforgiveable. She should have regarded him as an afflicted being, and not have been this slave to mere eyesight, like a child. To follow him and entreat him to return was her first thought. But on making inquiries she found that nobody had seen him: he had silently disappeared.

More than this, to undo the scene of last night was impossible. Her terror had been too plain, and he was a man unlikely to be coaxed back by her efforts to do her duty. She went and confessed to her parents all that had occurred; which, indeed, soon became known to more persons than those of her own family.

The year passed, and he did not return; and it was doubted if he were alive. Barbara's contrition for her unconquerable repugnance was now such that she longed to build a church-aisle, or erect a monument, and devote herself to deeds of charity for the remainder of her days. To that end she made inquiry of the excellent parson under whom she sat on Sundays, at a vertical distance of a dozen feet. But he could only adjust his wig and tap his snuff-box; for such was the lukewarm state of religion in those days, that not an aisle, steeple, porch, east window, Ten-Commandment board, lion-and-unicorn, or brass candlestick, was required anywhere at all in the neighbourhood as a votive offering from a distracted soul—the last century contrasting greatly in this respect with the happy times in which we live, when urgent appeals for contributions to such objects pour in by every morning's post, and nearly all churches have been made to look like new pennies. As the poor lady could not ease her conscience this way, she determined at least to be charitable, and soon had the satisfaction of finding her porch thronged every morning by the raggedest, idlest, most drunken, hypocritical, and worthless tramps in Christendom.

But human hearts are as prone to change as the leaves of the creeper on the wall, and in the course of time, hearing nothing of her husband, Barbara could sit unmoved whilst her mother and friends said in her hearing, 'Well, what has happened is for the best.' She began to think so herself, for even now she could not summon up that lopped and mutilated form without a shiver, though whenever her mind flew back to her early wedded days, and the man who had stood beside her then, a thrill of tenderness moved her, which if quickened by his living presence might have become strong. She was young and inexperienced, and had hardly on his late return grown out of the capricious fancies of girlhood.

But he did not come again, and when she thought of his word that he would return once more, if living, and how unlikely he was to break his word, she gave him up for dead. So did her parents; so also did another person—that man of silence, of irresistible incisiveness, of still countenance, who was as awake as seven sentinels when he seemed to be as sound asleep as the figures on his family monument. Lord Uplandtowers, though not yet thirty, had chuckled like a caustic fogey of threescore when he heard of Barbara's terror and flight at her husband's return, and of the latter's prompt departure. He felt pretty sure, however, that Willowes, despite his hurt feelings, would have reappeared to claim his bright-eyed property if he had been alive at the end of the twelve months.

As there was no husband to live with her, Barbara had relinquished the house prepared for them by her father, and taken up her abode anew at Chene Manor, as in the days of her girlhood. By degrees the episode with Edmond Willowes seemed but a fevered dream, and as the months grew to years Lord Uplandtowers' friendship with the people at Chene—which had somewhat cooled after Barbara's elopement—revived considerably, and he again became a frequent visitor there. He could not make the most trivial alteration or improvement at Knollingwood Hall, where he lived, without riding off to consult with his friend Sir John at Chene; and thus putting himself frequently under her eyes, Barbara grew accustomed to him, and talked to him as freely as to a brother. She even began to look up to him as a person of authority, judgement, and prudence; and though his severity on the bench towards poachers, smugglers, and turnip-stealers was matter of common notoriety, she trusted that much of what was said might be misrepresentation.

Thus they lived on till her husband's absence had stretched to years, and there could be no longer any doubt of his death. A passionless manner of renewing his addresses seemed no longer out of place in Lord Uplandtowers. Barbara did not love him, but hers was essentially one of those sweet-pea or with-wind natures which require a twig of stouter fibre than its own to hang upon and bloom. Now, too, she was older, and admitted to herself that a man whose ancestor had run scores of Saracens through and through in fighting for the site of the Holy Sepulchre was a more desirable husband, socially considered, than one who could only claim with certainty to know that his father and grandfather were respectable burgesses.

Sir John took occasion to inform her that she might legally consider herself a widow; and, in brief, Lord Uplandtowers carried his point with her, and she married him, though he could never get her to own that she loved him as she had loved Willowes. In my childhood I knew an old lady whose mother saw the wedding, and she said that when Lord and Lady Uplandtowers drove away from her father's house in the evening it was in a coach-and-four, and that my lady was dressed in green and silver, and wore the gayest hat and feather that ever were seen; though whether it was that the green did not suit her complexion, or otherwise, the Countess looked pale, and the reverse of blooming. After their marriage her husband took her to London, and she saw the gaieties of a season there; then they returned to Knollingwood Hall, and thus a year passed away.

Before their marriage her husband had seemed to care but little about her inability to love him passionately. 'Only let me win you,' he had said, 'and I will submit to all that.' But now her lack of warmth seemed to irritate him, and he conducted himself towards her with a resentfulness which led to her passing many hours with him in painful silence. The heir-presumptive to the title was a remote relative, whom Lord Uplandtowers did not exclude from the dislike he entertained towards many persons and things besides, and he had set his mind upon a lineal successor. He blamed her much that there was no promise of this, and asked her what she was good for.

On a particular day in her gloomy life a letter, addressed to her as Mrs Willowes, reached Lady Uplandtowers from an unexpected quarter. A sculptor in Pisa, knowing nothing of her second marriage, informed her that the long-delayed life-size statue of Mr Willowes, which, when her husband left that city, he had been directed to retain till it was sent for, was still in his studio. As his commission had not wholly been paid, and the statue was taking up room he could ill spare, he should be glad to have the debt cleared off, and directions where to forward the figure. Arriving at a time when the Countess was beginning to have little secrets (of a harmless kind, it is true) from her husband, by reason of their growing estrangement, she replied to this letter without saying a word to Lord Uplandtowers, sending off the balance that was owing to the sculptor, and telling him to despatch the statue to her without delay.

It was some weeks before it arrived at Knollingwood Hall, and, by a singular coincidence, during the interval she received the first absolutely conclusive tidings of her Edmond's death. It had taken place years before, in a foreign land, about six months after their parting, and had been induced by the sufferings he had already undergone, coupled with much depression of spirit, which had caused him to succumb to a slight ailment. The news was sent her in a brief and formal letter from some relative of Willowes's in another part of England.

Her grief took the form of passionate pity for his misfortunes, and of reproach to herself for never having been able to conquer her aversion to his latter image by recollection of what Nature had originally made him. The sad spectacle that had gone from earth had never been her Edmond at all to her. O that she could have met him as he was at first! Thus Barbara thought. It was only a few days later that a waggon with two horses, containing an immense packing-case, was seen at breakfast-time both by Barbara and her husband to drive round to the back of the house, and by-and-by they were informed that a case labelled 'Sculpture' had arrived for her ladyship.

'What can that be?' said Lord Uplandtowers.

'It is the statue of poor Edmond, which belongs to me, but has never been sent till now,' she answered.

'Where are you going to put it?' asked he.

'I have not decided,' said the Countess. 'Anywhere, so that it will not annoy you.'

'Oh, it won't annoy me,' says he.

When it had been unpacked in a back room of the house, they went to examine it. The statue was a full-length figure, in the purest Carrara marble, representing Edmond Willowes in all his original beauty, as he had stood at parting from her when about to set out on his travels; a specimen of manhood almost perfect in every line and contour. The work had been carried out with absolute fidelity.

'Phoebus-Apollo, sure,' said the Earl of Uplandtowers, who had never seen Willowes, real or represented, till now.

Barbara did not hear him. She was standing in a sort of trance before the first husband, as if she had no consciousness of the other husband at her side. The mutilated features of Willowes had disappeared from her mind's eye; this perfect being was really the man she had loved, and not that later pitiable figure; in whom tenderness and truth should have seen this image always, but had not done so.

It was not till Lord Uplandtowers said roughly, 'Are you going to stay here all the morning worshipping him?' that she roused herself.

Her husband had not till now the least suspicion that Edmond Willowes originally looked thus, and he thought how deep would have been his jealousy years ago if Willowes had been known to him. Returning to the Hall in the afternoon he found his wife in the gallery, whither the statue had been brought.

She was lost in reverie before it, just as in the morning.

'What are you doing?' he asked.

She started and turned. 'I am looking at my husb—my statue, to see if it is well done,' she stammered. 'Why should I not?'

'There's no reason why,' he said. 'What are you going to do with the monstrous thing? It can't stand here for ever.'

'I don't wish it,' she said. 'I'll find a place.'

In her boudoir there was a deep recess, and while the Earl was absent from home for a few days in the following week, she hired joiners from the village, who under her directions enclosed the recess with a panelled door. Into the tabernacle thus formed she had the statue placed, fastening the door with a lock, the key of which she kept in her pocket.

When her husband returned he missed the statue from the gallery, and, concluding that it had been put away out of deference to his feelings, made no remark. Yet at moments he noticed something on his lady's face which he had never noticed there before. He could not construe it; it was a sort of silent ecstasy, a reserved beatification. What had become of the statue he could not divine, and growing more and more curious, looked about here and there for it till, thinking of her private room, he went towards that spot. After knocking he heard the shutting of a door, and the click of a key; but when he entered his wife was sitting at work, on what was in those days called knotting. Lord Uplandtowers' eye fell upon the newly-painted door where the recess had formerly been.

'You have been carpentering in my absence then, Barbara,' he said carelessly.

'Yes, Uplandtowers.'

'Why did you go putting up such a tasteless enclosure as that—spoiling the handsome arch of the alcove?'

'I wanted more closet-room; and I thought that as this was my own apartment—'

'Of course,' he returned. Lord Uplandtowers knew now where the statue of young Willowes was.

One night, or rather in the smallest hours of the morning, he missed the Countess from his side. Not being a man of nervous imaginings he fell asleep again before he had much considered the matter, and the next morning had forgotten the incident. But a few nights later the same circumstances occurred. This time he fully roused himself; but before he had moved to search for her she returned to the chamber in her dressing-gown, carrying a candle, which she extinguished as she approached, deeming him asleep. He could discover from her breathing that she was strangely moved; but not on this occasion either did he reveal that he had seen her. Presently, when she had lain down, affecting to wake, he asked her some trivial questions. 'Yes, *Edmond*,' she replied absently.

Lord Uplandtowers became convinced that she was in the habit of leaving the chamber in this queer way more frequently than he had observed, and he determined to watch. The next midnight he feigned deep sleep, and shortly after perceived her stealthily rise and let herself out of the room in the dark. He slipped on some clothing and followed. At the further end of the corridor, where the clash of flint and steel would be out of the hearing of one in the bedchamber, she struck a light. He stepped aside into an empty room till she had lit a taper and had passed on to her boudoir. In a minute or two he followed. Arrived at the door of the boudoir, he beheld the door of the private recess open, and Barbara within it, standing with her arms clasped tightly round the neck of her Edmond, and her mouth on his. The shawl which she had thrown round her nightclothes had slipped from her shoulders, and her long white robe and pale face lent her the blanched appearance of a second statue embracing the first. Between her kisses, she apostrophized it in a low murmur of infantine tenderness:

'My only love—how could I be so cruel to you, my perfect one—so good and true—I am ever faithful to you, despite my seeming infidelity! I always think of you—dream of you—during the long hours of the day, and in the night-watches! O Edmond, I am always yours!' Such words as these, intermingled with sobs, and streaming tears, and dishevelled hair, testified to an intensity of feeling in his wife which Lord Uplandtowers had not dreamed of her possessing.

'Ha, ha!' says he to himself. 'This is where we evaporate—this is where my hopes of a successor in the title dissolve—ha! ha! This must be seen to, verily!'

Lord Uplandtowers was a subtle man when once he set himself to strategy; though in the present instance he never thought of the simple stratagem of constant tenderness. Nor did he enter the room and surprise his wife as a blunderer would have done, but went back to his chamber as silently as he had left it. When the Countess returned thither, shaken by spent sobs and sighs, he appeared to be soundly sleeping as usual. The next day he began his countermoves by making inquiries as to the whereabouts of the tutor who had travelled with his wife's first husband; this gentleman, he found, was now master of a grammar-school at no great distance from Knollingwood. At the first convenient moment Lord Uplandtowers went thither and obtained an interview with the said gentleman. The schoolmaster was much gratified by a visit from such an influential neighbour, and was ready to communicate anything that his lordship desired to know.

After some general conversation on the school and its progress, the visitor observed that he believed the schoolmaster had once travelled a good deal with the unfortunate Mr Willowes, and had been with him on the occasion of his accident. He, Lord Uplandtowers, was interested in knowing what had really happened at that time, and had often thought of inquiring. And then the Earl not only heard by word of mouth as much as he wished to know, but, their chat becoming more intimate, the schoolmaster drew upon paper a sketch of the disfigured head, explaining with bated breath various details in the representation.

'It was very strange and terrible!' said Lord Uplandtowers, taking the sketch in his hand. 'Neither nose nor ears, nor lips scarcely!'

A poor man in the town nearest to Knollingwood Hall, who combined the art of sign-painting with ingenious mechanical occupations, was sent for by Lord Uplandtowers to come to the Hall on a day in that week when the Countess had gone on a short visit to her parents. His employer made the man understand that the business in which his assistance was demanded was to be considered private, and money insured the observance of this request. The lock of the cupboard was picked, and the ingenious mechanic and painter, assisted by the schoolmaster's sketch, which Lord Uplandtowers had put in his pocket, set to work upon the god-like countenance of the statue under my lord's direction. What the fire had maimed in the original the chisel maimed in the copy. It was a fiendish disfigurement, ruthlessly carried out, and was rendered still more shocking by being tinted to the hues of life, as life had been after the wreck.

Six hours after, when the workman was gone, Lord Uplandtowers looked upon the result, and smiled grimly, and said:

'A statue should represent a man as he appeared in life, and that's as he appeared. Ha! ha! But 'tis done to good purpose, and not idly.'

He locked the door of the closet with a skeleton key, and went his way to fetch the Countess home.

That night she slept, but he kept awake. According to the tale, she murmured soft words in her dream; and he knew that the tender converse of her imaginings was held with one whom he had supplanted but in name. At the end of her dream the Countess of Uplandtowers awoke and arose, and then the enactment of former nights was repeated. Her husband remained still and listened. Two strokes sounded from the clock in the pediment without, when, leaving the chamber-door ajar, she passed along the corridor to the other end, where, as usual, she obtained a light. So deep was the silence that he could even from his bed hear her softly blowing the tinder to a glow after striking the steel. She moved on into the boudoir, and he heard, or fancied he heard, the turning of the key in the closet-door. The next moment there came from that direction a loud and prolonged shriek, which resounded to the furthest corners of the house. It was repeated, and there was the noise of a heavy fall.

Lord Uplandtowers sprang out of bed. He hastened along the dark corridor to the door of the boudoir, which stood ajar, and, by the light of the candle within, saw his poor young Countess lying in a heap in her nightdress on the floor of the closet. When he reached her side he found that she had fainted, much to the relief of his fears that matters were worse. He quickly shut up and locked in the hated image which had done the mischief, and lifted his wife in his arms, where in a few instants she opened her eyes. Pressing her face to his without saying a word, he carried her back to her room, endeavouring as he went to disperse her terrors by a laugh in her ear, oddly compounded of causticity, predilection, and brutality.

'Ho—ho—ho!' says he: 'Frightened, dear one, hey? What a baby 'tis! Only a joke, sure, Barbara—a splendid joke! But a baby should not go to closets at midnight to look for the ghost of the dear departed! If it do it must expect to be terrified at his aspect—ho—ho—ho!'

When she was in her bed-chamber, and had quite come to herself, though her nerves were still much shaken, he spoke to her more sternly. 'Now, my lady, answer me: do you love him—eh?'

'No—no!' she faltered, shuddering, with her expanded eyes fixed on her husband. 'He is too terrible—no, no!'

'You are sure?'

'Quite sure!' replied the poor broken-spirited Countess.

But her natural elasticity asserted itself. Next morning he again inquired of her: 'Do you love him now?' She quailed under his gaze, but did not reply.

'That means that you do still, by God!' he continued.

'It means that I will not tell an untruth, and do not wish to incense my lord,' she answered, with dignity.

'Then suppose we go and have another look at him?' As he spoke, he suddenly took her by the wrist, and turned as if to lead her towards the ghastly closet.

'No—no! O—no!' she cried, and her desperate wriggle out of his hand revealed that the fright of the night had left more impression upon her delicate soul than superficially appeared.

'Another dose or two, and she will be cured,' he said to himself.

It was now so generally known that the Earl and Countess were not in accord, that he took no great trouble to disguise his deeds in relation to this matter. During the day he ordered four men with ropes and rollers to attend him in the boudoir. When they arrived, the closet was open, and the upper part of the statue tied up in canvas. He had it taken to the sleeping-chamber. What followed is more or less matter of conjecture. The story, as told to me, goes on to say that, when Lady Uplandtowers retired with him that night, she saw facing the foot of the heavy oak four-poster, a tall dark wardrobe, which had not stood there before; but she did not ask what its presence meant.

'I have had a little whim,' he explained when they were in the dark.

'Have you?' says she.

'To erect a little shrine, as it may be called.'

'A little shrine?'

'Yes; to one whom we both equally adore—eh? I'll show you what it contains.'

He pulled a cord which hung covered by the bedcurtains, and the doors of the wardrobe slowly opened, disclosing that the shelves within had been removed throughout, and the interior adapted to receive the ghastly figure, which stood there as it had stood in the boudoir, but with a wax candle burning on each side of it to throw the cropped and distorted features into relief. She clutched him, uttered a low scream, and buried her head in the bedclothes. 'O, take it away—please take it away!' she implored.

'All in good time; namely, when you love me best,' he returned calmly. 'You don't quite yet—eh?'

'I don't know—I think—O Uplandtowers, have mercy—I cannot bear it—O, in pity, take it away!'

'Nonsense; one gets accustomed to anything. Take another gaze.'

In short, he allowed the doors to remain unclosed at the foot of the bed, and the wax-tapers burning; and such was the strange fascination of the grisly exhibition that a morbid curiosity took possession of the Countess as she lay, and, at his repeated request, she did again look out from the coverlet, shuddered, hid her eyes, and looked again, all the while begging him to take it away, or it would drive her out of her senses. But he would not do so yet, and the wardrobe was not locked till dawn.

The scene was repeated the next night. Firm in enforcing his ferocious correctives, he continued the treatment till the nerves of the poor lady were quivering in agony under the virtuous tortures inflicted by her lord, to bring her truant heart back to faithfulness.

The third night, when the scene had opened as usual, and she lay staring with immense wild eyes at the horrid fascination, on a sudden she gave an unnatural laugh; she laughed more and more, staring at the image, till she literally shrieked with laughter: then there was silence, and he found her to have become insensible. He thought she had fainted, but soon saw that the event was worse: she was in an epileptic fit. He started up, dismayed by the sense that, like many other subtle personages, he had been too exacting for his own interests. Such love as he was capable of, though rather a selfish gloating than a cherishing solicitude, was fanned into life on the instant. He closed the wardrobe with the pulley, clasped her in his arms, took her gently to the window, and did all he could to restore her.

It was a long time before the Countess came to herself, and when she did so, a considerable change seemed to have taken place in her emotions. She flung her arms around him, and with gasps of fear abjectly kissed him many times, at last bursting into tears. She had never wept in this scene before.

'You'll take it away, dearest—you will!' she begged plaintively.

'If you love me.'

'I do—oh, I do!'

'And hate him, and his memory?'

'Yes—yes!'

'Thoroughly?'

'I cannot endure recollection of him!' cried the poor Countess slavishly. 'It fills me with shame—how could I ever be so depraved! I'll never behave badly again, Uplandtowers; and you will never put the hated statue again before my eyes?'

He felt that he could promise with perfect safety. 'Never,' said he.

'And then I'll love you,' she returned eagerly, as if dreading lest the scourge should be applied anew. 'And I'll never, never dream of thinking a single thought that seems like faithlessness to my marriage vow.'

The strange thing now was that this fictitious love wrung from her by terror took on, through mere habit of enactment, a certain quality of reality. A servile mood of attachment to the Earl became distinctly visible in her contemporaneously with an actual dislike for her late husband's memory. The mood of attachment grew and continued when the statue was removed. A permanent revulsion was operant in her, which intensified as time wore on. How fright could have effected such a change of idiosyncrasy learned physicians alone can say; but I believe such cases of reactionary instinct are not unknown.

The upshot was that the cure became so permanent as to be itself a new disease. She clung to him so tightly that she would not willingly be out of his sight for a moment. She would have no sitting-room apart from his, though she could not help starting when he entered suddenly to her. Her eyes were well-nigh always fixed upon him. If he drove out, she wished to go with him; his slightest civilities to other women made her frantically jealous; till at length her very fidelity became a burden to him, absorbing his time, and curtailing his liberty, and causing him to curse and swear. If he ever spoke sharply to her now, she did not revenge herself by flying off to a mental world of her own; all that affection for another, which had provided her with a resource, was now a cold black cinder.

From that time the life of this scared and enervated lady—whose existence might have been developed to so much higher purpose but for the ignoble ambition of her parents and the conventions of the time—was one of obsequious amativeness towards a perverse and cruel man. Little personal events came to her in quick succession— half a dozen, eight, nine, ten such events, in brief, she bore him no less than eleven children in the nine following years, but half of them came prematurely into the world, or died a few days old; only one, a girl, attained to maturity; she in after years became the wife of the Honourable Mr Beltonleigh, who was created Lord d'Almaine, as may be remembered.

There was no living son and heir. At length, completely worn out in mind and body, Lady Uplandtowers was taken abroad by her husband, to try the effect of a more genial climate upon her wasted frame. But nothing availed to strengthen her, and she died at Florence, a few months after her arrival in Italy.

Contrary to expectation, the Earl of Uplandtowers did not marry again. Such affection as existed in him—strange, hard, brutal as it was—seemed untransferable, and the title, as is known, passed at his death to his nephew. Perhaps it may not be so generally known that, during the enlargement of the Hall for the sixth Earl, while digging in the grounds for the new foundations, the broken fragments of a marble statue were unearthed. They were submitted to various anti-quaries, who said that, so far as the damaged pieces would allow them to form an opinion, the statue seemed to be that of a mutilated Roman satyr; or, if not, an allegorical figure of Death. Only one or two old inhabitants guessed whose statue those fragments had composed.

I should have added that, shortly after the death of the Countess, an excellent sermon was preached by the Dean of Melchester, the subject of which, though names were not mentioned, was unquestion-ably suggested by the aforesaid events. He dwelt upon the folly of indulgence in sensuous love for a handsome form merely; and showed that the only rational and virtuous growths of that affection were those based upon intrinsic worth. In the case of the tender but somewhat shallow lady whose life I have related, there is no doubt that an infatuation for the person of young Willowes was the chief feeling that induced her to marry him; which was the more deplor-able in that his beauty, by all tradition, was the least of his recom-mendations, every report bearing out the inference that he must have been a man of steadfast nature, bright intelligence, and promising life.

MARCEL SCHWOB

Bloody Blanche

When Guillaume de Flavy grew weary of warfare and politics, he decided to increase his fortunes by taking a wife. He was a big strong man, broad-shouldered, with a hairy and bosomy chest. He could grab two armed knights, one with each hand, and force them both to the ground. He used to strap on his leggings and go around his lands in person, right through the mire, clapping his heavy hand upon the backs of the muddied men who stooped among the furrows. His broad face was flushed with the blood that always throbbed at his temples; and he used to crack the bones between his teeth when eating meat.

One day, riding within the borders of his meadows near Rheims, he saw the fields belonging to Robert d'Ovrebreuc. He dismounted and entered the great hall of the house. The enormous chests arranged along the walls, each one big enough to climb into, looked shabby; the dining table was rickety, the fire-irons were rusty, and the spit was coated with dirt an inch thick. Here and there he noticed a cobbler's apron, awls, and some flat hammers; and there was a man sitting cross-legged in a corner darning a coarse linen shirt. But then, squatting on the hearthstones, staring directly at him in surprise, with golden hair strewn about her pallid face, a little girl turned her head towards Guillaume de Flavy. She might have been ten years old: her chest was flat, her limbs scrawny, her hands tiny; but her mouth was a woman's, sliced across her pale face like a bloody gash.

It was Blanche d'Ovrebreuc, whose father had within the last few days succeeded to the title of vicomte d'Acy. Hump-backed and long in the beard, his hands now fit only for handling tools, he regarded his fiefs with the startled and worried appearance of a man handling a dangerous object. The English squire Jacques de Béthune, who served under Luxembourg, had already come asking for his daughter, but her father was undecided, not knowing whether he could expect a better offer. The estate he had inherited was saddled with debts of three hundred thousand crowns, the late vicomte d'Acy having himself frittered away a good ten thousand. Perhaps the English or the Luxemburgers could take care of that.

But it was Guillaume de Flavy who carried little Blanche away. He paid off the debts in order to keep hold of the lands. Once he had wed her legally, he promised to delay their true marriage for three years. And so, being an impressive-looking man, he got his hands on d'Acy's estates and on this scrawny, lawless child. Three months later little Blanche was wandering around the castle like a diseased cat, scowling through deadened eyes, having undergone the cruel nuptials of Guillaume de Flavy.

She did not, and could not, understand, being so very different in years and in nature. The man was hard on her, as he was on his barber: at mealtimes, when he had wiped his mouth on the back of his hand, he flung the food he no longer wanted in the grovelling barber's face. He yelled and cursed continually, keeping his wine and victuals in his own clutches. He would gather all the plates in front of him, leaving Blanche's father and mother at each end of the table. The mother was already feeble-minded and skeletal—she lived on for a while, scarcely ever eating or speaking, old and incoherent, then became sickly pale, and died. The father, wasting away as if he had taken poison, signed some deeds in Flavy's favour, under the influence of drink: he had given up his debt-encumbered estates, and now rubbed his hands together purring over his handsome pension. But now that he was no longer fed, he wanted money. The poor frightened creature protested feebly, and composed in his trembling hand a list of complaints to the king. Guillaume intercepted these papers; the old man wailed, and the servants put him in a dungeon. Letting some daylight into it a month later, they found a dried-up corpse, its teeth stuck into a shoe from which the rats had gnawed away the toe.

Little Blanche became uncommonly greedy. She would eat sweets until she dropped, and her cruel red mouth was stuffed with plump pies and cream. Leaning over the table with her eyes up against her food, always staring glassily, she would gobble away at great speed; then she would throw back her head and gulp down great mouthfuls of Burgundy, bringing a visible wave of pleasure through her face. She would upend a goblet of wine down into her gaping mouth, hold it in her puffed-up cheeks without swallowing, and squirt it out into the faces of the guests like a living fountain. After the meal, she would stagger to her feet, fuddled with drink, and do it against the wall standing up like a man.

These habits appealed to Aurbandac the Bastard, a swarthy and sinister man whose eyebrows met in a straight line over his nose. He often came to see Flavy, who was a kinsman, and whose lands he coveted impatiently. Lithe, wiry, strong as steel in arms and legs, he cunningly sized up Guillaume's cumbersome body. But little Blanche was not aroused by him; so he delicately raised the subject of her clothes, expressing his surprise to see her still wearing her wedding gown, for he could tell that she had grown since then. He mentioned some young townswomen who had scarlet dresses of Mechlin lace and squirrel-fur linings, with long sleeves and a hood trailing red or green silks down to the ground from its elongated peak. She listened as if he were telling her about a doll's clothes. Then Aurbandac the Bastard picked up a glass to join her in a toast, and got her drinking and laughing, plying her with sweets and poking fun at her husband, so that she splashed the wine about like a bird bathing and flapping in a puddle.

The barber, his long face scarred by mutton-bones, leant between them, at the Bastard's ear. They plotted to seize the castle: it would be the Bastard's to keep, while the wife in her innocence would be anyone's, so long as she had the key to the cellar and the pantry.

One evening, Guillaume de Flavy injured his face, tripping on the threshold and opening up a wound across his cheek and nose. He called out for the barber, who instantly brought in strange-smelling medicated bandages. As the night wore on, Guillaume's face bulged up: his tightly stretched skin was turning white with brown flecks, his protruding eyes were running all the time, and his wound looked loathesomely gangrenous.

Throughout the next morning he stayed in an armchair, howling with pain. Little Blanche seemed to be so terrified that she forgot to drink; and from the other end of the room she watched Guillaume with her limpid eyes, while her bright red lips twitched feebly.

Hardly had Guillaume gone upstairs to bed, watched over by the squire Bastoigne, when the castle echoed with a thousand slight noises. Blanche listened, with one ear to the door and a finger pressed to her lips. A muffled clashing of coats of mail could be heard, the dull jarring of arms, the creaking of the grille to the heavy postern-gate, and an unaccustomed crackling in the courtyard; a number of mysterious lights from lanterns came and went. Meanwhile the pitch torches in the great hall where joints of meat were always served up burned with an upright flame, sending a long thread of smoke up through the placid air.

Blanche climbed the stairs to her husband's bedchamber on childish tiptoes; he was sleeping on his back, his puffed-up features heavily bandaged and facing the rafters. Bastoigne left, because Blanche made as if to get into bed. And in fact she did slip into it, clasping that fearsome head in her arms and fondling it. Guillaume was breathing with difficulty, in fitful gasps. Then little Blanche threw herself across him, snatched the pillow, held it firmly on to his swaddled face, and then slid open a Judas-trap above the bed, which was usually kept sealed up.

The swarthy head of the Bastard poked through it, as he crept in cautiously. With one bound, he was kneeling on Guillaume's chest, and he bludgeoned him twice, then three times, with a cloven staff he carried with him. The man burst out of the sheets, sending out a dreadful yell from his swollen mouth. But as Bastoigne opened the door, the barber emerged from under the bed and tackled him; and the Bastard slit Guillaume's throat with the broad dagger he wore on his belt. The corpse jerked upright and rolled on to the ground, pulling little Blanche with it; she stayed there on the floor, pinned down by the still-warm corpse, drenched in the tepid blood flowing from its throat—because her dress was caught under her dying husband, and she was not strong enough to pull herself free.

While the Bastard dashed to the window, the barber considerately helped little Blanche to her feet; and since Blanche d'Ovrebreuc, vicomtesse d'Acy, was a religious soul, she wiped her mouth and her husband's face with her Picardy hood, placed it over his swollen face, and recited in her childish voice three *Our Fathers* and one *Hail Mary*, amid the yelling of the Bastard's men, who were busy ransacking the coffers.

CHARLOTTE PERKINS STETSON

The Yellow Wall-Paper (1892)

It is very seldom that mere ordinary people like John and myself secure ancestral halls for the summer.

A colonial mansion, a hereditary estate, I would say a haunted house, and reach the height of romantic felicity—but that would be asking too much of fate!

Still I will proudly declare that there is something queer about it.

Else, why should it be let so cheaply? And why have stood so long untenanted?

John laughs at me, of course, but one expects that in marriage.

John is practical in the extreme. He has no patience with faith, an intense horror of superstition, and he scoffs openly at any talk of things not to be felt and seen and put down in figures.

John is a physician, and *perhaps*—(I would not say it to a living soul, of course, but this is dead paper and a great relief to my mind) —*perhaps* that is one reason I do not get well faster.

You see he does not believe I am sick!

And what can one do?

If a physician of high standing, and one's own husband, assures friends and relatives that there is really nothing the matter with one but temporary nervous depression—a slight hysterical tendency— what is one to do?

My brother is also a physician, and also of high standing, and he says the same thing.

So I take phosphates or phosphites—whichever it is, and tonics, and journeys, and air, and exercise, and am absolutely forbidden to 'work' until I am well again.

Personally, I disagree with their ideas.

Personally, I believe that congenial work, with excitement and change, would do me good.

But what is one to do?

I did write for a while in spite of them; but it *does* exhaust me a good deal—having to be so sly about it, or else meet with heavy opposition.

I sometimes fancy that in my condition if I had less opposition and more society and stimulus—but John says the very worst thing I can do is to think about my condition, and I confess it always makes me feel bad.

So I will let it alone and talk about the house.

The most beautiful place! It is quite alone, standing well back from the road, quite three miles from the village. It makes me think of English places that you read about, for there are hedges and walls and gates that lock, and lots of separate little houses for the gardeners and people.

There is a *delicious* garden! I never saw such a garden—large and shady, full of box-bordered paths, and lined with long grape-covered arbors with seats under them.

There were greenhouses, too, but they are all broken now.

There was some legal trouble, I believe, something about the heirs and coheirs; anyhow, the place has been empty for years.

That spoils my ghostliness, I am afraid, but I don't care—there is something strange about the house—I can feel it.

I even said so to John one moonlight evening, but he said what I felt was a *draught*, and shut the window.

I get unreasonably angry with John sometimes. I'm sure I never used to be so sensitive. I think it is due to this nervous condition.

But John says if I feel so, I shall neglect proper self-control; so I take pains to control myself—before him, at least, and that makes me very tired.

I don't like our room a bit. I wanted one downstairs that opened on the piazza and had roses all over the window, and such pretty old-fashioned chintz hangings! but John would not hear of it.

He said there was only one window and not room for two beds, and no near room for him if he took another.

He is very careful and loving, and hardly lets me stir without special direction.

I have a schedule prescription for each hour in the day; he takes all care from me, and so I feel basely ungrateful not to value it more.

He said we came here solely on my account, that I was to have perfect rest and all the air I could get. 'Your exercise depends on your strength, my dear,' said he, 'and your food somewhat on your appetite; but air you can absorb all the time.' So we took the nursery at the top of the house.

It is a big, airy room, the whole floor nearly, with windows that look all ways, and air and sunshine galore. It was nursery first and then playroom and gymnasium, I should judge; for the windows are barred for little children, and there are rings and things in the walls.

The paint and paper look as if a boys' school had used it. It is stripped off—the paper—in great patches all around the head of my bed, about as far as I can reach, and in a great place on the other side of the room low down. I never saw a worse paper in my life.

One of those sprawling flamboyant patterns committing every artistic sin.

It is dull enough to confuse the eye in following, pronounced enough to constantly irritate and provoke study, and when you follow the lame uncertain curves for a little distance they suddenly commit suicide—plunge off at outrageous angles, destroy themselves in unheard of contradictions.

The color is repellent, almost revolting; a smouldering unclean yellow, strangely faded by the slow-turning sunlight.

It is a dull yet lurid orange in some places, a sickly sulphur tint in others.

No wonder the children hated it! I should hate it myself if I had to live in this room long.

There comes John, and I must put this away,—he hates to have me write a word.

We have been here two weeks, and I haven't felt like writing before, since that first day.

I am sitting by the window now, up in this atrocious nursery, and there is nothing to hinder my writing as much as I please, save lack of strength.

John is away all day, and even some nights when his cases are serious.

I am glad my case is not serious!

But these nervous troubles are dreadfully depressing.

John does not know how much I really suffer. He knows there is no *reason* to suffer, and that satisfies him.

Of course it is only nervousness. It does weigh on me so not to do my duty in any way!

I meant to be such a help to John, such a real rest and comfort, and here I am a comparative burden already!

Nobody would believe what an effort it is to do what little I am able,—to dress and entertain, and order things.

It is fortunate Mary is so good with the baby. Such a dear baby!

And yet I *cannot* be with him, it makes me so nervous.

I suppose John never was nervous in his life. He laughs at me so about this wall-paper!

At first he meant to repaper the room, but afterwards he said that I was letting it get the better of me, and that nothing was worse for a nervous patient than to give way to such fancies.

He said that after the wall-paper was changed it would be the heavy bedstead, and then the barred windows, and then that gate at the head of the stairs, and so on.

'You know the place is doing you good,' he said, 'and really, dear, I don't care to renovate the house just for a three months' rental.'

'Then do let us go downstairs,' I said, 'there are such pretty rooms there.'

Then he took me in his arms and called me a blessed little goose, and said he would go down to the cellar, if I wished, and have it whitewashed into the bargain.

But he is right enough about the beds and windows and things.

It is an airy and comfortable room as any one need wish, and, of course, I would not be so silly as to make him uncomfortable just for a whim.

I'm really getting quite fond of the big room, all but that horrid paper.

Out of one window I can see the garden, those mysterious deep-shaded arbors, the riotous old-fashioned flowers, and bushes and gnarly trees.

Out of another I get a lovely view of the bay and a little private wharf belonging to the estate. There is a beautiful shaded lane that runs down there from the house. I always fancy I see people walking in these numerous paths and arbors, but John has cautioned me not to give way to fancy in the least. He says that with my imaginative power and habit of story-making, a nervous weakness like mine is sure to lead to all manner of excited fancies, and that I ought to use my will and good sense to check the tendency. So I try.

I think sometimes that if I were only well enough to write a little it would relieve the press of ideas and rest me.

But I find I get pretty tired when I try.

It is so discouraging not to have any advice and companionship about my work. When I get really well, John says we will ask Cousin Henry and Julia down for a long visit; but he says he would as soon put fireworks in my pillow-case as to let me have those stimulating people about now.

I wish I could get well faster.

But I must not think about that. This paper looks to me as if it *knew* what a vicious influence it had!

There is a recurrent spot where the pattern lolls like a broken neck and two bulbous eyes stare at you upside down.

I get positively angry with the impertinence of it and the ever-lastingness. Up and down and sideways they crawl, and those absurd, unblinking eyes are everywhere. There is one place where two breadths didn't match, and the eyes go all up and down the line, one a little higher than the other.

I never saw so much expression in an inanimate thing before, and we all know how much expression they have! I used to lie awake as a child and get more entertainment and terror out of blank walls and plain furniture than most children could find in a toy-store.

I remember what a kindly wink the knobs of our big, old bureau used to have, and there was one chair that always seemed like a strong friend.

I used to feel that if any of the other things looked too fierce I could always hop into that chair and be safe.

The furniture in this room is no worse than inharmonious, however, for we had to bring it all from downstairs. I suppose when this was used as a playroom they had to take the nursery things out, and no wonder! I never saw such ravages as the children have made here.

The wall-paper, as I said before, is torn off in spots, and it sticketh closer than a brother—they must have had perseverance as well as hatred.

Then the floor is scratched and gouged and splintered, the plaster itself is dug out here and there, and this great heavy bed which is all we found in the room, looks as if it had been through the wars.

But I don't mind it a bit—only the paper.

There comes John's sister. Such a dear girl as she is, and so careful of me! I must not let her find me writing.

She is a perfect and enthusiastic housekeeper, and hopes for no better profession. I verily believe she thinks it is the writing which made me sick!

But I can write when she is out, and see her a long way off from these windows.

There is one that commands the road, a lovely shaded winding road, and one that just looks off over the country. A lovely country, too, full of great elms and velvet meadows.

This wall-paper has a kind of sub-pattern in a different shade, a particularly irritating one, for you can only see it in certain lights, and not clearly then.

But in the places where it isn't faded and where the sun is just so—I can see a strange, provoking, formless sort of figure, that seems to skulk about behind that silly and conspicuous front design.

There's sister on the stairs!

* * *

Well, the Fourth of July is over! The people are all gone and I am tired out. John thought it might do me good to see a little company, so we just had mother and Nellie and the children down for a week.

Of course I didn't do a thing. Jennie sees to everything now.

But it tired me all the same.

John says if I don't pick up faster he shall send me to Weir Mitchell in the fall.

But I don't want to go there at all. I had a friend who was in his hands once, and she says he is just like John and my brother, only more so!

Besides, it is such an undertaking to go so far.

I don't feel as if it was worth while to turn my hand over for anything, and I'm getting dreadfully fretful and querulous.

I cry at nothing, and cry most of the time.

Of course I don't when John is here, or anybody else, but when I am alone.

And I am alone a good deal just now. John is kept in town very often by serious cases, and Jennie is good and lets me alone when I want her to.

So I walk a little in the garden or down that lovely lane, sit on the porch under the roses, and lie down up here a good deal.

I'm getting really fond of the room in spite of the wall-paper. Perhaps *because* of the wall-paper.

It dwells in my mind so!

I lie here on this great immovable bed—it is nailed down, I believe—and follow that pattern about by the hour. It is as good as gymnastics, I assure you. I start, we'll say, at the bottom, down in the corner over there where it has not been touched, and I determine for the thousandth time that I *will* follow that pointless pattern to some sort of a conclusion.

I know a little of the principle of design, and I know this thing was not arranged on any laws of radiation, or alternation, or repetition, or symmetry, or anything else that I ever heard of.

It is repeated, of course, by the breadths, but not otherwise.

Looked at in one way each breadth stands alone, the bloated curves and flourishes—a kind of 'debased Romanesque' with *delirium tremens*—go waddling up and down in isolated columns of fatuity.

But, on the other hand, they connect diagonally, and the sprawling outlines run off in great slanting waves of optic horror, like a lot of wallowing seaweeds in full chase.

254

The whole thing goes horizontally, too, at least it seems so, and I exhaust myself in trying to distinguish the order of its going in that direction.

They have used a horizontal breadth for a frieze, and that adds wonderfully to the confusion.

There is one end of the room where it is almost intact, and there, when the crosslights fade and the low sun shines directly upon it, I can almost fancy radiation after all,—the interminable grotesques seem to form around a common center and rush off in headlong plunges of equal distraction.

It makes me tired to follow it. I will take a nap I guess.

I don't know why I should write this.

I don't want to.

I don't feel able.

And I know John would think it absurd. But I *must* say what I feel and think in some way—it is such a relief!

But the effort is getting to be greater than the relief.

Half the time now I am awfully lazy, and lie down ever so much.

John says I mustn't lose my strength, and has me take cod liver oil and lots of tonics and things, to say nothing of ale and wine and rare meat.

Dear John! He loves me very dearly, and hates to have me sick. I tried to have a real earnest reasonable talk with him the other day, and tell him how I wish he would let me go and make a visit to Cousin Henry and Julia.

But he said I wasn't able to go, nor able to stand it after I got there; and I did not make out a very good case for myself, for I was crying before I had finished.

It is getting to be a great effort for me to think straight. Just this nervous weakness I suppose.

And dear John gathered me up in his arms, and just carried me upstairs and laid me on the bed, and sat by me and read to me till it tired my head.

He said I was his darling and his comfort and all he had, and that I must take care of myself for his sake, and keep well.

He says no one but myself can help me out of it, that I must use my will and self-control and not let any silly fancies run away with me.

There's one comfort, the baby is well and happy, and does not have to occupy this nursery with the horrid wall-paper.

If we had not used it, that blessed child would have! What a fortunate escape! Why, I wouldn't have a child of mine, an impressionable little thing, live in such a room for worlds.

I never thought of it before, but it is lucky that John kept me here after all, I can stand it so much easier than a baby, you see.

Of course I never mention it to them any more—I am too wise,—but I keep watch of it all the same.

There are things in that paper that nobody knows but me, or ever will.

Behind that outside pattern the dim shapes get clearer every day.

It is always the same shape, only very numerous.

And it is like a woman stooping down and creeping about behind that pattern. I don't like it a bit. I wonder—I begin to think—I wish John would take me away from here!

It is so hard to talk with John about my case, because he is so wise, and because he loves me so.

But I tried it last night.

It was moonlight. The moon shines in all around just as the sun does.

I hate to see it sometimes, it creeps so slowly, and always comes in by one window or another.

John was asleep and I hated to waken him, so I kept still and watched the moonlight on that undulating wall-paper till I felt creepy.

The faint figure behind seemed to shake the pattern, just as if she wanted to get out.

I got up softly and went to feel and see if the paper *did* move, and when I came back John was awake.

'What is it, little girl?' he said. 'Don't go walking about like that —you'll get cold.'

I thought it was a good time to talk, so I told him that I really was not gaining here, and that I wished he would take me away.

'Why darling!' said he, 'our lease will be up in three weeks, and I can't see how to leave before.'

'The repairs are not done at home, and I cannot possibly leave town just now. Of course if you were in any danger, I could and would, but you really are better, dear, whether you can see it or not. I am a doctor, dear, and I know. You are gaining flesh and color, your appetite is better, I feel really much easier about you.'

'I don't weigh a bit more,' said I, 'nor as much; and my appetite may be better in the evening when you are here, but it is worse in the morning when you are away!'

'Bless her little heart!' said he with a big hug, 'she shall be as sick as she pleases! But now let's improve the shining hours by going to sleep, and talk about it in the morning!'

'And you won't go away?' I asked gloomily.

'Why, how can I, dear? It is only three weeks more and then we will take a nice little trip of a few days while Jennie is getting the house ready. Really dear you are better!'

'Better in body perhaps—' I began, and stopped short, for he sat up straight and looked at me with such a stern, reproachful look that I could not say another word.

'My darling,' said he, 'I beg of you, for my sake and for our child's sake, as well as for your own, that you will never for one instant let that idea enter your mind! There is nothing so dangerous, so fascinating, to a temperament like yours. It is a false and foolish fancy. Can you not trust me as a physician when I tell you so?'

So of course I said no more on that score, and we went to sleep before long. He thought I was asleep first, but I wasn't, and lay there for hours trying to decide whether that front pattern and the back pattern really did move together or separately.

On a pattern like this, by daylight, there is a lack of sequence, a defiance of law, that is a constant irritant to a normal mind.

The color is hideous enough, and unreliable enough, and infuriating enough, but the pattern is torturing.

You think you have mastered it, but just as you get well underway in following, it turns a back-somersault and there you are. It slaps you in the face, knocks you down, and tramples upon you. It is like a bad dream.

The outside pattern is a florid arabesque, reminding one of a fungus. If you can imagine a toadstool in joints, an interminable string of toadstools, budding and sprouting in endless convolutions—why, that is something like it.

That is, sometimes!

There is one marked peculiarity about this paper, a thing nobody seems to notice but myself, and that is that it changes as the light changes.

When the sun shoots in through the east window—I always watch for that first long, straight ray—it changes so quickly that I never can quite believe it.

That is why I watch it always.

By moonlight—the moon shines in all night when there is a moon—I wouldn't know it was the same paper.

At night in any kind of light, in twilight, candle light, lamplight, and worst of all by moonlight, it becomes bars! The outside pattern I mean, and the woman behind it is as plain as can be.

I didn't realize for a long time what the thing was that showed behind, that dim sub-pattern, but now I am quite sure it is a woman.

By daylight she is subdued, quiet. I fancy it is the pattern that keeps her so still. It is so puzzling. It keeps me quiet by the hour.

I lie down ever so much now. John says it is good for me, and to sleep all I can.

Indeed he started the habit by making me lie down for an hour after each meal.

It is a very bad habit I am convinced, for you see I don't sleep.

And that cultivates deceit, for I don't tell them I'm awake—O no!

The fact is I am getting a little afraid of John.

He seems very queer sometimes, and even Jennie has an inexplicable look.

It strikes me occasionally, just as a scientific hypothesis,—that perhaps it is the paper!

I have watched John when he did not know I was looking, and come into the room suddenly on the most innocent excuses, and I've caught him several times *looking at the paper!* And Jennie too. I caught Jennie with her hand on it once.

She didn't know I was in the room, and when I asked her in a quiet, a very quiet voice, with the most restrained manner possible, what she was doing with the paper—she turned around as if she had been caught stealing, and looked quite angry—asked me why I should frighten her so!

Then she said that the paper stained everything it touched, that she had found yellow smooches on all my clothes and John's, and she wished we would be more careful!

Did not that sound innocent? But I know she was studying that pattern, and I am determined that nobody shall find it out but myself!

Life is very much more exciting now than it used to be. You see I have something more to expect, to look forward to, to watch. I really do eat better, and am more quiet than I was.

John is so pleased to see me improve! He laughed a little the other day, and said I seemed to be flourishing in spite of my wall-paper.

I turned it off with a laugh. I had no intention of telling him it was *because* of the wall-paper—he would make fun of me. He might even want to take me away.

I don't want to leave now until I have found it out. There is a week more, and I think that will be enough.

I'm feeling ever so much better! I don't sleep much at night, for it is so interesting to watch developments; but I sleep a good deal in the daytime.

In the daytime it is tiresome and perplexing.

There are always new shoots on the fungus, and new shades of yellow all over it. I cannot keep count of them, though I have tried conscientiously.

It is the strangest yellow, that wall-paper! It makes me think of all the yellow things I ever saw—not beautiful ones like buttercups, but old foul, bad yellow things.

But there is something else about that paper—the smell! I noticed it the moment we came into the room, but with so much air and sun it was not bad. Now we have had a week of fog and rain, and whether the windows are open or not, the smell is here.

It creeps all over the house.

I find it hovering in the dining-room, skulking in the parlor, hiding in the hall, lying in wait for me on the stairs.

It gets into my hair.

Even when I go to ride, if I turn my head suddenly and surprise it—there is that smell!

Such a peculiar odor, too! I have spent hours in trying to analyze it, to find what it smelled like.

It is not bad—at first, and very gentle, but quite the subtlest, most enduring odor I ever met.

In this damp weather it is awful, I wake up in the night and find it hanging over me.

It used to disturb me at first. I thought seriously of burning the house—to reach the smell.

But now I am used to it. The only thing I can think of that it is like is the *color* of the paper! A yellow smell.

There is a very funny mark on this wall, low down, near the mopboard. A streak that runs round the room. It goes behind every piece of furniture, except the bed, a long, straight, even *smooch*, as if it had been rubbed over and over.

I wonder how it was done and who did it, and what they did it for. Round and round and round—round and round and round—it makes me dizzy!

I really have discovered something at last.

Through watching so much at night, when it changes so, I have finally found out.

The front pattern *does* move—and no wonder! The woman behind shakes it!

Sometimes I think there are a great many women behind, and sometimes only one, and she crawls around fast, and her crawling shakes it all over.

Then in the very bright spots she keeps still, and in the very shady spots she just takes hold of the bars and shakes them hard.

And she is all the time trying to climb through. But nobody could climb through that pattern—it strangles so; I think that is why it has so many heads.

They get through, and then the pattern strangles them off and turns them upside down, and makes their eyes white!

If those heads were covered or taken off it would not be half so bad.

I think that woman gets out in the daytime!

And I'll tell you why—privately—I've seen her!

I can see her out of every one of my windows!

It is the same woman, I know, for she is always creeping, and most women do not creep by daylight.

I see her on that long road under the trees, creeping along, and when a carriage comes she hides under the blackberry vines.

I don't blame her a bit. It must be very humiliating to be caught creeping by daylight!

I always lock the door when I creep by daylight. I can't do it at night, for I know John would suspect something at once.

And John is so queer now, that I don't want to irritate him. I wish he would take another room! Besides, I don't want anybody to get that woman out at night but myself.

I often wonder if I could see her out of all the windows at once.

But, turn as fast as I can, I can only see out of one at one time.

And though I always see her, she *may* be able to creep faster than I can turn!

I have watched her sometimes away off in the open country, creeping as fast as a cloud shadow in a high wind.

If only that top pattern could be gotten off from the under one! I mean to try it, little by little.

I have found out another funny thing, but I shan't tell it this time! It does not do to trust people too much.

There are only two more days to get this paper off, and I believe John is beginning to notice. I don't like the look in his eyes.

And I heard him ask Jennie a lot of professional questions about me. She had a very good report to give.

She said I slept a good deal in the daytime.

John knows I don't sleep very well at night, for all I'm so quiet!

He asked me all sorts of questions, too, and pretended to be very loving and kind.

As if I couldn't see through him!

Still, I don't wonder he acts so, sleeping under this paper for three months.

It only interests me, but I feel sure John and Jennie are secretly affected by it.

Hurrah! This is the last day, but it is enough. John to stay in town over night, and won't be out until this evening.

Jennie wanted to sleep with me—the sly thing! but I told her I should undoubtedly rest better for a night all alone.

That was clever, for really I wasn't alone a bit! As soon as it was moonlight and that poor thing began to crawl and shake the pattern, I got up and ran to help her.

I pulled and she shook, I shook and she pulled, and before morning we had peeled off yards of that paper.

A strip about as high as my head and half around the room.

And then when the sun came and that awful pattern began to laugh at me, I declared I would finish it to-day!

We go away to-morrow, and they are moving all my furniture down again to leave things as they were before.

Jennie looked at the wall in amazement, but I told her merrily that I did it out of pure spite at the vicious thing.

She laughed and said she wouldn't mind doing it herself, but I must not get tired.

How she betrayed herself that time!

But I am here, and no person touches this paper but me,—not *alive!*

She tried to get me out of the room—it was too patent! But I said it was so quiet and empty and clean now that I believed I would lie down again and sleep all I could; and not to wake me even for dinner—I would call when I woke.

So now she is gone, and the servants are gone, and the things are gone, and there is nothing left but that great bedstead nailed down, with the canvas mattress we found on it.

We shall sleep downstairs tonight, and take the boat home to-morrow.

I quite enjoy the room, now it is bare again.

How those children did tear about here!

This bedstead is fairly gnawed!

But I must get to work.

I have locked the door and thrown the key down into the front path.

I don't want to go out, and I don't want to have anybody come in, till John comes.

I want to astonish him.

I've got a rope up here that even Jennie did not find. If that woman does get out, and tries to get away, I can tie her!

But I forgot I could not reach far without anything to stand on!

This bed will *not* move!

I tried to lift and push it until I was lame, and then I got so angry I bit off a little piece at one corner—but it hurt my teeth.

Then I peeled off all the paper I could reach standing on the floor. It sticks horribly and the pattern just enjoys it! All those strangled heads and bulbous eyes and waddling fungus growths just shriek with derision!

I am getting angry enough to do something desperate. To jump out of the window would be admirable exercise, but the bars are too strong even to try.

Besides I wouldn't do it. Of course not. I know well enough that a step like that is improper and might be misconstrued.

I don't like to *look* out of the windows even—there are so many of those creeping women, and they creep so fast.

I wonder if they all come out of that wall-paper as I did?

But I am securely fastened now by my well-hidden rope—you don't get *me* out in the road there!

I suppose I shall have to get back behind the pattern when it comes night, and that is hard!

It is so pleasant to be out in this great room and creep around as I please!

I don't want to go outside. I won't, even if Jennie asks me to.

For outside you have to creep on the ground, and everything is green instead of yellow.

But here I can creep smoothly on the floor, and my shoulder just fits in that long smooch around the wall, so I cannot lose my way.

Why there's John at the door!

It is no use, young man, you can't open it!

How he does call and pound!

Now he's crying for an axe.

It would be a shame to break down that beautiful door!

'John dear!' said I in the gentlest voice, 'the key is down by the front steps, under a plantain leaf!'

That silenced him for a few moments.

Then he said—very quietly indeed, 'Open the door, my darling!'

'I can't,' said I. 'The key is down by the front door under a plantain leaf!'

And then I said it again, several times, very gently and slowly, and said it so often that he had to go and see, and he got it of course, and came in. He stopped short by the door.

'What is the matter?' he cried. 'For God's sake, what are you doing!'

I kept on creeping just the same, but I looked at him over my shoulder.

'I've got out at last,' said I, 'in spite of you and Jane. And I've pulled off most of the paper, so you can't put me back!'

Now why should that man have fainted? But he did, and right across my path by the wall, so that I had to creep over him every time!

ARTHUR CONAN DOYLE

The Adventure of the Speckled Band (1892)

In glancing over my notes of the seventy odd cases in which I have during the last eight years studied the methods of my friend Sherlock Holmes, I find many tragic, some comic, a large number merely strange, but none commonplace; for, working as he did rather for the love of his art than for the acquirement of wealth, he refused to associate himself with any investigation which did not tend towards the unusual, and even the fantastic. Of all these varied cases, however, I cannot recall any which presented more singular features than that which was associated with the well-known Surrey family of the Roylotts of Stoke Moran. The events in question occurred in the early days of my association with Holmes, when we were sharing rooms as bachelors, in Baker Street. It is possible that I might have placed them upon record before, but a promise of secrecy was made at the time, from which I have only been freed during the last month by the untimely death of the lady to whom the pledge was given. It is perhaps as well that the facts should now come to light, for I have reasons to know there are widespread rumours as to the death of Dr Grimesby Roylott which tend to make the matter even more terrible than the truth.

It was early in April, in the year '83, that I woke one morning to find Sherlock Holmes standing, fully dressed, by the side of my bed. He was a late riser as a rule, and, as the clock on the mantelpiece showed me that it was only a quarter past seven, I blinked up at him in some surprise, and perhaps just a little resentment, for I was myself regular in my habits.

'Very sorry to knock you up, Watson,' said he, 'but it's the common lot this morning. Mrs Hudson has been knocked up, she retorted upon me, and I on you.'

'What is it, then? A fire?'

'No, a client. It seems that a young lady has arrived in a considerable state of excitement, who insists upon seeing me. She is waiting now in the sitting-room. Now, when young ladies wander about the metropolis at this hour of the morning, and knock sleepy people up out of their beds, I presume that it is something very pressing which they have to communicate. Should it prove to be an interesting case, you would, I am sure, wish to follow it from the outset. I thought at any rate that I should call you, and give you the chance.'

'My dear fellow, I would not miss it for anything.'

I had no keener pleasure than in following Holmes in his professional investigations, and in admiring the rapid deductions, as swift as intuitions, and yet always founded on a logical basis, with which he unravelled the problems which were submitted to him. I rapidly threw on my clothes, and was ready in a few minutes to accompany my friend down to the sitting-room. A lady dressed in black and heavily veiled, who had been sitting in the window, rose as we entered.

'Good morning, madam,' said Holmes cheerily. 'My name is Sherlock Holmes. This is my intimate friend and associate, Dr Watson, before whom you can speak as freely as before myself. Ha, I am glad to see that Mrs Hudson has had the good sense to light the fire. Pray draw up to it, and I shall order you a cup of hot coffee, for I observe that you are shivering.'

'It is not cold which makes me shiver,' said the woman in a low voice, changing her seat as requested.

'What then?'

'It is fear, Mr Holmes. It is terror.' She raised her veil as she spoke, and we could see that she was indeed in a pitiable state of agitation, her face all drawn and grey, with restless, frightened eyes, like those of some hunted animal. Her features and figure were those of a woman of thirty, but her hair was shot with premature grey, and her expression was weary and haggard. Sherlock Holmes ran her over with one of his quick, all-comprehensive glances.

'You must not fear,' said he soothingly, bending forward and patting her forearm. 'We shall soon set matters right, I have no doubt. You have come in by train this morning, I see.'

'You know me, then?'

'No, but I observe the second half of a return ticket in the palm of your left glove. You must have started early and yet you had a good drive in a dog-cart, along heavy roads, before you reached the station.'

The lady gave a violent start, and stared in bewilderment at my companion.

'There is no mystery, my dear madam,' said he, smiling. 'The left arm of your jacket is spattered with mud in no less than seven places. The marks are perfectly fresh. There is no vehicle save a dog-cart which throws up mud in that way, and then only when you sit on the left-hand side of the driver.'

'Whatever your reasons may be, you are perfectly correct,' said she. 'I started from home before six, reached Leatherhead at twenty past, and came in by the first train to Waterloo. Sir, I can stand this strain no longer, I shall go mad if it continues. I have no one to turn to—none, save only one, who cares for me, and he, poor fellow, can be of little aid. I have heard of you, Mr Holmes; I have heard of you from Mrs Farintosh, whom you helped in the hour of her sore need. It was from her that I had your address. Oh, sir, do you not think you could help me too, and at least throw a little light through the dense darkness which surrounds me? At present it is out of my power to reward you for your services, but in a month or two I shall be married, with the control of my own income, and then at least you shall not find me ungrateful.'

Holmes turned to his desk, and unlocking it, drew out a small case-book which he consulted.

'Farintosh,' said he. 'Ah, yes, I recall the case; it was concerned with an opal tiara. I think it was before your time, Watson. I can only say, madam, that I shall be happy to devote the same care to your case as I did to that of your friend. As to reward, my profession is its reward; but you are at liberty to defray whatever expenses I may be put to, at the time which suits you best. And now I beg that you will lay before us everything that may help us in forming an opinion upon the matter.'

'Alas!' replied our visitor. 'The very horror of my situation lies in the fact that my fears are so vague, and my suspicions depend so entirely upon small points, which might seem trivial to another, that even he to whom of all others I have a right to look for help and advice looks upon all that I tell him about it as the fancies of a nervous woman. He does not say so, but I can read it from his soothing answers and averted eyes. But I have heard, Mr Holmes, that you can see deeply into the manifold wickedness of the human heart. You may advise me how to walk amid the dangers which encompass me.'

'I am all attention, madam.'

'My name is Helen Stoner, and I am living with my stepfather, who is the last survivor of one of the oldest Saxon families in England, the Roylotts of Stoke Moran, on the Western border of Surrey.'

Holmes nodded his head. 'The name is familiar to me,' said he.

'The family was at one time among the richest in England, and the estate extended over the borders into Berkshire in the north, and Hampshire in the west. In the last century, however, four successive heirs were of a dissolute and wasteful disposition, and the family ruin was eventually completed by a gambler, in the days of the Regency. Nothing was left save a few acres of ground and the two-hundred-year-old house, which is itself crushed under a heavy mortgage. The last squire dragged out his existence there, living the horrible life of an aristocratic pauper; but his only son, my stepfather, seeing that he must adapt himself to the new conditions, obtained an advance from a relative, which enabled him to take a medical degree, and went out to Calcutta, where, by his professional skill and his force of character, he established a large practice. In a fit of anger, however, caused by some robberies which had been perpetrated in the house, he beat his native butler to death, and narrowly escaped a capital sentence. As it was, he suffered a long term of imprisonment, and afterwards returned to England a morose and disappointed man.

'When Dr Roylott was in India he married my mother, Mrs Stoner, the young widow of Major-General Stoner, of the Bengal Artillery. My sister Julia and I were twins, and we were only two years old at the time of my mother's remarriage. She had a considerable sum of money, not less than a thousand a year, and this she bequeathed to Dr Roylott entirely whilst we resided with him, with a provision that a certain annual sum should be allowed to each of us in the event of our marriage. Shortly after our return to England my mother died— she was killed eight years ago in a railway accident near Crewe. Dr Roylott then abandoned his attempts to establish himself in practice in London, and took us to live with him in the ancestral house at Stoke Moran. The money which my mother had left was enough for all our wants, and there seemed no obstacle to our happiness.

'But a terrible change came over our stepfather about this time. Instead of making friends and exchanging visits with our neighbours, who had at first been overjoyed to see a Roylott of Stoke Moran back in the old family seat, he shut himself up in his house, and seldom came out save to indulge in ferocious quarrels with whoever might cross his path. Violence of temper approaching to mania has been hereditary in the men of the family, and in my stepfather's case it had, I believe, been intensified by his long residence in the tropics. A series of disgraceful brawls took place, two of which ended in the police-court, until at last he became the terror of the village, and the folks would fly at his approach, for he is a man of immense strength, and absolutely uncontrollable in his anger.

'Last week he hurled the local blacksmith over a parapet into a stream and it was only by paying over all the money that I could gather together that I was able to avert another public exposure. He had no friends at all save the wandering gipsies, and he would give these vagabonds leave to encamp upon the few acres of bramble-covered land which represent the family estate, and would accept in return the hospitality of their tents, wandering away with them sometimes for weeks on end. He has a passion also for Indian animals, which are sent over to him by a correspondent, and he has at this moment a cheetah and a baboon, which wander freely over his grounds, and are feared by the villagers almost as much as their master.

'You can imagine from what I say that my poor sister Julia and I had no great pleasure in our lives. No servant would stay with us, and for a long time we did all the work of the house. She was but thirty at the time of her death, and yet her hair had already begun to whiten, even as mine has.'

'Your sister is dead, then?'

'She died just two years ago, and it is of her death that I wish to speak to you. You can understand that, living the life which I have described, we were little likely to see anyone of our own age and position. We had, however, an aunt, my mother's maiden sister, Miss Honoria Westphail, who lives near Harrow, and we were occasionally allowed to pay short visits at this lady's house. Julia went there at Christmas two years ago, and met there a half-pay Major of Marines, to whom she became engaged. My stepfather learned of the engagement when my sister returned, and offered no objection to the marriage; but within a fortnight of the day which had been fixed for the wedding, the terrible event occurred which has deprived me of my only companion.'

Sherlock Holmes had been leaning back in his chair with his eyes closed, and his head sunk in a cushion, but he half opened his lids now, and glanced across at his visitor.

'Pray be precise as to details,' said he.

'It is easy for me to be so, for every event of that dreadful time is seared into my memory. The manor house is, as I have already said, very old, and only one wing is now inhabited. The bedrooms in this wing are on the ground floor, the sitting-rooms being in the central block of the buildings. Of these bedrooms the first is Dr Roylott's, the second my sister's, and the third my own. There is no communication between them, but they all open out into the same corridor. Do I make myself plain?'

'Perfectly so.'

'The windows of the three rooms open out upon the lawn. That fatal night Dr Roylott had gone to his room early, though we knew that he had not retired to rest, for my sister was troubled by the smell of the strong Indian cigars which it was his custom to smoke. She left her room, therefore, and came into mine, where she sat for some time, chatting about her approaching wedding. At eleven o'clock she rose to leave me, but she paused at the door and looked back.

'"Tell me, Helen," said she, "have you ever heard anyone whistle in the dead of the night?"

'"Never," said I.

'"I suppose that you could not possibly whistle yourself in your sleep?"

'"Certainly not. But why?"

'"Because during the last few nights I have always, about three in the morning, heard a low clear whistle. I am a light sleeper, and it has awakened me. I cannot tell where it came from—perhaps from the next room, perhaps from the lawn. I thought that I would just ask you whether you had heard it."

'"No, I have not. It must be those wretched gipsies in the plantation."

'"Very likely. And yet if it were on the lawn I wonder that you did not hear it also."

'"Ah, but I sleep more heavily than you."

'"Well, it is of no great consequence, at any rate," she smiled back at me, closed my door, and a few moments later I heard her key turn in the lock.'

'Indeed,' said Holmes. 'Was it your custom always to lock yourselves in at night?'

'Always.'

'And why?'

'I think that I mentioned to you that the Doctor kept a cheetah and a baboon. We had no feeling of security unless our doors were locked.'

'Quite so. Pray proceed with your statement.'

'I could not sleep that night. A vague feeling of impending misfortune impressed me. My sister and I, you will recollect, were twins, and you know how subtle are the links which bind two souls which are so closely allied. It was a wild night. The wind was howling outside, and the rain was beating and splashing against the windows. Suddenly, amidst all the hubbub of the gale, there burst forth the wild scream of a terrified woman. I knew that it was my sister's voice. I sprang from my bed, wrapped a shawl round me, and rushed into the corridor. As I opened my door I seemed to hear a low whistle, such as my sister described, and a few moments later a clanging sound, as if a mass of metal had fallen. As I ran down the passage my sister's door was unlocked, and revolved slowly upon its hinges. I stared at it horror-stricken, not knowing what was about to issue from it. By the light of the corridor lamp I saw my sister appear at the opening, her face blanched with terror, her hands groping for help, her whole figure swaying to and fro like that of a drunkard. I ran to her and threw my arms round her, but at that moment her knees seemed to give way and she fell to the ground. She writhed as one who is in terrible pain, and her limbs were dreadfully convulsed. At first I thought that she had not recognized me, but as I bent over her she suddenly shrieked out in a voice which I shall never forget, "Oh, my God! Helen! It was the band! The speckled band!" There was something else which she would fain have said, and she stabbed with her finger into the air in the direction of the Doctor's room, but a fresh convulsion seized her and choked her words. I rushed out, calling loudly for my stepfather, and I met him hastening from his room in his dressing-gown. When he reached my sister's side she was unconscious, and though he poured brandy down her throat, and sent for medical aid from the village, all efforts were in vain, for she slowly sank and died without having recovered her consciousness. Such was the dreadful end of my beloved sister.'

'One moment,' said Holmes: 'are you sure about this whistle and metallic sound? Could you swear to it?'

'That was what the county coroner asked me at the inquiry. It is my strong impression that I heard it, and yet among the crash of the gale, and the creaking of an old house, I may possibly have been deceived.'

'Was your sister dressed?'

'No, she was in her nightdress. In her right hand was found the charred stump of a match, and in her left a matchbox.'

'Showing that she had struck a light and looked about her when the alarm took place. That is important. And what conclusions did the coroner come to?'

'He investigated the case with great care, for Dr Roylott's conduct had long been notorious in the county, but he was unable to find any satisfactory cause of death. My evidence showed that the door had been fastened upon the inner side, and the windows were blocked by old-fashioned shutters with broad iron bars, which were secured every night. The walls were carefully sounded, and were shown to be quite solid all round, and the flooring was also thoroughly examined, with the same result. The chimney is wide, but is barred up by four large staples. It is certain, therefore, that my sister was quite alone when she met her end. Besides, there were no marks of any violence upon her.'

'How about poison?'

'The doctors examined her for it, but without success.'

'What do you think that this unfortunate lady died of, then?'

'It is my belief that she died of pure fear and nervous shock, though what it was which frightened her I cannot imagine.'

'Were there gipsies in the plantation at the time?'

'Yes, there are nearly always some there.'

'Ah, and what did you gather from this allusion to a band—a speckled band?'

'Sometimes I have thought that it was merely the wild talk of delirium, sometimes that it may have referred to some band of people, perhaps to these very gipsies in the plantation. I do not know whether the spotted handkerchiefs which so many of them wear over their heads might have suggested the strange adjective which she used.'

Holmes shook his head like a man who is far from being satisfied.

'These are very deep waters,' said he; 'pray go on with your narrative.'

'Two years have passed since then, and my life has been until lately lonelier than ever. A month ago, however, a dear friend, whom I have known for many years, has done me the honour to ask my hand in marriage. His name is Armitage—Percy Armitage—the second son of Mr Armitage, of Crane Water, near Reading. My stepfather has offered no opposition to the match, and we are to be married in the course of the spring. Two days ago some repairs were started in the west wing of the building, and my bedroom wall has been pierced, so that I have had to move into the chamber in which my sister died, and to sleep in the very bed in which she slept. Imagine, then, my thrill of terror when last night, as I lay awake, thinking over her terrible fate, I suddenly heard in the silence of the night the low whistle which had been the herald of her own death. I sprang up and lit the lamp, but nothing was to be seen in the room. I was too shaken to go to bed again, however, so I dressed, and as soon as it was daylight I slipped down, got a dog-cart at the Crown Inn, which is opposite, and drove to Leatherhead, from whence I have come on this morning, with the one object of seeing you and asking your advice.'

'You have done wisely,' said my friend. 'But have you told me all?'

#2

'Yes, all.'

'Miss Stoner, you have not. You are screening your stepfather.'

'Why, what do you mean?'

For answer Holmes pushed back the frill of black lace which fringed the hand that lay upon our visitor's knee. Five little livid spots, the marks of four fingers and a thumb, were printed upon the white wrist.

'You have been cruelly used,' said Holmes.

The lady coloured deeply, and covered over her injured wrist. 'He is a hard man,' she said, 'and perhaps he hardly knows his own strength.'

There was a long silence, during which Holmes leaned his chin upon his hands and stared into the crackling fire.

'This is very deep business,' he said at last. 'There are a thousand details which I should desire to know before I decide upon our course of action. Yet we have not a moment to lose. If we were to come to Stoke Moran today, would it be possible for us to see over these rooms without the knowledge of your stepfather?'

'As it happens, he spoke of coming into town today upon some most important business. It is probable that he will be away all day, and that there would be nothing to disturb you. We have a house-keeper now, but she is old and foolish, and I could easily get her out of the way.'

'Excellent. You are not averse to this trip, Watson?'

'By no means.'

'Then we shall both come. What are you going to do yourself?'

'I have one or two things which I would wish to do now that I am in town. But I shall return by the twelve o'clock train, so as to be there in time for your coming.'

'And you may expect us early in the afternoon. I have myself some small business matters to attend to. Will you not wait and breakfast?'

'No, I must go. My heart is lightened already since I have confided my trouble to you. I shall look forward to seeing you again this afternoon.' She dropped her thick black veil over her face, and glided from the room.

'And what do you think of it all, Watson?' asked Sherlock Holmes, leaning back in his chair.

'It seems to me to be a most dark and sinister business.'

'Dark enough and sinister enough.'

'Yet if the lady is correct in saying that the flooring and walls are sound, and that the door, window, and chimney are impassable, then her sister must have been undoubtedly alone when she met her mysterious end.'

'What becomes, then, of these nocturnal whistles, and what of the very peculiar words of the dying woman?'

'I cannot think.'

'When you combine the ideas of whistles at night, the presence of a band of gipsies who are on intimate terms with this old doctor, the fact that we have every reason to believe that the doctor has an interest in preventing his stepdaughter's marriage, the dying allusion to a band, and finally, the fact that Miss Helen Stoner heard a metallic clang, which might have been caused by one of those metal bars which secured the shutters falling back into their place, I think there is good ground to think that the mystery may be cleared along those lines.'

'But what, then, did the gipsies do?'

'I cannot imagine.'

'I see many objections to any such a theory.'

'And so do I. It is precisely for that reason that we are going to Stoke Moran this day. I want to see whether the objections are fatal, or if they may be explained away. But what, in the name of the devil!'

The ejaculation had been drawn from my companion by the fact that our door had been suddenly dashed open, and that a huge man framed himself in the aperture. His costume was a peculiar mixture of the professional and of the agricultural, having a black top-hat, a long frock-coat, and a pair of high gaiters, with a hunting-crop swinging in his hand. So tall was he that his hat actually brushed the cross-bar of the doorway, and his breadth seemed to span it across from side to side. A large face, seared with a thousand wrinkles, burned yellow with the sun, and marked with every evil passion, was turned from one to the other of us, while his deep-set, bile-shot eyes, and the high thin fleshless nose, gave him somewhat the resemblance to a fierce old bird of prey.

'Which of you is Holmes?' asked this apparition.

'My name, sir, but you have the advantage of me,' said my companion quietly.

'I am Dr Grimesby Roylott, of Stoke Moran.'

'Indeed, Doctor,' said Holmes blandly. 'Pray take a seat.'

'I will do nothing of the kind. My stepdaughter has been here. I have traced her. What has she been saying to you?'

'It is a little cold for the time of the year,' said Holmes.

'What has she been saying to you?' screamed the old man furiously.

'But I have heard that the crocuses promise well,' continued my companion imperturbably.

'Ha! You put me off, do you?' said our new visitor, taking a step forward, and shaking his hunting-crop. 'I know you, you scoundrel! I have heard of you before. You are Holmes the meddler.'

My friend smiled.

'Holmes the busybody!'

His smile broadened.

'Holmes the Scotland Yard jack-in-office.'

Holmes chuckled heartily. 'Your conversation is most entertaining,' said he. 'When you go out close the door, for there is a decided draught.'

'I will go when I have had my say. Don't you dare to meddle with my affairs. I know that Miss Stoner has been here—I traced her! I am a dangerous man to fall foul of! See here.' He stepped swiftly forward, seized the poker, and bent it into a curve with his huge brown hands.

'See that you keep yourself out of my grip,' he snarled, and hurling the twisted poker into the fireplace, he strode out of the room.

'He seems a very amiable person,' said Holmes, laughing. 'I am not quite so bulky, but if he had remained I might have shown him that my grip was not much more feeble than his own.' As he spoke he picked up the steel poker, and with a sudden effort straightened it out again.

'Fancy his having the insolence to confound me with the official detective force! This incident gives zest to our investigation, however, and I only trust that our little friend will not suffer from her imprudence in allowing this brute to trace her. And now, Watson, we shall order breakfast, and afterwards I shall walk down to Doctors' Commons, where I hope to get some data which may help us in this matter.'

It was nearly one o'clock when Sherlock Holmes returned from his excursion. He held in his hand a sheet of blue paper, scrawled over with notes and figures.

'I have seen the will of the deceased wife,' said he. 'To determine its exact meaning I have been obliged to work out the present prices of the investments with which it is concerned. The total income, which at the time of the wife's death was little short of £1,100, is now through the fall in agricultural prices not more than £750. Each daughter can claim an income of £250, in case of marriage. It is evident, therefore, that if both girls had married, this beauty would have had a mere pittance, while even one of them would cripple him to a serious extent. My morning's work has not been wasted, since it has proved that he has the very strongest motives for standing in the way of anything of the sort. And now, Watson, this is too serious for dawdling, especially as the old man is aware that we are interesting ourselves in his affairs, so if you are ready we shall call a cab and drive to Waterloo. I should be very much obliged if you would slip your revolver into your pocket. An Eley's No. 2 is an excellent argument with gentlemen who can twist steel pokers into knots. That and a toothbrush are, I think, all that we need.'

At Waterloo we were fortunate in catching a train for Leatherhead, where we hired a trap at the station inn, and drove for four or five miles through the lovely Surrey lanes. It was a perfect day, with a bright sun and a few fleecy clouds in the heavens. The trees and wayside hedges were just throwing out their first green shoots, and the air was full of the pleasant smell of the moist earth. To me at least there was a strange contrast between the sweet promise of the spring and this sinister quest upon which we were engaged. My companion sat in front of the trap, his arms folded, his hat pulled down over his eyes, and his chin sunk upon his breast, buried in the deepest thought. Suddenly, however, he started, tapped me on the shoulder, and pointed over the meadows.

'Look there!' said he.

A heavily timbered park stretched up in a gentle slope, thickening into a grove at the highest point. From amidst the branches there jutted out the grey gables and high roof-tree of a very old mansion.

'Stoke Moran?' said he.

'Yes, sir, that be the house of Dr Grimesby Roylott,' remarked the driver.

'There is some building going on there,' said Holmes: 'that is where we are going.'

'There's the village,' said the driver, pointing to a cluster of roofs some distance to the left; 'but if you want to get to the house, you'll find it shorter to go over this stile, and so by the footpath over the fields. There it is, where the lady is walking.'

'And the lady, I fancy, is Miss Stoner,' observed Holmes, shading his eyes. 'Yes, I think we had better do as you suggest.'

We got off, paid our fare, and the trap rattled back on its way to Leatherhead.

'I thought it as well,' said Holmes, as we climbed the stile, 'that this fellow should think we had come here as architects, or on some definite business. It may stop his gossip. Good afternoon,

Miss Stoner. You see that we have been as good as our word.'

Our client of the morning had hurried forward to meet us with a face which spoke her joy. 'I have been waiting so eagerly for you,' she cried, shaking hands with us warmly. 'All has turned out splendidly. Dr Roylott has gone to town, and it is unlikely that he will be back before evening.'

'We have had the pleasure of making the Doctor's acquaintance,' said Holmes, and in a few words he sketched out what had occurred. Miss Stoner turned white to the lips as she listened.

'Good heavens!' she cried, 'he has followed me, then.'

'So it appears.'

'He is so cunning that I never know when I am safe from him. What will he say when he returns?'

'He must guard himself, for he may find that there is someone more cunning than himself upon his track. You must lock yourself from him tonight. If he is violent, we shall take you away to your aunt's at Harrow. Now, we must make the best use of our time, so kindly take us at once to the rooms which we are to examine.'

The building was of grey, lichen-blotched stone, with a high central portion, and two curving wings, like the claws of a crab, thrown out on each side. In one of these wings the windows were broken, and blocked with wooden boards, while the roof was partly caved in, a picture of ruin. The central portion was in little better repair, but the right-hand block was comparatively modern, and the blinds in the windows, with the blue smoke curling up from the chimneys, showed that this was where the family resided. Some scaffolding had been erected against the end wall, and the stonework had been broken into, but there were no signs of any workmen at the moment of our visit. Holmes walked slowly up and down the ill-trimmed lawn, and examined with deep attention the outsides of the windows.

'This, I take it, belongs to the room in which you used to sleep, the centre one to your sister's, and the one next to the main building to Dr Roylott's chamber?'

'Exactly so. But I am now sleeping in the middle one.'

'Pending the alterations, as I understand. By the way, there does not seem to be any very pressing need for repairs at that end wall.'

'There were none. I believe that it was an excuse to move me from my room.'

'Ah! that is suggestive. Now, on the other side of this narrow wing runs the corridor from which these three rooms open. There are windows in it, of course?'

'Yes, but very small ones. Too narrow for anyone to pass through.'

'As you both locked your doors at night, your rooms were un-approachable from that side. Now, would you have the kindness to go into your room, and to bar your shutters.'

Miss Stoner did so, and Holmes, after a careful examination through the open window, endeavoured in every way to force the shutter open, but without success. There was no slit through which a knife could be passed to raise the bar. Then with his lens he tested the hinges, but they were of solid iron, built firmly into the massive masonry. 'Hum!' said he, scratching his chin in some perplexity, 'my theory certainly presents some difficulties. No one could pass these shutters if they were bolted. Well, we shall see if the inside throws any light upon the matter.'

A small side-door led into the whitewashed corridor from which the three bedrooms opened. Holmes refused to examine the third chamber, so we passed at once to the second, that in which Miss Stoner was now sleeping, and in which her sister had met her fate. It was a homely little room, with a low ceiling and a gaping fireplace, after the fashion of old country houses. A brown chest of drawers stood in one corner, a narrow white-counter-paned bed in another, and a dressing-table on the left-hand side of the window. These articles, with two small wickerwork chairs, made up all the furniture in the room, save for a square of Wilton carpet in the centre. The boards round and the panelling of the walls were brown, worm-eaten oak, so old and discoloured that it may have dated from the original building of the house. Holmes drew one of the chairs into a corner and sat silent, while his eyes travelled round and round and up and down, taking in every detail of the apartment.

'Where does that bell communicate with?' he asked at last, pointing to a thick bell-rope which hung down beside the bed, the tassel actually lying upon the pillow.

'It goes to the housekeeper's room.'

'It looks newer than the other things?'

'Yes, it was only put there a couple of years ago.'

'Your sister asked for it, I suppose?'

'No, I never heard of her using it. We used always to get what we wanted for ourselves.'

'Indeed, it seemed unnecessary to put so nice a bell-pull there. You will excuse me for a few minutes while I satisfy myself as to this floor.' He threw himself down upon his face with his lens in his hand, and crawled swiftly backwards and forwards, examining minutely the cracks between the boards. Then he did the same with the woodwork with which the chamber was panelled. Finally he walked over to the bed and spent some time in staring at it, and in running his eye up and down the wall. Finally he took the bell-rope in his hand and gave it a brisk tug.

'Why, it's a dummy,' said he.

'Won't it ring?'

'No, it is not even attached to a wire. This is very interesting. You can see now that it is fastened to a hook just above where the little opening of the ventilator is.'

'How very absurd! I never noticed that before.'

'Very strange!' muttered Holmes, pulling at the rope. 'There are one or two very singular points about this room. For example, what a fool a builder must be to open a ventilator in another room, when, with the same trouble, he might have communicated with the outside air!'

'That is also quite modern,' said the lady.

'Done about the same time as the bell-rope?' remarked Holmes.

'Yes, there were several little changes carried out about that time.'

'They seem to have been of a most interesting character—dummy bell-ropes, and ventilators which do not ventilate. With your permission, Miss Stoner, we shall now carry our researches into the inner apartment.'

Dr Grimesby Roylott's chamber was larger than that of his step-daughter, but was as plainly furnished. A camp bed, a small wooden shelf full of books, mostly of a technical character, an armchair beside the bed, a plain wooden chair against the wall, a round table, and a large iron safe were the principal things which met the eye. Holmes walked slowly round and examined each and all of them with the keenest interest.

'What's in here?' he asked, tapping the safe.

'My stepfather's business papers.'

'Oh! you have seen inside then?'

'Only once, some years ago. I remember that it was full of papers.'

'There isn't a cat in it, for example?'

'No. What a strange idea!'

'Well, look at this!' He took up a small saucer of milk which stood on the top of it.

'No; we don't keep a cat. But there is a cheetah and a baboon.'

'Ah, yes, of course! Well, a cheetah is just a big cat, and yet a saucer of milk does not go very far in satisfying its wants, I daresay. There is one point which I should wish to determine.' He squatted down in front of the wooden chair, and examined the seat of it with the greatest attention.

'Thank you. That is quite settled,' said he, rising and putting his lens in his pocket. 'Hello! here is something interesting!'

The object which had caught his eye was a small dog lash hung on one corner of the bed. The lash, however, was curled upon itself, and tied so as to make a loop of whipcord.

'What do you make of that, Watson?'

'It's a common enough lash. But I don't know why it should be tied.'

'That is not quite so common, is it? Ah, me! it's a wicked world, and when a clever man turns his brain to crime it is the worst of all. I think that I have seen enough now, Miss Stoner, and, with your permission, we shall walk out upon the lawn.'

I had never seen my friend's face so grim, or his brow so dark, as it was when we turned from the scene of his investigation. We had walked several times up and down the lawn, neither Miss Stoner nor myself liking to break in upon his thoughts before he roused himself from his reverie.

'It is very essential, Miss Stoner,' said he, 'that you should absolutely follow my advice in every respect.'

'I shall most certainly do so.'

'The matter is too serious for any hesitation. Your life may depend upon your compliance.'

'I assure you that I am in your hands.'

'In the first place, both my friend and I must spend the night in your room.'

Both Miss Stoner and I gazed at him in astonishment.

'Yes, it must be so. Let me explain. I believe that that is the village inn over there?'

'Yes, that is the "Crown".'

'Very good. Your windows would be visible from there?'

'Certainly.'

'You must confine yourself in your room, on pretence of a headache, when your stepfather comes back. Then when you hear him retire for the night, you must open the shutters of your window, undo the hasp, put your lamp there as a signal to us, and then withdraw with everything which you are likely to want into the room which you used to occupy. I have no doubt that, in spite of the repairs, you could manage there for one night.'

'Oh, yes, easily.'

'The rest you will leave in our hands.'

'But what will you do?'

'We shall spend the night in your room, and we shall investigate the cause of this noise which has disturbed you.'

'I believe, Mr Holmes, that you have already made up your mind,' said Miss Stoner, laying her hand upon my companion's sleeve.

'Perhaps I have.'

'Then for pity's sake tell me what was the cause of my sister's death.'

'I should prefer to have clearer proofs before I speak.'

'You can at least tell me whether my own thought is correct, and if she died from some sudden fright.'

'No, I do not think so. I think that there was probably some more tangible cause. And now, Miss Stoner, we must leave you, for if Dr Roylott returned and saw us, our journey would be in vain. Good-bye, and be brave, for if you will do what I have told you, you may rest assured that we shall soon drive away the dangers that threaten you.'

Sherlock Holmes and I had no difficulty in engaging a bedroom and sitting-room at the Crown Inn. They were on the upper floor, and from our window we could command a view of the avenue gate, and of the inhabited wing of Stoke Moran Manor House. At dusk we saw Dr Grimesby Roylott drive past, his huge form looming up beside the little figure of the lad who drove him. The boy had some slight difficulty in undoing the heavy iron gates, and we heard the hoarse roar of the Doctor's voice, and saw the fury with which he shook his clenched fists at him. The trap drove on, and a few minutes later we saw a sudden light spring up among the trees as the lamp was lit in one of the sitting-rooms.

'Do you know, Watson,' said Holmes, as we sat together in the gathering darkness, 'I have really some scruples as to taking you tonight. There is a distinct element of danger.'

'Can I be of assistance?'

'Your presence might be invaluable.'

'Then I shall certainly come.'

'It is very kind of you.'

'You speak of danger. You have evidently seen more in these rooms than was visible to me.'

'No, but I fancy that I may have deduced a little more. I imagine that you saw all that I did.'

'I saw nothing remarkable save the bell-rope, and what purpose that could answer I confess is more than I can imagine.'

'You saw the ventilator, too?'

'Yes, but I do not think that it is such a very unusual thing to have a small opening between two rooms. It was so small a rat could hardly pass through.'

'I knew that we should find a ventilator before ever we came to Stoke Moran.'

'My dear Holmes!'

'Oh, yes, I did. You remember in her statement she said that her sister could smell Dr Roylott's cigar. Now, of course that suggests at once that there must be a communication between the two rooms. It could only be a small one, or it would have been remarked upon at the coroner's inquiry. I deduced a ventilator.'

'But what harm can there be in that?'

'Well, there is at least a curious coincidence of dates. A ventilator is made, a cord is hung, and a lady who sleeps in the bed dies. Does not that strike you?'

'I cannot as yet see any connection.'

'Did you observe anything very peculiar about that bed?'

'No.'

'It was clamped to the floor. Did you ever see a bed fastened like that before?'

'I cannot say that I have.'

'The lady could not move her bed. It must always be in the same relative position to the ventilator and to the rope—for so we may call it, since it was clearly never meant for a bell-pull.'

'Holmes,' I cried, 'I seem to see dimly what you are hitting at. We are only just in time to prevent some subtle and horrible crime.'

'Subtle enough and horrible enough. When a doctor does go wrong he is the first of criminals. He has nerve and he has knowledge. Palmer and Pritchard were among the heads of their profession. This man strikes even deeper, but, I think, Watson, that we shall be able to strike deeper still. But we shall have horrors enough before the night is over: for goodness' sake let us have a quiet pipe, and turn our minds for a few hours to something more cheerful.'

About nine o'clock the light among the trees was extinguished, and all was dark in the direction of the Manor House. Two hours passed slowly away, and then, suddenly, just at the stroke of eleven, a single bright light shone out right in front of us.

'That is our signal,' said Holmes, springing to his feet; 'it comes from the middle window.'

As we passed out he exchanged a few words with the landlord, explaining that we were going on a late visit to an acquaintance, and that it was possible that we might spend the night there. A moment later we were out on the dark road, a chill wind blowing in our faces, and one yellow light twinkling in front of us through the gloom to guide us on our sombre errand.

There was little difficulty in entering the grounds, for unrepaired breaches gaped in the old park wall. Making our way among the trees, we reached the lawn, crossed it, and were about to enter through the window, when out from a clump of laurel bushes there darted what seemed to be a hideous and distorted child, who threw itself on the grass with writhing limbs, and then ran swiftly across the lawn into the darkness.

'My God!' I whispered, 'did you see it?'

Holmes was for the moment as startled as I. His hand closed like a vice upon my wrist in his agitation. Then he broke into a low laugh, and put his lips to my ear.

'It is a nice household,' he murmured, 'that is the baboon.'

I had forgotten the strange pets which the doctor affected. There was a cheetah, too; perhaps we might find it upon our shoulders at any moment. I confess that I felt easier in my mind when, after following Holmes's example and slipping off my shoes, I found myself inside the bedroom. My companion noiselessly closed the shutters, moved the lamp on to the table, and cast his eyes round the room. All was as we had seen it in the day-time. Then creeping up to me and making a trumpet of his hand, he whispered into my ear again so gently that it was all that I could do to distinguish the words:

'The least sound would be fatal to our plans.'

I nodded to show that I had heard.

'We must sit without a light. He would see it through the ventilator.'

I nodded again.

'Do not go to sleep; your very life may depend upon it. Have your pistol ready in case we should need it. I will sit on the side of the bed, and you in that chair.'

I took out my revolver and laid it on the corner of the table.

Holmes had brought up a long thin cane, and this he placed upon the bed beside him. By it he laid the box of matches and the stump of a candle. Then he turned down the lamp and we were left in darkness.

How shall I ever forget that dreadful vigil? I could not hear a sound, not even the drawing of a breath, and yet I knew that my companion sat open-eyed, within a few feet of me, in the same state of nervous tension in which I was myself. The shutters cut off the least ray of light, and we waited in absolute darkness. From outside came the occasional cry of a nightbird, and once at our very window a long drawn, cat-like whine, which told us that the cheetah was indeed at liberty. Far away we could hear the deep tones of the parish clock, which boomed out every quarter of an hour. How long they seemed, those quarters! Twelve o'clock, and one, and two, and three, and still we sat waiting silently for whatever might befall.

Suddenly there was the momentary gleam of a light up in the direction of the ventilator, which vanished immediately, but was succeeded by a strong smell of burning oil and heated metal. Someone in the next room had lit a dark lantern. I heard a gentle sound of movement, and then all was silent once more, though the smell grew stronger. For half an hour I sat with straining ears. Then suddenly another sound became audible—a very gentle, soothing sound, like that of a small jet of steam escaping continually from a kettle. The instant that we heard it, Holmes sprang from the bed, struck a match, and lashed furiously with his cane at the bell-pull.

'You see it, Watson?' he yelled. 'You see it?'

But I saw nothing. At the moment when Holmes struck the light I heard a low, clear whistle, but the sudden glare flashing into my weary eyes made it impossible for me to tell what it was at which my friend lashed so savagely. I could, however, see that his face was deadly pale, and filled with horror and loathing.

He had ceased to strike, and was gazing up at the ventilator, when suddenly there broke from the silence of the night the most horrible cry to which I have ever listened. It swelled up louder and louder, a hoarse yell of pain and fear and anger all mingled in the one dreadful shriek. They say that away down in the village, and even in the distant parsonage, that cry raised the sleepers from their beds. It struck cold to our hearts, and I stood gazing at Holmes, and he at me, until the last echoes of it had died away into the silence from which it rose.

'What can it mean?' I gasped.

'It means that it is all over,' Holmes answered. 'And perhaps, after all, it is for the best. Take your pistol, and we shall enter Dr Roylott's room.'

With a grave face he lit the lamp, and led the way down the corridor. Twice he struck at the chamber door without any reply from within. Then he turned the handle and entered, I at his heels, with the cocked pistol in my hand.

It was a singular sight which met our eyes. On the table stood a dark lantern with the shutter half open, throwing a brilliant beam of light upon the iron safe, the door of which was ajar. Beside this table, on the wooden chair, sat Dr Grimesby Roylott, clad in a long grey dressing-gown, his bare ankles protruding beneath, and his feet thrust into red heelless Turkish slippers. Across his lap lay the short stock with the long lash which we had noticed during the day. His chin was cocked upwards, and his eyes were fixed in a dreadful rigid stare at the corner of the ceiling. Round his brow he had a peculiar yellow band, with brownish speckles, which seemed to be bound tight round his head. As we entered he made neither sound nor motion.

'The band! the speckled band!' whispered Holmes.

I took a step forward: in an instant his strange headgear began to move, and there reared itself from among his hair the squat diamond-shaped head and puffed neck of a loathsome serpent.

'It is a swamp adder!' cried Holmes—'the deadliest snake in India. He has died within ten seconds of being bitten. Violence does, in truth, recoil upon the violent, and the schemer falls into the pit which he digs for another. Let us thrust this creature back into its den, and we can then remove Miss Stoner to some place of shelter, and let the county police know what has happened.'

As he spoke he drew the dog whip swiftly from the dead man's lap, and throwing the noose round the reptile's neck, he drew it from its horrid perch, and carrying it at arm's length, threw it into the iron safe, which he closed upon it.

Such are the true facts of the death of Dr Grimesby Roylott, of Stoke Moran. It is not necessary that I should prolong a narrative which has already run to too great a length, by telling how we broke the sad news to the terrified girl, how we conveyed her by the morning train to the care of her good aunt at Harrow, of how the slow process of official inquiry came to the conclusion that the Doctor met his fate while indiscreetly playing with a dangerous pet. The little which I had yet to learn of the case was told me by Sherlock Holmes as we travelled back next day.

'I had,' said he, 'come to an entirely erroneous conclusion, which shows, my dear Watson, how dangerous it always is to reason from insufficient data. The presence of the gipsies, and the use of the word "band", which was used by the poor girl, no doubt, to explain the appearance which she had caught a horrid glimpse of by the light of her match, were sufficient to put me upon an entirely wrong scent. I can only claim the merit that I instantly reconsidered my position when, however, it became clear to me that whatever danger threatened an occupant of the room could not come either from the window or the door. My attention was speedily drawn, as I have already remarked to you, to this ventilator, and to the bell-rope which hung down to the bed. The discovery that this was a dummy, and that the bed was clamped to the floor, instantly gave rise to the suspicion that the rope was there as a bridge for something passing through the hole, and coming to the bed. The idea of a snake instantly occurred to me, and when I coupled it with my knowledge that the Doctor was furnished with a supply of creatures from India, I felt that I was probably on the right track. The idea of using a form of poison which could not possibly be discovered by any chemical test was just such a one as would occur to a clever and ruthless man who had an Eastern training. The rapidity with which such a poison would take effect would also, from his point of view, be an advantage. It would be a sharp-eyed coroner indeed who could distinguish the two little dark punctures which would show where the poison fangs had done their work. Then I thought of the whistle. Of course, he must recall the snake before the morning light revealed it to the victim. He had trained it, probably by the use of the milk which we saw, to return to him when summoned. He would put it through the ventilator at the hour that he thought best, with the certainty that it would crawl down the rope, and land on the bed. It might or might not bite the occupant, perhaps she might escape every night for a week, but sooner or later she must fall a victim.

'I had come to these conclusions before ever I had entered his room. An inspection of his chair showed me that he had been in the habit of standing on it, which, of course, would be necessary in order that he should reach the ventilator. The sight of the safe, the saucer of milk, and the loop of whipcord were really enough to finally dispel any doubts which may have remained. The metallic clang heard by Miss Stoner was obviously caused by her father hastily closing the door of his safe upon its terrible occupant. Having once made up my mind, you know the steps which I took in order to put the matter to the proof. I heard the creature hiss, as I have no doubt that you did also, and I instantly lit the light and attacked it.'

'With the result of driving it through the ventilator.'

'And also with the result of causing it to turn upon its master at the other side. Some of the blows of my cane came home, and roused its snakish temper, so that it flew upon the first person it saw. In this way I am no doubt indirectly responsible for Dr Grimesby Roylott's death, and I cannot say that it is likely to weigh very heavily upon my conscience.'

E. N E S B I T

Hurst of Hurstcote

We were at Eton together, and afterwards at Christ Church, and I always got on very well with him; but somehow he was a man about whom none of the other men cared very much. There was always something strange and secret about him; even at Eton he liked grubbing among books and trying chemical experiments better than cricket or the boats. That sort of thing would make any boy unpopular. At Oxford, it wasn't merely his studious ways and his love of science that went against him; it was a certain habit he had of gazing at us through narrowing lids, as though he were looking at us more from the outside than any human being has a right to look at any other, and a bored air of belonging to another and a higher race, whenever we talked the ordinary chatter about athletics and the Schools.

A wild paper on 'Black Magic', which he read to the Essay Society, filled to overflowing the cup of his College's contempt for him. I suppose no man was ever so much disliked for so little cause.

When we went down I noticed—for I knew his people at home—that the sentiment of dislike which he excited in most men was curiously in contrast to the emotions which he inspired in women. They all liked him, listened to him with rapt attention, talked of him with undisguised enthusiasm. I watched their strange infatuation with calmness for several years, but the day came when he met Kate Danvers, and then I was not calm any more. She behaved like all the rest of the women, and to her, quite suddenly, Hurst threw the handkerchief. He was not Hurst of Hurstcote then, but his family was good, and his means not despicable, so he and she were conditionally engaged. People said it was a poor match for the beauty of the county; and her people, I know, hoped she would think better of it. As for me—well, this is not the story of my life, but of his. I need only say that I thought him a lucky man.

I went to town to complete the studies that were to make me MD; Hurst went abroad, to Paris or Leipzig or somewhere, to study hypnotism and prepare notes for his book on 'Black Magic'. This came out in the autumn, and had a strange and brilliant success.

Hurst became famous, famous as men do become nowadays. His writings were asked for by all the big periodicals. His future seemed assured. In the spring they were married; I was not present at the wedding. The practice my father had bought for me in London claimed all my time, I said.

It was more than a year after their marriage that I had a letter from Hurst.

Congratulate me, old man! Crowds of uncles and cousins have died, and I am Hurst of Hurstcote, which God wot I never thought to be. The place is all to pieces, but we can't live anywhere else. If you can get away about September, come down and see us. We shall be installed. I have everything now that I ever longed for—Hurstcote—cradle of our race—and all that, the only woman in the world for my wife, and—But that's enough for any man, surely.

JOHN HURST OF HURSTCOTE

Of course I knew Hurstcote. Who does not? Hurstcote, which seventy years ago was one of the most perfect, as well as the finest, brick Tudor mansions in England. The Hurst who lived there seventy years ago noticed one day that his chimneys smoked, and called in a Hastings architect. 'Your chimneys', said the local man, 'are beyond me, but with the timbers and lead of your castle I can build you a snug little house in the corner of your park, much more suitable for a residence than this old brick building.' So they gutted Hurstcote, and built the new house, and faced it with stucco. All of which things you will find written in the Guide to Sussex. Hurstcote, when I had seen it, had been the merest shell. How would Hurst make it habitable? Even if he had inherited much money with the castle, and intended to restore the building, that would be a work of years, not months. What would he do?

In September I went to see.

Hurst met me at Pevensey Station.

'Let's walk up,' he said; 'there's a cart to bring your traps. Eh, but it's good to see you again, Bernard!'

It was good to see him again. And to see him so changed. And so changed for good, too. He was much stouter, and no longer wore the untidy ill-fitting clothes of the old days. He was rather smartly got up in grey stockings and knee-breeches, and wore a velvet shooting-jacket. But the most noteworthy change was in his face; it bore no more the eager, inquiring, half-scornful, half-tolerant look that had won him such ill-will at Oxford. His face now was the face of a man completely at peace with himself and with the world.

'How well you look!' I said, as we walked along the level winding road through the still marshes.

'How much better, you mean!' he laughed. 'I know it. Bernard you'll hardly believe it, but I'm on the way to be a popular man!'

He had not lost his old knack of reading one's thoughts.

'Don't trouble yourself to find the polite answer to that,' he hastened to add. 'No one knows as well as I how unpopular I was; and no one knows so well why,' he added, in a very low voice. 'However,' he went on gaily, 'unpopularity is a thing of the past. The folk hereabout call on us, and condole with us on our hutch. A thing of the past, as I said—but what a past it was, eh! You're the only man who ever liked me. You don't know what that's been to me many a dark day and night. When the others were—you know—it was like a hand holding mine, to think of you. I've always thought I was sure of one soul in the world to stand by me.'

'Yes,' I said—'yes.'

He flung his arm over my shoulder with a frank, boyish gesture of affection, quite foreign to his nature as I had known it.

'And I know why you didn't come to our wedding,' he went on; 'but that's all right now, isn't it?'

'Yes,' I said again, for indeed it was. There are brown eyes in the world, after all, as well as blue, and one pair of brown that meant heaven to me as the blue had never done.

'That's well,' Hurst answered, and we walked on in satisfied silence, till we passed across the furze-crowned ridge, and went down the hill to Hurstcote. It lies in the hollow, ringed round by its moat, its dark red walls showing the sky behind them. There was no welcoming sparkle of early litten candle, only the pale amber of the September evening shining through the gaunt unglazed windows.

Three planks and a rough handrail had replaced the old drawbridge. We passed across the moat, and Hurst pulled a knotted rope that hung beside the great iron-bound door. A bell clanged loudly inside. In the moment we spent there, waiting, Hurst pushed back a briar that was trailing across the arch, and let it fall outside the handrail.

'Nature is too much with us here,' he said, laughing. 'The clematis spends its time tripping one up, or clawing at one's hair, and we are always expecting the ivy to force itself through the window and make an uninvited third at our dinner-table.'

Then the great door of Hurstcote Castle swung back, and there stood Kate, a thousand times sweeter and more beautiful than ever. I looked at her with momentary terror and dazzlement. She was indeed much more beautiful than any woman with brown eyes could be. My heart almost stopped beating.

With life or death in the balance: Right!

To be beautiful is not the same thing as to be dear, thank God. I went forward and took her hand with a free heart.

It was a pleasant fortnight I spent with them. They had had one tower completely repaired, and in its queer eight-sided rooms we lived, when we were not out among the marshes, or by the blue sea at Pevensey.

Mrs Hurst had made the rooms quaintly charming by a medley of Liberty stuffs and Wardour Street furniture. The grassy space within the castle walls, with its underground passages, its crumbling heaps of masonry, overgrown with lush creepers, was better than any garden. There we met the fresh morning; there we lounged through lazy noons; there the grey evenings found us.

I have never seen any two married people so utterly, so undisguisedly in love as these were. I, the third, had no embarrassment in so being—for their love had in it a completeness, a childish abandonment, to which the presence of a third—a friend—was no burden. A happiness, reflected from theirs, shone on me. The days went by, dreamlike, and brought the eve of my return to London, and to the commonplaces of life.

We were sitting in the courtyard; Hurst had gone to the village to post some letters. A big moon was just showing over the battlements, when Mrs Hurst shivered.

'It's late,' she said, 'and cold; the summer is gone. Let us go in.' So we went in to the little warm room, where a wood fire flickered on a brick hearth, and a shaded lamp was already glowing softly. Here we sat on the cushioned seat in the open window, and looked out through the lozenge panes at the gold moon, and ah! the light of her making ghosts in the white mist that rose thick and heavy from the moat.

'I am so sorry you are going,' she said presently; 'but you will come and skate on the moat with us at Christmas, won't you? We mean to have a medieval Christmas. You don't know what that is? Neither do I; but John does. He is very, very wise.'

'Yes,' I answered, 'he used to know many things that most men don't even dream of as possible to know.'

She was silent a minute, and then shivered again. I picked up the shawl she had thrown down when we came in, and put it round her.

'Thank you! I think—don't you?—that there are some things one is not meant to know, and some one is meant *not* to know. You see the distinction?'

'I suppose so—yes.'

'Did it never frighten you in the old days,' she went on, 'to see that John would never—was always——'

'But he has given all that up now?'

'Oh yes, ever since our honeymoon. Do you know, he used to mesmerise me. It was horrible. And that book of his—'

'I didn't know you believed in Black Magic.'

'Oh, I don't—not the least bit. I never was at all superstitious, you know. But those things always frighten me just as much as if I believed in them. And besides—I think they are wicked; but John ——Ah, there he is! Let's go and meet him.'

His dark figure was outlined against the sky behind the hill. She wrapped the soft shawl more closely around her, and we went out in the moonlight to meet her husband.

The next morning when I entered the room I found that it lacked its chief ornament. The sparkling white and silver breakfast accessories were there, but for the deft white hands and kindly welcoming blue eyes of my hostess I looked in vain. At ten minutes past nine Hurst came in looking horribly worried, and more like his old self than I had ever expected to see him.

'I say, old man,' he said hurriedly, 'are you really set on going back to town today—because Kate's awfully queer? I can't think what's wrong. I want you to see her after breakfast.'

I reflected a minute. 'I can stay if I send a wire,' I said.

'I wish you would, then,' Hurst said, wringing my hand and turning away; 'she's been off her head most of the night, talking the most astounding nonsense. You must see her after breakfast. Will you pour out the coffee?'

'I'll see her now, if you like,' I said, and he led me up the winding stair to the room at the top of the tower.

I found her quite sensible, but very feverish. I wrote a prescription, and rode Hurst's mare over to Eastbourne to get it made up. When I got back she was worse. It seemed to be a sort of aggravated marsh fever. I reproached myself with having let her sit by the open window the night before. But I remembered with some satisfaction that I had told Hurst that the place was not quite healthy. I only wished I had insisted on it more strongly.

For the first day or two I thought it was merely a touch of marsh fever, that would pass off with no more worse consequence than a little weakness; but on the third day I perceived that she would die.

Hurst met me as I came from her bedside, stood aside on the narrow landing for me to pass, and followed me down into the little sitting-room, which, deprived for three days of her presence, already bore the air of a room long deserted. He came in after me and shut the door.

'You're wrong,' he said abruptly, reading my thoughts as usual; 'she won't die—she can't die.'

'She will,' I bluntly answered, for I am no believer in that worst refinement of torture known as 'breaking bad news gently'. 'Send for any other man you choose. I'll consult with the whole College of Physicians if you like. But nothing short of a miracle can save her.'

'And you don't believe in miracles,' he answered quietly. 'I do, you see.'

'My dear old fellow, don't buoy yourself up with false hopes. I know my trade; I wish I could believe I didn't! Go back to her now; you have not very long to be together.'

I wrung his hand; he returned the pressure, but said almost cheerfully—

'You know your trade, old man, but there are some things you don't know. Mine, for instance—I mean my wife's constitution. Now I know that thoroughly. And you mark my words—she won't die. You might as well say *I* was not long for this world.'

'*You*,' I said with a touch of annoyance; 'you're good for another thirty or forty years.'

'Exactly so,' he rejoined quickly, 'and so is she. Her life's as good as mine, you'll see—she won't die.'

At dusk on the next day she died. He was with her; he had not left her since he had told me that she would not die. He was sitting by her holding her hand. She had been unconscious for some time, when suddenly she dragged her hand from his, raised herself in bed, and cried out in a tone of acutest anguish—

'John! John! Let me go! For Heaven's sake let me go!'

Then she fell back dead.

He would not understand—would not believe; he still sat by her, holding her hand, and calling on her by every name that love could teach him. I began to fear for his brain. He would not leave her, so by-and-by I brought him a cup of coffee in which I had mixed a strong opiate. In about an hour I went back and found him fast asleep with his face on the pillow close by the face of his dead wife. The gardener and I carried him down to my bedroom, and I sent for a woman from the village. He slept for twelve hours. When he awoke his first words were—

'She is not dead! I must go to her!'

I hoped that the sight of her—pale, and beautiful, and still—with the white asters about her, and her cold hands crossed on her breast, would convince him; but no. He looked at her and said—

'Bernard, you're no fool; you know as well as I do that this is not death. Why treat it so? It is some form of catalepsy. If she should awake and find herself like this the shock might destroy her reason.'

And, to the horror of the woman from the village, he flung the asters on to the floor, covered the body with blankets, and sent for hot-water bottles.

I was now quite convinced that his brain was affected, and I saw plainly enough that he would never consent to take the necessary steps for the funeral.

I began to wonder whether I had not better send for another doctor, for I felt that I did not care to try the opiate again on my own responsibility, and something must be done about the funeral.

I spent a day in considering the matter—a day passed by John Hurst beside his wife's body. Then I made up my mind to try all my powers to bring him to reason, and to this end I went once more into the chamber of death. I found Hurst talking wildly, in low whispers. He seemed to be talking to some one who was not there. He did not know me, and suffered himself to be led away. He was, in fact, in the first stage of brain fever. I actually blessed his illness, because it opened a way out of the dilemma in which I found myself. I wired for a trained nurse from town, and for the local undertaker. In a week she was buried, and John Hurst still lay unconscious and unheeding; but I did not look forward to his first renewal of consciousness.

Yet his first conscious words were not the inquiry I dreaded. He only asked whether he had been ill long, and what had been the matter. When I had told him, he just nodded and went off to sleep again.

A few evenings later I found him excited and feverish, but quite himself, mentally. I said as much to him in answer to a question which he put to me—

'There's no brain disturbance now? I'm not mad or anything?'

'No, no, my dear fellow. Everything is as it should be.'

'Then,' he answered slowly, 'I must get up and go to her.'

My worst fears were realized.

In moments of intense mental strain the truth sometimes overpowers all one's better resolves. It sounds brutal, horrible. I don't know what I meant to say; what I said was—

'You can't; she's buried.'

He sprang up in bed, and I caught him by the shoulders.

'Then it's true!' he cried, 'and I'm not mad. Oh, great God in heaven, let me go to her; let me go! It's true! It's true!'

I held him fast, and spoke.

'I am strong—you know that. You are weak and ill; you are quite in my power—we're old friends, and there's nothing I wouldn't do to serve you. Tell me what you mean; I will do anything you wish.' This I said to soothe him.

'Let me go to her,' he said again.

'Tell me all about it,' I repeated. 'You are too ill to go to her. I will go, if you can collect yourself and tell me why. You could not walk five yards.'

He looked at me doubtfully.

'You'll help me? You won't say I'm mad, and have me shut up? You'll help me?'

'Yes, yes—I swear it!' All the time I was wondering what I should do to keep him from his mad purpose.

He lay back on his pillows, white and ghastly; his thin features and sunken eyes showed hawklike above the rough growth of his four weeks' beard. I took his hand. His pulse was rapid, and his lean fingers clenched themselves round mine.

'Look here,' he said, 'I don't know——There aren't any words to tell you how true it is. I am not mad, I am not wandering. I am as sane as you are. Now listen, and if you've a human heart in you, you'll help me. When I married her I gave up hypnotism and all the old studies; she hated the whole business. But before I gave it up I hypnotised her, and when she was completely under my control I forbade her soul to leave its body till my time came to die.'

I breathed more freely. Now I understood why he had said, 'She *cannot* die.'

'My dear old man,' I said gently, 'dismiss these fancies, and face your grief boldly. You can't control the great facts of life and death by hypnotism. She is dead; she is dead, and her body lies in its place. But her soul is with God who gave it.'

'No!' he cried, with such strength as the fever had left him. 'No! no! Ever since I have been ill I have seen her, every day, every night, and always wringing her hands and moaning, "Let me go, John—let me go".'

'Those were her last words, indeed,' I said; 'it is natural that they should haunt you. See, you bade her soul not leave her body. It has left it, for she is dead.'

His answer came almost in a whisper, borne on the wings of a long breathless pause.

'*She is dead, but her soul has not left her body.*'

I held his hand more closely, still debating what I should do.

'She comes to me,' he went on; 'she comes to me continually. She does not reproach, but she implores, "Let me go, John—let me go!" And I have no more power now; I cannot let her go, I cannot reach her. I can do nothing, nothing. Ah!' he cried, with a sudden sharp change of voice that thrilled through me to the ends of my fingers and feet: 'Ah, Kate, my life, I will come to you! No, no, you shan't be left alone among the dead. I am coming, my sweet.'

He reached his arms out towards the door with a look of longing and love, so really, so patently addressed to a sentient presence, that I turned sharply to see if, in truth, perhaps——Nothing—of course—nothing.

'She is dead,' I repeated stupidly. 'I was obliged to bury her.'

A shudder ran through him.

'I must go and see for myself,' he said.

Then I knew—all in a minute—what to do.

'I will go,' I said. 'I will open her coffin, and if she is not—is not as other dead folk, I will bring her body back to this house.'

'Will you go now?' he asked, with set lips.

It was nigh on midnight. I looked into his eyes.

'Yes, now,' I said; 'but you must swear to lie still till I return.'

'I swear it.' I saw I could trust him, and I went to wake the nurse. He called weakly after me, 'There's a lantern in the tool-shed—and, Bernard——'

'Yes, my poor old chap.'

'There's a screwdriver in the sideboard drawer.'

I think until he said that I really meant to go. I am not accustomed to lie, even to mad people, and I think I meant it till then.

He leaned on his elbow, and looked at me with wide open eyes.

'Think,' he said, 'what she must feel. Out of the body, and yet tied to it, all alone among the dead. Oh, make haste, make haste; for if I am not mad, and I have really fettered her soul, there is but one way!'

'And that is?'

'I must die too. Her soul can leave her body when I die.'

I called the nurse, and left him. I went out, and across the wold to the church, but I did not go in. I carried the screwdriver and the lantern, lest he should send the nurse to see if I had taken them. I leaned on the churchyard wall, and thought of her. I had loved the woman, and I remembered it in that hour.

As soon as I dared I went back to him—remember I believed him mad—and told the lie that I thought would give him most ease.

'Well?' he said eagerly, as I entered.

I signed to the nurse to leave us.

'There is no hope,' I said. 'You will not see your wife again till you meet her in heaven.'

I laid down the screwdriver and the lantern, and sat down by him.

'You have seen her?'

'Yes.'

'And there's no doubt?'

'There is no doubt.'

'Then I *am* mad; but you're a good fellow, Bernard, and I'll never forget it in this world or the next.'

He seemed calmer, and fell asleep with my hand on his. His last word was a 'Thank you', that cut me like a knife.

When I went into his room next morning he was gone. But on his pillow a letter lay, painfully scrawled in pencil, and addressed to me.

'You lied. Perhaps you meant kindly. You didn't understand. She is not dead. She has been with me again. Though her soul may not leave her body, thank God it can still speak to mine. That vault—it is worse than a mere churchyard grave. Good-bye.'

I ran all the way to the church, and entered by the open door. The air was chill and dank after the crisp October sunlight. The stone that closed the vault of the Hursts of Hurstcote had been raised, and was lying beside the dark gaping hole in the chancel floor. The nurse, who had followed me, came in before I could shake off the horror that held me moveless. We both went down into the vault. Weak, exhausted by illness and sorrow, John Hurst had yet found strength to follow his love to the grave. I tell you he had crossed that wold alone, in the grey of the chill dawn; alone he had raised the stone and had gone down to her. He had opened her coffin, and he lay on the floor of the vault with his wife's body in his arms.

He had been dead some hours.

The brown eyes filled with tears when I told my wife this story.

'You were quite right, he was mad,' she said. 'Poor things! poor lovers!'

But sometimes when I wake in the grey morning, and, between waking and sleeping, think of all those things that I must shut out from my sleeping and my waking thoughts, I wonder was I right or was he? Was he mad, or was I idiotically incredulous? For—and it is this thing that haunts me—when I found them dead together in the vault, she had been buried five weeks. But the body that lay in John Hurst's arms, among the mouldering coffins of the Hursts of Hurstcote, was perfect and beautiful as when first he clasped her in his arms, a bride.

III

The Twentieth Century

A Vine on a House

About three miles from the little town of Norton, in Missouri, on the road leading to Maysville, stands an old house that was last occupied by a family named Harding. Since 1886 no one has lived in it, nor is anyone likely to live in it again. Time and the disfavor of persons dwelling thereabout are converting it into a rather picturesque ruin. An observer unacquainted with its history would hardly put it into the category of 'haunted houses,' yet in all the region round such is its evil reputation. Its windows are without glass, its doorways without doors; there are wide breaches in the shingle roof, and for lack of paint the weatherboarding is a dun gray. But these unfailing signs of the supernatural are partly concealed and greatly softened by the abundant foliage of a large vine overrunning the entire structure. This vine—of a species which no botanist has ever been able to name—has an important part in the story of the house.

The Harding family consisted of Robert Harding, his wife Matilda, Miss Julia Went, who was her sister, and two young children. Robert Harding was a silent, cold-mannered man who made no friends in the neighborhood and apparently cared to make none. He was about forty years old, frugal and industrious, and made a living from the little farm which is now overgrown with brush and brambles. He and his sister-in-law were rather tabooed by their neighbors, who seemed to think that they were seen too frequently together—not entirely their fault, for at these times they evidently did not challenge observation. The moral code of rural Missouri is stern and exacting.

Mrs Harding was a gentle, sad-eyed woman, lacking a left foot.

At some time in 1884 it became known that she had gone to visit her mother in Iowa. That was what her husband said in reply to inquiries, and his manner of saying it did not encourage further questioning. She never came back, and two years later, without selling his farm or anything that was his, or appointing an agent to look after his interests, or removing his household goods, Harding, with the rest of the family, left the country. Nobody knew whither he went; nobody at that time cared. Naturally, whatever was movable about the place soon disappeared and the deserted house became 'haunted' in the manner of its kind.

One summer evening, four or five years later, the Revd J. Gruber, of Norton, and a Maysville attorney named Hyatt met on horseback in front of the Harding place. Having business matters to discuss, they hitched their animals and going to the house sat on the porch to talk. Some humorous reference to the somber reputation of the place was made and forgotten as soon as uttered, and they talked of their business affairs until it grew almost dark. The evening was oppressively warm, the air stagnant.

Presently both men started from their seats in surprise: a long vine that covered half the front of the house and dangled its branches from the edge of the porch above them was visibly and audibly agitated, shaking violently in every stem and leaf.

'We shall have a storm,' Hyatt exclaimed.

Gruber said nothing, but silently directed the other's attention to the foliage of adjacent trees, which showed no movement; even the delicate tips of the boughs silhouetted against the clear sky were motionless. They hastily passed down the steps to what had been a lawn and looked upward at the vine, whose entire length was now visible. It continued in violent agitation, yet they could discern no disturbing cause.

'Let us leave,' said the minister.

And leave they did. Forgetting that they had been traveling in opposite directions, they rode away together. They went to Norton, where they related their strange experience to several discreet friends. The next evening, at about the same hour, accompanied by two others whose names are not recalled, they were again on the porch of the Harding house, and again the mysterious phenomenon occurred: the vine was violently agitated while under the closest scrutiny from root to tip, nor did their combined strength applied to the trunk serve to still it. After an hour's observation they retreated, no less wise, it is thought, than when they had come.

No great time was required for these singular facts to rouse the curiosity of the entire neighborhood. By day and by night crowds of persons assembled at the Harding house 'seeking a sign'. It does not appear that any found it, yet so credible were the witnesses mentioned that none doubted the reality of the 'manifestations' to which they testified.

By either a happy inspiration or some destructive design, it was one day proposed—nobody appeared to know from whom the suggestion came—to dig up the vine, and after a good deal of debate this was done. Nothing was found but the root, yet nothing could have been more strange!

For five or six feet from the trunk, which had at the surface of the ground a diameter of several inches, it ran downward, single and straight, into a loose, friable earth; then it divided and subdivided into rootlets, fibers and filaments, most curiously interwoven. When carefully freed from soil they showed a singular formation. In their ramifications and doublings back upon themselves they made a compact network, having in size and shape an amazing resemblance to the human figure. Head, trunk and limbs were there; even the fingers and toes were distinctly defined; and many professed to see in the distribution and arrangement of the fibers in the globular mass representing the head a grotesque suggestion of a face. The figure was horizontal; the smaller roots had begun to unite at the breast.

In point of resemblance to the human form this image was imperfect. At about ten inches from one of the knees, the *cilia* forming that leg had abruptly doubled backward and inward upon their course of growth. The figure lacked the left foot.

There was but one inference—the obvious one; but in the ensuing excitement as many courses of action were proposed as there were incapable counselors. The matter was settled by the sheriff of the county, who as the lawful custodian of the abandoned estate ordered the root replaced and the excavation filled with the earth that had been removed.

Later inquiry brought out only one fact of relevancy and significance: Mrs Harding had never visited her relatives in Iowa, nor did they know that she was supposed to have done so.

Of Robert Harding and the rest of his family nothing is known. The house retains its evil reputation, but the replanted vine is as orderly and well-behaved a vegetable as a nervous person could wish to sit under of a pleasant night, when the katydids grate out their immemorial revelation and the distant whippoorwill signifies his notion of what ought to be done about it.

ELLEN GLASGOW

Jordan's End

At the fork of the road there was the dead tree where buzzards were roosting, and through its boughs I saw the last flare of the sunset. On either side the November woods were flung in broken masses against the sky. When I stopped they appeared to move closer and surround me with vague, glimmering shapes. It seemed to me that I had been driving for hours; yet the ancient negro who brought the message had told me to follow the Old Stage Road till I came to Buzzard's Tree at the fork. 'F'om dar on hit's moughty nigh ter Marse Jur'dn's place,' the old man had assured me, adding tremulously, 'en young Miss she sez you mus' comes jes' ez quick ez you kin.' I was young then (that was more than thirty years ago), and I was just beginning the practice of medicine in one of the more remote counties of Virginia.

My mare stopped, and leaning out, I gazed down each winding road, where it branched off, under half bared boughs, into the autumnal haze of the distance. In a little while the red would fade from the sky, and the chill night would find me still hesitating between those dubious ways which seemed to stretch into an immense solitude. While I waited uncertainly there was a stir in the boughs overhead, and a buzzard's feather floated down and settled slowly on the robe over my knees. In the effort to drive off depression, I laughed aloud and addressed my mare in a jocular tone:

'We'll choose the most God-forsaken of the two, and see where it leads us.'

To my surprise the words brought an answer from the trees at my back. 'If you're goin' to Isham's store, keep on the Old Stage Road,' piped a voice from the underbrush.

Turning quickly, I saw the dwarfed figure of a very old man, with a hunched back, who was dragging a load of pine knots out of the woods. Though he was so stooped that his head reached scarcely higher than my wheel, he appeared to possess unusual vigour for one of his age and infirmities. He was dressed in a rough overcoat of some wood brown shade, beneath which I could see his overalls of blue jeans. Under a thatch of grizzled hair his shrewd little eyes twinkled cunningly, and his bristly chin jutted so far forward that it barely escaped the descending curve of his nose. I remember thinking that he could not be far from a hundred; his skin was so wrinkled and weather-beaten that, at a distance, I had mistaken him for a negro.

I bowed politely. 'Thank you, but I am going to Jordan's End,' I replied.

He cackled softly. 'Then you take the bad road. Thar's Jur'dn's turn-out.' He pointed to the sunken trail, deep in mud, on the right. 'An' if you ain't objectin' to a little comp'ny, I'd be obleeged if you'd give me a lift. I'm bound thar on my own o' count, an' it's a long ways to tote these here lightwood knots.'

While I drew back my robe and made room for him, I watched him heave the load of resinous pine into the buggy, and then scramble with agility to his place at my side.

'My name is Peterkin,' he remarked by way of introduction. 'They call me Father Peterkin along o' the gran'child'en.' He was a garrulous soul, I suspected, and would not be averse to imparting the information I wanted.

'There's not much travel this way,' I began, as we turned out of the cleared space into the deep tunnel of the trees. Immediately the twilight enveloped us, though now and then the dusky glow in the sky was still visible. The air was sharp with the tang of autumn; with the effluvium of rotting leaves, the drift of wood smoke, the ripe flavour of crushed apples.

'Thar's nary a stranger, thoughten he was a doctor, been to Jur'dn's End as fur back as I kin recollect. Ain't you the new doctor?'

'Yes, I am the doctor.' I glanced down at the gnomelike shape in the wood brown overcoat. 'Is it much farther?'

'Naw, suh, we're all but thar jest as soon as we come out of Whitten woods.'

'If the road is so little travelled, how do you happen to be going there?'

Without turning his head, the old man wagged his crescent shaped profile. 'Oh, I live on the place. My son Tony works a slice of the farm on shares, and I manage to lend a hand at the harvest or corn shuckin', and, now-and-agen, with the cider. The old gentleman used to run the place that away afore he went deranged, an' now that the young one is laid up, thar ain't nobody to look arter the farm but Miss Judith. Them old ladies don't count. Thar's three of 'em, but they're all addle-brained an' look as if the buzzards had picked 'em. I reckon that comes from bein' shut up with crazy folks in that thar old tumbledown house. The roof ain't been patched fur so long that the shingles have most rotted away, an' thar's times, Tony says, when you kin skearcely hear yo' years fur the rumpus the wrens an' rats are makin' overhead.'

'What is the trouble with them—the Jordans, I mean?'

'Jest run to seed, suh, I reckon.'

'Is there no man of the family left?'

For a minute Father Peterkin made no reply. Then he shifted the bundle of pine knots, and responded warily. 'Young Alan, he's still livin' on the old place, but I hear he's been took now, an' is goin' the way of all the rest of 'em. 'Tis a hard trial for Miss Judith, po' young thing, an' with a boy nine year old that's the very spit an' image of his pa. Wall, wall, I kin recollect away back yonder when old Mr Timothy Jur'dn was the proudest man anywhar aroun' in these parts; but arter the War things sorter begun to go down hill with him, and he was obleeged to draw in his horns.'

'Is he still living?'

The old man shook his head. 'Mebbe he is, an' mebbe he ain't. Nobody knows but the Jur'dn's, an' they ain't tellin' fur the axin'.'

'I suppose it was this Miss Judith who sent for me?'

''Twould most likely be she, suh. She was one of the Yardlys that lived over yonder at Yardly's Field; an' when young Mr Alan begun to take notice of her, 'twas the first time sence way back that one of the Jur'dn's had gone courtin' outside the family. That's the reason the blood went bad like it did, I reckon. Thar's a sayin' down aroun' here that Jur'dn an' Jur'dn won't mix.' The name was invariably called Jurdin by all classes; but I had already discovered that names are rarely pronounced as they are spelled in Virginia.

'Have they been married long?'

'Ten year or so, suh. I remember as well as if 'twas yestiddy the day young Alan brought her home as a bride, an' thar warn't a soul besides the three daft old ladies to welcome her. They drove over in my son Tony's old buggy, though 'twas spick an' span then. I was goin' to the house on an arrant, an' I was standin' right down thar at the ice pond when they come by. She hadn't been much in these parts, an' none of us had ever seed her afore. When she looked up at young Alan her face was pink all over and her eyes war shinin' bright as the moon. Then the front do' opened an' them old ladies, as black as crows, flocked out on the po'ch. Thar never was anybody as peart-lookin' as Miss Judith was when she come here; but soon arterwards she begun to peak an' pine, though she never lost her sperits an' went mopin' roun' like all the other women folks at Jur'dn's End. They married sudden, an' folks do say she didn't know nothin' about the family, an' young Alan didn't know much mo' than she did. The old ladies had kep' the secret away from him, sorter believin' that what you don't know cyarn' hurt you. Anyways they never let it leak out tell arter his chile was born. Thar ain't never been but that one, an' old Aunt Jerusly declars he was born with a caul over his face, so mebbe things will be all right fur him in the long run.'

'But who are the old ladies? Are their husbands living?'

When Father Peterkin answered the question he had dropped his voice to a hoarse murmur. 'Deranged. All gone deranged,' he replied.

I shivered, for a chill depression seemed to emanate from the November woods. As we drove on, I remembered grim tales of enchanted forests filled with evil faces and whispering voices. The scents of wood earth and rotting leaves invaded my brain like a magic spell. On either side the forest was as still as death. Not a leaf quivered, not a bird moved, not a small wild creature stirred in the underbrush. Only the glossy leaves and the scarlet berries of the holly appeared alive amid the bare interlacing branches of the trees. I began to long for an autumn clearing and the red light of the afterglow.

'Are they living or dead?' I asked presently.

'I've hearn strange tattle,' answered the old man nervously, 'but nobody kin tell. Folks do say as young Alan's pa is shut up in a padded place, and that his gran'pa died thar arter thirty years. His uncles went crazy too, an' the daftness is beginnin' to crop out in the women. Up tell now it has been mostly the men. One time I remember old Mr Peter Jur'dn tryin' to burn down the place in the dead of the night. Thar's the end of the wood, suh. If you'll jest let me down here, I'll be gittin' along home across the old-field, an' thanky too.'

At last the woods ended abruptly on the edge of an abandoned field which was thickly sown with scrub pine and broomsedge. The glow in the sky had faded now to a thin yellow-green, and a melancholy twilight pervaded the landscape. In this twilight I looked over the few sheep huddled together on the ragged lawn, and saw the old brick house crumbling beneath its rank growth of ivy. As I drew nearer I had the feeling that the surrounding desolation brooded there like some sinister influence.

Forlorn as it appeared at this first approach, I surmised that Jordan's End must have possessed once charm as well as distinction. The proportions of the Georgian front were impressive, and there was beauty of design in the quaint doorway, and in the steps of rounded stone which were brocaded now with a pattern of emerald moss. But the whole place was badly in need of repair. Looking up, as I stopped, I saw that the eaves were falling away, that crumbled shutters were sagging from loosened hinges, that odd scraps of hemp sacking or oil cloth were stuffed into windows where panes were missing. When I stepped on the floor of the porch, I felt the rotting boards give way under my feet.

After thundering vainly on the door, I descended the steps, and followed the beaten path that led round the west wing of the house. When I had passed an old boxwood tree at the corner, I saw a woman and a boy of nine years or so come out of a shed, which I took to be the smoke-house, and begin to gather chips from the woodpile. The woman carried a basket made of splits on her arm, and while she stooped to fill this, she talked to the child in a soft musical voice. Then, at a sound that I made, she put the basket aside, and rising to her feet, faced me in the pallid light from the sky. Her head was thrown back, and over her dress of some dark calico, a tattered gray shawl clung to her figure. That was thirty years ago; I am not young any longer; I have been in many countries since then, and looked on many women; but her face, with that wan light on it, is the last one I shall forget in my life. Beauty! Why, that woman will be beautiful when she is a skeleton, was the thought that flashed into my mind.

She was very tall, and so thin that her flesh seemed faintly luminous, as if an inward light pierced the transparent substance. It was the beauty, not of earth, but of triumphant spirit. Perfection, I suppose, is the rarest thing we achieve in this world of incessant compromise with inferior forms; yet the woman who stood there in that ruined place appeared to me to have stepped straight out of legend or allegory. The contour of her face was Italian in its pure oval; her hair swept in wings of dusk above her clear forehead; and, from the faintly shadowed hollows beneath her brows, the eyes that looked at me were purple-black, like dark pansies.

'I had given you up,' she began in a low voice, as if she were afraid of being overheard. 'You are the doctor?'

'Yes, I am the doctor. I took the wrong road and lost my way. Are you Mrs Jordan?'

She bowed her head. 'Mrs Alan Jordan. There are three Mrs Jordans besides myself. My husband's grandmother and the wives of his two uncles.'

'And it is your husband who is ill?'

'My husband, yes. I wrote a few days ago to Doctor Carstairs.' (Thirty years ago Carstairs, of Baltimore, was the leading alienist in

the country.) 'He is coming to-morrow morning; but last night my
husband was so restless that I sent for you to-day.' Her rich voice,
vibrating with suppressed feeling, made me think of stained glass
windows and low organ music.

'Before we go in,' I asked, 'will you tell me as much as you can?'

Instead of replying to my request, she turned and laid her hand on
the boy's shoulder. 'Take the chips to Aunt Agatha, Benjamin,' she
said, 'and tell her that the doctor has come.'

While the child picked up the basket and ran up the sunken steps
to the door, she watched him with breathless anxiety. Not until he
had disappeared into the hall did she lift her eyes to my face again.
Then, without answering my question, she murmured, with a sigh
which was like the voice of that autumn evening, 'We were once
happy here.' She was trying, I realized, to steel her heart against the
despair that threatened it.

My gaze swept the obscure horizon, and returned to the mouldering woodpile where we were standing. The yellow-green had faded
from the sky, and the only light came from the house where a few
scattered lamps were burning. Through the open door I could see
the hall, as bare as if the house were empty, and the spiral staircase
which crawled to the upper story. A fine old place once, but repulsive
now in its abject decay, like some young blood of former days who
has grown senile.

'Have you managed to wring a living out of the land?' I asked,
because I could think of no words that were less compassionate.

'At first a poor one,' she answered slowly. 'We worked hard,
harder than any negro in the fields, to keep things together, but we
were happy. Then three years ago this illness came, and after that
everything went against us. In the beginning it was simply brooding, a
kind of melancholy, and we tried to ward it off by pretending that it
was not real, that we imagined it. Only of late, when it became so
much worse, have we admitted the truth, have we faced the reality—'

This passionate murmur, which had almost the effect of a chant
rising out of the loneliness, was addressed, not to me, but to some
abstract and implacable power. While she uttered it her composure
was like the tranquillity of the dead. She did not lift her hand to hold
her shawl, which was slipping unnoticed from her shoulders, and her
eyes, so like dark flowers in their softness, did not leave my face.

'If you will tell me all, perhaps I may be able to help you,' I said.

'But you know our story,' she responded. 'You must have heard it.'

'Then it is true? Heredity, intermarriage, insanity?'

She did not wince at the bluntness of my speech. 'My husband's grandfather is in an asylum, still living after almost thirty years. His father—my husband's, I mean—died there a few years ago. Two of his uncles are there. When it began I don't know, or how far back it reaches. We have never talked of it. We have tried always to forget it—Even now I cannot put the thing into words—My husband's mother died of a broken heart, but the grandmother and the two others are still living. You will see them when you go into the house. They are old women now, and they feel nothing.'

'And there have been other cases?'

'I do not know. Are not four enough?'

'Do you know if it has assumed always the same form?' I was trying to be as brief as I could.

She flinched, and I saw that her unnatural calm was shaken at last. 'The same, I believe. In the beginning there is melancholy, moping, Grandmother calls it, and then—' She flung out her arms with a despairing gesture, and I was reminded again of some tragic figure of legend.

'I know, I know.' I was young, and in spite of my pride, my voice trembled. 'Has there been in any case partial recovery, recurring at intervals?'

'In his grandfather's case, yes. In the others none. With them it has been hopeless from the beginning.'

'And Carstairs is coming?'

'In the morning. I should have waited, but last night—Her voice broke, and she drew the tattered shawl about her with a shiver. 'Last night something happened. Something happened,' she repeated, and could not go on. Then, collecting her strength with an effort which made her tremble like a blade of grass in the wind, she continued more quietly, 'Today he has been better. For the first time he has slept, and I have been able to leave him. Two of the hands from the fields are in the room.' Her tone changed suddenly, and a note of energy passed into it. Some obscure resolution brought a tinge of colour to her pale cheek. 'I must know,' she added, 'if this is as hopeless as all the others.'

I took a step toward the house. 'Carstairs's opinion is worth as much as that of any man living,' I answered.

'But will he tell me the truth?'

I shook my head. 'He will tell you what he thinks. No man's judgment is infallible.'

Turning away from me, she moved with an energetic step to the house. As I followed her into the hall the threshold creaked under my tread, and I was visited by an apprehension, or, if you prefer, by a superstitious dread of the floor above. Oh, I got over that kind of thing before I was many years older; though in the end I gave up medicine, you know, and turned to literature as a safer outlet for a suppressed imagination.

But the dread was there at that moment, and it was not lessened by the glimpse I caught, at the foot of the spiral staircase, of a scantily furnished room, where three lean black-robed figures, as impassive as the Fates, were grouped in front of a wood fire. They were doing something with their hands. Knitting, crocheting, or plaiting straw?

At the head of the stairs the woman stopped and looked back at me. The light from the kerosene lamp on the wall fell over her, and I was struck afresh not only by the alien splendour of her beauty, but even more by the look of consecration, of impassioned fidelity that illumined her face.

'He is very strong,' she said in a whisper. 'Until this trouble came on him he had never had a day's illness in his life. We hoped that hard work, not having time to brood, might save us; but it has only brought the thing we feared sooner.'

There was a question in her eyes, and I responded in the same subdued tone. 'His health, you say, is good?' What else was there for me to ask when I understood everything?

A shudder ran through her frame. 'We used to think that a blessing, but now—' She broke off and then added in a lifeless voice, 'We keep two field hands in the room day and night, lest one should forget to watch the fire, or fall asleep.'

A sound came from a room at the end of the hall, and, without finishing her sentence, she moved swiftly toward the closed door. The apprehension, the dread, or whatever you choose to call it, was so strong upon me, that I was seized by an impulse to turn and retreat down the spiral staircase. Yes, I know why some men turn cowards in battle.

'I have come back, Alan,' she said in a voice that wrung my heartstrings.

The room was dimly lighted; and for a minute after I entered, I could see nothing clearly except the ruddy glow of the wood fire in front of which two negroes were seated on low wooden stools. They had kindly faces, these men; there was a primitive humanity in their features, which might have been modelled out of the dark earth of the fields.

Looking round the next minute, I saw that a young man was sitting away from the fire, huddled over in a cretonne-covered chair with a high back and deep wings. At our entrance the negroes glanced up with surprise; but the man in the winged chair neither lifted his head nor turned his eyes in our direction. He sat there, lost within the impenetrable wilderness of the insane, as remote from us and from the sound of our voices as if he were the inhabitant of an invisible world. His head was sunk forward; his eyes were staring fixedly at some image we could not see; his fingers, moving restlessly, were plaiting and unplaiting the fringe of a plaid shawl. Distraught as he was, he still possessed the dignity of mere physical perfection. At his full height he must have measured not under six feet three; his hair was the colour of ripe wheat, and his eyes, in spite of their fixed gaze, were as blue as the sky after rain. And this was only the beginning, I realized. With that constitution, that physical frame, he might live to be ninety.

'Alan!' breathed his wife again in her pleading murmur.

If he heard her voice, he gave no sign of it. Only when she crossed the room and bent over his chair, he put out his hand, with a gesture of irritation, and pushed her away, as if she were a veil of smoke which came between him and the object at which he was looking. Then his hand fell back to its old place, and he resumed his mechanical plaiting of the fringe.

The woman lifted her eyes to mine. 'His father did that for twenty years,' she said in a whisper that was scarcely more than a sigh of anguish.

When I had made my brief examination, we left the room as we had come, and descended the stairs together. The three old women were still sitting in front of the wood fire. I do not think they had moved since we went upstairs; but, as we reached the hall below, one of them, the youngest, I imagine, rose from her chair, and came out to join us. She was crocheting something soft and small, an infant's sacque, I perceived as she approached, of pink wool. The ball had rolled from her lap as she stood up, and it trailed after her now, like a woolen rose, on the bare floor. When the skein pulled at her, she turned back and stooped to pick up the ball, which she rewound with caressing fingers. Good God, an infant's sacque in that house!

'Is it the same thing?' she asked.

'Hush!' responded the younger woman kindly. Turning to me she added, 'We cannot talk here,' and opening the door, passed out on the porch. Not until we had reached the lawn, and walked in silence to where my buggy stood beneath an old locust tree, did she speak again.

Then she said only, 'You know now?'

'Yes, I know,' I replied, averting my eyes from her face while I gave my directions as briefly as I could. 'I will leave an opiate,' I said. 'To-morrow, if Carstairs should not come, send for me again. If he does come,' I added, 'I will talk to him and see you afterward.'

'Thank you,' she answered gently; and taking the bottle from my hand, she turned away and walked quickly back to the house.

I watched her as long as I could; and then getting into my buggy, I turned my mare's head toward the woods, and drove by moonlight, past Buzzard's Tree and over the Old Stage Road, to my home. 'I will see Carstairs to-morrow,' was my last thought that night before I slept.

But, after all, I saw Carstairs only for a minute as he was taking the train. Life at its beginning and its end had filled my morning; and when at last I reached the little station, Carstairs had paid his visit, and was waiting on the platform for the approaching express. At first he showed a disposition to question me about the shooting, but as soon as I was able to make my errand clear, his jovial face clouded.

'So you've been there?' he said. 'They didn't tell me. An interesting case, if it were not for that poor woman. Incurable, I'm afraid, when you consider the predisposing causes. The race is pretty well deteriorated, I suppose. God! what isolation! I've advised her to send him away. There are three others, they tell me, at Staunton.'

The train came; he jumped on it, and was whisked away while I gazed after him. After all, I was none the wiser because of the great reputation of Carstairs.

All that day I heard nothing more from Jordan's End; and then, early next morning, the same decrepit negro brought me a message.

'Young Miss, she tole me ter ax you ter come along wid me jes' ez soon ez you kin git ready.'

'I'll start at once, Uncle, and I'll take you with me.'

My mare and buggy stood at the door. All I needed to do was to put on my overcoat, pick up my hat, and leave word, for a possible patient, that I should return before noon. I knew the road now, and I told myself, as I set out, that I would make as quick a trip as I could. For two nights I had been haunted by the memory of that man in the armchair, plaiting and unplaiting the fringe of the plaid shawl. And his father had done that, the woman had told me, for twenty years!

It was a brown autumn morning, raw, windless, with an overcast sky and a peculiar illusion of nearness about the distance. A high wind had blown all night, but at dawn it had dropped suddenly, and now there was not so much as a ripple in the broomsedge. Over the fields, when we came out of the woods, the thin trails of blue smoke were as motionless as cobwebs. The lawn surrounding the house looked smaller than it had appeared to me in the twilight, as if the barren fields had drawn closer since my last visit. Under the trees, where the few sheep were browsing, the piles of leaves lay in wind-rifts along the sunken walk and against the wings of the house.

When I knocked the door was opened immediately by one of the old women, who held a streamer of black cloth or rusty crape in her hands.

'You may go straight upstairs,' she croaked; and, without waiting for an explanation, I entered the hall quickly, and ran up the stairs.

The door of the room was closed, and I opened it noiselessly, and stepped over the threshold. My first sensation, as I entered, was one of cold. Then I saw that the windows were wide open, and that the room seemed to be full of people, though, as I made out presently, there was no one there except Alan Jordan's wife, her little son, the two old aunts, and an aged crone of a negress. On the bed there was something under a yellowed sheet of fine linen (what the negroes call 'a burial sheet', I suppose), which had been handed down from some more affluent generation.

When I went over, after a minute, and turned down one corner of the covering, I saw that my patient of the other evening was dead. Not a line of pain marred his features, not a thread of gray dimmed the wheaten gold of his hair. So he must have looked, I thought, when she first loved him. He had gone from life, not old, enfeebled and repulsive, but enveloped still in the romantic illusion of their passion.

As I entered, the two old women, who had been fussing about the bed, drew back to make way for me, but the witch of a negress did not pause in the weird chant, an incantation of some sort, which she was mumbling. From the rag carpet in front of the empty fireplace, the boy, with his father's hair and his mother's eyes, gazed at me silently, broodingly, as if I were trespassing; and by the open window, with her eyes on the ashen November day, the young wife stood as motionless as a statue. While I looked at her a redbird flew out of the boughs of a cedar, and she followed it with her eyes.

'You sent for me?' I said to her.

She did not turn. She was beyond the reach of my voice, of any voice, I imagine; but one of the palsied old women answered my question.

'He was like this when we found him this morning,' she said. 'He had a bad night, and Judith and the two hands were up with him until daybreak. Then he seemed to fall asleep, and Judith sent the hands, turn about, to get their breakfast.'

While she spoke my eyes were on the bottle I had left there. Two nights ago it had been full, and now it stood empty, without a cork, on the mantelpiece. They had not even thrown it away. It was typical of the pervading inertia of the place that the bottle should still be standing there awaiting my visit.

For an instant the shock held me speechless; when at last I found my voice it was to ask mechanically:

'When did it happen?'

The old woman who had spoken took up the story. 'Nobody knows. We have not touched him. No one but Judith has gone near him.' Her words trailed off into unintelligible muttering. If she had ever had her wits about her, I dare-say fifty years at Jordan's End had unsettled them completely.

I turned to the woman at the window. Against the gray sky and the black intersecting branches of the cedar, her head, with its austere perfection, was surrounded by that visionary air of legend. So Antigone might have looked on the day of her sacrifice, I reflected. I had never seen a creature who appeared so withdrawn, so detached, from all human associations. It was as if some spiritual isolation divided her from her kind.

'I can do nothing,' I said.

For the first time she looked at me, and her eyes were unfathomable. 'No, you can do nothing,' she answered. 'He is safely dead.'

The negress was still crooning on; the other old women were fussing helplessly. It was impossible in their presence, I felt, to put in words the thing I had to say.

'Will you come downstairs with me?' I asked. 'Outside of this house?'

Turning quietly, she spoke to the boy. 'Run out and play, dear. He would have wished it.'

Then, without a glance toward the bed, or the old women gathered about it, she followed me over the threshold, down the stairs, and out on the deserted lawn. The ashen day could not touch her, I saw then. She was either so remote from it, or so completely a part of it, that she was impervious to its sadness. Her white face did not become more pallid as the light struck it; her tragic eyes did not grow deeper; her frail figure under the thin shawl did not shiver in the raw air. She felt nothing, I realized suddenly.

Wrapped in that silence as in a cloak, she walked across the windrifts of leaves to where my mare was waiting. Her step was so slow, so unhurried, that I remember thinking she moved like one who had all eternity before her. Oh, one has strange impressions, you know, at such moments!

In the middle of the lawn, where the trees had been stripped bare in the night, and the leaves were piled in long mounds like double graves, she stopped and looked in my face. The air was so still that the whole place might have been in a trance or asleep. Not a branch moved, not a leaf rustled on the ground, not a sparrow twittered in the ivy; and even the few sheep stood motionless, as if they were under a spell. Farther away, beyond the sea of broomsedge, where no wind stirred, I saw the flat desolation of the landscape. Nothing moved on the earth, but high above, under the leaden clouds, a buzzard was sailing.

I moistened my lips before I spoke. 'God knows I want to help you!' At the back of my brain a hideous question was drumming. How had it happened? Could she have killed him? Had that delicate creature nerved her will to the unspeakable act? It was incredible. It was inconceivable. And yet....

'The worst is over,' she answered quietly, with that tearless agony which is so much more terrible than any outburst of grief.

'Whatever happens, I can never go through the worst again. Once in the beginning he wanted to die. His great fear was that he might live too long, until it was too late to save himself. I made him wait then. I held him back by a promise.'

So she had killed him, I thought. Then she went on steadily, after a minute, and I doubted again.

'Thank God, it was easier for him than he feared it would be,' she murmured.

No, it was not conceivable. He must have bribed one of the negroes. But who had stood by and watched without intercepting? Who had been in the room? Well, either way! 'I will do all I can to help you,' I said.

Her gaze did not waver. 'There is so little that any one can do now,' she responded, as if she had not understood what I meant. Suddenly, without the warning of a sob, a cry of despair went out of her, as if it were torn from her breast. 'He was my life,' she cried, 'and I must go on!'

So full of agony was the sound that it seemed to pass like a gust of wind over the broomsedge. I waited until the emptiness had opened and closed over it. Then I asked as quietly as I could:

'What will you do now?'

She collected herself with a shudder of pain. 'As long as the old people live, I am tied here. I must bear it out to the end. When they die, I shall go away and find work. I am sending my boy to school. Doctor Carstairs will look after him, and he will help me when the time comes. While my boy needs me, there is no release.'

While I listened to her, I knew that the question on my lips would never be uttered. I should always remain ignorant of the truth. The thing I feared most, standing there alone with her, was that some accident might solve the mystery before I could escape. My eyes left her face and wandered over the dead leaves at our feet. No, I had nothing to ask her.

'Shall I come again?' That was all.

She shook her head. 'Not unless I send for you. If I need you, I will send for you,' she answered; but in my heart I knew that she would never send for me.

I held out my hand, but she did not take it; and I felt that she meant me to understand, by her refusal, that she was beyond all consolation and all companionship. She was nearer to the bleak sky and the deserted fields than she was to her kind.

As she turned away, the shawl slipped from her shoulders to the dead leaves over which she was walking; but she did not stoop to recover it, nor did I make a movement to follow her. Long after she had entered the house I stood there, gazing down on the garment that she had dropped. Then climbing into my buggy, I drove slowly across the field and into the woods.

H. P. LOVECRAFT

The Outsider

That night the Baron dreamt of many a wo;
And all his warrior-guests, with shade and form
Of witch, and demon, and large coffin-worm,
Were long be-nightmared.
KEATS

Unhappy is he to whom the memories of childhood bring only fear and sadness. Wretched is he who looks back upon lone hours in vast and dismal chambers with brown hangings and maddening rows of antique books, or upon awed watches in twilight groves of grotesque, gigantic, and vine-encumbered trees that silently wave twisted branches far aloft. Such a lot the gods gave to me—to me, the dazed, the disappointed; the barren, the broken. And yet I am strangely content and cling desperately to those sere memories, when my mind momentarily threatens to reach beyond to *the other.*

I know not where I was born, save that the castle was infinitely old and infinitely horrible, full of dark passages and having high ceilings where the eye could find only cobwebs and shadows. The stones in the crumbling corridors seemed always hideously damp, and there was an accursed smell everywhere, as of the piled-up corpses of dead generations. It was never light, so that I used sometimes to light candles and gaze steadily at them for relief, nor was there any sun outdoors, since the terrible trees grew high above the topmost accessible tower. There was one black tower which reached above the trees into the unknown outer sky, but that was partly ruined and could not be ascended save by a well-nigh impossible climb up the sheer wall, stone by stone.

I must have lived years in this place, but I cannot measure the time. Beings must have cared for my needs, yet I cannot recall any person except myself, or anything alive but the noiseless rats and bats and spiders. I think that whoever nursed me must have been shockingly aged, since my first conception of a living person was that of somebody mockingly like myself, yet distorted, shrivelled, and decaying like the castle. To me there was nothing grotesque in the bones and skeletons that strewed some of the stone crypts deep down among the foundations. I fantastically associated these things with everyday events, and thought them more natural than the coloured pictures of living beings which I found in many of the mouldy books. From such books I learned all that I know. No teacher urged or guided me, and I do not recall hearing any human voice in all those years—not even my own; for although I had read of speech, I had never thought to try to speak aloud. My aspect was a matter equally unthought of, for there were no mirrors in the castle, and I merely regarded myself by instinct as akin to the youthful figures I saw drawn and painted in the books. I felt conscious of youth because I remembered so little.

Outside, across the putrid moat and under the dark mute trees, I would often lie and dream for hours about what I read in the books; and would longingly picture myself amidst gay crowds in the sunny world beyond the endless forests. Once I tried to escape from the forest, but as I went farther from the castle the shade grew denser and the air more filled with brooding fear; so that I ran frantically back lest I lose my way in a labyrinth of nighted silence.

So through endless twilights I dreamed and waited, though I knew not what I waited for. Then in the shadowy solitude my longing for light grew so frantic that I could rest no more, and I lifted entreating hands to the single black ruined tower that reached above the forest into the unknown outer sky. And at last I resolved to scale that tower, fall though I might; since it were better to glimpse the sky and perish, than to live without ever beholding day.

In the dank twilight I climbed the worn and aged stone stairs till I reached the level where they ceased, and thereafter clung perilously to small footholds leading upward. Ghastly and terrible was that dead, stairless cylinder of rock; black, ruined, and deserted, and sinister with startled bats whose wings made no noise. But more ghastly and terrible still was the slowness of my progress; for climb as I might, the darkness overhead grew no thinner, and a new chill as of haunted and venerable mould assailed me. I shivered as I wondered why I did not reach the light, and would have looked down had I dared. I fancied that night had come suddenly upon me, and vainly groped with one free hand for a window embrasure, that I might peer out and above, and try to judge the height I had attained.

All at once, after an infinity of awesome, sightless, crawling up that concave and desperate precipice, I felt my head touch a solid thing, and I knew I must have gained the roof, or at least some kind of floor. In the darkness I raised my free hand and tested the barrier, finding it stone and immovable. Then came a deadly circuit of the tower, clinging to whatever holds the slimy wall could give; till finally my testing hand found the barrier yielding, and I turned upward again, pushing the slab or door with my head as I used both hands in my fearful ascent. There was no light revealed above, and as my hands went higher I knew that my climb was for the nonce ended; since the slab was the trapdoor of an aperture leading to a level stone surface of greater circumference than the lower tower, no doubt the floor of some lofty and capacious observation chamber. I crawled through carefully, and tried to prevent the heavy slab from falling back into place, but failed in the latter attempt. As I lay exhausted on the stone floor I heard the eerie echoes of its fall, hoped when necessary to pry it up again.

Believing I was now at prodigious height, far above the accursed branches of the wood, I dragged myself up from the floor and fumbled about for windows, that I might look for the first time upon the sky, and the moon and stars of which I had read. But on every hand I was disappointed; since all that I found were vast shelves of marble, bearing odious oblong boxes of disturbing size. More and more I reflected, and wondered what hoary secrets might abide in this high apartment so many aeons cut off from the castle below. Then unexpectedly my hands came upon a doorway, where hung a portal of stone, rough with strange chiselling. Trying it, I found it locked; but with a supreme burst of strength I overcame all obstacles and dragged it open inward. As I did so there came to me the purest ecstasy I have ever known; for shining tranquilly through an ornate grating of iron, and down a short stone passageway of steps that ascended from the newly found doorway, was the radiant full moon, which I had never before seen save in dreams and in vague visions I dared not call memories.

Fancying now that I had attained the very pinnacle of the castle, I commenced to rush up the few steps beyond the door; but the sudden veiling of the moon by a cloud caused me to stumble, and I felt my way more slowly in the dark. It was still very dark when I reached the grating—which I tried carefully and found unlocked, but which I did not open for fear of falling from the amazing height to which I had climbed. Then the moon came out.

Most demoniacal of all shocks is that of the abysmally unexpected and grotesquely unbelievable. Nothing I had before undergone could compare in terror with what I now saw; with the bizarre marvels that sight implied. The sight itself was as simple as it was stupefying, for it was merely this: instead of a dizzying prospect of treetops seen from a lofty eminence, there stretched around me on the level through the grating nothing less than *the solid ground*, decked and diversified by marble slabs and columns, and overshadowed by an ancient stone church, whose ruined spire gleamed spectrally in the moonlight.

Half unconscious, I opened the grating and staggered out upon the white gravel path that stretched away in two directions. My mind, stunned and chaotic as it was, still held the frantic craving for light; and not even the fantastic wonder which had happened could stay my course. I neither knew nor cared whether my experience was insanity, dreaming, or magic; but was determined to gaze on brilliance and gaiety at any cost. I knew not who I was or what I was, or what my surroundings might be; though as I continued to stumble along I became conscious of a kind of fearsome latent memory that made my progress not wholly fortuitous. I passed under an arch out of that region of slabs and columns, and wandered through the open country; sometimes following the visible road, but sometimes leaving it curiously to tread across meadows where only occasional ruins bespoke the ancient presence of a forgotten road. Once I swam across a swift river where crumbling, mossy masonry told of a bridge long vanished.

Over two hours must have passed before I reached what seemed to be my goal, a venerable ivied castle in a thickly wooded park, maddeningly familiar, yet full of perplexing strangeness to me. I saw that the moat was filled in, and that some of the well-known towers were demolished; whilst new wings existed to confuse the beholder. But what I observed with chief interest and delight were the open windows—gorgeously ablaze with light and sending forth sound of the gayest revelry. Advancing to one of these I looked in and saw an oddly dressed company indeed; making merry, and speaking brightly to one another. I had never, seemingly, heard human speech before and could guess only vaguely what was said. Some of the faces seemed to hold expressions that brought up incredibly remote recollections, others were utterly alien.

I now stepped through the low window into the brilliantly lighted room, stepping as I did so from my single bright moment of hope to my blackest convulsion of despair and realization. The nightmare was quick to come, for as I entered, there occurred immediately one of the most terrifying demonstrations I had ever conceived. Scarcely had I crossed the sill when there descended upon the whole company a sudden and unheralded fear of hideous intensity, distorting every face and evoking the most horrible screams from nearly every throat.

Flight was universal, and in the clamour and panic several fell in a swoon and were dragged away by their madly fleeing companions. Many covered their eyes with their hands, and plunged blindly and awkwardly in their race to escape, overturning furniture and stumbling against the walls before they managed to reach one of the many doors.

The cries were shocking; and as I stood in the brilliant apartment alone and dazed, listening to their vanishing echoes, I trembled at the thought of what might be lurking near me unseen. At a casual inspection the room seemed deserted, but when I moved towards one of the alcoves I thought I detected a presence there—a hint of motion beyond the golden-arched doorway leading to another and somewhat similar room. As I approached the arch I began to perceive the presence more clearly; and then, with the first and last sound I ever uttered—a ghastly ululation that revolted me almost as poignantly as its noxious cause—I beheld in full, frightful vividness the inconceivable, indescribable, and unmentionable monstrosity which had by its simple appearance changed a merry company to a herd of delirious fugitives.

I cannot even hint what it was like, for it was a compound of all that is unclean, uncanny, unwelcome, abnormal, and detestable. It was the ghoulish shade of decay, antiquity, and dissolution; the putrid, dripping eidolon of unwholesome revelation, the awful baring of that which the merciful earth should always hide. God knows it was not of this world—or no longer of this world—yet to my horror I saw in its eaten-away and bone-revealing outlines a leering, abhorrent travesty on the human shape; and in its mouldy, disintegrating apparel an unspeakable quality that chilled me even more.

I was almost paralysed, but not too much so to make a feeble effort towards flight; a backward stumble which failed to break the spell in which the nameless, voiceless monster held me. My eyes bewitched by the glassy orbs which stared loathsomely into them, refused to close; though they were mercifully blurred, and showed the terrible object but indistinctly after the first shock. I tried to raise my hand to shut out the sight, yet so stunned were my nerves that my arm could not fully obey my will. The attempt, however, was enough to disturb my balance; so that I had to stagger forward several steps to avoid falling. As I did so I became suddenly and agonizingly aware of the *nearness* of the carrion thing, whose hideous hollow breathing I half fancied I could hear. Nearly mad, I found myself yet able to throw out a hand to ward off the foetid apparition which pressed so close; when in one cataclysmic second of cosmic nightmarishness and hellish accident *my fingers touched the rotting outstretched paw of the monster beneath the golden arch.*

I did not shriek, but all the fiendish ghouls that ride the nightwind shrieked for me as in that same second there crashed down upon my mind a single fleeting avalanche of soul-annihilating memory. I knew in that second all that had been; I remembered beyond the frightful castle and the trees, and recognized the altered edifice in which I now stood; I recognized, most terrible of all, the unholy abomination that stood leering before me as I withdrew my sullied fingers from its own.

But in the cosmos there is balm as well as bitterness, and that balm is nepenthe. In the supreme horror of that second I forgot what had horrified me, and the burst of black memory vanished in a chaos of echoing images. In a dream I fled from that haunted and accursed pile, and ran swiftly and silently in the moonlight. When I returned to the churchyard place of marble and went down the steps I found the stone trap-door immovable; but I was not sorry, for I had hated the antique castle and the trees. Now I ride with the mocking and friendly ghouls on the night-wind, and play by day amongst the catacombs of Nephren-Ka in the sealed and unknown valley of Hadoth by the Nile. I know that light is not for me, save that of the moon over the rock tombs of Neb, nor any gaiety save the unnamed feasts of Nitokris beneath the Great Pyramid; yet in my new wildness and freedom I almost welcome the bitterness of alienage.

For although nepenthe has calmed me, I know always that I am an outsider; a stranger in this century and among those who are still men. This I have known ever since I stretched out my fingers to the abomination within that great gilded frame; stretched out my fingers and touched *a cold and unyielding surface of polished glass.*

WILLIAM   FAULKNER

A Rose for Emily

I

When Miss Emily Grierson died, our whole town went to her funeral: the men through a sort of respectful affection for a fallen monument, the women mostly out of curiosity to see the inside of her house, which no one save an old man-servant—a combined gardener and cook—had seen in at least ten years.

It was a big, squarish frame house that had once been white, decorated with cupolas and spires and scrolled balconies in the heavily lightsome style of the seventies, set on what had once been our most select street. But garages and cotton gins had encroached and obliterated even the august names of that neighborhood; only Miss Emily's house was left, lifting its stubborn and coquettish decay above the cotton wagons and the gasoline pumps—an eyesore among eyesores. And now Miss Emily had gone to join the representatives of those august names where they lay in the cedar-bemused cemetery among the ranked and anonymous graves of Union and Confederate soldiers who fell at the battle of Jefferson.

Alive, Miss Emily had been a tradition, a duty, and a care; a sort of hereditary obligation upon the town, dating from that day in 1894 when Colonel Sartoris, the mayor—he who fathered the edict that no Negro woman should appear on the streets without an apron—remitted her taxes, the dispensation dating from the death of her father on into perpetuity. Not that Miss Emily would have accepted charity. Colonel Sartoris invented an involved tale to the effect that Miss Emily's father had loaned money to the town, which the town, as a matter of business, preferred this way of repaying. Only a man of Colonel Sartoris' generation and thought could have invented it, and only a woman could have believed it.

When the next generation, with its more modern ideas, became mayors and aldermen, this arrangement created some little dissatisfaction. On the first of the year they mailed her a tax notice. February came, and there was no reply. They wrote her a formal letter, asking her to call at the sheriff's office at her convenience. A week later the mayor wrote her himself, offering to call or to send his car for her, and received in reply a note on paper of an archaic shape, in a thin, flowing calligraphy in faded ink, to the effect that she no longer went out at all. The tax notice was also enclosed, without comment.

They called a special meeting of the Board of Aldermen. A deputation waited upon her, knocked at the door through which no visitor had passed since she ceased giving china-painting lessons eight or ten years earlier. They were admitted by the old Negro into a dim hall from which a stairway mounted into still more shadow. It smelled of dust and disuse—a close, dank smell. The Negro led them into the parlor. It was furnished in heavy, leather-covered furniture. When the Negro opened the blinds of one window, they could see that the leather was cracked; and when they sat down, a faint dust rose sluggishly about their thighs, spinning with slow motes in the single sun-ray. On a tarnished gilt easel before the fireplace stood a crayon portrait of Miss Emily's father.

They rose when she entered—a small, fat woman in black, with a thin gold chain descending to her waist and vanishing into her belt, leaning on an ebony cane with a tarnished gold head. Her skeleton was small and spare; perhaps that was why what would have been merely plumpness in another was obesity in her. She looked bloated, like a body long submerged in motionless water, and of that pallid hue. Her eyes, lost in the fatty ridges of her face, looked like two small pieces of coal pressed into a lump of dough as they moved from one face to another while the visitors stated their errand.

She did not ask them to sit. She just stood in the door and listened quietly until the spokesman came to a stumbling halt. Then they could hear the invisible watch ticking at the end of the gold chain.

Her voice was dry and cold. 'I have no taxes in Jefferson. Colonel Sartoris explained it to me. Perhaps one of you can gain access to the city records and satisfy yourselves.'

'But we have. We are the city authorities, Miss Emily. Didn't you get a notice from the sheriff, signed by him?'

'I received a paper, yes,' Miss Emily said. 'Perhaps he considers himself the sheriff . . . I have no taxes in Jefferson.'

'But there is nothing on the books to show that, you see. We must go by the—'

'See Colonel Sartoris. I have no taxes in Jefferson.'

'But, Miss Emily—'

'See Colonel Sartoris.' (Colonel Sartoris had been dead almost ten years.) 'I have no taxes in Jefferson. Tobe!' The Negro appeared. 'Show these gentlemen out.'

II

So she vanquished them, horse and foot, just as she had vanquished their fathers thirty years before about the smell. That was two years after her father's death and a short time after her sweetheart—the one we believed would marry her—had deserted her. After her father's death she went out very little; after her sweetheart went away, people hardly saw her at all. A few of the ladies had the temerity to call, but were not received, and the only sign of life about the place was the Negro man—a young man then—going in and out with a market basket.

'Just as if a man—any man—could keep a kitchen properly,' the ladies said; so they were not surprised when the smell developed. It was another link between the gross, teeming world and the high and mighty Griersons.

A neighbor, a woman, complained to the mayor, Judge Stevens, eighty years old.

'But what will you have me do about it, madam?' he said.

'Why, send her word to stop it,' the woman said. 'Isn't there a law?'

'I'm sure that won't be necessary,' Judge Stevens said. 'It's probably just a snake or a rat that nigger of hers killed in the yard. I'll speak to him about it.'

The next day he received two more complaints, one from a man who came in diffident deprecation. 'We really must do something about it, Judge. I'd be the last one in the world to bother Miss Emily, but we've got to do something.' That night the Board of Aldermen met—three graybeards and one younger man, a member of the rising generation.

'It's simple enough,' he said. 'Send her word to have her place cleaned up. Give her a certain time to do it in, and if she don't . . .'

'Dammit, sir,' Judge Stevens said, 'will you accuse a lady to her face of smelling bad?'

So the next night, after midnight, four men crossed Miss Emily's lawn and slunk about the house like burglars, sniffing along the base of the brickwork and at the cellar openings while one of them performed a regular sowing motion with his hand out of a sack slung from his shoulder. They broke open the cellar door and sprinkled lime there, and in all the outbuildings. As they recrossed the lawn, a window that had been dark was lighted and Miss Emily sat in it, the light behind her, and her upright torso motionless as that of an idol. They crept quietly across the lawn and into the shadow of the locusts that lined the street. After a week or two the smell went away.

That was when people had begun to feel really sorry for her. People in our town, remembering how old lady Wyatt, her great-aunt, had gone completely crazy at last, believed that the Griersons held themselves a little too high for what they really were. None of the young men were quite good enough for Miss Emily and such. We had long thought of them as a tableau, Miss Emily a slender figure in white in the background, her father a spraddled silhouette in the foreground, his back to her and clutching a horsewhip, the two of them framed by the back-flung front door. So when she got to be thirty and was still single, we were not pleased exactly, but vindicated; even with insanity in the family she wouldn't have turned down all of her chances if they had really materialized.

When her father died, it got about that the house was all that was left to her; and in a way, people were glad. At last they could pity Miss Emily. Being left alone, and a pauper, she had become humanized. Now she too would know the old thrill and the old despair of a penny more or less.

The day after his death all the ladies prepared to call at the house and offer condolence and aid, as is our custom. Miss Emily met them at the door, dressed as usual and with no trace of grief on her face. She told them that her father was not dead. She did that for three days, with the ministers calling on her, and the doctors, trying to persuade her to let them dispose of the body. Just as they were about to resort to law and force, she broke down, and they buried her father quickly.

We did not say she was crazy then. We believed she had to do that. We remembered all the young men her father had driven away, and we knew that with nothing left, she would have to cling to that which had robbed her, as people will.

III

She was sick for a long time. When we saw her again, her hair was cut short, making her look like a girl, with a vague resemblance to those angels in colored church windows—sort of tragic and serene.

The town had just let the contracts for paving the sidewalks, and in the summer after her father's death they began the work. The construction company came with niggers and mules and machinery, and a foreman named Homer Barron, a Yankee—a big, dark, ready man, with a big voice and eyes lighter than his face. The little boys would follow in groups to hear him cuss the niggers, and the niggers singing in time to the rise and fall of picks. Pretty soon he knew everybody in town. Whenever you heard a lot of laughing anywhere about the square, Homer Barron would be in the center of the group. Presently we began to see him and Miss Emily on Sunday afternoons driving in the yellow-wheeled buggy and the matched team of bays from the livery stable.

At first we were glad that Miss Emily would have an interest, because the ladies all said, 'Of course a Grierson would not think seriously of a Northerner, a day laborer.' But there were still others, older people, who said that even grief could not cause a real lady to forget *noblesse oblige*—without calling it *noblesse oblige*. They just said, 'Poor Emily. Her kinsfolk should come to her.' She had some kin in Alabama; but years ago her father had fallen out with them over the estate of old lady Wyatt, the crazy woman, and there was no communication between the two families. They had not even been represented at the funeral.

And as soon as the old people said, 'Poor Emily,' the whispering began. 'Do you suppose it's really so?' they said to one another. 'Of course it is. What else could . . .' This behind their hands; rustling of craned silk and satin behind jalousies closed upon the sun of Sunday afternoon as the thin, swift clop-clop-clop of the matched team passed: 'Poor Emily.'

She carried her head high enough—even when we believed that she was fallen. It was as if she demanded more than ever the recognition of her dignity as the last Grierson; as if it had wanted that touch of earthiness to reaffirm her imperviousness. Like when she bought the rat poison, the arsenic. That was over a year after they had begun to say 'Poor Emily,' and while the two female cousins were visiting her.

'I want some poison,' she said to the druggist. She was over thirty then, still a slight woman, though thinner than usual, with cold, haughty black eyes in a face the flesh of which was strained across the temples and about the eye-sockets as you imagine a lighthouse-keeper's face ought to look. 'I want some poison,' she said.

'Yes, Miss Emily. What kind? For rats and such? I'd recom—'

'I want the best you have. I don't care what kind.'

The druggist named several. 'They'll kill anything up to an elephant. But what you want is—'

'Arsenic,' Miss Emily said. 'Is that a good one?'

'Is . . . arsenic? Yes, ma'am. But what you want—'

'I want arsenic.'

The druggist looked down at her. She looked back at him, erect, her face like a strained flag. 'Why, of course,' the druggist said. 'If that's what you want. But the law requires you to tell what you are going to use it for.'

Miss Emily just stared at him, her head tilted back in order to look him eye for eye, until he looked away and went and got the arsenic and wrapped it up. The Negro delivery boy brought her the package; the druggist didn't come back. When she opened the package at home there was written on the box, under the skull and bones: 'For rats.'

IV

So the next day we all said, 'She will kill herself'; and we said it would be the best thing. When she had first begun to be seen with Homer Barron, we had said, 'She will marry him.' Then we said, 'She will persuade him yet,' because Homer himself had remarked—he liked men, and it was known that he drank with the younger men in the Elks' Club—that he was not a marrying man. Later we said, 'Poor Emily' behind the jalousies as they passed on Sunday afternoon in the glittering buggy, Miss Emily with her head high and Homer Barron with his hat cocked and a cigar in his teeth, reins and whip in a yellow glove.

Then some of the ladies began to say that it was a disgrace to the town and a bad example to the young people. The men did not want to interfere, but at last the ladies forced the Baptist minister—Miss Emily's people were Episcopal—to call upon her. He would never divulge what happened during that interview, but he refused to go back again. The next Sunday they again drove about the streets, and the following day the minister's wife wrote to Miss Emily's relations in Alabama.

So she had blood-kin under her roof again and we sat back to watch developments. At first nothing happened. Then we were sure that they were to be married. We learned that Miss Emily had been to the jeweler's and ordered a man's toilet set in silver, with the letters H. B. on each piece. Two days later we learned that she had bought a complete outfit of men's clothing, including a nightshirt, and we said, 'They are married.' We were really glad. We were glad because the two female cousins were even more Grierson than Miss Emily had ever been.

So we were not surprised when Homer Barron—the streets had been finished some time since—was gone. We were a little disappointed that there was not a public blowing-off, but we believed that he had gone on to prepare for Miss Emily's coming, or to give her a chance to get rid of the cousins. (By that time it was a cabal, and we were all Miss Emily's allies to help circumvent the cousins.) Sure enough, after another week they departed. And, as we had expected all along, within three days Homer Barron was back in town. A neighbor saw the Negro man admit him at the kitchen door at dusk one evening.

And that was the last we saw of Homer Barron. And of Miss Emily for some time. The Negro man went in and out with the market basket, but the front door remained closed. Now and then we would see her at a window for a moment, as the men did that night when they sprinkled the lime, but for almost six months she did not appear on the streets. Then we knew that this was to be expected too; as if that quality of her father which had thwarted her woman's life so many times had been too virulent and too furious to die.

When we next saw Miss Emily, she had grown fat and her hair was turning gray. During the next few years it grew grayer and grayer until it attained an even pepper-and-salt iron-gray, when it ceased turning. Up to the day of her death at seventy-four it was still that vigorous iron-gray, like the hair of an active man.

From that time on her front door remained closed, save for a period of six or seven years, when she was about forty, during which she gave lessons in china-painting. She fitted up a studio in one of the downstairs rooms, where the daughters and granddaughters of Colonel Sartoris' contemporaries were sent to her with the same regularity and in the same spirit that they were sent to church on Sundays with a twenty-five-cent piece for the collection plate. Meanwhile her taxes had been remitted.

Then the newer generation became the backbone and the spirit of the town, and the painting pupils grew up and fell away and did not send their children to her with boxes of color and tedious brushes and pictures cut from the ladies' magazines. The front door closed upon the last one and remained closed for good. When the town got free postal delivery, Miss Emily alone refused to let them fasten the metal numbers above her door and attach a mailbox to it. She would not listen to them.

Daily, monthly, yearly we watched the Negro grow grayer and

more stooped, going in and out with the market basket. Each December we sent her a tax notice, which would be returned by the post office a week later, unclaimed. Now and then we would see her in one of the downstairs windows—she had evidently shut up the top floor of the house—like the carven torso of an idol in a niche, looking or not looking at us, we could never tell which. Thus she passed from generation to generation—dear, inescapable, impervious, tranquil, and perverse.

And so she died. Fell ill in the house filled with dust and shadows, with only a doddering Negro man to wait on her. We did not even know she was sick; we had long since given up trying to get any information from the Negro. He talked to no one, probably not even to her, for his voice had grown harsh and rusty, as if from disuse.

She died in one of the downstairs rooms, in a heavy walnut bed with a curtain, her gray head propped on a pillow yellow and moldy with age and lack of sunlight.

V

The Negro met the first of the ladies at the front door and let them in, with their hushed, sibilant voices and their quick, curious glances, and then he disappeared. He walked right through the house and out the back and was not seen again.

The two female cousins came at once. They held the funeral on the second day, with the town coming to look at Miss Emily beneath a mass of bought flowers, with the crayon face of her father musing profoundly above the bier and the ladies sibilant and macabre; and the very old men—some in their brushed Confederate uniforms—on the porch and the lawn, talking of Miss Emily as if she had been a contemporary of theirs, believing that they had danced with her and courted her perhaps, confusing time with its mathematical progression, as the old do, to whom all the past is not a diminishing road but, instead, a huge meadow which no winter ever quite touches, divided from them now by the narrow bottle-neck of the most recent decade of years.

Already we knew that there was one room in that region above stairs which no one had seen in forty years, and which would have to be forced. They waited until Miss Emily was decently in the ground before they opened it.

The violence of breaking down the door seemed to fill this room with pervading dust. A thin, acrid pall as of the tomb seemed to lie everywhere upon this room decked and furnished as for a bridal: upon the valance curtains of faded rose color, upon the rose-shaded lights, upon the dressing table, upon the delicate array of crystal and the man's toilet things backed with tarnished silver, silver so tarnished that the monogram was obscured. Among them lay a collar and tie, as if they had just been removed, which, lifted, left upon the surface a pale crescent in the dust. Upon a chair hung the suit, carefully folded; beneath it the two mute shoes and the discarded socks.

The man himself lay in the bed.

For a long while we just stood there, looking down at the profound and fleshless grin. The body had apparently once lain in the attitude of an embrace, but now the long sleep that outlasts love, that conquers even the grimace of love, had cuckolded him. What was left of him, rotted beneath what was left of the nightshirt, had become inextricable from the bed in which he lay; and upon him and upon the pillow beside him lay that even coating of the patient and biding dust.

Then we noticed that in the second pillow was the indentation of a head. One of us lifted something from it, and leaning forward, that faint and invisible dust dry and acrid in the nostrils, we saw a long strand of iron-gray hair.

CLARK ASHTON SMITH

A Rendezvous in Averoigne

Gerard de l'Automne was meditating the rimes of a new ballade in honor of Fleurette, as he followed the leaf-arrased pathway toward Vyones through the woodland of Averoigne. Since he was on his way to meet Fleurette, who had promised to keep a rendezvous among the oaks and beeches like any peasant girl, Gerard himself made better progress than the ballade. His love was at that stage which, even for a professional troubadour, is more productive of distraction than inspiration; and he was recurrently absorbed in a meditation upon other than merely verbal felicities.

The grass and trees had assumed the fresh enamel of a mediaeval May; the turf was figured with little blossoms of azure and white and yellow, like an ornate broidery; and there was a pebbly stream that murmured beside the way, as if the voices of undines were parleying deliciously beneath its waters. The sun-lulled air was laden with a wafture of youth and romance; and the longing that welled from the heart of Gerard seemed to mingle mystically with the balsams of the wood.

Gerard was a *trouvère* whose scant years and many wanderings had brought him a certain renown. After the fashion of his kind he had roamed from court to court, from chateau to chateau; and he was now the guest of the Comte de la Frênaie, whose high castle held dominion over half the surrounding forest. Visiting one day that quaint cathedral town, Vyones, which lies so near to the ancient wood of Averoigne, Gerard had seen Fleurette, the daughter of a well-to-do mercer named Guillaume Cochin; and had become more sincerely enamored of her blond piquancy than was to be expected from one who had been so frequently susceptible in such matters. He had managed to make his feelings known to her; and, after a month of *billets-doux*, ballads, and stolen interviews contrived by the help of a complaisant waiting-woman, she had made this woodland tryst with him in the absence of her father from Vyones. Accompanied by her maid and a man-servant, she was to leave the town early that after-noon and meet Gerard under a certain beech-tree of enormous age and size. The servants would then withdraw discreetly; and the lovers, to all intents and purposes, would be alone. It was not likely that they would be seen or interrupted; for the gnarled and immemorial wood possessed an ill-repute among the peasantry. Somewhere in this wood there was the ruinous and haunted Chateau des Faussesflammes; and, also, there was a double tomb, within which the Sieur Hugh du Malinbois and his chatelaine, who were notorious for sorcery in their time, had lain unconsecrated for more than two hundred years. Of these, and their phantoms, there were grisly tales; and there were stories of *loup-garous* and goblins, of fays and devils and vampires that infested Averoigne. But to these tales Gerard had given little heed, considering it improbable that such creatures would fare abroad in open daylight. The madcap Fleurette had professed herself unafraid also; but it had been necessary to promise the servants a substantial *pourboire*, since they shared fully the local superstitions.

Gerard had wholly forgotten the legendry of Averoigne, as he hastened along the sun-flecked path. He was nearing the appointed beech-tree, which a turn of the path would soon reveal; and his pulses quickened and became tremulous, as he wondered if Fleurette had already reached the trysting-place. He abandoned all effort to continue his ballade, which, in the three miles he had walked from La Frênaie, had not progressed beyond the middle of a tentative first stanza.

His thoughts were such as would befit an ardent and impatient lover. They were now interrupted by a shrill scream that rose to an unendurable pitch of fear and horror, issuing from the green stillness of the pines beside the way. Startled, he peered at the thick branches; and as the scream fell back to silence, he heard the sound of dull and hurrying footfalls, and a scuffling as of several bodies. Again the scream arose. It was plainly the voice of a woman in some distressful peril. Loosening his dagger in its sheath, and clutching more firmly a long hornbeam staff which he had brought with him as a protection against the vipers which were said to lurk in Averoigne, he plunged without hesitation or premeditation among the low-hanging boughs from which the voice had seemed to emerge.

In a small open space beyond the trees, he saw a woman who was struggling with three ruffians of exceptionally brutal and evil aspect. Even in the haste and vehemence of the moment, Gerard realized that he had never before seen such men or such a woman. The woman was clad in a gown of emerald green that matched her eyes; in her face was the pallor of dead things, together with a faery beauty; and her lips were dyed as with the scarlet of newly flowing blood.

The men were dark as Moors, and their eyes were red slits of flame beneath oblique brows with animal-like bristles. There was something very peculiar in the shape of their feet; but Gerard did not realize the exact nature of the peculiarity till long afterward. Then he remembered that all of them were seemingly club-footed, though they were able to move with surpassing agility. Somehow, he could never recall what sort of clothing they had worn.

The woman turned a beseeching gaze upon Gerard as he sprang forth from amid the boughs. The men, however, did not seem to heed his coming; though one of them caught in a hairy clutch the hands which the woman sought to reach toward her rescuer.

Lifting his staff, Gerard rushed upon the ruffians. He struck a tremendous blow at the head of the nearest one—a blow that should have leveled the fellow to earth. But the staff came down on unresisting air, and Gerard staggered and almost fell headlong in trying to recover his equilibrium. Dazed and uncomprehending, he saw the knot of struggling figures had vanished utterly. At least, the three men had vanished; but from the middle branches of a tall pine beyond the open space, the death-white features of the woman smiled upon him for a moment with faint, inscrutable guile ere they melted among the needles.

Gerard understood now; and he shivered as he crossed himself. He had been deluded by phantoms or demons, doubtless for no good purpose; he had been the gull of a questionable enchantment. Plainly there was something after all in the legends he had heard, in the ill-renown of the forest of Averoigne.

He retraced his way toward the path he had been following. But when he thought to reach again the spot from which he had heard that shrill unearthly scream, he saw that there was no longer a path; nor, indeed, any feature of the forest which he could remember or recognize. The foliage about him no longer displayed a brilliant verdure; it was sad and funereal, and the trees themselves were either cypress-like, or were already sere with autumn or decay. In lieu of the purling brook there lay before him a tarn of waters that were dark and dull as clotting blood, and which gave back no reflection of the brown autumnal sedges that trailed therein like the hair of suicides, and the skeletons of rotting osiers that writhed above them.

Now, beyond all question, Gerard knew that he was the victim of an evil enchantment. In answering that beguileful cry for succor, he had exposed himself to the spell, had been lured within the circle of its power. He could not know what forces of wizardry or demonry had willed to draw him thus; but he knew that his situation was fraught with supernatural menace. He gripped the hornbeam staff more tightly in his hand, and prayed to all the saints he could remember, as he peered about for some tangible bodily presence of ill.

The scene was utterly desolate and lifeless, like a place where cadavers might keep their tryst with demons. Nothing stirred, not even a dead leaf; and there was no whisper of dry grass or foliage, no song of birds nor murmuring of bees, no sigh nor chuckle of water. The corpse-gray heavens above seemed never to have held a sun; and the chill, unchanging light was without source or destination, without beams or shadows.

Gerard surveyed his environment with a cautious eye; and the more he looked the less he liked it: for some new and disagreeable detail was manifest at every glance. There were moving lights in the wood that vanished if he eyed them intently; there were drowned faces in the tarn that came and went like livid bubbles before he could discern their features. And, peering across the lake, he wondered why he had not seen the many-turreted castle of hoary stone whose nearer walls were based in the dead waters. It was so gray and still and vasty, that it seemed to have stood for incomputable ages between the stagnant tarn and the equally stagnant heavens. It was ancienter than the world, it was older than the light: it was coeval with fear and darkness; and a horror dwelt upon it and crept unseen but palpable along its bastions.

There was no sign of life about the castle; and no banners flew above its turrets or its donjon. But Gerard knew, as surely as if a voice had spoken aloud to warn him, that here was the fountainhead of the sorcery by which he had been beguiled. A growing panic whispered in his brain, he seemed to hear the rustle of malignant plumes, the mutter of demonian threats and plottings. He turned, and fled among the funereal trees.

Amid his dismay and bewilderment, even as he fled, he thought of Fleurette and wondered if she were awaiting him at their place of rendezvous, or if she and her companions had also been enticed and led astray in a realm of damnable unrealities. He renewed his prayers, and implored the saints for her safety as well as his own.

The forest through which he ran was a maze of bafflement and eeriness. There were no landmarks, there were no tracks of animals or men; and the swart cypresses and sere autumnal trees grew thicker and thicker as if some malevolent will were marshalling them against his progress. The boughs were like implacable arms that strove to retard him; he could have sworn that he felt them twine about him with the strength and suppleness of living things. He fought them, insanely, desperately. And seemed to hear a crackling of infernal laughter in their twigs as he fought. At last, with a sob of relief, he broke through into a sort of trail. Along this trail, in the mad hope of eventual escape, he ran like one whom a fiend pursues; and after a short interval he came again to the shores of the tarn, above whose motionless waters the high and hoary turrets of that time-forgotten castle were still dominant. Again he turned and fled; and once more, after similar wanderings and like struggles, he came back to the inevitable tarn.

With a leaden sinking of his heart, as into some ultimate slough of despair and terror, he resigned himself and made no further effort to escape. His very will was benumbed, was crushed down as by the incumbence of a superior volition that would no longer permit his puny recalcitrance. He was unable to resist when a strong and hateful compulsion drew his footsteps along the margent of the tarn toward the looming castle.

When he came nearer, he saw that the edifice was surrounded by a moat whose waters were stagnant as those of the lake, and were mantled with the iridescent scum of corruption. The drawbridge was down and the gates were open, as if to receive an expected guest. But still there was no sign of human occupancy; and the walls of the great gray building were silent as those of a sepulcher. And more tomb-like even than the rest was the square and overtowering bulk of the mighty donjon.

Impelled by the same power that had drawn him along the lake-shore, Gerard crossed the drawbridge and passed beneath the frowning barbican into a vacant courtyard. Barred windows looked blankly down; and at the opposite end of the court a door stood mysteriously open, revealing a dark hall. As he approached the doorway, he saw that a man was standing on the threshold; though a moment previous he could have sworn that it was untenanted by any visible form.

Gerard had retained his hornbeam staff; and though his reason told him that such a weapon was futile against any supernatural foe, some obscure instinct prompted him to clasp it valiantly as he neared the waiting figure on the sill.

The man was inordinately tall and cadaverous, and was dressed in black garments of a superannuate mode. His lips were strangely red amid his bluish beard and the mortuary whiteness of his face. They were like the lips of the woman who, with her assailants, had disappeared in a manner so dubious when Gerard had approached them. His eyes were pale and luminous as marsh-lights; and Gerard shuddered at his gaze and at the cold, ironic smile of his scarlet lips that seemed to reserve a world of secrets all too dreadful and hideous to be disclosed.

'I am the Sieur du Malinbois,' the man announced. His tones were both unctuous and hollow, and served to increase the repugnance felt by the young troubadour. And when his lips parted, Gerard had a glimpse of teeth that were unnaturally small and were pointed like the fangs of some fierce animal.

'Fortune has willed that you should become my guest,' the man went on. 'The hospitality which I can proffer you is rough and inadequate, and it may be that you will find my abode a trifle dismal. But at least I can assure you of a welcome no less ready than sincere.'

'I thank you for your kind offer,' said Gerard. 'But I have an appointment with a friend; and I seem in some unaccountable manner to have lost my way. I should be profoundly grateful if you would direct me toward Vyones. There should be a path not far from here; and I have been so stupid as to stray from it.'

The words rang empty and hopeless in his own ears even as he uttered them; and the name that his strange host had given—the Sieur du Malinbois—was haunting his mind like the funereal accents of a knell; though he could not recall at that moment the macabre and spectral ideas which the name tended to evoke.

'Unfortunately, there are no paths from my chateau to Vyones,' the stranger replied. 'As for your rendezvous, it will be kept in another manner, at another place, than the one appointed. I must therefore insist that you accept my hospitality. Enter, I pray; but leave your hornbeam staff at the door. You will have no need of it any longer.'

Gerard thought that he made a moue of distaste and aversion with his over-red lips as he spoke the last sentences; and that his eyes lingered on the staff with an obscure apprehensiveness. And the strange emphasis of his words and demeanor served to awaken other fantasmal and macabre thoughts in Gerard's brain; though he could not formulate them fully till afterward. And somehow he was prompted to retain the weapon, no matter how useless it might be against an enemy of spectral or diabolic nature. So he said:

'I must crave your indulgence if I retain the staff. I have made a vow to carry it with me, in my right hand or never beyond arm's reach, till I have slain two vipers.'

'That is a queer vow,' rejoined his host. 'However, bring it with you if you like. It is of no matter to me if you choose to encumber yourself with a wooden stick.'

He turned abruptly, motioning Gerard to follow him. The troubadour obeyed unwillingly, with one rearward glance at the vacant heavens and the empty courtyard. He saw with no great surprise that a sudden and furtive darkness had closed in upon the chateau without moon or star, as if it had been merely waiting for him to enter before it descended. It was thick as the folds of a cerecloth, it was airless and stifling like the gloom of a sepulcher that has been sealed for ages; and Gerard was aware of a veritable oppression, a corporeal and psychic difficulty in breathing, as he crossed the threshold.

He saw that cressets were now burning in the dim hall to which his host had admitted him; though he had not perceived the time and agency of their lighting. The illumination they afforded was singularly vague and indistinct, and the thronging shadows of the hall were unexplainably numerous, and moved with a mysterious disquiet; though the flames themselves were still as tapers that burn for the dead in a windless vault.

At the end of the passage, the Sieur du Malinbois flung open a heavy door of dark and somber wood. Beyond, in what was plainly the eating-room of the chateau, several people were seated about a long table by the light of cressets no less dreary and dismal than those in the hall. In the strange, uncertain glow, their faces were touched with a gloomy dubiety, with a lurid distortion; and it seemed to Gerard that shadows hardly distinguishable from the figures were gathered around the board. But nevertheless he recognized the woman in the emerald green who had vanished in so doubtful a fashion amid the pines when Gerard answered her call for succor. At one side, looking very pale and forlorn and frightened, was Fleurette Cochin. At the lower end reserved for retainers and inferiors, there sat the maid and the man-servant who had accompanied Fleurette to her rendezvous with Gerard.

The Sieur du Malinbois turned to the troubadour with a smile of sardonic amusement.

'I believe you have already met everyone assembled,' he observed. 'But you have not yet been formally presented to my wife, Agathe, who is presiding over the board. Agathe, I bring to you Gerard de l'Automne, a young troubadour of much note and merit.'

The woman nodded slightly, without speaking, and pointed to a chair opposite Fleurette. Gerard seated himself, and the Sieur du Malinbois assumed according to feudal custom a place at the head of the table beside his wife.

Now, for the first time, Gerard noticed that there were servitors who came and went in the room, setting upon the table various wines and viands. The servitors were preternaturally swift and noiseless, and somehow it was very difficult to be sure of their precise features or their costumes. They seemed to walk in an adumbration of sinister insoluble twilight. But the troubadour was disturbed by a feeling that they resembled the swart demoniac ruffians who had disappeared together with the woman in green when he approached them.

The meal that ensued was a weird and funereal affair. A sense of insuperable constraint, of smothering horror and hideous oppression, was upon Gerard; and though he wanted to ask Fleurette a hundred questions, and also demand an explanation of sundry matters from his host and hostess, he was totally unable to frame the words or to utter them. He could only look at Fleurette, and read in her eyes a duplication of his own helpless bewilderment and nightmare thralldom. Nothing was said by the Sieur du Malinbois and his lady, who were exchanging glances of a secret and baleful intelligence all through the meal; and Fleurette's maid and man-servant were obviously paralyzed by terror, like birds beneath the hypnotic gaze of deadly serpents.

The foods were rich and of strange savor; and the wines were fabulously old, and seemed to retain in their topaz or violet depths the unextinguished fire of buried centuries. But Gerard and Fleurette could barely touch them; and they saw that the Sieur du Malinbois and his lady did not eat or drink at all. The gloom of the chamber deepened; the servitors became more furtive and spectral in their movements; the stifling air was laden with unformulable menace, was constrained by the spell of a black and lethal necromancy. Above the aromas of the rare foods, the bouquets of the antique wines, there crept forth the choking mustiness of hidden vaults and embalmed centurial corruption, together with the ghostly spice of a strange perfume that seemed to emanate from the person of the chatelaine. And now Gerard was remembering many tales from the legendry of Averoigne, which he had heard and disregarded; was recalling the story of a Sieur du Malinbois and his lady, the last of the name and the most evil, who had been buried somewhere in this forest hundreds of years ago; and whose tomb was shunned by the peasantry since they were said to continue their sorceries even in death. He wondered what influence had bedrugged his memory, that he had not recalled it wholly when he had first heard the name. And he was remembering other things and other stories, all of which confirmed his instinctive belief regarding the nature of the people into whose hands he had fallen. Also, he recalled a folklore superstition concerning the use to which a wooden stake can be put; and realized why the Sieur du Malinbois had shown a peculiar interest in the hornbeam staff. Gerard had laid the staff beside his chair when he sat down; and he was reassured to find that it had not vanished. Very quietly and unobtrusively, he placed his foot upon it.

The uncanny meal came to an end; and the host and his chatelaine arose.

'I shall now conduct you to your rooms,' said the Sieur du Malinbois, including all of his guests in a dark, inscrutable glance. 'Each of you can have a separate chamber, if you so desire; or Fleurette Cochin and her maid Angelique can remain together; and the manservant Raoul can sleep in the same room with Messire Gerard.'

A preference for the latter procedure was voiced by Fleurette and the troubadour. The thought of uncompanioned solitude in that castle of timeless midnight and nameless mystery was abhorrent to an insupportable degree.

The four were now led to their respective chambers, on opposite sides of a hall whose length was but indeterminately revealed by the dismal lights. Fleurette and Gerard bade each other a dismayed and reluctant good-night beneath the constraining eye of their host. Their rendezvous was hardly the one which they had thought to keep; and both were overwhelmed by the supernatural situation amid whose dubious horrors and ineluctable sorceries they had somehow become involved. And no sooner had Gerard left Fleurette than he began to curse himself for a poltroon because he had not refused to part from her side; and he marvelled at the spell of drug-like involition that had bedrowsed all his faculties. It seemed that his will was not his own, but had been thrust down and throttled by an alien power.

The room assigned to Gerard and Raoul was furnished with a couch, and a great bed whose curtains were of antique fashion and fabric. It was lighted with tapers that had a funereal suggestion in their form, and which burned dully in an air that was stagnant with the mustiness of dead years.

'May you sleep soundly,' said the Sieur du Malinbois. The smile that accompanied and followed the words was no less unpleasant than the oily and sepulchral tone in which they were uttered. The troubadour and the servant were conscious of profound relief when he went out and closed the leaden-clanging door. And their relief was hardly diminished even when they heard the click of a key in the lock.

Gerard was now inspecting the room; and he went to the one window, through whose small and deep-set panes he could see only the pressing darkness of a night that was veritably solid, as if the whole place were buried beneath the earth and were closed in by clinging mold. Then, with an excess of unsmothered rage at his separation from Fleurette, he ran to the door and hurled himself against it, he beat upon it with his clenched fists, but in vain. Realizing his folly, and desisting at last, he turned to Raoul.

'Well, Raoul,' he said, 'what do you think of all this?'

Raoul crossed himself before he answered; and his face had assumed the vizard of a mortal fear.

'I think, Messire,' he finally replied, 'that we have all been decoyed by a malefic sorcery; and that you, myself, the demoiselle Fleurette, and the maid Angelique, are all in deadly peril of both soul and body.'

'That, also, is my thought,' said Gerard. 'And I believe it would be well that you and I should sleep only by turns; and that he who keeps vigil should retain in his hands my hornbeam staff, whose end I shall now sharpen with my dagger. I am sure that you know the manner in which it should be employed if there are any intruders; for if such should come, there would be no doubt as to their character and their intentions. We are in a castle which has no legitimate existence, as the guests of people who have been dead, or supposedly dead, for more than two hundred years. And such people, when they stir abroad, are prone to habits which I need not specify.'

'Yes, Messire.' Raoul shuddered; but he watched the sharpening of the staff with considerable interest. Gerard whittled the hard wood to a lance-like point, and hid the shavings carefully. He even carved the outline of a little cross near the middle of the staff, thinking that this might increase its efficacy or save it from molestation. Then, with the staff in his hand, he sat down upon the bed, where he could survey the little room from between the curtains.

'You can sleep first, Raoul.' He indicated the couch, which was near the door.

The two conversed in a fitful manner for some minutes. After hearing Raoul's tale of how Fleurette, Angelique and himself had been led astray by the sobbing of a woman amid the pines, and had been unable to retrace their way, the troubadour changed the theme. And henceforth he spoke idly and of matters remote from his real preoccupations, to fight down his torturing concern for the safety of Fleurette. Suddenly he became aware that Raoul had ceased to reply; and saw that the servant had fallen asleep on the couch. At the same time an irresistible drowsiness surged upon Gerard himself in spite of all his volition, in spite of the eldritch terrors and forebodings that still murmured in his brain. He heard through his growing hebetude a whisper as of shadowy wings in the castle halls; he caught the sibilation of ominous voices, like those of familiars that respond to the summoning of wizards; and he seemed to hear, even in the vaults and towers and remote chambers, the tread of feet that were hurrying on malign and secret errands. But oblivion was around him like the meshes of a sable net; and it closed in relentlessly upon his troubled mind, and drowned the alarms of his agitated senses.

When Gerard awoke at length, the tapers had burned to their sockets; and a sad and sunless daylight was filtering through the window. The staff was still in his hand; and though his senses were still dull with the strange slumber that had drugged them, he felt that he was unharmed. But peering between the curtains, he saw that Raoul was lying mortally pale and lifeless on the couch, with the air and look of an exhausted moribund.

He crossed the room, and stooped above the servant. There was a small red wound on Raoul's neck; and his pulses were slow and feeble, like those of one who has lost a great amount of blood. His very appearance was withered and vein-drawn. And a phantom spice arose from the couch—a lingering wraith of the perfume worn by the chatelaine Agathe.

Gerard succeeded at last in arousing the man; but Raoul was very weak and drowsy. He could remember nothing of what had happened during the night; and his horror was pitiful to behold when he realized the truth.

'It will be your turn next, Messire,' he cried. 'These vampires mean to hold us here amid their unhallowed necromancies till they have drained us of our last drop of blood. Their spells are like mandragora or the sleepy sirups of Cathay; and no man can keep awake in their despite.'

Gerard was trying the door; and somewhat to his surprise he found it unlocked. The departing vampire had been careless, in the lethargy of her repletion. The castle was very still; and it seemed to Gerard that the animating spirit of evil was now quiescent; that the shadowy wings of horror and malignity, the feet that had sped on baleful errands, the summoning sorcerers, the responding familiars, were all lulled in a temporary slumber.

He opened the door, he tiptoed along the deserted hall, and knocked at the portal of the chamber allotted to Fleurette and her maid. Fleurette, fully dressed, answered his knock immediately; and he caught her in his arms without a word, searching her wan face with a tender anxiety. Over her shoulder he could see the maid Angelique, who was sitting listlessly on the bed with a mark on her white neck similar to the wound that had been suffered by Raoul. He knew, even before Fleurette began to speak, that the nocturnal experiences of the demoiselle and her maid had been identical with those of himself and the man-servant.

While he tried to comfort Fleurette and reassure her, his thoughts were now busy with a rather curious problem. No one was abroad in the castle; and it was more than probable that the Sieur du Malinbois and his lady were both asleep after the nocturnal feast which they had undoubtedly enjoyed. Gerard pictured to himself the place and the fashion of their slumber; and he grew even more reflective as certain possibilities occurred to him.

'Be of good cheer, sweetheart,' he said to Fleurette. 'It is in my mind that we may soon escape from this abominable mesh of enchantments. But I must leave you for a little and speak again with Raoul, whose help I shall require in a certain matter.'

He went back to his own chamber. The man-servant was sitting on the couch and was crossing himself feebly and muttering prayers with a faint, hollow voice.

'Raoul,' said the troubadour a little sternly, 'you must gather all your strength and come with me. Amid the gloomy walls that surround us, the somber ancient halls, the high towers and the heavy bastions, there is but one thing that veritably exists; and all the rest is a fabric of illusion. We must find the reality whereof I speak, and deal with it like true and valiant Christians. Come, we will now search the castle ere the lord and chatelaine shall awaken from their vampire lethargy.'

He led the way along the devious corridors with a swiftness that betokened much forethought. He had reconstructed in his mind the hoary pile of battlements and turrets as he had seen them on the previous day; and he felt that the great donjon, being the center and stronghold of the edifice, might well be the place which he sought. With the sharpened staff in his hand, with Raoul lagging bloodlessly at his heels, he passed the doors of many secret rooms, the many windows that gave on the blindness of an inner court, and came at last to the lower storey of the donjon-keep.

It was a large, bare room, entirely built of stone, and illumined only by narrow slits high up in the wall, that had been designed for the use of archers. The place was very dim; but Gerard could see the glimmering outlines of an object not ordinarily to be looked for in such a situation, that arose from the middle of the floor. It was a tomb of marble; and stepping nearer, he saw that it was strangely weatherworn and was blotched by lichens of gray and yellow, such as flourish only within access of the sun. The slab that covered it was doubly broad and massive, and would require the full strength of two men to lift.

Raoul was staring stupidly at the tomb. 'What now, Messire?' he queried.

'You and I, Raoul, are about to intrude upon the bedchamber of our host and hostess.'

At his direction, Raoul seized one end of the slab; and he himself took the other. With a mighty effort that strained their bones and sinews to the cracking-point, they sought to remove it; but the slab hardly stirred. At length, by grasping the same end in unison, they were able to tilt the slab; and it slid away and dropped to the floor with a thunderous crash. Within, there were two open coffins, one of which contained the Sieur Hugh du Malinbois and the other his lady Agathe. Both of them appeared to be slumbering peacefully as infants; a look of tranquil evil, of pacified malignity, was imprinted upon their features; and their lips were dyed with a fresher scarlet than before.

Without hesitation or delay, Gerard plunged the lancelike end of his staff into the bosom of the Sieur du Malinbois. The body crumbled as if it were wrought of ashes kneaded and painted to human semblance; and a slight odor as of age-old corruption arose to the nostrils of Gerard. Then the troubadour pierced in like manner the bosom of the chatelaine. And simultaneously with her dissolution, the walls and floor of the donjon seemed to dissolve like a sullen vapor, they rolled away on every side with a shock as of unheard thunder. With a sense of weird vertigo and confusion Gerard and Raoul saw that the whole chateau had vanished like the towers and battlements of a bygone storm; that the dead lake and its rotting shores no longer offered their malefic illusions to the eye. They were standing in a forest glade, in the full unshadowed light of the afternoon sun; and all that remained of the dismal castle was the lichen-mantled tomb that stood open beside them. Fleurette and her maid were a little distance away; and Gerard ran to the mercer's daughter and took her in his arms. She was dazed with wonderment, like one who emerges from the nightlong labyrinth of an evil dream, and finds that all is well.

'I think, sweetheart,' said Gerard, 'that our next rendezvous will not be interrupted by the Sieur du Malinbois and his chatelaine.'

But Fleurette was still bemused with wonder, and could only respond to his words with a kiss.

ISAK DINESEN

The Monkey

I

𝕴n a few of the Lutheran countries of northern Europe there are still in existence places which make use of the name convent, and are governed by a prioress or chanoiness, although they are of no religious nature. They are retreats for unmarried ladies and widows of noble birth who here pass the autumn and winter days of their lives in a dignified and comfortable routine, according to the traditions of the houses. Many of these institutions are extremely wealthy, own great stretches of land, and have had during the centuries inheritances and legacies bequested to them. A proud and kindly spirit of past feudal times seems to dwell in the stately buildings and to guide the existence of the communities.

The Virgin Prioress of Closter Seven, under whose hands the convent prospered from the year 1818 to that of 1845, had a little grey monkey which had been given her by her cousin, Admiral von Schreckenstein, on his return from Zanzibar, and of which she was very fond. When she was at her card table, a place where she spent some of her happiest hours, the monkey was wont to sit on the back of her chair, and to follow with its glittering eyes the course of the cards as they were dealt out and taken in. At other times it would be found, in the early mornings, on top of the step-ladder in the library, pulling out brittle folios a hundred years old, and scattering over the black-and-white marble floor browned leaves dealing with strategy, princely marriage contracts, and witches' trials.

In a different society the monkey might not have been popular. But the convent of Closter Seven held, coordinately with its estimable female population, a whole world of pets of all sorts, and was well aware of the order of precedence therein. There were here parrots and cockatoos, small dogs, graceful cats from all parts of the world, a white Angora goat, like that of Esmeralda, and a purple-eyed young fallow deer. There was even a tortoise which was supposed to be more than a hundred years old. The old ladies therefore showed a forbearance with the whims of the Prioress's favourite, much like that which courtiers of a petticoat-governed court of the old days, conscious of their own frailty, might have shown towards the caprices of a royal *maîtresse-en-titre*.

From time to time, particularly in the autumn, when nuts were ripening in the hedges along the roads and in the large forests that surrounded the convent, it happened that the Prioress's monkey would feel the call of a freer life and would disappear for a few weeks or a month, to come back of its own accord when the night frosts set in. The children of the villages belonging to Closter Seven would then come upon it running across the road or sitting in a tree, from where it watched them attentively. But when they gathered around it and started to bombard it with chestnuts from their pockets, it would roll its eyes and grind its teeth at them, and finish by swiftly mounting the branches to disappear in the crowns of the forest.

It was the general opinion, or a standing joke amongst the ladies of the convent, that the Prioress, during these periods would become silent and the victim of a particular restlessness, and would seem loth to act in the affairs of the house, in which at ordinary times she showed great vigour. Amongst themselves they called the monkey her *Geheimrat*, and they rejoiced when it was to be seen again in her drawing-room, a little chilled after its stay in the woods.

Upon a fine October day, when the monkey had in this way been missing for some weeks, the Prioress's young nephew and godson, who was a lieutenant in the Royal Guards, arrived unexpectedly at the convent.

The Prioress was held in high respect by all her relations, and had in her time presented at the font many babies of her own noble blood, but this young man was her favourite amongst them. He was a graceful boy of twenty-two, with dark hair and blue eyes. Although he was a younger son, he was fortunately situated in life. He was the preferred child of his mother, who had come from Russia and had been an heiress; he had made a fine career. He had friends everywhere in that world that is of any significance.

On his arrival at the convent he did not, however, look like a young man under a lucky star. He came, as already said, in headlong hurry and unannounced, and the ladies with whom he exchanged a few words while waiting for admission to his aunt, and who were all fond of him, noticed that he was pale and looked deadly tired as if under some great agitation of mind.

They were not unaware, either, that he might have reason to be so.

Although Closter Seven was a small world of its own, and moved in a particular atmosphere of peace and immutability, news of the greater world outside reached it with surprising quickness, for each of the ladies had her own watchful and zealous correspondents there. Thus these cloistered women knew, just as well as the people in the centre of things, that during the last month clouds of strange and sinister nature had been gathering over the heads of that very regiment and circle of friends to which the boy belonged. A sanctimonious clique of the capital, led by the Court-Chaplain, of all people, who had the ear of high personages had, under pretence of moral indignation, lifted their voices against these young flowers of the land, and nobody knew for certain, or could even imagine, what might come out of that.

The ladies had not discussed these happenings much amongst themselves, but the librarian of the convent, who was a theologian and a scholar, had been dragged away into more than one *tête-à-tête*, and encouraged to give his opinion on the problem. From him they had learnt to connect it somehow with those romantic and sacred shores of ancient Greece which they had till now held in high esteem. Remembering their young days, when everything Greek had been *le dernier cri*, and frocks and coiffures had been named *à la grecque*, they wondered—Could the expression be used also to designate anything so little related to their young ladies' dreams of refinement? They had loved those frocks, they had waltzed with princes in them; now they thought of them with uneasiness.

Few things could have stirred their natures more deeply. It was not only the impudence of the heroes of the pulpit and the quill attacking warriors which revolted the old daughters of a fighting race, or the presentiment of trouble and much woe that worried them, but something in the matter which went deeper than that. To all of them it had been a fundamental article of faith that woman's loveliness and charm, which they themselves represented in their own sphere and according to their gifts, must constitute the highest inspiration and prize of life. In their own individual cases the world might have spread snares in order to capture this prize of their being at less cost than they meant it to, or there might have been a strange misunderstanding, a lack of appreciation, on the part of the world, but still the dogma held good. To hear it disputed now meant to them what it would mean to a miser to be told that gold no longer had absolute value, or to a mystic to have it asserted that the Lord was not present in the Eucharist. Had they known that it might ever be called into question, all these lives, which were now so nearly finished, might have come to look very different. To a few proud old maids, who had the strategic instincts of their breed developed to the full, these new conceptions came very hard. So might have come, to a gallant and faithful old general who through a long campaign, in loyalty to higher orders, had stood strictly upon the defensive, the information that an offensive would have been the right and approved move.

Still in the midst of their inquietude every one of the old women would have liked to have heard more of this strange heresy, as if, after all, the tender and dangerous emotions of the human heart were, even within their own safe seclusion, by right their domain. It was as if the tall bouquets of dried flowers in front of the convent's pier glasses had stirred and claimed authority when a question of floriculture was being raised.

They gave the pale boy an unsure welcome, as if he might have been either one of Herod's child martyrs, or a young priest of black magic, still within hope of conversion, and when he walked up the broad stair which led to the Prioress's rooms, they evaded one another's eyes.

The Prioress received her nephew within her lofty parlour. Its three tall windows looked out, between heavy curtains which had on them borders of flower garlands done in cross-stitch, over the lawns and avenues of the autumnal garden. From the damask-clad walls her long-departed father and mother gazed down, out of broad gilt frames, with military gravity and youthful grace, powdered and laced for some great court occasion. Those two had been the young man's friends since he was a baby, yet today he was struck and surprised by a puzzled, even a worried, look upon their faces. It seemed to him also, for a moment, that there was a certain strange and disquieting smell in the room, mixed with that of the incense sticks, which were being burned more amply than usual. Was this, he thought, a new aspect of the catastrophal tendencies of his existence?

The boy, while taking in the whole well-known and harmonious atmosphere, did not want or dare to waste time. After he had kissed his aunt's hand, enquired after her health and the monkey, and given her the news of his own people in town, he came straight to the matter which had brought him to Closter Seven.

'Aunt Cathinka,' he said, 'I have come to you because you have always been so good to me. I should like'—here he swallowed to keep his rebellious heart in place, knowing how little indeed it would like it—'to marry, and I hope that you will give me your advice and help.'

347

II

The boy was well aware that under ordinary circumstances nothing that he could have said could possibly have pleased the old woman better. Thus did life, he thought, manage to satisfy its taste for parody, even in relation to people like his aunt, whom in his own heart he had named after the Chinese goddess Kuan-Yin, the deity of mercy and benignant subtlety. He thought that in this case she would suffer from the irony of destiny more than he himself, and it made him feel sorry for her.

On his way to the convent, driving through the forests and little villages, past long stretches of stubble-fields on which large flocks of geese were feeding, herded by bare-legged children and young girls, he had been trying to imagine how the meeting between his aunt and himself would be likely to develop. Knowing the old lady's weakness for little Latin phrases, he had wondered if he would get from her lips *Et tu, Brute,* or a decided *Discite justitiam moniti, et non temnere divos.* Perhaps she would say *Ad sanitatem gradus est novisse morbum*— that would be a better sign.

After a moment he looked straight at the old lady's face. Her high-backed chair was in the chiaroscuro of the lace curtain, while he had on him the full light of the afternoon sun. From the shade her luminous eyes met his, and made him look away, and this dumb play was repeated twice over.

'*Mon cher enfant,*' she said at last in a gentle voice which gave him the impression of firmness, although it had in it a curious little shiver, 'it has long been a prayer of my heart that you should make this decision. On what help an old woman, outside the world, can give you, dear Boris, you can surely rely.'

Boris looked up with smiling eyes in a white face. After a terribly agitated week, and a row of wild scenes which his mother's love and jealousy had caused, he felt like a person who is, from a flooded town, taken up into a boat. As soon as he could speak he said: 'It is all for you to decide, Aunt Cathinka,' trusting that the sweetness of power would call out all the generosity of the old woman's nature.

She kept her eyes on him, kindly. They took possession of him as if she had actually been drawing him to her bosom, or even within the closer circle of her heart. She held her little handkerchief to her mouth, a gesture common with her when she was moved. She would help him, he felt, but she had something to say first.

'What is it,' she said very slowly, in the manner of a sibylla, 'which is bought dearly, offered for nothing, and then most often refused?—

Experience, old people's experience. If the children of Adam and Eve had been prepared to make use of their parents' experience, the world would have been behaving sensibly six thousand years ago. I will give you my experience of life in a little pill, sugar-coated by poetry to make it go down: "For as of all the ways of life but one—the path of duty—leads to happiness."' Boris sat silent for a moment. 'Aunt Cathinka,' he said at last, 'why should there be only one way? I know that good people think so, and I was taught it myself at my confirmation, but still the motto of our family is: "Find a way or make it." Neither can you read any cookery book which will not give you at least three or four ways of making a chicken ragout, or more. And when Columbus sailed out and discovered America,' he went on, because these were thoughts which had occupied him lately, and the Prioress was a friend of his to whom he could venture to express them, 'he really did so to find the back way to the Indies, and it was considered a heroic exploit.' 'Ah,' said the Prioress with great energy, 'Dr Sass, who was the parson of Closter Seven in the seventeenth century, maintained that in paradise, until the time of the fall, the whole world was flat, the back-curtain of the Lord, and that it was the devil who invented a third dimension. Thus are the words "straight", "square", and "flat" the words of noblemen, but the apple was an orb, and the sin of our first parents, the attempt at getting around God. I myself much prefer the art of painting to sculpture.' Boris did not contradict her. His own taste differed from hers here, but she might be right. Up to now he had congratulated himself upon his talent for enjoying life from all sides, but lately he had come to consider it a doubtful blessing. It was to this, he thought, that he owed what seemed to be his fate: to get everything he wanted at a time when he no longer wanted it. He knew from experience how a wild craving for an orgy, or music, or the sea, or confidence might, before there had been time for its fulfilment, have ceased to exist—as in the case of a star, of which the light only reaches the earth long after it has itself gone under—so that at the moment when his wish was about to be granted him, only a bullfight, or the life of a peasant ploughing his land in the rain, would satisfy the hunger of his soul.

The Prioress looked him up and down, and said:

> *Straight is the line of duty,*
> *Curved is the line of beauty.*
> *Follow the straight line; thou shalt see*
> *The curved line ever follows thee.*

The boy thought the poem over.

349

A decanter of wine and some fruit were at this moment brought in for him, and as he understood that she wanted him to keep quiet, he drank two glasses, which did him good, and in silence peeled the famous silky pears of Closter Seven, and picked the dim black grapes off their stems one by one. Without looking at his aunt he could follow all her thoughts. The dramatic urgency for quick action, which might have frightened another person of her age, did not upset her in the least. She had amongst her ancestors great lords of war who had prepared campaigns with skill, but who had also had it in them to give over at the right moment to pure inspiration.

He understood that for her in these moments her red parlour was filled with young virgins of high birth—dark and fair, slim and junoesque, good housekeepers, good horsewomen, granddaughters of schoolmates and friends of her youth—a muster-roll of young femininity, who could hide no excellency or shortcoming from her clear eyes. Spiritually she was licking her lips, like an old connoisseur walking through his cellar, and Boris himself followed her in thought, like the butler who is holding the candle.

Just then the door opened and the Prioress's old servant came in again, this time with a letter on a silver tray, which he presented to her. She took it with a hand that trembled a little, as if she could not very well take in any more catastrophe, read it through, read it again, and coloured faintly. 'It is all right, Johann,' she said, keeping the letter in her silken lap.

She sat for a little while in deep thought. Then she turned to the boy, her dark eyes clear as glass. 'You have come through my new fir plantation,' she said with the animation of a person talking about a hobby. 'What do you think of it?' The planting and upkeep of forests were indeed among her greatest interests in life. They talked for some time pleasantly of trees. There was nothing for your health, she said, like forest air. She herself was never able to pass a good night in town or amongst fields, but to lie down at night knowing that you had the trees around you for miles, their roots so deep in the earth, their crowns moving in the dark, she considered to be one of the delights of life. The forest had always done Boris good when he had been staying at Closter Seven as a child. Even now he would notice a difference when he had been in town for a long time, and she wished that she could get him down more often.—'And who, Boris,' she said with a sudden skip of thought and a bright and determined benevolence, 'who, now that we come to talk about it, could indeed make you a better wife than that great friend of yours and mine, little Athena Hopballehus?'

No name could in this connection have come more unexpectedly to Boris. He was too surprised to answer. The phrase itself sounded absurd to him. He had never heard Athena described as little, and he remembered her as being half an inch taller than himself. But that the Prioress should speak of her as a great friend showed a complete change of spirit, for he was sure that ever since their neighbour's daughter had grown up, his aunt and his mother, who were rarely of one mind, had been joining forces to keep him and Athena apart.

As his mind turned from this unaccountable veering on the part of the old lady to the effect which it might have upon his own destiny, he found that he did not dislike the idea. The burlesque he had always liked, and it might even be an extravaganza of the first water to bring Athena to town as his wife. So when he looked at his aunt he had the face of a child. 'I have the greatest faith in your judgement, Aunt Cathinka,' he said.

The Prioress now spoke very slowly, not looking at him, as if she did not want any impressions from other minds to intermingle with her own. 'We will not waste time, Boris,' she said. 'That has never been my habit once my mind was made up.' And that means, never at all, Boris thought. 'You go and change into your uniform, and I will in the meantime write a letter to the old Count. I will tell him how you have made me your confidante in this matter of your heart, upon which the happiness of your life depends, and in which your dear mother has not been able to give you her sympathy. And you, you must be ready to go within half an hour.'

'Do you think, Aunt Cathinka, that Athena will have me?' asked Boris as he rose to go. He was always quick to feel sorry for other people. Now, looking out over the garden and seeing two of the old ladies emerge, in galoshes, from one of the avenues, wherein they had been taking their afternoon walk, he felt sorry for Athena for merely existing. 'Athena,' the Prioress was saying, 'has never had an offer of marriage in her life. I doubt if, for the last year, she has seen any man but Pastor Rosenquist, who comes to play chess with her papa. She has heard my ladies discuss the brilliant marriages which you might have made if you had wanted to. If Athena will not have you, my little Boris,' she said, and smiled at him very sweetly, 'I will.'

Boris kissed her hand for this, and reflected what an excellent arrangement it might prove to be, and then all at once he got such a terrible impression of strength and cunning that it was as if he had touched an electric eel. Women, he thought, when they are old enough to have done with the business of being women, and can let loose their strength, must be the most powerful creatures in the whole world. He gazed at his aunt's refined face.

No, it would not do, he thought.

III

Boris drove from Closter Seven in the Prioress's britzska, with her letter upon his heart, looking the ideal young hero of romance. The news of his errand had spread mysteriously in the convent, as if it had been a new kind of incense, and had gone straight to the hearts of the old ladies. Two or three of them were sitting in the sun on the long terrace to see him go, and a particular friend of his, a corpulent old maid, bleached by having been kept for fifty years from all the lights of life, stood beside his carriage to hand him three long-stemmed white asters from her little winter garden. Thus had gone away, thirty years ago, the young man she loved, and then he had been killed at Jena. A gentle melancholy veiled her always, and her lady companion said of her: 'The Countess Anastasia has a heavy cross. The love of eating is a heavy cross.' But it was the memory of this last parting of theirs that had kept her eyes, in her puny face, bright like light blue enamel. She felt at the moment the resurrection of an entire destiny, and handed him her flowers as if they had been some part of it, mysteriously come to life in a second round, as if they had been her three unborn daughters, now tall and marriageable, joining his journey in the quality of bridesmaids.

Boris had left his servant at the convent, for he knew him to be in love with one of the lady's maids, and it seemed to him that he ought now to show sympathy towards all legitimate lovemaking. He wished to be alone. Solitude was always a pleasure to him, and he never had much opportunity for it. Lately he seemed never to have been alone at all. When people were not at him, working upon his feelings with all their might, they had still succeeded in making him take up their line of thought, until he felt those convolutions of the brain which had to do with these matters aching as if they were worn out. Even on his way down to the convent he had been made to think the thoughts of other people. Now, he thought with great contentment, for an hour he could think whatever he liked.

The road from Closter Seven to Hopballehus rises more than five hundred feet and winds through tall pine forest. From time to time this opens and affords a magnificent view over large stretches of land below. Now in the afternoon sun the trunks of the fir trees were burning red, and the landscape far away seemed cool, all blue and pale gold. Boris was able now to believe what the old gardener at the convent had told him when he was a child: that he had once seen, about this time of the year and the day, a herd of unicorns come out of the woods to graze upon the sunny slopes, the white and dappled mares, rosy in the sun, treading daintily and looking around for their young, the old stallion, darker roan, sniffing and pawing the ground. The air here smelled of fir leaves and toadstools, and was so fresh that it made him yawn. And yet, he thought, it was different from the freshness of spring; the courage and gaiety of it were tinged with despair. It was the finale of the symphony.

⌐ subtale

He remembered how he had, upon a May evening not six months ago, been taken into the young heart of spring, as now into the sad heart of autumn. He and a young friend of his had amused themselves by wandering for three weeks about the country, visiting places where nobody had known them to be. They had travelled in a caravan, carrying with them a little theatre of dolls, and had given performances of plays which they made up themselves in the villages that they came through. The air had been filled with sweet smells, the nightingales had been raving within the bird cherries, the moon stood high, not much paler than the sky of those nights of spring.

One night they had come, very tired, to a farmhouse in a grass field, and had been given a large bed in a room that had in it a grandfather's clock and a dim looking-glass. Just as the clock was striking twelve, three quite young girls appeared on the threshold in their shifts, each with a lighted candle in her hand, but the night was so clear that the little flames looked only like little drops of the moon. They clearly did not know that two wayfaring young men had been taken in and given the large bedroom, and the guests watched them in deep silence from behind the hangings of the big bed. Without looking at one another, without a word, one by one they dropped their slight garments on the floor and quite naked they walked up to the mirror and looked into it, the candle held high overhead, absorbed in the picture. Then they blew out their candles, and in the same solemn silence they walked backward to the door, their long hair hanging down, got into their shifts, and disappeared. The nightingales kept on singing outside, in a green bush near the window. The two boys remembered that this was Walpurgis Night, and decided that what they had witnessed was some witchcraft by which these girls had hoped to catch a glimpse of their future husbands.

He had not been up this way for a long time, not since, as a child, he had gone with the Prioress in her landaulet to pay a call at her neighbour's. He recognized the curves, but they had shrunk, and he fell to meditating upon the subject of change.

The real difference between God and human beings, he thought, was that God cannot stand continuance. No sooner has he created a season of a year, or a time of the day, than he wishes for something quite different, and sweeps it all away. No sooner was one a young man, and happy at that, than the nature of things would rush one into marriage, martyrdom or old age. And human beings cleave to the existing state of things. All their lives they are striving to hold the moment fast, and are up against a *force majeure*. Their art is nothing but the attempt to catch by all means the one particular moment, one mood, one light, the momentary beauty of one woman or one flower, and make it everlasting. It is all wrong, he thought, to imagine paradise as a never-changing state of bliss. It will probably, on the contrary, turn out to be, in the true spirit of God, an incessant up and down, a whirlpool of change. Only you may yourself, by that time, have become one with God, and have taken to liking it. He thought with deep sadness of all the young men who had been, through the ages, perfect in beauty and vigour—young Pharaohs with clean-cut faces hunting in chariots along the Nile, young Chinese sages, silk-clad, reading within the live shade of willows—who had been changed, against their wishes, into supporters of society, fathers-in-law, authorities on food and morals. All this was sad.

A turning of the road and a long vista cut through the wood brought him face to face with Hopballehus, still at a distance. The old architect of two hundred years ago had succeeded in building something so enormous that it fell in with nature, and might have been a little formation of the grey rock. To someone now standing on the terrace, Boris thought, I and the britzska and the grey and black horses would look diminutive, hardly distinguishable.

The sight of the house turned his thoughts towards it. It had always appealed to his imagination. Even now when he had not seen it for years, it would happen that he would dream of it at night. It was in itself a fantastic place, resting upon a large plateau, with miles of avenues around it, rows of statues and fountains, built in late baroque and now baroquely dilapidated and more than half a ruin. It seemed a sort of Olympus, more Olympic still for the doom which was hanging over it. The existence therein of the old Count and his daughter had about it something Olympic as well. They lived, but how they got through the twenty-four hours of their day and night must remain a mystery to humans. The old Count, who had once been a brilliant diplomatist, a scientist and a poet, had for many years been absorbed in a great lawsuit which he had going on in Poland, and which he had inherited from his father and grandfather. If he could win it, it would give him back the immense riches and estates that had once belonged to his family, but it was known that he could never win it, and it was only ruining him with ever greater speed. He lived in those gigantic worries as in clouds which made all his movements dim. Boris had at times wondered what the world looked like to his daughter. Money, if she had ever seen it, he knew to hold no place in her life; no more did society or what is called the pleasures of life, and he wondered if she had ever heard of love. God knows, he thought, if she has ever looked at herself in a glass.

The light carriage swished through the layers of fallen leaves upon the terrace. In places they lay so thick that they half covered the stone balusters and reached the knees of Diana's stag. But the trees were bare; only here and there a single golden leaf trembled high upon the black twigs. Following the curve of the road, Boris's carriage came straight upon the main terrace and the house, majestic as the Sphinx herself in the sunset. The light of the setting sun seemed to have soaked into the dull masses of stone. They reddened and glowed with it until the whole place became a mysterious, a glorified, abode, in which the tall windows shone like a row of evening stars.

Boris got out of the britzska in front of the mighty stone stairs and walked towards them, feeling for his letter. Nothing stirred in the house. It was like walking into a cathedral. And, he thought, by the time that I get into that carriage once more, what will everything be like to me?

IV

At this moment the heavy doors above the stairs were flung open, and the old Count appeared at the top step, standing like Samson when in his wrath he broke down the temple of the Philistines.

He was always a striking figure, short in the legs and with the torso of a giant, his mighty head surrounded by a mane of wild grey hair, like a poet's or a lion's. But today he seemed strangely inspired, in the grip of some tremendous emotion, swaying where he stood. He remained for a moment immovable, scrutinizing his visitor, like an old man gorilla outside his lair, ready for the attack; then he came down the stairs upon the young man, imposing upon him a presence such as the Lord himself might have shown had he descended, for once, the ladder of Jacob.

Good God, thought Boris, as he walked up the steps to meet him, this old man knows all, and is going to kill me. He had a glimpse of the old Count's face, filled with wild triumph, the light eyes aflame. The next moment he felt his arms around him, and his body trembling against his own.

'Boris!' he cried, 'Boris, my child,' for he had known the boy from childhood, and had, Boris was aware, once been one of his beautiful mother's adorers, 'welcome. Welcome here today. Do you know?' 'Know?' said Boris. 'I have won my case,' said the old man. Boris stared at him. 'I have won my case in Poland,' he repeated. 'Lariki, Lipnika, Parnov Grabovo—they are all mine, as they were the old people's.'

'I congratulate you,' said Boris, slowly, his thoughts strangely put into motion. 'With all my heart. This is unexpected news indeed!' The old Count thanked him many times, and showed him the letter from his lawyer, which he had just received, and was still holding in his hand. As he was talking to the boy he spoke slowly at first, seeking for his words, as a man out of the habit of speech, but as he went on he recovered his old voice and speech that had in the old days charmed so many people. 'A great passion, Boris,' he said, 'such as does really and truly devour your heart and soul, you cannot feel for individual beings. Perhaps you cannot feel it for anything which is capable of loving you in return. Those officers who have loved their armies, those lords who have loved their soil, they can talk about passion. My God, I have had the whole weight of the land of Hopballehus upon my chest at night, when I imagined that I had been leading it into a lost battle. But this,' he said, drawing a deep breath, 'this is happiness.' Boris understood that it was not the thought of his riches which filled the soul of the old man, but the triumph of right over wrong, the righteousness of the entire universe being, to him, concentrated in his own figure. He began to explain the judgement in detail, still with one hand upon the young man's shoulder, and Boris felt that he was welcome to his heart as a friend who could listen. 'Come in, come in, Boris,' he said, 'we will drink a glass together, you and I, from the wine which I have put aside for today. Our good Pastor is here. I sent for him when I got the letter, to keep me company, as I did not know that you would be coming.'

Within the prodigious hall, richly ornamented with black marble, a small corner was made habitable by a few chairs and a table, covered with the Count's books and papers. Above it was a gigantic picture, much darkened by age, an equestrian portrait of an old lord of the house, holding himself very calm upon a rearing horse with a small head, and pointing with a roll of paper towards a battlefield depicted in the distance under the belly of the horse. Pastor Rosenquist, a short man with red cheeks, who had for many years been the spiritual guide of the family, and whom Boris knew well, was sitting in one of the chairs apparently in deep thought. The happenings of the day had brought disorder in his theories, which was to him a more serious disaster than if the parsonage had burnt down. He had suffered from poverty and misfortunes all his life, and had in the course of time come to live upon a system of spiritual bookkeeping according to which earthly trials became an investment, drawing interest in the other world. His own personal account, he knew, was made up in very small change, but he had taken a great interest in the old Count's sorrows, and had looked upon him as a favourite of the Lord's, whose treasures were all the time accumulating in the new Jerusalem, like to sapphires, chrysoprase and amethyst propagating on their own. Now he was upset and did not know what to think, which to him was a terrible condition. He had sought comfort in the book of Job, but even there the figures would not agree, Behemoth and Leviathan coming in upon an account of losses and profits of their own. The whole affair seemed to him in the nature of a gift, which, according to Ecclesiastes, destroyeth the heart, and he could not get away from the thought that this old man whom he loved was in the bad way of anticipating his income.

'Now I would,' said the old Count, when he had fetched and opened the golden bottle, 'that my poor father and my dear grandfather were here with us to drink this wine. I have felt, as I have lain awake at night, that they have kept awake with me within their sarcophagi below. I am happy,' he went on as, still standing, he lifted his glass, 'that it be the son of Abunde'—that was his old name for Boris's mother—'who drinks here with me tonight.' In the exuberance of his heart he patted Boris's cheek with tenderness, while his face radiated a gentleness which had been in exile for years; and the boy, who knew a good thing when he saw it, envied the old man his innocence of heart. 'And to our good Pastor,' the Count said, turning to him. 'My friend, you have shed tears of sympathy in this house. They arise now as wine.'

The old Count's manner heightened Pastor Rosenquist's uneasiness. It seemed to him that only a frivolous heart could move with such ease in a new atmosphere, forgetting the old. Brought up himself upon a system of examinations and promotions, he was not prepared to understand a race reared upon the laws of luck in war and court favour, adjusted for the unforeseen and accustomed to the unexpected, for whom to be safe, or even saved, seems the least necessary of all things. Then again came into his mind the words of the Scripture—'He saith amongst the trumpets, ha, ha!'—and he thought that perhaps after all his old friend was all right. 'Yes, yes,' he said, smiling, 'water has certainly been changed into wine, once. It is without doubt a good drink. But you know what our good peasants hold: that wine-begotten children will end badly. So, we have reason to fear, will wine-begotten hopes and moods. Though that,' he added, 'would not, of course, apply to the children of the wedding of Cana, of which I was just speaking.'

'At Lariki,' said the Count, 'there is hung, in the ceiling of the gateway, a hunting horn in an iron chain. My grandfather's grandfather was a man of herculean strength. When in the evening he rode through the gate, he used to take hold of the horn, and lifting himself and his horse from the ground, he blew it. I have known that I could do the same, but I thought I should never ride through that gate. Athena might do it, too,' he added thoughtfully.

He refilled his glasses. 'How is it that you came here today?' he asked Boris, beaming upon him and his gala uniform, as if his coming had been a unique exploit. 'What brings you to Hopballehus?' Boris felt the old man's openness reflected in his own heart, like a blue sky in the sea. He looked into his friend's face. 'I came here today,' he said, 'to ask Athena to marry me.' The old man gave him a great luminous glance. 'To ask Athena to marry you!' he exclaimed. 'You came here today for that?' He stood for a moment, deeply moved. 'The ways of God are strange indeed,' he said. Pastor Rosenquist rose from his chair and sat down again, to arrange his accounts.

When the old Count spoke again he was much changed. The intoxication was gone, and he seemed to have collected the forces of his nature in good order. It was this balance which had given him a name in the old days, when he had, as a young man of the Embassy in Paris, upon the first night of his tragedy, *The Undine*, fought a duel with pistols in the *entr'acte*.

'Boris, my child,' he said, 'you have come here to change my heart. I have been living with my face towards the past, or for this hour of victory. This moment is the first in which I have thought of the future. I see that I shall have to come down from a pinnacle to walk along a road. Your words are opening up a great vista to me. What am I to be? The patriarch of Hopballehus, crowning virtuous village maidens? Grandpapa, planting apple trees? Ave, Hopballehus. *Naturi te salutem.*'

Boris remembered the Prioress's letter, and told the old man how he had called at Closter Seven on his way. The Count inquired after the lady, and, always keen on all sorts of papers, he put on his glasses and became absorbed in the letter. Boris sat and drank his wine in a happy mood. During the last week he had come to doubt whether life ever held anything pleasant at all. Now his reception in the old Count's house was to him a show of the most enjoyable kind, and he always moved with ease from one mood to another.

When the Count had finished the reading, he laid the letter down and, keeping his folded hands upon it, he sat for a long time silent.

'I give you,' he said at last slowly and solemnly, 'my blessing. First I give it to the son of your mother—and of your father—secondly to the young man who, as I see now, has loved so long against all. And finally I feel that you have been sent, Boris, by stronger hands than your own tonight.

'I give you, in Athena, the key of my whole world. Athena,' he repeated, as if it gave him joy to pronounce his daughter's name, 'is herself like a hunting-horn in the woods.' And as if, without knowing it himself, some strange and sad memory of his youth had taken possession of him, he added, almost in a whisper, '*Dieu, que le son du cor est triste au fond du bois.*'

V

While they had been talking, a strong wind had sprung up outside. The day had been still. This blowing weather had come with the dusk, like an animal of the night. It swept along the long walls, around the corners of the house, and whirled the dead leaves up in the air. In the midst of it, Athena, who had been outspanning the horse from Pastor Rosenquist's trap in the stables, was heard to cross the terrace and come up the stairs.

The old Count, whose eyes had been dwelling on Boris's face, made a sudden movement, as if he had been alarmed by something he did not himself understand. 'Do not speak to her tonight,' he said. 'You will understand: our friend, the Pastor, Athena and myself have had so many evenings here, together. Let this be the last of them. I will tell her myself, and you, my dear son, come back to Hopballehus tomorrow morning.' Boris thought this a good plan. As the Count spoke, his daughter came into the room, still in her big cloak.

Athena was a strong young woman of eighteen, six feet high and broad in proportion, with a pair of shoulders which could lift and carry a sack of wheat. At forty she would be enormous, but now she was too young to be fat, and straight as a larch tree. Beneath her flaming hair her noble forehead was white as milk; lower down her face was, like her broad wrists, covered with freckles. Still she was so fair and clear of skin that she seemed to lighten up the hall on entering it, with the light that you will get inside a room when the snow is lying outside. Her clear eyes had a darker ring around the iris—a pair of eyes for a young lioness or eagle—otherwise the strong young creature's countenance was peaceful, and her round face had that expression of attention and reserve which is ordinarily found in the faces of people who are hard of hearing. When he had been with her, Boris had sometimes thought of the old ballad about the giant's daughter, who finds a man in the wood, and, surprised and pleased, takes him home to play with. The giant orders her to let him go, telling her that she will only break him.

The giant himself, the old Count, showed her an old-fashioned chivalrousness which appeared to Boris like a rather noble old coin, dug out of the ground, and keeping its gold value, even when no more current. It was said that the Count had been, in his young days, one of the lovers of Princess Pauline Borghese, who was the loveliest woman of her time. He had seen Venus Anadyomene face to face, and for the sake of that vision gave homage to the likeness of the goddess, even where it was more clumsily cut in wood or stone. With no claim to beauty, Athena had grown up in an atmosphere of incense burnt to woman's loveliness.

She blinked a little at the light and the stranger, and indeed Boris, in his white uniform and high golden collar, his pomatumed curls like a halo in the light, was a striking meteor in the great dim room. Still, safe in her great strength, she asked him—standing, as was her habit, on one leg, like a big stork—of news of his aunt, and the ladies of Closter Seven. She knew very few people, and for these old women, who had given her much good advice, though she had shocked them a little by growing up so unromantically big, she had, Boris thought, the sort of admiration that a peasant's child at a fair has for the skilled and spangled tight-rope dancers. If she marries me, he thought, as he stood and talked to her, his voice sweet as a song, with the fond gaze of the old Count upon her face and his, she will be susceptible to my tricks; but is my married life to be an everlasting fair? And if ever I drop from my rope, will she pick me up, or just turn her back and leave?

She bid him let the Prioress know that she had seen her monkey a few nights ago, on the terrace of Hopballehus, sitting upon the socle of Venus's statue, in the place where a small Cupid, now broken, used to be. Talking about the monkey, she asked him if he did not think it curious that her father's solicitor in Poland had a monkey of the same kind, which had also come from Zanzibar. The old Count started to speak of the Wendish idols, from whose country his own family originally came, and of which the goddess of love had the face and façade of a beautiful woman, while, if you turned her around, she presented at the back the image of a monkey. How, he asked, had these wild Nordic tribes come to know about monkeys? Might there have lived monkeys in the sombre pine forests of Wenden a thousand years ago?

'No, that is not possible,' said Pastor Rosenquist. 'It would always have been too cold. But there are certain symbols which seem to have been the common property of all pagan iconoclasts. It would be worth studying; it might be due to the idea of original sin.'

But how, asked Athena, did they know, in the case of that goddess of love, which was the front and which the back?

Boris here ordered his carriage, and took leave of the party. The old Count seemed to be sorry to send him away and repentant of his hardness to a lover. He apologized for the bad weather of Hopballehus, held the youth's hand with tears in his eyes, and told Athena to see him out. Pastor Rosenquist, on the other hand, could not but be pleased by the departure of anyone who looked so much like an angel without being one.

Athena walked out on the terrace with Boris. In the light of his carriage lanterns her big cloak, blowing about her, threw strange shadows upon the gravel, like a pair of large wings. Over the vast lawn, iron grey in the moonlight, the moon herself appeared and disappeared in a stormy sky.

Boris felt at this moment really sorry to be leaving Hopballehus. The chaotic world of the place had reminded him of his childhood, and seemed to him infinitely preferable to the existence of clockwork order which he would find at the convent. He stood a little in silence, near Athena. The clouds were parted, and a few of the constellations of stars stood clear in the sky. The Great Bear preached its lesson: Keep your individuality in the crowd. 'Do you ever think of the bear hunt?' Boris asked Athena. The children had not been allowed to take part in it, but they had stolen away together, and had joined the Count's huntsmen, on a very hot July day, high up in the hills. Two spotted dogs had been killed, and he remembered the terrible tumult of the fight, and the quick movements of the huge ragged brown beast within the thicket of firs and ferns, and one glimpse of its furious roaring face, the red tongue hanging out.

'Yes, I do, sometimes,' said Athena, her eyes, with his, in the skies, on a stellar bear hunt. 'It was the bear which the peasants called the Empress Catherine. She had killed five men.'

'Are you still a Republican, Athena?' he asked. 'One time you wanted to cut off the heads of all the tyrants of Europe.'

The colour of Athena's face, in the light of the lamp, heightened. 'Yes,' she said, 'I am a Republican. I have read the history of the French Revolution. The kings and priests were lazy and licentious, cruel to the people, but those men who called themselves "the Mountain" and put on the red Phrygian bonnet were courageous. Danton was a true patriot, and I should have liked to meet him; so was the Abbé Sieyès.' She warmed to her subject in the night air. 'I should like to see that place in Paris where the guillotine stood,' she said.

'And to wear the Phrygian bonnet?' Boris asked her. Athena nodded shortly, collecting her thoughts. Then, as if meaning to be sure to bring the truth home to him, she broke into some lines of verse, herself, as she went on, carried away by the pathos of the words:

> *O Corse à cheveux plats, que la France était belle*
> *au grand soleil de Messidor.*
> *C'était une cavale indomptable et rebelle,*
> *sans freins d'acier, ni rênes d'or.*
> *Une jument sauvage, à la croupe rustique,*
> *fumant encore du sang des rois.*
> *Mais fière, et d'un pied libre heurtant le sol antique,*
> *libre, pour la première fois!*

As Boris drove away from Hopballehus the wind was blowing strong. The moon was racing the heavens behind wild thin clouds; the air was cold. It must be near the freezing-point, he thought. His lanterns chased the trees and their shadows and threw them to all sides around him. A large dry branch from a tree was suddenly blown down, and crashed in front of his shying horses. He thought, alone in the dark, of the three people in the hall of Hopballehus, and laughed.

As he drove on, below him in the valley lights leapt up. As if they were playing with him they appeared between the trees, looked him straight in the face and went off again. A large group of lights came in sight, like a reflection, on the earth, of the Pleiades. Those were the lamps of Closter Seven.

And suddenly it came upon him that somewhere something was not right, was quite wrong and out of order. Strange powers were out tonight. The feeling was so strong and distinct that it was as if an ice-cold hand had passed for a moment over his scalp. His hair rose a little upon his head. For a few minutes he was really and genuinely afraid, struck by an extraordinary terror. In this strange turbulence of the night, and the wild life of dead things all around him, he felt himself, his britzska, and his grey and black horses terribly and absurdly small, exposed and unsafe.

As he turned into the long avenue of Closter Seven, his lamps suddenly shone into a pair of glinting eyes. A very small shadow ran across the road and was gone into the deeper black shadows of the Prioress's shrubbery.

On his arrival at the convent he was told that the Prioress had gone to bed. To have, Boris thought, all her strength on hand in the morning.

The supper table was laid for him in his aunt's private dining-room, which she had just lately redecorated. Before it had been white, with ornaments of stucco perhaps a hundred years old. Now it was prettily covered with a wall paper whose pattern, upon a buff background, presented various scenes of oriental life. A girl danced under a palm tree, beating a tambourine, while old men in red and blue turbans and long beards looked on. A sultan held his court of justice under a golden canopy, and a hunting party on horseback, preceded by its greyhounds and Negro dog-boys, passed a ruin. The Prioress had also done away with the old-fashioned candlesticks, and had the table lighted by tall, brightly modern, Carcel lamps of blue china, painted with pink roses. In the warm and cosy room he supped by himself. Like, he thought, Don Giovanni in the last act of the opera. 'Until the Commandante comes,' his thoughts added on their own. He stole a glance at the window. The wind was still singing outside, but the disquieting night had been shut out by the heavy drawn curtains.

VI

The aunt and the nephew had breakfast together in pleasant harmony, from time to time gazing, within the Prioress's silver samovar, at their own faces curiously distorted. A little shining sun also showed itself therein, for the day that followed the stormy night was clear and serene. The wind had wandered on to other neighbourhoods, leaving the gardens of Closter Seven airy and bare.

Boris had recorded to the old lady the happenings at Hopballehus, and she had listened with great content and a deep interest in the fate of her old neighbour and friend. She could hardly refrain from letting her imagination flutter amongst the glories of the boy's future, but it was done so gracefully that the old Count and Athena might have been present.

'I feel, my dear,' she said, 'that now Athena ought to travel and see a little of the world. When I was her age, Papa took me to Rome and Paris, and I met many celebrities. What a pleasure to a man of talent to accompany that highly gifted child to those places, and show her life.'

'Yes,' said Boris, pouring himself out some more coffee, 'she told me yesterday that she wanted to see Paris.'

'Naturally,' said the Prioress. 'The dear child has never owned a Paris bonnet in her life. At Lariki,' she went on, her thoughts running pleasantly to and fro, there is splendid bear-hunting, and wild boars. I can well imagine your divinity, spear in hand. At Lipnika the cellar is stored with Tokay, presented to one old lord by the Empress Maria Theresa. Athena will pour it out with the generous hand of her family. At Patnov Grabovo are found the famous row of *jets d'eaux* which were constructed by the great Danish astronomer Ole Roemer, the same who made the *grandes eaux* of Versailles.'

While they were thus playing about with the happy possibilities of life, old Johann had brought in two letters, which had arrived at the same time, although the one for the Prioress had come by post, and Boris's letter had been brought by a groom from Hopballehus. Boris, on looking up after having read a few lines, noticed the hard and fine little smile on the face of the old lady, absorbed in her reading. She will not smile for long, he thought.

The old Count's letter ran as follows:

I am writing you, my dear Boris, because Athena refuses to do so. I am taking hold of my pen in deep distress and repentance; indeed I have come to know that desire to cover my head with ashes, of which the old writers talk.

I have to tell you that my daughter has rejected your suit, which last night seemed to me to crown the benefactions of destiny towards my house. She surely feels no reluctance towards this alliance in particular, but she tells me that she will never marry, and that it is even impossible for her to consider the question at all.

In a way it is right that it should be I who write you this letter. For in this misfortune the guilt is mine, the responsibility rests with me.

I, who have had this young life in my hand, have made her strong youth my torchbearer on my descent to the sepulchral chamber. Step by step, as I have gone downwards, her shoulder has been my support, and she has never failed me. Now she will not—she cannot—look up.

The peasants of our province have the saying that no child born in wedlock can look straight at the sun; only bastards are capable of it. Alas, how much is my poor Athena my legitimate child, the legitimate child of my race and its fate! She is so far from being able to look straight at the sun, that she fears no darkness whatever, but her eyes are hurt by light. I have made of my young dove, a bird of the night.

She had been to me both son and daughter, and I have in my mind seen her wearing the old coats of armour of Hopballehus. Too late I now realize that she is wearing it, not as the young St George fighting the dragons, but as Azrael, the angel of death, of our house. Indeed, she has shut herself up therein, and for all the coming years of her life, she will refuse to lay it aside.

I have never sinned against the past, but I see now that I have been sinning against the future; rightly it will have none of me. Upon Athena's maiden grave I shall be laying down flowers for those unborn generations in whose faces I had for a moment, my dear child, thought to see your features. In asking your forgiveness I shall be asking the forgiveness of much doomed energy, talent and beauty, of lost laurels and myrtles. The ashes which I strew on my head is theirs! . . .

Boris handed the letter to the Prioress without words, and leaned his chin in his hand to watch her face while she read it. He nearly got more than he asked for. She became so deadly white that he feared that she was going to faint or die, while red flames sprang out on her face as if somebody had struck her across it with a whip. King Solomon, it is known, shut up the most prominent demons of Jewry in bottles, sealed them, and had them sunk to the bottom of the sea. What goings on, down there, of impotent fury! Alike, Boris thought, to the dumb struggles within the narrow and wooden chests of old women, sealed up by the Solomonic wax of their education. Probably her sight failed her, and the red damask parlour grew black before her eyes, for she laid down the letter before she could have had time to finish it.

'What! what!' she said in a hoarse and hardly audible voice, 'what does the Poet write to you?' She gasped for air, raised her right hand, and shook her trembling forefinger in the air. 'She will not marry you!' she exclaimed.

'She will not marry at all, Aunt,' said Boris to console her.

'No? Not at all?' sneered the old lady. 'A Diana, is she that? But would you not have made a nice little Actæon, my poor Boris? And all that you have offered her—the position, the influence, the future—that means nothing to her? What is it she wants to be?' She looked into the letter, but in her agony she was holding it, bewildered, upside down. 'A stone figure upon a sarcophagus—in the dark, in silence, for ever? Here we have a fanatical virgin, *en plein dix-neuvième siècle? Vraiment tu n'as pas de la chance!* There is no *horror vaccui* here.'

'The law of the *horror vacui*,' Boris, who was really frightened, said to distract her, 'does not hold good more than thirty-two feet up.'

'More than what?' asked the Prioress.

'Thirty-two feet,' he said. The Prioress shrugged her shoulders.

She turned her glinting eyes on him, pulling the letter, which she had received by the post, half up from her silk pocket, and putting it back again. 'She will have nothing,' she said slowly, 'and you will give nothing. It seems to me, in all modesty, that you are well paired. I myself, giving you my blessing, have got nothing to say. That was already in the rules of my forefathers: "Where nothing is, *le Seigneur a perdu son droit*." You, Boris, you will have to go back to Court, and to the old Dowager Queen and her Chaplain, by the way you came. For,' she added, still more slowly, 'where we have entered in, there also we withdraw.' These words impressed the old woman herself more than they did her nephew, who had heard them before. She became very silent.

Boris began to feel really uncomfortable, and desired to put an end to the conversation. He could understand quite well that she wanted him to suffer. While she had been happy she had liked to have happy people around her. Now, tortured, she had to surround herself with the sort of substance which was within herself, or, as in the vacuum of which she had been talking, she would be crushed. But in his particular case she had such strong allies in the very circumstances. It was true that he had not yet realized what Athena's refusal would mean to him. If the old woman would go on beating him like this with all her might, all the misery of the last weeks would be returned upon his head again. Suddenly the Prioress turned from him and went up to the window, as if she meant to throw herself out.

In the midst of his own individual distress Boris could not hold his thoughts from the other two persons within this trinity of theirs. Perhaps Athena was walking the pine forests of Hopballehus, her face as wildly set as that of the old woman in her parlour. In his mind he saw himself in his white uniform, as a marionette, pulled alternately by the deadly determined old lady and the deadly determined young lady. How was it that things meant so much to them? What forces did these impassionate people have within them to make them prefer death to surrender? Very likely he had himself as strong tastes in the matter of this marriage as anybody, but still he did not clench his hands or lose his power of speech.

The Prioress turned from the window and came up to him. She was all changed, and carried no implements of the rack with her. On the contrary she seemed to bring a garland to crown his head. She looked so much lighter, that it was really as if she had been throwing a weight away, out of the window, and was now gracefully floating an inch above the ground.

'Dear Boris,' she said, 'Athena still has a heart. She owes it to the old playfellow of her childhood to see him, to give him a chance of speaking to her, and to answer him by word of mouth. I will tell her all this, and send the letter back at once. The daughter of Hopballehus has a sense of duty. She will come.'

'Where?' asked Boris.

'Here,' said the Prioress.

'When?' asked Boris, looking around.

'This evening, for supper,' said his aunt. She was smiling, a gentle, even waggish little smile, and still her mouth seemed to get smaller and smaller, like a very dainty little rosebud. 'Athena,' she said, 'must not leave Closter Seven tomorrow without being—' She paused a little, looked to the right and left, and then at him. 'Ours!' she said, smiling, in a little whisper. Boris looked at her. Her face was fresh as that of a young girl.

'My child, my dear child,' she exclaimed, in a sudden outburst of deep, gentle passion, 'nothing, nothing must stand in the way of your happiness!'

VII

This great supper of seduction, which was to remain a landmark in the existence of the banqueters, was served in the Prioress's dining-room, and groups of oriental statesmen and dancers watched it from the walls. The table was prettily decorated with camellias from the orangery, and upon the snow-white tablecloth, amongst the clear crystal glasses, the old green wineglasses threw delicate little shadows, like the spirit of a pine forest in summer. The Prioress had on a grey taffeta frock with very rare lace, a white lace cap with streamers, and her large old diamond eardrops and brooches. The heroic strength of soul of old women, Boris thought, who with great taste and trouble make themselves beautiful—more beautiful, perhaps, than they have ever been as young women—and who still can hold no hope of awakening any desire in the hearts of men, is like that of a righteous man working at his good deeds even after he has abandoned his faith in a heavenly reward.

The food was very good, and they had one of the famous carp of Closter Seven, cooked in a way which was kept a secret of the convent. Old Johann poured out the wine very freely, and before they had come to the marzipan and crystallized fruit, the convives of this quiet and dignified meal of an old and a young maid and a rejected lover, were all three of them more than a little drunk.

Athena was slightly drunk in the everyday sense of the word. She had drunk very little wine in her life, and had never tasted champagne, and with the amounts which the hostess of the supper party poured into her, she ought rightly not to have been able to stand on her legs. But she had behind her a long row of ancestors who had in their time lain under all the heavy old oak tables of the province, and who now came to the assistance of the daughter of their race. Still the wine went to her head. It gave her a rose on each cheek, and very bright eyes, and let loose new forces of her nature. She came to swell over a little in her feeling of invincibility, like a young captain advancing into fire, with a high courage, overbearingly.

Boris, who could drink more than most people, and who till the end remained the most sober of the party, was drunk in a more spiritual way. The deepest and truest thing in the nature of the young man was his great love for the stage and all its ways. His mother, as a maiden, had had the same grand passion, and had fought a mighty combat with her parents in Russia to go on to the stage, and lost it. Her son had no need to fight anybody. He was not dogmatic enough to believe that you must have boards and footlights to be within the theatre; he carried the stage with him in his heart. As a very young boy he had played many ladies' roles in amateur theatricals, and the famous old stage manager Paccazina had burst into tears on seeing him as Antigone, so much did he remind him of Mars. To him the theatre was real life. As long as he could not act, he was puzzled by the world and uncertain what to do with it; but as an actor he was his true self, and as soon as he could see a situation in the light of the theatre, he would feel at home in it. He did not shirk tragedy, and would perform with good grace in a pastoral, if it were asked of him.

There was something in this way of thinking that he had which exasperated his mother, in spite of her old sympathies for the art, for she suspected him of having in his heart very little preference for the role of a promising and popular young officer. He was, she thought, prepared to give it up at any moment should a role that would appeal more strongly to him present itself, be it that of an outcast or martyr, or, possibly, the tragic part of a youth ascending the scaffold. She had sometimes wanted to cry to him, contrarily to the Old Cordelier: Oh, my child, you fear too little unpopularity, exile and death! Still she could not herself help admiring him in his favourite roles, nor, even, at times taking up a role herself in an ensemble with him, and these performances of theirs might embrace a very wide scale.

Tonight Paccazina would have delighted in him; he had never played better. Out of gratitude to his godmother, he had resolved to do his best. He had laid his mask with great care in front of his mirror, and had exchanged his uniform for that black colour which he considered more appropriate to his part. In itself he always preferred the role of the unhappy, to that of the successful, lover. The wine helped him on, as did the faces of his fellow-players, including old Johann, who wore on his closed countenance a discreet shine of happiness. But he was himself in his own heart carried away by the situation, by the action of the play and by his own talents. He was on the boards, the curtain was up, every moment was precious, and he needed no *souffleur*.

As he looked at Athena on his left hand, he was pleased with his *jeune première* of the night. Now that they were upon the stage together he read her like a book.

He quite understood the deep impression which his proposal had made upon the mind of the girl. It had not flattered her; it had probably at the moment made her very angry. And the fact that any live person could in this way break in upon the proud isolation of her life had given her a shock. He agreed with her about it. Having lived all his life with people who were never alone, he had become sensitive to her atmosphere of solitude. It had happened to himself, at times, to be entirely alone on a night, dreaming, not of familiar persons or things, but of scenes and people wholly his own creation, and the recollection of such nights he would cherish in his mind. What was now at the moment bewildering the girl was the fact that the enemy approached her in such an extremely gentle manner, and that the offender was asking for consolation. As Boris grew conscious of these feelings of hers, he accentuated the sweetness and sadness of his behaviour.

It was probably such a new thing to Athena to feel fear that it had a strange attraction for her. It was doubtful, he thought, whether anything but the scent of some sort of danger could have brought her to Closter Seven on this night. Of what is she afraid? he thought. Of being made happy by my aunt and me? This is this tragic maiden's prayer: From being a success at court, a happy, congratulated bride, a mother of a promising family, good Lord, deliver me. As a tragic actor of a high standard himself, he applauded her.

The presence of some unknown danger, he felt, was impressed upon the girl by the Prioress's manner towards her. The old woman had been her friend before, but a severe friend. Most of what the girl had said and done had till now been wrong here at the convent, and she had always known that in a benevolent way the old lady had wanted to put her in a cage. Tonight the old eyes dwelt upon her with sweet content, what she said was received with little smiles as gentle as caresses. The cage had been put out of sight. This special sort of incense, offered to her individually, was as unknown to Athena as the champagne itself, and as it was now being burnt at her from her right and her left, she might have felt a difficulty in breathing within the comfortable dining-room of Closter Seven, had she not felt so sure that the door behind her would open, whenever she wanted it, to the woods of Hopballehus.

Boris, who knew more about that door, lifted his eyelashes, soft as mimosa leaves, upon her flaming face. Had her father called her a bird of the night, the eyes of which are hurt by the light? He himself was now walking, slowly, backwards in front of her, carrying some sort of chandelier which twinkled at her. She blinked a little at the light, but she came on.

The Prioress was drunk with some secret joy which remained a mystery to the other convives of her supper party and which glinted in the dark. From time to time she dabbed her eyes or her mouth with her little, delicately perfumed, lace handkerchief.

VIII

'My great-grandmother,' said the Prioress in the course of the conversation, 'was, in her second marriage, ambassadress to Paris, and lived there for twenty years. This was under the Regency. She has written down in her memoirs, how, during the Christmas of 1727, the Holy Family came to Paris and were known to stay there for twelve hours. The entire building of the stable of Bethlehem had mysteriously been moved, even with the crib and the pots in which St Joseph had been cooking the spiced beer for the Virgin, to a garden of a small convent, called du Saint Esprit. The ox and the ass were themselves transported, together with the straw upon the floor. When the nuns reported the miracle at the Court of Versailles, it was kept from the public, for they feared that it might presage a judgement upon the lewdness of the rulers of France. But the Regent went in great state, with all his jewels on, together with his daughter, the Duchess of Berri, the Cardinal Dubois, and a few selected ladies and gentlemen of the Court, to do homage to the Mother of God and her husband. My great-grandmother was allowed, because of the high esteem in which she was held at Court, to come with them as the only foreigner, and she preserved to the end of her days the furred robe of brocade, with a long train, which she wore on the occasion.

'The Regent had been highly moved and agitated by the news. At the sight of the Virgin he went into a strange ecstasy. He swayed and uttered little screams. You will know that the beauty of the Mother of the Lord, while without equal, was of such a kind that it could awaken no sort of earthly desire. This the Duke of Orléans had never experienced before, and he did not know what to do. At last he asked her, in turn blushing scarlet and deadly pale, to come to a supper at the Berri's, where he would have such food and wine served as had never been seen before, and to which he would make the Comte de Noircy come, and Madame de Parabère.

'The Duchess of Berri was at the time in *grossesse*, and evil tongues had it that this was by her father, the Regent. She threw herself at the feet of the Virgin. "Oh, dear sweet Virgin," she cried, "forgive me. You would never have done it, I know. But if I could only tell you what a deadly, what a damnably dull Court this is!" Fascinated by the beauty of the child she dried her tears and asked for permission to touch it. "Like strawberries and cream," she exclaimed, "like strawberries à la Zelma Kuntz." Cardinal Dubois saluted St Joseph with extreme politeness. He considered that this saint would not often be bothering the Almighty with supplications, but when he did so, he would be heard, as the Lord owed him much. The Regent fell upon my great-grandmother's neck, all in tears, and cried: "She will never, never come. Oh, Madame—you, who are a virtuous woman, tell me what in the world to do." All this is in my great-grandmother's memoirs.'

They talked about travels, and the Prioress entertained them with many pleasant reminiscences of her young days. She was in high spirits, her old face freshly coloured under the lace of her cap. From time to time she made use of a little gesture peculiar to her, of daintily scratching herself here and there with her delicately pointed little finger. 'You are lucky, my little friend,' she said to Athena. 'To you the world is like a bride, and each particular unveiling is a surprise and a delight. Alas, we, who have celebrated our golden wedding with it, are prudent in our inquisitiveness.'

'I should like,' said Athena, 'to go to India, where the King of Ava is now fighting the English General Amhurst. He has, Pastor Rosenquist has told me, tigers with his army, which are taught to fight the enemy along with it.' In her excited state of mind she overturned her glass, breaking the stem of it, and the wine flowed over the tablecloth.

'I should like,' said Boris, who did not want to talk of Pastor Rosenquist, in whom he suspected an antagonist—beware, his mind told him, of people who have in the course of their lives neither taken part in an orgy nor gone through the experience of childbirth, for they are dangerous people—'to go away and live upon a forlorn island, far from other people. There is nothing for which you feel such a great longing as for the sea. The passion of man for the sea,' he went on, his dark eyes on Athena's face, 'is unselfish. He cannot cultivate it; its water he cannot drink; in it he dies. Still, far from the sea you feel part of your own soul dying, disappearing, like a jellyfish thrown on dry land.'

'On the sea!' the Prioress cried. 'Going on the sea! Ah, never, never.' Her deep disgust drove the blood to her face until it became quite pink and her eyes shone. Boris was impressed, as he had been before, by the intensity of all women's aversion to anything nautical. He had himself as a boy tried to run away from home to be a sailor. But nothing, he thought, makes a woman flare up in a deadly hostility as quickly as talk of the sea. From the first smell of sea water to the contact with salted and tarred ropes, they loathe and shun it and all its ways; and perhaps the Church might have kept the sex in order by painting them a maritime, an ashen-grey and frigid waving hell. For fire they fear not, looking upon it as an ally to whom they have long done service. But to talk to them of the sea is like talking of the devil. By the time when the rule of woman shall have made the land inhabitable to man, he will have to take to the sea for peace, for women will rather die than follow him there.

A sweet pudding was served to them, and the Prioress, with a neat *gourmandise*, picked out a few of the cloves in it and ate them. 'This is a very lovable smell and taste,' she said, 'and the fragrance of a clove grove unbelievably delightful in the midday sun, or when the evening breeze fans the spiced currents of air all over the land. Try a few of them. It is incense to the stomach.'

'Where do they come from, Madame my Aunt?' asked Athena, who, in accordance with the tradition of the province, was used to address her in this way.

'From Zanzibar,' said the Prioress. A gentle melancholy seemed for a few minutes to sink over her as she sat in deep thought, nibbling at her cloves.

Boris, in the meantime, had been looking at Athena, and had let a fantasy take hold of his mind. He thought that she must have a lovely, an exquisitely beautiful, skeleton. She would lie in the ground like a piece of matchless lace, a work of art in ivory, and in a hundred years might be dug up and turn the heads of old archaeologists. Every bone was in place, as finely finished as a violin. Less frivolous than the traditional old libertine who in his thoughts undresses the women with whom he sups Boris liberated the maiden of her strong and fresh flesh together with her clothes, and imagined that he might be very happy with her, that he might even fall in love with her, could he have her in her beautiful bones alone. He fancied her thus, creating a sensation on horseback, or trailing her long dresses through the halls and galleries at Court, with the famous tiara of her family, now in Poland, upon her polished skull. Many human relations, he thought, would be infinitely easier if they could be carried out in the bones only.

'The King of Ava,' said the Prioress, awakening from the soft reveries into which she had been sunk, 'had, in the city of Yandabu— so I have been told by those who have been there—a large menagerie. As in all his country he had none but the elephants of India, the Sultan of Zanzibar presented him with an African elephant, which is much bigger and more magnificent than the rotund, domesticated Indian beasts. They are indeed wonderful animals. They rule the highlands of East Africa, and the ivory traders who sell their mighty tusks at the ivory market have many tales of their strength and ferocity. The elephants of Yandabu and their herdsmen were terrified of the Sultan's elephant—such as Africa always frightens Asia—and in the end they made the King have him put in chains and a barred house built for him in the menagerie. But from that time, on moonlit nights, the whole city of Yandabu began to swarm with the shades of the elephants of Africa, wandering about the place and waving their large shadow-ears in the streets. The natives of Yandabu believed that these shadow-elephants were able to walk along the bottom of the ocean, and to come up beside the landing place of the boats. No people dared any more be out in the town after dark had fallen. Still they could not break the cage of the captive elephant.

'The hearts of animals in cages,' the Prioress went on, 'become grated, as upon a grill, upon the shadows of the bars. Oh, the grated hearts of caged animals!' she exclaimed with terrible energy.

'Still,' she said after a moment, her face changing, with a little giggle at the bottom of her voice, 'it served those elephants right. They were great tyrants when in their own country. No other animal could have its own way for them.'

'And what became of the Sultan's elephant?' Athena asked.

'He died, he died,' said the old woman, licking her lips.

'In the cage?' asked Athena.

'Yes. In the cage,' the Prioress answered.

Athena laid her folded hands upon the table, with exactly the gesture of the old Count after he had read the Prioress's letter. She looked around the room. The bright colour sank from her face. The supper was finished, and they had nearly emptied their glasses of port.

'I think, my Aunt,' she said, 'that with your permission I will now go to bed. I feel very tired.'

'What?' said the Prioress. 'Indeed you must not deprive us of the pleasure of your company yet, my nutmeg. I was going to withdraw myself now, but I want you two old friends to have a little talk on this night. Surely you promised Boris that—the dear boy.'

'Yes, but that must be tomorrow morning,' Athena said, 'for I believe that I have drunk too much of the good wine. Look, my hand is not even steady when I put it on this table.' The Prioress stared at the girl. She probably felt, Boris thought, that she ought not to have talked about cages, that she had here made her one *faux pas* of the evening.

Athena looked at Boris, and he felt that he had obtained this slight success: that she was sorry to part from him. Altogether she probably realized that she was making an abrupt retreat from the battle, and regretted it, but under the circumstances she considered it the best move. Boris felt her straight glance as a decoration received before the front. It was not a high decoration, but in this campaign he could not expect more. The girl bid a very kind good night to the Prioress, curtseyed to her, and was gone.

The Prioress turned in great agitation to her nephew. 'Do not let her go away,' she said to him. 'Follow her. Take hold of her. Do not waste your time.'

'Let us leave her alone,' said Boris. 'That girl has spoken the truth. She will not have me.'

The double rebelliousness in the two young people, the happiness of whose lives she was arranging, seemed to make the Prioress lose speech, or faith in speech. She and Boris remained together in the room for perhaps five minutes more, and it seemed to Boris, when he afterwards thought of it, that their intercourse had been carried out entirely in pantomime.

The Prioress stood quite still and looked at the young man, and he really did not know whether within the next seconds she would kill him or kiss him. She did neither. She laughed a little in his face, and fumbling in her pocket she drew out the letter which she had received in the morning, and gave it to him to read.

This letter was a last deadly blow upon the boy's head. It was written by the Prioress's friend, who was the first lady of honour of the Dowager Queen. With deep compassion for his aunt she gave, in very dark colours, the latest news of the capital. His name had been brought up, he had even been pointed out particularly by the Court Chaplain, as one of the corrupters of youth in the case. It was clear that he was at this moment standing upon the brink of an abyss, and that unless he could get this marriage of his through, he should fall over and disappear.

He stood for a little while, his face changed by pain. His whole being rose against being dragged from his star part of the evening, and the elegiac mood of a lover, back to this reality that he loathed. As he looked up to give back the letter to his aunt he found her standing quite close to him. She lifted one hand, keeping her elbow close to her body, and pointed towards the door.

'Aunt Cathinka,' said Boris, 'you do not know, perhaps, but there is a limit to the effects of will-power in a man.'

The old woman kept staring at him. She stretched out her dry delicate little hand and touched him. Her face twisted in a wry little grimace. After a moment she moved around to the back of the room and brought back a bottle and a small glass. Very carefully she filled the glass, handed it to him, and nodded her head two or three times. In sheer despair he emptied it.

The glass was filled with a liquor of the colour of very old dark amber. It had an acrid and rank taste. Acrid and rank were also the old dark-amber eyes of the woman, watching him over the rim of her glass. As he drank, she laughed. Then she spoke. Boris, strangely enough, afterwards remembered these words, which he did not understand: 'Help him now, you good Faru,' she said.

When he had left the room, after a second or two she very gently closed the door after him.

IX

Now this might be the hour for tears, to move the proud beauty's heart, Boris thought. He remembered the tales of that gruesome gang of pilgrims, the old hangmen, who are said to have been wandering over Europe in the twelfth century, visiting the holy places. They carried with them the attributes of their trade: thumbscrews, whips, irons and tongs, and these people, it was said, were able to weep whenever they wanted to. 'Yes,' the boy said to himself, 'but I have not hewed up, flayed and fried alive enough people for that. A few I have, of course, as we all have; but I am only a young hangman for all that—a hangman's apprentice—and the gift of weeping whenever I want to, I have not attained.'

He walked down the long white corridor, which led to Athena's room. It had on his left hand a row of old portraits of ladies, and on the right a row of tall windows. The floor was laid with black and white marble tiles, and the whole place looked seriously at him in the nocturnal light. He heard his own footfall, fatal to others and to himself. He looked out of one of the windows as he passed it. The moon stood high in the heavens, clear and cold, but the trees of the park and the lawns lay in a silvery mist. There outside was the whole noble blue universe, full of things, in which the earth swam onward amongst thousands of stars, some near and others far away. O world, he thought, O rich world. Into his hot brain was thrown a long-forgotten verse:

> *Athena, my high mistress, on Apollon's bidding,*
> *Here I come to thee.*
> *Much experienced, and tried in many things.*
> *A house, inhabited by strangers, strangely changed.*
> *Thus have I wandered far on land, and on the sea . . .*

He had come to the door. He turned the handle, and went in.

Of all the memories, which afterwards Boris carried with him from this night, the memory of the transition from the colouring and light of the corridor to that of the room was the longest lasting.

The Prioress's state guest room was large and square, with windows, upon which the curtains were now drawn, on the two walls. The whole room was hung with rose silks, and in the depths of it the crimson draperies of the four-poster bed glowed in the shade. There were two pink-globed lamps, solicitously lighted by the Prioress's maid. The floor had a wine-coloured carpet with roses in it, which, near the lamps, seemed to be drinking in the light, and farther from them looked like pools of dark crimson into which one would not like to walk. The room was filled with the scent of incense and flowers. A large bouquet decorated the table near the bed.

Boris knew at once what it was that he felt like. He had at one time, when he had been on a visit to Madrid, been much addicted to bull fights. He was familiar with the moment when the bull is, from his dark waiting-room underneath the tribune, rushed into the dazzling sunlight of the arena, with the many hundred eyes around it. So was he himself in a moment hurled from the black and white corridor, of quiet moonlight, into this red atmosphere. His blood leapt up to his brain; he hardly knew where he was. With failing breath he wondered if this was an effect of the Prioress's love potion. He did not know either whether Athena was now to be the disembowelled horse, which would be dragged out of the arena, having no more will of its own, or the matador who was to lay him low. One or the other she would be—he could meet nobody else in this place.

Athena was standing in the middle of the room. She had taken off her frock and was dressed only in a white chemise and white pantalettes. She looked like a sturdy young sailor boy about to swab the deck. She turned as he came in, and stared at him.

Boris had been afraid, when imagining the development of the situation, that he would not be able to keep himself from laughing. This risibility of his had before now been his ruin in tender situations. But at the moment he ran no such risk. He was as much in earnest as the girl herself. He had, before he knew where he was, taken hold of one of her wrists and drawn her towards him. Their breaths met and mingled, they were both baring their teeth a little in a sort of perplexed smile or challenge.

'Athena,' he said, 'I have loved you all my life. You know that without you I shall dry up and shrink, there shall be nothing left of me. Stoop to me, throw me back in the deep. Have mercy on me.'

For a moment the light-eyed girl stared at him, bewildered. Then she drew herself up as a snake does when it is ready to strike. That she did not attempt to cry for help showed him that she had a clearer understanding of the situation, and of the fact that she had no friend in the house, than he had given her credit for; or perhaps her young broad breast harboured sheer love of combat. The next moment she struck out. Her powerful, swift and direct fist hit him in the mouth and knocked out two of his teeth. The pain and the smell and taste of the blood which filled his mouth sent him beside himself. He let her go to try for a stronger hold, and immediately they were in each other's arms, in an embrace of life and death.

At this same moment Boris's heart leapt up within him and sang aloud, like a bird which swings itself to the top of a tree and there bursts into song. Nothing happier in all the world could have happened to him. He had not known how this conflict between them was to be solved, but she had known it; and as a coast sinks around a ship which takes the open sea, so did all the worries of his life sink around this release of all his being. His existence up to now had given him very little opportunity for fury. Now he gave his heart up to the rapture of it. His soul laughed like the souls of those old Teutons to whom the lust of anger was in itself the highest voluptuousness, and who demanded nothing better of their paradise than the capacity for being killed once a day.

He could not have fought another young man, were he one of the Einherjar of Valhalla, as he fought this girl. All hunters of big game will know that there is a difference between hunting the wild boar or buffalo, however dangerous they may be, and hunting the carnivora, who, if successful, will eat you up at the end of the contest. Boris, on a visit to his Russian relations, had seen his horse devoured by a pack of wolves. After that, none of the Prioress's raging wild elephants could have called forth the same feeling in him. The old, wild love, which sympathy cannot grant, which contrast and adversity inspire, filled him altogether.

If the shadows of the young women who had clung to him, and out of whose soft arms the fickle lover had torn himself, had been at this moment gathered within the Prioress's rose-coloured guest room, they would have felt the pride of their sex satisfied in the contemplation of his mortal pursuit of this maiden who now strove less to escape than to kill him. They tumbled to and fro for a few seconds, and one of the lamps was turned over, fell down, and went out. Then the struggle stabilized itself. They ceased moving and stood clasped together, swaying a little until they found their foothold, the balance of the one so dependent upon and amalgamated with that of the other that neither knew clearly where his own body ended and that of his adversary began. They were breathing hard. Her breath in his face was fragrant as an apple. The blood kept coming into his mouth.

The girl had no feminine inspiration to scratch or bite. Like a young she-bear, she relied on her great strength, and in weight she scored a little. Against his attempts to bend her knees she stood up as straight as a tree. By a sudden movement she got her hands on his throat. He was holding her close to him, her elbows pressed to her sides. Her posture was that of a warrior, clinging to the hilt of his lifted sword, taking a vital vow. He had not known the power of her hands and wrists. Gasping for air, his mouth full of blood, he saw the whole room swaying from one side to another. Red and black flecks swam in front of him. At this moment he struck out for a last triumph. He forced her head forward with the hand that he had at the back of her neck, and pressed his mouth to hers. His teeth grated against her teeth.

Instantly he felt, through his whole body, which was clinging to hers from the knees to the lips, the terrible effect which his kiss had on the girl. She, surely, had never been kissed in her life, she had not even heard or read of a kiss. The force used against her made her whole being rise in a mortal disgust. As if he had run a rapier straight through her, the blood sank from her face, her body stiffened in his arms like that of a slow-worm, when you hit it. Then all the strength and suppleness which he had been fighting seemed to roll back and withdraw, as a wave withdraws from a bather. He saw her eyes grow dim, her face, so close to his, fade to a dead white. She went down so suddenly that he came down with her, like a drowning man tied to a weight. His face was thrown against hers.

He got up on his knees, wondering if she were dead. As he found that she was not, he lifted her, after a moment, with difficulty, and laid her upon her bed. She was indeed now like a stone effigy of a mail-clad knight, felled in battle. Her face had preserved its expression of deadly disgust. He watched her for a little while, very still himself. He did not know that his own face had the same expression. Had the thought of the Court Chaplain been with him, had the Court Chaplain been with him in the flesh, it could not have stirred him. His spirit had gone almost as definitely as hers. There was no more effect of the wine in him; none, either, of the Prioress's love philtre, which perhaps was not calculated for more than one great effort. He wiped his bleeding mouth and left the room.

Within his own room and bed he came to wonder whether the maiden would, upon her awakening, lament her lost innocence. He laughed to himself in the dark, and it seemed to him that a thin, shrill laughter, like to the shoot of hot steam from a boiling kettle, was echoing his own somewhere in the great house, in the dark.

X

In the morning the Prioress sent for Boris. He was a little frightened when he saw her, for she seemed to have shrunk. She filled up neither her clothes nor her armchair, and he wondered what sort of night hours had passed over her head in her lonely bed to have squeezed out her strength like this. If all this, he thought, is to go on much longer, there will be nothing left of her. But probably I am looking worse than she myself. Still, she appeared to be in high spirits, and pleased to have got hold of him, as if she had been, somehow, in fear that he might have run away. She told him to sit down. 'I have sent for Athena as well,' she said.

Boris was content that she did not ask him any questions. His mouth had swelled badly, and hurt him when he had to speak. While waiting he thought of the Vicomte de Valmont, who loved *de passion, les mines de lendemain*. Would the unusual in the circumstances have given this particular morrow an additional charm in the eyes of the matter-of-fact old conqueror of a hundred years ago? Or was it not more likely that he would have considered the romantic values of the situation to be all nonsense? Athena's arrival put an end to his reflections.

She was wearing the same great grey cloak in which he had seen her at Hopballehus, and seemed about to depart. She did indeed so much give the impression of having turned her back on Closter Seven, and of being already away from it, that he felt somehow left out in the cold. As she looked slowly around, he was deeply struck by her appearance. She seemed to be well on her way to that purified state of the skeleton in which he had imagined her on the night before. She had in reality a death's-head upon her strong shoulders. Her eyes, grown paler in themselves, lay in black holes. She had given up her habit of standing on one leg, as if it now required both her legs to keep her upright and in balance. Confronted by the Prioress, who had still much keen life in her face, she might well have been an accused in the felon's dock, brought straight from the vaults of a dungeon, and from the rack.

Boris at this moment wondered whether it would be better for her that he should tell her all, and assure her that he had done her no harm and would not be likely ever to do her any; in fact, that she had come out of their trial of strength with the honours of war. But he thought it would not. If you prepare yourself, he considered, for lifting a leaden weight, and are deceived by a painted cardboard, your arms come out of joint. In his admiration for her skeleton he was the last person to wish this to happen to her. It was better for her to carry the weight. This maiden, he thought, who could not, who would not, be made happy, let her now have her fill. Like to an artist who has got his statue in the crucible and finds himself short of metals, and who seizes the gold and silver from his treasury, from his table, from his women's caskets to hurl it in, so he had thrown his being, body and soul, into the fatal soundings of her nature. Now she must make out of it what she could.

The Prioress, looking in turn at one and then at the other of the young people, spoke to the girl.

'I have been informed,' she said in a dull and hard voice, 'by Boris of what has happened here in the night. I do not forgive him. It is a horrible deed to seduce a maiden. But I know that he was goaded on, and also that a candid repentance extenuates the crime. But you, Athena, a girl of your blood and your upbringing—what have you done? You, who must have known your own nature, you ought never to have come here.'

'No, no, Madame my Aunt,' said Athena, looking straight at the old woman, 'I came here because you invited me, and you told me that it was my duty to come. Now I go away again, and if you do not like to think of me, you need not.'

'Ah, no,' said the Prioress, 'such a thing you cannot do. It is terrible to me that this has happened within the walls of Closter Seven. You know me very little if you think I shall not have it repaired. Would I show so little friendship towards your father, who is a nobleman? Till this wrong has been expiated, you shall not depart.'

Athena first seemed to let this pass for what it was worth and did not answer. Then she asked: 'How is it to be repaired?'

'We must be thankful,' said the Prioress, 'that Boris, guilty as he be, has still a sense of duty left. He will marry you even now.' With these words she shot at her nephew a little hard and shining glance, which startled him, as if she had touched him once more.

'Yes, but I will not marry him,' said Athena.

The Prioress had by now a highly glowing colour in her face. 'How is it,' she asked in a shrill voice, 'that you refuse an honourable offer, of which your father approves, to accept, in the middle of the night, the love that you had rejected?'

'I do not think,' said Athena, 'that it matters whether a thing happens in the day or the night.'

'And if you have a child?' cried the Prioress.

'What!' said Athena.

The Prioress subdued her blazing passion with a wonderful strength of spirit. 'I pity you as much as I condemn you,' she said. 'And if you have a child, unfortunate girl?'

Athena's world was evidently tumbling down to the right and left of her, like a position under heavy gun fire, but still she stood up straight. 'What?' she asked. 'Shall I have a child from that?'

The old woman looked hard at her. 'Athena,' she said after a moment, with the first particle of gentleness which she had, during the conversation, shown towards the girl, 'the last thing I wish is to destroy what innocence you may still have left. But it is more than likely that you will have a child.'

'If I have a child,' said Athena, from her quaking earth thrusting at the heaven, 'my father will teach him astronomy.'

Boris leaned his elbow on the table and his face in his hand to hide it. For the life of him he could not help laughing. This deadly pale and still maiden was not beaten. A good deal of her pallor and immobility might be due to the wine and the exertion of the night, and God only knew if they would ever get her into their power. She had in her the magnet, the maelstrom quality of drawing everything which came inside her circle of consciousness into her own being and making it one with herself. It was a capacity, he thought, which had very likely been a characteristic of the martyrs, and which may well have aggravated the Great Inquisitor, and even the Emperor Nero himself, to the brink of madness. The tortures, the stake, the lions, they made their own, and thereby conveyed to them a great harmonious beauty; but the torturer they left outside. No matter what efforts he made to possess them, they stood in no relation to him, and in fact deprived him of existence. They were like the lion's den, into which all tracks were seen to lead, while none came out; or like the river, which drowns blood or filth in its own being, and flows on. Here, just as the conquering old woman and young man had believed the situation to be closing around her, the girl was about to ride away from Closter Seven, like to Samson when he lifted upon his shoulders the doors of Gaza, the two posts, bars and all, and carried them to the top of the hill that is before Hebron. And if she should really become aware of him, would the giant's daughter, he wondered, carry him with her upon the palm of her hand to Hopballehus, and make him groom her unicorns? Again a verse from Euripides ran through his head, and he felt that it must be the wine of the previous night and the whole agitation around him which now caused him, in this way, to mix up the classics with Scripture and with the legends of his province, for ordinarily he did not do that sort of thing:

> *Oh, Pallas, saviour of my house, I was bereft*
> *of Fatherland, and thou hast given me a home again therein.*
> *It shall be said*
> *in Hellas: Lo, the man is an Argive once more,*
> *and dwells again within his father's heritance . . .*

'And what of the honour of your house?' asked the Prioress with a deadly calm. 'Who do you think, Athena, of the daughters of Hopballehus, has, before you, been breeding bastards?'

At these words all Athena's blood rushed to her face until it flamed darker than her flaming hair. She took a step towards the old lady.

'My child,' she cried in a low tone, but with the lioness's roar deep within her voice, from head to foot the offended daughter of a mighty race, 'would my child be that?'

'You are ignorant, Athena,' said the old woman. 'Unless Boris marries you, what can your child be but a bastard?' Brave as the Prioress was, she probably realized that the girl, if she wished to, could crush her between her fingers. She kept her quick eyes on Boris, who did not feel called upon to interfere in the women's discussion of his child.

Athena did not move. She stood for a few moments quite still. 'Now,' she said at length, 'I will go back to Hopballehus, and speak with my father, and ask his advice about all this.'

'No,' said the Prioress again, 'that is not as it should be. If you tell your father of what you have done, you will break his heart. I will not let that happen. And who knows, if you go now, if Boris will still be ready to marry you when you meet again? No, Athena, you must marry Boris, and you must never let your father know of what has happened here. These two things you shall promise me. Then you can go.'

'Good,' said Athena. 'I will never tell Papa of anything. And as to Boris, I promise you that I shall marry him. But, Madame my Aunt, when we are married, and whenever I can do so, I shall kill him. I came near to killing him last night; he can tell you that. These three things I promise you. Then I will go.'

After Athena's words there was a long pause. The three people in the room had enough in their own thoughts, without speech, to occupy them.

In this silence was heard a hard and sharp knocking upon the pane of one of the windows. Boris now realized that he had heard it before, during the course of their talk, without paying any attention to it. Now it was repeated three or four times.

He became really aware of it at the sight of the extraordinary effect which the sound had upon his aunt. She had, like himself, been too absorbed in the debate to listen. Now it attracted her attention and she was immediately struck by a deadly terror. She glanced towards the window and grew white as a corpse. Her arms and legs moved in little jerks, her eyes darted up and down the walls, like a rat that is shut up and cannot get out. Boris turned to the window to find out what was frightening her. He had not known that anything could really do so. Upon the stone sill outside, the monkey was crouching together, its face close to the glass.

He rose to open the window for it. 'No! No!' shrieked the old woman in a paroxysm of horror. The knocking went on. The monkey obviously had something in its hand with which it was beating against the pane. The Prioress got up from her chair. She swayed in raising herself, but once on her legs she seemed alert and ready to run. But at the next moment the glass of the window fell crashing to the floor and the monkey jumped into the room.

Instantly, without looking around, as if escaping from the flames of an advancing fire, the Prioress, gathering up the front of her silk frock with her two hands, ran, threw herself, towards the door. On finding it closed, she did not give herself time to open it. With the most surprising, most wonderful, lightness and swiftness she heaved herself straight up along the frame, and at the next moment was sitting squeezed together upon the sculptured cornice, shivering in a horrible passion, and grinding her teeth at the party on the floor. But the monkey followed her. As quickly as she had done it, it squirmed up the doorcase and was stretching out its hand to seize her when she deftly slid down the opposite side of the doorframe. Still holding her frock with both hands, and bending double, as if ready to drop on all fours, madly, as if blinded by fright, she dashed along the wall. But still the monkey followed her, and it was quicker than she. It jumped upon her, got hold of her lace cap, and tore it from her head. The face which she turned towards the young people was already transformed, shrivelled and wrinkled, and of dark-brown colour. There was a few moments' wild whirling fight. Boris made a movement to throw himself into it, to save his aunt. But already at the next moment, in the middle of the red damask parlour, under the eyes of the old powdered general and his wife, in the broad daylight and before their eyes, a change, a metamorphosis, was taking place and was consummated.

The old woman with whom they had been talking was, writhing and dishevelled, forced to the floor; she was scrunched and changed. Where she had been, a monkey was now crouching and whining, altogether beaten, trying to take refuge in a corner of the room. And where the monkey had been jumping about, rose, a little out of breath from the effort, her face still a deep rose, the true Prioress of Closter Seven.

The monkey crawled into the shade of the back of the room and for a little while continued its whimpering and twitching. Then, shaking off its misfortunes, it jumped in a light and graceful leap on to a pedestal, which supported the marble head of the philosopher Immanuel Kant, and from there it watched, with its glittering eyes, the behaviour of the three people in the room.

The Prioress took up her little handkerchief and held it to her eyes. For a few minutes she found no words, but her deportment was as quietly dignified and kindly as the young people had always remembered it.

They had been following the course of events, too much paralysed by surprise to speak, move, or even look at each other. Now, as out of the terrible tornado which had been reigning in the room, calm was again descending, they found themselves close to each other. They turned around and looked into each other's faces.

This time Athena's luciferous eyes within their deep dark sockets did not exactly take Boris into possession. She was aware of him as a being outside herself; even the memory of their fight was clearly to be found in her clear limpid gaze. But she was, in this look, laying down another law, a command which was not to be broken: from now, between, on the one side, her and him, who had been present together at the happenings of the last minutes, and, on the other side, the rest of the world, which had not been there, an insurmountable line would be for ever drawn.

The Prioress lowered the handkerchief from her face, and in a soft and sweeping movement sat down in her large arm-chair. She looked at the young man and the girl.

'*Discite justitiam, et non temnere divos,*' she said.

(gooh)

F. M. MAYOR

Miss de Mannering of Asham

Oct. 9

My dear Evelyn,

As you say you really are interested in this experience of mine, I am
doing what you asked, and writing you an account of it. You can accept
it as a token of friendship for, to tell you the truth, I had been trying to
forget it, whatever it was. I hope in the end to bring myself to the belief
that I never had it, but at present my remembrance is more vivid than I
care for.

Yours affectionately
MARGARET LATIMER

You remember my friend, Kate Ware? She had been ill, and she
asked me to stay in lodgings with her at an East Coast resort. 'It is
simply Brixton-by-the-Sea, with a dash of Kensington,' Kate wrote,
'but I ought to go, because my aunt lives there, and likes to see me.
So come, if you can bear it.'

'I think we might take a day off,' said Kate one morning, after we
had been there a week. 'Too much front makes me think there really
is no England but this. Let's have some sandwiches, and bicycle out
as far away as we can.'

We came to a wayside inn, so quiet, so undisturbed, so cheerful in
its quietness, that we felt at last we had found the soothing and rest
we were in need of. Yes, I suppose our nerves were a little unstrung;
at any rate, being high school mistresses, we knew what nerves were.
But hitherto I have felt capable of controlling mine, only, as Hamlet
says, I have bad dreams. And Kate is rather strange by nature; I do
not think her nerves make her any stranger.

'Now,' said Kate, when we had finished our meal—she always
settles everything—'I propose we borrow the pony here, and have a
drive. I don't like desecrating these solitary lanes, which have existed
for generations and generations before bicycles, with anything more
modern than Tommy.'

Kate generally wants to have a map, and know exactly where she is
going, but to-day we agreed to take the first turn to the left, and see
where it led to. It was a sleepy afternoon, and Tommy trotted so

gently that we were all three dozing, before we had gone a mile or two. Then we came to what had been magnificent wrought iron gates with stone pillars on either side. The pillars were now ruined, and the wall beyond was falling down. Kate said, 'Let's go in.' I said it was private, but we did go in.

We came into an avenue of laurels, resembling the sepulchral shrubberies with which our fathers and our fathers' fathers loved to surround their residences, only those were generally more serpentine. It must have been there many years, and had had time to grow so high as to block out almost all the sky. It was very narrow, and the dankness, the closeness, the black ground that never gets dry, which have always oppressed me in such places, seemed almost intolerable here. I thought we should never get out to the small piece of white light we saw at the end of it. At the same time I dreaded what I expected to find there; one of those great, lugubrious, black mausoleums of a mansion, which so often are the complement of the shrubbery. But this avenue seemed to have been planted at haphazard, for it led only to another gate, and that opened on a neglected park. We saw before us an expanse of unfertile-looking grass, and then the horizon was completely hidden by ridges of very heavy greenish-black trees. There were other trees scattered about; they looked very old, and some had been struck by lightning. I felt sorry for their wounds; it seemed as if no one cared whether they lived or died.

There was a small church standing at the left-hand corner of the park, so small that it must have been a chapel for the private worship of the owners of the park; but we thought they could not have valued their church, for there was actually no path to it, nothing but grass, long, rank and damp.

I do not know when it was that I became so certain that I abhorred parks, but I remember it came over me very strongly all of a sudden. I was extremely anxious that Kate should not know what I felt. However, I said to her that grandeur was oppressive, and that after all I preferred small gardens.

'Yes,' said Kate, 'one might feel too much enclosed, if one lived in a park, as if one could never get out, and as if other things. . . .'

Here Kate stopped. I asked her to go on, and she said that was all she had to say. I don't know if you want to hear these minute details, but nearly everything I have to tell you is merely a succession of minute details. I remember looking up at the sky, because I wanted to keep my eyes away from the distant trees. I did not like to see them—it seems a very poor reason for a woman of thirty-eight—

because they were so black. When I was six years old, I was afraid of black, and also, though I loved the country, I used to feel a sense of fear and isolation, if the sun was not shining, and I was alone in a large field; but then a child's mind is open to every terror, or rather it creates a terror out of everything. I thought I had as much forgotten that condition as if I had never known it. I should have supposed the weight of my many grown-up years would have defended me, but I assure you that I felt all at once that I was—what after all we are—as much at the mercy of the universe as an insect.

I remember when I looked up at the sky I observed that it had changed. As we were coming it had had the ordinary pale no-colour aspect, which it bears for quite half the days in the year. Some people grumble at it, but it is very English, and if you do not like it, or more than like it, relish it, you cannot really relish England. The sky had now that strange appearance to which days in the north are liable; I do not think they know anything about it in Italy or the south of France. It is a fancy of mine that the sudden strangeness and wildness one finds in our literature is due to these days; it is something to compensate us for them.

If I said the day was dying, you would think of beautiful sunsets, and certainly the day could not be dying, for it was only three o'clock in the afternoon, but it looked ill; and the grey of the atmosphere was not that silvery grey, which I think the sweetest of all the skies in the year, but an unwholesome grey, which made the trees look blacker still. I should have felt it a relief if only it had begun to rain, then there would have been a noise; it was so utterly silent.

Just as I was wondering where I should turn my eyes next, Tommy came to a sudden stop, and nearly jerked us out of the cart. 'Clever,' said Kate, 'you're letting Tommy stumble.'

But it was simply that Tommy would not go on. He was such a mild little pony too, anxious, as Kate said, to do everything one asked, before one asked him.

'Tommy's frightened,' said Kate. 'He's all trembling and sweating.'

Kate got out, and tried to soothe him, but for some time it was very little good.

'It's another snub for the men of science,' said Kate. 'Tommy sees an angel in the way. Animals are very odd you know. Haven't you noticed dogs scurrying past ghosts in the twilight? I am so glad we haven't got their faculties.'

Then Tommy all at once surprised us by going on as quietly as before.

We drove a little further, and we came to the hall. It was built

150 years before the mausoleum period, but it could not well have been drearier, though it must formerly have been a noble Jacobean mansion. It was not that it looked out of repair; a house can be very cheerful, in fact rather more cheerful, if it is shabby. And here there was a terrace with greenhouse plants in stucco vases placed at intervals, and also a clean-shaven lawn, so that man must have been there recently; nevertheless it seemed as if it had been abandoned for years.

I cannot tell you how relieved I was when a respectable young man in shirt sleeves made his appearance. It is Kate generally who talks to strangers, but the moment he was in sight I felt I must cling to him, as a protection. I felt Tommy and Kate had no protection.

I apologized for trespassing in private grounds.

'No trespassing at all, miss, I'm sure.' He went on to say he wished it happened oftener, Colonel Winterton, the owner, being hardly ever there, only liking to keep the place up with servants, and 'if there wasn't a number of us to make it lively, one room being shut up and all,' he really did not know—

It did not seem right to encourage him on the subject of a shut-up room; we changed the conversation, and asked him about the church.

He said it was a very ancient church, and there was tombs and that, people came a wonderful way to see. Not that he cared much about them himself.

Kate, who is fond of sight-seeing, declared she would visit the church.

I would not go, though I should like to have seen the tombs. I said I must hold the pony. The young man said he was a groom, and would hold the pony for us. Then I said I was tired: Kate said she would go alone. She started.

'Don't go down there, miss,' said the groom, 'the grass is so wet. Round by the right it's better.'

His way looked the same as hers to me, but Kate followed his advice.

I talked to the groom while Kate was away, and I was glad to hear that he liked the pictures in reason, and that his father was a saddler, living in the High Street of some small town. This was cheerful and distracting to my thoughts, and I had managed to become so much interested that it was the young man who said, 'There's the lady coming back.'

'Well,' I said, 'what was the church like?'

'It was locked,' Kate answered, 'however, it was nice outside.'

'But Kate,' I said, 'how pale you are!'

'Of course I am,' said Kate. 'I always am.'

The young man hastened to ask if he should get Kate a glass of water.

'Oh dear no, thank you,' said Kate. 'But I think we might be going now. Is there any other road out? I don't want to drive exactly the same way back.'

There was, and we set off. As soon as we had said good-bye to the young man, Kate began: 'About Grace Martin; what do you think of her chances for the Certificate?' and we talked about the Certificate until we got back to the inn. As to that oppressed feeling, I could hardly imagine now what it was. It had passed, and the world seemed its usual dear, safe self, irritating and comfortable. It was clearing up, and the trees and hedges looked as they generally look at the end of August. They were dusty and a little shabby, showing here and there a red leaf, occasional bits of toadflax, and all those little yellow flowers whose names one forgets, but to which one turns tenderly in recollection, when seeing the beauty of foreign lands. My thoughts broke away from our conversation now and then to wonder what I could possibly have been afraid of.

They gave us tea at Tommy's home, and the innkeeper's wife was glad to have some conversation.

'Yes, the poor old Hall, it seems a pity the Colonel coming down so seldom. He only bought it seven years ago, and he seems tired of it already, and then only bringing gentlemen. Gentlemen spend more, but I always think there's more life with ladies. It's changed hands so often. Yes, there's a shut-up room. They say it was something about a housemaid many years ago and a baby, if you'll excuse my mentioning it, but I'm sure I couldn't say. If you listen to all the tales in a village like this, in a little place you know, one says one thing and one another. I come from Norwich myself.'

'The church looks rather dismal,' said Kate. 'The churchyard is so overgrown.'

'Yes, poor Mr Fuller, he's a nice gentleman, though he is so high. First when he come there was great goings on, services and antics. He says to me, "Tell me, Mrs Gage, is that why the people don't come?" "Oh," I says, "well, of course, I've been about, and seen life, so whether it's high or low, I just take no notice." I said that to put him off, poor gentleman, because it wasn't that. They won't come at all hardly after dark, particularly November; December it's better again; and for his communion service, what he sets his heart on so, we have such a small party, sometimes hardly more than two or three, and then he gets so downhearted. He seems to have lost all his spirit now.'

'But why is it better in December?'

'I'm sure I couldn't tell you, miss, but they always say those things is worse in November. I always heard my grandfather say that.'

I had rather expected that what I had forgotten in the day would come back at night, and about two, when I was reading *Framley Parsonage* with all possible resolution, I heard a knock at the door, and Kate came in.

'I saw your light,' said she. 'I can't sleep either. I think you felt uncomfortable in the park too, didn't you? Your face betrays you rather easily, you know. Going to the church, at least not going first of all, but as I got near the church, and the churchyard—ugh! However, I am *not* going to be conquered by a thought, and I mean to go there to-morrow. Still, I think, if you don't very much mind, I should like to sleep in here.'

I asked her to get into my bed.

'Thank you, I will,' said she. 'It's very good of you, Margaret, for I'm sure you loathe sharing somebody's bed as much as I do, but things being as they are—'

The next morning Kate was studying the guidebook at breakfast.

'Here we are,' said she. '"Asham Hall is a fine Jacobean mansion. The church, which is situated in the park, was originally the private chapel of the de Mannerings. Many members of the family are buried there, and their tombs are well worth a visit. The inscriptions in Norman French are of particular interest. The keys can be obtained from the sexton." Nothing about the shut-up room; I suppose we could hardly hope for it. We must see the tombs, don't you think so?'

Kate was one who very rarely showed her feelings, and I knew better than to refer to last night.

We bicycled to the Hall. It was a very sweet, bright windy morning, such a morning as would have pleased Wordsworth, I think, and may have brought forth many a poem from him.

'Now,' said Kate, 'when we get into the park, we'll walk our bicycles over the grass to the church.'

I began: then exactly the same feeling came over me as before, only this time there could be nothing in calm, beautiful nature to have produced it. The trees, though dark, did not look at all sinister, but stately and benignant, as they often do in late August, and early September. Whatever it was, it was within me. I felt I could not go to the church.

'You go on alone,' I said.

'You'd better come,' said Kate. 'I know just what you feel, but it will be worse here by yourself.'

'I think perhaps I won't,' I said.

'Very well,' said Kate. 'Bicycle on and meet me at the other gate.'

I said I was a coward, and Kate said she did not think it mattered being a coward. I meant to start at once, but I found something wrong with the bicycle. It took quite half an hour to repair, but as I was repairing it all my oppression passed, and I felt light and at ease. By the time I was ready, Kate had visited the tombs, and was coming out of the church door. I looked at her going down the path, and saw there was another woman in the churchyard. She was walking rather slowly. She came up behind Kate, then passed quite close to Kate on her left side. I was too far off to see her face. I felt thankful Kate had someone with her. I mounted; when I looked again the woman was gone.

I met Kate outside the church. She always had odd eyes; now they had a glittering look, half scared and half excited, which made me very uncomfortable. I asked her if she had spoken to the woman about the church.

'What woman? Where?' said Kate.

'The one in the churchyard just now.'

'I didn't see anyone.'

'You must have. She passed quite close to you.'

'Did she?' said Kate. 'She passed on my left side then?'

'Yes, she did. How did you know?'

'Oh, I don't know. We give the keys in here, and let's bicycle home fast, it's turned so cold.'

I always think Kate rather manlike, and she was manlike in her extreme moodiness. If anything of any sort went wrong, she clothed herself in a mood, and became impenetrable. Such a mood came on her now.

'I don't know why I never will tell things at the time,' said Kate next day. It was raining, and we were sitting over a nice little fire after tea. 'It's a sign of great feebleness of mind, I think. However, if you like to hear about Asham Church, you shall. I saw the tombs, and they are all that they should be. I hope the de Mannerings were worthy of them. But the church; perhaps being a clergyman's daughter made me take it so much to heart, but there was a filthy old carpet rolled up on the altar, all the draperies are full of holes, the paint is coming off, part of the chancel rail is broken, and it seems an abode of insects. I did not know there were such forsaken churches in England. That rather spoilt the tombs for me, also an uncomfortable idea that I did not want to look behind me; I don't know what I thought I was going to see. However, I gave every tomb its due.

Then, when I was in the churchyard, I had the same feeling as last time; I could not get it out of my head that something I did not like was going to happen the next minute. Then I had that sensation, which books call the blood running chill; that really means, I think, a catch in one's heart as if one cannot breathe; and at the same time I had such an acute consciousness of someone standing at my left side that I almost felt I was being pushed, no one being there at all, you understand. That lasted a second, I should think, but after that I felt as if I were an intruder in the churchyard, and had better go.'

One afternoon a week later, the great-aunt of the smart townlike landlady at our lodgings came to clear away tea. First of all she was deferential and overwhelmed, but I have never known anyone have such a way with old ladies and gentlemen of the agricultural classes as Kate. In a few moments Mrs Croucher was sitting on the sofa with Kate beside her.

'Asham Hall,' said she. 'Why, my dear mother was sewing maid there, when she was a girl. Oh dear me, yes, the times she's told me about it all. Oh, it's a beautiful place, and them lovely laurels in the avenue, where Miss de Mannering was so fond of walking. It was the old gentleman, Mr de Mannering, he planted them; they was to have gone right up to the Hall, so they say. There was to be wonderful improvements, he was to have pulled down the old Hall and built something better, and then he hadn't the money. Yes, even then it was going down, for Mr William, that was the only son, that lived abroad, he was so wild. Yes, my mother was there in the family's time, not with them things which hev a-took it since.'

'You don't think much of Colonel Winterton, then?'

'Oh, I daresay he's a kind sort of gentleman, they say he's very free at Christmas with coals and that, but them new people they comes and goes, it stands to reason they can't be like the family. In the village we calls them jumped-up bit-of-a-things, but I'm sure I've nothing to say against Colonel Winterton.'

'Are there any of the family still here?'

'Oh no, mum. They've all gone. Some says there's a Mr de Mannering still in America, but he's never been near the place.'

'It's very sad when the old families go,' said Kate sympathetically.

'Oh, it is, mum. Poor old Mr de Mannering; but the place wasn't sold till after his death. My mother, she did feel it.'

'Was there a room shut up in your mother's time, Mrs Croucher?'

'Not when she first went there, mum.'

'It was a housemaid, wasn't it?'

'Not a housemaid,' with a look of important mystery. 'That's what they say, and it's better it *should* be said; I shouldn't tell it to everybody, but I don't mind telling a lady like you; it wasn't a housemaid at all.'

'Not a housemaid?'

'No; my mother's often told me. Miss de Mannering, she was a very high lady, well, she was a lady that *was* a lady, if you catch my meaning, and she must have been six or seven and forty, when she was took with her last illness. And the night before she died, my mother was sitting sewing in Mrs Packe's room (she was the lady's maid, my mother was sewing maid, you know) and she heard Doctor Mason say, "Don't take any notice of what Miss de Mannering says, Mrs Packe. People get very odd fancies, when they're ill," he says. And she says, "No, sir, I won't," and she comes straight to my mother, and she says, "If you could hear the way she's a-going on. 'Oh, my baby,' she says, 'if I could have seen him smile. Oh, if he had lived just one day, one hour, even one moment.' I says to her, says Mrs Packe to my mother, 'Your baby, ma'am, whatever are you talking about?' It was such a peculiar thing for her to say," says Mrs Packe. "Don't you think so, Bessie?" Bessie was my mother. "I'm sure I don't know," says my mother; she never liked Mrs Packe. "Miss de Mannering didn't take no notice," Mrs Packe went on, "then she says, 'If only I'd buried him in the churchyard.' So I says to her, 'But where did you bury him then, ma'am?' and fancy! she turns round, and looks at me, and she says, 'I burnt him.'" Well, that's the truth, that's what my mother told me, and she always said, my mother did, Mrs Packe had no call to repeat such a thing.'

'I think your mother was quite right,' said Kate. 'Burnt! Poor Miss de Mannering must have been delirious. It is such a frightful. . . .'

'No, my mother didn't like carrying tales about the family,' said Mrs Croucher, engaged on quite a different line of thought. And whether it was that she had heard the story so often, or whether it was that they are still more inured to horrors in the country—I have observed far stranger things happen in the country than in the town—Mrs Croucher did not seem to have any idea that she was relating what was terrible. On the contrary, I think she found it homely, recalling a happy part of her childhood.

'Then,' went on Mrs Croucher, 'Mrs Packe, she says to my mother, "You come and hear her," she says, and my mother says, "I don't like to, whatever would she say?" "Oh," says Mrs Packe, "she don't take any notice of anything, you come and peep in at the door." "So I went," my mother says, "and I just peeped in, but I couldn't see anything, only just Miss de Mannering lying in bed, for there was no candle, only the firelight. Only I heard Miss de Mannering give a terrible sigh, and say very faint, but you could hear her quite plain, 'Oh, if only I'd buried him in the churchyard'. I wouldn't stay any longer," says my mother, "and Miss de Mannering died at seven in the evening next day." Whenever my mother spoke of it to me, she always said, "I only regretted going into her room once, and that was all my life. It was taking a liberty, which never should have been took." '

'But,' said Kate, framing the question with difficulty, 'did anybody—? Had anybody had a suspicion that Miss de Mannering—?'

'No, mum. Miss de Mannering was always very reserved, she was not a lady that was at all free in her ways like some ladies; not like you are, if you'll excuse me, mum. Not that I mean she would have said anything to anyone of course, and she had no relations, no sisters, and they never had no company at the Hall, and the old gentleman, he'd married very late in life, so he was what you might call aged, and the servants was terrible afraid of him, his temper was so bad; even Miss de Mannering had a wonderful dread of him, they said.

'There was a deal of talk among the servants after what Mrs Packe said, and there was a housemaid, she'd been in the family a long time, and she remembered one winter years before, I daresay eighteen or twenty years before, Miss de Mannering was ailing, and she sent away her maid, and then she didn't sleep in her own room, but in a room in another part of the house not near anyone, that's the room they shut up, mum. And they remembered once she was ill for months and months, and her nurse that lived at Selby, when she was very old, she got a-talking as sometimes old people will, she died years after Miss de Mannering, and she let out what she would have done better to keep to herself.

'It wasn't long after Miss de Mannering's death they began to say you could see her come out of that there room, walk down the stairs, out at the front door, down through the park, along the avenue, and back again to the house, and then across the park to the churchyard. And of course they say she's trying to find a place for her baby. Then there's some as says Mr Northfield, what lived at Asham before Colonel Winterton came, he saw her. They say that's why he sold it. Mr Fuller they say he's spoke to her; they say that's why he's turned so quiet.

'Then there's some say, Miss Jarvis—she kept The Blue Boar in the village, when I was a girl—she used to say, that Miss Emily

Robinson, the daughter of Sir Thomas Robinson, who bought the place from Mr Seaton, who bought it after Mr de Mannering's death—he wasn't much of a "Sir" to my mind, just kept a draper's shop in London, the saying was—she was took very sudden with the heart disease, and was found dead, flat on her face in the avenue. Of course the tale was, she met Miss de Mannering and she laid a hand on her. The footman that was attending Miss Robinson—she was regular pomped up with pride *she* was, and always would have a footman after her—he says he *see* a woman quite plain come up behind her, and then she fell. He told Mr Jarvis. Poor Mrs Dicey—they was at the Hall before the Northfields—she went off sudden too at the end, but she was always sickly, and I don't hold with all those tales myself.

'But people will believe anything. Why, not long ago, well, perhaps twenty years ago, in Northfield's time, there was a footman got one of the housemaids into trouble, and of course there's new people about in the village since the family went, and they say the room was shut up along of *her*. It's really ridickerlous.'

'Did you ever see her, Mrs Croucher?'

'Not to say see her, mum, but more than once as I've been walking in the park, I've *heard* her quite plain behind me. That was in November. November is the month, as you very well know, mum,'—I could see Kate was gratified that it was supposed she should know—'and you could hear the leaves a-rustling as she walked. There's no need to be frightened, if you don't take no notice, and just walk straight on. They won't never harm you; they only gives you a chill.'

'Did your mother ever see her?'

'If she did, she never would say so. My mother wouldn't have any tales against Miss de Mannering. She said she never had any complaints to make. There was a young man treated my mother badly, and one day she was crying, and Miss de Mannering heard her, and she comes into the sewing-room, and she says, "What is it?" and my mother told her, and Miss de Mannering spoke very feeling, and said, "it's very sad, Bessie, but life is very sad." In general Miss de Mannering never spoke to anybody.

'My mother bought a picture of Miss de Mannering, if you young ladies would like to see it. Everything was in great confusion when Mr de Mannering died. Nothing had been touched for years, and there were all Miss de Mannering's dresses and her private things. No one had looked through them since her death. So what my mother could afford to buy she did, and she left them to me, and charged me to see they should never fall into hands that would not take care of them. There's a lot of writing I know, but I'm not much of a scholar myself, though my dear mother was, and I can't tell you what it's all about, not that my mother had read Miss de Mannering's papers, for she said that would never have been her place.'

Mrs Croucher went to her bedroom and brought us the papers and the portrait. It was a water-colour drawing dated Bath, 1805. The artist had done his best for Miss de Mannering with the blue sash to match the bit of blue sky, and the coral necklace to match her coral lips. The likeness presented to us was that of a young woman, dark, pale, thin, elegant, lady-like, long-nosed and plain. One gathers from pictures that such a type was not uncommon at that period. I should have been afraid of Miss de Mannering from her mouth and the turn of the head, they were so proud and aristocratic, but I loved her sad, timid eyes, which seemed appealing for kindness and protection.

Mrs Croucher was anxious to give Kate the portrait, 'for none of 'em don't care for my old things'. Kate refused. 'But after you are gone,' she said, for she knows that all such as Mrs Croucher are ready to discuss their deaths openly, 'if your niece will send her to me, I should like to have Miss de Mannering; I shall prize her very much.'

Then Mrs Croucher withdrew, 'for I shall be tiring your two young ladies with my talk'. It is rather touching how poor people, however old and feeble, think that everything will tire 'a lady', however young and robust.

We turned to Miss de Mannering's papers. It was strange to look at something, written over a century ago, so long put by and never read. I had a terrible sensation of intruding, but Kate said she thought, if we were going to be as fastidious as all that, life would never get on at all. So I have copied out the narrative for you. I am sure, if Mrs Croucher knew you, she would feel you worthy to share the signal honour she conferred on us.

MISS DE MANNERING'S NARRATIVE

It is now twenty-two years since, yet the events of the year 1805 are engraved upon my memory with greater accuracy than those of any other in my life. It is to escape their pressing so heavily upon my brain that I commit them to paper, confiding to the pages of a book what may never be related to a human friend.

Had my lot been one more in accordance with that of other young women of my position, I might have been preserved from the calamity which befell me. But we are in the hands of a merciful Creator, who appoints to each his course. I sinned of my own free will, nor do I seek to mitigate my sin. My mother, Lady Jane de Mannering, daughter of the Earl of Poveril, died when I was five years old. She entrusted me to the care of a faithful governess and nurse, and owing to their affectionate solicitude in childhood and girlhood I hardly missed a mother's care. Of my father I saw but little. He was violent and moody. My brother, fourteen years older than I, was already causing him the greatest anxiety by his dissipation. Some words of my father's, and a chance remark, lightly spoken in my hearing, made an ineffaceable impression on me. In the unusual solitude of my existence I had ample, too ample, leisure to brood over recollections which had best be forgotten. Cheerful thoughts, natural to my age, should have left them no room in my heart. When I was thirteen years old, my father said to me one day, 'I don't want you skulking here, you're too much of a Poveril. Everyone knows that a Poveril once, for all their pride, stooped to marry a French waiting-maid. That's why every man Jack of them is black and sallow, as you are.' I fled from the room in terror.

Another day Miss Fanshawe was talking with the governess of a young lady who had come to spend the afternoon with me. They were walking behind us, and I heard their conversation.

'Is not Miss Maynard beautiful?' said Miss Adams. 'I believe that golden hair and brilliant eye will make a sensation even in London. What a pity Miss de Mannering is so black! Fair beauties are all the rage they say, and her eyes are too small.'

'Beauty is a very desirable possession for a young woman,' said Miss Fanshawe, 'but one which is perhaps too highly valued. Anyone may have beauty; a milkmaid may have beauty; but there is an air of rank and breeding which outlasts beauty, and is, I believe, more prized by a man of fastidious taste. Such an air is possessed by Miss de Mannering in a remarkable degree.'

My kind, beloved Fan! but at fifteen how much rather would I have shared the gift possessed by milkmaids! From henceforth I was certain I should not please.

Miss Fanshawe, who never failed to give me the encouragement and confidence I lacked, died when I was seventeen and had reached the age which, above all others in a woman's life, requires the comfort and protection of a female friend. My father, more and more engrossed with money difficulties, made no arrangement for my introduction to the world. He had no relations, but my mother's sisters had several times invited me to visit them. My father however, who was on bad terms with the family, would not permit me to go. The most rigid economy was necessary. He would allow no guests to be invited, and therefore no invitations to be accepted. The Hall was situated in a very solitary part of the country, and it was rare indeed for any visitor to find his way thither. My brother was forbidden the house. Months, nay years passed, and I saw no one.

Suddenly my father said to me one day, 'You are twenty-five, so that cursed lawyer of the Poverils tells me; twenty-five, and not yet married. I have no money to leave you after my death. Write and tell your aunt at Bath that you will visit her, and she must find you a husband.'

Secluded from society as I had been, the prospect of leaving the Hall and being plunged into the world of fashion filled me with the utmost apprehension. 'I entreat you, sir, to excuse me,' I cried. 'Let me stay here. I ask nothing from you, but I cannot go to Bath.'

I fell on my knees before him, but he would take no denial, and a few weeks after I found myself at Bath.

My aunt, Lady Theresa Lindsay, a widow, was one of the gayest in that gay city, and especially this season, for she was introducing her daughter Miss Leonora.

My father had given me ten pounds to buy myself clothes for my visit, but, entirely inexperienced as I was, I acquitted myself ill.

'My dear creature,' said my cousin in a coaxing manner that could not wound. 'Poor Nancy in the scullery would blush to see herself like you. You must hide yourself completely from the world for the next few days like the monks of La Trappe, and put yourself in Mamma's hands and mine. After that time I doubt not Miss Sophia de Mannering will rival the fashionable toast Lady Charlotte Harper.'

My dear Leonora did all in her power to set me off to the best advantage, to praise and encourage me, and my formidable aunt was kind for my mother's sake. But my terror at the crowd of gentlemen, that filled my aunt's drawing-room, was not easily allayed.

'I tremble at their approach,' I said to Leonora.

'Tremble at their approach?' said Leonora. 'But it is their part to tremble at ours, my little cousin, to tremble with hopes that we shall be kind, or with fears that we shall not. I say my little cousin, because I am a giantess,' she was very tall and exquisitely beautiful, 'and also I am very old and experienced, and you are to look up to me in everything.'

I wished to have remained retired at the assemblies, but Leonora always sought me out, and presented her partners to me. But my awkwardness and embarrassment soon wearied them, and after such attentions as courtesy required they left me for more congenial company. Certainly I could not blame them; it was what I had anticipated. Yet the mortification wounded me and I said to my cousin, 'It is of no use, Leonora. I can never, never hope to please.'

'Those who fish diligently,' she replied, 'shall not go unrewarded. A gentleman said to me this evening, "Your cousin attracts me; she has so much countenance." Captain Phillimore is accounted a connoisseur in our sex. That is a large fish, and I congratulate you with all my heart.'

Captain Phillimore came constantly to my aunt's house. Once he entered into conversation with me. Afterwards he sought me out; at first I could not believe it possible, but again he sought me out, and yet again.

'Captain Phillimore is a connection not to be despised by the ancient house of de Mannering,' said my aunt. 'There are tales of his extravagance it is true, and other matters; but the family is wealthy, and of what man of fashion are not such tales related? Marriage will steady him.'

Weeks passed by. It was now April. My aunt was to leave Bath in a few days, and I was to return home; the season was drawing to its close. My aunt was giving a farewell reception to her friends. Captain Phillimore drew me into an anteroom adjoining one of the drawing-rooms. He told me that he loved me, that he had loved me from the moment he first saw me. He kissed me. Never, never can I forget the bliss of that moment. 'There are,' he said 'important reasons why our engagement must at present be known only to ourselves. As soon as it is possible I will apprise my father, and hasten to Asham to obtain Mr de Mannering's consent. Till then not a word to your aunt. It will be safest not even to correspond.' He told me that he had been summoned suddenly to join his regiment in Ireland and must leave Bath the following day. 'I must therefore see you once more before I go. The night is as warm as summer. Have you the resolution to meet me in an hour's time in the garden? We must enjoy a few minutes' solitude away from the teasing crowd.'

I, who was usually timid, had now no fears. I easily escaped unnoticed. The whole household was occupied with the reception. At the end of a long terrace there was an arbour. Here we met. He urged me to give myself entirely to him, using the wicked sophistries which had been circulated by the infidel philosophers of France; that marriage is a superstitious form with no value for the more enlightened of mankind. But alas, there was no need of sophistries. Whatever he had proposed, had he bidden me throw myself over a precipice, I should have obeyed. I loved him as no weak mortal should be loved. When his bright blue eye gazed into mine, and his hand caressed me, I sank before him as a worshipper before a shrine. With my eyes fully open I yielded to him.

I returned to the house. My absence had not been observed. My cousin came to my room, and said with her arch smile, 'I ask no question, I am too proud to beg for confidences. But I know what I know. Kiss me, and receive my blessing.'

I retired to rest, and could not sleep all night for feverish exaltation. It was not till the next day that I recognized my guilt. I hardly dared look my aunt and cousin in the face, but my demeanour passed unnoticed; for during the morning a Russian nobleman attached to the Imperial court, who had been paying Leonora great attentions, solicited her hand and was accepted. In the ensuing agitation I was forgotten, and my proposal that I should return to Asham a day or two earlier was welcomed. My aunt was anxious to go to London without delay to begin preparations for the wedding.

She made me a cordial farewell, engaging me to accompany her to Bath next year. 'But, Mamma,' said Leonora, 'I think Captain Phillimore will have something to say to that. All I stipulate is that Captain and Mrs Phillimore shall be my first visitors at St Petersburgh.'

Their kindness went through me like a knife, and I returned to Asham with a heavy heart.

'Where is your husband?' was my father's greeting.

'I have none, sir,' said I.

'The more fool you,' he answered, and asked no further particulars of my visit.

Time passed on. Every day I hoped for the appearance of Captain Phillimore. In vain; he came not. Certainty was succeeded by hope, hope by doubt, doubt by dread. I would not, I could not despair. Ere long it was evident that I was to become a mother. The horror of this discovery, with my total ignorance of Captain Phillimore's whereabouts, caused me the most miserable perturbation. I walked continually with the fever of madness along the laurel avenue and in the Park. I went to the Church, hoping that there I might find consolation, but the memorials of former de Mannerings reminded me too painfully that I alone of all the women of the family had brought dishonour on our name.

I longed to pour out my misery to some human ear, even though I exposed my disgrace. There was but one in my solitude whom I could trust; my old nurse, who lived at Selby three miles off. I walked thither one summer evening, and with many tears I told her all. She mingled her tears with mine. I was her nursling, she did not shrink from me. All in her power she would do for me. She knew a discreet woman in Ipswich, whither she might arrange for me to go as my time approached, who would later take charge of the infant. She suggested all that could be done to allay suspicion in the household and village.

At first my aunt and cousin wrote constantly, and even after Leonora's marriage I continued to hear from Russia. My letters were short and cold. When I knew that I was to be a mother, I could not bear to have further communication with them. My aunt wrote to me kindly and reproachfully. I did not answer, and gradually all correspondence ceased. Yet their affectionate letters were all I had to cheer the misery of those ensuing months. I shall never forget them. Although it was now summer, the weather was almost continuously gloomy and tempestuous. There were many thunderstorms, which wrought havoc among our elm trees in the Park. The rushing of the wind at night through the heavy branches and the falling of the rain against my window gave me an indescribable feeling of apprehension, so that I hid my head under the bedclothes that I might hear nothing. Yet more terrible to me were the long days of August, when the leaden sky oppressed my spirit, and it seemed as if I and the world alike were dead. I struggled against the domination of such fancies, fancies perhaps not uncommon in my condition, and in general soothed by the tenderness of an indulgent husband. I could imagine such tenderness. Night and day Captain Phillimore was in my thoughts. No female pride came to my aid; I loved him more passionately than ever.

On the 20th November some ladies visited us at the Hall. We had a common bond in two cousins of theirs I had met frequently in Bath. They talked of our mutual acquaintance. At length Captain Phillimore's name was mentioned. Shall I ever forget those words? 'Have you heard the tale of Captain Phillimore, the all-conquering Captain Phillimore? Major Richardson, who was an intimate of his at Bath, told my brother that he said to him at the beginning of the season, "What do you bet me that in one season I shall successfully assault the virtue of the three most innocent and immaculate maids, old or young, in Bath? Easy virtue has no charms for me, I prefer the difficult, but my passion is for the impregnable," and Major Richardson assures my brother that Captain Phillimore won his bet. Mr de Mannering, we are telling very shocking scandals; three ladies of strict virtue fallen in one season at Bath. What is the world coming to?'

My father had appeared to pay little heed to their chatter, but he now burst forth, 'If any woman lets her virtue be assaulted by a rake, she's a rake herself. Should such a fate befall a daughter of mine, I should first horsewhip her, and then turn her from my doors.'

During this conversation I felt a stab at the heart, so that I could neither speak nor breathe. How it was my companions noticed nothing I cannot say. I dared not move, I dared not leave my seat to get a glass of water to relieve me. Yet I believe I remained outwardly at ease, and as soon as speech returned, I forced myself to say with tolerable composure, 'Major Richardson was paying great attention to Miss Burdett. Does your brother say anything of that affair?'

Shortly afterwards the ladies took their leave.

I retired to my room. I had moved to one in the most solitary part of the house, far from either my father or the servants. I tried in vain to calm myself, but each moment my fever became more uncontrollable. I dispatched a messenger to my nurse, begging her to come to me without delay. I longed to sob my sorrows out to her with her kind arms round me. The destruction of all my hopes was as nothing to the shattering of my idol. My love was dead, but though I might despise him, I could not, could not hate him.

Later in the day I was taken ill, and in the night my baby was born. My room was so isolated that I need have little fear of discovery. An unnatural strength seemed to be given me, so that I was able to do what was neccessary for my little one. He opened his eyes; the look on his innocent face exactly recalled my mother. My joy who shall describe? I was comforted with the fancy that in my hour of trial my mother was with me. I lay with my sweet babe in my arms, and kissed him a hundred times. The little tender cries were the most melodious music to my ears. But short-lived was my joy; my precious treasure was granted me but three brief hours. It was long ere I could bring myself to believe he had ceased to breathe. What could I do with the lovely waxen body? The horror that my privacy would be invaded, that some intruder should find my baby, and desecrate the sweet lifeless frame by questions and reproaches, was unendurable. I would have carried him to the churchyard, and dug the little grave with my own hands. But the first snow of the winter had been falling for some hours; it would be useless to venture forth.

The fire was still burning; I piled wood and coal upon it. I wrapped him in a cashmere handkerchief of my mother's; I repeated what I could remember of the funeral service, comforting and tranquillizing myself with its promises. I could not watch the flames destroy him. I fled to the other end of the room, and hid my face on the floor.

Afterwards I remember a confused feeling that I myself was burning and must escape the flames. I knew no more, till I opened my eyes and found myself lying on my bed, with my nurse near me, and our attached old Brooks, the village apothecary, sitting by my side.

'How do you feel yourself, Miss de Mannering?' said he.

'Have I been ill?'

'Very ill for many weeks,' said he, 'but I think we shall do very well now.'

My nurse told me that, as soon as my message had reached her, she had set out to walk to Asham, but the snow had impeded her progress, and she was forced to stop the night at an inn not far from Selby. She was up before dawn, and reached the Hall, as the servants were unbarring the shutters. She hastened to my room, and found me lying on the floor, overcome by a dangerous attack of fever. She tended me all the many weeks of my illness, and would allow none to come near me but the doctor, for throughout my delirium I spoke constantly of my child.

The doctor visited me daily. At first I was so weak that I hardly noticed him, but my strength increased, and with strength came remembrance. He said to me one morning, 'You have been brought from the brink of the grave, Miss de Mannering. I did not think it possible that we should have saved you.'

In the anguish of my spirit I could not refrain from crying out, 'Would God that I had died.'

'Nay,' said he, 'since your life has been spared, should you reject the gift from the hands of the Almighty?'

'Ah,' I said in bitterness. 'You do not know—'

'Yes, madam,' said he, looking earnestly upon me, 'I know all.'

I turned from him trembling.

'Do not fear,' he said. 'The knowledge will never be revealed.'

I remained with my face against the wall.

'My dear Madam,' he said with the utmost kindness. 'Do not turn from an old man, who has attended you since babyhood and your mother also. My father and my father before me doctored the de Mannerings, and I wish to do all in my power to serve you. A physician may sometimes give his humble aid to the soul as well as to the body. Let me recall to your suffering soul that all of us sinners are promised mercy through our Redeemer. I entreat you not to lose heart. Now for my proper domain, the body. You must not spend your period of convalescence in this inclement native county of ours. You must seek sun and warmth, and change of scene to cheer your mind.'

His benevolence touched me, and my tears fell fast. Amid tears I answered him, 'Alas, I am without friends; I have nowhere to go.'

'Do not let that discourage us,' he said with a smile, 'we shall devise a plan. Let me sit by my own fireside with my own glass of whisky, and I shall certainly devise a plan.'

By his generous exertions I went on a visit to his sister at Worthing. She watched over me with a mother's care, and I returned to Asham with my health restored. Peace came to my soul; I learnt to forgive him. The years passed in outward tranquillity, but in each succeeding November, or whenever the winds were high or the sky leaden, I would suffer, as I had suffered in the months preceding the birth of my child. My mind was filled with baseless fears, above all that I should not meet my baby in Heaven, because his body did not lie in consecrated ground. Nor were the assurances of my Reason and my Faith able to conjure the delusion: yet I had—

Here the writing stopped.

'Wait, though,' said Kate, 'there's a letter.' She read the following:

> 3 Hen and Chicken Court,
> Clerkenwell.
> March 7, 1810.

Madam,

I have been told that my days are numbered. Standing as I do on the confines of eternity, I venture to address you. Long have I desired to implore your forgiveness, but have not presumed so far. I entreat you not to spurn my letter. God knows you have cause to hate the name of him who betrayed you. Yes, Madam, my vows were false, but even at the time I faltered, as I encountered your trusting and affectionate gaze, and often during my subsequent career of debauchery has that vision appeared before me. Had I embraced the opportunity offered me by Destiny to link my happiness with one as innocent and confiding as yourself, I might have been spared the wretchedness which has been my portion.

> I am Madam, your obedient servant,
> Frederic Phillimore.

I could not speak for a minute; I was so engrossed with thinking what Miss de Mannering must have felt when she got that letter.

Kate said, 'I wonder what she wrote back to him. How often it has been folded and refolded, read and re-read, and do you see where words have got all smudged? I believe those are her tears, tears for that skunk!'

But I felt I could imagine better than Kate all that letter, with its stilted old-fashioned style, which makes it hard for us to believe the writer was in earnest, would have meant to Miss de Mannering.

'To-morrow is our last afternoon,' said Kate. 'What do you think,' coaxingly, 'of making a farewell visit to Asham?'

But though Miss de Mannering is a gentle ghost, I do not like ghosts; besides, now I know her secret, I *could* not intrude upon her. So we did not go to Asham again. Now we are back at school, and that is the end of my story.

FREDERICK COWLES

The Vampire of Kaldenstein

I

Since I was a lad I have been accustomed to spend my vacations wandering about the more remote parts of Europe. I have had some pleasant times in Italy, Spain, Norway, and southern France, but of all the countries I have explored in this fashion Germany is my favourite. It is an ideal holiday land for the lover of open-air life whose means are small and tastes simple, for the people are always so friendly and the inns are good and cheap. I have had many excellent holidays in Germany, but one will always stand out in my memory because of a very queer and remarkable experience which befell me.

It was in the summer of 1933, and I had practically made up my mind to go on a cruise to the Canaries with Donald Young. Then he caught a very childish complaint—the measles, in fact—and I was left to make my own arrangements. The idea of joining an organised cruise without a companion did not appeal to me. I am not a particularly sociable kind of person, and these cruises seem to be one round of dances, cocktail parties, and bridge drives. I was afraid of feeling like a fish out of water, so I decided to forgo the cruise. Instead I got out my maps of Germany and began to plan a walking tour.

Half the fun of a holiday is in the planning of it, and I suppose I decided on a particular part of the country and changed my mind half a dozen times. At first I fancied the Moselle Valley, then it was the Lahn. I toyed with the idea of the Black Forest, swung over to the Hartz Mountains, and then thought it might be fun to re-visit Saxony. Finally I fixed upon southern Bavaria, because I had never been there and it seemed better to break fresh ground.

Two days of third-class travel is tiring even for a hardened globe-trotter, and I arrived at Munich feeling thoroughly weary and sore. By some good chance I discovered the Inn of the Golden Apple, near the Hofgarten, where Peter Schmidt sells both good wine and good food, and has a few rooms for the accommodation of guests. Peter, who lived in Canada for ten years and speaks excellent English, knew exactly how I was feeling. He gave me a comfortable room for one Mark a night, served me with hot coffee and rolls, and recommended me to go to bed and stay there until I was completely rested. I took his advice, slept soundly for twelve hours, and awakened feeling as fresh as a daisy. A dish of roast pork and two glasses of lager beer completed the cure, and I sallied forth to see something of Munich.

The city is the fourth largest in Germany and has much of interest to show the visitor. The day was well advanced, but I managed to inspect the Frauen-Kirche with its fine stained glass, the old Rathaus, and the fourteenth-century church of St Peter, near the Marien-Platz. I looked in at the *Regina-Palast*, where a tea-dance was in progress, and then went back to the Golden Apple for dinner. Afterwards I attended a performance of *Die Meistersinger* at the National-Theater. It was past midnight when I retired to bed, and by then I had decided to stay in Munich for another day.

I won't bore you with a description of the things I saw and did on that second day. It was just the usual round of sights with nothing out of the ordinary.

After dinner Peter helped me to plan my tour. He revealed a very intimate knowledge of the Bavarian villages, and gave me a list of inns which eventually proved invaluable. It was he who suggested I should train to Rosenheim and begin my walk from there. We mapped out a route covering about two hundred miles and bringing me back to Munich at the end of fifteen days.

Well, to cut a long story short, I caught the early morning train to Rosenheim, and a deadly slow journey it was. It took nearly three hours to cover a distance of forty-six miles. The town itself is quite a cheerful place of the small industrial type, with a fifteenth-century church and a good museum of Bavarian paintings housed in an old chapel.

I did not linger there, but started off along the road to Traunstein— a pleasant road curving round the Chiem-See, the largest lake in Bavaria.

I spent the night at Traunstein and the next day pushed on to the old walled town of Mühldorf. From there I planned to make for Vilshofen by way of Pfarrkirchen. But I took a wrong turning and found myself in a small place called Gangkofen. The local innkeeper tried to be helpful and directed me to a field path which he said would prove a short cut to Pfarrkirchen. Evidently I misunderstood his instructions, for evening came and I was hopelessly lost in the heart of a range of low hills which were not marked on my map. Darkness was falling when I came upon a small village huddled under the shadow of a high cliff upon which stood a grey stone castle.

Fortunately the village possessed an inn—a primitive place but moderately comfortable. The landlord was an intelligent kind of chap and friendly enough, although he informed me that visitors were seldom seen in the district. The name of the hamlet was Kaldenstein.

I was served with a simple meal of goat's milk cheese, salad, coarse bread, and a bottle of thin red wine, and, having done justice to the spread, went for a short stroll.

The moon had risen and the castle stood out against a cloudless sky like some magic castle in a fairy tale. It was only a small building—square, with four turrets—but it was the most romantic-looking fortress I had ever seen. A light twinkled in one of the windows, so I knew the place was inhabited. A steep path and a flight of steps cut in the rock led up to it, and I half considered paying the Lord of Kaldenstein a late visit. Instead I returned to the inn and joined the few men who were drinking in the public room.

The company was mainly composed of folk of the labouring class, and although they were polite they had little of that friendly spirit one is accustomed to meet with in German villages. They seemed morose and unresponsive and I had the impression that they shared some dread secret. I did my best to engage them in conversation without success. Then, to get one of them to speak, I asked, 'Tell me, my friends, who lives in the castle on the hillside?'

The effect of the harmless question upon them was startling. Those who were drinking placed their beer-mugs on the table and gazed at me with consternation on their faces. Some made the sign of the cross, and one old chap hoarsely whispered, 'Silence, stranger. God forbid that he should hear.'

My inquiry seemed to have upset them altogether, and within ten minutes they all left in a body. I apologised to the landlord for any indiscretion I had been guilty of, and hoped my presence had not robbed him of custom.

He waved aside my excuses and assured me that the men would not have stayed long in any case.

'They are terrified of any mention of the castle,' he said, 'and consider it unlucky to even glance at the building after nightfall.'

'But why?' I inquired. 'Who lives there?'

'It is the home of Count Ludwig von Kaldenstein.'

'And how long has he lived up there?' I asked.

The man moved over to the door and carefully shut and barred it before he replied. Then he came over to my chair and whispered, 'He has been up there for nearly three hundred years.'

'Nonsense,' I exclaimed laughing. 'How can any man, be he count or peasant, live for three hundred years. I suppose you mean that his family has held the castle for that length of time?'

'I mean exactly what I say, young man,' answered the old fellow earnestly. 'The Count's family has held the castle for ten centuries, and the Count himself has dwelt in Burg Kaldenstein for nearly three hundred years.'

'But how can that be possible?'

'He is a vampire. Deep down in the castle rock are great vaults and in one of these the Count sleeps during the day so that the sunlight may not touch him. Only at night does he walk abroad.'

This was too fantastic for anything. I am afraid I smiled in a sceptical manner, but the poor landlord was obviously very serious, and I hesitated to make another remark that might wound his feelings. I finished my beer and got up to go to bed. As I was mounting the stairs my host called me back and grasping my arm said, 'Please, sir, let me beg you to keep your window closed. The night air of Kaldenstein is not healthy.'

On reaching my room I found the window already tightly shut, although the atmosphere was like that of an oven. Of course I opened it at once and leaned out to fill my lungs with fresh air. The window looked directly upon the castle and, in the clear light of the full moon, the building appeared more than ever like some dream of fairyland.

I was just drawing back into the room when I fancied I saw a black figure silhouetted against the sky on the summit of one of the turrets. Even as I watched it flapped enormous wings and soared into the night. It seemed too large for an eagle, but the moonlight has a queer trick of distorting shapes. I watched until it was only a tiny black speck in the far distance. Just then, from far away, a dog howled weirdly and mournfully.

Within a few moments I was ready for bed, and disregarding the inn-keeper's warning I left the window open. I took my electric flash-light from my rucksack and placed it on the small bedside table—a table above which hung a wooden crucifix.

I am usually asleep as soon as my head touches the pillow, but on this particular night I found it difficult to settle. The moonlight disturbed me and I tossed about vainly trying to get comfortable. I counted sheep until I was heartily sick of imagining the silly creatures passing through a gap in a hedge, but still sleep eluded me.

A clock in the house chimed the hour of midnight, and suddenly I had the unpleasant feeling that I was no longer alone. For a moment I felt frightened and then, overcoming my fear, I turned over. There, by the window and black against the moonlight, was the figure of a tall man. I started up in bed and groped for my flashlight. In doing so I knocked something from the wall. It was the little crucifix and my fingers closed over it almost as soon as it touched the table. From the direction of the window came a muttered curse, and I saw the figure poise itself on the sill and spring out into the night. In that brief moment I noticed one other thing—the man, whoever he was, cast no shadow. The moonlight seemed to stream right through him.

It must have been almost half an hour before I dared get out of bed and close the window. After that I fell asleep immediately and slept soundly until the maid called me at eight o'clock.

In the broad daylight the events of the night seemed too ridiculous to be true, and I decided that I had been the victim of some fantastic nightmare. In answer to the landlord's polite inquiry I vowed I had spent a most comfortable night, although I am afraid my looks must have belied the statement.

II

After breakfast I went out to explore the village. It was rather larger than it had appeared on the previous evening, some of the houses lying in a valley at the side of the road. There was even a small church, Romanesque in type and sadly in need of repair. I entered the building and was inspecting its gaudy high altar when a priest came in through a side door. He was a lean, ascetic-looking man, and at once gave me a friendly greeting. I returned his salutation and told him I was from England. He apologised for the obvious poverty of the building, pointed out some good fifteenth-century glass, a carved font of the same period, and a very pleasing statue of the Madonna.

Later, as I stood at the church door with him, I looked towards the castle and said, 'I wonder, Father, if the Lord of Kaldenstein will give me a welcome as friendly as the one I have received from you?'

'The Lord of Kaldenstein,' repeated the priest with a tremor in his voice. 'Surely you are not proposing to visit the castle?'

'That is my intention,' I replied. 'It looks a very interesting place and I should be sorry to leave this part of the world without seeing it.'

'Let me implore you not to attempt to enter that accursed place,' he pleaded. 'Visitors are not welcomed at Kaldenstein Castle. Besides that,' he went on with a change in his voice, 'there is nothing to see in the building.'

'What about the wonderful vaults in the cliff and the man who has lived in them for three hundred years?' I laughed.

The priest's face visibly blanched. 'Then you know of the vampire,' he said. 'Do not laugh at evil, my son. May God preserve us all from the living dead.' He made the sign of the Cross.

'But Father,' I cried, 'surely you do not believe in such a medieval superstition?'

'Every man believes what he knows to be true, and we of Kaldenstein can prove that no burial has taken place in the castle since 1645, when Count Feodor died, and his cousin Ludwig from Hungary inherited the estate.'

'Such a tale is too absurd,' I remonstrated. 'There must be some reasonable explanation of the mystery. It is unthinkable that a man who came to this place in 1645 can still be alive.'

'Much is possible to those who serve the devil,' answered the priest. 'Always throughout the history of the world evil has warred with good, and often triumphed. Kaldenstein Castle is the haunt of terrible, unnatural wickedness, and I urge you to keep as far away from it as you can.'

He bade me a courteous farewell, lifted his hand in a gentle benediction, and re-entered the church.

Now I must confess that the priest's words gave me a most uncomfortable feeling and made me think of my nightmare. Had it been a dream after all? Or could it have been the vampire himself seeking to make me one of his victims, and only being frustrated in his plan by my accidental gripping of the crucifix? These thoughts passed through my mind and I almost abandoned my resolve to seek admittance to the castle. Then I looked up again at the grey old walls gleaming in the morning sunshine, and laughed at my fears. No mythical monster of the Middle Ages was going to frighten me away. The priest was just as superstitious as his ignorant parishioners.

Whistling a popular song, I made my way up the village street and was soon climbing the narrow path which led to the castle. As the ascent became steeper the path gave place to a flight of steps which brought me on to a small plateau before the main door of the building. There was no sign of life about the place, but a ponderous bell hung before the entrance. I pulled a rusty chain and set the cracked thing jangling. The sound disturbed a colony of rooks in one of the turrets and started them chattering, but no human being appeared to answer my summons. Again I set the bell ringing. This time the echoes had hardly died away when I heard bolts being withdrawn. The great door creaked on its hinges, and an old man stood blinking in the sunlight.

'Who comes to Castle Kaldenstein?' he asked in a curious high-pitched voice, and I could see that he was half-blind.

'I am an English visitor,' I answered, 'and would like to see the Count.'

'His Excellency does not receive visitors,' was the reply, and the man made to close the door in my face.

'But is it not permitted that I should see over the castle?' I asked hurriedly. 'I am interested in medieval fortresses and should be sorry to leave Kaldenstein without inspecting this splendid building.'

The old fellow peered out at me, and in a hesitant voice said, 'There is little to see, sir, and I am afraid you would only be wasting your time.'

'Yet I should appreciate the privilege of a brief visit.' I argued, 'and I am sure the Count would not object. I do assure you I shall not be a nuisance and I have no desire to disturb His Excellency's privacy.'

'What is the hour?' asked the man.

I informed him that it was barely eleven o'clock. He muttered something about it being 'safe whilst the sun is in the sky', and motioned me to enter. I found myself in a bare hall, hung with rotting tapestry and smelling of damp and decay. At the end of the room was a canopied dais surmounted by a coat of arms.

'This is the main hall of the castle,' mumbled my guide, 'and it has witnessed many great historic scenes in the days of the great lords of Kaldenstein. Here Frederic, the sixth Count, put out the eyes of twelve Italian hostages, and afterwards had them driven over the edge of the cliff. Here Count August is said to have poisoned a prince of Wurttemburg, and then sat at a feast with the dead body.'

He went on with his tales of foul and treacherous deeds, and it was evident that the Counts of Kaldenstein must have been a very unsavoury lot. From the main hall he conducted me into a number of smaller rooms filled with mouldering furniture. His own quarters were in the north turret, but although he showed me over the whole building I saw no room in which his master could be. The old fellow opened every door without hesitation and it seemed that, except for himself, the castle was untenanted.

'But where is the Count's room?' I inquired as we returned to the main hall.

He looked confused for a moment and then replied, 'We have

certain underground apartments, and His Excellency uses one as his bed-chamber. You see he can rest there undisturbed.'

I thought that any room in the building would give him the quietness he required without having to seek peace in the bowels of the earth.

'And have you no private chapel?' I asked.

'The chapel is also below.'

I intimated that I was interested in chapels, and should very much like to see an example of an underground place of worship. The old man made several excuses, but at last consented to show me the crypt. Taking an old-fashioned lantern from a shelf he lit the candle in it, and lifting a portion of the tapestry from the wall, opened a hidden door. A sickly odour of damp corruption swept up at us. Muttering to himself he led the way down a flight of stone steps and along a passage hollowed in the rock. At the end of this was another door which admitted us to a large cavern furnished like a church. The place stank like a charnel-house, and the feeble light of the lantern only intensified the gloom. My guide led me towards the chancel and, lifting the light, pointed out a particularly revolting painting of Lazarus rising from the dead which hung above the altar. I moved forward to examine it more closely and found myself near another door.

'And what is beyond this?'

'Speak softly, sir,' he implored. 'It is the vault in which rest the mortal remains of the Lords of Kaldenstein.'

And whilst he was speaking I heard a sound from beyond that barrier—a sigh and the kind of noise that might be made by a person turning in his sleep.

I think the old servitor also heard it, for he grasped me with a trembling hand and led me out of the chapel. His flickering light went before me as I mounted the stairs, and I laughed sharply with relief as we stepped into the castle hall again. He gave me a quick look and said, 'That is all, sir. You see there is little of interest in this old building.'

I tried to press a five-mark piece into his hand, but he refused to accept it.

'Money is of no use to me, sir,' he whispered. 'I have nothing to spend it upon for I live with the dead. Give the coin to the priest in the village and ask him to say a Mass for me if you will.'

I promised it should be done as he desired and then, in some mad spirit of bravado, asked, 'And when does the Count receive visitors?'

'My master never receives visitors,' was the reply.

'But surely he is sometimes in the castle itself? He doesn't spend all his time in the vaults,' I urged.

'Usually after nightfall he sits in the hall for an hour or so, and sometimes walks on the battlements.'

'Then I shall be back to-night,' I cried. 'I owe it to His Excellency to pay my respects to him.'

The old man turned in the act of unfastening the door, and fixing his dim eyes upon my face said, 'Come not to Kaldenstein after the sun has set lest you find that which shall fill your heart with fear.'

'Don't try to frighten me with any of your hob-goblins,' I rudely replied. Then raising my voice I cried, 'To-night I shall wait upon the Count von Kaldenstein.'

The servant flung the door wide and the sunlight streamed into the mouldering building.

'If you come he will be ready to receive you,' he said, 'and remember that if you enter the castle again you do so of your own free will.'

III

By the time evening came my courage had quite evaporated and I wished I had taken the priest's advice and left Kaldenstein. But there is a streak of obstinacy in my make-up and, having vowed to visit the castle again, nothing could turn me from my purpose. I waited until dusk had fallen and, saying nothing to the inn-keeper of my intentions, made my way up the steep path to the fortress. The moon had not yet risen and I had to use my flash-light on the steps. I rang the cracked bell and the door opened almost immediately. There stood the old servant bowing a welcome.

'His Excellency will see you, sir,' he cried. 'Enter Kaldenstein Castle—enter of your own free will.'

For one second I hesitated. Something seemed to warn me to retreat whilst there was still time. Then I plucked up courage and stepped over the threshold.

A log fire was burning in the enormous grate and gave a more cheerful atmosphere to the gloomy apartment. Candles gleamed in the silver candelabra, and I saw that a man was sitting at the table on the dais. As I advanced he came down to greet me.

How shall I describe the Count of Kaldenstein? He was unusually tall, with a face of unnatural pallor. His hair was intensely black, and his hands delicately shaped but with very pointed fingers and long nails. His eyes impressed me most. As he crossed the room they seemed to glow with a red light, just as if the pupils were ringed with flame. However, his greeting was conventional enough.

'Welcome to my humble home, sir,' he said, bowing very low. 'I regret my inability to offer you a more hospitable welcome, but we live very frugally. It is seldom we entertain guests, and I am honoured that you should take the trouble to call upon me.'

I murmured some polite word of thanks, and he conducted me to a seat at the long table upon which stood a decanter and one glass.

'You will take wine?' he invited, and filled the glass to the brim. It was a rare old vintage, but I felt a little uncomfortable at having to drink alone.

'I trust you will excuse me for not joining you,' he said, evidently noticing my hesitant manner. 'I never drink wine.' He smiled, and I saw that his front teeth were long and sharply pointed.

'And now tell me,' he went on. 'What are you doing in this part of the world? Kaldenstein is rather off the beaten track and we seldom see strangers.'

I explained that I was on a walking tour and had missed my way to Pfarrkirchen. The Count laughed softly, and again showed his fang-like teeth.

'And so you came to Kaldenstein and of your own free will you have come to visit me.'

I began to dislike these references to my free will. The expression seemed to be a kind of formula. The servant had used it when I was leaving after my morning visit, and again when he had admitted me that evening, and now the Count was making use of it.

'How else should I come but of my own free will?' I asked sharply.

'In the bad old days of the past many have been brought to this castle by force. The only guests we welcome to-day are those who come willingly.'

All this time a queer sensation was gradually coming over me: I felt as if all my energy was being sapped from me and a deadly nausea was overpowering my senses. The Count went on uttering common-places, but his voice came from far away. I was conscious of his peculiar eyes gazing into mine. They grew larger and larger, and it seemed that I was looking into two wells of fire. And then, with a clumsy movement, I knocked my wine-glass over. The frail thing shattered to fragments, and the noise restored me to my senses. A splinter pierced my hand and a tiny pool of blood formed on the table. I sought for a handkerchief, but before I could produce it I was terrified by an unearthly howl which echoed through the vaulted hall.

The cry came from the lips of the Count, and in a moment he was bending over the blood on the table and licking it up with obvious relish. A more disgusting sight I have never witnessed, and, struggling to my feet, I made for the door.

But terror weakened my limbs, and the Count had overtaken me before I had covered many yards. His white hands grasped my arms and led me back to the chair I had vacated.

'My dear sir,' he said. 'I must beg you to excuse me for my discourtesy. The members of my family have always been peculiarly affected by the sight of blood. Call it an idiosyncrasy if you like, but it does at times make us behave like wild animals. I am grieved to have so far forgotten my manners as to behave in such a strange way before a guest. I assure you that I have sought to conquer this failing, and for that reason I keep away from my fellow-men.'

The explanation seemed plausible enough, but it filled me with horror and loathing—more especially as I could see a tiny globule of blood clinging to his mouth.

'I fear I am keeping Your Excellency from bed,' I suggested, 'and in any case I think it is time I got back to the inn.'

'Ah, no, my friend,' he replied. 'The night hours are the ones I enjoy best, and I shall be very grateful if you will remain with me until morning. The castle is a lonely place and your company will be a pleasant change. There is a room prepared for you in the south turret and to-morrow, who knows, there may be other guests to cheer us.'

A deadly fear gripped my heart and I staggered to my feet stammering, 'Let me go . . . Let me go. I must return to the village at once.'

'You cannot return to-night, for a storm is brewing and the cliff path will be unsafe.'

As he uttered these words he crossed to a window and, flinging it open, raised one arm towards the sky. As if in obedience to his gesture a flash of vivid lightning split the clouds, and a clap of thunder seemed to shake the castle. Then the rain came in a terrible deluge and a great wind howled across the mountains. The Count closed the casement and returned to the table.

'You see, my friend,' he chuckled, 'the very elements are against your return to the village. You must be satisfied with such poor hospitality as we can offer you for to-night at any rate.'

The red-rimmed eyes met mine, and again I felt my will being sapped from my body. His voice was no more than a whisper and seemed to come from far away.

'Follow me, and I will conduct you to your room. You are my guest for to-night.'

He took a candle from the table and, like a man in a trance, I followed him up a winding staircase, along an empty corridor, and into a cheerless room furnished with an ancient four-poster.

'Sleep well,' he said with a wicked leer. 'To-morrow night you shall have other company.'

The heavy door slammed behind him as he left me alone, and I heard a bolt being shot on the other side. Summoning what little strength was left in my body I hurled myself against the door. It was securely fastened and I was a prisoner. Through the keyhole came the Count's purring voice.

'Yes, you shall have other company to-morrow night. The Lords of Kaldenstein shall give you a hearty welcome to their ancestral home.'

A burst of mocking laughter died away in the distance as I fell to the floor in a dead faint.

IV

I must have recovered somewhat after a time and dragged myself to the bed and again sunk into unconsciousness, for when I came round daylight was streaming through the barred window of the room. I looked at my wrist watch. It was half-past three and, by the sun, it was afternoon, so the greater part of the day had passed.

I still felt weak, but struggled over to the window. It looked out upon the craggy slopes of the mountain and there was no human habitation in sight. With a moan I returned to the bed and tried to pray. I watched the patch of sunlight on the floor grow fainter and fainter until it had faded altogether. Then the shadows gathered and at last only the dim outline of the window remained.

The darkness filled my soul with a new terror and I lay on the bed in a cold, clammy sweat. Then I heard footsteps approaching, the door was flung open, and the Count entered bearing a candle.

'You must pardon me for what may seem shocking lack of manners on my part,' he exclaimed, 'but necessity compels me to keep to my chamber during the day. Now, however, I am able to offer you some entertainment.'

I tried to rise, but my limbs refused to function. With a mirthless laugh he placed one arm about my waist and lifted me with as little effort as if I were a baby. In this fashion he carried me across the corridor and down the stairs into the hall.

Only three candles burned on the table, and I could see little of the room for some moments after he had dumped me into a chair. Then, as my eyes became accustomed to the gloom, I realised that there were two other guests at that board. The feeble light flickered on their faces and I almost screamed with terror. I looked upon the ghastly countenances of dead men, every feature stamped with evil, and their eyes glowed with the same hellish light that shone in the Count's eyes.

'Allow me to introduce my uncle and my cousin,' said my gaoler. 'August von Kaldenstein and Feodor von Kaldenstein.'

'But,' I blurted out, 'I was told that Count Feodor died in 1645.'

The three terrible creatures laughed heartily as if I had recounted a good joke. Then August leaned over the table and pinched the fleshy part of my arm.

'He is full of good blood,' he chuckled. 'This feast has been long promised, Ludwig, but I think it has been worth waiting for.'

I must have fainted at that, and when I came to myself I was lying on the table and the three were bending over me. Their voices came in sibilant whispers.

'The throat must be mine,' said the Count. 'I claim the throat as my privilege.'

'It should be mine,' muttered August. 'I am the eldest and it is long since I fed. Yet I am content to have the breast.'

'The legs are mine,' croaked the third monster. 'Legs are always full of rich red blood.'

Their lips were drawn back like the lips of animals, and their white fangs gleamed in the candle-light. Suddenly a clanging sound disturbed the silence of the night. It was the castle bell. The creatures darted to the back of the dais and I could hear them muttering. Then the bell gave a more persistent peal.

'We are powerless against it,' the Count cried. 'Back to your retreat.'

His two companions vanished through the small door which led to the underground chapel, and the Count of Kaldenstein stood alone in the centre of the room. I raised myself into a sitting posture and, as I did so, I heard a strong voice calling beyond the main door.

'Open in the Name of God,' it thundered. 'Open by the power of the ever Blessed Sacrament of the altar.'

As if drawn by some overwhelming force the Count approached the door and loosened the bolts. It was immediately flung open and there stood the tall figure of the parish priest, bearing aloft something in a silver box like a watch. With him was the inn-keeper, and I could see the poor fellow was terrified. The two advanced into the hall, and the Count retreated before them.

'Thrice in ten years have I frustrated you by the power of God,' cried the priest. 'Thrice has the Holy Sacrament been carried into this house of sin. Be warned in time, accursed man. Back to your foul tomb, creature of Satan. Back, I command you.'

With a strange whimpering cry the Count vanished through the small door, and the priest came over and assisted me from the table. The inn-keeper produced a flask and forced some brandy between my lips, and I made an effort to stand.

'Foolish boy,' said the priest. 'You would not take my warning and see what your folly has brought you to.'

They helped me out of the castle and down the steps, but I collapsed before we reached the inn. I have a vague recollection of being helped into bed, and remember nothing more until I awakened in the morning.

The priest and the inn-keeper were awaiting me in the dining-room and we breakfasted together.

'What is the meaning of it all, Father?' I asked after the meal had been served.

'It is exactly as I told you,' was the reply. 'The Count of Kaldenstein is a vampire—he keeps the semblance of life in his evil body by drinking human blood. Eight years ago a headstrong youth, like yourself, determined to visit the castle. He did not return within reasonable time, and I had to save him from the clutches of the monster. Only by carrying with me the Body of Christ was I able to effect an entrance, and I was just in time. Then, two years later, a woman who professed to believe in neither God nor the Devil made up her mind to see the Count. Again I was forced to bear the Blessed Sacrament into the castle, and, by its power, overcame the forces of Satan. Two days since I watched you climb the cliff and saw, with relief, that you returned safely. But yesterday morning Heinrich came to inform me that your bed had not been slept in, and he was afraid the Count had got you. We waited until nightfall and then made our way up to the castle. The rest you know.'

'I can never thank you both sufficiently for the manner in which you saved me from those creatures,' I said.

'Creatures,' repeated the priest in a surprised voice. 'Surely there is only the Count? The servant does not share his master's blood-lust.'

'No, I did not see the servant after he had admitted me. But there were two others—August and Feodor.'

'August and Feodor,' he murmured. 'Then it is worse than we have ever dreamed. August died in 1572, and Feodor in 1645. Both were monsters of iniquity, but I did not suspect they were numbered among the living dead.'

'Father,' quavered the inn-keeper. 'We are not safe in our beds. Can we not call upon the government to rid us of these vampires?'

'The government would laugh at us,' was the reply. 'We must take the law into our own hands.'

'What is to be done?' I asked.

'I wonder if you have the courage to see this ghastly business through, and to witness a sight that will seem incredible?'

I assured him I was willing to do anything to help for I considered I owed my life to him.

'Then,' he said, 'I will return to the church for a few things and we will go up to the castle. Will you come with us, Heinrich?'

The inn-keeper hesitated just a moment, but it was evident that he had the greatest confidence in the priest, and he answered, 'Of course I will, Father.'

It was almost midday when we set off on our mysterious mission. The castle door stood wide open exactly as we had left it on the previous night, and the hall was deserted. We soon discovered the door under the tapestry and the priest, with a powerful electric torch in his hand, led the way down the damp steps. At the chapel door he paused and from his robes drew three crucifixes and a vessel of holy water. To each of us he handed one of the crosses, and sprinkled the door with the water. Then he opened it and we entered the cavern.

With hardly a glance at the altar and its gruesome painting he made his way to the entrance of the vault. It was locked, but he burst the catch with a powerful kick. A wave of fetid air leapt out at us and we staggered back. Then, lifting his crucifix before him and crying, 'In the Name of the Father, the Son, and the Holy Ghost,' the priest led us into the tomb. I do not know what I expected to see, but I gave a gasp of horror as the light revealed the interior of the place. In the centre, resting on a wooden bier, was the sleeping body of the Count of Kaldenstein. His red lips were parted in a smile, and his wicked eyes were half open.

Around the vault niches contained coffins, and the priest examined each in turn. Then he directed us to lift two of them to the floor. I noticed that one bore the name of August von Kaldenstein and the other that of Feodor. It took all our united strength to move the caskets, but at last we had them down. And all the time the eyes of the Count seemed to be watching us although he never moved.

'Now,' whispered the priest, 'the most ghastly part of the business begins.'

Producing a large screw-driver he began to prise off the lid of the first coffin. Soon it was loose and he motioned us to raise it. Inside was Count August looking exactly as I had seen him the previous night. His red-rimmed eyes were wide open and gleamed wickedly, but the stench of corruption hung about him. The priest set to work on the second casket, and soon revealed the body of Count Feodor with his matted hair hanging about his white face.

Then began a strange ceremony. Taking the crucifixes from us the priest laid them upon the breasts of the two bodies, and, producing his Breviary, recited some Latin prayers. Finally he stood back and flung holy water into the coffins. As the drops touched the leering corpses they appeared to writhe in agony, to swell as though they were about to burst, and then, before our eyes, they crumbled into dust. Silently we replaced the lids on the coffins and restored them to their niches.

'And now,' said the priest, 'we are powerless. Ludwig von Kaldenstein by evil arts has conquered death—for the time being at any rate, and we cannot treat him as we have treated these creatures whose vitality was only a semblance of life. We can but pray that God will curb the activities of this monster of sin.'

So saying he laid the third cross upon the Count's breast and sprinkling him with holy water uttered a Latin prayer. With that we left the vault but, as the door clanged behind us, something fell to the ground inside the place. It must have been the crucifix falling from the Count's breast.

We made our way up into the castle and never did God's good air taste sweeter. All this time we had seen no sign of the old servant and I suggested we should try to discover him. His quarters, I remembered, were in the north turret. There we found his crooked old body hanging by the neck from a beam in the roof. He had been dead for at least twenty-four hours, and the priest said that nothing could be done other than to notify his death to the proper quarter and arrange for the funeral to take place.

I am still puzzled about the mystery of Kaldenstein Castle. The fact that Count August and Count Feodor had become vampires after death, although it sounds fantastic enough, is more easily understandable than Count Ludwig's seeming immunity from death. The priest could not explain the matter and appeared to think that the Count might go on living and troubling the neighbourhood for an indefinite period.

One thing I do know. On that last night at Kaldenstein I opened my window before retiring to bed and looked out upon the castle. At the top of one of the turrets, clear in the bright moonlight, stood a black figure—the shadowy form of the Count of Kaldenstein.

Little more remains to be told. Of course my stay in the village threw all my plans out, and by the time I arrived back at Munich my tour had taken nearly twenty days. Peter Schmidt laughed at me and wondered what blue-eyed maiden had caused me to linger in some Bavarian village. I didn't tell him that the real causes of the delay had been two dead men, and a third who by all natural laws should have been dead long ago.

EUDORA WELTY

Clytie

It was late afternoon, with heavy silver clouds which looked bigger and wider than cotton fields, and presently it began to rain. Big round drops fell, still in the sunlight, on the hot tin sheds, and stained the white false fronts of the row of stores in the little town of Farr's Gin. A hen and her string of yellow chickens ran in great alarm across the road, the dust turned river-brown, and the birds flew down into it immediately, sitting out little pockets in which to take baths. The bird dogs got up from the doorways of the stores, shook themselves down to the tail, and went to lie inside. The few people standing with long shadows on the level road moved over into the post office. A little boy kicked his bare heels into the sides of his mule, which proceeded slowly through the town toward the country.

After everyone else had gone under cover, Miss Clytie Farr stood still in the road, peering ahead in her near-sighted way, and as wet as the little birds.

She usually came out of the old big house about this time in the afternoon, and hurried through the town. It used to be that she ran about on some pretext or other, and for a while she made soft-voiced explanations that nobody could hear, and after that she began to charge up bills, which the postmistress declared would never be paid any more than anyone else's, even if the Farrs were too good to associate with other people. But now Clytie came for nothing. She came every day, and no one spoke to her any more: she would be in such a hurry, and couldn't see who it was. And every Saturday they expected her to be run over, the way she darted out into the road with all the horses and trucks.

It might be simply that Miss Clytie's wits were all leaving her, said the ladies standing in the door to feel the cool, the way her sister's had left her; and she would just wait there to be told to go home. She would have to wring out everything she had on—the waist and the jumper skirt, and the long black stockings. On her head was one of the straw hats from the furnishing store, with an old black satin ribbon pinned to it to make it a better hat, and tied under the chin. Now, under the force of the rain, while the ladies watched, the hat slowly began to sag down on each side until it looked even more absurd and done for, like an old bonnet on a horse. And indeed it was with the patience almost of a beast that Miss Clytie stood there in the rain and stuck her long empty arms out a little from her sides, as if she were waiting for something to come along the road and drive her to shelter.

In a little while there was a clap of thunder.

'Miss Clytie! Go in out of the rain, Miss Clytie!' someone called.

The old maid did not look around, but clenched her hands and drew them up under her armpits, and sticking out her elbows like hen wings, she ran out of the street, her poor hat creaking and beating about her ears.

'Well, there goes Miss Clytie,' the ladies said, and one of them had a premonition about her.

Through the rushing water in the sunken path under the four wet black cedars, which smelled bitter as smoke, she ran to the house.

'Where the devil have you been?' called the older sister, Octavia, from an upper window.

Clytie looked up in time to see the curtain fall back.

She went inside, into the hall, and waited, shivering. It was very dark and bare. The only light was falling on the white sheet which covered the solitary piece of furniture, an organ. The red curtains over the parlor door, held back by ivory hands, were still as tree trunks in the airless house. Every window was closed, and every shade was down, though behind them the rain could still be heard.

Clytie took a match and advanced to the stair post, where the bronze cast of Hermes was holding up a gas fixture; and at once above this, lighted up, but quite still, like one of the unmovable relics of the house, Octavia stood waiting on the stairs.

She stood solidly before the violet-and-lemon-colored glass of the window on the landing, and her wrinkled, unresting fingers took hold of the diamond cornucopia she always wore in the bosom of her long black dress. It was an unwithered grand gesture of hers, fondling the cornucopia.

'It is not enough that we are waiting here—hungry,' Octavia was saying, while Clytie waited below. 'But you must sneak away and not answer when I call you. Go off and wander about the streets. Common—common—!'

'Never mind, Sister,' Clytie managed to say.

'But you alway return.'

'Of course . . .'

'Gerald is awake now, and so is Papa,' said Octavia, in the same vindictive voice—a loud voice, for she was usually calling.

Clytie went to the kitchen and lighted the kindling in the wood stove. As if she were freezing cold in June, she stood before its open door, and soon a look of interest and pleasure lighted her face, which had in the last years grown weather-beaten in spite of the straw hat. Now some dream was resumed. In the street she had been thinking about the face of a child she had just seen. The child, playing with another of the same age, chasing it with a toy pistol, had looked at her with such an open, serene, trusting expression as she passed by! With this small, peaceful face still in her mind, rosy like these flames, like an inspiration which drives all other thoughts away, Clytie had forgotten herself and had been obliged to stand where she was in the middle of the road. But the rain had come down, and someone had shouted at her, and she had not been able to reach the end of her meditations.

It had been a long time now, since Clytie had first begun to watch faces, and to think about them.

Anyone could have told you that there were not more than 150 people in Farr's Gin, 'counting Negroes'. Yet the number of faces seemed to Clytie almost infinite. She knew now to look slowly and carefully at a face; she was convinced that it was impossible to see it all at once. The first thing she discovered about a face was always that she had never seen it before. When she began to look at people's actual countenances there was no more familiarity in the world for her. The most profound, the most moving sight in the whole world must be a face. Was it possible to comprehend the eyes and the mouths of other people, which concealed she knew not what, and secretly asked for still another unknown thing? The mysterious smile of the old man who sold peanuts by the church gate returned to her; his face seemed for a moment to rest upon the iron door of the stove, set into the lion's mane. Other people said Mr Tom Bate's Boy, as he called himself, stared away with a face as clean-blank as a watermelon seed, but to Clytie, who observed grains of sand in his eyes and in his old yellow lashes, he might have come out of a desert, like an Egyptian.

But while she was thinking of Mr Tom Bate's Boy, there was a terrible gust of wind which struck her back, and she turned around. The long green window shade billowed and plunged. The kitchen window was wide open—she had done it herself. She closed it gently. Octavia, who never came all the way downstairs for any reason, would never have forgiven her for an open window, if she knew. Rain and sun signified ruin, in Octavia's mind. Going over the whole house, Clytie made sure that everything was safe. It was not that ruin in itself could distress Octavia. Ruin or encroachment, even upon priceless treasures and even in poverty, held no terror for her; it was simply some form of prying from without, and this she would not forgive. All of that was to be seen in her face.

Clytie cooked the three meals on the stove, for they all ate different things, and set the three trays. She had to carry them in proper order up the stairs. She frowned in concentration, for it was hard to keep all the dishes straight, to make them come out right in the end, as Old Lethy could have done. They had had to give up the cook long ago when their father suffered the first stroke. Their father had been fond of Old Lethy, she had been his nurse in childhood, and she had come back out of the country to see him when she heard he was dying. Old Lethy had come and knocked at the back door. And as usual, at the first disturbance, front or back, Octavia had peered down from behind the curtain and cried, 'Go away! Go away! What the devil have you come *here* for?' And although Old Lethy and their father had both pleaded that they might be allowed to see each other, Octavia had shouted as she always did, and sent the intruder away. Clytie had stood as usual, speechless in the kitchen, until finally she had repeated after her sister, 'Lethy, go away.' But their father had not died. He was, instead, paralyzed, blind, and able only to call out in unintelligible sounds and to swallow liquids. Lethy still would come to the back door now and then, but they never let her in, and the old man no longer heard or knew enough to beg to see her. There was only one caller admitted to his room. Once a week the barber came by appointment to shave him. On this occasion not a word was spoken by anyone.

Clytie went up to her father's room first and set the tray down on a little marble table they kept by his bed.

'I want to feed Papa,' said Octavia, taking the bowl from her hands.

'You fed him last time,' said Clytie.

Relinquishing the bowl, she looked down at the pointed face on the pillow. Tomorrow was the barber's day, and the sharp black points, at their longest, stuck out like needles all over the wasted cheeks. The old man's eyes were half closed. It was impossible to know what he felt. He looked as though he were really far away, neglected, free. . . . Octavia began to feed him.

Without taking her eyes from her father's face, Clytie suddenly began to speak in rapid, bitter words to her sister, the wildest words that came to her head. But soon she began to cry and gasp, like a small child who has been pushed by the big boys into the water.

'That is enough,' said Octavia.

But Clytie could not take her eyes from her father's unshaven face and his still-open mouth.

'And I'll feed him tomorrow if I want to,' said Octavia. She stood up. The thick hair, growing back after an illness and dyed almost purple, fell over her forehead. Beginning at her throat, the long accordion pleats which fell the length of her gown opened and closed over her breasts as she breathed. 'Have you forgotten Gerald?' she said. 'And I am hungry too.'

Clytie went back to the kitchen and brought her sister's supper.

Then she brought her brother's.

 Gerald's room was dark, and she had to push through the usual barricade. The smell of whisky was everywhere; it even flew up in the striking of the match when she lighted the jet.

'It's night,' said Clytie presently.

Gerald lay on his bed looking at her. In the bad light he resembled his father.

'There's some more coffee down in the kitchen,' said Clytie.

'Would you bring it to me?' Gerald asked. He stared at her in an exhausted, serious way.

She stooped and held him up. He drank the coffee while she bent over him with her eyes closed, resting.

Presently he pushed her away and fell back on the bed, and began to describe how nice it was when he had a little house of his own down the street, all new, with all conveniences, gas stove, electric lights, when he was married to Rosemary. Rosemary—she had given up a job in the next town, just to marry him. How had it happened that she had left him so soon? It meant nothing that he had threatened time and again to shoot her, it was nothing at all that he had pointed the gun against her breast. She had not understood. It was only that he had relished his contentment. He had only wanted to play with her. In a way he had wanted to show her that he loved her above life and death.

'Above life and death,' he repeated, closing his eyes.

Clytie did not make an answer, as Octavia always did during these scenes, which were bound to end in Gerald's tears.

Outside the closed window a mockingbird began to sing. Clytie held back the curtain and pressed her ear against the glass. The rain had stopped. The bird's song sounded in liquid drops down through the pitch-black trees and the night.

'Go to hell,' Gerald said. His head was under the pillow.

She took up the tray, and left Gerald with his face hidden. It was not necessary for her to look at any of their faces. It was their faces which came between.

Hurrying, she went down to the kitchen and began to eat her own supper.

Their faces came between her face and another. It was their faces which had come pushing in between, long ago, to hide some face that had looked back at her. And now it was hard to remember the way it looked, or the time when she had seen it first. It must have been when she was young. Yes, in a sort of arbor, hadn't she laughed, leaned forward . . . and that vision of a face—which was a little like all the other faces, the trusting child's, the innocent old traveler's, even the greedy barber's and Lethy's and the wandering peddlers' who one by one knocked and went unanswered at the door—and yet different, yet far more—this face had been very close to hers, almost familiar, almost accessible. And then the face of Octavia was thrust between, and at other times the apoplectic face of her father, the face of her brother Gerald and the face of her brother Henry with the bullet hole through the forehead. . . . It was purely for a resemblance to a vision that she examined the secret, mysterious, unrepeated faces she met in the street of Farr's Gin.

But there was always an interruption. If anyone spoke to her, she fled. If she saw she was going to meet someone on the street, she had been known to dart behind a bush and hold a small branch in front of her face until the person had gone by. When anyone called her by name, she turned first red, then white, and looked somehow, as one of the ladies in the store remarked, *disappointed*.

She was becoming more frightened all the time, too. People could tell because she never dressed up any more. For years, every once in a while, she would come out in what was called an 'outfit', all in hunter's green, a hat that came down around her face like a bucket, a green silk dress, even green shoes with pointed toes. She would wear the outfit all one day, if it was a pretty day, and then next morning she would be back in the faded jumper with her old hat tied under the chin, as if the outfit had been a dream. It had been a long time now since Clytie had dressed up so that you could see her coming.

Once in a while when a neighbor, trying to be kind or only being curious, would ask her opinion about anything—such as a pattern of crochet—she would not run away; but, giving a thin trapped smile, she would say in a childish voice, 'It's nice.' But, the ladies always added, nothing that came anywhere close to the Farrs' house was nice for long.

'It's nice,' said Clytie when the old lady next door showed her the new rosebush she had planted, all in bloom.

But before an hour was gone, she came running out of her house screaming, 'My sister Octavia says you take that rosebush up! My sister Octavia says you take the rosebush up and move it away from our fence! If you don't I'll kill you! You take it away.'

And on the other side of the Farrs lived a family with a little boy who was always playing in his yard. Octavia's cat would go under the fence, and he would take it and hold it in his arms. He had a song he sang to the Farrs' cat. Clytie would come running straight out of the house, flaming with her message from Octavia. 'Don't you do that! Don't you do that!' She would cry in anguish. 'If you do that again, I'll have to kill you!'

And she would run back to the vegetable patch and begin to curse. The cursing was new, and she cursed softly, like a singer going over a song for the first time. But it was something she could not stop. Words which at first horrified Clytie poured in a full, light stream from her throat, which soon, nevertheless, felt strangely relaxed and rested. She cursed all alone in the peace of the vegetable garden. Everybody said, in something like deprecation, that she was only imitating her older sister, who used to go out to that same garden and curse in that same way, years ago, but in a remarkably loud, commanding voice that could be heard in the post office.

Sometimes in the middle of her words Clytie glanced up to where Octavia, at her window, looked down at her. When she let the curtain drop at last, Clytie would be left there speechless.

Finally, in a gentleness compounded of fright and exhaustion and love, an overwhelming love, she would wander through the gate and out through the town, gradually beginning to move faster, until her long legs gathered a ridiculous, rushing speed. No one in town could have kept up with Miss Clytie, they said, giving them an even start.

She always ate rapidly, too, all alone in the kitchen, as she was eating now. She bit the meat savagely from the heavy silver fork and gnawed the little chicken bone until it was naked and clean.

Halfway upstairs, she remembered Gerald's second pot of coffee, and went back for it. After she had carried the other trays down again and washed the dishes, she did not forget to try all the doors and windows to make sure that everything was locked up absolutely tight.

The next morning, Clytie bit into smiling lips as she cooked breakfast. Far out past the secretly opened window a freight train was crossing the bridge in the sunlight. Some Negroes filed down the road going fishing, and Mr Tom Bate's Boy, who was going along, turned and looked at her through the window.

Gerald had appeared dressed and wearing his spectacles, and announced that he was going to the store today. The old Farr furnishing store did little business now, and people hardly missed Gerald when he did not come; in fact, they could hardly tell when he did because of the big boots strung on a wire, which almost hid the cagelike office. A little high-school girl could wait on anybody who came in.

Now Gerald entered the dining room.

'How are you this morning, Clytie?' he asked.

'Just fine, Gerald, how are you?'

'I'm going to the store,' he said.

He sat down stiffly, and she laid a place on the table before him.

From above, Octavia screamed, 'Where in the devil is my thimble, you stole my thimble, Clytie Farr, you carried it away, my little silver thimble!'

'It's started,' said Gerald intensely. Clytie saw his fine, thin, almost black lips spread in a crooked line. 'How can a man live in the house with women? How can he?'

He jumped up, and tore his napkin exactly in two. He walked out of the dining room without eating the first bite of his breakfast. She heard him going back upstairs into his room.

'My thimble!' screamed Octavia.

She waited one moment. Crouching eagerly, rather like a little squirrel, Clytie ate part of her breakfast over the stove before going up the stairs.

At nine Mr Bobo, the barber, knocked at the front door.

Without waiting, for they never answered the knock, he let himself in and advanced like a small general down the hall. There was the old organ that was never uncovered or played except for funerals, and then nobody was invited. He went ahead, under the arm of the tiptoed male statue and up the dark stairway. There they were, lined up at the head of the stairs, and they all looked at him with repulsion. My Bobo was convinced that they were every one mad. Gerald, even, had already been drinking, at nine o'clock in the morning.

Mr Bobo was short and had never been anything but proud of it, until he had started coming to this house once a week. But he did not enjoy looking up from below at the soft, long throats, the cold, repelled, high-reliefed faces of those Farrs. He could only imagine what one of those sisters would do to him if he made one move. (As if he would!) As soon as he arrived upstairs, they all went off and left him. He pushed out his chin and stood with his round legs wide apart, just looking around. The upstairs hall was absolutely bare. There was not even a chair to sit down in.

'Either they sell away their furniture in the dead of night,' said Mr Bobo to the people of Farr's Gin, 'or else they're just too plumb mean to use it.'

Mr Bobo stood and waited to be summoned, and wished he had never started coming to this house to shave old Mr Farr. But he had been so surprised to get a letter in the mail. The letter was on such old, yellowed paper that at first he thought it must have been written a thousand years ago and never delivered. It was signed 'Octavia Farr', and began without even calling him 'Dear Mr Bobo.' What it said was: 'Come to this residence at nine o'clock each Friday morning until further notice, where you will shave Mr James Farr.'

He thought he would go one time. And each time after that, he thought he would never go back—especially when he never knew when they would pay him anything. Of course, it was something to be the only person in Farr's Gin allowed inside the house (except for the undertaker, who had gone there when young Henry shot himself, but had never to that day spoken of it). It was not easy to shave a man as bad off as Mr Farr, either—not anything like as easy as to shave a corpse or even a fighting-drunk field hand. Suppose you were like this, Mr Bobo would say: you couldn't move your face; you couldn't hold up your chin, or tighten your jaw, or even bat your eyes when the razor came close. The trouble with Mr Farr was his face made no resistance to the razor. His face didn't hold.

'I'll never go back,' Mr Bobo always ended to his customers. 'Not even if they paid me. I've seen enough.'

Yet here he was again, waiting before the sickroom door.

'This is the last time,' he said. 'By God!'

And he wondered why the old man did not die.

Just then Miss Clytie came out of the room. There she came in her funny, sideways walk, and the closer she got to him the more slowly she moved.

'Now?' asked Mr Bobo nervously.

Clytie looked at his small, doubtful face. What fear raced through his little green eyes! His pitiful, greedy, small face—how very mournful it was, like a stray kitten's. What was it that this greedy little thing was so desperately needing?

Clytie came up to the barber and stopped. Instead of telling him that he might go in and shave her father, she put out her hand and with breathtaking gentleness touched the side of his face.

For an instant afterward, she stood looking at him inquiringly, and he stood like a statue, like the statue of Hermes.

Then both of them uttered a despairing cry. Mr Bobo turned and fled, waving his razor around in a circle, down the stairs and out the front door; and Clytie, pale as a ghost, stumbled against the railing. The terrible scent of bay rum, of hair tonic, the horrible moist scratch of an invisible beard, the dense, popping green eyes—what had she got hold of with her hand! She could hardly bear it—the thought of that face.

From the closed door to the sickroom came Octavia's shouting voice.

'Clytie! Clytie! You haven't brought Papa the rain water! Where in the devil is the rain water to shave Papa?'

Clytie moved obediently down the stairs.

Her brother Gerald threw open the door of his room and called after her, 'What now? This is a madhouse! Somebody was running past my room, I heard it. Where do you keep your men? Do you have to bring them home?' He slammed the door again, and she heard the barricade going up.

Clytie went through the lower hall and out the back door. She stood beside the old rain barrel and suddenly felt that this object, now, was her friend, just in time, and her arms almost circled it with impatient gratitude. The rain barrel was full. It bore a dark, heavy, penetrating fragrance, like ice and flowers and the dew of night.

Clytie swayed a little and looked into the slightly moving water. She thought she saw a face there.

Of course. It was the face she had been looking for, and from which she had been separated. As if to give a sign, the index finger of a hand lifted to touch the dark cheek.

Clytie leaned closer, as she had leaned down to touch the face of the barber.

It was a wavering, inscrutable face. The brows were drawn together as if in pain. The eyes were large, intent, almost avid, the nose ugly and discolored as if from weeping, the mouth old and closed from any speech. On either side of the head dark hair hung down in a disreputable and wild fashion. Everything about the face frightened and shocked her with its signs of waiting, of suffering.

For the second time that morning, Clytie recoiled, and as she did so, the other recoiled in the same way.

Too late, she recognized the face. She stood there completely sick

433

at heart, as though the poor, half-remembered vision had finally betrayed her.

'Clytie! Clytie! The water! The water!' came Octavia's monumental voice.

Clytie did the only thing she could think of to do. She bent her angular body further, and thrust her head into the barrel, under the water, through its glittering surface into the kind, featureless depth, and held it there.

When Old Lethy found her, she had fallen forward into the barrel, with her poor ladylike black-stockinged legs up-ended and hung apart like a pair of tongs.

RAY RUSSELL

Sardonicus *(1960)*

𝕴n the late summer of the year 18—, a gratifying series of professional successes had brought me to a state of such fatigue that I had begun seriously to contemplate a long rest on the Continent. I had not enjoyed a proper holiday in nearly three years, for, in addition to my regular practice, I had been deeply involved in a program of research, and so rewarding had been my progress in this special work (it concerned the ligaments and muscles, and could, it was my hope, be beneficially applied to certain varieties of paralysis) that I was loath to leave the city for more than a week at a time. Being unmarried, I lacked a solicitous wife who might have expressed concern over my health; thus it was that I had overworked myself to a point that a holiday had beome absolutely essential to my well-being; hence, the letter which was put in my hand one morning near the end of that summer was most welcome.

When it was first presented to me by my valet, at breakfast, I turned it over and over, feeling the weight of its fine paper which was almost of the heaviness and stiffness of parchment; pondering the large seal of scarlet wax upon which was imprinted a device of such complexity that it was difficult to decipher; examining finally the hand in which the address had been written: *Sir Robert Cargrave, Harley Street, London*. It was a feminine hand, that much was certain, and there was a curious touch of familiarity to its delicacy as well as to its clearness (this last an admirable quality far too uncommon in the handwriting of ladies). The fresh clarity of that hand—and where had I seen it before?—bespoke a directness that seemed contrary to the well-nigh unfathomable ornamentation of the seal, which, upon closer and more concentrated perusal, I at length concluded to be no more than a single 'S', but an 'S' whose writhing curls seemed almost to grin presumptuously at one, an 'S' which seemed to be constructed of little else than these grins, an 'S' of such vulgar pretension that I admit to having felt vexed for an instant, and then, in the next instant, foolish at my own vexation—for surely, I admonished myself, there are things a deal more vexing than a seal which you have encountered without distemper?

435

Smiling at my foible, I continued to weigh the letter in my hand, searching my mind for a friend or acquaintance whose name began with 'S'. There was old Shipley of the College of Surgeons; there was Lord Henry Stanton, my waggish and witty friend; and that was the extent of it. Was it Harry? He was seldom in one place for very long and was a faithful and gifted letterwriter. Yet Harry's bold hand was far from effeminate, and, moreover, he would not use such a seal—unless it were as a lark, as an antic jest between friends. My valet had told me, when he put the letter in my hand, that it had come not by the post but by special messenger, and although this intelligence had not struck me as remarkable at the time, it now fed my curiosity and I broke that vexing seal and unfolded the stiff, crackling paper.

The message within was written in that same clear, faintly familiar hand. My eye first traveled to the end to find the signature, but that signature—*Madam S.*—told me nothing, for I knew of no Madam S. among my circle.

I read the letter. It is before me now as I set down this account, and I shall copy it out verbatim:

My dear Sir Robert,

It has been close to seven years since last we met—indeed, at that time you were not yet Sir Robert at all, but plain Robert Cargrave (although some talk of imminent knighthood was in the air), and so I wonder if you will remember Maude Randall?

Remember Maude Randall! Dear Maude of the bell-like voice, of the chestnut hair and large brown eyes, of a temperament of such sweetness and vivacity that the young men of London had eyes for no one else. She was of good family, but during a stay in Paris there had been something about injudicious speculation by her father that had diminished the family fortunes to such an extent that the wretched man had taken his own life and the Randalls had vanished from London society altogether. Maude, or so I had heard, had married a foreign gentleman and had remained in Europe. It had been sad news, for no young man of London had ever had more doting eyes for Maude than had I, and it had pleased my fancy to think that my feelings were, at least in part, reciprocated. Remember Maude Randall? Yes, yes, I almost said aloud. And now, seven years later, she was 'Madam S.', writing in that same hand I had seen countless times on invitations. I continued to read:

I often think of you, for—although it may not be seemly to say it—the company of few gentlemen used to please me so much as yours, and the

London soirées given by my dear mother, at which you were present, are among my most cherished recollections now. But there! Frankness was always my failing, as Mother used to remind me. She, dear kind lady, survived less than a year after my poor father died, but I suppose you know this.

I am quite well, and we live in great comfort here, although we receive but rarely and are content with our own company most of the time. Mr S. is a gracious gentleman, but of quiet and retiring disposition, and throngs of people, parties, balls, etc., are retrograde to his temperament; thus it is a special joy to me that he has expressly asked me to invite you here to the castle for a fortnight—or, if I may give you his exact words: 'For a fortnight at least, but howsoever long as it please Sir Robert to stay among such drab folk as he will think us.' (You see, I told you he was gracious!)

I must have frowned while reading, for the words of Mr S. were not so much gracious, I thought, as egregious, and as vulgar as his absurd seal. Still, I held these feelings in check, for I knew that my emotions toward this man were not a little coloured by jealousy. He, after all, had wooed and won Maude Randall, a young lady of discernment and fine sensibilities: Could she have been capable of wedding an obsequious boor? I thought it not likely. And a castle! Such romantic grandeur! ... Invite you here to the castle ...' she had written, but where was 'here'? The letter's cover, since it had not come by the post, offered no clue; therefore I read on:

It was, indeed, only yesterday, in the course of conversation, that I was recalling my old life in London, and mentioned your name. Mr S., I thought, was, of a sudden, interested. 'Robert Cargrave?' he said. 'There is a well-known physician of that name, but I do not imagine it is the same gentleman.' I laughed and told him it *was* the same gentleman, and that I had known you before you had become so illustrious. 'Did you know him well?' Mr S. then asked me, and you will think me silly, but I must tell you that for a moment I assumed him to be jealous! Such was not the case, however, as further conversation proved. I told him you had been a friend of my family's and a frequent guest at our house. 'This is a most happy coincidence,' he said. 'I have long desired to meet Sir Robert Cargrave, and your past friendship with him furnishes you with an excellent opportunity to invite him here for a holiday.'

And so, Sir Robert, I am complying with his request—and at the same time obeying the dictates of my own inclination—by most cordially inviting you to visit us for as long as you choose. I entreat you to come, for we see so few people here and it would be a great pleasure to talk with someone from the old days and to hear the latest London gossip. Suffer me, then, to receive a letter from you at once. Mr S. does not trust the post, hence I have sent this by a servant of ours who was to be in London on special business; please relay your answer by way of him——

I rang for my man. 'Is the messenger who delivered this letter waiting for a reply?' I asked.

'He is sitting in the vestibule, Sir Robert,' he said.

'You should have told me.'

'Yes, sir.'

'At any rate, send him in now. I wish to see him.'

My man left, and it took me but a minute to dash off a quick note of acceptance. It was ready for the messenger when he was ushered into the room. I addressed him: 'You are in the employ of Madam——' I realized for the first time that I did not know her husband's name.

The servant—a taciturn fellow with Slavic features—spoke in a thick accent: 'I am in the employ of Mr Sardonicus, sir.'

Sardonicus! A name as flamboyant as the seal, I thought to myself. 'Then deliver this note, if you please, to Madam Sardonicus, immediately you return.'

He bowed slightly and took the note from my hand. 'I shall deliver it to my master straightway, sir,' he said.

His manner nettled me. I corrected him. 'To your mistress,' I said coldly.

'Madam Sardonicus will receive your message, sir,' he said.

I dismissed him, and only then did it strike me that I had not the faintest idea where the castle of Mr Sardonicus was located. I referred once again to Maude's letter:

'. . . Please relay your answer by way of him and pray make it affirmative, for I do hope to make your stay in —— a pleasant one.'

I consulted an atlas. The locality she mentioned, I discovered, was a district in a remote and mountainous region of Bohemia.

Filled with anticipation, I finished my breakfast with renewed appetite, and that very afternoon began to make arrangements for my journey.

I am not—as my friend Harry Stanton is—fond of travel for its own sake. Harry has often chided me on this account, calling me a dry-as-dust academician and 'an incorrigible Londoner'—which I suppose I am. For, in point of fact, few things are more tiresome to me than ships and trains and carriages; and although I have found deep enjoyment and spiritual profit in foreign cities, having arrived, the tedium of travel itself has often made me think twice before starting out on a long voyage.

Still, in less than a month after I had answered Maude's invitation, I found myself in her adopted homeland. Sojourning from London to Paris, thence to Berlin, finally to Bohemia, I was met at ———— by a coachman who spoke imperfect English but who managed, in his solemn fashion, to make known to me that he was a member of the staff at Castle Sardonicus. He placed at my disposal a coach drawn by two horses, and, after taking my bags, proceeded to drive me on the last leg of my journey.

Alone in the coach, I shivered, for the air was brisk and I was very tired. The road was full of ruts and stones, and the trip was far from smooth. Neither did I derive much pleasure by bending my glance to the view afforded by the windows, for the night was dark, and the country was, at any rate, wild and raw, not made for serene contemplation. The only sounds were the clatter of hooves and wheels, the creak of the coach, and the harsh, unmusical cries of unseen birds.

'We receive but rarely,' Maude had written, and now I told myself—Little wonder! in this ragged and, one might say, uninhabitable place, far from the graces of civilized society, who indeed is there to *be* received, or, for the matter of that, to receive one? I sighed, for the desolate landscape and the thought of what might prove a holiday devoid of refreshing incident, had combined to cloak my already wearied spirit in a melancholic humour.

It was when I was in this condition that Castle Sardonicus met my eye—a dense, hunched outline at first, then, with an instantaneous flicker of moonlight, a great gaping death's head, the sight of which made me inhale sharply. With the exhalation, I chuckled at myself. 'Come, come, Sir Robert,' I inwardly chided, 'it is, after all, but a castle, and you are not a green girl who starts at shadows and quails at midnight stories!'

The castle is situated at the terminus of a long and upward-winding mountain road. It presents a somewhat forbidding aspect to the world, for there is little about it to suggest gaiety or warmth or any of those qualities that might assure the wayfarer of welcome. Rather, this vast edifice of stone exudes an austerity, cold and repellent, a hint of ancient mysteries long buried, an effluvium of medieval dankness and decay. At night, and most particularly on nights when the moon is slim or cloud-enshrouded, it is a heavy blot upon the horizon, a shadow only, without feature save for its many-turreted outline; and should the moon be temporarily released from her cloudy confinement, her fugitive rays lend scant comfort, for they but serve to throw the castle into sudden, startling chiaroscuro, its windows fleetingly assuming the appearance of sightless though all-seeing orbs, its portcullis becoming for an instant a gaping mouth, its entire form striking the physical and the mental eye as would the sight of a giant skull.

But, though the castle had revealed itself to my sight, it was a full quarter of an hour before the coach had creaked its way up the steep and tortuous road to the great gate that barred the castle grounds from intruders. Of iron the gate was wrought—black it seemed in the scant illumination—and composed of intricate twists that led, every one of them, to a central, huge device, of many curves, which in the infrequent glints of moonglow appeared to smile metallically down, but which, upon gathering my reason about me, I made out to be no more than an enlarged edition of that presumptuous seal: a massive single 'S'. Behind it, at the end of the rutted road, stood the castle itself—dark, save for lights in two of its many windows.

Some words in a foreign tongue passed between my coachman and a person behind the gate. The gate was unlocked from within and swung open slowly, with a long rising shriek of rusted hinges; and the coach passed through.

As we drew near, the door of the castle was flung open and cheery light spilled out upon the road. The portcullis, which I had previously marked, was evidently a remnant from older days and now inactive. The coach drew to a halt, and I was greeted with great gravity by a butler whom I saw to be he who had carried Maude's invitation to London. I proffered him a nod of recognition. He acknowledged this and said, 'Sir Robert, Madam Sardonicus awaits you, and if you will be good enough to follow me, I will take you to her presence.' The coachman took charge of my bags, and I followed the butler into the castle.

It dated, I thought, to the twelfth or thirteenth century. Suits of armour—priceless relics, I ascertained them to be—stood about the vast halls; tapestries were in evidence throughout; strong, heavy, richly carved furniture was everywhere. The walls were of time-defying stone, great grey blocks of it. I was led into a kind of salon, with comfortable chairs, a tea table, and a spinet. Maude rose to greet me.

'Sir Robert,' she said softly, without smiling. 'How good to see you at last.'

I took her hand. 'Dear lady,' said I, 'we meet again.'

'You are looking well and prosperous,' she said.

'I am in good health, but just now rather tired from the journey.'

She gave me leave to sit, and did so herself, venturing the opinion that a meal and some wine would soon restore me. 'Mr Sardonicus will join us soon,' she added.

I spoke of her appearance, saying that she looked not a day older than when I last saw her in London. This was true, in regard to her physical self, for her face bore not a line, her skin was of the same freshness, and her glorious chestnut hair was still rich in colour and gleaming with health. But what I did not speak of was the change in her spirit. She who had been so gay and vivacious, the delight of soirées, was now distant and aloof, of serious mien, unsmiling. I was sorry to see this, but attributed it to the seven years that had passed since her carefree girlhood, to the loss of her loved parents, and even to the secluded life she now spent in this place.

'I am eager to meet your husband,' I said.

'And he, Sir Robert, is quite eager to meet you,' Maude assured me. 'He will be down presently. Meanwhile, do tell me how you have fared in the world.'

I spoke, with some modesty, I hope, of my successes in my chosen field, of the knighthood I had received from the Crown; I described my London apartment, laboratory, and office; I made mention of certain mutual friends, and generally gave her news of London life, speaking particularly of the theatre (for I knew Maude had loved it) and describing Mr Macready's farewell appearance as Macbeth at The Haymarket. When Maude had last been in London, there had been rumours of making an opera house out of Covent Garden theatre, and I told her that those plans had been carried through. I spoke of the London premiere of Mr Verdi's latest piece at Her Majesty's. At my mention of these theatres and performances, her eyes lit up, but she was not moved to comment until I spoke of the opera.

'The opera!' she sighed. 'Oh, Sir Robert, if you could but know how I miss it. The excitement of a premiere, the ladies and gentlemen in their finery, the thrilling sounds of the overture, and then the curtain rising——' She broke off, as if ashamed of her momentary transport. 'But I receive all the latest scores, and derive great satisfaction from playing and singing them to myself. I must order the new Verdi from Rome. It is called *Ernani*, you say?'

I nodded, adding, 'With your permission, I will attempt to play some of the more distinctive airs.'

'Oh, pray do, Sir Robert!' she said.

'You will find them, perhaps, excessively modern and dissonant.' I sat down at the spinet and played—just passably, I fear, and with some improvization when I could not remember the exact notes—a potpourri of melodies from the opera.

She applauded my playing. I urged her to play also, for she was an accomplished keyboard artist and possessed an agreeable voice, as well. She complied by playing the minuet from *Don Giovanni* and then singing the *Voi che sapete* from *Le Nozze di Figaro*. As I stood over her, watching her delicate hands move over the keys, hearing the pure, clear tones of her voice, all my old feelings washed over me in a rush, and my eyes smarted at the unalloyed sweetness and goodness of this lady. When she asked me to join her in the duet, *Là ci darem la mano*, I agreed to do it, although my voice is less than ordinary. On the second singing of the word '*mano*'—'hand'—I was seized by a vagrant impulse and took her left hand in my own. Her playing was hampered, of course, and the music limped for a few measures; and then, my face burning, I released her hand and we finished out the duet. Wisely, she neither rebuked me for my action nor gave me encouragement; rather, she acted as if the rash gesture had never been committed.

To mask my embarrassment, I now embarked upon some light chatter, designed to ease whatever tension existed between us; I spoke of many things, foolish things, for the most part, and even asked if Mr Sardonicus had later demonstrated any of the jealousy she had said, in her letter, that she had erroneously thought him to have exhibited. She laughed at this—and it brightened the room, for it was the first time her face had abandoned its grave expression; indeed, I was taken by the thought that this was the first display of human merriment I had marked since stepping into the coach—and she said, 'Oh, no! To the contrary, Mr Sardonicus said that the closer we had been in the old days, the more he would be pleased.'

This seemed an odd and even coarse thing for a man to say to his wife, and I jovially replied: 'I hope Mr Sardonicus was smiling when he said that.'

At once, Maude's own smile vanished from her face. She looked away from me and began to talk of other things. I was dumbfounded. Had my innocent remark given offence? It seemed not possible. A moment later, however, I knew the reason for her strange action, for a tall gentleman entered the room with a gliding step, and one look at him explained many things.

'Sir Robert Cargrave?' he asked, but he spoke with difficulty, certain sounds—such as the *b* in Robert and the *v* in Cargrave—being almost impossible for him to utter. To shape these sounds, the lips must be used, and the gentleman before me was the victim of some terrible affliction that had caused his lips to be pulled perpetually apart from each other, baring his teeth in a continuous ghastly smile. It was the same humourless grin I had seen once before: on the face of a person in the last throes of lockjaw. We physicians have a name for that chilling grimace, a Latin name, and as it entered my mind, it seemed to dispel yet another mystery, for the term we use to describe the lockjaw smile is: *Risus sardonicus*. A pallor approaching phosphorescence completed his astonishing appearance.

'Yes,' I replied, covering my shock at the sight of his face. 'Do I have the pleasure of addressing Mr Sardonicus?'

We shook hands. After an exchange of courtesies, he said, 'I have ordered dinner to be served in the large dining hall one hour hence. In the meantime, my valet will show you to your rooms, for I am sure you will wish to refresh yourself after your journey.'

'You are most kind.' The valet appeared–a man of grave countenance, like the butler and the coachman—and I followed him up a long flight of stone stairs. As I walked behind him, I reflected on the unsmiling faces in this castle, and no longer were they things of wonder. For who would be disposed to smile under the same roof with him who must smile forever? The most spontaneous of smiles would seem a mockery in the presence of that afflicted face. I was filled with pity for Maude's husband: of all God's creatures, man alone is blest with the ability to smile; but for the master of Castle Sardonicus, God's great blessing had become a terrible curse. As a physician, my pity was tempered with professional curiosity. His smile resembled the *risus* of lockjaw, but lockjaw is a mortal disease, and Mr Sardonicus, his skullish grin notwithstanding, was very much alive. I felt shame for some of my earlier uncharitable thoughts toward this gentleman, for surely such an unfortunate could be forgiven much. What bitterness must fester in his breast; what sharp despair gnaw at his inwards!

My rooms were spacious and certainly as comfortable as this dank stone housing could afford. A hot tub was prepared, for which my tired and dusty frame was most grateful. As I lay in it, I began to experience the pleasant pangs of appetite. I looked forward to dinner. After my bath, I put on fresh linen and a suit of evening clothes. Then, taking from my bag two small gifts for my host and hostess—a bottle of scent for Maude, a box of cigars for her husband—I left my rooms.

I was not so foolish as to expect to find my way, unaided, to the main dining hall; but since I was early, I intended to wander a bit and let the ancient magnificence of the castle impress itself upon me.

Tapestries bearing my host's 'S' were frequently displayed. They were remarkably new, their colours fresh, unlike the faded grandeur of their fellow tapestries. From this—and from Mr Sardonicus' lack of title—I deduced that the castle had not been inherited through a family line, but merely purchased by him, probably from an impoverished nobleman. Though not titled, Mr Sardonicus evidently possessed enormous wealth. I pondered its source. My ponderings were interrupted by the sound of Maude's voice.

I looked up. The acoustical effects in old castles are often strange— I had marked them in our own English castles—and though I stood near neither room nor door of any kind, I could hear Maude speaking in a distressed tone. I was standing at an open window which overlooked a kind of courtyard. Across this court, a window was likewise open. I took this to be the window of Maude's room; her voice was in some way being amplified and transported by the circumstantial shape of the courtyard and the positions of the two windows. By listening very attentively, I could make out most of her words.

She was saying, 'I shan't. You must not ask me. It is unseemly.' And then the voice of her husband replied: 'You shall and will, madam. In my castle, it is I who decide what is seemly or unseemly. Not you.' I was embarrassed at overhearing this private discussion on what was obviously a painful subject, so I made to draw away from the window that I might hear no more, but was restrained by the sound of my own name on Maude's lips. 'I have treated Sir Robert with courtesy,' she said. 'You must treat him with more than courtesy,' Mr Sardonicus responded. 'You must treat him with warmth. You must rekindle in his breast those affections he felt for you in other days . . .'

I could listen no longer. The exchange was vile. I drew away from the window. What manner of creature was this Sardonicus who threw his wife into the arms of other men? As a practitioner of medicine, a man dedicated to healing the ills of humankind, I had brought myself to learn many things about the minds of men, as well as about their bodies. I fully believed that, in some future time, physicians would heal the body by way of the mind, for it is in that *terra incognita* that all secrets lie hidden. I knew that love has many masks; masks of submission and of oppression; and even more terrible masks that make Nature a stranger to herself and 'turn the truth of God into a lie,' as St Paul wrote. There is even a kind of love, if it can be elevated by that name, that derives its keenest pleasure from the sight of the beloved in the arms of another. These are unpleasant observations, which may one day be codified and studied by healers, but which, until then, may not be thought on for too long, lest the mind grow morbid and stagger under its load of repugnance.

With a heavy heart, I sought out a servant and asked to be taken to the dining hall. It was some distance away, and by the time I arrived there, Sardonicus and his lady were already at table, awaiting me. He arose, and with that revolting smile, indicated a chair; she also arose, and took my arm, addressing me as 'Dear Sir Robert' and leading me to my place. Her touch, which at any previous time would have gladdened me, I now found distinctly not to my liking.

A hollow joviality hung over the dinner table throughout the meal. Maude's laughter struck me as giddy and false; Sardonicus drank too much wine and his speech became even more indistinct. I contrived to talk on trivial subjects, repeating some anecdotes about the London theatre which I had hitherto related to Maude, and describing Mr Macready's interpretation of Macbeth.

'Some actors,' said Sardonicus, 'interpret the Scottish chieftain as a creature compounded of pure evil, unmingled with good qualities of any kind. Such interpretations are often criticized by those who feel no human being can be so unremittingly evil. Do you agree, Sir Robert?'

'No,' I said evenly; then, looking Sardonicus full in the face, I added, 'I believe it is entirely possible for a man to possess not a single one of the virtues, to be a dæmon in human flesh.' Quickly, I embarked upon a discussion of the character of Iago, who took ghoulish delight in tormenting his fellow man.

The dinner was, I suppose, first rate, and the wine an honorable vintage, but I confess to tasting little of what was placed before me. At the end of the meal, Maude left us for a time and Sardonicus escorted me into the library, whither he ordered brandy to be brought. He opened the box of cigars, expressed his admiration of them and gratitude for them, and offered them to me. I took one and we both smoked. The smoking of the cigar made Sardonicus look even more grotesque: being unable to hold it in his lips, he clenched it in his constantly visible teeth, creating a unique spectacle. Brandy was served; I partook of it freely, though I am not customarily given to heavy drinking, for I now deemed it to be beneficial to my dampened spirits.

'You used the word "ghoulish" a few moments ago, Sir Robert,' said Sardonicus. 'It is one of those words one uses so easily in conversation—one utters it without stopping to think of its meaning.

445

But, in my opinion, it is not a word to be used lightly. When one uses it, one should have in one's mind a firm, unwavering picture of a ghoul.'

'Perhaps I did,' I said.

'Perhaps,' he admitted. 'And perhaps not. Let us obtain a precise definition of the word.' He arose and walked to one of the bookcases that lined the room's walls. He reached for a large two-volume dictionary. 'Let me see,' he murmured. 'We desire Volume One, from A to M, do we not? Now then: "ghee"..."gherkin"... "ghetto" ... "ghoom" (an odd word, eh, Sir Robert? "To search for game in the dark")..."ghost"...ah, "ghoul!" "Among Eastern nations, an imaginary evil being who robs graves and feeds upon corpses." One might say, then, that he ghooms?' Sardonicus chuckled. He returned to his chair and helped himself to more brandy. 'When you described Iago's actions as "ghoulish",' he continued, 'did you think of him as the inhabitant of an Eastern nation? Or an imaginary being as against the reality of Othello and Desdemona? And did you mean seriously to suggest that it was his custom to rob graves and then to feed upon the disgusting nourishment he found therein?'

'I used the word in a figurative sense,' I replied.

'Ah,' said Sardonicus. 'This is because you are English and do not believe in ghouls. Were you a Middle-European, as am I, you would believe in their existence, and would not be tempted to use the word other than literally. In my country—I was born in Poland—we understood such things. I, in point of fact, have known a ghoul.' He paused for a moment and looked at me, then said, 'You English are so blasé. Nothing shocks you. I sit here and tell you a thing of dreadful import and you do not even blink your eyes. Can it be because you do not believe me?'

'It would be churlish to doubt the word of my host,' I replied.

'And an Englishman may be many things, but never a churl, eh, Sir Robert? Let me refill your glass, my friend, and then let me tell you about ghouls—which, by the way, are by no means imaginary, as that stupid lexicon would have us to think, and which are not restricted to Eastern nations. Neither do they—necessarily—feed upon carrion flesh, although they are interested, *most* interested, in the repellent contents of graves. Let me tell you a story from my own country, Sir Robert, a story that—if I have any gift at all as a spinner of tales— will create in you a profound belief in ghouls. You will be entertained, I hope, but I also hope you will add to your learning. You will learn, for example, how low a human being can sink, how truly *monstrous* a man can become.'

* * *

'You must transport your mind,' said Sardonicus, 'back a few years
and to a rural region of my homeland. You must become acquainted
with a family of country folk—hard-working, law-abiding, God-
fearing, of moderate means—the head of which was a simple, good
man named Tadeusz Boleslawski. He was an even-tempered personage, kindly disposed to all men, the loving husband of a devoted
wife and father of five strong boys. He was also a firm churchman,
seldom even taking the Lord's name in vain. The painted women
who plied their trade in certain elaborate houses of the nearest
large city, Warsaw, held no attraction for him, though several of his
masculine neighbours, on their visits to the metropolis, succumbed to
such blandishments with tidal regularity. Neither did he drink in
excess: a glass of beer with his evening meal, a toast or two in wine
on special occasions. No: hard liquor, strong language, fast women—
these were not the weaknesses of Tadeusz Boleslawski. His weakness
was gambling.

'Every month he would make the trip to Warsaw, to sell his
produce at the markets and to buy certain necessaries for his home.
While his comrades visited the drinking and wenching houses,
Tadeusz would attend strictly to business affairs—except for one
minor deviation. He would purchase a lottery ticket, place it securely
in a small, tight pocket of his best waistcoat—which he wore only on
Sundays and on his trips to the city—then put it completely out of his
mind until the following month, when, on reaching the city, he would
remove it from his pocket and closely scan the posted list of winners.
Then, after methodically tearing the ticket to shreds (for Tadeusz
never lived to win a lottery), he would purchase another. This was a
ritual with him; he performed it every month for twenty-three years,
and the fact that he never won did not discourage him. His wife knew
of this habit, but since it was the good man's only flaw, she never
remarked upon it.'

Outside, I could hear the wind howling dismally. I took more
brandy as Sardonicus continued:

'Years passed; three of the five sons married; two (Henryk and
Marek, the youngest) were still living with their parents, when
Tadeusz—who had been of sturdy health—collapsed one day in the
fields and died. I will spare you an account of the family's grief; how
the married sons returned with their wives to attend the obsequies; of
the burial in the small graveyard of that community. The good man
had left few possessions, but these few were divided, according to his

written wish, among his survivors, with the largest share going, of course, to the eldest son. Though this was custom, the other sons could not help feeling a trifle disgruntled, but they held their peace for the most part—especially the youngest, Marek, who was perhaps the most amiable of them and a lad who was by nature quiet and interested in improving his lot through the learning he found in books.

'Imagine, sir, the amazement of the widow when, a full three weeks after the interment of her husband, she received word by men returning from Warsaw that the lottery ticket Tadeusz had purchased had now been selected as the winner. It was a remarkable irony, of course, but conditions had grown hard for the poor woman, and would grow harder with her husband dead, so she had no time to reflect upon that irony. She set about looking through her husband's possessions for the lottery ticket. Drawers were emptied upon the floor; boxes and cupboards were ransacked; the family Bible was shaken out; years before, Tadeusz had been in the habit of temporarily hiding money under a loose floorboard in the bedroom—this cavity was thoroughly but vainly plumbed. The sons were sent for: among the few personal effects they had been bequeathed, did the ticket languish there? In the snuff box? In any article of clothing?

'And at that, Sir Robert, the eldest son leapt up. "An article of clothing!" he cried. "Father always wore his Sunday waist-coat to the city when he purchased the lottery tickets—the very waistcoat in which he was buried!"

'"Yes, yes!" the other sons chorused, saving Marek, and plans began to be laid for the exhuming of the dead man. But the widow spoke firmly: "Your father rests peacefully," she said. "He must not be disturbed. No amount of gold would soothe our hearts if we disturbed him." The sons protested with vehemence, but the widow stood her ground. "No son of mine will profane his father's grave—unless he first kills his mother!" Grumbling, the sons withdrew their plans. But that night, Marek awoke to find his mother gone from the house. He was frightened, for this was not like her. Intuition sent him to the graveyard, where he found her, keeping a lonely vigil over the grave of her husband, protecting him from the greed of grave robbers. Marek implored her to come out of the cold, to return home; she at first refused; only when Marek offered to keep vigil all night himself did she relent and return home, leaving her youngest son to guard the grave from profanation.

'Marek waited a full hour. Then he produced from under his shirt a small shovel. He was a strong boy, and the greed of a youngest son who has been deprived of inheritance lent added strength to his arms.

He dug relentlessly, stopping seldom for rest, until finally the coffin was uncovered. He raised the creaking lid. An overpowering fœtor filled his nostrils and nearly made him faint. Gathering courage, he searched the pockets of the mouldering waistcoat.

'The moon proved to be his undoing, Sir Robert. For suddenly its rays, hitherto hidden, struck the face of his father, and at the sight of that face, the boy recoiled and went reeling against the wall of the grave, the breath forced from his body. Now, you must know that the mere sight of his father—even in an advanced state of decomposition—he had steeled himself to withstand; but what he had *not* foreseen——'

Here, Sardonicus leaned close to me and his pallid, grinning head filled my vision. 'What he had not foreseen, my dear sir, was that the face of his father, in the rigour of death, would look directly and hideously upon him.' Sardonicus' voice became an ophidian hiss. 'And, Sir Robert,' he added, 'most terrible and most unforeseen of all, the dead lips were drawn back from the teeth *in a constant and soul-shattering smile!*'

I know not whether it was the ghastliness of his story, or the sight of his hideous face so close to mine, or the cheerless keening of the wind outside, or the brandy I had consumed, or all of these in combination; but when Sardonicus uttered those last words, my heart was clutched by a cold hand, and for a moment—a long moment ripped from the texture of time—I was convinced beyond doubt and beyond logic that the face I looked into was the face of that cadaver, reanimated by obscure arts, to walk among the living, dead though not dead.

The moment of horror passed, at length, and reason triumphed. Sardonicus, considerably affected by his own tale, sat back in his chair, trembling. Before too long, he spoke again:

'The remembrance of that night, Sir Robert, though it is now many years past, fills me still with dread. You will appreciate this when I tell you what you have perhaps already guessed—that *I* am that ghoulish son, Marek.'

I had not guessed it; but since I had no wish to tell him that I had for an instant thought he was the dead father, I said nothing.

'When my senses returned,' said Sardonicus, 'I scrambled out of the grave and ran as swiftly as my limbs would carry me. I had reached the gate of the graveyard when I was smitten by the fact that I had not accomplished the purpose of my mission—the lottery ticket remained in may father's pocket!'

'But surely——' I started to say.

'Surely I ignored the fact and continued to run? No, Sir Robert. My terror notwithstanding, I halted, and forced myself to retrace those hasty steps. My fear notwithstanding, I descended once more into that noisome grave. My disgust notwithstanding, I reached into the pocket of my decaying father's waistcoat and extracted the ticket! I need hardly add that, this time, I averted my eyes from his face.

'But the horror was not behind me. Indeed, it had only begun. I reached my home at a late hour, and my family was asleep. For this I was grateful, since my clothes were covered with soil and I still trembled from my fearful experience. I quietly poured water into a basin and prepared to wash some of the graveyard dirt from my face and hands. In performing my ablutions, I looked up into a mirror—*and screamed so loudly as to wake the entire house*!

'My face was as you see it now, a replica of my dead father's: the lips drawn back in a perpetual, mocking grin. I tried to close my mouth. I could not. The muscles were immovable, as if held in the gelid rigour of death. I could hear my family stirring at my scream, and since I did not wish them to look upon me, I ran from the house—never, Sir Robert, to return.

'As I wandered the rural roads, my mind sought the cause of the affliction that had been visited upon me. Though but a country lad, I had read much and I had a blunt, rational mind that was not susceptible to the easy explanations of the supernatural. I would not believe that God had placed a malediction upon me to punish me for my act. I would not believe that some black force from beyond the grave had reached out to stamp my face. At length, I began to believe it was the massive shock that had forced my face to its present state, and that my great guilt had helped to shape it even as my father's dead face was shaped. Shock and guilt: strong powers not from God above or the Fiend below, but from within my own breast, my own brain, my own soul.

'Let me bring this history to a hasty close, Sir Robert. You need only know that, despite my blighted face, I redeemed the lottery ticket and thus gained an amount of money that will not seem large to you, but which was more than I had ever seen before that time. It was the fulcrum from which I plied the lever that was to make me, by dint of shrewd speculation, one of the richest men in Central Europe. Naturally, I sought out physicians and begged them to restore my face to its previous state. None succeeded, though I offered them vast sums. My face remained fixed in this damnable unceasing smile, and my heart knew the most profound despair imaginable. I could not even pronounce my own name! By a dreadful irony, the initial letters of my first and last names were impossible for my frozen lips to form. This seemed the final indignity. I will admit to you that, at this period, I was perilously near the brink of self-destruction. But the spirit of preservation prevailed, and I was saved from that course. I changed my name. I had read of the *Risus sardonicus*, and its horrible aptness appealed to my bitter mind, so I became Sardonicus—a name I can pronounce with no difficulty.'

Sardonicus paused and sipped his brandy. 'You are wondering,' he then said, 'in what way my story concerns you.'

I could guess, but I said: 'I am.'

'Sir Robert,' he said, 'you are known throughout the medical world. Most laymen, perhaps, have not heard of you; but a layman such as I, a layman who avidly follows the medical journals for tidings of any recent discoveries in the curing of paralyzed muscles, has heard of you again and again. Your researches into these problems have earned you high professional regard; indeed, they have earned you a knighthood. For some time, it has been in my mind to visit London and seek you out. I have consulted many physicians, renowned men—Keller in Berlin, Morignac in Paris, Buonagente in Milan—and none have been able to help me. My despair has been utter. It prevented me from making the long journey to England. But when I heard—sublime coincidence!—that my own wife had been acquainted with you, I took heart. Sir Robert, I entreat you to heal me, to lift from me this curse, to make me look once more like a man, that I may walk in the sun again, among my fellow human beings, as one of them, rather than as a fearsome gargoyle to be shunned and feared and ridiculed. Surely you cannot, *will* not deny me?'

My feelings for Sardonicus, pendulum-like, again swung toward his favour. His story, his plight, had rent my heart, and I reverted to my earlier opinion that such a man should be forgiven much. The strange overheard conversation between Maude and him was momentarily forgotten. I said, 'I will examine you, Mr Sardonicus. You were right to ask me. We must never abandon hope.'

He clasped his hands together. 'Ah, Sir! May you be blest forever!'

I performed the examination then and there. Although I did not tell him this, never had I encountered muscles as rigid as those of his face. They could only be compared to stone, so inflexible were they. Still, I said, 'Tomorrow we will begin treatment. Heat and massage.'

'These have been tried,' he said, hopelessly.

'Massage differs from one pair of hands to another,' I replied. 'I have had success with my own techniques, and therefore place faith in them. Be comforted then, sir, and share my faith.'

He seized my hand in his. 'I do,' he said. 'I must. For if you—if even *you*, Sir Robert Cargrave, fail me . . .' He did not complete the sentence, but his eyes assumed an aspect so bitter, so full of hate, so strangely cold yet flaming, that they floated in my dreams that night.

I slept not well, awakening many times in a fever compounded of drink and turbulent emotions. When the first rays of morning crept on to my pillow, I arose, little refreshed. After a cold tub and a light breakfast in my room, I went below to the salon whence music issued. Maude was already there, playing a pretty little piece upon the spinet. She looked up and greeted me. 'Good morning, Sir Robert. Do you know the music of Mr Gottschalk? He is an American pianist: this is his *Maiden's Blush*. Amiable, is it not?'

'Most amiable,' I replied, dutifully, although I was in no mood for the embroideries of *politesse*.

Maude soon finished the piece and closed the album. She turned to me and said, in a serious tone, 'I have been told what you are going to do for my poor husband, Sir Robert. I can scarce express my gratitude.'

'There is no need to express it,' I assured her. 'As a physician—as well as your old friend—I could not do less. I hope you understand, however, that a cure is not a certainty. I will try, and I will try to the limit of my powers, but beyond that I can promise nothing.'

Her eyes shone with supplication: 'Oh, cure him, Sir Robert! That I beg of you!'

'I understand your feelings, madam,' I said, 'It is fitting that you should hope so fervently for his recovery; a devoted wife could feel no other way.'

'Oh, sir,' she said, and into her voice crept now a harshness, 'you misunderstand. My fervent hope springs from unalloyed selfishness.'

'How may that be?' I asked.

'If you do not succeed in curing him,' she told me, 'I will suffer.'

'I understand that, but——'

'No, you do not understand,' she said. 'But I can tell you little more without offending. Some things are better left unspoken. Suffice it to be said that, in order to urge you toward an ultimate effort, to the "limit of your powers" as you have just said, my husband intends to hold over your head the threat of my punishment.'

'This is monstrous!' I cried. 'It cannot be tolerated. But in what manner, pray, would he dare punish you? Surely he would not beat you?'

'I wish he would be content with a mere beating,' she groaned, 'but his cleverness knows a keener torture. No, he holds over me—and over you, through me—a punishment far greater; a punishment (believe me!) so loathsome to the sensibilities, so unequivocably vile and degraded, that my mind shrinks from contemplating it. Spare me your further questions, sir, I implore you; for to describe it would plunge me into an abyss of humiliation and shame!'

She broke into sobbing, and tears coursed down her cheeks. No longer able to restrain my tender feelings for her, I flew to her side and took her hands in mine. 'Maude,' I said, 'may I call you that? In the past I addressed you only as Miss Randall; at present I may only call you Madam Sardonicus; but in my heart—then as now—you are, you always have been, you always will be, simply Maude, my own dear Maude!'

'Robert,' she sighed; 'dearest Robert. I have yearned to hear my Christian name from your lips all these long years.'

'The warmth we feel,' I said, 'may never, with honour, reach fulfillment. But—trust me, dearest Maude!—I will in some wise deliver you from the tyranny of that creature: this I vow!'

'I have no hope,' she said, 'save in you. Whether I go on as I am, or am subjected to an unspeakable horror, rests with you. My fate is in your hands—these strong, healing hands, Robert.' Her voice dropped to a whisper: 'Fail me not! Oh fail me not!'

'Govern your fears,' I said. 'Return to your music. Be of good spirits; or, if you cannot, make a show of it. I go now to treat your husband, and also to confront him with what you have told me.'

'Do not!' she cried. 'Do not, I beseech you, Robert; lest, in the event of your failure, he devise foul embellishments upon the agonies into which he will cast me!'

'Very well,' I said, 'I will not speak of this to him. But my heart aches to learn the nature of the torments you fear.'

'Ask no more, Robert, she said, turning away. 'Go to my husband. Cure him. Then I will no longer fear those torments.'

I pressed her dear hand and left the salon.

Sardonicus awaited me in his chambers. Thither, quantities of hot water and stacks of towels had been brought by the servants, upon my orders. Sardonicus was stripped to the waist, displaying a trunk strong and of good musculature, but with the same near-phosphorescent pallor of his face. It was, I now understood, the pallor of one who has avoided daylight for years. 'As you see, sir,' he greeted me, 'I am ready for your ministrations.'

I bade him recline upon his couch, and began the treatment.

Never have I worked so long with so little reward. After alternating applications of heat and of massage, over a period of three and a quarter hours, I had made no progress. The muscles of his face were still as stiff as marble; they had not relaxed for an instant. I was mortally tired. He ordered our luncheon brought to us in his chambers, and after a short respite, I began again. The clock tolled six when I at last sank into a chair, shaking with exhaustion and strain. His face was exactly as before.

'What remains to be done, sir?' he asked me.

'I will not deceive you,' I said. 'It is beyond my skill to alleviate your condition. I can do no more.'

He rose swiftly from the couch. 'You *must* do more!' he shrieked. 'You are my last hope!'

'Sir,' I said, 'new medical discoveries are ever being made. Place your trust in Him who created you——'

'Cease that detestable gibberish at once!' he snapped. 'Your puling sentiments sicken me! Resume the treatment.'

I refused. 'I have applied all my knowledge, all my art, to your affliction,' I assured him. 'To resume the treatment would be idle and foolish, for—as you have divined—the condition is a product of your own mind.'

'At dinner last night,' countered Sardonicus, 'we spoke of the character of Macbeth. Do you not remember the words he addressed to *his* doctor?—

> 'Canst thou not minister to a mind diseas'd;
> Pluck from the memory a rooted sorrow;
> Raze out the written troubles of the brain;
> And with some sweet oblivious antidote
> Cleanse the stuff'd bosom of that perilous stuff
> Which weighs upon the heart?'

'I remember them,' I said; 'and I remember, as well, the doctor's reply: "*Therein the patient must minister to himself.*"' I arose and started for the door.

'One moment, Sir Robert,' he said. I turned. 'Forgive my precipitate outburst a moment ago. However, the mental nature of my affliction notwithstanding, and even though this mode of treatment has failed, surely there are other treatments?'

'None,' I said, 'that have been sufficiently tested. None I would venture to use upon a human body.'

'Ah!' he cried. 'Then other treatments *do* exist!'

I shrugged. 'Think not of them, sir. They are at present unavailable to you.' I pitied him, and added: 'I am sorry.'

'Doctor!' he said; 'I implore you to use whatever treatments exist, be they ever so untried!'

'They are fraught with danger,' I said.

'Danger?' He laughed. 'Danger of what? Of disfigurement? Surely no man has ever been more disfigured than I! Of death? I am willing to gamble my life!'

'*I* am not willing to gamble your life,' I said. 'All lives are precious. Even yours.'

'Sir Robert, I will pay you a thousand pounds.'

'This is not a question of money.'

'Five thousand pounds, Sir Robert, *ten* thousand!'

'No.'

He sank onto the couch. 'Very well,' he said. 'Then I will offer you the ultimate inducement.'

'Were it a million pounds,' I said, 'you could not sway me.'

'The inducement I speak of,' he said, 'is not money. Will you hear?'

I sat down. 'Speak, sir,' I said, 'since that is your wish. But nothing will persuade me to use a treatment that might cost you your life.'

'Sir Robert,' he said, after a pause, 'yestereve, when I came down to meet you for the first time, I heard happy sounds in the salon. You were singing a charming melody with my wife. Later, I could not help but notice the character of your glances toward her . . .'

'They were not reciprocated, sir,' I told him, 'and herewith I offer you a most abject apology for my unbecoming conduct.'

'You obscure my point,' he said. 'You are a friend of hers, from the old days in London; at that period, you felt an ardent affection for her, I would guess. This is not surprising: for she is a lady whose face and form promise voluptuous delights and yet a lady whose manner is most decorous and correct. I would guess further: that your ardour has not diminished over the years; that, at the sight of her, the embers have burst into a flame. No, sir, hear me out. What would you say, Sir Robert, were I to tell you—that you may quench that flame?'

I frowned. 'Your meaning, sir?——'

'Must I speak even more plainly? I am offering you a golden opportunity to requite the love that burns in your heart. To requite it in a single night, if that will suffice you, or over an extended period of weeks, months; a year, if you will; as long as you need——'

'Scoundrel!' I roared, leaping up.

He heeded me not, but went on speaking: '. . . As my guest, Sir Robert! I offer you a veritable Oriental paradise of unlimited raptures!' He laughed, then entered into a catalogue of his wife's excellences. 'Consider, sir,' he said, 'that matchless bosom, like alabaster which has been imbued with the pink of the rose, those creamy limbs——'

'Enough!' I cried. 'I will hear no more of your foulness.' I strode to the door.

'Yes, you will, Sir Robert,' he said immediately. 'You will hear a good deal more of my foulness. You will hear what I plan to do to your beloved Maude, should you fail to relieve me of this deformity.'

Again, I stopped and turned. I said nothing, but waited for him to speak further.

'I perceive that I have caught your interest,' he said. 'Hear me: for if you think I spoke foully before, you will soon be forced to agree that my earlier words were, by comparison, as blameless as *The Book of Common Prayer*. If rewards do not tempt you, then threats may coerce you. In fine, Maude will be punished if you fail, Sir Robert.'

'She is an innocent.'

'Just so. Hence, the more exquisite and insupportable to you should be the thought of her punishment.'

My mind reeled. I could not believe such words were being uttered.

'Deep in the bowels of this old castle,' said Sardonicus, 'are dungeons. Suppose I were to tell you that my intention is to drag my wife thither and stretch her smooth body to unendurable length upon the rack——'

'You would not dare!' I cried.

'My daring or lack of it is not the issue here. I speak of the rack only that I may go on to assure you that Maude would *infinitely prefer* that dreadful machine to the punishment I have in truth designed for her. I will describe it to you. You will wish to be seated, I think.'

'I will stand,' I said.

'As you please.' Sardonicus himself sat down. 'Perhaps you have marveled at the very fact of Maude's marriage to me. When the world was so full of personable men—men like yourself, who adored her— why did she choose to wed a monster, a creature abhorrent to the eyes and who did not, moreover, have any redeeming grace of spiritual beauty, or kindness, or charm?

'I first met Maude Randall in Paris. I say "met," but it would be truer to simply say I saw her—from my hotel window, in fact. Even in Paris society, which abounds in ladies of remarkable pulchritude, she was to be remarked upon. You perhaps would say I fell in love with her, but I dislike that word "love", and will merely say that the sight of her smote my senses with most agreeable emphasis. I decided to make her mine. But how? By presenting my irresistibly handsome face to her view? Hardly. I began methodically: I hired secret operatives to find out everything about her and about her mother and father—both of whom were then alive. I discovered that her father was in the habit of speculating, so I saw to it that he received some supposedly trustworthy but very bad advice. He speculated heavily and was instantly ruined. I must admit I had not planned his consequent suicide, but when that melancholy event occurred, I rejoiced, for it worked to my advantage. I presented myself to the bereaved widow and daughter, telling them the excellent qualities of Mr Randall were widely known in the world of affairs and that I considered myself almost a close friend. I offered to help them in any possible way. By dint of excessive humility and persuasiveness, I won their trust and succeeded in diminishing their aversion to my face. This, you must understand, from first to last, occupied a period of many months. I spoke nothing of marriage, made no sign of affection toward the daughter for at least six of these months; when I did— again, with great respect and restraint—she gently refused me. I retreated gracefully, saying only that I hoped I might remain her and her mother's friend. She replied that she sincerely shared that hope, for, although she could never look upon me as an object of love, she indeed considered me a true friend. The mother, who pined excessively after the death of the father, soon expired: another incident unplanned but welcomed by me. Now the lovely child was alone in the world in a foreign city, with no money, no one to guide her, no one to fall back upon—save kindly Mr Sardonicus. I waited many weeks, then I proposed marriage again. For several days, she continued to decline the offer, but her declinations grew weaker and weaker until, at length, on one day, she said this to me:

'"Sir, I esteem you highly as a friend and benefactor, but my other feelings toward you have not changed. If you could be satisfied with such a singular condition; if you could agree to enter into marriage with a lady and yet look upon her as no more than a companion of kindred spirit; if the prospect of a dispassionate and childless marriage does not repulse you—as well it might—then, sir, my unhappy circumstances would compel me to accept your kind offer."

'Instantly, I told her my regard for her was of the purest and most elevated variety; that the urgings of the flesh were unknown to me; that I lived on a spiritual plane and desired only her sweet and stimulating companionship through the years. All this, of course, was a lie. The diametric opposite was true. But I hoped, by this false-hood, to lure her into marriage; after which, by slow and strategic process, I could bring about her submission and my rapture. She still was hesitant; for, as she frankly told me, she believed that love was a noble and integral part of marriage; and that marriage without it could be only a hollow thing; and that though I knew not the urgings of the flesh, she could not with honesty say the same of herself. Yet she reiterated that, so far as my own person was concerned, a platonic relationship was all that could ever exist between us. I calmed her misgivings. We were married not long after.

'And now, Sir Robert, I will tell you a surprising thing. I have confessed myself partial to earthly pleasures; as a physician and as a man of the world, you are aware that a gentleman of strong appetites may not curb them for very long without fomenting turmoil and distress in his bosom. And yet, sir, not once in the years of our marriage—not *once*, I say—have I been able to persuade or cajole my wife into relenting and breaking the stringent terms of our marriage agreement. Each time I have attempted, she has recoiled from me with horror and disgust. This is not because of an abhorrence of all fleshly things—by her own admission—but because of my monstrous face.

'Perhaps now you will better understand the vital necessity for this cure. And perhaps also you will understand the full extent of Maude's suffering should you fail to effect that cure. For, mark me well: if you fail, my wife will be made to become a true wife to me—by main force, and not for one fleeting hour, but every day and every night of her life, whensoever I say, in whatsoever manner I choose to express my conjugal privilege!' As an afterthought, he added, 'I am by nature imaginative.'

I had been shocked into silence. I could only look upon him with disbelief. He spoke again:

'If you deem it a light punishment, Sir Robert, then you do not know the depth of her loathing for my person, you do not know the revulsion that wells up inside her when I but place my fingers upon her arm, you do not know what mastery of her very gorge is required of her when I kiss her hand. Think, then; think of the abomina-tion she would feel were my attentions to grow more ardent, more demanding! It would unseat her mind, sir; of that I am sure, for she would as soon embrace a reptile.'

Sardonicus arose and put on his shirt. 'I suggest we both begin dressing for dinner,' he said. 'Whilst you are dressing, reflect. Ask yourself, Sir Robert: could you ever again look upon yourself with other than shame and loathing if you were to sacrifice the beautiful and blameless Maude Randall on an altar of the grossest depravity? Consider how ill you would sleep in your London bed, night after night, knowing what she was suffering at that very moment; suffering because *you* abandoned her, because *you* allowed her to become an entertainment for a monster.'

The days that passed after that time were, in the main, tedious yet filled with anxiety. During them, certain supplies were being brought from London and other places; Sardonicus spared no expense in procuring for me everything I said was necessary to the treatment. I avoided his society as much as I could, shunning even his table, and instructing the servants to bring my meals to my rooms. On the other hand, I sought out the company of Maude, endeavouring to comfort her and allay her fears. In those hours when her husband was occupied with business affairs, we talked together in the salon, and played music. Thus, they were days spotted with small pleasures that seemed the greater for having been snatched in the shadow of wretchedness.

I grew to know Maude, in that time, better than I had ever known her in London. Adversity stripped the layers of ceremony from our congress, and we spoke directly. I came to know her warmth, but I came to know her strength, too. I spoke outright of my love, though in the next breath I assured her I was aware of the hopelessness of that love. I did not tell her of the 'reward' her husband had offered me—and which I had refused—and I was gladdened to learn (as I did by indirection) that Sardonicus, though he had abjured her to be excessively cordial to me, had not revealed the ultimate and ignoble purpose of that cordiality.

'Robert,' she said once, 'is it likely that he will be cured?'

I did not tell her how unlikely it was. 'For your sake, Maude,' I said, 'I will persevere more than I have ever done in my life.'

At length, a day arrived when all the necessaries had been gathered: some plants from the New World, certain equipment from London, and a vital instrument from Scotland. I worked long and late, in complete solitude, distilling a needed liquor from the plants. The next day, dogs were brought to me alive, and carried out dead. Three days after that, a dog left my laboratory alive and my distilling labours came to an end.

I informed Sardonicus that I was ready to administer the treatment. He came to my laboratory, and I imagined there was almost a gloating triumph in his immobile smile. 'Such are the fruits of concentrated effort,' he said. 'Man is an indolent creature, but light the fire of fear under him, and of what miracles is he not capable!'

'Speak not of miracles,' I said, 'though prayers would do you no harm now, for you will soon be in peril of your life.' I motioned him toward a table and bade him lie upon it. He did so, and I commenced explaining the treatment to him. 'The explorer Magellan,' I said, 'wrote of a substance used on darts by the savage inhabitants of the South American continent. It killed instantly, dropping large animals in their tracks. The substance was derived from certain plants, and is, in essence, the same substance I have been occupied in extracting these past days.'

'A poison, sir Robert?' he asked, wryly.

'When used full strength,' I said, 'it kills by bringing about a *total* relaxation of the muscles—particularly the muscles of the lungs and heart. I have long thought that a dilution of that poison might beneficially slacken the rigidly tensed muscles of paralyzed patients.'

'Most ingenious, sir,' he said.

'I must warn you,' I went on, 'that this distillment has never been used on a human subject. It may kill you. I must, perforce, urge you again not to insist upon its use; to accept your lot; and to remove the threat of punishment you now hold over your wife's head.'

'You seek to frighten me, Doctor,' chuckled Sardonicus; 'to plant distrust in my bosom. But I fear you not—an English knight and a respected physician would never do a deed so dishonourable as to wittingly kill a patient under his care. You would be hamstrung by your gentleman's code as well as by your professional oath. Your virtues are, in short, my vices' best ally.'

I bristled. 'I am no murderer such as you,' I said. 'If you force me to use this treatment, I will do everything in my power to ensure its success. But I cannot conceal from you the possibility of your death.'

'See to it that I live,' he said flatly, 'for if I die, my men will kill both you and my wife. They will not kill you quickly. See to it, also, that I am cured—lest Maude be subjected to a fate she fears more than the slowest of tortures.' I said nothing. 'Then bring me this elixir straightway,' he said, 'and let me drink it off and make an end of this!'

'It is not to be drunk,' I told him.

He laughed. 'Is it your plan to smear it on darts, like the savages?'

'Your jest is most apposite,' I said. 'I indeed plan to introduce it into your body by means of a sharp instrument—a new instrument not yet widely known, that was sent me from Scotland. The original suggestion was put forth in the University of Oxford some two hundred years ago by Dr Christopher Wren, but only recently, through development by my friend, Dr Wood of Edinburgh, has it seemed practical. It is no more than a syringe'—I showed him the instrument—'attached to a needle; but the needle is hollow, so that, when it punctures the skin, it may carry healing drugs directly into the bloodstream.'

'The medical arts will never cease earning my admiration,' said Sardonicus.

I filled the syringe. My patient said, 'Wait.'

'Are you afraid?' I asked.

'Since that memorable night in my father's grave,' he replied, 'I have not known fear. I had a surfeit of it then; it will last out my lifetime. No: I simply wish to give instructions to one of my men.' He arose from the table, and, going to the door, told one of his helots to bring Madam Sardonicus to the laboratory.

'Why must she be here?' I asked.

'The sight of her,' he said, 'may serve you as a remembrancer of what awaits her in the event of my death, or of that other punishment she may expect should your treatment prove ineffectual.'

Maude was brought into our presence. She looked upon my equipment—the bubbling retorts and tubes, the pointed syringe—with amazement and fright. I began to explain the principle of the treatment to her, but Sardonicus interrupted: 'Madam is not one of your students, Sir Robert; it is not necessary she know these details. Delay no longer; begin at once!'

He stretched out upon the table again, fixing his eyes upon me. I proffered Maude a comforting look, and walked over to my patient. He did not wince as I drove the needle of the syringe into the left, and then the right, side of his face. 'Now, sir,' I said—and the tremor in my voice surprised me—'we must wait a period of ten minutes.' I joined Maude, and talked to her in low tones, keeping my eyes always upon my patient. He stared at the ceiling; his face remained solidified in that unholy grin. Precisely ten minutes later, a short gasp escaped him; I rushed to his side, and Maude followed close behind me.

We watched with consuming fascination as that clenched face slowly softened, relaxed, changed; the lips drawing closer and closer to each other, gradually covering those naked teeth and gums, the graven creases unfolding and becoming smooth. Before a minute had passed, we were looking down upon the face of a serenely handsome man. His eyes flashed with pleasure, and he made as if to speak.

'No,' I said, 'do not attempt speech yet. The muscles of your face are so slackened that it is beyond your power, at present, to move your lips. This condition will pass.' My voice rang with exultation, and for the moment our enmity was forgotten. He nodded, then leapt from the table and dashed to a mirror which hung on a wall nearby. Though his face could not yet express his joy, his whole body seemed to unfurl in a great gesture of triumph and a muffled cry of happiness burst in his throat.

He turned and seized my hand; then he looked full into Maude's face. After a moment, she said, 'I am happy for you, sir,' and looked away. A rasping laugh sounded in his throat, and he walked to my work bench, tore a leaf from one of my notebooks, and scribbled upon it. This he handed to Maude, who read it and passed it over to me. The writing said: *Fear not, lady. You will not be obliged to endure my embraces. I know full well that the restored beauty of my face will weigh not a jot in the balance of your attraction and repugnance. By this document, I dissolve our pristine marriage. You who have been a wife only in name are no longer even that. I give you your freedom.*

I looked up from my reading. Sardonicus had been writing again. He ripped another leaf from the notebook and handed it directly to me. It read: *This paper is your safe conduct out of the castle and into the village. Gold is yours for the asking, but I doubt if your English scruples will countenance the accepting of my money. I will expect you to have quit these premises before morning, taking her with you.*

'We will be gone within the hour,' I told him, and guided Maude toward the door. Before we left the room, I turned for the last time to Sardonicus.

'For your unclean threats,' I said; 'for the indirect but no less vicious murder of this lady's parents; for the defiling of your own father's grave; for the greed and inhumanity that moved you even before your blighted face provided you with an excuse for your conduct; for these and for what crimes unknown to me blacken your ledger—accept this token of my censure and detestation.' I struck him forcibly on the face. He did not respond. He was standing there in the laboratory when I left the room with Maude.

This strange account should probably end here. No more can be said of its central character, for neither Maude nor I saw him or heard of him after that night. And of us two, nothing need be imparted other than the happy knowledge that we have been most contentedly married for the past 12 years and are the parents of a sturdy boy and two girls who are the lovely images of their mother.

However, I have mentioned my friend Lord Henry Stanton, the inveterate traveler and faithful letterwriter, and I must copy out now a portion of a missive I received from him only a week since, and which, in point of fact, has been the agent that has prompted me to unfold this whole history of Mr Sardonicus:

'...But, my dear Bobbie,' wrote Stanton,

in truth there is small pleasure to be found in this part of the world, and I shall be glad to see London again. The excitements and the drama have all departed (if, indeed, they ever existed) and one must content one's self with the stories told at the hearthstones of inns, with the flames crackling and the mulled wine agreeably stinging one's throat. The natives here are most fond of harrowing stories, tales of gore and grue, of ghosts and ghouls and ghastly events, and I must confess a partiality to such entertainments myself. They will show you a stain on a wall and tell you it is the blood of a murdered innocent who met her death there fifty years before: no amount of washing will ever remove that stain, they tell you in sepulchral tones, and indeed it deepens and darkens on a certain day of the year, the anniversary of her violent passing. One is expected to nod gravely, of course, and one does, if one wishes to encourage the telling of more stories. Back in the eleventh century, you will be apprised, a battalion of foreign invaders were vanquished by the skeletons of long-dead patriots who arose from their tombs to defend their homeland and then returned to the earth when the enemy had been driven from their borders. (And since they are able to show you the very graves of these lively bones, how can one disbelieve them, Bobbie?) Or they will point to a desolate skull of a castle (the country here abounds in such depressing piles) and tell you of the spectral tyrant who, a scant dozen years before, despaired and died alone there. Deserted by the minions who had always hated him, the frightening creature roamed the village, livid and emaciated, his mind shattered, mutely imploring the succour of even the lowliest beggars. I say *mutely*, and that is the best part of this tall tale: for, as they tell it around the fire, these inventive folk, this poor unfortunate could not speak, could not eat, and could not drink. You ask why? For the simple reason that, though he clawed most horribly at his own face, and though he enlisted the aid of strong men—he was absolutely unable to open his mouth. Cursed by Lucifer, they say, he thirsted and starved in the midst of plenty, surrounded by kegs of drink and tables full of the choicest viands, suffering the tortures of Tantalus, until he finally died. Ah, Bobbie! the efforts of our novelists are pale stuff compared to this! English *literateurs* have not the shameless wild imaginations of these people! I will never again read Mrs Radcliffe with pleasure, I assure you, and the ghost of King Hamlet will, from this day hence, strike no terror to my soul, and will fill my heart with but paltry pity. Still, I have journeyed in foreign climes quite enough for one trip, and I long for England and that good English dullness which is relieved only by you and your dear lady (to whom you must commend me most warmly). Until next month, I remain,

Your wayward friend,
Harry Stanton (Bohemia, March, 18—)'

Now, it would not be a difficult feat for the mind to instantly assume that the unfortunate man in that last tale was Sardonicus—indeed, it is for that reason that I have not yet shewn Stanton's letter to Maude: for she, albeit she deeply loathed Sardonicus, is of such a compassionate and susceptible nature that she would grieve to hear of him suffering a death so horrible. But I am a man of science, and I do not form conclusions on such gossamer evidence. Harry did not mention the province of Bohemia that is supposed to have been the stage of that terrible drama; and his letter, though written in Bohemia, was not mailed by Harry until he reached Berlin, so the postmark tells me nothing. Castles like that of Sardonicus are not singular in Bohemia—Harry himself says the country 'abounds in such depressing piles'—so I plan to suspend conclusive thoughts on the matter until I welcome Harry home and can elicit from him details of the precise locality.

For if that 'desolate skull of a castle' *is* Castle Sardonicus, and if the story of the starving man is to be believed, then I will be struck by an awesome and curious thing:

Five days I occupied myself in extracting a liquor from the South American plants. During those days, dogs were carried dead from my laboratory. I had deliberately killed the poor creatures with the undiluted poison, in order to impress Sardonicus with its deadliness. I never intended to—and, in fact, never did—prepare a safe dilution of that lethal drug, for its properties were too unknown, its potentiality too dangerous. The liquid I injected into Sardonicus was pure, distilled water—nothing more. This had always been my plan. The ordering of *materia medica* from far-flung lands was but an elaborate façade designed to work not upon the physical part of Sardonicus, but upon his mind; for after Keller, Morignac, Buonagente, and my own massaging techniques had failed, I was convinced that it was only through his mind that his body could be cured. It was necessary to persuade him, however, that he was receiving a powerful medicament. His mind, I had hoped, would provide the rest—as, in truth, it did.

If the tale of the 'spectral tyrant' prove true, then we must look upon the human mind with wonderment and terror. For, in that case, there was nothing—nothing corporeal—to prevent the wretched creature from opening his mouth and eating his fill. Alone in that castle, food aplenty at his fingertips, he had suffered a dire punishment which came upon him—to paraphrase Sardonicus' very words—*not from God above or the Fiend below, but from within his own breast, his own brain, his own soul.*

self-punished?

ALEJANDRA PIZARNIK

The Bloody Countess

> The criminal does not make beauty; he himself is the authentic beauty.
> JEAN-PAUL SARTRE

There is a book by Valentine Penrose which documents the life of a real and unusual character: the Countess Bathory, murderer of more than six hundred young girls. The Countess Bathory's sexual perversion and her madness are so obvious that Valentine Penrose disregards them and concentrates instead on the convulsive beauty of the character.

It is not easy to show this sort of beauty. Valentine Penrose, however, succeeded because she played admirably with the aesthetic value of this lugubrious story. She inscribes the underground kingdom of Erzebet Bathory within the walls of her torture chamber, and the chamber within her medieval castle. Here the sinister beauty of nocturnal creatures is summed up in this silent lady of legendary paleness, mad eyes, and hair the sumptuous colour of ravens.

A well-known philosopher includes cries in the category of silence—cries, moans, curses, form 'a silent substance'. The substance of this underworld is evil. Sitting on her throne, the countess watches the tortures and listens to the cries. Her old and horrible maids are wordless figures that bring in fire, knives, needles, irons; they torture the girls, and later bury them. With their iron and knives, these two old women are themselves the instruments of a possession. This dark ceremony has a single silent spectator.

I. THE IRON MAIDEN

> ... among red laughter of glistening lips and monstrous gestures of mechanical women.
> RENÉ DAUMAL

There was once in Nuremberg a famous automaton known as the Iron Maiden. The Countess Bathory bought a copy for her torture chamber in Csejthe Castle. This clockwork doll was of the size and colour of a human creature. Naked, painted, covered in jewels, with blond hair that reached down to the ground, it had a mechanical device that allowed it to curve its lips into a smile, and to move its eyes.

The Countess, sitting on her throne, watches.

For the Maiden to spring into action it is necessary to touch some of the precious stones in its necklace. It responds immediately with horrible creaking sounds and very slowly lifts its white arms which close in a perfect embrace around whatever happens to be next to it—in this case, a girl. The automaton holds her in its arms and now no one will be able to uncouple the living body from the body of iron, both equally beautiful. Suddenly the painted breasts of the Iron Maiden open, and five daggers appear that pierce her struggling companion whose hair is as long as its own.

Once the sacrifice is over another stone in the necklace is touched: the arms drop, the smile and the eyes fall shut, and the murderess becomes once again the Maiden, motionless in its coffin.

II. DEATH BY WATER

> He is standing. And he is standing as absolutely and definitely as if he were sitting.
> WITOLD GOMBROWICZ

The road is covered in snow and, inside the coach, the sombre lady wrapped in furs feels bored. Suddenly she calls out the name of one of the girls in her train. The girl is brought to her: the Countess bites her frantically and sticks needles in her flesh. A while later the procession abandons the wounded girl in the snow. The girl tries to run away. She is pursued, captured and pulled back into the coach. A little further along the road they halt: the Countess has ordered cold water. Now the girl is naked, standing in the snow. Night has fallen. A circle of torches surrounds her, held out by impassive footmen. They pour water over the body and the water turns to ice. (The Countess observes this from inside the coach.) The girl attempts one last slight gesture, trying to move closer to the torches—the only source of warmth. More water is poured over her, and there she remains, for ever standing, upright, dead.

III. THE LETHAL CAGE

> . . . scarlet and black wounds burst upon the splendid flesh.
> ARTHUR RIMBAUD

Lined with knives and adorned with sharp iron blades, it can hold one human body, and can be lifted by means of a pulley. The ceremony of the cage takes place in this manner:

Dorko the maid drags in by the hair a naked young girl, shuts her up in the cage and lifts it high into the air. The Lady of These Ruins appears, a sleepwalker in white. Slowly and silently she sits upon a footstool placed underneath the contraption.

A red-hot poker in her hand, Dorko taunts the prisoner who, drawing back (and this is the ingenuity of the cage) stabs herself against the sharp irons while her blood falls upon the pale woman who dispassionately receives it, her eyes fixed on nothing, as in a daze. When the lady recovers from the trance, she slowly leaves the room. There have been two transformations: her white dress is now red, and where a girl once stood a corpse now lies.

IV. CLASSICAL TORTURE

> Unblemished fruit, untouched by worm or frost,
> whose firm, polished skin cries out to be bitten!
> BAUDELAIRE

Except for a few baroque refinements—like the Iron Maiden, death by water, or the cage—the Countess restricted herself to a monotonously classic style of torture that can be summed up as follows:

Several tall, beautiful, strong girls were selected—their ages had to be between 12 and 18—and dragged into the torture chamber where, dressed in white upon her throne, the countess awaited them. After binding their hands, the servants would whip the girls until the skin of their bodies ripped and they became a mass of swollen wounds; then the servants would burn them with red-hot pokers; cut their fingers with scissors or shears; pierce their wounds; stab them with daggers (if the Countess grew tired of hearing the cries they would sew their mouths up; if one of the girls fainted too soon they would revive her by burning paper soaked in oil between her legs). The blood spurted like fountains and the white dress of the nocturnal lady would turn red. So red, that she would have to go up to her room and change (what would she think about during this brief intermission?). The walls and the ceiling of the chamber would also turn red.

Not always would the lady remain idle while the others busied themselves around her. Sometimes she would lend a hand, and then, impetuously, tear at the flesh—in the most sensitive places—with tiny silver pincers; or she would stick needles, cut the skin between the fingers, press red-hot spoons and irons against the soles of the feet, use the whip (once, during one of her excursions, she ordered her servants to hold up a girl who had just died and kept on whipping her even though she was dead); she also murdered several by means of icy water (using a method invented by Darvulia, the witch; it consisted of plunging a girl into freezing water and leaving her there overnight). Finally, when she was sick, she would have the girls brought to her bedside and she would bite them.

During her erotic seizures she would hurl blasphemous insults at her victims. Blasphemous insults and cries like the baying of a she-wolf were her means of expression as she stalked, in a passion, the gloomy rooms. But nothing was more ghastly than her laugh. (I recapitulate: the medieval castle, the torture chamber, the tender young girls, the old and horrible servants, the beautiful madwoman laughing in a wicked ecstasy provoked by the suffering of others.) Her last words, before letting herself fall into a final faint, would be: 'More, ever more, harder, harder!'

Not always was the day innocent, the night guilty. During the morning or the afternoon, young seamstresses would bring dresses for the Countess, and this would lead to innumerable scenes of cruelty. Without exception, Dorko would find mistakes in the sewing and would select two or three guilty victims (at this point the Countess's doleful eyes would glisten). The punishment of the seamstresses—and of the young maids in general—would vary. If the Countess happened to be in one of her rare good moods, Dorko would simply strip the victims who would continue to work, naked, under the Countess's eyes, in large rooms full of black cats. The girls bore this painless punishment in agonizing amazement, because they never believed it to be possible. Darkly, they must have felt terribly humiliated because their nakedness forced them into a kind of animal world, a feeling heightened by the fully clothed 'human' presence of the Countess, watching them. This scene led me to think of Death—Death as in old allegories, as in the Dance of Death. To strip naked is a prerogative of Death; another is the incessant watching over the creatures it has dispossessed. But there is more: sexual climax forces us into death-like gestures and expressions (gasping and writhing as in agony, cries and moans of paroxysm). If the sexual act implies a sort of death, Erzebet Bathory needed the visible, elementary, coarse

469

death, to succeed in dying that other phantom death we call orgasm. But, who is Death? A figure that harrows and wastes wherever and however it pleases. This is also a possible description of the Countess Bathory. Never did anyone wish so hard not to grow old; I mean, to die. That is why, perhaps, she acted and played the role of Death. Because, how can Death possibly die?

Let us return to the seamstresses and the maids. If Erzebet woke up wrothful, she would not be satisfied with her *tableaux vivants*, but:

To the one who had stolen a coin she would repay with the same coin . . . red-hot, which the girl had to hold tight in her hand.

To the one who had talked during working hours, the Countess herself would sew her mouth shut, or otherwise would open her mouth and stretch it until the lips tore.

She also used the poker with which she would indiscriminately burn cheeks, breasts, tongues. . . .

When the punishments took place in Erzebet's chamber, at night-time, it was necessary to spread large quantities of ashes around her bed, to allow the noble lady to cross without difficulties the vast pools of blood.

V. ON THE STRENGTH OF A NAME

And cold madness wandered aimlessly about the house.
MILOSZ

The name of Bathory—in the power of which Erzebet believed, as if it were an extraordinary talisman—was an illustrious one from the very early days of the Hungarian Empire. It was not by chance that the family coat-of-arms displayed the teeth of a wolf, because the Bathory were cruel, fearless, and lustful. The many marriages that took place between blood relations contributed, perhaps, to the hereditary aberrations and diseases: epilepsy, gout, lust. It is not at all unlikely that Erzebet herself was an epileptic: she seemed possessed by seizures as unexpected as her terrible migraines and pains in the eyes (which she conjured away by placing a wounded pigeon, still alive, on her forehead).

The Countess's family was not unworthy of its ancestral fame. Her uncle Istvan, for instance, was so utterly mad that he would mistake summer for winter, and would have himself drawn in a sleigh along the burning sands that were, in his mind, roads covered with snow. Or consider her cousin Gabor, whose incestuous passion was reciprocated by his sister's. But the most charming of all was the celebrated aunt Klara. She had four husbands (the first two perished by her hand) and died a melodramatic death: she was caught in the arms of a casual acquaintance by her lover, a Turkish Pasha: the intruder was roasted on a spit and aunt Klara was raped (if this verb may be used in her respect) by the entire Turkish garrison. This however did not cause her death: on the contrary, her rapists—tired perhaps of having their way with her—finally had to stab her. She used to pick up her lovers along the Hungarian roads, and would not mind sprawling on a bed where she had previously slaughtered one of her female attendants.

By the time the Countess reached the age of forty, the Bathory had diminished or consumed themselves either through madness or through death. They became almost sensible, thereby losing the interest they had until then provoked in Erzebet.

VI. A WARRIOR BRIDEGROOM

When the warrior took me in his arms
   I felt the fire of pleasure . . .
THE ANGLO-SAXON ELEGY (VIII CEN.)

In 1575, at the age of fifteen, Erzebet married Ferencz Nadasdy, a soldier of great courage. This simple soul never found out that the lady who inspired him with a certain love tinged by fear was in fact a monster. He would come to her in the brief respites between battles, drenched in horse-sweat and blood—the norms of hygiene had not yet been firmly established—and this probably stirred the emotions of the delicate Erzebet, always dressed in rich cloths and perfumed with costly scents.

One day, walking through the castle gardens, Nadasdy saw a naked girl tied to a tree. She was covered in honey: flies and ants crawled all over her, and she was sobbing. The Countess explained that the girl was purging the sin of having stolen some fruit. Nadasdy laughed candidly, as if she had told him a joke.

The soldier would not allow anyone to bother him with stories about his wife, stories of bites, needles, etc. A serious mistake: even as a newly-wed, during those crises whose formula was the Bathory's secret, Erzebet would prick her servants with long needles; and when, felled by her terrible migraines, she was forced to lie in bed, she would gnaw their shoulders and chew on the bits of flesh she had been able to extract. As if by magic, the girl's shrieks would soothe her pain.

But all this is child's play—a young girl's play. During her husband's life she never committed murder.

VII. THE MELANCHOLY MIRROR

Everything is mirror!
OCTAVIO PAZ

The Countess would spend her days in front of her large dark mirror; a famous mirror she had designed herself. It was so comfortable that it even had supports on which to lean one's arms, so as to be able to stand for many hours in front of it without feeling tired. We can suppose that while believing she had designed a mirror, Erzebet had in fact designed the plans for her lair. And now we can understand why only the most grippingly sad music of her gypsy orchestra, or dangerous hunting parties, or the violent perfume of the magic herbs in the witch's hut or—above all—the cellars flooded with human blood, could spark something resembling life in her perfect face. Because no one has more thirst for earth, for blood, and for ferocious sexuality than the creatures who inhabit cold mirrors. And on the subject of mirrors: the rumours concerning her alleged homosexuality were never confirmed. Was this allegation unconscious, or, on the contrary, did she accept it naturally, as simply another right to which she was entitled? Essentially she lived deep within an exclusively female world. There were only women during her nights of crime. And a few details are obviously revealing: for instance, in the torture chamber, during the moments of greatest tension, she herself used to plunge a burning candle into the sex of her victim. There are also testimonies which speak of less solitary pleasures. One of the servants said during the trial that an aristocratic and mysterious lady dressed as a young man would visit the Countess. On one occasion she saw them together, torturing a girl. But we do not know whether they shared any pleasures other than the sadistic ones.

More on the theme of the mirror: even though we are not concerned with *explaining* this sinister figure, it is necessary to dwell on the fact that she suffered from that sixteenth-century sickness: melancholia.

An unchangeable colour rules over the melancholic: his dwelling is a space the colour of mourning. Nothing happens in it. No one intrudes. It is a bare stage where the inert *I* is assisted by the *I* suffering from that inertia. The latter wishes to free the former, but all efforts fail, as Theseus would have failed had he been not only himself, but also the Minotaur; to kill him then, he would have had to kill himself. But there are fleeting remedies: sexual pleasures, for instance, can, for a brief moment, obliterate the silent gallery of echoes and mirrors that constitutes the melancholic soul. Even more: they can illuminate the funeral chamber and transform it into a sort of musical box with gaily-coloured figurines that sing and dance deliciously. Afterwards, when the music winds down, the soul will return to immobility and silence. The music box is not a gratuitous comparison. Melancholia is, I believe, a musical problem: a dissonance, a change in rhythm. While on the *outside* everything happens with the vertiginous rhythm of a cataract, on the *inside* is the exhausted *adagio* of drops of water falling from time to tired time. For this reason the *outside*, seen from the melancholic *inside*, appears absurd and unreal, and constitutes 'the farce we must all play'. But for an instant—because of a wild music, or a drug, or the sexual act carried to its climax—the very slow rhythm of the melancholic soul does not only rise to that of the outside world: it overtakes it with an ineffably blissful exorbitance, and the soul then thrills animated by delirious new energies.

The melancholic soul sees Time as suspended before and after the fatally ephemeral violence. And yet the truth is that time is never suspended, but it grows as slowly as the fingernails of the dead. Between two silences or two deaths, the prodigious, brief moment of speed takes on the various forms of lust: from an innocent intoxication to sexual perversions and even murder.

I think of Erzebet Bathory and her nights whose rhythms are measured by the cries of adolescent girls. I see a portrait of the Countess: the sombre and beautiful lady resembles the allegories of Melancholia represented in old engravings. I also recall that in her time, a melancholic person was a person possessed by the Devil.

VIII. BLACK MAGIC

> ... who kills the sun in order to install the reign of darkest night.
> ANTONIN ARTAUD

Erzebet's greatest obsession had always been to keep old age at bay, at any cost. Her total devotion to the arts of black magic was aimed at preserving—intact for all eternity—the 'sweet bird' of her youth.

The magical herbs, the incantations, the amulets, even the blood baths had, in her eyes, a medicinal function: to immobilize her beauty in order to become, for ever and ever, *a dream of stone*. She always lived surrounded by talismans. In her years of crime she chose one single talisman which contained an ancient and filthy parchment on which was written in special ink, a prayer for her own personal use. She carried it close to her heart, underneath her costly dresses, and in the midst of a celebration, she would touch it surreptitiously. I translate the prayer:

Help me, oh Isten; and you also, all-powerful cloud. Protect me, Erzebet, and grant me long life. Oh cloud, I am in danger. Send me ninety cats, for you are the supreme mistress of cats. Order them to assemble here from all their dwelling-places: from the mountains, from the waters, from the rivers, from the gutters and from the oceans. Tell them to come quickly and bite the heart of —— and also the heart of —— and of ——. And to also bite and rip the heart of Megyery, the Red. And keep Erzebet from all evil.

The blanks were to be filled with the names of those whose hearts she wanted bitten.

In 1604 Erzebet became a widow and met Darvulia. Darvulia was exactly like the woodland witch who frightens us in children's tales. Very old, irascible, always surrounded by black cats, Darvulia fully responded to Erzebet's fascination: within the Countess's eyes the witch found a new version of the evil powers buried in the poisons of the forest and in the coldness of the moon. Darvulia's black magic wrought itself in the Countess's black silence. She initiated her to even crueller games; she taught her to look upon death, and the *meaning* of looking upon death. She incited her to seek death and blood in a literal sense: that is, to love them for their own sake, without fear.

IX. BLOOD BATHS

If you go bathing, Juanilla, tell me to what baths you go.
CANCIONERO OF UPSALA

This rumour existed: since the arrival of Darvulia, the Countess, in order to preserve her comeliness, took baths of human blood. True: Darvulia, being a witch, believed in the invigorating powers of the 'human fluid'. She proclaimed the merits of young girls' blood—especially if they were virgins—to vanquish the demon of senility, and the Countess accepted the treatment as meekly as if it had been a salt bath. Therefore, in the torture chamber, Dorko applied herself to slicing veins and arteries; the blood was collected in pitchers and, when the victims were bled dry, Dorko would pour the red warm liquid over the body of the waiting Countess—ever so quiet, ever so white, ever so erect, ever so silent.

In spite of her unchangeable beauty, Time inflicted upon her some of the vulgar signs of its passing. Towards 1610 Darvulia mysteriously disappeared and Erzebet, almost fifty, complained to her new witch about the uselessness of the blood baths. In fact, more than complain, she threatened to kill her if she did not stop at once the encroaching and execrable signs of old age. The witch argued that Darvulia's method had not worked because plebeian blood had been used. She assured—or prophesied—that changing the colour of the blood, using blue blood instead of red, would ensure the fast retreat of old age. Here began the hunt for the daughters of gentlemen. To attract them, Erzebet's minions would argue that the Lady of Csejthe, alone in her lonely castle, could not resign herself to her solitude. And how to banish solitude? Filling the dark halls with young girls of good families who, in exchange for happy company, would receive lessons in fine manners and learn how to behave exquisitely in society. A fortnight later, of the twenty-five 'pupils' who had hurried to become aristocrats, only two were left: one died some time later, bled white; the other managed to take her life.

X. THE CASTLE OF CSEJTHE

The stone walk is paved with dark cries.
PIERRE-JEAN JOUVE

A castle of grey stones, few windows, square towers, underground mazes; a castle high upon a cliff, a hillside of dry windblown weeds, of woods full of white beasts in winter and dark beasts in summer; a castle that Erzebet Bathory loved for the doleful silence of its walls which muffled every cry.

The Countess's room, cold and badly lit by a lamp of jasmine oil, reeked of blood, and the cellars reeked of dead bodies. Had she wanted to, she could have carried out her work in broad daylight and murdered the girls under the sun, but she was fascinated by the gloom of her dungeon. The gloom which matched so keenly her terrible eroticism of stone, snow, and walls. She loved her maze-shaped dungeon, the archetypical hell of our fears; the viscous, insecure space where we are unprotected and can get lost.

What did she do with all of her days and nights, there, in the loneliness of Csejthe? Of her nights we know something. During the day, the Countess would not leave the side of her two old servants, two creatures escaped from a painting by Goya: the dirty, malodorous, incredibly ugly and perverse Dorko and Jo Ilona. They would try to amuse her with domestic tales to which she paid no attention, and yet she needed the continuous and abominable chatter. Another way of passing time was to contemplate her jewels, to look at herself in her famous mirror, to change her dresses fifteen times a day. Gifted with a great practical sense, she saw to it that the underground cellars were always well supplied; she also concerned herself with her daughters' future—her daughters who always lived so far away from her; she administered her fortune with intelligence, and she occupied herself with all the little details that rule the profane order of our lives.

XI. SEVERE MEASURES

> ... the law, cold and aloof by its very nature, has no access to the passions that might justify the cruel act of murder.
> SADE

For six years the Countess murdered with impunity. During those years there had been countless rumours about her. But the name of Bathory, not only illustrious but also diligently protected by the Hapsburgs, frightened her possible accusers.

Towards 1610 the king had in his hands the most sinister reports—together with proofs—concerning the Countess. After much hesitation he decided to act. He ordered the powerful Thurzo, Count Palatine, to investigate the tragic events at Csejthe and to punish the guilty parties.

At the head of a contingent of armed men, Thurzo arrived unannounced at the castle. In the cellar, cluttered with the remains of the previous night's bloody ceremony, he found a beautiful mangled corpse and two young girls who lay dying. But that was not all. He smelt the smell of the dead; he saw the walls splattered with blood; he saw the Iron Maiden, the cage, the instruments of torture, bowls of dried blood, the cells—and in one of them a group of girls who were waiting their turn to die and who told him that after many days of fasting they had been served roast flesh that had once belonged to the bodies of their companions.

The Countess, without denying Thurzo's accusations, declared that these acts were all within her rights as a noble woman of ancient lineage. To which the Count Palatine replied: 'Countess, I condemn you to life imprisonment within your castle walls.'

Deep in his heart, Thurzo must have told himself that the Countess should be beheaded, but such an exemplary punishment would have been frowned upon, because it affected not only the Bathory family, but also the nobility in general. In the meantime, a notebook was found in the Countess's room, filled with the names and descriptions of her 610 victims in her handwriting. The followers of Erzebet, when brought before the judge, confessed to unthinkable deeds, and perished on the stake.

Around her the prison grew. The doors and windows of her room were walled up; only a small opening was left in one of the walls to allow her to receive her food. And when everything was ready, four gallows were erected on the four corners of the castle to indicate that within those walls lived a creature condemned to death.

In this way she lived for three years, almost wasting away with cold and hunger. She never showed the slightest sign of repentance. She never understood why she had been condemned. On August 21, 1614, a contemporary historian wrote: 'She died at dawn, abandoned by everyone.'

She was never afraid, she never trembled. And no compassion, no sympathy or admiration may be felt for her. Only a certain astonishment at the enormity of the horror, a fascination with a white dress that turns red, with the idea of total laceration, with the imagination of a silence starred with cries in which everything reflects an unacceptable beauty.

Like Sade in his writings, and Gilles de Rais in his crimes, the Countess Bathory reached beyond all limits the uttermost pit of unfettered passions. She is yet another proof that the absolute freedom of the human creature is horrible.

Translated by Alberto Manguel

JORGE LUIS BORGES

The Gospel According to Mark

hese events took place at La Colorada ranch, in the southern part of the township of Junín, during the last days of March 1928. The protagonist was a medical student named Baltasar Espinosa. We may describe him, for now, as one of the common run of young men from Buenos Aires, with nothing more noteworthy about him than an almost unlimited kindness and a capacity for public speaking that had earned him several prizes at the English school in Ramos Mejía. He did not like arguing, and preferred having his listener rather than himself in the right. Although he was fascinated by the probabilities of chance in any game he played, he was a bad player because it gave him no pleasure to win. His wide intelligence was undirected; at the age of thirty-three, he still lacked credit for graduation, by one course—the course to which he was most drawn. His father, who was a freethinker (like all the gentlemen of his day), had introduced him to the lessons of Herbert Spencer, but his mother, before leaving on a trip to Montevideo, once asked him to say the Lord's Prayer and make the sign of the cross every night. Through the years, he had never gone back on that promise.

Espinosa was not lacking in spirit; one day, with more indifference than anger, he had exchanged two or three punches with a group of fellow-students who were trying to force him to take part in a university demonstration. Owing to an acquiescent nature, he was full of opinions, or habits of mind, that were questionable: Argentina mattered less to him than a fear that in other parts of the world people might think of us as Indians; he worshipped France but despised the French; he thought little of Americans but approved the fact that there were tall buildings, like theirs, in Buenos Aires; he believed the gauchos of the plains to be better riders than those of hill or mountain country. When his cousin Daniel invited him to spend the summer months out at La Colorada, he said yes at once—not because he was really fond of the country, but more out of his natural complacency and also because it was easier to say yes than to dream up reasons for saying no.

The ranch's main house was big and slightly run-down; the

quarters of the foreman, whose name was Gutre, were close by. The Gutres were three: the father, an unusually uncouth son, and a daughter of uncertain paternity. They were tall, strong, and bony, and had hair that was on the reddish side and faces that showed traces of Indian blood. They were barely articulate. The foreman's wife had died years before.

There in the country, Espinosa began learning things he never knew, or even suspected—for example, that you do not gallop a horse when approaching settlements, and that you never go out riding except for some special purpose. In time, he was to come to tell the birds apart by their calls.

After a few days, Daniel had to leave for Buenos Aires to close a deal on some cattle. At most, this bit of business might take him a week. Espinosa, who was already somewhat weary of hearing about his cousin's incessant luck with women and his tireless interest in the minute details of men's fashion, preferred staying on at the ranch with his textbooks. But the heat was unbearable, and even the night brought no relief. One morning at daybreak, thunder woke him. Outside, the wind was rocking the Australian pines. Listening to the first heavy drops of rain, Espinosa thanked God. All at once, cold air rolled in. That afternoon, the Salado overflowed its banks.

The next day, looking out over the flooded fields from the gallery of the main house, Baltasar Espinosa thought that the stock metaphor comparing the pampa to the sea was not altogether false—at least, not that morning—though W. H. Hudson had remarked that the sea seems wider because we view it from a ship's deck and not from a horse or from eye level.

The rain did not let up. The Gutres, helped or hindered by Espinosa, the town dweller, rescued a good part of the livestock, but many animals were drowned. There were four roads leading to La Colorada; all of them were under water. On the third day, when a leak threatened the foreman's house, Espinosa gave the Gutres a room near the tool shed, at the back of the main house. This drew them all closer; they ate together in the big dining-room. Conversation turned out to be difficult. The Gutres, who knew so much about country things, were hard put to it to explain them. One night, Espinosa asked them if people still remembered the Indian raids from back when the frontier command was located there in Junín. They told him yes, but they would have given the same answer to a question about the beheading of Charles I. Espinosa recalled his father's saying that almost every case of longevity that was cited in the country was really a case of bad memory or of a dim notion of dates.

Gauchos are apt to be ignorant of the year of their birth or of the name of the man who begot them.

In the whole house, there was apparently no other reading matter than a set of the *Farm Journal*, a handbook of veterinary medicine, a deluxe edition of the Uruguayan epic *Tabaré*, a *History of Shorthorn Cattle in Argentina*, a number of erotic or detective stories, and a recent novel called *Don Segundo Sombra*. Espinosa, trying in some way to bridge the inevitable after-dinner gap, read a couple of chapters of this novel to the Gutres, none of whom could read or write. Unfortunately, the foreman had been a cattle drover, and the doings of the hero, another cattle drover, failed to whet his interest. He said that the work was light, that drovers always travelled with a packhorse that carried everything they needed, and that, had he not been a drover, he would never have seen such far-flung places as the Laguna de Gómez, the town of Bragado, and the spread of the Núñez family in Chacabuco. There was a guitar in the kitchen; the ranch hands, before the time of the events I am describing, used to sit around in a circle. Someone would tune the instrument without ever getting around to playing it. This was known as a guitarfest.

Espinosa, who had grown a beard, began dallying in front of the mirror to study his new face, and he smiled to think how, back in Buenos Aires, he would bore his friends by telling them the story of the Salado flood. Strangely enough, he missed places he never frequented and never would: a corner of Cabrera Street on which there was a mailbox; one of the cement lions of a gateway on Jujuy Street, a few blocks from the Plaza del Once; an old bar-room with a tiled floor, whose exact whereabouts he was unsure of. As for his brothers and his father, they would already have learned from Daniel that he was isolated—etymologically, the word was perfect—by the floodwaters.

Exploring the house, still hemmed in by the watery waste, Espinosa came across an English Bible. Among the black pages at the end, the Guthries—such was their original name—had left a handwritten record of their lineage. They were natives of Inverness; had reached the New World, no doubt as common labourers, in the early part of the nineteenth century; and had intermarried with Indians. The chronicle broke off sometime during the eighteen-seventies, when they no longer knew how to write. After a few generations, they had forgotten English; their Spanish, at the time Espinosa knew them, gave them trouble. They lacked any religious faith, but there survived in their blood, like faint tracks, the rigid fanaticism of the Calvinist and the superstitions of the pampa Indian. Espinosa later told them of his find, but they barely took notice.

Leafing through the volume, his fingers opened it at the beginning of the Gospel according to St Mark. As an exercise in translation, and maybe to find out whether the Gutres understood any of it, Espinosa decided to begin reading them that text after their evening meal. It surprised him that they listened attentively, absorbed. Maybe the gold letters on the cover lent the book authority. It's still there in their blood, Espinosa thought. It also occurred to him that the generations of men, throughout recorded time, have always told and retold two stories—that of a lost ship which searches the Mediterranean seas for a dearly loved island, and that of a god who is crucified on Golgotha. Remembering his lessons in elocution from his schooldays in Ramos Mejía, Espinosa got to his feet when he came to the parables.

The Gutres took to bolting their barbecued meat and their sardines so as not to delay the Gospel. A pet lamb that the girl adorned with a small blue ribbon had injured itself on a strand of barbed wire. To stop the bleeding, the three had wanted to apply a cobweb to the wound, but Espinosa treated the animal with some pills. The gratitude that this treatment awakened in them took him aback. (Not trusting the Gutres at first, he'd hidden away in one of his books the two hundred and forty pesos he had brought with him.) Now, the owner of the place away, Espinosa took over and gave timid orders, which were immediately obeyed. The Gutres, as if lost without him, liked following him from room to room and along the gallery that ran around the house. While he read to them, he noticed that they were secretly stealing the crumbs he had dropped on the table. One evening, he caught them unawares, talking about him respectfully, in very few words.

Having finished the Gospel according to St Mark, he wanted to read another of the three Gospels that remained, but the father asked him to repeat the one he had just read, so that they could understand it better. Espinosa felt that they were like children, to whom repetition is more pleasing than variations or novelty. That night—this is not to be wondered at—he dreamed of the Flood; the hammer blows of the building of the ark woke him up, and he thought that perhaps they were thunder. In fact, the rain, which had let up, started again. The cold was bitter. The Gutres had told him that the storm had damaged the roof of the tool shed, and that they would show it to him when the beams were fixed. No longer a stranger now, he was treated by them with special attention, almost to the point of spoiling him.

481

None of them liked coffee, but for him there was always a small cup into which they heaped sugar.

The new storm had broken out on a Tuesday. Thursday night, Espinosa was awakened by a soft knock at his door, which—just in case—he always kept locked. He got out of bed and opened it; there was the girl. In the dark he could hardly make her out, but by her footsteps he could tell she was barefoot, and moments later, in bed, that she must have come all the way from the other end of the house naked. She did not embrace him or speak a single word; she lay beside him, trembling. It was the first time she had known a man. When she left, she did not kiss him; Espinosa realized that he didn't even know her name. For some reason that he did not want to pry into, he made up his mind that upon returning to Buenos Aires he would tell no one about what had taken place.

The next day began like the previous ones, except that the father spoke to Espinosa and asked him if Christ had let Himself be killed so as to save all other men on earth. Espinosa, who was a freethinker but who felt committed to what he had read to the Gutres, answered, 'Yes, to save everyone from Hell.'

Gutre then asked, 'What's Hell?'

'A place under the ground where souls burn and burn.'

'And the Roman soldiers who hammered in the nails—were they saved, too?'

'Yes,' said Espinosa, whose theology was rather dim.

All along, he was afraid that the foreman might ask him about what had gone on the night before with his daughter. After lunch, they asked him to read the last chapters over again.

Espinosa slept a long nap that afternoon. It was a light sleep, disturbed by persistent hammering and by vague premonitions. Towards evening, he got up and went out onto the gallery. He said, as if thinking aloud, 'The waters have dropped. It won't be long now.'

'It won't be long now,' Gutre repeated, like an echo.

The three had been following him. Bowing their knees to the stone pavement, they asked his blessing. Then they mocked at him, spat on him, and shoved him towards the back part of the house. The girl wept. Espinosa understood what awaited him on the other side of the door. When they opened it, he saw a patch of sky. A bird sang out. A goldfinch, he thought. The shed was without a roof; they had pulled down the beams to make the cross.

ANGELA CARTER

The Lady of the House of Love

At last the revenants became so troublesome the peasants abandoned the village and it fell solely into the possession of subtle and vindictive inhabitants who manifest their presences by shadows that fall almost imperceptibly awry, too many shadows, even at midday, shadows that have no source in anything visible; by the sound, sometimes, of sobbing in a derelict bedroom where a cracked mirror suspended from a wall does not reflect a presence; by a sense of unease that will afflict the traveller unwise enough to pause to drink from the fountain in the square that still gushes spring water from a faucet stuck in a stone lion's mouth. A cat prowls in a weedy garden; he grins and spits, arches his back, bounces away from an intangible on four fear-stiffened legs. Now all shun the village below the château in which the beautiful somnambulist helplessly perpetuates her ancestral crimes.

Wearing an antique bridal gown, the beautiful queen of the vampires sits all alone in her dark, high house under the eyes of the portraits of her demented and atrocious ancestors, each one of whom, through her, projects a baleful posthumous existence; she counts out the Tarot cards, ceaselessly construing a constellation of possibilities as if the random fall of the cards on the red plush tablecloth before her could precipitate her from her chill, shuttered room into a country of perpetual summer and obliterate the perennial sadness of a girl who is both death and the maiden.

Her voice is filled with distant sonorities, like reverberations in a cave: now you are at the place of annihilation, now you are at the place of annihilation. And she is herself a cave full of echoes, she is a system of repetitions, she is a closed circuit. 'Can a bird sing only the song it knows or can it learn a new song?' She draws her long, sharp fingernail across the bars of the cage in which her pet lark sings, striking a plangent twang like that of the plucked heartstrings of a woman of metal. Her hair falls down like tears.

The castle is mostly given over to ghostly occupants but she herself has her own suite of drawing-room and bedroom. Closely barred shutters and heavy velvet curtains keep out every leak of natural light.

There is a round table on a single leg covered with a red plush cloth on which she lays out her inevitable Tarot; this room is never more than faintly illuminated by a heavily shaded lamp on the mantelpiece and the dark red figured wallpaper is obscurely, distressingly patterned by the rain that drives in through the neglected roof and leaves behind it random areas of staining, ominous marks like those left on the sheets by dead lovers. Depredations of rot and fungus everywhere. The unlit chandelier is so heavy with dust the individual prisms no longer show any shapes; industrious spiders have woven canopies in the corners of this ornate and rotting place, have trapped the porcelain vases on the mantelpiece in soft grey nets. But the mistress of all this disintegration notices nothing.

She sits in a chair covered in moth-ravaged burgundy velvet at the low, round table and distributes the cards; sometimes the lark sings, but more often remains a sullen mound of drab feathers. Sometimes the Countess will wake it for a brief cadenza by strumming the bars of its cage; she likes to hear it announce how it cannot escape.

She rises when the sun sets and goes immediately to her table where she plays her game of patience until she grows hungry, until she becomes ravenous. She is so beautiful she is unnatural; her beauty is an abnormality, a deformity, for none of her features exhibit any of those touching imperfections that reconcile us to the imperfection of the human condition. Her beauty is a symptom of her disorder, of her soullessness.

The white hands of the tenebrous belle deal the hand of destiny. Her fingernails are longer than those of the mandarins of ancient China and each is pared to a fine point. These and teeth as fine and white as spikes of spun sugar are the visible signs of the destiny she wistfully attempts to evade via the arcana; her claws and teeth have been sharpened on centuries of corpses, she is the last bud of the poison tree that sprang from the loins of Vlad the Impaler who picnicked on corpses in the forests of Transylvania.

The walls of her bedroom are hung with black satin, embroidered with tears of pearl. At the room's four corners are funerary urns and bowls which emit slumbrous, pungent fumes of incense. In the centre is an elaborate catafalque, in ebony, surrounded by long candles in enormous silver candlesticks. In a white lace négligé stained a little with blood, the Countess climbs up on her catafalque at dawn each morning and lies down in an open coffin.

A chignoned priest of the Orthodox faith staked out her wicked father at a Carpathian crossroad before her milk teeth grew. Just as they staked him out, the fatal Count cried: 'Nosferatu is dead;

long live Nosferatu!' Now she possesses all the haunted forests and mysterious habitations of his vast domain; she is the hereditary commandant of the army of shadows who camp in the village below her château, who penetrate the woods in the form of owls, bats and foxes, who make the milk curdle and the butter refuse to come, who ride the horses all night on a wild hunt so they are sacks of skin and bone in the morning, who milk the cows dry and, especially, torment pubescent girls with fainting fits, disorders of the blood, diseases of the imagination.

But the Countess herself is indifferent to her own weird authority, as if she were dreaming it. In her dream, she would like to be human; but she does not know if that is possible. The Tarot always shows the same configuration: always she turns up La Papesse, La Mort, La Tour Abolie, wisdom, death, dissolution.

On moonless nights, her keeper lets her out into the garden. This garden, an exceedingly sombre place, bears a strong resemblance to a burial ground and all the roses her dead mother planted have grown up into a huge, spiked wall that incarcerates her in the castle of her inheritance. When the back door opens, the Countess will sniff the air and howl. She drops, now, on all fours. Crouching, quivering, she catches the scent of her prey. Delicious crunch of the fragile bones of rabbits and small, furry things she pursues with fleet, four-footed speed; she will creep home, whimpering, with blood smeared on her cheeks. She pours water from the ewer in her bedroom into the bowl, she washes her face with the wincing, fastidious gestures of a cat.

The voracious margin of huntress's nights in the gloomy garden, crouch and pounce, surrounds her habitual tormented somnambulism, her life or imitation of life. The eyes of this nocturnal creature enlarge and glow. All claws and teeth, she strikes, she gorges; but nothing can console her for the ghastliness of her condition, nothing. She resorts to the magic comfort of the Tarot pack and shuffles the cards, lays them out, reads them, gathers them up with a sigh, shuffles them again, constantly constructing hypotheses about a future which is irreversible.

An old mute looks after her, to make sure she never sees the sun, that all day she stays in her coffin, to keep mirrors and all reflective surfaces away from her—in short, to perform all the functions of the servants of vampires. Everything about this beautiful and ghastly lady is as it should be, queen of night, queen of terror—except her horrible reluctance for the role.

Nevertheless, if an unwise adventurer pauses in the square of the deserted village to refresh himself at the fountain, a crone in a black dress and white apron presently emerges from a house. She will invite you with smiles and gestures; you will follow her. The Countess wants fresh meat. When she was a little girl, she was like a fox and contented herself entirely with baby rabbits that squeaked piteously as she bit into their necks with a nauseated voluptuousness, with voles and fieldmice that palpitated for a bare moment between her embroidress's fingers. But now she is a woman, she must have men. If you stop too long beside the giggling fountain, you will be led by the hand to the Countess's larder.

All day, she lies in her coffin in her négligé of blood-stained lace. When the sun drops behind the mountain, she yawns and stirs and puts on the only dress she has, her mother's wedding dress, to sit and read her cards until she grows hungry. She loathes the food she eats; she would have liked to take the rabbits home with her, feed them on lettuce, pet them and make them a nest in her red-and-black chinoiserie escritoire, but hunger always overcomes her. She sinks her teeth into the neck where an artery throbs with fear; she will drop the deflated skin from which she has extracted all the nourishment with a small cry of both pain and disgust. And it is the same with the shepherd boys and gipsy lads who, ignorant or foolhardy, come to wash the dust from their feet in the water of the fountain; the Countess's governess brings them into the drawing room where the cards on the table always show the Grim Reaper. The Countess herself will serve them coffee in tiny cracked, precious cups, and little sugar cakes. The hobbledehoys sit with a spilling cup in one hand and a biscuit in the other, gaping at the Countess in her satin finery as she pours from a silver pot and chatters distractedly to put them at their fatal ease. A certain desolate stillness of her eyes indicates she is inconsolable. She would like to caress their lean brown cheeks and stroke their ragged hair. When she takes them by the hand and leads them to her bedroom, they can scarcely believe their luck.

Afterwards, her governess will tidy the remains into a neat pile and wrap it in its own discarded clothes. This mortal parcel she then discreetly buries in the garden. The blood on the Countess's cheeks will be mixed with tears; her keeper probes her fingernails for her with a little silver toothpick, to get rid of the fragments of skin and bone that have lodged there

> Fee fie fo fum
> I smell the blood of an Englishman.

One hot, ripe summer in the pubescent years of the present century, a young officer in the British army, blond, blue-eyed, heavy-muscled, visiting friends in Vienna, decided to spend the remainder of his furlough exploring the little-known uplands of Romania. When he quixotically decided to travel the rutted cart-tracks by bicycle, he saw all the humour of it: 'on two wheels in the land of the vampires'. So, laughing, he sets out on his adventure.

He has the special quality of virginity, most and least ambiguous of states: ignorance, yet at the same time, power in potentia, and, furthermore, unknowingness, which is not the same as ignorance. He is more than he knows—and has about him, besides, the special glamour of that generation for whom history has already prepared a special, exemplary fate in the trenches of France. This being, rooted in change and time, is about to collide with the timeless Gothic eternity of the vampires, for whom all is as it has always been and will be, whose cards always fall in the same pattern.

Although so young, he is also rational. He has chosen the most rational mode of transport in the world for his trip round the Carpathians. To ride a bicycle is in itself some protection against superstitious fears, since the bicycle is the product of pure reason applied to motion. Geometry at the service of man! Give me two spheres and a straight line and I will show you how far I can take them. Voltaire himself might have invented the bicycle, since it contributes so much to man's welfare and nothing at all to his bane. Beneficial to the health, it emits no harmful fumes and permits only the most decorous speeds. How can a bicycle ever be an implement of harm?

A single kiss woke up the Sleeping Beauty in the Wood.

The waxen fingers of the Countess, fingers of a holy image, turn up the card called Les Amoureux. Never, never before ... never before has the Countess cast herself a fate involving love. She shakes, she trembles, her great eyes close beneath her finely veined, nervously fluttering eyelids; the lovely cartomancer has, this time, the first time, dealt herself a hand of love and death.

> Be he alive or be he dead
> I'll grind his bones to make my bread.

At the mauvish beginnings of evening, the English m'sieu toils up the hill to the village he glimpsed from a great way off; he must dismount and push his bicycle before him, the path too steep to ride. He hopes to find a friendly inn to rest the night; he's hot, hungry, thirsty, weary, dusty ... At first, such disappointment, to discover the roofs of all the cottages caved in and tall weeds thrusting through the piles of fallen tiles, shutters hanging disconsolately from their hinges, an entirely uninhabited place. And the rank vegetation whispers, as if foul secrets, here, where, if one were sufficiently imaginative, one could almost imagine twisted faces appearing momentarily beneath the crumbling eaves ... but the adventure of it all, and the consolation of the poignant brightness of the hollyhocks still bravely blooming in the shaggy gardens, and the beauty of the flaming sunset, all these considerations soon overcame his disappointment, even assuaged the faint unease he'd felt. And the fountain where the village women used to wash their clothes still gushed out bright, clear water; he gratefully washed his feet and hands, applied his mouth to the faucet, then let the icy stream run over his face.

When he raised his dripping, gratified head from the lion's mouth, he saw, silently arrived beside him in the square, an old woman who smiled eagerly, almost conciliatorily at him. She wore a black dress and a white apron, with a housekeeper's key ring at the waist; her grey hair was neatly coiled in a chignon beneath the white linen headdress worn by elderly women of that region. She bobbed a curtsy at the young man and beckoned him to follow her. When he hesitated, she pointed towards the great bulk of the mansion above them, whose façade loured over the village, rubbed her stomach, pointed to her mouth, rubbed her stomach again, clearly miming an invitation to supper. Then she beckoned him again, this time turning determinedly upon her heel as though she would brook no opposition.

A great, intoxicated surge of the heavy scent of red roses blew into his face as soon as they left the village, inducing a sensuous vertigo; a blast of rich, faintly corrupt sweetness strong enough almost, to fell him. Too many roses. Too many roses bloomed on enormous thickets that lined the path, thickets bristling with thorns, and the flowers themselves were almost too luxuriant, their huge congregations of plush petals somehow obscene in their excess, their whorled, tightly budded cores outrageous in their implications. The mansion emerged grudgingly out of this jungle.

In the subtle and haunting light of the setting sun, that golden light rich with nostalgia for the day that is just past, the sombre visage of the place, part manor house, part fortified farmhouse, immense, rambling, a dilapidated eagle's nest atop the crag down which its attendant village meandered, reminded him of childhood tales on winter evenings, when he and his brothers and sisters scared themselves half out of their wits with ghost stories set in just such places and then had to have candles to light them up newly terrifying stairs to bed. He could almost have regretted accepting the crone's unspoken invitation; but now, standing before the door of time-eroded oak while she selected a huge iron key from the clanking ringful at her waist, he knew it was too late to turn back and brusquely reminded himself he was no child, now, to be frightened of his own fancies.

The old lady unlocked the door, which swung back on melodramatically creaking hinges, and fussily took charge of his bicycle, in spite of his protests. He felt a certain involuntary sinking of the heart to see his beautiful two-wheeled symbol of rationality vanish into the dark entrails of the mansion, to, no doubt, some damp outhouse where they would not oil it or check its tyres. But, in for a penny, in for a pound—in his youth and strength and blond beauty, in the invisible, even unacknowledged pentacle of his virginity, the young man stepped over the threshold of Nosferatu's castle and did not shiver in the blast of cold air, as from the mouth of a grave, that emanated from the lightless, cavernous interior.

The crone took him to a little chamber where there was a black oak table spread with a clean white cloth and this cloth was carefully laid with heavy silverware, a little tarnished, as if someone with foul breath had breathed on it, but laid with one place only. Curiouser and curiouser; invited to the castle for dinner, now he must dine alone. All the same, he sat down as she had bid him. Although it was not yet dark outside, the curtains were closely drawn and only the sparing light trickling from a single oil lamp showed him how dismal his surroundings were. The crone bustled about to get him a bottle of wine and a glass from an ancient cabinet of wormy oak; while he bemusedly drank his wine, she disappeared but soon returned bearing a steaming platter of the local spiced meat stew with dumplings, and a shank of black bread. He was hungry after his long day's ride, he ate heartily and polished his plate with the crust, but this coarse food was hardly the entertainment he'd expected from the gentry and he was puzzled by the assessing glint in the dumb woman's eyes as she watched him eating.

But she darted off to get him a second helping as soon as he'd finished the first one and she seemed so friendly and helpful, besides, that he knew he could count on a bed for the night in the castle, as well as his supper, so he sharply reprimanded himself for his own childish lack of enthusiasm for the eerie silence, the clammy chill of the place.

When he'd put away the second plateful, the old woman came and gestured he should leave the table and follow her once again. She made a pantomime of drinking; he deduced he was now invited to take after-dinner coffee in another room with some more elevated member of the household who had not wished to dine with him but, all the same, wanted to make his acquaintance. An honour, no doubt; in deference to his host's opinion of himself, he straightened his tie, brushed the crumbs from his tweed jacket.

He was surprised to find how ruinous the interior of the house was—cobwebs, worm-eaten beams, crumbling plaster; but the mute crone resolutely wound him on the reel of her lantern down endless corridors, up winding staircases, through the galleries where the painted eyes of family portraits briefly flickered as they passed, eyes that belonged, he noticed, to faces, one and all, of a quite memorable beastliness. At last she paused and, behind the door where they'd halted, he heard a faint, metallic twang as of, perhaps, a chord struck on a harpsichord. And then, wonderfully, the liquid cascade of the song of a lark, bringing to him, in the heart—had he but known it—of Juliet's tomb, all the freshness of morning.

The crone rapped with her knuckles on the panels; the most seductively caressing voice he had ever heard in his life softly called out, in heavily accented French, the adopted language of the Romanian aristocracy: 'Entrez.'

First of all, he saw only a shape, a shape imbued with a faint luminosity since it caught and reflected in its yellowed surfaces what little light there was in the ill-lit room; this shape resolved itself into that of, of all things, a hoop-skirted dress of white satin draped here and there with lace, a dress fifty or sixty years out of fashion but once, obviously, intended for a wedding. And then he saw the girl who wore the dress, a girl with the fragility of the skeleton of a moth, so thin, so frail that her dress seemed to him to hang suspended, as if untenanted in the dank air, a fabulous lending, a self-articulated garment in which she lived like a ghost in a machine. All the light in the room came from a low-burning lamp with a thick greenish shade on a distant mantelpiece; the crone who accompanied him shielded her lantern with her hand, as if to protect her mistress from too suddenly seeing, or their guest from too suddenly seeing her.

So that it was little by little, as his eyes grew accustomed to the half-dark, that he saw how beautiful and how very young the bedizened scarecrow was, and he thought of a child dressing up in her mother's clothes, perhaps a child putting on the clothes of a dead mother in order to bring her, however briefly, to life again.

The Countess stood behind a low table, beside a pretty, silly, gilt-and-wire birdcage, hands outstretched in a distracted attitude that was almost one of flight; she looked as startled by their entry as if she had not requested it. With her stark white face, her lovely death's head surrounded by long dark hair that fell down as straight as if it were soaking wet, she looked like a shipwrecked bride. Her huge dark eyes almost broke his heart with their waiflike, lost look; yet he was disturbed, almost repelled, by her extraordinarily fleshy mouth, a mouth with wide, full prominent lips of a vibrant purplish-crimson, a morbid mouth. Even—but he put the thought away from him immediately—a whore's mouth. She shivered all the time, a starveling chill, a malarial agitation of the bones. He thought she must be only sixteen or seventeen years old, no more, with the hectic, unhealthy beauty of a consumptive. She was the châtelaine of all this decay.

With many tender precautions, the crone now raised the light she held to show his hostess her guest's face. At that, the Countess let out a faint, mewing cry and made a blind, appalled gesture with her hands, as if pushing him away, so that she knocked against the table and a butterfly dazzle of painted cards fell to the floor. Her mouth formed a round 'o' of woe, she swayed a little and then sank into her chair, where she lay as if now scarcely capable of moving. A bewildering reception. Tsk'ing under her breath, the crone busily poked about on the table until she found an enormous pair of dark green glasses, such as blind beggars wear, and perched them on the Countess's nose.

He went forward to pick up her cards for her from a carpet that, he saw to his surprise, was part rotted away, partly encroached upon by all kinds of virulent-looking fungi. He retrieved the cards and shuffled them carelessly together, for they meant nothing to him, though they seemed strange playthings for a young girl. What a grisly picture of a capering skeleton! He covered it up with a happier one—of two young lovers, smiling at one another, and put her toys back into a hand so slender you could almost see the frail net of bone beneath the translucent skin, a hand with fingernails as long, as finely pointed, as banjo picks.

At his touch, she seemed to revive a little and almost smiled, raising herself upright.

'Coffee,' she said. 'You must have coffee.' And scooped up her cards into a pile so that the crone could set before her a silver spirit kettle, a silver coffee pot, cream jug, sugar basin, cups ready on a silver tray, a strange touch of elegance, even if discoloured, in this devastated interior whose mistress ethereally shone as if with her own blighted, submarine radiance.

The crone found him a chair and, tittering noiselessly, departed, leaving the room a little darker.

While the young lady attended to the coffee-making, he had time to contemplate with some distaste a further series of family portraits which decorated the stained and peeling walls of the room; these livid faces all seemed contorted with a febrile madness and the blubber lips, the huge, demented eyes that all had in common bore a disquieting resemblance to those of the hapless victim of inbreeding now patiently filtering her fragrant brew, even if some rare grace has so finely transformed those features when it came to her case. The lark, its chorus done, had long ago fallen silent; no sound but the chink of silver on china. Soon, she held out to him a tiny cup of rose-painted china.

'Welcome,' she said in her voice with the rushing sonorities of the ocean in it, a voice that seemed to come elsewhere than from her white, still throat. 'Welcome to my château. I rarely receive visitors and that's a misfortune since nothing animates me half as much as the presence of a stranger ... This place is so lonely, now the village is deserted, and my one companion, alas, she cannot speak. Often I am so silent that I think I, too, will soon forget how to do so and nobody here will ever talk any more.'

She offered him a sugar biscuit from a Limoges plate; her fingernails struck carillons from the antique china. Her voice, issuing from those red lips like the obese roses in her garden, lips that do not move—her voice is curiously disembodied; she is like a doll, he thought, a ventriloquist's doll, or, more, like a great, ingenious piece of clockwork. For she seemed inadequately powered by some slow energy of which she was not in control; as if she had been wound up years ago, when she was born, and now the mechanism was inexorably running down and would leave her lifeless. This idea that she might be an automaton, made of white velvet and black fur, that could not move of its own accord, never quite deserted him; indeed, it deeply moved his heart. The carnival air of her white dress emphasized her unreality, like a sad Columbine who lost her way in the wood a long time ago and never reached the fair.

'And the light. I must apologize for the lack of light ... a hereditary affliction of the eyes ...'

Her blind spectacles gave him his handsome face back to himself twice over; if he presented himself to her naked face, he would dazzle her like the sun she is forbidden to look at because it would shrivel her up at once, poor night bird, poor butcher bird.

Vous serez ma proie.

You have such a fine throat, m'sieu, like a column of marble. When you came through the door retaining about you all the golden light of the summer's day of which I know nothing, nothing, the card called 'Les Amoureux' had just emerged from the tumbling chaos of imagery before me; it seemed to me you had stepped off the card into my darkness and, for a moment, I thought, perhaps, you might irradiate it.

I do not mean to hurt you. I shall wait for you in my bride's dress in the dark.

The bridegroom is come, he will go into the chamber which has been prepared for him.

I am condemned to solitude and dark; I do not mean to hurt you.

I will be very gentle.

(And could love free me from the shadows? Can a bird sing only the song it knows, or can it learn a new song?)

See, how I'm ready for you. I've always been ready for you; I've been waiting for you in my wedding dress, why have you delayed for so long . . . it will all be over very quickly.

You will feel no pain, my darling.

She herself is a haunted house. She does not possess herself; her ancestors sometimes come and peer out of the windows of her eyes and that is very frightening. She has the mysterious solitude of ambiguous states; she hovers in a no-man's land between life and death, sleeping and waking, behind the hedge of spiked flowers, Nosferatu's sanguinary rosebud. The beastly forebears on the walls condemn her to a perpetual repetition of their passions.

(One kiss, however, and only one, woke up the Sleeping Beauty in the Wood.)

Nervously, to conceal her inner voices, she keeps up a front of inconsequential chatter in French while her ancestors leer and grimace on the walls; however hard she tries to think of any other, she only knows of one kind of consummation.

He was struck, once again, by the birdlike, predatory claws which tipped her marvellous hands; the sense of strangeness that had been growing on him since he buried his head under the streaming water in the village, since he entered the dark portals of the fatal castle, now fully overcame him. Had he been a cat, he would have bounced backwards from her hands on four fear-stiffened legs, but he is not a cat: he is a hero.

A fundamental disbelief in what he sees before him sustains him, even in the boudoir of Countess Nosferatu herself; he would have said, perhaps, that there are some things which, even if they *are* true, we should not believe possible. He might have said: it is folly to believe one's eyes. Not so much that he does not believe in her;

he can see her, she is real. If she takes off her dark glasses, from her eyes will stream all the images that populate this vampire-haunted land, but, since he himself is immune to shadow, due to his virginity—he does not yet know what there is to be afraid of—and due to his heroism, which makes him like the sun, he sees before him, first and foremost, an inbred, highly strung girl child, fatherless, motherless, kept in the dark too long and pale as a plant that never sees the light, half-blinded by some hereditary condition of the eyes. And though he feels unease, he cannot feel terror; so he is like the boy in the fairy tale, who does not know how to shudder, and not spooks, ghouls, beasties, the Devil himself and all his retinue could do the trick.

This lack of imagination gives his heroism to the hero.

He will learn to shudder in the trenches. But this girl cannot make him shudder.

Now it is dark. Bats swoop and squeak outside the tightly shuttered windows. The coffee is all drunk, the sugar biscuits eaten. Her chatter comes trickling and diminishing to a stop; she twists her fingers together, picks at the lace of her dress, shifts nervously in her chair. Owls shriek; the impedimenta of her condition squeak and gibber all around us. Now you are at the place of annihilation, now you are at the place of annihilation. She turns her head away from the blue beams of his eyes; she knows no other consummation than the only one she can offer him. She has not eaten for three days. It is dinner-time. It is bedtime.

> Suivez-moi.
> Je vous attendais.
> Vous serez ma proie.

The raven caws on the accursed roof. 'Dinnertime, dinnertime,' clang the portraits on the walls. A ghastly hunger gnaws her entrails; she has waited for him all her life without knowing it.

The handsome bicyclist, scarcely believing his luck, will follow her into her bedroom; the candles around her sacrificial altar burn with a low, clear flame, light catches on the silver tears stitched to the wall. She will assure him, in the very voice of temptation: 'My clothes have but to fall and you will see before you a succession of mysteries.'

She has no mouth with which to kiss, no hands with which to caress, only the fangs and talons of a beast of prey. To touch the mineral sheen of the flesh revealed in the cool candle gleam is to invite her fatal embrace; in her low, sweet voice, she will croon the lullaby of the House of Nosferatu.

Embraces, kisses; your golden head, of a lion, although I have never seen a lion, only imagined one, of the sun, even if I've only seen the picture of the sun on the Tarot card, your golden head of the lover whom I dreamed would one day free me, this head will fall back, its eyes roll upwards in a spasm you will mistake for that of love and not of death. The bridegroom bleeds on my inverted marriage bed. Stark and dead, poor bicyclist; he has paid the price of a night with the Countess and some think it too high a fee while some do not.

Tomorrow, her keeper will bury his bones under her roses. The food her roses feed on gives them their rich colour, their swooning odour, that breathes lasciviously of forbidden pleasures.

Suivez-moi.

'Suivez-moi!'

The handsome bicyclist, fearful for his hostess's health, her sanity, gingerly follows her hysterical imperiousness into the other room; he would like to take her into his arms and protect her from the ancestors who leer down from the walls.

What a macabre bedroom!

His colonel, an old goat with jaded appetites, had given him the visiting card of a brothel in Paris where, the satyr assured him, ten louis would buy just such a lugubrious bedroom, with a naked girl upon a coffin; offstage, the brothel pianist played the *Dies Irae* on a harmonium and, amidst all the perfumes of the embalming parlour, the customer took his necrophiliac pleasure of a pretended corpse. He had good-naturedly refused the old man's offer of such an initiation; how can he now take criminal advantage of the disordered girl with fever-hot, bone-dry, taloned hands and eyes that deny all the erotic promises of her body with their terror, their sadness, their dreadful, balked tenderness?

So delicate and damned, poor thing. Quite damned.

Yet I do believe she scarcely knows what she is doing.

She is shaking as if her limbs were not efficiently joined together, as if she might shake into pieces. She raises her hands to unfasten the neck of her dress and her eyes well with tears, they trickle down beneath the rim of her dark glasses. She can't take off her mother's wedding dress unless she takes off her dark glasses; she has fumbled the ritual, it is no longer inexorable. The mechanism within her fails her, now, when she needs it most. When she takes off the dark glasses, they slip from her fingers and smash to pieces on the tiled floor. There is no room in her drama for improvisation; and this unexpected, mundane noise of breaking glass breaks the wicked spell in the room, entirely. She gapes blindly down at the splinters and ineffectively smears the tears across her face with her fist. What is she to do now?

When she kneels to try to gather the fragments of glass together, a sharp sliver pierces deeply into the pad of her thumb; she cries out, sharp, real. She kneels among the broken glass and watches the bright bead of blood form a drop. She has never seen her own blood before, not her *own* blood. It exercises upon her an awed fascination.

Into this vile and murderous room, the handsome bicyclist brings the innocent remedies of the nursery; in himself, by his presence, he is an exorcism. He gently takes her hand away from her and dabs the blood with his own handkerchief, but still it spurts out. And so he puts his mouth to the wound. He will kiss it better for her, as her mother, had she lived, would have done.

All the silver tears fall from the wall with a flimsy tinkle. Her painted ancestors turn away their eyes and grind their fangs.

How can she bear the pain of becoming human?

The end of exile is the end of being.

He was awakened by larksong. The shutters, the curtains, even the long-sealed windows of the horrid bedroom were all opened up and light and air streamed in; now you could see how tawdry it all was, how thin and cheap the satin, the catafalque not ebony at all but black-painted paper stretched on struts of wood, as in the theatre. The wind had blown droves of petals from the roses outside into the room and this crimson residue swirled fragrantly about the floor. The candles had burnt out and she must have set her pet lark free because it perched on the edge of the silly coffin to sing him its ecstatic morning song. His bones were stiff and aching, he'd slept on the floor with his bundled-up jacket for a pillow, after he'd put her to bed.

But now there was no trace of her to be seen, except, lightly tossed across the crumpled black satin bedcover, a lace négligé lightly soiled with blood, as it might be from a woman's menses, and a rose that must have come from the fierce bushes nodding through the window. The air was heavy with incense and roses and made him cough. The Countess must have got up early to enjoy the sunshine, slipped outside to gather him a rose. He got to his feet, coaxed the lark on to his wrist and took it to the window. At first, it exhibited the reluctance for the sky of a long-caged thing, but, when he tossed it up on to the currents of the air, it spread its wings and was up and away into the clear blue bowl of the heavens; he watched its trajectory with a lift of joy in his heart.

Then he padded into the boudoir, his mind busy with plans. We shall take her to Zurich, to a clinic; she will be treated for nervous hysteria. Then to an eye specialist, for her photophobia, and to a dentist to put her teeth into better shape. Any competent manicurist will deal with her claws. We shall turn her into the lovely girl she is; I shall cure her of all these nightmares.

The heavy curtains are pulled back, to let in brilliant fusillades of early morning light; in the desolation of the boudoir, she sits at her round table in her white dress, with the cards laid out before her. She has dropped off to sleep over the cards of destiny that are so fingered, so soiled, so worn by constant shuffling that you can no longer make the image out on any single one of them.

She is not sleeping.

In death, she looked far older, less beautiful and so, for the first time, fully human.

I will vanish in the morning light; I was only an invention of darkness.

And I leave you as a souvenir the dark, fanged rose I plucked from between my thighs, like a flower laid on a grave. On a grave.

My keeper will attend to everything.

Nosferatu always attends his own obsequies; she will not go to the graveyard unattended. And now the crone materialized, weeping, and roughly gestured him to begone. After a search in some foul-smelling outhouses, he discovered his bicycle and, abandoning his holiday, rode directly to Bucharest where, at the poste restante, he found a telegram summoning him to rejoin his regiment at once. Much later, when he changed back into uniform in his quarters, he discovered he still had the Countess's rose, he must have tucked it into the breast pocket of his cycling jacket after he had found her body. Curiously enough, although he had brought it so far away from Romania, the flower did not seem to be quite dead and, on impulse, because the girl had been so lovely and her death so unexpected and pathetic, he decided to try and resurrect her rose. He filled his tooth glass with water from the carafe on his locker and popped the rose into it, so that its withered head floated on the surface.

When he returned from the mess that evening, the heavy fragrance of Count Nosferatu's roses drifted down the stone corridor of the barracks to greet him, and his spartan quarters brimmed with the reeling odour of a glowing, velvet, monstrous flower whose petals had regained all their former bloom and elasticity, their corrupt, brilliant, baleful splendour.

Next day, his regiment embarked for France.

JOYCE CAROL OATES

Secret Observations on the Goat-Girl

At the edge of my father's property, in an abandoned corncrib, there lives a strange creature—a goat-child—a girl—my age—with no name that we know—and no mother or father or companions. She has a long narrow head and immense slanted eyes, albino-pale, and an expression that seems to be perpetually startled. The veins of her eyes glow a faint warm pulsing pink and the irises are animal-slits, vertical, very black. Sometimes she suns herself in the open doorway, her slender front legs tucked neatly beneath her, her head alert and uplifted. Sometimes she grazes in the back pasture. Though we children are forbidden to know about her we frequently spy on her, and laugh to see her down on all fours, *grazing as animals do*—yet in an awkward improvised posture, as if she were a child playing at being a goat.

But of course she *is* an animal and frightening to see.

Her small body is covered in coarse white hairs, wavy, slightly curly, longest around her temples and at the nape of her neck. Her ears are frankly goatish, pert and oversized and sensitive to the slightest sound. (If we creep up in the underbrush to spy on her, she always hears us—her ears prick up and tremble—though she doesn't seem to see us. Which is why some of us have come to believe that the goat-girl is blind.)

Her nose, like her ears, is goatish: snubbed and flat with wide dark nostrils. But her eyes are human eyes. Thickly lashed and beautiful. Except they are so very pale. The tiny blood vessels are exposed which is why they look pink; I wonder, does the sunshine hurt her? . . . do tears form in her eyes? (Of my eight brothers and sisters it is the older, for some reason, who argue that the goat-girl is blind and should be put out of her misery. One of my sisters has night-mares about her—about her strange staring eyes—though she has seen the goat-girl only once, and then from a distance of at least fifteen feet. Oh the nasty thing, she says, half sobbing, the filthy thing!—Father should have it butchered.)

But we all speak in whispers. Because we are forbidden to know.

Since the goat-girl came to live at the edge of our property my mother rarely leaves the house. In fact she rarely comes downstairs now. Sometimes she wears a robe over her nightgown and doesn't brush out her hair and pin it up the way she used to, sometimes she hurries out of the room if one of us comes in. Her laughter is faint and shrill.

Her fingers are cold to the touch. She doesn't embrace us any longer.

Father doesn't admonish her because, as he says, he loves her too deeply. But he often avoids her. And of course he is very busy with his travels—he is sometimes absent for weeks at a time.

Shame, shame!—the villagers whisper.

But never so that any of us can hear.

The goat-girl cannot speak as human beings do, nor does she make goat noises. For the most part she is silent. But she is capable of a strangulated mew, a bleating whine, and, sometimes at night, a questioning cry that is human in its intonation and rhythm, though of course it is incomprehensible, and disturbing to hear. To some of us it sounds pleading, to others angry and accusing. Of course no one ever replies.

The goat-girl eats grass, grain, vegetables the farm workers have tossed into her pen—gnarled and knotted carrots, wormy turnips, blackened potatoes. One day I slipped away from the house to bring her a piece of my birthday cake (angel food with pink frosting and a sprinkling of silver 'stars')—I left it wrapped in a napkin near the corncrib but as far as I knew she never approached it: she is very shy by daylight.

(Except when she believes no one is near. Then you should see how delightful she is, playing in the meadow, trotting and frisking about, kicking up her little hooves!—exactly like any young animal, without a worry in the world.)

The goat-girl has no name, just as she has no mother or father. But she is a girl and so it seems cruel to call her *it*. I will baptize her Astrid because the name makes me think of snow and the goat-girl's hair is snowy white.

The years pass and the goat-girl continues to live in the old corn-crib at the edge of our property. No one speaks of her—no one wonders at the fact that she has grown very little since she came to live with us. (When I was nine years old I thought the goat-girl was my age exactly and that she would grow along with me, like a sister. But I must have been mistaken.)

Mother no longer comes downstairs at all. It is possible that people have forgotten her in the village. My brothers and sisters and I would forget her too except for her rapid footsteps overhead and her occasional laughter. Sometimes we hear doors being slammed upstairs—my parents' voices—dim and muffled—the words never audible.

Father asks us to pray for Mother. Which of course we have been doing all along.

By night the goat-girl becomes a nocturnal creature and loses her shyness in a way that is surprising. She leaves the safety of her pen, leaves her little pasture, and prowls anywhere she wishes. Sometimes we hear her outside our windows—her cautious hooves in the grass, her low bleating murmur. I wish I could describe the sound she makes!—it is gentle, it is pleading, it is reproachful, it is trembling with rage—a fluid wordless questioning—like music without words—*Why? How long? Who?*—stirring us from sleep.

Now I see that, by moonlight, the goat-girl is terrifying to watch. Many times I have crept from my bed to look down at her, through my gauzy curtains, protected (I believe) by the dark, and have been frightened by her stiff little body, her defiant posture, her glaring pale eyes. I want to cry out—Please don't hate me!—Please don't wish me harm!—but of course I say nothing, not even a whisper. I draw back from the window and tiptoe to my bed and try to sleep and in the morning it might be that the goat-girl appeared to all my brothers and sisters during the night. . . . But I wasn't asleep, I didn't dream, I try to explain, I saw her myself; but they say mockingly, No, no, you were dreaming too, you are no different from the rest of us, it wouldn't dare come this close to the house.

She isn't *it*, I tell them. Her name is Astrid.

Father dreams of her death but is too weak to order it, so my oldest brother plans to arrange for the butchering as soon as he comes to maturity. Until then the goat-girl lives quietly and happily enough at the edge of our property, sunning herself in good weather, browsing in the pasture, frisking and gamboling about. Singing her plaintive little mew to herself. Trespassing by moonlight. One day soon I will creep as close as possible to look into her eyes, to judge if they are human or not, if they are blind.

She has grown very little over the years but her haunches are muscular, her nearly human shoulders, neck, and head are more defined, sometimes I see her child-soul pushing up out of her goat body like a swimmer emerging from a frothy white sea, about to gasp for air, blink and gape in amazement.

Astrid! I will call. Sister!

But she won't know her name.

PATRICK McGRATH

Blood Disease

This is probably how it happened: William Clack-Herman, the anthropologist (popularly known as 'Congo Bill') was doing field research on the kinship systems of the pygmies of the equatorial rain forest. One afternoon he was sitting outside his hut of mongongo leaves, writing up his notes, when a mosquito bit him. It is only the female that makes the blood meal, for she needs it to boost her egg output. From the thorny tip of her mouthparts she unsheathed a slender stylus, and having sliced neatly through Bill's skin tissue, pierced a tiny blood vessel. Bill noticed nothing. Two powerful pumps in the insect's head began to draw off blood while simultaneously hundreds of tiny parasites were discharged into his bloodstream. Within half-an-hour, when the mosquito had long since returned to the water, the parasites were safely established in his liver. For six days they multiplied, asexually, and then on the morning of the seventh they burst out and invaded the red blood cells. Within a relatively short period of time Congo Bill was exhibiting all the classical symptoms of malaria. He was delirious; he suffered from chills, vomiting, and diarrhea; and his spleen was dangerously enlarged. He was also alone—the pygmies had deserted him, had melted deeper into the gloom of the rain forest. An essentially nomadic people, they could not wait for Bill to recover, nor could they take him with them. So there he lay, shivering and feverish by turns, on a narrow camp bed in a dark hut in the depths of a chartless jungle.

How he made it back is a fascinating story, but not immediately relevant to the events that concern us here. Make it back he did; but the Congo Bill who docked at Southampton one morning in the summer of 1934 was not the vigorous young man who'd left for Africa a year previously. He was haggard and thin now, and forced to walk with a stick. His flesh was discolored, and his fingers trembled constantly. He looked, in short, like a man who was dying. When at last he stepped gingerly down the gangway, one steward was at his elbow and another close behind, carrying a large bamboo cage. Huddled in the corner of the cage was a small black-and-white

Colobus monkey that the anthropologist had befriended before leaving the Congo for the last time. He intended to give it to his son, Frank.

Virginia Clack-Herman was considerably shocked at her husband's frailty; and the fact that he could speak only in a hoarse whisper certainly added pathos to their reunion. Frank, then aged nine, did not recognize his father, and accepted with some unease the monkey; and then the three of them, with the monkey, made their way very slowly through the customs shed and out to the car. There were at the time no strict regulations regarding the quarantining of monkeys.

The journey from Southampton was uneventful. Virginia drove, and Bill sat beside her with a rug over his knees and slept most of the way. Frank sat in the back; the bamboo cage was placed on the seat beside him, and the little monkey sat hunkered inside it, alert but unmoving. From time to time the boy's eyes were drawn to the monkey's; they were both, clearly, perplexed and slightly alarmed. Congo Bill muttered as he dozed, and Virginia, stony-faced, kept her eyes on the road.

It was a warm day, and in the sunshine of the late afternoon the cornfields of Berkshire rippled about them like a golden sea; and then, just as Virginia began to wonder where they would break the journey, from out of this sea heaved a big inn, Tudor in construction, with steeply gabled roofs and black beams criss-crossed on the white-plastered walls beneath the eaves. This was the Blue Bat; since destroyed by fire, in the early Thirties it boasted good beds, a fine kitchen, and an extensive cellar.

Virginia pulled off the main road and into the forecourt of the inn. Servants appeared; suitcases were carried in and the car taken round to the garages. Some minutes later, a cream-colored roadster pulled in beside it. The owner of this car was Ronald Dexter. He was traveling with his valet, an old man called Clutch.

Ronald Dexter was a gentleman of independent means who had never had to work a day in his life. He was an elegant, witty chap with sleek black hair, parted high, brushed straight back from his forehead, and gleaming with oil. Half-an-hour later he stepped out of his bathroom and found Clutch laying out his evening clothes. He slipped into a dressing gown, sank into an armchair, lit his pipe—and sighed, for Clutch was running a small silver crucifix with great care along the seams of his garments. A curious-looking man, Clutch, he had a remarkable head, disproportionately large for his body and completely hairless. The skull was a perfect dome, and the tight-stretched skin of it an almost translucent shade of yellow-brown finely engraved with subcutaneous blue-black veins. The overall impression he gave was of a monstrous fetus, or else some type of prehistoric man, a Neanderthal perhaps, in whom the millennia had deposited deep strains of racial wisdom—though he wore, of course, the tailcoat and gray pin-striped trousers of his profession. He was stooped and frail now, and Ronald had long since given up interfering with the bizarre superstitions he practiced. When he was finished, he tucked the crucifix into an inside pocket and turned, nodding, to his master.

'Do you imagine, Clutch,' said Ronald, 'that I shall be set upon by vampires?'

'One cannot be too careful,' replied the old man. 'We are not in London, sir.'

'No indeed,' said Ronald, as the put-put-put of a tractor came drifting across the cornfields. 'This is wild country.'

'Will there be anything else, sir?'

Ronald told him there was nothing else, and Clutch left the room, closing the door softly behind him. At precisely the same instant, just down the corridor, Virginia Clack-Herman, who was a tall, spirited woman with a rich laugh and scarlet-painted fingernails, was sitting before her mirror clad only in stockings and slip, the latter a silky, sleeveless undergarment with thin shoulder straps and a delicate border of patterned lacework at the breast. A cigarette burned in the ashtray beside her, its tendril of smoke coiling away through casement windows thrown open to the warmth of the early evening. She was plucking her eyebrows with a pair of silver tweezers, and in the bathroom that connected their rooms she could hear her husband shuffling about and talking to himself. With her head close to the glass, the fingers of her left hand splayed upon her forehead, she clamped the twin pincers about a hair. Her lips were parted, her teeth locked; all at once she plucked out the hair; her eyes fired up and a single tear started from the left one. Simultaneously, Congo Bill dropped his hairbrushes, and as they bounced on the tiles Virginia cast a glance at the bathroom door. She turned back to the mirror and prepared to pluck a second hair. Bill's mumble rose and fell like the distant drone of public prayer. Oh, to come back to her so utterly ruined, like one of the walking dead! Out came another hair; the eyebrows arched thin as filaments, flaring a fraction as they neared the nose. Satisfied, she dabbed at her left eye with a small handkerchief and then, still facing the glass, she closed her eyes and clenched her fists and sat rigidly for a moment in an attitude of bitter mortification. But when Congo Bill came in, several minutes later, with his shirt cuffs flapping pathetically about his wrists and asked her to fasten his links, she displayed only warm concern. 'Of course, darling,' she murmured, as she rose from her dressing table and pecked his cheek, leaving a very light impression of red lips upon the yellowing skin.

'I wonder,' whispered Congo Bill, 'how that monkey's doing.'

In point of fact the monkey was not doing at all well. Even as his father asked the question, young Frank had his face pressed flush to the bamboo cage, in a corner of which the monkey lay curled up and very still. 'Are you sick?' he whispered. He inserted a finger through the bars. 'Little monkey,' he cooed, poking it. There was no response. Frank straightened up and turned away from the cage with his lips pressed tight together. From the public bar below came a sudden gust of laughter. He opened the door of the cage, reached in, and retrieved the monkey. It was dead. He laid its little head against his shoulder and stroked the matted, scurfy fur for a moment. A flea hopped onto his wrist and bit him. He opened a drawer and took out the sheet of tissue paper lining it; in this he wrapped the little corpse, then tucked it down the front of his shirt, crossed the bedroom, and opened the door. The corridor was deserted, and he stepped out.

Ronald Dexter had already ordered when the door of the Blue Bat's shadowy, wood-paneled dining room swung slowly open and an attractive woman entered with a shuffling figure whose evening clothes hung like shrouds upon his wasted body. Ronald, who hated to dine alone, assumed they were father and daughter, and wondered if he could tempt them to join him. There were no other guests in the dining room; in fact, there were no other guests in the Blue Bat at all.

'Excuse me,' he said, rising to his feet with a charming smile. 'Good lord! Virginia!'

Bill and Virginia paused, turned, and scrutinized him. 'Ronald!' cried Virginia at last. 'Ronald Dexter! Darling, you remember Ronald Dexter?'

Congo Bill did not remember Ronald Dexter, with whom Virginia had been friendly before her marriage. The two were in fact very distantly related, on her mother's side, and in the few moments of theater that followed, Virginia recapped the rather tenuous blood relationship they shared. Congo Bill participated minimally in all this, his appetite for 'extraordinary coincidences' much dampened by the malaria. Ronald was altogether delighted, and his pleasure was shot through with an undeniable charge of sexual excitement—for despite their consanguinity the two were instantly, and strongly, attracted to each other.

There was no question now but that they must eat together, and so, in a flurry of small talk, and continuing expressions of pleasure that they should meet again in such odd circumstances, they sat down. Behind Congo Bill's chair the empty fireplace was hidden from view by a low woven screen, and above the mantelpiece the eyes of a large stag's head with sixteen-pointed antlers glittered glassily in the gloom of the encroaching dusk. Food arrived, and wine, and Ronald proposed a toast to homecomings and reunions. Congo Bill's hand trembled as he lifted a glass of claret to his bloodless lips. They drank, and there followed a brief, slightly uncomfortable silence. Ronald turned to Congo Bill, fishing for a conversational gambit. 'See much cricket in Africa?' he said.

'None at all,' whispered Congo Bill, dabbing his lips with a starched white napkin and staining it with wine.

'I don't suppose they have much time for cricket, do they darling?' said Virginia, brightly, 'what with all the hunting and gathering they have to do.' She turned to Ronald. 'They're quite primitive, you know; practically living in the Stone Age.'

'That must have been refreshing,' said Ronald. 'One grows so weary of decency and good manners, don't you agree, Virginia? Don't you sometimes wish we could indulge our impulses with unrestrained spontaneity, like savages?' His eyes flashed in the candlelight; Virginia took his meaning all too clearly.

'Oh, but we must have manners,' she said; 'otherwise we'll return to a state of nature, and I don't think we'd do terribly well at it.'

'Bill would,' said Ronald. 'He can cope in jungles.'

'You must be mad!' cried Virginia. 'Just look at the state of him! I'm sorry, darling,' she added, laying slender, red-nailed fingers on Congo Bill's bony wrist. 'But you must admit, equatorial Africa did get the better of you this time.'

'Malaria,' began Congo Bill; but Ronald cut him short. 'On the other hand,' he reflected, 'I suppose even the savages have manners, don't they? Rather different from ours, of course, but the same principle—which wife you sleep with tonight, who gets the best bit of the elephant—'

'Pygmies,' whispered Congo Bill, but Ronald had not finished.

'Manners are what distinguish us from the animals,' he said, 'so I suppose the more of them we have the better. What?'

Virginia laughed aloud at this. She opened her mouth and gave full, free tongue to an unrestrained peal of mirth that rang like clashing bells through that dusk-laden dining room. How lovely she was! thought Ronald. Exquisitely made up, perfectly at ease. Her dress was of dead-white satin and cut extremely low. She was wearing a rope of pearls; her face was as white as her pearls, and her lips a vivid scarlet. Quite spontaneously, as her laughter subsided, she leaned across the table and pressed Ronald's hand. At the touch of her fingers his blood turned hot and rapid. He promptly suggested that they take their brandy in the saloon bar. Virginia agreed, rose gracefully, and linking one arm in her husband's and the other in Ronald's, shuffled them off toward the door.

Clutch, meanwhile, having left his master's room, frowning, uneasy, conscious of some subtly malignant influence at work in the inn, had made his way downstairs and into the public bar. He took a seat at a small table in the corner and nursed a bottle of Guinness. There were perhaps twenty people gathered in the bar—local farm laborers they appeared, fat, sallow people, many with a yellowish tinge to their pallor. They were clustered about a wooden trapdoor in the center of the flagged floor, a trapdoor which stood upright on its hinges, a chain on either side stretched taut to hooks in the opening. The ceiling was low, and spanned by thick black beams, and though the air was thick with tobacco smoke a rising moon was visible through the uncurtained window. And then a weak and ragged cheer erupted as from the cellar beneath appeared the head of the landlord of the Blue Bat, Kevin Pander, a young man but, like his customers, very fat, and pale, and sallow-skinned. Wheezing badly, he ascended the cellar stairs with a hogshead of ale on one shoulder and a wooden crate containing two dozen bottles of beer dangling, clinking, from his white and hamlike palm. His wrists and ankles were bagged and swollen with accumulated body fluids, but he came up like a god, an asthmatic Bacchus ascending from the netherworld, and paused, breathing heavily, at the top of the steps. Then he kicked the trapdoor down behind him and it slammed shut with a great bang. Congo Bill, sunk in a black leather armchair in the saloon bar, sat up in considerable distress. 'Darling, what is it?' said Virginia.

'Must go up,' he whispered. 'The noise . . .' Clearly, the sounds from the public bar had awakened some African memory, a memory profoundly disturbing to the fragile nervous system of the debilitated anthropologist. Virginia, glancing at Ronald, helped her husband to his feet and led him off toward the stairs. At precisely the same instant, Clutch realized with a thrill of horror what was wrong with the people in the public bar: pernicious anemia.

*   *   *

Frank tiptoed out of his bedroom with the wrapped dead monkey stuffed down his shirt. He did not make for the main staircase, for he was quite sure that his parents would veto the ceremony that he had decided privately to conduct. Instead he went to the other end of the corridor, to a door with a large key protruding from the lock. He turned the key and pushed open the door, and found himself on a dusty, uncarpeted back stairway. A small high window filmed over with cobwebs admitted what dim light was still to be had from the day. He crossed the landing and began to descend the stairs, which were steep, narrow, and, in the gloom, quite treacherous. Reaching the lower floor, he found a long passage at the far end of which stood another door. But barely had he begun to advance along the passage when he heard footsteps on the stairs he had just descended. He stood for a moment frozen in an agony of terrified indecision. As luck would have it, the wall of the passage was not entirely without a place of concealment: there was a shallow, rounded depression, no more than two feet high and two feet deep, quite close to where he was standing. He rapidly squeezed himself into this depression and huddled there like a fetus in a womb, with the dead monkey tucked in his lap like a second fetus, a fetus of the second order. Thus he waited as the descending step grew louder on the stairs.

It reached the bottom and paused. It was like no ordinary footstep; rather, a slow, heavy clump-clump-clump. To the small boy crouched in his womblike hiding hole, with his little heart hammering fit to burst, it was a very terrible sound indeed. It began to advance along the passage. Clump-clump-clump. Closer and closer. Eyes wide, fists clenched, Frank waited. He needed to go to the bathroom very badly. Clump-clump. Go past! Hurry! screamed a voice in the boy's head. Clump. It stopped. Frank glanced sideways in terror. He saw an orthopedic boot, an ugly big black one with a pair of metal braces ascending either side of a slim white ankle to a stout belt buckled halfway up the calf. And then a head, upside down, dropped into view, its red hair fanning out in waves upon the dusty boards. 'What are you doing in there?' it said from an upside-down mouth.

'I'm hiding,' said Frank.

'What from?'

'You.'

Late that night, when Congo Bill lay heavily sedated in sleep, and the moon hung suspended like a silver ball over the black bulk of the Blue Bat, and a susurrus of night breezes whispered through the palely gleaming cornfields like a ghost, Ronald Dexter, in silk pajamas, rustled softly along the corridor and tapped on Virginia's door. Farther along the corridor, in the deep shadows, another door creaked open just a crack; it was Frank's. 'Come,' came a voice, and Ronald slipped into Virginia's room. Frank frowned, and then tiptoed away in the opposite direction, to the door at the end of the corridor. He carried in his trouser pocket the large key that opened that door. A moment later he was on the back stairs, and lit by the moonlight glowing through the cob-webbed window over the staircase, he quickly descended.

He was on his way to meet the girl in the orthopedic boot. She was eleven years old and her name was Meg Pander; she was the landlord's daughter. 'What's that?' she had said, earlier, pointing at the lump under Frank's shirt as he scrambled out of the depression in the wall of the passage. Frank had pulled out the bundle and folded back the wrapping to show her the dead monkey. She had taken it from him and cradled it in her arms, cooing gently.

'I want to bury it out in the fields,' said Frank.

'I know a better place,' said the girl.

'Where?'

'In the cellar.'

Frank thought about this. 'All right,' he said.

'We can't go there now. Meet me here at midnight.'

'All right.'

'You better let me keep the monkey,' she said.

Frank was not the only one to see Ronald Dexter enter his mother's bedroom. Two men from the public bar, flabby men with waxy skin and big, soft faces as round and pale as the rising moon, and a predisposition to breathlessness, were lurking in the shadows. They said nothing, as the minutes passed, but they were not silent: the corridor was filled, like a living thing, with the wheeze and gasp of their laboring lungs. Nearby lay Congo Bill, who had returned in the depths of his sleeping mind to the eerie twilight of the rain forest, where huge trunks of mahogany and African walnut reared two hundred feet over his head to form a densely woven canopy that effectively blocked out all sunlight, while underfoot, moldering gently, the forest floor deadened all sound, and a heavy, ominous silence clung to the place, a silence broken only occasionally by the manic chatter of a troop of Colobus monkeys . . . But even as Congo Bill relived in dream his last fevered journey through that dim and silent forest, Ronald Dexter was rising from his (Bill's) wife's bed and slipping on his silk pajamas. With a few last whispered words, a few last caresses, he left Virginia's bedroom and with a soft click! carefully closed her door. The soft click was succeeded by a crisp crack! and a brief ringing sound, as one of the fat men emerged from the shadows and hit him very hard on the back of the head with a length of metal piping. The pipe bounced off the skull and Ronald wobbled for a moment and then collapsed into a limp heap on the floor. The first man lifted him by the armpits, the second from under the knees, and then they shuffled rapidly off down the corridor, panting heavily, as Ronald's head lolled on his shoulder and his fingers dragged limply along the carpet.

Meg had finished dressing the body of the dead monkey when Frank reached her room shortly after midnight. It was a small, low-ceilinged servant's room, massively dominated by the bedstead, a vast Victorian contraption of dark, lacquered wood with an extremely thick mattress and a Gothic headboard all crockets and gargoyles. High in the wall above the bed was set a single small window, and upon its broad sill burned a candle by the wavering flame of which Frank could see, on the bed, the monkey stretched out in a tiny gown of white lace such as an infant might have worn for its christening or, as in this instance, burial. Meg herself was sitting very straight in a hard-backed chair beside the bed with her hands folded on a small black prayer book in her lap. She turned to Frank with a solemn face.

'God took your monkey away,' she whispered.

Frank grinned, rather uncertainly.

'He's in Jesus' bosom now.'

Frank absently scratched his wrist where the flea had bitten him. A small crusty scab, reddish-black in color, had begun to form there. On Meg's washstand stood a large jar full of clear fluid, and something floated in the fluid that he could not quite identify in the candlelight, but it looked organic.

'We have to go to the cellar now,' said Meg. She stood up and stamped her orthopedic boot four or five times on the floor. 'My leg keeps going to sleep,' she said, 'Will you get the candle down?'

So Frank climbed onto the bed and retrieved the candle from the windowsill while Meg laid the monkey gently in a cardboard shoe box lined with the tissue Frank had taken earlier from the drawer in his bedroom.

They made their way to the door at the end of the passage, then out into the yard at the back of the inn. Clinging to the shadows, they crept around the building; the walls and out-buildings of the Blue

Bat glimmered in the fullness of the moonlight, and from far across the fields came the muted barking of a dog on a distant farm. Meg held Frank's hand firmly in her own as she edged down a flight of worn stone steps at the bottom of which damp grass and moss struggled up through the cracks between ancient paving stones. Directly before them stood a very low green door with peeling paintwork and rusting studs. Meg lifted the door on its hinges and it slowly scraped inwards; a moment later the pair were crouched in the musty darkness of the cellar, the door pushed firmly closed and the candle flickering on the ground between them and throwing up a strange light onto their pale, excited faces.

Congo Bill meanwhile was blindly crashing through the jungle in a state of deep delirium. He had lost his quinine in an accident on the river two weeks previously, and now the fever roiled and seethed unchecked within him. Delicate screens of misty lichen hung from the branches, and through these he clawed his wild way as brightly colored birds shrieked from the foliage high overhead, and the Colobus monkeys chattered derisively from dappled tree trunks wreathed with vines. On through the damp gloom of the forest he charged, till his strength at last started to flag. It was then that he saw Virginia. She was standing beside a sunlit pool some thirty or forty yards from him, wearing a simple summer frock and waving a large straw hat with a tilted brim and a cluster of bright fake cherries fastened to the band. Congo Bill stared at her for a few seconds, clutching the thick tendril of a climbing liana that twisted about a huge-trunked ebony tree smothered in flowering orchids. Upon the pool the few shafts of sunlight that penetrated the foliage overhead picked diamonds of light which trembled and shimmered in such a way that Virginia seemed to evanesce momentarily and then re-materialize, more clearly than before, still slowly waving her straw hat at him. Then she turned and moved round the pool and into the trees, and Congo Bill, stumbling after her, cried 'Wait!' as her dappled form danced away among the shifting shadows of the forest. 'Wait!' cried Congo Bill, as he staggered toward the pool.

And even as he did so, Virginia was drifting into sleep, her limbs languid and heavy, her whole drowsy being suffused with the lingering glow of deep and recent sexual pleasure. She sank into sleep, dreamless sleep, and as the curtains stirred slightly in the warm night breeze, a single broad shaft of moonlight drifted languidly across her bed and touched with silvered fingers the ridges and hummocks of the white sheet spread over her now-slumbering form.

*   *   *

Frank and Meg had penetrated the membrane of the cellar. With their feebly glimmering candle they crept forward from post to post toward the center, where they could hear a low murmur of human voices. Toward the source of the murmur the two children crept with stealth and trembling. They extinguished the candle; Meg still carried the dead monkey in its cardboard coffin. They ascended a shallow wooden staircase and squirmed forward along a damp planked platform between big-bellied barrels reeking of tar and ale; reaching the edge of the platform, they gazed down upon the men and women from the public bar, who were seated about a screened lamp, waiting. Barely had the children settled, side by side on their bellies with their chins cupped in their hands, to watch, when the trapdoor in the cellar roof was hauled open and voices were heard from the public bar above. For a moment there was confused bustle in the cellar; and then, with fresh lamps lit, two men descended carrying between them a supine form in silk pajamas.

'What are they going to do with him?' whispered Frank.

'I expect Daddy wants his blood.'

'Oh, crikey!' breathed the boy, and in his mind a series of images rapidly unfolded of opened sarcophagi and ghoulish creatures neither dead nor alive. In fact, the explanation for the events in the cellar was quite straightforward, in scientific terms. Clutch was right: these people suffered from pernicious anemia, a disease which, if untreated, produces a chemical imbalance in the organism that can manifest in a craving for fresh blood. It has this in common with malaria, that in both diseases there is disintegration of the red blood cells, though malaria for some reason has never produced a sense of group identity among its victims. This is not true of pernicious anemia. The Blue Bat was in fact both haven and refuge to a small cell of untreated anemics, and had been for five years, ever since Kevin Pander had watched his wife sicken and die of the disease. This trauma had brought about what is clinically termed an *iatrophobic reaction* in the young innkeeper, a pathological dread of doctors, with the result that when he detected the first symptoms in himself he did not seek treatment, but instead began to gather about him a cadre of anemics who, like him, were prepared to live and die beyond the pale of contemporary medical practice; beyond, indeed, the law. For five years these committed anemics had maintained a sporadic supply of fresh blood in the cellar, and there they were to be found, outside normal licensing hours, sipping the good red corpuscles their own bodies so desperately lacked. The Blue Bat's clientele being what it was, almost all of this blood came from members of the upper classes. The fall of the Roman Empire has been attributed in part to malarial epidemics, and also to the effects of pernicious anemia caused by lead in the plumbing. Whether these facts played any part in Pander's elaborate delusional system is not known; the psychopathology of that disturbed young man is fortunately beyond the scope of this narrative.

And so the limp Ronald Dexter was stripped of his pajamas, and then—after his pale, naked body had aroused a spontaneous gasp of appreciation from the assembled company—his ankles were lashed together with a length of stout twine, and the twine slipped into an iron ring attached to a rope which ran to a pulley block fixed to a hook set into a thick beam overhead. Several of the men then took up the rope hanging from the pulley block, and with no small effort managed by a series of heaves to hoist Dexter aloft, and there he hung, quite comatose, and twisting gently, as Kevin Pander lashed the end of the rope to a pair of thick nails driven into an upright post for that purpose. A trellis table was then positioned beneath the dangling man, and upon the table was set a wooden keg bound with hoops of steel.

All this work had produced a greatly intensified respiration among the anemics, and even those who had not participated were panting in short, hoarse, shallow gasps, such was the excitement that now crackled almost palpably in the depths of the body of the inn. To young Frank, on his platform, the whole nightmarish scene had assumed a distinct patina of unreality; as the bulky figures moved about in the lamplight, their shadows against the stacked barrels and massy beams took on huge, monstrous proportions, and he watched like a spectator of cinema, suspended in the darkness in wordless captivation. He was barely conscious of the mounting excitement in the girl beside him as she followed her father's activity. Then Kevin Pander suddenly seized Ronald by the hair and sliced open his throat; and as the young man's blood came pumping out, young Meg trembled all over and rose onto her knees and gazed with wide, shining eyes, her palms pressed together at her breast as if in prayer. Kevin Pander released Ronald's hair and stepped back, lifting high the dripping razor then bringing it to his lips while two of the other men took hold of the violently convulsing body so as not to lose a drop, and the rest looked on with little piggy eyes that gleamed in the lamplight, the only sound now the hiss and pant of their flaccid lungs.

At length Ronald ceased twitching, and the spurts dwindled to a thick drip, faintly audible amid the wheezing. The keg was tapped, and now, his gestures inflected with theatricality, Kevin Pander drew off a small amount of the contents into a glass and, to a subdued murmur of approval, held it up before him. In the obscurity the blood was black. He tossed it down his throat; then, his heavy eyelids sliding over his eyes until he resembled a latter-day satyr, lacking only hoofs and horns, and his blood-smeared lips parting in a voluptuary's grin, he said something that produced a perceptible twitch of ardor in the assembly's collective body. And where, you may wonder—though now, of course, it was too late for him to be of any assistance to his master—was Clutch all this time?

A cell without a nucleus is a ruin, and when Congo Bill stumbled into an abandoned pygmy camp there was nobody there to greet him but a ghost; and the ghost in the ruin was Virginia. She smiled shyly at him from the entrance to one of the huts, then disappeared into its dark interior. He managed to drag himself in after her, and collapsed in the cool gloom onto the floor. Illness, according to the pygmies, passes through the following stages: first one is hot, then feverish, then ill, then dead, then absolutely dead, and finally, dead forever. When a small hunting group came through late the following day they found Congo Bill dead. He was not, however, dead forever, nor even absolutely dead, and they set about nursing him with medicines derived from plants growing wild in the forest. At this time, the 1930s, these people enjoyed an existence which to most Westerners would seem utopian. Utterly at peace with the forest that sustained and sheltered them, they lived without chiefs and had no need of a belief in evil spirits. The state of nature was, for them, a state of grace—a functioning anarchy within a benign and generous environment. Not surprisingly, they sang constant songs of praise to the forest that provided for them with such abundance. They were singing these songs when, having seen Bill through his crisis, they carried him into the *Station de Chasse* on a litter, and handed him over to the resident Belgian colonial.

Had he known what was occurring in the depths of the Blue Bat, Congo Bill would doubtless have wished to return to the paradise he had briefly known among the people of the forest. By this stage Ronald Dexter was no more than a desiccated envelope of flesh, an empty thing—*bule*, as the pygmies would have said; but the anemics were by no means satisfied. When, some time later, Virginia was awakened by the sounds of heavy breathing, she opened her eyes to find herself surrounded by large pale women whose eyes glittered at her with an unnatural brilliance. Without further ado she was dragged screaming from her bed; Congo Bill, deeply sedated and ignorant of her plight, slept on in the next room, reliving the happiness and innocent plenty he had known among the pygmies. Help was in fact on its way, thanks to Clutch; the only question was, would it get there in time?

Yes, Clutch had known the anemics for what they were after only a few minutes in the public bar. He was an old man, and he had seen many strange things in his long life. He doubted he would have been listened to if he'd raised the alarm earlier; so he had hiked off toward Reading, where somebody at the Royal Berkshire Hospital, he felt sure, would take his story seriously. By a stroke of good fortune the physician on duty was a man called Gland who'd once read a paper on iatrophobia and sanguinivorous dementia (bloodlust) in pernicious anemia, and within minutes a small fleet of ambulances was racing through the moonlit countryside, klaxons wailing, toward the Blue Bat. But even as they did so, Virginia, in a filmy summer nightgown, was being hustled across the public bar toward the yawning trapdoor, where, in the darkness below, Kevin Pander awaited her with horrible relish.

It was when he saw his mother being manhandled down the cellar steps that the bubble of suspended disbelief in which young Frank had witnessed the atrocity perpetrated on Ronald Dexter was finally punctured. His whole body stiffened; he turned to Meg, and she immediately gripped him hard by the wrists. 'Don't make a sound,' she hissed, 'or they'll drink your blood too.'

'That's my mother,' he hissed back. 'I must help her.'

'You can't.'

'I must!'

'They'll cut your throat!'

'I don't care—'

Then suddenly Frank broke off, his gaze burning on the shoe box. Meg's eyes followed his; in stupefied amazement they saw the lid move. Then it was still. Then it moved again, and this time it rose slowly, then slid off, onto the planks, and the dead monkey in its white lace gown sat up stiffly and turned its little head toward them. The two children were barely conscious of the scuffling, of the muffled screams, that issued from the cellar beyond, where the anemics were leering at Virginia and making vulgar remarks. She was not a person in their eyes, merely a blood vessel, a blood bank, to be plundered and consumed like all her kind. The monkey (which was dead but not, clearly, dead forever) rubbed its eyes with tiny paws, and with a small sob Meg seized it up and clutched it to her chest.

Frank saw his chance; he was on his feet and down the stairs, and running at the assembled anemics. 'You leave my mother alone!' he screamed. 'You take your hands off her!' Kevin Pander, chuckling hoarsely, seized the child, then passed him to another man, who held him still and smothered his mouth with a fat white hand. There was jocular murmuring among the anemics about this, all conducted in a rich, slurry Berkshire dialect, while Kevin Pander began stropping his razor on a stout strip of leather nailed to a post. Virginia had also been muzzled by her captors; her limbs jerked and her eyes blazed with desperation as she struggled in vain to get close to her son.

Then the trellis was being hauled over and a number of men took hold of the two Clack-Hermans to steady them over the keg when their bodies began the series of involuntary spasms that predictably ensue when the carotid arteries are sliced. Close by, Ronald turned slowly on his hook. Kevin Pander touched the razor's edge to his tongue. Apparently satisfied, he stepped forward. He was not smiling now. It was a tense moment, for it very much looked as though Clutch had failed, that he was going to be too late.

Congo Bill was in pretty bad shape when they brought him out of the forest, and it was generally agreed that a few more hours would have seen the end of him. He had the pygmies to thank, then, for saving his life. Fortified with quinine, he was shipped down the Congo to Léopoldville (as it was then called), where he rested up for some weeks before going on to the coast to board a liner for home. It was in Léopoldville that he bought the monkey. His prognosis was somewhat gloomy—periodic relapses were predicted, accompanied by general enfeeblement and, because of the large number of red blood cells destroyed in the successive paroxysms of fever, a chronic anemic condition. In fact, he could look forward to the life of a semi-invalid, and how Virginia would adapt to that was a cause of some anxiety to him as he crossed the Atlantic—though, as matters stand at this point, the question may well have been academic. He was also filled with deep regret that he would never again do anthropological fieldwork, never again set foot in the equatorial rain forest. Curious irony, he reflected, that the forest in which he had known his deepest tranquility was the same forest in which he had contracted the disease that drove him out forever.

An hour later Dr George Gland stood in the public bar of the Blue Bat with a small man in a gray raincoat. This was a detective from the Berkshire County Constabulary, a man called Limp, and he was smoking a pipe. The trapdoor was up on its chains, and policemen and forensic experts moved silently and purposefully up and down the cellar stairs. The anemics had already been led away to waiting ambulances, bound, first, for the Royal Berkshire Hospital, where they would begin a course of painful injections of liver extract, which was how the disease was treated in 1934. The two men were watching Clutch, who sat at a table nearby with his great brown head in his hands, mourning the death of his master, whose drained corpse lay on the floor beneath a white sheet. Sad to say, Ronald was not the only corpse on the flagstone floor of the public bar; beside him lay Virginia, also sheeted, and beside her lay the pathetic remains of little Frank. Clutch had, in fact, come too late, and the three white sheets bore silent and tragic testimony to his failure. Suddenly Limp removed the pipe from his mouth and, turning to the doctor, pointed it at him, wet stem forward. 'He had a girl!' he exclaimed.

'Who?'

'Pander,' said Limp. 'Pander had a little girl—a cripple—she wore one of those boots.'

'An orthopedic boot?' said Gland. 'A girl in an orthopedic boot?'

Upstairs, a uniformed policeman was knocking on Congo Bill's locked bedroom door. Slowly the anthropologist was roused from his dream, which was almost over anyway. 'Who is it?' he cried, irritably, in a hoarse whisper.

'Police. Open the door please, Dr Clack-Herman.'

Congo Bill sat up in bed, his withered, yellowing face pouched and wrinkled with annoyance and sickness and sleep. 'What do you want?' he mumbled.

'Open the door please, Doctor,' came the voice.

'Wait.' Slowly he eased himself out of bed, sitting a moment on the edge of the mattress to get his breath. What on earth would the police want, in the middle of the night? He reached for his stick, and slipped his feet into a pair of slippers. His dressing gown lay tossed on a chair beneath the window. He levered himself up off the bed and shuffled across the room. Picking up his dressing gown, he glanced through the curtains. The moon had gone down, and it was the hour before the dawn, that strange, haunted hour between the blackness of the night and the first pale flush of sunrise, and the sky had turned an eerie electric blue. His eye was caught by a movement in the fields, and he saw that it was a girl, a young girl, far out among the glowing cornstalks and limping away from the inn toward a copse of trees that bristled blackly against the blue light on the brow of a distant low hill. Tiny as she was in the distance, he could make out, on her shoulder, the little black-and-white Colobus monkey. He frowned, as he tied the cord of his dressing gown. Why was she taking Frank's monkey to the trees?

'Doctor.'

'I'm coming,' whispered Congo Bill, turning toward the door, faintly disturbed; 'I'm awake now.'

ISABEL ALLENDE

If You Touched My Heart

Amadeo Peralta was raised in the midst of his father's gang and, like all the men of his family, grew up to be a ruffian. His father believed that school was for cissies; you don't need books to get ahead in life, he always said, just balls and quick wits, and that was why he trained his boys to be rough and ready. With time, nevertheless, he realized that the world was changing very rapidly and that his business affairs needed to be more firmly anchored. The era of undisguised plunder had been replaced by one of corruption and bribery; it was time to administer his wealth by using modern criteria, and to improve his image. He called his sons together and assigned them the task of establishing friendships with influential persons and of learning the legal tricks that would allow them to continue to prosper without danger of losing their impunity. He also encouraged them to find sweethearts among the old-line families and in this way see whether they could cleanse the Peralta name of all its stains of mud and blood. By then Amadeo was thirty-two years old; the habit of seducing girls and then abandoning them was deeply ingrained; the idea of marriage was not at all to his liking but he did not dare disobey his father. He began to court the daughter of a wealthy landowner whose family had lived in the same place for six generations. Despite her suitor's murky reputation, the girl accepted, for she was not very attractive and was afraid of ending up an old maid. Then began one of those tedious provincial engagements. Wretched in a white linen suit and polished boots, Amadeo came every day to visit his fiancée beneath the hawk-like eye of his future mother-in-law or some aunt, and while the young lady served coffee and *guayaba* sweets he would peek at his watch, calculating the earliest moment to make his departure.

A few weeks before the wedding, Amadeo Peralta had to make a business trip through the provinces and found himself in Agua Santa, one of those towns where nobody stays and whose name travellers rarely recall. He was walking down a narrow street at the hour of the siesta, cursing the heat and the oppressive, cloying odour of mango marmalade in the air, when he heard a crystalline sound like water purling between stones; it was coming from a modest house with paint flaked by the sun and rain like most of the houses in that town. Through the ornamental iron grille he glimpsed an entryway of dark paving stones and whitewashed walls, then a patio and, beyond, the surprising vision of a young girl sitting cross-legged on the ground and cradling a blond wood psaltery on her knees. For a while he stood and watched her.

'Come here, sweet thing,' he called, finally. She looked up, and despite the distance he could see the startled eyes and uncertain smile in a still-childish face. 'Come with me,' Amadeo asked— implored—in a hoarse voice.

She hesitated. The last notes lingered like a question in the air of the patio. Peralta called again. The girl stood up and walked towards him; he slipped his hand through the iron grille, shot the bolt, opened the gate, and seized her hand, all the while reciting his entire repertoire of seduction: he swore that he had seen her in his dreams, that he had been looking for her all his life, that he could not let her go, and that she was the woman fate had meant for him—all of which he could have omitted because the girl was simple and even though she may have been enchanted by the tone of his voice she did not understand the meaning of his words. Hortensia was her name and she had just turned fifteen; her body was turned for its first embrace, though she was unable to put a name to the restlessness and tremors that shook it. It was so easy for Peralta to lead her to his car and drive to a nearby clearing that an hour later he had completely forgotten her. He did not recognize her even when a week later she suddenly appeared at his house, one hundred and forty kilometres away, wearing a simple yellow cotton dress and canvas espadrilles, her psaltery under her arm, and inflamed with the fever of love.

Forty-seven years later, when Hortensia was rescued from the pit in which she had been entombed and newspapermen travelled from every corner of the nation to photograph her, not even she could remember her name or how she had got there.

The reporters accosted Amadeo Peralta: 'Why did you keep her locked up like a miserable beast?'

'Because I felt like it,' he replied calmly. By then he was eighty, and as lucid as ever; he could not understand this belated outcry over something that had happened so long ago.

He was not inclined to offer explanations. He was a man of authority, a patriarch, a great-grandfather; no one dared look him in the eye; even priests greeted him with bowed head. During the course of his long life he had multiplied the fortune he inherited from his father; he had become the owner of all the land from the ruins of the Spanish fort to the state line, and then had launched himself on a political career that made him the most powerful cacique in the territory. He had married the landowner's ugly daughter and sired nine legitimate descendants with her and an indefinite number of bastards with other women, none of whom he remembered since he had a heart hardened to love. The only woman he could not entirely discard was Hortensia; she stuck in his consciousness like a persistent nightmare. After the brief encounter in the tall grass of an empty lot, he had returned to his home, his work, and his insipid, well-bred fiancée. It was Hortensia who had searched until she found *him*; it was she who had planted herself before him and clung to his shirt with the terrifying submission of a slave. This is a fine kettle of fish, he had thought; here I am about to get married with all this hoopla and to-do, and now this idiot girl turns up on my doorstep. He wanted to be rid of her, and yet when he saw her in her yellow dress, with those entreating eyes, it seemed a waste not to take advantage of the opportunity, and he decided to hide her while he found a solution.

And so, by carelessness, really, Hortensia ended up in the cellar of an old sugar mill that belonged to the Peraltas, where she was to remain for a lifetime. It was a large room, dank, and dark, suffocating in summer and in the dry season often cold at night, furnished with a few sticks of furniture and a straw pallet. Amadeo Peralta never took time to make her more comfortable, despite his occasionally feeding a fantasy of making the girl a concubine from an oriental tale, clad in gauzy robes and surrounded with peacock feathers, brocade tented ceilings, stained-glass lamps, gilded furniture with spiral feet, and thick rugs where he could walk barefoot. He might actually have done it had Hortensia reminded him of his promises, but she was like a wild bird, one of those blind guacharos that live in the depths of caves: all she needed was a little food and water. The yellow dress rotted away and she was left naked.

'He loves me; he has always loved me,' she declared when she was rescued by neighbours. After being locked up for so many years she had lost the use of words and her voice came out in spurts like the croak of a woman on her deathbed.

For a few weeks, Amadeo had spent a lot of time in the cellar with her, satisfying an appetite he thought insatiable. Fearing that she would be discovered, and jealous even of his own eyes, he did not want to expose her to daylight and allowed only a pale ray to enter through the tiny hole that provided ventilation. In the darkness, they coupled frenziedly, their skin burning and their hearts impatient as carnivorous crabs. In that cavern all odours and tastes were heightened to the extreme. When they touched, each entered the other's being and sank into the other's most secret desires. There, voices resounded in repeated echoes; the walls returned amplified murmurs and kisses. The cellar became a sealed flask in which they wallowed like playful twins swimming in amniotic fluid, two swollen, stupefied foetuses. For days they were lost in an absolute intimacy they confused with love.

When Hortensia fell asleep, her lover went out to look for food and before she awakened returned with renewed energy to resume the cycle of caresses. They should have made love to each other until they died of desire; they should have devoured one another or flamed like mirrored torches, but that was not to be. What happened instead was more predictable and ordinary, much less grandiose. Before a month had passed, Amadeo Peralta tired of the games, which they were beginning to repeat; he sensed the dampness eating into his joints, and he began to feel the attraction of things outside the walls of that grotto. It was time to return to the world of the living and to pick up the reins of his destiny.

'You wait for me here. I'm going out and get very rich. I'll bring you gifts and dresses and jewels fit for a queen,' he told her as he said goodbye.

'I want children,' said Hortensia.

'Children, no; but you shall have dolls.'

In the months that followed, Peralta forgot about the dresses, the jewels, and the dolls. He visited Hortensia when he thought of her, not always to make love, sometimes merely to hear her play some old melody on her psaltery; he liked to watch her bent over the instrument, strumming chords. Sometimes he was in such a rush that he did not even speak; he filled her water jugs, left her a sack filled with provisions, and departed. Once he forgot about her for nine days, and found her on the verge of death; he realized then the need to find someone to help care for his prisoner, because his family, his travels, his business, and his social engagements occupied all his time. He chose a tight-mouthed Indian woman to fill that role. She kept the key to the padlock, and regularly came to clean the cell and scrape away the lichens growing on Hortensia's body like pale delicate flowers almost invisible to the naked eye and redolent of tilled soil and neglected things.

'Weren't you ever sorry for that poor woman?' they asked when they arrested her as well, charging her with complicity in the kidnapping. She refused to answer but stared straight ahead with expressionless eyes and spat a black stream of tobacco.

No, she had felt no pity for her; she believed the woman had a calling to be a slave and was happy being one, or else had been born an idiot and like others in her situation was better locked up than exposed to the jeers and perils of the street. Hortensia had done nothing to change her jailer's opinion; she never exhibited any curiosity about the world, she made no attempt to be outside for fresh air, and she complained about nothing. She never seemed bored; her mind had stopped at some moment in her childhood, and solitude in no way disturbed her. She was, in fact, turning into a subterranean creature. There in her tomb her senses grew sharp and she learned to see the invisible; she was surrounded by hallucinatory spirits who led her by the hand to other universes. She left behind a body huddled in a corner and travelled through starry space like a messenger particle, living in a dark land beyond reason. Had she had a mirror, she would have been terrified by her appearance; as she could not see herself, however, she was not witness to her deterioration: she was unaware of the scales sprouting from her skin, or the silkworms that had spun a nest in her long, tangled hair, or the lead-coloured clouds covering eyes already dead from peering into shadows. She did not feel her ears growing to capture external sounds, even the faintest and most distant, like the laughter of children at school recess, the ice-cream vendor's bell, birds in flight, or the murmuring river. Nor did she realize that her legs, once graceful and firm, were growing twisted as they adjusted to moving in that confined space, to crawling, nor that her toenails were thickening like an animal's hooves, her bones changing into tubes of glass, her belly caving in, and a hump forming on her back. Only her hands, forever occupied with the psaltery, maintained their shape and size, although her fingers had forgotten the melodies they had once known and now extracted from the instrument the unvoiced sob trapped in her breast. From a distance, Hortensia resembled a tragic circus monkey; on closer view, she inspired infinite pity. She was totally ignorant of the malignant transformations taking place; in her mind she held intact the image of herself as the young girl she had last seen reflected in the window of Amadeo Peralta's automobile the day he had driven her to this lair. She believed she was as pretty as ever, and continued to act as if she were; the memory of beauty crouched deep inside her and only if someone approached very close would he have glimpsed it beneath the external façade of a prehistoric dwarf.

All the while, Amadeo Peralta, rich and feared, cast the net of his power across the region. Every Sunday he sat at the head of a long table occupied by his sons and nephews, cronies and accomplices, and special guests such as politicians and generals whom he treated with a hearty cordiality tinged with sufficient arrogance to remind everyone who was master here. Behind his back, people whispered about his victims, about how many he had ruined or caused to disappear, about bribes to authorities; there was talk that he had made half his fortune from smuggling, but no one was disposed to seek the proof of his transgressions. It was also rumoured that Peralta kept a woman prisoner in a cellar. That aspect of his black deeds was repeated with more conviction even than stories of his crooked dealings; in fact, many people knew about it, and with time it became an open secret.

One afternoon on a very hot day, three young boys played hookey from school to swim in the river. They spent a couple of hours splashing around on the muddy bank and then wandered off towards the old Peralta sugar mill that had been closed two generations earlier when cane ceased to be a profitable crop. The mill had the reputation of being haunted; people said you could hear sounds of devils, and many had seen a dishevelled old witch invoking the spirits of dead slaves. Excited by their adventure, the boys crept onto the property and approached the mill. Soon they were daring enough to enter the ruins; they ran through large rooms with thick adobe walls and termite-riddled beams; they picked their way through weeds growing from the floor, mounds of rubbish and dog shit, rotted roof tiles, and snakes' nests. Making jokes to work up their courage, egging each other on, they came to the huge roofless room that contained the ruined sugar presses; here rain and sun had created an impossible garden, and the boys thought they could detect a lingering scent of sugar and sweat. Just as they were growing bolder they heard, clear as a bell, the notes of a monstrous song. Trembling, they almost retreated, but the lure of horror was stronger than their fear, and they huddled there, listening, as the last note drilled into their foreheads. Gradually, they were released from their paralysis; their fear evaporated and they began looking for the source of those weird sounds so different from any music they had ever known. They discovered a small trap door in the floor, closed with a lock they could not open. They rattled the wood planks that sealed the entrance and were struck in the face by an indescribable odour that reminded them of a caged beast. They called but no one answered; they heard only a hoarse panting on the other side. Finally they ran home to shout the news that they had discovered the door to hell.

The children's uproar could not be stilled, and thus the neighbours finally proved what they had suspected for decades. First the boys' mothers came to peer through the cracks in the trap door; they, too, heard the terrible notes of the psaltery, so different from the banal melody that had attracted Amadeo Peralta the day he had paused in a small alley in Agua Santa to dry the sweat from his forehead. The mothers were followed by throngs of curious and, last of all, after a crowd had already gathered, came the police and firemen, who chopped open the door and descended into the hole with their lamps and equipment. In the cave they found a naked creature with flaccid skin hanging in pallid folds; this apparition had tangled grey hair that dragged the floor, and moaned in terror of the noise and light. It was Hortensia, glowing with a mother-of-pearl phosphorescence under the steady beams of the firefighters' lanterns; she was nearly blind, her teeth had rotted away, and her legs were so weak she could barely stand. The only sign of her human origins was the ancient psaltery clasped to her breast.

The news stirred indignation throughout the country. Television screens and newspapers displayed pictures of the woman rescued from the hole where she had spent her life, now, at least, half-clothed in a cloak someone had tossed around her shoulders. In only a few hours, the indifference that had surrounded the prisoner for almost half a century was converted into a passion to avenge and succour her. Neighbours improvised lynch parties for Amadeo Peralta; they stormed his house, dragged him out, and had the Guard not arrived in time, would have torn him limb from limb in the plaza. To assuage their guilt for having ignored Hortensia for so many years, everyone wanted to do something for her. They collected money to provide her a pension, they gathered tons of clothing and medicine she did not need, and several welfare organizations were given the task of scraping the filth from her body, cutting her hair, and outfitting her from head to toe, so she looked like an ordinary old lady. The nuns offered her a bed in a shelter for indigents, and for several months kept her tied up to prevent her from running back to her cellar, until finally she grew accustomed to daylight and resigned to living with other human beings.

Taking advantage of the public furore fanned by the press, Amadeo Peralta's numerous enemies finally gathered courage to launch an attack against him. Authorities who for years had overlooked his abuses fell upon him with the full fury of the law. The story occupied everyone's attention long enough to see the former caudillo in prison, and then faded and died away. Rejected by family and friends, a symbol of all that is abominable and abject, harassed by both jailers and companions-in-misfortune, Peralta spent the rest of his days in prison. He remained in his cell, never venturing into the courtyard with the other inmates. From there, he could hear the sounds from the street.

Every day at ten in the morning, Hortensia, with the faltering step of a madwoman, tottered down to the prison where she handed the guard at the gate a warm saucepan for the prisoner.

'He almost never left me hungry,' she would tell the guard in an apologetic tone. Then she would sit in the street to play her psaltery, wresting from it moans of agony impossible to bear. In the hope of distracting her or silencing her, some passers-by gave her money.

Crouched on the other side of the wall, Amadeo Peralta heard those sounds that seemed to issue from the depths of the earth and course through every nerve in his body. This daily castigation must mean something, but he could not remember what. From time to time he felt something like a stab of guilt, but immediately his memory failed and images of the past evaporated in a dense mist. He did not know why he was in that tomb, and gradually he forgot the world of light and lost himself in his misfortune.

NOTES

'Sir Bertrand, a Fragment', by Anna Laetitia Aikin (1743–1824, later known under her married name—Mrs Barbauld—as a significant poet and literary editor) was first published in the collection *Miscellaneous Pieces in Prose* (1773), written with her brother John Aikin.

'The Poisoner of Montremos' is a new title that I have given to a tale which first appeared in *The Lady's Magazine* for March 1791 under the simple heading 'Remarkable Narrative', prefaced by a notice that 'Richard Cumberland esq. who about eight years since was, for some time, resident in Spain in the quality of secretary to our embassy there, gives the following remarkable narrative'. Richard Cumberland (1732–1811) was a diplomat, playwright, and novelist.

'The Friar's Tale' appeared anonymously in three instalments in *The Lady's Magazine* in 1792.

'Raymond: A Fragment' appeared under the pseudonym 'Juvenis' (Latin: a young man or woman) in *The Lady's Magazine* for February 1799.

'The Parricide Punished' appeared in the *Monthly Mirror* for May 1799. The French publication referred to in the prefatory note appears to have been a miscellany published in London in 1782.

'The Ruins of the Abbey of Fitz-Martin', with its embedded tale 'The Bleeding Nun of St Catherine's', was published in a chapbook collection of short Gothic fragments entitled *Romances and Gothic Tales* in 1801.

'The Vindictive Monk; or The Fatal Ring' by Isaac Crookenden appeared in his chapbook collection *Romantic Tales*, published in London in 1802. In very condensed form, its plot bears some resemblance to that of Ann Radcliffe's *The Italian* (1797). A version of this tale has appeared in Peter Haining's anthology *The Shilling Shockers* (1978), although in heavily amended and modernized form. Reprinted here for the first time is Crookenden's original version.

'The Astrologer's Prediction; or The Maniac's Fate' appeared in a collection entitled *Legends of Terror* published in London in 1826.

'Andreas Vesalius the Anatomist' is an English version of 'Don Andréa Vésalius, l'anatomiste' by Petrus Borel (Joseph Petrus Borel d'Hauterive,

1809–59), which appeared in his collection of tales, *Champavert: contes immoraux* in 1833. Borel was a minor French poet and novelist in the Romantic literary circles around Gautier and Nerval. The tale appears here in a new English translation by the editor of this volume. The Latin titles given by Borel to the tale's short chapters may be translated as follows: I. A people of iron; II. A dance, a riot, a death; III. What I have chosen, I cannot perform; IV. A home defiled; V. The workshop; VI. Denouement; VII. The story concluded.

'Lady Eltringham; or, the Castle of Ratcliffe Cross' was first published under the name J. Wadham in a penny-dreadful magazine boldly entitled *The Calendar of Horrors! Weekly Register of the Terrific, Wonderful, Instructive, Legendary, Extraordinary, and Fictitious*, in July 1836.

'The Fall of the House of Usher' by Edgar Allan Poe (1809–49) was first published in *Burton's Gentleman's Magazine and American Monthly Review* in September 1839 (the poem 'The Haunted Palace' having been published earlier in the same year in the *Baltimore Museum*). Poe included the tale in his collection of *Tales of the Grotesque and Arabesque* (1840), and revised it for his subsequent collection, *Tales* (1845). The text reproduced here is the revised 1845 version. Poe remains the undisputed master of the shorter Gothic tale, having given it a new intensity of psychological conviction. 'The Fall of the House of Usher' in particular stands as a classic exhibition of Gothic effects.

'A Chapter in the History of a Tyrone Family' by Joseph Sheridan Le Fanu (1814–73) was first published in the *Dublin University Magazine* in October 1839. Le Fanu, a Dublin journalist and novelist, later became celebrated as a master of Irish Gothic writing for his novel *Uncle Silas* (1864) and his collection of uncanny tales *In a Glass Darkly* (1872). This tale has an additional interest as a possible source for the story of Rochester and Bertha Mason in Charlotte Brontë's *Jane Eyre* (1847). Although Charlotte Brontë denied the influence, her father is known to have been a reader of the *Dublin University Magazine*. Le Fanu's tale was one of a series of narratives supposedly collected and bequeathed to his executors by Francis Purcell, a parish priest and collector of local folk-tales.

'Rappaccini's Daughter' by Nathaniel Hawthorne (1804–64) was first published in the New York monthly journal *The Democratic Review* in December 1844. Hawthorne reprinted it in his collection *Mosses from an Old Manse* (1846). Hawthorne's many teasingly ambiguous fables and tales are the foundation for the great American tradition of the short story, while his short novel *The Scarlet Letter* (1850) is one of the finest American novels. The Gothic side of his art is displayed at greater length in the novel *The House of the Seven Gables* (1851), which is based on the curse hanging over an ancestral mansion in Salem.

'Selina Sedilia' by Bret Harte (1836–1902) was first published in the weekly magazine *The Californian* in August 1865, as part of Harte's series of parodied 'condensed novels', later collected in *Condensed Novels and Other Papers* (1867). The victims of this parody are the leading English 'sensation' novelists of the early 1860s, Mary Elizabeth Braddon (whose popular novel *Lady Audley's Secret* appeared in 1862) and Mrs Henry Wood (author of the equally successful *East Lynne* in 1861). Along with Wilkie Collins, these novelists specialized in elaborate plots involving concealed poisonings and forgeries, often with a distinctly Gothic flavour. Another notable tale in the same sequence is Harte's 'Miss Mix' (1865), which sends up the Gothic extravagance of Charlotte Brontë's *Jane Eyre*.

'Jean-ah Poquelin' by George Washington Cable (1844–1925) was first published in *Scribner's Monthly* in May 1875, and then appeared in the collection of Cable's Louisiana tales, *Old Creole Days* (1879), that established him as one of the leading writers of the 'local color' movement in American fiction.

'Olalla' by Robert Louis Stevenson (1850–94) first appeared in the Christmas number of *The Court and Society Review* in 1885, before being reprinted in Stevenson's collection *The Merry Men* (1887).

'Barbara of the House of Grebe' by Thomas Hardy (1840–1928) first appeared in his sequence of Dorset tales *A Group of Noble Dames* in 1891.

'Bloody Blanche' is an English version of 'Blanche la sanglante' by Marcel Schwob (1867–1905), which appeared in Schwob's collection of tales entitled *Le Roi au masque d'or* in 1892. Schwob was an active literary participant in the French *décadence* of the 1890s. A Jewish Parisian, he associated himself variously with Jarry, Wilde, Valery, and Stevenson. The tale appears here in a new English translation by the editor of this volume.

'The Yellow Wall-Paper' by Charlotte Perkins Stetson (1860–1935, born Charlotte Anna Perkins, and later known as Charlotte Perkins Gilman after her second marriage in 1900) was first published in the *New England Magazine* in January 1892. The story's basis is autobiographical: the author went through a post-natal depression following the birth of her daughter in 1885, and her husband Charles Stetson put her in the care of the noted neurologist Dr S. Weir Mitchell, who prescribed a stifling regime of domestic inactivity. She later made her name as one of the leading American feminist writers of her day, in manifestos including *Women and Economics* (1898) and the Utopian novel *Herland* (1915).

'The Adventure of the Speckled Band' by Arthur Conan Doyle (1859–1930) was first published in the *Strand* magazine in February 1892, and then reprinted in Conan Doyle's first collection of Sherlock Holmes stories, *The Adventures of Sherlock Holmes*, in the same year. The Gothic strain in Doyle's fiction surfaces in several other Sherlock Holmes tales, and in his lesser-known novels, notably *The Firm of Girdlestone* (1890).

'Hurst of Hurstcote' by E. Nesbit (Edith Nesbit, 1858–1924) appeared in Nesbit's collection of ghost stories, *Something Wrong* in 1893. Better known for her many children's books including *The Railway Children* (1906), Nesbit also wrote several works for adults, and took part in the work of the Fabian Society along with her philandering husband Hubert Bland and her close friend George Bernard Shaw.

'A Vine on a House' by Ambrose Bierce (1842–1914?) first appeared in the New York magazine *Cosmopolitan* in September 1905, and was then reprinted along with several other haunted-house tales in the third volume of Bierce's *Collected Works*, published in 1909.

'Jordan's End' by Ellen Glasgow (1874–1945) appeared in *The Shadowy Third and Other Stories* (1923). Copyright 1923 by Doubleday, Page and Company and renewed 1951 by First and Merchants National Bank of Richmond, Virginia. Reprinted by permission of Harcourt Brace Jovanovich Inc. Glasgow was a prolific writer, best known for her novel *Barren Ground* (1925). Most of her fiction is set in her native state of Virginia.

'The Outsider' by H. P. Lovecraft (1890–1937) was first published in the April 1926 issue of the magazine *Weird Tales*, and was reprinted in the same magazine in 1931. Copyright 1926, 1939, 1945 by August Derleth and Donald Wandrei, © renewed 1973 by the Estate of H. P. Lovecraft. Reprinted by permission of Scott Meredith Literary Agency, Inc., agents for the Estate. It later appeared in Lovecraft's posthumous collection *The Outsider and Others* in 1939. In his work for popular magazines, Lovecraft evolved a uniquely sinister mythology of lost races and subterranean slime that has made him something of a founding father of modern fantasy writing.

'A Rose for Emily' by William Faulkner (1897–1962) was first published in the New York magazine *Forum* in April 1930, and subsequently appeared in Faulkner's collection of stories *These 13* in 1931. From *Collected Stories of William Faulkner*, copyright 1930 and © renewed 1958 by William Faulkner, reproduced by permission of Curtis Brown Ltd., London, and Random House, Inc. Faulkner's many novels and stories, which have given him a major international reputation, revolve around the declining dynasties of the American South, and the life of his home town—Oxford, Mississippi—in particular. The strong Gothic element of his imagination is especially evident in his horror-novel *Sanctuary* (1931) and in his masterpiece, *Absolom, Absalom!* (1936).

'A Rendezvous in Averoigne' by Clark Ashton Smith (1893–1961) first appeared in the April/May issue of the magazine *Weird Tales* in 1931, and was reprinted in Smith's collection of tales *Out of Space and Time* in 1942. Copyright 1931 by Popular Fiction Publishing Co., copyright 1942 by Clark Ashton Smith. Reprinted by permission of Ralph M. Vicinanza Ltd. A Californian writer influenced partly by H. P. Lovecraft, Smith wrote several tales of science fiction and fantasy, and published four volumes of poetry.

'The Monkey' by Isak Dinesen (pseudonym of Karen Blixen, 1885–1962) appeared in her first book, *Seven Gothic Tales*, in 1934. Copyright 1934 by Harrison Smith and Robert Haas, Inc., and renewed 1962 by Isak Dinesen. Reprinted by permission of Random House Inc., and the Rungstedlund Foundation, Denmark. Although now better known for her memoir of her life in Kenya, *Out of Africa* (1937; published under her own name), her finest work is in her tales, with their aristocratic eccentricity and stylishly romantic settings; later collections include *Winter's Tales* (1942) and *Last Tales* (1957). Baroness Blixen (as she became by marriage to her cousin in 1914) was Danish by birth, but wrote most of her published work in English before producing Danish versions. The highly allusive style of 'The Monkey' perhaps calls for a few explanatory notes on quotations and foreign phrases:

The German title *Geheimrat* applied to the monkey on p. 345 means 'privy councillor'.

The Latin maxim *Discite justitiam* ... on p. 348 is a quotation from Virgil's *Aeneid*, meaning 'Be warned: learn justice, and not to scorn the gods'. This injunction recurs in briefer form at the end of the tale.

The Latin maxim *Ad sanitatem* ... on p. 348 means 'To know one's sickness is a step towards health'.

The English verses quoted by the Prioress on p. 349 are from 'Duty', a nineteenth-century jingle by William Maccall.

On p. 358, the Count's Latin exclamation *Naturi te salutem* is, strictly speaking, meaningless as it stands. It should almost certainly read *Naturi te saluant* ('Those about to be born salute you')—a deliberate inversion of the traditional greeting of the gladiators to the Emperor at the Roman games (*Morituri te saluant*: 'Those who are about to die salute you').

The French verse line spoken by Boris on p. 359 is quoted from Alfred de Vigny's poem 'Le Cor', and translates as 'God, how sad is the sound of the horn in the depths of the wood'.

The French verses recited by Athena on p. 362, in tribute to the revolutionary inspiration of Napoleon Bonaparte, are quoted, with some changes of punctuation, from the poem 'L'idole' by Auguste Barbier.

The 'long-forgotten verse' recalled by Boris on p. 376 is in fact a jumble of fragmentary quotations beginning with part of a speech made by Orestes to the goddess Athena in the *Eumenides* of Aeschylus.

The reference on p. 380 to 'the Vicomte de Valmont, who loved *de passion, les mines de lendemain*' ('in passionate affairs, the faces made on the morning after') alludes to the charming villain of Laclos's novel *Les Liaisons dangereuses* (1782), a cynical master of the arts of seduction.

Notes

The 'verse from Euripides' recalled by Boris on p. 382 is not in fact from Euripides at all, but is a sequence of lines spoken by Orestes in the *Eumenides* of Aeschylus, uttered in thanks to the goddess Athena for releasing him from the curse of the Furies.

'Miss de Mannering of Asham' by F. M. Mayor (Flora MacDonald Mayor, 1872–1932) appeared in her posthumous collection of stories, *The Room Opposite* (1935). Mayor's best-known work is the novel *The Rector's Daughter* (1924).

'The Vampire of Kaldenstein' by Frederick Cowles (1900–48) was published in Cowles's collection of tales *The Night Wind Howls* (1938). This and his other ghost-story collection *The Horror of Abbot's Grange* (1936) enjoy a high reputation among connoisseurs of supernatural fiction. Reprinted by permission of Michael W. Cowles.

'Clytie' by Eudora Welty (b. 1909) was first published in the *Southern Review* in 1941, and was reprinted in the same year in Welty's first collection of stories, *A Curtain of Green*. Copyright 1941, © 1969 by Eudora Welty, reprinted by permission of Marion Boyars Publishers Ltd., and Harcourt Brace Jovanovich, Inc. Welty's fiction, set chiefly in her native Mississippi, has long been prominent in the so-called 'Southern Gothic' school. In addition to the tales gathered in *Collected Stories* (1981), she has published five novels, including *The Robber Bridegroom* (1942) and *The Ponder Heart* (1954).

'Sardonicus' by Ray Russell first appeared in *Playboy* magazine in 1961, and was reprinted in the same year in Russell's collection *Sardonicus and Other Stories*. Copyright © 1960, © 1988 by Ray Russell. Used by permission of the author. In a slightly revised form, it later formed part of a trilogy of tales published as *Unholy Trinity* (1967).

'The Bloody Countess' by Alejandra Pizarnik (1936–72) is a translation by Alberto Manguel of the Argentine surrealist poet's narrative 'Acerca de la condesa sangrienta', first published in Spanish in 1968. Copyright © 1968 by Alejandra Pizarnik. Translation © 1986 by Alberto Manguel. Reprinted by permission of Clarkson N. Potter, Inc., a division of Crown Publishers, Inc., and the Lucinda Vardey Agency Ltd., Toronto. The story is founded on well-established historical accounts of the Hungarian mass-murderess, upon which a number of books and films have also been based. The book referred to at the start of this piece is Valentine Penrose's *Erzsébet Báthory, la comtesse sanglante*, which was published in Paris in 1962, before being translated into English in 1970. Manguel's English version of Pizarnik's story appeared in his anthology *Other Fires: Stories from the Women of Latin America* (1986).

'The Gospel According to Mark' by Jorge Luis Borges (1899–1986) first appeared in Spanish in Borges' collection of short fictions, *El informe de Brodie* (1970), which was published in an English translation by Borges and Norman Thomas di Giovanni as *Doctor Brodie's Report* in 1972. Copyright © Emece Editores S.A., and Norman Thomas di Giovanni, 1970, 1971, 1972. Used by permission of the publisher, Dutton, an imprint of New American Library, a division of Penguin Books USA Inc., and by permission of Penguin Books (UK) Ltd. An outstanding figure in Argentine literature, Borges has had, through his short prose works (which he preferred to call 'fictions' rather than tales), a major international impact upon modern fiction. His most important collections are *Ficciones* (1944) and *El Aleph* (1949).

'The Lady of the House of Love' by Angela Carter (1940–92) comes from her widely admired collection of subversively revised adult fairy-tales, *The Bloody Chamber* (1979). Copyright © Angela Carter, 1979. Reprinted by permission of Victor Gollancz Ltd., Rogers, Coleridge & White Ltd. The sumptuously stylish exploration of Gothic and macabre themes recurs in Carter's novels, notably *Heroes and Villains* (1969) and *The Infernal Desire Machines of Doctor Hoffman* (1972).

'Secret Observations on the Goat-Girl' by Joyce Carol Oates (b. 1938) appeared in her collection of short stories, *The Assignation*, in 1988. Copyright © 1988 by The Ontario Review Inc. First published by The Ecco Press in 1988. Reprinted by permission. In addition to her many novels and volumes of poems and essays, Oates has published several collections of short stories, most of them strangely sinister in atmosphere.

'Blood Disease' by Patrick McGrath appeared in his collection of tales, *Blood and Water* in 1988. Copyright © Patrick McGrath, 1988. Reprinted by permission of the Jane Gregory Agency and Penguin Books Ltd. Brought up in the notorious English psychiatric institution of Broadmoor, where his father was a medical superintendent, McGrath has spent his adult life in Canada and New York. His short novel *The Grotesque* (1989) continues in the vein of black humour and Gothic pastiche found in his tales.

'If You Touched My Heart' by Isabel Allende (b. 1942) comes from the collection *The Stories of Eva Luna* (1991), translated from the Spanish by Margaret Sayers Peden. Copyright © 1989 by Isabel Allende. English translation © 1991 by Macmillan Publishing Co. Reprinted by permission of Key Porter Books Ltd., Ontario, and Atheneum Publishers, an imprint of Macmillan Publ. Co. The other works of this Chilean novelist are *The House of the Spirits* (1985), *Of Love and Shadows* (1987), and *Eva Luna* (1988).